ARTHURIAN
LEGENDS

ARTHURIAN LEGENDS

EDITED BY
MIKE ASHLEY

CASTLE BOOKS

Originally published as *The Mammoth Book of Arthurian Legends*

This edition published in 2002 by
CASTLE BOOKS
A division of Book Sales, Inc.
114 Northfield Avenue
Edison, New Jersey 08837

This edition published by arrangement with and permission of
Carroll & Graf Publishers, Inc.
161 William Street
New York, New York 10038

First published in the UK by Robinson Publishing 1998

First Carroll & Graf edition 1998

Collection and editorial material copyright © Mike Ashley 1998

ISBN: 0-7858-1518-X

Printed in the United States of America

CONTENTS

Sources and Acknowledgements

I must once again thank Dr Lawrence Mendelsburg for his help in the compilation of this book and in particular for providing the texts for "The Quest of the Saracen Beast" and "Sir Marrok". Acknowledgements are accorded to the following for the rights to reprint the stories in this anthology.

"The Dog's Story" © 1996 by Eleanor Arnason, first published in *Asimov's Science Fiction*, May 1996. Reprinted by permission of the Virginia Kidd Agency, Inc., on behalf of the author.

"The Romance of Tristan and Iseult" © 1913 by Hilaire Belloc. Reprinted by permission of The Peters Fraser and Dunlop Group Limited on behalf of the Estate of Hilaire Belloc.

"Madoc the Door Ward" © 1998 by Douglas Carmichael. First publication, original to this anthology. Printed by permission of the author.

"The Isle of Avalon" © 1998 by Phil Carradice. First publication, original to this anthology. Printed by permission of the author.

"The Pretender" © 1996 by Stephen Dedman, first published in *Realms of Fantasy*, February 1997. Reprinted by permission of the author.

"The Winning of the Kingdom" by Geoffrey of Monmouth is based upon the translation by Sebastian Evans (London: Dent, 1912) and has been freely adapted by the editor. This version is © 1998 by Mike Ashley.

"Sir Percivale of Wales" © 1953 by Roger Lancelyn Green, first published in *King Arthur and His Knights of the Round Table* (London: Penguin Books, 1953). Reprinted by permission of Richard Lancelyn Green.

"The Lady of Belec" © 1989 by Phyllis Ann Karr, first published in *The Pendragon Chronicles* (London: Robinson Books, 1989) and *Weird Tales*, Winter 1989/90. Reprinted by permission of the author.

"Guinevere and Lancelot" © 1909 by Arthur Machen, first published in *T. P.'s Weekly* 2 April 1909 as "Many-Tower'd Camelot" and reprinted in *Notes and Queries* (London: Spurr & Swift, 1926). Reprinted by permission of A. M. Heath & Company, Ltd., on behalf of the author's estate.

"The Quest of the Saracen Beast" © 1950 by Theodore Goodridge Roberts, first published in *The Blue Book*, November 1950. Copyright expired 1976. No record of copyright renewal.

"Ravens' Meat" © 1998 by Fay Sampson. First publication, original to this anthology. Printed by permission of the author.

"The Knight with the Two Swords" © 1976 by Elaine Steinbeck, from *The Acts of King Arthur and His Noble Knights* by John Steinbeck (New York: Farrar, Straus & Giroux, 1976; London: William Heinemann, 1977).

Reprinted by permission of William Heinemann and Farrar, Straus & Giroux, Inc.

"Sir Gawain and the Green Knight" © 1981 by Rosemary Sutcliff, from *The Sword and the Circle* (London: The Bodley Head, 1981). Reprinted by permission of The Bodley Head and David Higham Associates on behalf of the author's estate.

"The Temptation of Launcelot" © 1998 by Peter Valentine Timlett. First publication, original to this anthology. Printed by permission of the author.

"The Quiet Monk" © 1988 by Jane Yolen, first published in *Isaac Asimov's Science Fiction Magazine*, March 1988. Reprinted by permission of the author and the author's agent, Curtis Brown, Ltd.

"The Carle of Carlisle" © 1998 by Ron Tiner. First publication, original to this anthology. Printed by permission of the author.

All other stories and translations are in the public domain.

Introduction:
THE ENDURING MYTH

Mike Ashley

The fascination with King Arthur, Merlin and the knights of the Round Table continues to absorb generation after generation, and has done for over a thousand years. Once hooked, it is impossible to get free because the story has so many different aspects.

To begin with there's the mystery of who Arthur really was. Was there a man behind the myth and, if so, who was he? And if he was real, what about Guinevere and Merlin and Lancelot and all of the others? Were they real too?

Then there is the story of adventure. Arthur and his knights were all mighty heroes undertaking chivalrous quests against evil men and savage beasts. The Arthurian legends were amongst the first tales of heroic fantasy, a field which in the last few decades has become the most popular of all genres.

Then there are the tales of romance and intrigue. Arthur's love for Guinevere; his incestuous relationship with his sister, or half-sister, Morgan. Guinevere's love for Lancelot and Arthur's eventual betrayal. And we must not forget the magic and mystery of Merlin and Morgan le Fay.

The legends have something for everyone, and that's what I've tried to bring together in this collection. Some of you may be aware that I have produced a series of Arthurian anthologies which looked at different aspects of the legend. The first was *The Pendragon Chronicles*, which followed through the life of Arthur. Then came *The Camelot Chronicles* which looked at the wider world of the Arthurian legend. These were followed by *The*

Merlin Chronicles, which focused on the magical elements of the legend, *The Chronicles of the Holy Grail*, which looked at the mystical aspects of the ultimate quest, and finally *The Chronicles of the Round Table*, which brought together adventure stories of many of the knights.

The first two of these anthologies are now out of print, and my publisher asked me if I'd produce an omnibus volume. I said I'd do more than that. I didn't just want to reprint the two volumes as one, because that wouldn't offer anything new. What I suggested was bringing together a volume that included a mixture of old and new stories which focused on the very heart of the Arthurian legends. To this end I have selected a few stories from those first two volumes, but for the most part this book contains stories not previously reprinted. These include brand new stories, plus others either not previously published in book form or long out of print and now rare collector's items.

The stories follow the Arthurian legend from the days before Arthur's birth, through the episode of the sword-in-the-stone and his conquest of the kingdom, to the creation of the Knights of the Round Table and many of their adventures, to Arthur's fate at the Battle of Camlann. There are even a couple of stories that take us beyond Arthur's death to later echoes of the legend.

Most of the stories follow the traditional tale of Arthur, as we know it from Malory's *Mort d'Arthur*, though I have in each case selected what I believe to be the best or most expressive example of that work. And so there are stories here from such diverse writers as John Steinbeck and Howard Pyle, Hilaire Belloc and Andrew Lang, Arthur Machen and Rosemary Sutcliff. But I also wanted stories that looked at the lesser known legends and introduced a fresh twist to some of the tales. Thus you will find some very interesting retellings by Ron Tiner and Douglas Carmichael, Fay Sampson and Eleanor Arnason, Jane Yolen and Phyllis Anne Karr. There's also a surprising Afterword which throws an entirely new light on the legend.

In between the stories I've woven a narrative which links the stories together and takes us through the Arthurian world. If this is the first time you've read anything about King Arthur and his Knights, then I envy you the thrill of discovery. If it is not the first time, then may I welcome you back to this most enduring of all legends. I hope you all find something that stirs the imagination.

The Start of the Legend

THE FIRST PENDRAGON

Sir James Knowles

What fascinates me about the Arthurian legends is that they do have
a basis in historical fact. We know that when Rome, battered on
all sides by barbarian armies, withdrew their support from Britain
in AD 410 it soon became a lawless land. Lowland Britain found
itself under attack from the Irish to the west, the Picts in the north,
and the various Germanic tribes – those we generally call Saxons –
in the east and south. Within a generation what was left of society in
Britain had totally broken down. There were massacres, famine and
plague. Those who clung to the "civilized" Roman way of life found
it difficult to survive the onslaught, but eventually they fought back.
They looked for a leader amongst their own tribes and the first to
emerge was a man history records as Vortigern. That, though, was
a title which meant High King. It is likely that his real name (or at
least his Romanised one) was Vitalinus, and that his royal palace
was at Gloucester. Vitalinus attempted to bring some control back
to Britain and organized the local tribes; but power went to his head
and there were many who regarded him as a despot. A rival chieftain
called Ambrosius Aurelianus challenged Vitalinus. All this happened
around the period 430–40, still a generation or two before Arthur.
However over the centuries, time has telescoped it into a much
shorter period, and the following story of Vortigern, Ambrosius,
the young Merlin and Uther Pendragon is related as happening in
the years just prior to Arthur's birth.

I was keen to open this anthology with a story by James
Knowles (1831–1908), who was knighted in 1903. Along with
Lord Tennyson, who is also represented in this anthology, Knowles
was the first to re-introduce the Arthurian myth to the Victorian

audience, and certainly the first to recreate Malory in narrative story form. His book The Story of King Arthur and His Knights *(1862) attracted the attention of Tennyson, and a strong bond of interest was forged between them, to explore the symbolism of the Arthurian legend. Knowles was an architect for much of his life – he designed the Grosvenor Hotel opposite Victoria Station – though he also founded the Metaphysical Society in 1869 and was editor of the journals* Contemporary Review *and* Nineteenth Century.

King Vortigern the usurper sat upon his throne in London, when, suddenly, upon a certain day, ran in a breathless messenger, and cried aloud – "Arise, Lord King, for the enemy is come; even Ambrosius and Uther, upon whose throne thou sittest – and full twenty thousand with them – and they have sworn by a great oath, Lord, to slay thee, ere this year be done; and even now they march towards thee as the north wind of winter for bitterness and haste."

At those words Vortigern's face grew white as ashes, and, rising in confusion and disorder, he sent for all the best artificers and craftsmen and mechanics, and commanded them vehemently to go and build him straightway in the furthest west of his lands a great and strong castle, where he might fly for refuge and escape the vengeance of his master's sons – "and, moreover," cried he, "let the work be done within a hundred days from now, or I will surely spare no life amongst you all."

Then all the host of craftsmen, fearing for their lives, found out a proper site whereon to build the tower, and eagerly began to lay in the foundations. But no sooner were the walls raised up above the ground than all their work was overwhelmed and broken down by night invisibly, no man perceiving how, or by whom, or what. And the same thing happening again, and yet again, all the workmen, full of terror, sought out the king, and threw themselves upon their faces before him, beseeching him to interfere and help them or to deliver them from their dreadful work.

Filled with mixed rage and fear, the king called for the astrologers and wizards, and took counsel with them what these things might be, and how to overcome them. The wizards worked their spells and incantations, and in the end declared that nothing but the blood of a youth born without mortal father, smeared on the foundations of the castle, could avail to make it stand. Messengers were therefore sent forthwith through all the land to find, if it were possible, such a child. And, as some of them went down a certain village street, they saw a band of lads fighting and quarrelling, and heard them shout at one – "Avaunt, thou imp! – avaunt! Son of no mortal man! go, find thy father, and leave us in peace."

At that the messengers looked steadfastly on the lad, and asked who he was. One said his name was Merlin; another, that his birth and parentage were known by no man; a third, that the foul fiend alone was his father. Hearing the things, the officers seized Merlin, and carried him before the king by force.

But no sooner was he brought to him than he asked in a loud voice, for what cause he was thus dragged there?

"My magicians," answered Vortigern, "told me to seek out a man that had no human father, and to sprinkle my castle with his blood, that it may stand."

"Order those magicians," said Merlin, "to come before me, and I will convict them of a lie."

The king was astonished at his words, but commanded the magicians to come and sit down before Merlin, who cried to them—

"Because ye know not what it is that hinders the foundation of the castle, ye have advised my blood for a cement to it, as if that would avail; but tell me now rather what there is below that ground, for something there is surely underneath that will not suffer the tower to stand?"

The wizards at these words began to fear, and made no answer. Then said Merlin to the king—

"I pray, Lord, that workmen may be ordered to dig deep down into the ground till they shall come to a great pool of water."

This then was done, and the pool discovered far beneath the surface of the ground.

Then, turning again to the magicians, Merlin said, "Tell me now, false sycophants, what there is underneath that pool?" – but they were silent. Then said he to the king, "Command this pool to be drained, and at the bottom shall be found two dragons, great and huge, which now are sleeping, but which at night awake and fight and tear each other. At their great struggle all the ground shakes and trembles, and so casts down thy towers, which, therefore, never yet could find secure foundations."

The king was amazed at these words, but commanded the pool to be forthwith drained; and surely at the bottom of it did they presently discover the two dragons, fast asleep, as Merlin had declared.

But Vortigern sat upon the brink of the pool till night to see what else would happen.

Then those two dragons, one of which was white, the other red, rose up and came near one another, and began a sore fight, and cast forth fire with their breath. But the white dragon had the advantage, and chased the other to the end of the lake. And he, for grief at his flight, turned back upon his foe, and renewed the combat, and forced him to retire in turn. But in the end the red dragon was worsted, and the white dragon disappeared no man knew where.

When their battle was done, the king desired Merlin to tell him what it meant. Whereat he, bursting into tears, cried out this prophecy, which first foretold the coming of King Arthur.

"Woe to the red dragon, which figureth the British nation, for his banishment cometh quickly; his lurking-holes shall be seized by the white dragon – the Saxon whom thou, O king, hast called to the land. The mountains shall be levelled as the valleys, and the rivers of the valleys shall run blood; cities shall be burned, and churches laid in ruins; till at length the oppressed shall turn for a season and prevail against the strangers. For a Boar of Cornwall shall arise and rend them, and trample their necks beneath his feet. The island shall be subject to his power, and he shall take the forests of Gaul. The house of Romulus shall dread him – all the world shall fear him – and his end shall no man know; he shall be immortal in the mouths of the people, and his works shall be food to those that tell them.

"But as for thee, O Vortigern, flee thou the sons of Constantine, for they shall burn thee in thy tower. For thine own ruin wast thou traitor to their father, and didst bring the Saxon heathens to the land. Aurelius and Uther are even now upon thee to revenge their father's murder; and the brood of the white dragon shall waste thy country, and shall lick thy blood. Find out some refuge, if thou wilt! but who may escape the doom of God?"

The king heard all this, trembling greatly; and, convicted of his sins, said nothing in reply. Only he hasted the builders of his tower by day and night, and rested not till he had fled thereto.

In the meantime, Aurelius, the rightful king, was hailed with joy by the Britons, who flocked to his standard, and prayed to be led against the Saxons. But he, till he had first killed Vortigern, would begin no other war. He marched therefore to Cambria, and came before the tower which the usurper had built. Then, crying out to all his knights, "Avenge ye on him who hath ruined Britain and slain my father and your king!" he rushed with many thousands at the castle walls. But, being driven back again and yet again, at length he thought of fire, and ordered blazing brands to be cast into the building from all sides. These finding soon a proper fuel, ceased not to rage, till spreading to a mighty conflagration, they burned down the tower and Vortigern within it.

Then did Aurelius turn his strength against Hengist and the Saxons, and, defeating them in many places, weakened their power for a long season, so that the land had peace.

Anon the king, making many journeys to and fro, restoring ruined churches and, creating order, came to the monastery near Salisbury, where all those British knights lay buried who had been slain there by the treachery of Hengist. For when in former times Hengist had made a solemn truce with Vortigern, to meet in peace and settle terms, whereby himself and all his Saxons should depart from Britain, the Saxon soldiers carried every one of them beneath his garment a long dagger, and, at a given signal, fell upon the Britons, and slew them, to the number of nearly five hundred.

The sight of the place where the dead lay moved Aurelius to great sorrow, and he cast about in his mind how to make a worthy tomb over so many noble martyrs, who had died there for their country.

When he had in vain consulted many craftsmen and builders, he sent, by the advice of the archbishop, for Merlin, and asked him what to do. "If you would honour the burying-place of these men," said Merlin, "with an everlasting monument, send for the Giants' Dance which is in Killaraus, a mountain in Ireland; for there is a structure of stone there which none of this age could raise without a perfect knowledge of the arts. They are stones of a vast size and wondrous nature, and if they can be placed here as they are there, round this spot of ground, they will stand for ever."

At these words of Merlin, Aurelius burst into laughter, and said, "How is it possible to remove such vast stones from so great a distance, as if Britain, also, had no stones fit for the work?"

"I pray the king," said Merlin, "to forbear vain laughter; what I have said is true, for those stones are mystical and have healing virtues. The giants of old brought them from the furthest coast of Africa, and placed them in Ireland while they lived in that country: and their design was to make baths in them, for use in time of grievous illness. For if they washed the stones and put the sick into the water, it certainly healed them, as also it did them that were wounded in battle; and there is no stone among them but hath the same virtue still."

When the Britons heard this, they resolved to send for the stones, and to make war upon the people of Ireland if they offered to withhold them. So, when they had chosen Uther the king's brother for their chief, they set sail, to the number of 15,000 men, and came to Ireland. There Gillomanius, the king, withstood them fiercely, and not till after a great battle could they approach the Giants' Dance, the sight of which filled them with joy and admiration. But when they sought to move the stones, the strength of all the army was in vain, until Merlin, laughing at their failures, contrived machines of wondrous cunning, which took them down with ease, and placed them in the ships.

When they had brought the whole to Salisbury, Aurelius, with the crown upon his head, kept for four days the feast of Pentecost with royal pomp; and in the midst of all the clergy and the people, Merlin raised up the stones, and set them round the sepulchre of the knights and barons, as they stood in the mountains of Ireland.

Then was the monument called "Stonehenge," which stands, as all men know, upon the plain of Salisbury to this very day.

Soon thereafter it befell that Aurelius was slain by poison at Winchester, and was himself buried within the Giants' Dance.

At the same time came forth a comet of amazing size and brightness, darting out a beam, at the end whereof was a cloud of fire shaped like a dragon, from whose mouth went out two rays, one stretching over Gaul, the other ending in seven lesser rays over the Irish sea.

At the appearance of this star a great dread fell upon the people, and Uther, marching into Cambria against the son of Vortigern, himself was very troubled to learn what it might mean. Then Merlin, being called before him, cried with a loud voice: "O mighty loss! O stricken Britain! Alas! the great prince is gone from us. Aurelius Ambrosius is dead, whose death will be ours also, unless God help us. Haste, therefore, noble Uther, to destroy the enemy; the victory shall be thine, and thou shalt be king of all Britain. For the star with the fiery dragon signifies thyself; and the ray over Gaul portends that thou shalt have a son, most mighty, whom all those kingdoms shall obey which the ray covers."

Thus, for the second time, did Merlin foretell the coming of King Arthur. And Uther, when he was made king, remembered Merlin's words, and caused two dragons to be made in gold, in likeness of the dragon he had seen in the star. One of these he gave to Winchester Cathedral, and had the other carried into all his wars before him, whence he was ever after called Uther Pendragon, or the dragon's head.

Now, when Uther Pendragon had passed through all the land, and settled it – and even voyaged into all the countries of the Scots, and tamed the fierceness of that rebel people – he came to London, and ministered justice there. And it befell at a certain great banquet and high feast which the king made at Easter-tide, there came, with many other earls and barons, Gorloïs, Duke of Cornwall, and his wife Igerna, who was the most famous beauty in all Britain. And soon thereafter, Gorloïs being slain in battle, Uther determined to make Igerna his own wife. But in order to do this, and enable him to come to her – for she was shut up in the high castle of Tintagil, on the furthest coast of Cornwall – the king sent for Merlin, to take counsel with him and to pray his help. This, therefore, Merlin promised him on one condition – namely, that the king should give him up the first son born of the marriage. For Merlin by his arts foreknew that this firstborn should be the long-wished prince, King Arthur.

When Uther, therefore, was at length happily wedded, Merlin came to the castle on a certain day, and said, "Sir, thou must now provide thee for the nourishing of thy child."

And the king, nothing doubting, said, "Be it as thou wilt."

"I know a lord of thine in this land," said Merlin, "who is a man both true and faithful; let him have the nourishing of the child. His name is Sir Ector, and he hath fair possessions both in England and in Wales. When, therefore, the child is born, let him be delivered unto me, unchristened, at yonder postern-gate, and I will bestow him in the care of this good knight."

So when the child was born, the king bid two knights and two ladies to take it, bound in rich cloth of gold, and deliver it to a poor man whom they should discover at the postern-gate. And the child being delivered thus to Merlin, who himself took the guise of a poor man, was carried by him to a holy priest and christened by the name of Arthur, and then was taken to Sir Ector's house, and nourished at Sir Ector's wife's own breasts. And in the same house he remained privily for many years, no man soever knowing where he was, save Merlin and the king.

Anon it befell that the king was seized by a lingering distemper, and the Saxon heathens, taking their occasion, came back from over sea, and swarmed upon the land, wasting it with fire and sword. When Uther heard thereof, he fell into a greater rage than his weakness could bear, and commanded all his nobles to come before him, that he might upbraid them for their cowardice. And when he had sharply and hotly rebuked them, he swore that he himself, nigh unto death although he lay, would lead them forth against the enemy. Then causing a horse-litter to be made, in which he might be carried – for he was too faint and weak to ride – he went up with all his army swiftly against the Saxons.

But they, when they heard that Uther was coming in a litter, disdained to fight with him, saying it would be shame for brave men to fight with one half dead. So they retired into their city; and, as it were in scorn of danger, left the gates wide open. But Uther straightway commanding his men to assault the town, they did so without loss of time, and had already reached the gates, when the Saxons, repenting too late of their haughty pride, rushed forth to the defence. The battle raged till night, and was begun again next day; but at last, their leaders, Octa and Eosa, being slain, the Saxons turned their backs and fled, leaving the Britons a full triumph.

The king at this felt so great joy, that, whereas before he could scarce raise himself without help, he now sat upright in his litter by himself, and said, with a laughing and merry face, "They called me the half-dead king, and so indeed I was; but victory to me half dead is better than defeat and the best health. For to die with honour is far better than to live disgraced."

But the Saxons, although thus defeated, were ready still for war. Uther would have pursued them; but his illness had by now so grown, that his knights and barons kept him from the adventure. Whereat the enemy took courage, and left nothing undone to destroy the land; until, descending to the vilest treachery, they resolved to kill the king by poison.

To this end, as he lay sick at Verulam, they sent and poisoned stealthily a spring of clear water, whence he was wont to drink daily; and so, on the very next day, he was taken with the pains of death, as were also a hundred others after him, before the villainy was discovered, and heaps of earth thrown over the well.

The knights and barons, full of sorrow, now took counsel together, and came to Merlin for his help to learn the king's will before he died, for he was by this time speechless. "Sirs, there is no remedy," said Merlin, "and God's will must be done; but be ye all tomorrow before him, for God will make him speak before he die."

So on the morrow all the barons, with Merlin, stood round the bedside of the king; and Merlin said aloud to Uther, "Lord, shall thy son Arthur be the king of all this realm after thy days?"

Then Uther Pendragon turned him about, and said, in the hearing of them all, "God's blessing and mine be upon him. I bid him pray for my soul, and also that he claim my crown, or forfeit all my blessing;" and with those words he died.

Then came together all the bishops and the clergy, and great multitudes of people, and bewailed the king; and carrying his body to the convent of Ambrius, they buried it close by his brother's grave, within the "Giants' Dance."

THE WINNING
OF KINGHOOD

Howard Pyle

We know nothing about the childhood of the real Arthur. Whoever he was he was almost certain to belong to one of the royal families of Britain in the fifth or sixth centuries, even if he never became a king in his own right. The few scant records that do survive from those early days refer to him as a dux bellorum, *or "duke of battles," in other words a military general. It would have been impossible though for such a war leader not to have been of royal blood, so we can imagine that the real Arthur was raised at court, perhaps the younger son of a king. He would not be thus expected to become king himself but would be trained instead in all the art and practice of war, in which he was to excel.*

In the Arthurian legend, Arthur is an illegitimate son and is fostered out to be raised by Sir Ector, who provides his military training, whilst Merlin tutors him in the religious arts. It is fifteen years before Arthur is introduced back into the world in the memorable episode of the sword in the stone.

Howard Pyle (1853–1911) was an American writer and artist who established a reputation for his children's books which he wrote and elaborately illustrated. These began with The Merry Adventures of Robin Hood *in 1883, before he turned to a series inspired by the Arthurian legends:* The Story of King Arthur and His Knights *(1903),* The Story of the Champions of the Round Table *(1905),* The Story of Lancelot and His Companions *(1907) and* The Story of the Grail and the Passing of Arthur *(1911). His style was mock medieval, rather like his contemporary William*

Morris, which becomes infectious after a while even if he does use some antiquated words, like hight *which means* named. *Of all the versions of the sword-in-the-stone that I have read, this one captures the atmosphere by far the best.*

I

In ancient days there lived a very noble King, named Uther-Pendragon, and he became Overlord of all of Britain. This King was very greatly aided unto the achievement of the Pendragonship of the realm by the help of two men, who rendered him great assistance in all that he did. The one of these men was a certain very powerful enchanter and sometime prophet known to men as Merlin the Wise; and he gave very good counsel unto Uther-Pendragon. The other man was an excellent noble and renowned knight, hight Ulfius (who was thought by many to be the greatest leader in war of any man then alive); and he gave Uther-Pendragon aid and advice in battle. So, with the help of Merlin and Sir Ulfius, Uther-Pendragon was able to overcome all of his enemies and to become King of the entire realm.

After Uther-Pendragon had ruled his kingdom for a number of years he took to wife a certain beautiful and gentle lady, hight Igraine. This noble dame was the widow of Gerlois, the Duke of Tintegal; by which prince she had two daughters – one of whom was named Margaise and the other Morgana le Fay. And Morgana le Fay was a famous sorceress. These daughters the Queen brought with her to the Court of Uther-Pendragon after she had married that puissant King, and there Margaise was wedded to King Urien of Gore, and Morgana le Fay was wedded to King Lot of Orkney.

Now after awhile Uther-Pendragon and Queen Igraine had a son born unto them, and he was very beautiful and of great size and strength of bone. And whilst the child still lay wrapped in his swaddling clothes and lying in a cradle of gold and ultramarine, Merlin came to Uther-Pendragon with a spirit of prophecy strong upon him (for such was often the case with him), and, speaking in that spirit of prophecy, he said, "Lord, it is given unto me to foresee that thou shalt shortly fall sick of a fever and that thou shalt maybe die of a violent sweat that will follow thereon. Now, should such a dolorous thing befall us all, this young child (who is, certes, the hope of all this realm) will be in very great danger of his life; for many enemies will assuredly rise up with design to seize upon him for the sake of his inheritance, and either he will be slain or else he will be held in captivity from which he shall hardly hope to escape. Wherefore, I do beseech thee, Lord, that thou wilt permit Sir Ulfius and myself to presently convey the child away unto some place of safe refuge, where he may be hidden in secret until he groweth to manhood and is able to guard himself from such dangers as may threaten him."

When Merlin had made an end of speaking thus, Uther-Pendragon made reply with a very steadfast countenance in this wise: "Merlin, so far as my death is concerned—when my time cometh to die I believe God will give me grace to meet my end with entire cheerfulness; for, certes, my lot is in that wise no different from that of any other man who hath been born of woman. But touching the matter of this young child, if thy prophecy be true, then his danger is very great, and it would be well that he should be conveyed hence to some place of safe harborage as thou dost advise. Wherefore, I pray thee to perform they will in this affair, bearing in thy heart the consideration that the child is the most precious inheritance which I shall leave unto this land."

All this, as was said, Uther-Pendragon spake with great calmness and equanimity of spirit. And Merlin did as he had advised, and he and Sir Ulfius conveyed the child away by night, and no one but they wist whither the babe had been taken. And shortly afterward Uther-Pendragon was seized with the sickness as Merlin had foretold, and he died exactly as Merlin had feared that he would die; wherefore it was very well that the child had been taken to a place of safety.

And after Uther-Pendragon had departed from this life, it was likewise as Merlin had feared, for all the realm fell into great disorder. For each lesser king contended against his fellow for overlordship, and wicked knights and barons harried the highways as they listed and there levied toll with great cruelty upon helpless wayfarers. For some such travellers they took prisoners and held for ransom, whiles others they slew because they had no ransom to pay. So it was a very common sight to see a dead man lying by the roadside, if you should venture to make a journey upon some business or other. Thus it befell that, after awhile, all that dolorous land groaned with the trouble that lay upon it.

Thus there passed nearly eighteen years in such great affliction, and then one day the Archbishop of Canterbury summoned Merlin to him and bespake him in this wise: "Merlin, men say that thou art the wisest man in all the world. Canst thou not find some means to heal the distractions of this woeful realm? Bend thou thy wisdom to this matter and choose thou a king who shall be a fit overlord for us, so that we may enjoy happiness of life once more as we did in the days of Uther-Pendragon."

Then Merlin lifted up his countenance upon the Archbishop, and spake in this wise: "My lord, the spirit of prophecy that lieth upon me sometimes moveth me now to say that I do perceive that this country is soon to have a king who shall be wiser and greater and more worthy of praise than was even Uther-Pendragon. And he shall bring order and peace where is now disorder and war. Moreover, I may tell you that this King shall be of Uther-Pendragon's own full blood-royal."

To this the Archbishop said: "What thou tellest me, Merlin, is a wonderfully strange thing. But in this spirit of prophecy canst thou not foretell when this King is to come? And canst thou tell how we shall know him when he appeareth amongst us? For many lesser kings there are who would fain be overlord of this land, and many such there are who deem themselves fit to rule over all the others. How then shall we know the real King from those who may proclaim themselves to be the rightful king?"

"My lord Archbishop," quoth Merlin, "if I have thy leave for to exert my magic I shall set an adventure which, if any man achieve it, all the world shall straightway know that he is the rightful King and overlord of this realm." And to this the Archbishop said, "Merlin, I bid thee do whatsoever may seem to thee to be right in this affair." And Merlin said, "I will do so."

So Merlin caused by magic that a huge marble stone, four square, should suddenly appear in an open place before the cathedral door. And upon this block of marble he caused it to be that there should stand an anvil and into the anvil he caused it that there should be thrust a great naked sword midway deep of the blade. And this sword was the most wonderful that any man had ever seen, for the blade was of blue steel and extraordinarily bright and glistering. And the hilt was of gold, chased and carved with marvellous cunning, and inlaid with a great number of precious stones, so that it shone with wonderful brightness in the sunlight. And about the sword were written these words in letters of gold:

Whoso Pulleth Out this Sword from the Anvil
That same is Rightwise King-Born of England.

So a great many people came and gazed upon that sword and marvelled at it exceedingly, for its like had never before been beheld upon the earth.

Then, when Merlin had accomplished this miracle, he bade the Archbishop to call together all the chief people of that land upon Christmas-tide; and he bade the Archbishop to command that every man should make assay to draw out the sword, for that he who should succeed in drawing it forth out of the anvil should be rightwise King of Britain.

So the Archbishop did according as Merlin said; and this was the marvel of the marble stone and the anvil, of which same anyone may easily read for himself in that book written a very long while ago by Robert de Boron, which is called Le Roman de Merlin.

Now when the mandate of the Lord Archbishop went forth, summoning all the chief people of the land to the assay of that miracle (for, indeed, it was a miracle to draw forth a sword-blade out of an anvil of solid iron), all the realm became immediately cast into a great ferment, so that each man asked his fellow, "Who shall draw forth that sword, and who shall be our King?" Some thought it would be King Lot and others thought it would be King Urien of Gore (these being the sons-in-law unto Uther-Pendragon); some thought that it would be King Leodegrance of Camiliard, and others that it would be King Ryence of North Wales; some thought it would be this king and others that it would be that king; for all the world was divided into different parties who thought according to their liking.

Then, as Christmastide drew nigh, it presently appeared as though the entire world was wending its way to London Town, for the highways and the by-ways became filled with wayfarers – kings and lords and knights and ladies and esquires and pages and men-at-arms – all betaking their way whither the assay was to be made of that adventure of the sword and the anvil. Every inn and castle was filled so full of travellers that it was a marvel how so many folk could be contained within their compass, and everywhere were tents and pavilions pitched along the wayside for the accommodation of those who could not find shelter within doors.

But when the Archbishop beheld the multitudes that were assembling, he said to Merlin, "Indeed, Merlin, it would be a very singular thing if among all these great kings and noble, honorable lords we should not find some one worthy of being the King of this realm."

Unto which the Merlin smiled and said, "Marvel not, my lord, if among all those who appear to be so extraordinarily worthy there shall not be found one who is worthy; and marvel not if, among all those who are unknown, there shall arise one who shall approve himself to be entirely worthy." And the Archbishop pondered Merlin's words.

II

It happened that among those worthies who were summoned unto London Town by the mandate of the Archbishop as above recounted, there was a certain knight, very honorable and of high estate, by name Sir Ector of Bonmaison – surnamed the Trustworthy Knight, because of the fidelity with which he kept the counsel of those who confided in him, and because he always performed unto all men, whether of high or low degree, that which he promised to undertake, without defalcation as to the same. So this noble and excellent knight was held in great regard by all those who knew him; for not only was he thus honorable in conduct but he was, besides, of very high estate, being possessed of seven castles in Wales and in the adjoining country north thereof, and likewise of certain fruitful tracts of land with villages appertaining thereunto, and also of sundry forests of great extent, both in the north country and the west. This very noble knight had two sons; the elder of these was Sir Kay, a young knight of great valor and promise, and already well renowned in the Courts of Chivalry because of several very honorable deeds of worthy achievement in arms which he had performed; the other was a young lad of eighteen years of age, by name Arthur, who at that time was serving with good repute as Sir Kay's esquire-at-arms.

Now when Sir Ector of Bonmaison received by messenger the mandate of the Archbishop, he immediately summoned these two sons unto him and bade them to prepare straightway for to go with him to London Town, and they did so. And in the same manner he bade a great number of retainers and esquires and pages for to make them ready, and they likewise did so. Thus, with a very considerable array at arms and with great show of circumstance, Sir Ector of Bonmaison betook his way unto London Town in obedience to the commands of the Archbishop.

So, when he had come thither he took up his inn in a certain field where many other noble knights and puissant lords had already established themselves, and there he set up a very fair pavilion of green silk, and erected his banner emblazoned with the device of his house; to wit, a gryphon, black, upon a field of green.

And upon this field were a great multitude of other pavilions of many different colors, and over above each pavilion was the pennant and the banner of that puissant lord to whom the pavilion belonged. Wherefore, because of the multitude of these pennants and banners the sky was at places well-nigh hidden with the gaudy colors of the fluttering flags.

Among the great lords who had come thither in pursuance to the Archbishop's summons were many very famous kings and queens and noblemen of high degree. For there was King Lot of Orkney, who had taken to wife a step-daughter of Uther-Pendragon, and there was King Uriens of Gore, who had taken to wife another step-daughter of that great king, and there was King Ban, and King Bors, and King Ryance, and King Leodegrance and many others of like degree, for there were no less than twelve kings and seven dukes, so that, what with their court of lords and ladies and esquires and pages in attendance, the town of London had hardly ever seen the like before that day.

Now the Archbishop of Canterbury, having in mind the extraordinary state of the occasion that had brought so many kings and dukes and high lords unto that adventure of the sword and the anvil, had commanded that there should be a very stately and noble tournament proclaimed. Like wise he commanded that this contest at arms should be held in a certain field nigh to the great cathedral, three days before that assay should be made of the sword and the anvil (which same was to be undertaken, as aforesaid, upon Christmas day). To this tournament were bidden all knights who were of sufficient birth, condition, and quality for to fit them to take part therein. Accordingly, very many exalted knights made application for admission, and that in such numbers that three heralds were kept very busy looking into their pretensions unto the right of battle. For these heralds examined the escutcheons and the rolls of lineage of all applicants with great care and circumspection.

Now when Sir Kay received news of this tournament he went to where his father was, and when he stood before his face he spake in this wise: "Sire, being thy son and of such very high condition both as to birth and estate as I have inherited from thee, I find that I have an extraordinary desire to imperil my body in this tourney. Accordingly, if so be I may approve my quality as to knighthood before this college of heralds, it will maybe be to thy great honor and credit, and to the honor and credit of our house if I should undertake this adventure. Wherefore I do crave thy leave to do as I have a mind."

Unto these Sir Ector made reply: "My son, thou hast my leave for to enter this honorable contest, and I do hope that God will give thee a great deal of strength, and likewise such grace of spirit that thou mayst achieve honor to thyself and credit to us who are of thy blood."

So Sir Kay departed with very great joy and immediately went to that congress of heralds and submitted his pretensions unto them. And, after they had duly examined into his claims to knighthood, they entered his name as a knight-contestant according to his desire; and at this Sir Kay was filled with great content and joy of heart.

So, when his name had been enrolled upon the list of combatants, Sir Kay chose his young brother Arthur for to be his esquire-at-arms and to carry his spear and pennant before him into the field of battle, and Arthur was also made exceedingly glad because of the honor that had befallen him and his brother.

Now, the day having arrived when this tourney was to be held, a very huge concourse of people gathered together to witness that noble and courtly assault at arms. For at that time London was, as aforesaid, extraordinarily full of nobility and knighthood, wherefore it was reckoned that not less than twenty thousand lords and ladies (besides those twelve kings and their courts and seven dukes and their courts) were assembled in the lists circumadjacent to the field of battle for to witness the performance of those chosen knights. And those noble people sat so close together, and so filled the seats and benches assigned to them, that it appeared as though an entirely solid wall of human souls surrounded that meadow where the battle was to be fought. And, indeed, any knight might well be moved to do his uttermost upon such a great occasion with the eyes of so many beautiful dames and noble lords gazing upon his performances. Wherefore the hearts of all the knights attendant were greatly expanded with emulation to overturn their enemies into the dust.

In the centre of this wonderful court of lords and ladies there was erected the stall and the throne of the lord Archbishop himself. Above the throne was a canopy of purple cloth emblazoned with silver lilies, and the throne itself was hung all about with purple cloth of velvet, embroidered, alternately, with the figure of St. George in gold, and with silver crosses of St. George surrounded by golden halos. Here the lord Archbishop himself sat in great estate and pomp, being surrounded by a very exalted court of clerks of high degree and also of knights of honorable estate, so that all that centre of the field glistered with the splendor of gold and silver embroidery, and was made beautiful by various colors of rich apparel and bright with fine armor of excellent workmanship. And, indeed, such was the stateliness of all these circumstances that very few who were there had ever seen so noble a preparation for battle as that which they then beheld.

Now, when all that great assembly were in their places and everything had been prepared in due wise, an herald came and stood forth before the enstalled throne of the Archbishop and blew a very strong, loud blast upon a trumpet. At that signal the turnpikes of the lists were immediately opened and two parties of knights-contestant entered therein – the one party at the northern extremity of the meadow of battle and the other party at the southern extremity thereof. Then immediately all that lone field was a-glitter with the bright-shining splendor of the sunlight upon polished armor and accoutrements. So these two parties took up their station, each at such a place as had been assigned unto them – the one to the north and the other to the south.

Now the party with which Sir Kay had cast his lot was at the north of the field, and that company was fourscore and thirteen in number; and the other party stood at the south end of the field, and that company was fourscore and sixteen in number. But though the party with whom Sir Kay had attached himself numbered less by three than the other party, yet was it the stronger by some degree because that there were a number of knights of great strength and renown in that company. Indeed it may be here mentioned that two of those knights afterward became companions in very good credit of the round table – to wit: Sir Mador de la Porte, and Sir Bedevere – which latter was the last who saw King Arthur alive upon this earth.

So, when all was prepared according to the ordination of the tournament, and when those knights-contestant had made themselves ready in all ways that were necessary, and when they had dressed their spears and their shields in such a manner as befitted knights about to enter serious battle, the herald set his trumpet to his lips a second time and blew upon it with might and main. Then, having sounded this blast, he waited for a while and then he blew upon the trumpet again.

And, upon that blast, each of those parties of knights quitted its station and rushed forth in great tumult against the other party, and that with such noise and fury that the whole earth groaned beneath the feet of the war-horses, and trembled and shook as with an earthquake.

So those two companies met, the one against the other, in the midst of the field, and the roar of breaking lances was so terrible that those who heard it were astonished and appalled at the sound. For several fair dames swooned away with terror of the noise, and others shrieked aloud; for not only was there that great uproar, but the air was altogether filled with the splinters of ash wood that flew about.

In that famous assault threescore and ten very noble and honorable knights were overthrown, many of them being trampled beneath the hoofs of the horses; wherefore, when the two companies withdrew in retreat each to his station the ground was beheld to be covered all over with broken fragments of lances and with cantels of armor, and many knights were seen to be wofully lying in the midst of all that wreck. And some of these champions strove to arise and could not, while others lay altogether quiet as though in death. To these ran divers esquires and pages in great numbers, and lifted up the fallen men and bare them away to places of safe harborage. And likewise attendants ran and gathered up the cantels of armor and the broken spears, and bare them away to the barriers, so that, by and by, the field was altogether cleared once more.

Then all those who gazed down upon that meadow gave loud acclaim with great joyousness of heart, for such a noble and glorious contest at arms in friendly assay had hardly ever been beheld in all that realm before.

Now turn we unto Sir Kay; for in this assault he had conducted himself with such credit that no knight who was there had done better than he, and maybe no one had done so well as he. For, though two opponents at once had directed their spears against him, yet he had successfully resisted their assault. And one of those two he smote so violently in the midst of his defences that he had lifted that assailant entirely over the crupper of the horse which he rode, and had flung him down to the distance of half a spear's length behind his steed, so that the fallen knight had rolled thrice over in the dust ere he ceased to fall.

And when those of Sir Kay's party who were nigh to him beheld what he did, they gave him loud and vehement acclaim, and that in such measure that Sir Kay was wonderfully well satisfied and pleased at heart.

And, indeed, it is to be said that at that time there was hardly any knight in all the world who was so excellent in deeds of arms as Sir Kay. And though there afterward came knights of much greater renown and of more glorious achievement (as shall be hereinafter recorded in good season), yet at that time Sir Kay was reckoned by many to be one of the most wonderfully puissant knights (whether errant or in battle) in all of that realm.

So was that course of the combat run to the great pleasure and satisfaction of all who beheld it, and more especially of Sir Kay and his friends. And after it had been completed the two parties in array returned each to its assigned station once more.

And when they had come there, each knight delivered up his spear unto his esquire. For the assault which was next to be made was to be undertaken with swords, wherefore all lances and other weapons were to be put away; such being the order of that courteous and gentle bout at arms.

Accordingly, when the herald again blew upon his trumpet, each knight drew his weapon with such readiness for battle that there was a great splendor of blades all flashing in the air at once. And when the herald blew a second time each party pushed forward to the contest with great nobleness of heart and eagerness of spirit, every knight being moved with intent to engage his oppugnant with all the might and main that lay in him.

Then immediately began so fierce a battle that if those knights had been very enemies of long standing instead of friendly contestants, the blows which they delivered the one upon the other could not have been more vehement as to strength or more astonishing to gaze upon.

And in this affair likewise Sir Kay approved himself to be so extraordinary a champion that his like was nowhere to be seen in all that field; for he violently smote down five knights, the one after the other, ere he was stayed in his advance.

Wherefore, beholding him to be doing work of such a sort, several of the knights of the other party endeavored to come at him with intent to meet him in his advance.

Amongst these was a certain knight, hight Sir Balamorgineas, who was so huge of frame that he rode head and shoulders above any other knight. And he was possessed of such extraordinary strength that it was believed that he could successfully withstand the assault of three ordinary knights at one time. Wherefore when this knight beheld the work that Sir Kay did, he cried out to him, "Ho! ho! Sir Knight of the black gryphon, turn thou hitherward and do a battle with me!"

Now when Sir Kay beheld Sir Balamorgineas to be minded to come against him in that wise – very threateningly and minded to do him battle – he turned him toward his enemy with great cheerfulness of spirit. For at that time Sir Kay was very full of youthful fire and reckoned nothing of assaulting any enemy who might demand battle of him.

(So it was at that time. But it after befell, when he became Seneschal, and when other and mightier knights appeared at the court of the King, that he would sometimes avoid an encounter with such a knight as Sir Launcelot, or Sir Pellias, or Sir Marhaus, or Sir Gawaine, if he might do so with credit to his honor.)

So, being very full of the spirit of youth, he turned him with great lustiness of heart, altogether inflamed with the eagerness and fury of battle. And he cried out in a great voice, "Very well, I will do battle with thee, and I will cast thee down like thy fellows!" And therewith he smote with wonderful fierceness at Sir Balamorgineas, and that with all his might. And Sir Balamorgineas received the stroke upon his helmet and was altogether bewildered by the fury thereof, for he had never felt its like before that time. Wherefore his brains swam so light that it was necessary for him to hold to the horn of his saddle to save himself from falling.

But it was a great pity for Sir Kay that, with the fierceness of the blow, his sword-blade snapped short at the haft, flying so high in the air that it appeared to overtop the turrets of the cathedral in its flight. Yet so it happened, and thus it befell that Sir Kay was left without any weapon. Yet it was thought that, because of that stroke, he had Sir Balamorgineas entirely at his mercy, and that if he could have struck another blow with his sword he might easily have overcome him.

But as it was, Sir Balamorgineas presently so far recovered himself that he perceived his enemy to be altogether at his mercy; wherefore, being filled beyond measure with rage because of the blow he had received, he pushed against Sir Kay with intent to smite him down in a violent assault.

In this pass it would maybe have gone very ill with Sir Kay but that three of his companions in arms, perceiving the extreme peril in which he lay, thrust in betwixt him and Sir Balamorgineas with intent to take upon themselves the assault of that knight and so to save Sir Kay from overthrow. This they did with such success that Sir Kay was able to push out from the press and to escape to the barriers without suffering any further harm at the hands of his enemies.

Now when he reached the barrier, his esquire, young Arthur, came running to him with a goblet of spiced wine. And Sir Kay opened the umbril of his helmet for to drink, for he was athirst beyond measure. And, lo! his face was all covered over with blood and sweat, and he was so a-drought with battle that his tongue clave to the roof of his mouth and he could not speak. But when he had drunk of the draught that Arthur gave him, his tongue was loosened and he cried out to the young man in a loud and violent voice: "Ho! ho! Brother, get me another sword for to do battle, for I am assuredly winning for our house much glory this day!" And Arthur said, "Where shall I get thee a sword?" And Kay said, "Make haste unto our father's pavilion and fetch me thence another sword, for this which I have is broken." And Arthur said, "I will do so with all speed," and thereupon he set hand to the barrier and leaped over it into the alleyway beyond. And he ran down the alleyway with all the speed that he was able with intent to fulfill that task which his brother had bidden him to undertake; and with like speed he ran to that pavilion that his father had set up in the meadows.

But when he came to the pavilion of Sir Ector he found no one there, for all the attendants had betaken themselves unto the tournament. And neither could he find any sword fit for his brother's handling, wherefore he was put to a great pass to know what to do in that matter.

In this extremity he bethought him of that sword that stood thrust into the anvil before the cathedral, and it appeared to him that such a sword as that would suit his brother's purposes very well. Wherefore he said to himself, "I will go thither and get that sword if I am able to do so, for it will assuredly do very well for my brother for to finish his battle withal." Whereupon he ran with all speed to the cathedral. And when he had come there he discovered that no one was there upon guard at the block of marble, as had heretofore been the case, for all who had been upon guard had betaken themselves unto the contest of arms that was toward. And the anvil and the sword stood where he could reach them. So, there being no one to stay young Arthur, he leaped up upon the block of marble and laid his hands unto the hilt of the sword. And he bent his body and drew upon the sword very strongly, and, lo! it came forth from the anvil with wonderful smoothness and ease, and he held the sword in his hand, and it was his.

And when he had got the sword in that way, he wrapped it in his cloak so that no one might see it (for it shone with an exceeding brightness and splendor) and he leaped down from the block of marble stone and hastened with it unto the field of battle.

Now when Arthur had entered into that meadow once more, he found Sir Kay awaiting his coming with great impatience of spirit. And when Sir Kay saw him he cried out, very vehemently, "Hast thou got a sword?" And Arthur said, "Yea, I have one here." Thereupon he opened his cloak and showed Sir Kay what sword it was he had brought.

Now when Sir Kay beheld the sword he immediately knew it, and he wist not what to think or what to say, wherefore he stood for a while, like one turned into a stone, looking upon that sword. Then in a while he said, in a very strange voice "Where got ye that sword?" And Arthur looked upon his brother and he beheld that his countenance was greatly disturbed, and that his face was altogether as white as wax. And he said, "Brother, what ails thee that thou lookest so strangely. I will tell the entire truth. I could find no sword in our father's pavilion, wherefore I bethought me of that sword that stood in the anvil upon the marble cube before the cathedral. So I went thither and made assay for to draw it forth, and it came forth with wonderful ease. So, when I had drawn it out, I wrapped it in my cloak and brought it hither unto thee as thou beholdest."

Then Sir Kay turned his thoughts inward and communed with himself in this wise, "Lo! my brother Arthur is as yet hardly more than a child. And he is, moreover, exceedingly innocent. Therefore he knoweth not what he hath done in this nor what the doing thereof signifieth. Now, since he hath achieved this weapon, why should I not myself lay claim to that achievement, and so obtain the glory which it signifieth." Whereupon he presently aroused himself, and he said to Arthur, "Give the sword and the cloak to me," and Arthur did as his brother commanded. And when he had done so Sir Kay said to him, "Tell no man of this but keep it privy in thine own heart. Meantime go thou to our father where he sits at the lists and bid come straightaway unto the pavilion where we have taken up our inn."

And Arthur did as Sir Kay commanded him, greatly possessed with wonder that his brother should be so disturbed in spirit as he had appeared to be. For he wist not what he had done in drawing out that sword from the anvil, nor did he know of what great things should arise from that little thing, for so it is in this world that a man sometimes approves himself to be worthy of such a great trust as that, and yet, in lowliness of spirit, he is yet altogether unaware that he is worthy thereof. And so it was with young Arthur at that time.

III

So Arthur made haste to that part of the lists where Sir Ector sat with the people of his household. And he stood before his father and said, "Sire, my brother Kay hath sent me hitherward for to bid thee come straightway unto the pavilion where we have taken up our inn. And, truly, I think something very extraordinary hath befallen, for my brother Kay hath such a countenance as I never saw him wear."

Then Sir Ector marvelled very greatly what it was that should cause Sir Kay to quit that battle and to summon him at such a time, wherefore he arose from where he sat and went with Arthur. And they went to the pavilion, and when he had come there, behold! Sir Kay was standing in the midst of the pavilion. And Sir Ector saw that his face was as white as ashes of wood and that his eyes shone with a wonderful brightness. And Sir Ector said, "My son, what ails thee?" whereunto Sir Kay made reply, "Sire, here is a very wonderful matter." Therewith he took his father by the hand and brought him to the table that stood in the pavilion. And upon the table there lay a cloak and there was something within the cloak. Then Sir Kay opened the cloak and, lo! there lay the sword of the anvil, and the hilt thereof and the blade thereof glistered with exceeding splendor.

And Sir Ector immediately knew that sword and whence it came. Wherefore he was filled with such astonishment that he wist not what to do. And for a while his tongue refused to speak, and after a while he found speech and cried out aloud in a great voice, "What is this that mine eyes behold!"

To this Sir Kay made reply, "Sire. I have that sword which stood a while since embedded in the anvil that stands upon the cube of marble stone before the great cathedral. Wherefore I demand that thou tellest me what this may foretend?"

Then Sir Ector said, "How came you by that sword?"

And for a while Sir Kay was silent, but after a while he said, "Sire, I brake my sword in that battle which of late I fought, whereupon I found me this sword in its stead."

Then Sir Ector was altogether bemazed and knew not whether to believe what his ears heard. And after awhile he said, "If so be that thou didst draw forth this sword from the anvil, then it must also be that thou art rightwise King of Britain, for so the saying of the sword proclaimeth. But if thou didst indeed draw it forth from the anvil, then it will be that thou shalt as easily be able for to thrust it back again into that place from whence thou didst take it."

At this a great trouble of spirit fell upon Sir Kay, and he cried out in a very loud voice, "Who may do such a thing as that, and who could perform so great a miracle as to thrust a sword into solid iron." Whereunto Sir Ector made reply, "Such a miracle is no greater than the miracle that thou hast performed in drawing it out from its embedment. For who ever heard that a man could draw forth a sword from a place and yet would not thrust it back whence he drew it?"

Then Sir Kay wist not what to say to his father, and he greatly feared that he should not be able to perform that miracle. But, nevertheless, he took what comfort to himself he was able, saying, "If my young brother Arthur was able to perform this miracle why should I not do a miracle of a like sort, for, assuredly, I am not less worthy than he. Wherefore if he drew the sword forth with such ease, it may be that I with equal ease shall be able to thrust it back into its place again." Accordingly he took such comfort to himself in these thoughts as he was able.

So he wrapped the sword in the cloak again, and when he had done so he and Sir Ector went forth from the pavilion and betook their way unto where was the marble stone and the anvil before the cathedral. And Arthur went with his father and his brother and they forebade him not. And when they had come to that place where the sword had been, Sir Kay mounted upon the cube of marble stone and beheld the face of the anvil And lo! the face of the anvil was altogether smooth and without a scratch or scar of any sort. And Sir Kay said to himself, "What is this my father would have me do! What man is there in life who could thrust a sword-blade into a solid anvil of iron?" But, ne'theless, he could not withdraw from that impossible undertaking, but was constrained to assay that miracle, wherefore he set the point of the sword to the iron and bore upon it with all his strength. But it was impossible for him to accomplish that thing, and though he endeavored with all his might with the sword against the face of the anvil, yet did he not pierce the iron even to the breadth of a hair.

So, after he had thus assayed for a great while, he at last ceased what he did and came down from where he stood. And he said to his father, "Sire, no man in life may perform that miracle."

Unto this Sir Ector made reply, "How is it possible then that thou couldst have drawn out that sword as thou sayst and yet cannot put it back again?"

Then young Arthur lifted up his voice and said, "My father, have I thy leave to speak?" And Sir Ector said, "Speak, my son." And Arthur said, "I would that I might assay to handle that sword?" Whereunto Sir Ector replied, "By what authority wouldst thou handle that sword?" And Arthur said, "Because it was I who drew that sword forth from the anvil for my brother. Wherefore, as thou sayest, to draw it forth is not more difficult than to thrust it back again. So I believe that I shall be able to set it back into the iron whence I drew it."

Then Sir Ector gazed upon young Arthur in such a strange manner that Arthur wist not why he looked at him in that wise. Wherefore he cried out, "Sire, why dost thou gaze so strangely upon me? Has thou anger against me?" Whereunto Sir Ector made reply, "In the sight of God, my son, I have no anger against thee." Then he said, "If thou hast a desire to handle the sword, thou mayst assuredly make assay of that miracle."

So Arthur took the sword from his brother Kay and he leaped up upon the marble stone. And he set the point of the sword upon the anvil and bare very strongly upon it and lo! the sword penetrated very smoothly into the centre of the anvil until it stood midway deep therein, and there it stood fast. And after he had performed that miracle he drew the sword forth again very swiftly and easily, and then thrust it back again once more as he had done before.

But when Sir Ector beheld what Arthur did, he cried out in a voice of exceeding loudness, "Lord! Lord! what is the miracle mine eyes behold!" And when Arthur came down from the cube of marble stone, Sir Ector kneeled down before him and set his hands together, palm to palm.

But when Arthur beheld what his father did, he cried out aloud like one in a great measure of pain; and he said, "My father! my father! why dost thou kneel down to me?"

To him Sir Ector made reply, "I am not thy father, and now it is made manifest that thou art assuredly of very exalted race and that the blood of kings flows in thy veins, else thou couldst not have handled that sword as thou hast done."

Then Arthur fell a-weeping beyond all measure and he cried out as with great agony of spirit, "Father! father! what is this thou sayst? I beseech thee to arise and not to kneel unto me."

So Sir Ector arose from his knees and stood before the face of

Arthur, and he said, "Arthur, why dost thou weep?" And Arthur said, "Because I am afeard."

Now all this while Sir Kay had stood near by and he could neither move nor speak, but stood like one entranced, and he said to himself, "What is this? Is my brother a King?"

Then Sir Ector spake, saying, "Arthur, the time hath come for thee to know thyself, for the true circumstances of thy life have, heretofore, been altogether hidden from thee.

"Now I do confess everything to thee in this wise: that eighteen year ago there came to me a certain man very wise and high in favor with Uther-Pendragon and that man was the Enchanter Merlin. And Merlin showed me the signet ring of Uther-Pendragon and he commanded me by virtue of that ring that I should be at a certain assigned place at a particular time which he nominated; and the place which he assigned was the postern gate of Uther-Pendragon's castle; and the time which he named was midnight of that very day.

"And he bade me tell no man aught concerning those things which he communicated to me, and so I kept his counsel as he desired me to do.

"So I went to that postern gate at midnight as Merlin had commanded, and at that place there came unto me Merlin and another man, and the other man was Sir Ulfius, who was the chief knight of Uther-Pendragon's household. And I tell thee that these two worthies stood nigher unto Uther-Pendragon than any other men in all of the world.

"Now when those two came unto me, I perceived that Merlin bare in his arms a certain thing wrapped in a scarlet mantle of fine texture. And he opened the folds of the mantle and, lo! I beheld a child not long born and wrapped in swaddling clothes. And I saw the child in the light of a lanthorn which Sir Ulfius bare, and I perceived that he was very fair of face and large of bone – and thou wert that child.

"Then Merlin commanded me in this wise: that I was to take that child and that I should rear him as mine own; and he said that the child was to be called by the name of Arthur; and he said that no one in all the world was to know otherwise than that the child was mine own. And I told Merlin that I would do as he would have me, whereupon I took the child and bare it away with me. And I proclaimed that the child was mine own, and all over the world believed my words, wherefore no one ever knew otherwise than that thou wert mine own son. And that lady who was my wife, when she died she took that secret with her unto Paradise,

and since then until now no one in all the world knew aught of
this matter but I and those two aforementioned worthies.

"Nor have I until now ever known aught of who was thy father;
but now I do suspect who he was and that thou hast in thy veins
very high and kingly blood. And I do have in mind that perhaps
thy father was Uther-Pendragon himself. For who but the son of
Uther-Pendragon could have drawn forth that sword from out of
the anvil as thou hast done?"

Then, when Arthur heard that saying of his father's, he cried out
in a very loud and vehement voice, "Woe! Woe! Woe!" – saying
that word three times. And Sir Ector said, "Arthur, why art thou
woful?" And Arthur said, "Because I have lost my father, for I
would rather have my father than be a King!"

Now as these things passed, there came unto that place two men,
very tall and of a wonderfully noble and haughty appearance. And
when these two men had come nigh to where they were, Arthur
and Sir Ector and Sir Kay perceived that one of them was the
Enchanter Merlin and that the other was Sir Ulfius – for those
two men were very famous and well known unto all the world.
And when those two had come to where were the three, Merlin
spake, saying, "What cheer?" And Sir Ector made answer, "Here
is cheer of a very wonderful sort; for, behold, Merlin! this is that
child that thou didst bring unto me eighteen years ago, and, lo!
thou seest he hath grown unto manhood."

Then Merlin said, "Sir Ector, I know very well who is this youth,
for I have kept diligent watch over him for all this time. And I
know that in him lieth the hope of Britain. Moreover, I tell thee
that even to-day within the surface of an enchanted looking-glass
I have beheld all that he hath done since the morning; and I know
how he drew forth the sword from the anvil, and how he thrust it
back again; and I know how he drew it forth and thrust it back a
second time. And I know all that thou hast been saying unto him
this while; wherefore I also do now avouch that thou hast told
him the very truth. And, lo! the spirit of prophecy is upon me
and I do foresee into the future that thou, Arthur, shall become
the greatest and most famous King that ever lived in Britain; and
I do foresee that many knights of extraordinary excellence shall
gather about thee and that men shall tell of their marvellous deeds
as long as this land shall continue, and I do foresee that through
these knights thy reign shall be full of splendor and glory; and I
do foresee that the most marvellous adventure of the Holy Grail
shall be achieved by three of the knights of thy Court, and that

to thy lasting renown, who shall be the King under whose reign the holy cup shall be achieved. All these things I foresee; and, lo! the time is now at hand when the glory of thy House shall again be made manifest unto the world, and all the people of this land shall rejoice in thee and thy kinghood. Wherefore, Sir Ector, for these three days to come, I do charge it upon thee that thou do guard this young man as the apple of thine eye, for in him doth lie the hope and salvation of all this realm."

Then Sir Ector lifted up his voice and cried unto Arthur, "A boon! a boon!" And Arthur said, "Alas! how is this? Dost thou, my father, ask a boon of me who may have all in the world that is mine to give? Ask what thou wilt and it is thine!" Then Sir Ector said, "I do beseech this of thee: that when thou art King thy brother Kay may be Seneschal of all this realm." And Arthur said, "It shall be as thou dost ask." And he said, "As for thee, it shall be still better with thee, for thou shalt be my father unto the end!" Whereupon so saying, he took Sir Ector's head into his hands and he kissed Sir Ector upon the forehead and upon the cheeks, and so sealed his plighted word.

But all this while Sir Kay had stood like unto one struck by thunder, and he wist not whether to be uplifted unto the skies or to be cast down into the depths, that his young brother should thus have been passed by him and exalted unto that extraordinary altitude of fortune. Wherefore he stood like to one bereft of life and motion.

And let it here be said that Arthur fulfilled all that he had thus promised to his father – for, in after times, he made Sir Kay his Seneschal, and Sir Ector was to him a father until the day of his death, which same befell five years from that time.

IV

So when the morning of Christmas day had come, many thousands of folk of all qualities, both gentle and simple, gathered together in front of the cathedral for to behold the assay of that sword.

Now there had been a canopy of embroidered cloth of divers colors spread above the sword and the anvil, and a platform had been built around about the cube of marble stone. And nigh unto that place there had been a throne for the Archbishop established; for the Archbishop was to overlook that assay and to see that every circumstance was fulfilled with due equity and circumspection.

So, when the morning was half gone by, the Archbishop himself came with great pomp of estate and took his seat upon the high throne that had been placed for him, and all his court of clerks and knights gathered about him, so that he presented a very proud and excellent appearance of courtliness.

Now unto that assay there had gathered nineteen kings and sixteen dukes, and each of these was of such noble and exalted estate that he entertained high hopes that he would that day be approved before the world to be the right king and overlord of all Britain. Wherefore after the Archbishop had established himself upon his throne, there came several of these and made demand that he should straightway put that matter to the test. So the Archbishop commanded his herald for to sound a trumpet, and to bid all who had the right to make assay of the sword to come unto that adventure, and the herald did according as the Archbishop ordered.

And when the herald had sounded his trumpet there immediately appeared the first of those kings to make trial of the sword, and he who came was King Lot of Orkney and the Isles. With King Lot there came eleven knights and five esquires, so that he appeared in very noble estate before the eyes of all. And when King Lot had arrived at that place, he mounted the platform. And first he saluted the Archbishop, and then he laid his hands to the pommel of the sword in the sight of all. And he bent his body and drew upon the sword with great strength, but he could not move the blade in the anvil even so much as the breadth of a hair, for it stood as fast as the iron in which it was planted. And after that first assay he tried three times more, but still he was altogether unable to move the blade in the iron. Then, after that he had thus four times made assay, he ceased his endeavor and came down from that place. And he was filled with great anger and indignation that he had not succeeded in his endeavor.

And after King Lot there came his brother-in-law, King Urien of Gore, and he also made assay in the same wise as King Lot had done. But neither did he succeed any better than that other king. And after King Urien there came King Fion of Scotland, and after King Fion there came King Mark of Cornwall, and after King Mark there came King Ryence of North Wales, and after King Ryence there came King Leodegrance of Cameliard, and after him came all those other kings and dukes before numerated, and not one of all these was able to move the blade. And some of these high and mighty lords were filled with anger and indignation that they had not succeeded, and others were ashamed that they had failed in that undertaking before the eyes of all those who looked upon them. But whether they were angry or whether they were ashamed it in no wise helped their case.

Now when all the kings and dukes had thus failed in that adventure, the people who were there were very much astonished, and they said to one another, "How is this? If all those kings and dukes of very exalted estate have failed to achieve that adventure, who then may hope to succeed? For here have been all those who were most worthy of that high honor, and all have tried to draw that sword and all have failed. Who then is there now to come after these who may hope to succeed?"

And, likewise, those kings and dukes spoke together in the same manner. And by and by there came six of the most worthy – to wit, King Lot, King Urien, King Pellinore, King Ban, King Ryence, and Duke Clarence of Northumberland – and these stood before the throne of the Archbishop and spake to him in this wise: "Sir, here have all the kings and dukes of this realm striven before you for to draw forth that sword, and lo! not one of all those who have undertaken that thing hath succeeded in his undertaking. What, then, may we understand but that the enchanter Merlin hath set this adventure for to bring shame and discredit upon all of us who are here, and upon you, who are the head of the church in this realm? For who in all the world may hope to draw forth a sword-blade out from a bed of solid iron? Behold! it is beyond the power of any man. Is it not then plain to be seen that Merlin hath made a mock of us all? Now, therefore, lest all this great congregation should have been called here in vain, we do beseech you of your wisdom that you presently choose the one from among the kings here gathered, who may be best fitted to be overlord of this realm. And when ye shall have chosen him, we will promise to obey him in all things whatsoever he may ordain. Verily, such a choice as that will be better worth while than to spend time in this foolish task of striving to draw forth a sword out of an anvil which no man in all the world may draw forth."

Then was the Archbishop much troubled in spirit, for he said to himself, "Can it be sooth that Merlin hath deceived me, and hath made a mock of me and of all these kings and lordly folk? Surely this cannot be. For Merlin is passing wise, and he would not make a mock of all the realm for the sake of so sorry a jest as this would be. Certes he hath some intent in this of which we know naught, being of less wisdom than he – wherefore I will be patient for a while longer." Accordingly, having communed thus within himself, he spake aloud in this wise to those seven high lords: "Messires," he said, "I have yet faith that Merlin hath not deceived us, wherefore I pray your patience for one little while longer. For if, in the time a man may count five hundred twice over, no one cometh forward to perform this task, then will I, at your behest, proceed to choose one from amongst you and will proclaim him King and Overlord of all." For the Archbishop had faith that Merlin was about to immediately declare a king before them all.

Now leave we these and turn we unto Arthur and his father and brother.

For Merlin had bidden those three to abide in their pavilion until such time as he thought would be fit for them to come out thence. And that time being now come, Merlin and Sir Ulfius went to the pavilion of Sir Ector, and Merlin said, "Arthur, arise and come forth, for now the hour is come for thee to assay before the whole world that miracle which thou didst of late execute in privacy." So Arthur did as Merlin bade him to do, and he came forth from the pavilion with his father and his brother, and, lo! he was like one who walked in a dream.

So they five went down from thence toward the cathedral and unto that place of assay. And when they had come to the congregation there assembled, the people made way for them, greatly marvelling and saying to one another, "Who are these with the Enchanter Merlin and Sir Ulfius, and whence come they?" For all the world knew Merlin and Sir Ulfius, and they wist that here was something very extraordinary about to happen. And Arthur was clad all in flame-colored raiment embroidered with threads of silver, so that others of the people said, "Certes, that youth is very fair for to look upon; now who may he be?"

But Merlin said no word to any man, but he brought Arthur through the press unto that place where the Archbishop sat; and the press made way for him so that he was not stayed in his going. And when the Archbishop beheld Merlin come thus with those others, he arose and said, "Merlin, who are these whom thou bringest unto us, and what is their business here?" And Merlin said, "Lord, here is one come to make the assay of yonder sword." And the Archbishop said, "Which one is he?" and Merlin said, "This is he," and he laid his hand upon Arthur.

Then the Archbishop looked upon Arthur and he beheld that the youth was very comely of face, wherefore his heart went out unto Arthur and he loved him a very great deal. And the Archbishop said, "Merlin, by what right doth this young man come hither?"

And Merlin made reply, "Lord, he cometh hither by the best right that there is in the world; for he who standeth before thee clad in red is the true son of Uther-Pendragon and of his lawful wife, Queen Igraine."

Then the Archbishop cried out aloud in great amazement and those who stood nigh and who heard what Merlin said were so astonished that they wist not what to think. And the Archbishop said, "Merlin, what is this that thou tellest me? For who, until now, in all the world hath ever heard that Uther-Pendragon had a son?"

Unto this Merlin made reply: "No one hath ever known of such a thing until now, only a very few. For it was in this wise: When this child was born the spirit of prophecy lay upon me and I foresaw that Uther-Pendragon would die before a very great while. Wherefore I feared that the enemies of the King would lay violent hands upon the young child for the sake of his inheritance. So, at the King's behest, I and another took the young child from his mother and gave him unto a third, and that man received the kingly child and maintained him ever since as his own son. And as to the truth of these things there are others here who may attest the verity of them – for he who was with me when the young child was taken from his mother was Sir Ulfius, and he to whom he was entrusted was Sir Ector of Bonmaison – and those two witnesses, who are without any reproach, will avouch to the verity of that which I have asserted, for here they stand before thee to certify unto what I have said."

And Sir Ulfius and Sir Ector said, "All that Merlin hath spoken is true, and thereunto we do pledge our most faithful and sacred word of honor."

Then the Archbishop said, "Who is there may doubt the word of such honorable witnesses?" And he looked upon Arthur and smiled upon him.

Then Arthur said, "Have I then thy leave, Lord, to handle yonder sword?" And the Archbishop said, "Thou hast my leave, and may the grace of God go with thee to do thy endeavor."

Thereupon Arthur went to the cube of marble stone and he laid his hands upon the haft of the sword that was thrust into the anvil. And he bent his body and drew very strongly and, lo! the sword came forth with great ease and very smoothly. And when he had got the sword into his hands, he swung it about his head so that it flashed like lightning. And after he had swung it thus thrice about his head, he set the point thereof against the face of the anvil and bore upon it very strongly, and, behold! the sword slid very smoothly back again into that place where it had aforetime stood; and when it was there, midway deep, it stood fast where it was. And thus did Arthur successfully accomplish that marvellous miracle of the sword in the eyes of all the world.

Now when the people who were congregated at that place beheld this miracle performed before their faces, they lifted up their voices all together, and shouted so vehemently and with so huge a tumult of outcry that it was as though the whole earth rocked and trembled with the sound of their shouting.

And whiles they so shouted Arthur took hold of the sword again and drew it forth and swung it again, and again drave it back into the anvil. And when he had done that he drew it forth a third time and did the same thing as before. Thus it was that all those who were there beheld that miracle performed three times over.

And all the kings and dukes who were there were filled with great amazement, and they wist not what to think or to say when they beheld one who was little more than a boy perform that undertaking in which the best of them had failed. And some of them, seeing that miracle, were willing to acknowledge Arthur because of it, but others would not acknowledge him. These withdrew themselves and stood aloof; and as they stood thus apart, they said among themselves: "What is this and who can accredit such a thing that a beardless boy should be set before us all and should be made King and overlord of this great realm for to govern us. Nay! nay! we will have none of him for our King." And others said, "Is it not apparent that Merlin and Sir Ulfius are thus exalting this unknown boy so that they may elevate themselves along with him?" Thus these discontented kings spake among themselves, and of all of them the most bitter were King Lot and King Urien, who were brothers by marriage with Arthur.

Now when the Archbishop perceived the discontent of these kings and dukes, he said to them, "How now, Messires! Are ye not satisfied?" And they said, "We are not satisfied." And the Archbishop said, "What would ye have?" And they said, "We would have another sort of king for Britain than a beardless boy of whom no one knoweth and of whose birthright there are only three men to attest." And the Archbishop said, "What of that? Hath he not performed the miracle that ye yourselves assayed and failed to perform?"

But these high and mighty lords would not be satisfied, but with angry and averted faces they went away from that place, filled with wrath and indignation.

But others of these kings and dukes came and saluted Arthur and paid him court, giving him joy of that which he had achieved; and the chiefest of those who came thus unto him in friendliness was King Leodegrance of Cameliard. And all the multitude acknowledged him and crowded around that place shouting so that it sounded like to the noise of thunder.

Now all this while Sir Ector and Sir Kay had stood upon one side. And they were greatly weighed down by sorrow; for it appeared to them that Arthur had, of a sudden, been uplifted so far from their estate that they might never hope to approach him more. For now he was of kingly consequence and they but common knights. And, after awhile, Arthur beheld them where they stood with downcast looks, whereupon he straightway went to them and took first one and then the other by the hand and kissed each upon the cheek. Thereupon they were again very glad at being thus uplifted unto him.

And when Arthur departed from that place, great crowds of people followed after him so that the streets were altogether filled with the press of people. And the multitude continually gave him loud acclaim as the chosen King of England, and those who were nearest to him sought to touch the hem of his garments; wherefore the heart of Arthur was exceedingly uplifted with great joy and gladness, so that his soul took wing and flew like a bird into the sky.

THE WINNING
OF THE KINGDOM

Geoffrey of Monmouth

The person who first popularized the Arthurian story was Geoffrey of Monmouth who lived from c.1100 to 1155. In 1136, or thereabouts, he completed his Historia Regum Britanniae *or* The History of the Kings of Britain *which was a chronicle of the rulers of Britain from the earliest times down to the last British king, Cadwaladr in the seventh century. At the time Geoffrey's book was the equivalent of a best seller and the section that everyone loved was that dealing with the adventures of King Arthur. Geoffrey maintained that he was simply translating into Latin a book presented to him by the Archdeacon of Oxford which had been written in Celtic. This original manuscript has never come to light and many claim that Geoffrey made most of it up. Certainly Geoffrey knew how to tell a good story, and he no doubt embellished what he could for the benefit of his Norman masters. But did he make it all up? His book is totally unusable as history, since he gets even the simplest facts wrong, while many details are in the wrong order. Yet there are enough facts scattered through the book to suggest he was drawing on something. He doubtless relied much on the oral tradition. Despite his epithet, Geoffrey was more likely of Breton stock than Welsh, and the Arthurian legend was strong in Brittany – it was from the Breton legends in fact that Chrétien de Troyes later developed his Arthurian romances. The end result is a collection of snippets of fact hidden amongst great waves of fancy. The following extract tells how Arthur won his kingdom after he was elected to the kingship. What is important here is that Geoffrey did attempt to set his story of Arthur into an historical context, at a time when Britain was beset with military attacks from the Saxons, Picts and Irish (or Scots as they were then called), which Thomas Malory made no attempt to do. This episode, therefore, is probably the closest we'll get to an historical base for Arthur amongst the legends.*

After the death of Uther Pendragon the barons of Britain came together from their many provinces to the city of Silchester and there prevailed upon Dubricius, Archbishop of the City of Legions, that he should crown as their king, Arthur, the son of Uther. Much was the need upon them because when the Saxons learned of Uther's death they invited their fellow countrymen from Germany and under their leader, Duke Colgrin, were intent upon exterminating the Britons. They had already entirely subdued all that part of the island which stretches from the river Humber north as far as the sea at Caithness.

Dubricius lamented over the calamities befalling the land, called together his fellow bishops and bestowed the crown of the realm upon Arthur. At that time Arthur was a youth of fifteen years, of a courage and generosity beyond compare. His inborn goodness gave him such grace that he was beloved by almost all the peoples in the land. After his coronation he followed the ancient tradition of bestowing gifts upon his subjects and so free was he with his bounty that he ran short. But Arthur was brave as well as bountiful and he determined that he would not be lacking for long and would harry the Saxons so that he might recover their treasure to reward those retainers who served his own household. He rapidly had the courage of his conviction and he summoned together all the youths who had pledged allegiance to him and marched first on York.

As soon as Colgrin became aware of this he assembled together his army of Saxons, Scots and Picts and came with a mighty multitude to meet Arthur by the river Douglas where, by the time the battle came to an end, the greater part of both armies had been put to the sword. Arthur, however, won the day and, after pursuing Colgrin as far as York, besieged him within the city.

At that time Colgrin's brother, Baldulf, was camped by the coast awaiting the arrival of Duke Cheldric who was bringing reinforcements from Germany. Learning of his brother's plight,

Baldulf marched immediately upon York with six thousand men and decided to travel overnight so as to surprise Arthur. But Arthur was aware of Baldulf's plan and ordered Cador, Duke of Cornwall, to set off that same night with six hundred cavalry and three thousand soldiers. Cador surrounded the road down with the enemy was marching and took them by surprise. Many of Baldulf's men were cut to pieces and those who survived were forced to flee. Baldulf was distressed beyond measure that he was unable to help his brother and he pondered how he might make contact, so that between them they could devise a plan. Once he had assessed all other alternatives he shaved off his hair and beard, changed into the garb of a minstrel and strode up and down within the camp pretending to be a harpist. As no one suspected him he was able, little by little, to draw close to the city walls until he was able to make himself known to the besieged whereupon they lowered ropes and hauled him up into the city and reunited him with his brother, who was overjoyed.

However, neither Baldulf or Colgrin were able to determine a plan of escape and just as they were despairing news came to them that Duke Cheldric had landed with over six hundred ships full of stout warriors. When Arthur's counsellors heard of this they advised him to raise the siege for it would be dangerous to commit themselves to facing so large a force.

Arthur accepted the advice of his counsellors and withdrew his army to London. There his summoned all of the clergy and chief men of his realm and sought their advice. At last, by common agreement, they sent messengers to Hoel, King of Armorica, with news of the calamitous affairs in Britain. Hoel was Arthur's cousin, born to Boudic, king of the Armorican Britons. As soon as Hoel heard of his uncle's plight he ordered his fleet to be made ready and with fifteen thousand soldiers set sail at the next fair wind and landed at Southampton. Arthur welcomed him with all due honours and each man embraced the other over and over again.

A few days later they set forth for the city of Caerlindcoit, otherwise called Lincoln, which was under siege by the pagans and which lies on a hill between two rivers in the province of Lindsey. No sooner had they arrived than they did battle with the Saxons and the slaughter was great, for upon that day fell six thousand of them, some drowned in the rivers and some struck by deadly weapons. The surviving Saxons were dismayed, forsook the siege and fled. But Arthur pursued them relentlessly until they had reached the forest of Caledon where the enemy reassembled and did their best to make a stand. When the battle began they caused havoc amongst the British, defending themselves like men and avoiding the arrows of the Britons in the shelter given by the trees. When Arthur realized this he ordered that the trees in that part of the forest be felled and the trunks used to create a barrier in a circle about them, so that the Saxons might be beleaguered and starve to death. Arthur ordered his men to patrol the forest and stop the Saxons escaping. After three days the Saxons, lacking all food and dying of hunger begged permission to be freed on the understanding that they would leave behind all that they had pillaged, that they would return to Germany with nought but their ships, and would send Arthur further tribute from Germany. After taking counsel Arthur agreed to the terms and, taking hostages, allowed them to depart.

However, no sooner had the Saxons departed in their ships than they forsook their promise and turned back to Britain landing on the coast near Totnes. They took possession of the land, ravaged the countryside as far as the Severn Sea and killed a great many of the locals. They then marched upon Bath and laid siege to the city. When news of this reached Arthur he was both astonished and furious at their effrontery. He hanged the hostages without more ado and abandoned the expedition he had planned to repress the Picts and the Scots, and he hastened with his army to disperse the siege. Arthur was saddened that he had to leave behind his cousin Hoel in Alclud who was very ill. At length he reached Somerset and approached the siege. He spoke to his men: "For that these Saxons, of most impious and hateful name, have disdained to keep faith with me, I, keeping faith with my God, will endeavour this day to wreak revenge upon them for the blood of my countrymen. To arms, therefore, my warriors, to arms, and fall upon these traitors like men, for of a certain, with Christ's help, we cannot fail of victory!"

When Arthur had spoken, the holy Dubricius, Archbishop of the City of Legions, climbed to the top of a hill and cried out with a loud voice:

"You men, who are different from these Saxons by your Christian faith, take heed and be mindful of the loyalty you owe to your country and your fellow countrymen whose slaughter, by the treachery of the pagans, shall be an everlasting disgrace to you unless you do your utmost to defend them. Fight therefore for your country and if it be

that death overtakes you, suffer it willingly for your country's sake, for death itself is victory and a healing unto the soul, for he that shall have died for his fellow man does offer himself as a living sacrifice to God, and there is no doubt that hereafter he will follow in the footsteps of Christ who lay down His own life for His brothers. Therefore, whomsoever amongst you shall be slain in this battle, that death shall be as full penance and absolution of all his sins, provided he receives it willingly."

Thereupon, inspired by the words of the blessed Dubricius, Arthur's men hurried to arm themselves. Arthur himself put on a leather jerkin worthy of so noble a king, and placed upon his head a golden helmet with a crest carved in the semblance of a dragon. Across his shoulders he bore the shield that was named Pridwen; upon the inside of which was painted the image of the Blessed Mary, Mother of God, so that he might be constantly reminded of her. He girded himself with Caliburn, that best of swords, forged in the Isle of Avalon; and in his right hand he held his spear called Rón, a tall lance, stout and sturdy for slaughter.

Then Arthur organized his troops into companies and made assault upon the Saxons who, as usual, were ranked in wedge-shaped battalions. All that day they resisted the British advance. Finally, just verging on sunset, the Saxons occupied a nearby hill that might serve as a camp where they felt secure in their numbers. The next morning Arthur led an assault on the hill, losing many of his men on the way as the Saxons could inflict injuries more easily from their higher advantage. Yet the Britons reached the summit of the hill and engaged the enemy in hand-to-hand combat. The Saxons stood shoulder to shoulder and strove with all their endeavour to stand their ground. And so the battle continued almost all day until, at length, Arthur became angry at the slowness of his advance. He drew forth his sword Caliburn, cried aloud the name of the Blessed Mary, and charged forward at full speed into the thickest part of the enemy's ranks. Whomsoever he touched, calling upon God as he did so, he slew with a single blow; nor did he once slacken in his onslaught until he had slain four hundred and seventy men single-handed with his sword Caliburn. When the Britons beheld this, they followed him in close rank dealing slaughter on every side. Colgrin and Baldulf his brother fell amongst the first, and many thousands fell besides. When Cheldric saw the danger he fled with what troops remained.

With the King having won the victory, he ordered Cador, Duke of Cornwall, to pursue the enemy while he himself hastened his march back to Albany, for word had reached him that the Scots and the Picts were besieging Hoel in the city of Alclud, where he had laid sick and in ill health.

In the meanwhile the Duke of Cornwall, accompanied by ten thousand men, started from Bath, but was not minded at the outset to pursue the fleeing Saxons but deemed it better to make all speed to gain hold of their ships and thus prevent them from embarking. Once he had seized their boats he manned them with his best soldiers who could be trusted to ensure that no pagans came aboard. Then he made best haste to follow Arthur's orders and pursue the enemy, slaying all he overtook without mercy. As a consequence the Saxons, who had but a short time previously fought the Britons with the fury of a double thunderbolt, now sneaked away with fear in their hearts, seeking refuge in the depths of the forest, or into the mountains and caves, anywhere where they might gain some time. But they could find no hiding places and, with all shelter failing, they brought their shattered troops to the Isle of Thanet. There the Duke of Cornwall followed hard upon their heels and renewed the slaughter, smiting them down without mercy until after Cheldric had been slain. Only then did he take hostages and force the remainder to surrender.

With peace restored, Cador marched to Alclud where Arthur had already freed the town from the oppression of the barbarians. Arthur now led his army into Moray where the Scots and Picts were beleaguered, having sought refuge here after three battles against Arthur and Hoel and having three times suffered defeat. When the enemy had reached Loch Lomond they occupied the islands in the lake, thinking to find safe refuge. The lake contains sixty islands and receives the water of sixty rivers, although only a single river flows from it to the sea. Upon these islands are sixty crags, each of which bears an eyrie of eagles that gather here each year. These eagles are known to foretell of any prodigious event that is about to happen by all of them emitting a shrill scream together. Thus to these islands did the enemy flee, but to little avail. Arthur collected together a fleet and sailed around the river inlets for fifteen days, besieging the enemy until they began to die of hunger in their thousands.

While Arthur was killing the Picts and Scots in this way, Guillamur, the King of Ireland, arrived with a fleet and a large army of barbarians to bring help to those under siege. Arthur was obliged to raise the siege and turn his forces upon the Irish, whom he cut to pieces without mercy and forced to return to their own land. Having defeated the Irish he turned his attention again to the Scots and Picts, determined to wipe them out completely with the utmost cruelty. He spared no one, inasmuch as that at length all of the bishops of the miserable country, together with all their clergy, came unto Arthur barefoot, clutching the relics of their saints and the sacraments of their church, imploring the King's mercy for the safety of their people. They prayed for him to have pity on their forsaken people for he had inflicted enough suffering on them, and there was no need to slaughter the remaining few to the last man. They requested that the King allow them to retain a small tract of land whereon they would toil under perpetual bondage. When they had beseeched the King in such a way he was moved to tears and he agreed to their wishes and granted them his pardon.

With these matters ended, Hoel explored the loch and marvelled that there were so many islands, rivers and eyries and that there was the same number of each. And while he marvelled thus Arthur told him of another lake in the same province that was yet more marvellous. "It lies not far hence," he explained, "and it is twenty feet in breadth and the same measure in length, but is only five feet deep. Yet within this square, whether it is natural or man-made, there are four breeds of fish, and each fish will only be found in its one corner and not in the others.

"Moreover," Arthur continued, "there is a lake in Wales near the Severn known to the locals as Linligwan which, when the sea flows into it, is swallowed up as in a bottomless pit, and the lake never appears to be any more full despite the waters that flow into it. Yet when the tide ebbs away the lake spouts forth the waters it had swallowed as high as a mountain. If the people of that region should come near to the lake with their faces turned towards it so that the spray falls upon their clothing they will find it difficult to escape being sucked into the pool. Yet should they face away from the pool they need have no fear, even if they stand on the very brink."

With the Scots and Picts pardoned, Arthur made for York, there to celebrate the coming Christmas festival. But as he rode into the city he was grieved to see the churches in such a state of desolation. Samson, the Archbishop, had been driven out along with all the other holy men. The fury of the pagans had been so great that the half-burned churches no longer served for worship. Arthur immediately summoned an assembly of the clergy and the people and appointed his own chaplain, Pyramus, to the See. He re-built the churches and created religious convents for both men and women. He also restored to their titles the barons who had been driven out by the Saxons.

In York were three brothers born of the blood royal, Lot, Urian and Angusel, who had ruled as princes in these parts before the Saxon victories. Arthur was mindful of restoring them to their honours as he had with the barons. He therefore restored the kingship of the Scots to Angusel; the kingship of the people of Moray to Urian; and to Lot, who in the days of Aurelius Ambrosius had married Arthur's own sister and had become the father of Gawain and Mordred, he restored to the dukedom of Lothian and related territories.

At last, when he had re-established the state of the whole country in its ancient dignity he took unto him a wife born of a noble Roman family, by name Guinevere who, brought up and nurtured in the household of Duke Cador, did surpass in beauty all the other damsels in the entire island.

THE KNIGHT WITH
THE TWO SWORDS

John Steinbeck

Once Arthur has won his kingdom the legend takes over completely.
All we can surmise from the historical record, such as it is, is that
Arthur won such a decisive victory over the Saxons at Badon
(sometime between AD 495 and 516) that they retreated and
left Britain in relative peace for many years – the figures vary
from between twenty-five to forty. Certainly this does seem to be
true. There were significant advances by the Germanic invaders
in southern Britain and along the eastern coastline in the period
up to about AD 500 and then nothing further until about AD
540, when the Saxons began to emerge in strength to drive the
British back across Britain into the western and northern corners
in Scotland, Cumbria, Wales and Cornwall, and across the sea to
Brittany. There the Celtic races survived, and it was in all these areas
that the Arthurian legends grew and developed over the centuries
into a rich tapestry of tales which have become the single largest
hero-focused set of legends in existence. For much of the rest of
this book we are entirely in the land of legend.

John Steinbeck (1902–68) may, at first glance, seem out of place
in this volume, but Malory's Morte d' Arthur was special to him.
It was the first book he ever read and it captivated him. "Perhaps
a passionate love for the English language opened to me from this
one book," he later wrote. In 1958, after two years of reading
and research, Steinbeck began a modern translation of Malory.
"I wanted to set them down in plain present-day speech for my
own young sons, and for other sons not so young. If I can do this

and keep the wonder and magic, I shall be pleased and gratified."
Steinbeck did not complete the task, for he became so intoxicated
with it that it grew from a modern rendition to a major revision.
The completed portions were published as The Acts of King Arthur
and His Noble Knights *(1976), from which I have selected this early*
episode of the blood-crazed Sir Balin.

In the long and lawless time after Uther Pendragon's death and
before his son Arthur became king, in England and Wales, in
Cornwall and Scotland and the Outer Isles, many lords took
lawless power to themselves, and some of them refused to give
it up, so that Arthur's first kingly years were given to restoring
his realm by law, by order, and by force of arms.

One of his most persistent enemies was the Lord Royns of Wales
whose growing strength in the west and north was a constant threat
to the kingdom.

When Arthur held court at London, a faithful Knight rode in
with the news that Royns in his arrogance had raised a large army
and invaded the land, burning crops and houses and killing Arthur's
subjects as he came.

"If this is true, I must protect my people," Arthur said.

"It is true enough," said the Knight. "I myself saw the invaders
and their destructive work."

"Then I must fight this Royns and destroy him," said the king.
And he sent out an order to all loyal lords and knights and gentlemen
of arms to meet in general council at Camelot, where plans would be
made to defend the kingdom.

And when the barons and the knights had gathered and sat in
the great hall below the king, a damsel came before them saying
she was sent by the great lady Lyle of Avalon.

"What message do you bring?" asked Arthur.

Then the damsel opened her richly furred cloak and it was seen
that from her belt there hung a noble sword.

The king said, "It is not seemly for a maiden to go armed. Why
do you wear a sword?"

"I wear it because I have no choice," the damsel said. "And I
must wear it until it is taken from me by a knight who is brave and
honorable, of good repute and without stain. Only such a knight

may draw this sword from his scabbard. I have been to the camp of Lord Royns where I was told were good knights, but neither he nor any of his followers could draw the blade."

Arthur said, "Here are good men, and I myself will try to draw it, not that I am the best, but because if I try first my barons and knights will feel free to follow me."

Then Arthur grasped sheath and girdle and pulled eagerly at the sword, but it did not move.

"Sir," said the damsel, "You need not use strength. It will come out easily in the hands of the knight for whom it is destined."

Arthur turned to his men and said, "Now all of you try it one by one."

The damsel said, "Be sure, you who try, that you have no shame or guile or treachery before you try. Only a clean and unstained knight may draw it and he must be of noble blood on both his mother's and his father's side."

Then most of the gathered knights attempted to draw the sword and none succeeded. Then the maiden said sadly, "I believed that here I would find blameless men and the best knights in the world."

Arthur was displeased and he said, "These are as good or better knights than you will find anywhere. I am unhappy that it is not their fortune to help you."

A knight named Sir Balin of Northumberland had remained apart. It had been his misfortune in fair fight to kill a cousin of the king, and the quarrel being mis-represented, he had been a prisoner for half a year. Only recently had some of his friends explained the matter and had him released. He watched the trial anxiously, but because he had been in prison and because he was poor and his clothing worn and dirty, he did not come forward until all had tried and the damsel was ready to depart. Only then did Sir Balin call to her, saying, "Lady, I beg you out of your courtesy to let me try. I know I am poorly dressed, but I feel in my heart that I may succeed."

The damsel looked at his ragged cloak and she could not believe him a man of honor and of noble blood. She said, "Sir, why do you wish to put me to more pain when all of these noble knights have failed?"

Sir Balin said, "Fair lady, a man's worth is not in his clothing. Manhood and honor are hidden inside. And sometimes virtues are not known to everyone."

"That is the truth," said the damsel, "and I thank you for reminding me. Here, grasp the sword and see what you can do."

Then Balin went to her and drew the sword easily, and he looked at the shining blade and it pleased him very much. Then the king and many others applauded Sir Balin, but some of the knights were filled with jealous spite.

The damsel said, "You must be the best and most blameless knight I have found or you could not have done it. Now, gentle and courteous knight, please give me the sword again."

"No," said Balin, "I like this sword, and I will keep it until someone is able to take it from me by force."

"Do not keep it," the damsel cried. "It is not wise to keep it. If you do, you will use it to kill the best friend and the man you love best in the world. That sword will destroy you."

Balin said, "I will accept any adventure God sends me, Lady, but I will not return the sword to you."

"Then in a short time you will be sorry for it," the lady said. "I do not want the sword for myself. If you take it, the sword will destroy you and I pity you."

Then Sir Balin sent for his horse and armor and he begged the king's permission to depart.

Arthur said, "Do not leave us now. I know you are angered by your unjust imprisonment, but false evidence was brought against you. If I had known your honor and your bravery, I would have acted differently. Now, if you will stay in my court and in this fellowship, I will advance you and make amends."

"I thank Your Highness," said Balin. "Your bounty is well known. I have no resentment toward you, but I must go away and I beg that your grace may go with me."

"I am not glad of your departure," said the king. "I ask you, good sir, not to be long away from us. We shall welcome your return and I will repay you for the injustice done against you."

"God thank your good grace," replied the knight, and he made ready to depart. And there were some jealous men in the court who whispered that witchcraft rather than knightly virtue was responsible for his good fortune.

While Balin armed himself and his horse, the Lady of the Lake rode into Arthur's court, and she was richly dressed and well mounted. She saluted the king and then reminded him of the gift he had promised her when she gave him the sword of the lake.

"I remember my promise," said Arthur, "but I have forgotten the name of the sword, if you ever told it to me."

"It is called Excalibur," the lady said, "and that means Cut Steel."

"Thank you, lady," said the king. "And now, what gift do you ask? I will give you anything in my power."

Then the lady said savagely, "I want two heads – that of the knight who drew the sword and the head of the damsel who brought it here. I will not be content until I have both heads. That knight killed my brother and the damsel caused my father's death. This is my demand."

The king was taken aback at the ferocity. He said, "I cannot in honor kill these two for your vengeance. Ask for anything else and I will give it."

"I ask for nothing else," said the lady.

Now Balin was ready to depart and he saw the Lady of the Lake and knew her for the one who by secret craft had brought death to his mother three years before. And when he was told that she had demanded his head, he strode near to her and cried, "You are an evil thing. You want my head? I shall have yours." And he drew his sword and slashed her head from her body with one stroke.

"What have you done?" Arthur cried. "You have brought shame to me and to my court. I was in this lady's debt, and moreover she was under my protection. I can never forgive this outrage."

"My Lord," said Balin, "I am sorry for your displeasure, but not for my deed. This was an evil witch. By enchantment and sorcery she killed many good knights, and by craft and false-hood she caused my mother to be burned to death."

The king said, "No matter what your reason, you had no right to do this and in my presence. It was an ugly deed and an insult to me. Now leave my court. You are no longer welcome here."

Then Balin took up the head of the Lady of the Lake by the hair and carried it to his lodging, where his squire awaited him, and they mounted their horses and rode out of the town.

And Balin said, "I want you to take this head to my friends and relatives in Northumberland. Tell them my most dangerous enemy is dead. Tell them that I am free from prison and how I got this second sword."

"I am sad that you have done this," said the squire. "You are greatly to blame for losing the friendship of the king. No one doubts your courage, but you are a headstrong knight and when you choose a way you cannot change your course even if it lead to your destruction. That is your fault and your destiny."

Then Balin said, "I have thought of a way to win the king's affection. I will ride to the camp of his enemy Lord Royns and

I will kill him or be killed. If it should happen that I win, King Arthur will be my friend again."

The squire shook his head at such a desperate plan, but he said, "Sir, where shall I meet you?"

"In King Arthur's court," said Balin confidently, and he sent his squire away.

Meanwhile, the king and all his followers were sad and shamed at Balin's deed and they buried the Lady of the Lake richly and with all ceremony.

In the court at that time there was a knight who was most jealous of Balin for his success in drawing the magic sword. He was Sir Launceor, son of the King of Ireland, a proud and ambitious man who believed himself to be one of the best knights in the world. He asked the king's permission to ride after Sir Balin to avenge the insult to Arthur's dignity.

The king said, "Go – and do your best. I am angry with Balin. Wipe out the outrage to my court."

And when Sir Launceor had gone to his quarters, to make ready for the field, Merlin came before King Arthur, and he heard how the sword was drawn and how the Lady of the Lake was slaughtered.

The Merlin looked at the damsel of the sword who had remained in the court. And Merlin said, "Look at this damsel standing here. She is a false and evil woman and she cannot deny it. She has a brother, a brave knight and a good and true man. This damsel loved a knight and became his paramour. And her brother, to wipe away the shame, challenged her lover and killed him in fair fight. Then in her rage, this damsel took his sword to the lady Lyle of Avalon and asked help to be revenged on her own brother."

And Merlin said, "The lady Lyle took the sword and cast a spell on it and laid a curse on it. Only the best and the bravest of knights would be able to draw it from its sheath, and he who drew it would kill his brother with it." And Merlin turned again on the damsel. "This was your spiteful reason for coming here," he said. "Don't deny it. I know it as well as you do. I wish to God you had not come, for wherever you go you carry harm and death.

"The knight who drew the sword is the best and bravest, and the sword he drew will destroy him. For everything he does will turn to bitterness and death through no fault of his own. The curse of the sword has become his fate. My Lord," Merlin said to the king, "that good knight has little time to live, but before he dies he will do you a service you will long remember." And King Arthur listened in sad wonder.

By now Sir Launceor of Ireland had armed himself at all points. He dressed his shield on his shoulder and took a spear in his hand and he urged his horse at utmost speed along the path Sir Balin had taken. It was not long before he overtook his enemy on the top of a mountain. And Sir Launceor shouted, "Stop where you are or I will make you stop. Your shield will not protect you now."

Balin answered lightly, "You might better have remained at home. A man who threatens his enemy often finds his promise turns back on himself. From what court do you come?"

"From King Arthur's court," said the Irish knight. "And I come to avenge the insult you have put on the king this day."

Sir Balin said, "If I must fight you, I must. But believe me, sir, I am grieved that I have injured the king or any of his court. I know your duty is plain, but before we fight, know that I had no choice. The Lady of the Lake not only did me mortal injury but demanded my life as well."

Sir Launceor said, "Enough of talking. Make ready, for only one of us will leave this field."

Then they couched their spears and thundered together, and Launceor's spear splintered, but Balin's lanced through shield and armor and chest and the Irish knight went crashing to the ground. When Balin had turned his horse and drawn his sword, he saw his enemy lying dead on the grass. And then he heard galloping hooves and he saw a damsel ride toward them as fast as she could. When she drew up and saw Sir Launceor dead, she burst into wild sorrow.

"Balin!" she cried. "Two bodies you have killed in one heart and two hearts in one body and two souls you have released." Then she dismounted and took up her lover's sword and fell fainting to the ground. And when her senses returned she screamed her sorrow and Balin was filled with pain. He went to her and tried to take the sword from her, but she clung to it so desperately that for fear he might hurt her he released his hold. Then suddenly she reversed the sword and placed the pommel on the ground and drove her body on the point, and the blade pierced her and she died.

Balin stood with heavy heart and he was ashamed that he had caused her death. And he cried aloud, "What love there must have been between these two, and I have destroyed them!" He could not bear the sight of them, and he mounted and rode sadly away toward the forest.

In the distance he saw a knight approaching, and when he could see the device on the shield, Balin knew it was his brother, Balan. And when they met they tore off their helmets and kissed each other and wept for joy.

Balan said, "My brother, I could not have hoped to meet you so soon. I came upon a man at the castle of the four catapults, and he told me that you were released from prison and that he had seen you in King Arthur's court and I rode from Northumberland to look for you."

Then Balin told his brother about the damsel and the sword and how he had killed the Lady of the Lake and so angered the king, and he said, "Yonder a knight lies dead who was sent after me, and beside him his love who destroyed herself, and I am heavy-hearted and grieved."

"It is a sad thing," Balan said, "but you are a knight and you know you must accept whatever God ordains for you."

"I know that," said Balin, "but I am sorrowful that King Arthur is displeased with me. He is the best and greatest king who reigns on earth. And I will get back his love or leave my life."

"How will you do that, my brother?"

"I will tell you," said Balin. "King Arthur's enemy, Lord Royns, has laid siege to the castle Terrabil in Cornwall. I will ride there and prove my honor and courage against him."

"I hope it may be," Balan said. "I will go with you and venture my life with yours as a brother should."

"How good it is that you are here, dear brother," Balin said. "Let us ride on together."

As they talked a dwarf came riding from the direction of Camelot, and when he saw the bodies of the knight and his beloved damsel he tore his hair and cried out to the brothers, "Which of you has done this deed?"

"What right have you to ask?" said Balan.

"Because I want to know."

And Balin answered him, "It was I. I killed the knight in fair combat in self-defense and the damsel destroyed herself in sorrow, and I am grieved. For her sake I will serve all women while I live."

The dwarf said, "You have done great damage to yourself. This dead knight was the son of the King of Ireland. His kin will take vengeance on you. They will follow you all over the world until they have killed you."

"That does not frighten me," said Balin. "My pain is that I have doubly displeased my lord King Arthur by killing his knight."

Then King Mark of Cornwall came riding by and saw the bodies, and when he was told the story of the death, he said, "They must have loved each other truly. And I will see that they have a tomb in their memory." Then he ordered his men to pitch their tents and he searched the country for a place to bury the lovers. In a church nearby he had a great stone raised from the floor in front of the high altar and he buried the knight and his damsel together, and when the stone was lowered back, King Mark had words carved on it saying, "Here lies Sir Launceor, son of Ireland's king, slain in combat with Sir Balin and beside him his love the lady Colombe, who in sorrow slew herself with her lover's sword."

Merlin entered the church and he said to Balin, "Why did you not save this lady's life?"

"I swear I could not," said Balin, "I tried to save her but she was too quick."

"I am sorry for you," Merlin said. "In punishment for the death you are destined to strike the saddest blow since the lance pierced the side of our Lord Jesus Christ. With your stroke you will wound the best knight living and you will bring poverty and misery and despair to three kingdoms."

And Balin cried out, "This can't be true. If I believed it I would kill myself now and make you a liar."

"But you will not," said Merlin.

"What is my sin?" Balin demanded.

"Ill fortune," said Merlin. "Some call it fate." And suddenly he vanished.

And after a time the brothers took leave of King Mark.

"First, tell me your names," he asked.

And Balan answered, "You see that he wears two swords. Call him the Knight with the Two Swords."

Then the two brothers took their way towards the camp of Royns. And on a broad and windswept moor they came upon a stranger muffled in a cloak who asked them where they were going.

"Why should we tell you?" they replied, and Balin said, "Tell us your name, stranger."

"Why should I, when you are secret?" said the man.

"It's an evil sign when a man will not tell his name," said Balan.

"Think what you wish," the stranger said. "What would you think if I told you that you ride to find Lord Royns and that you will fail without my help?"

"I would think that you are Merlin, and if you are, I would ask your help."

"You must be brave, for you will need courage," said Merlin.

Sir Balin said, "Don't worry about courage. We will do what we can."

They came to the edge of a forest and dismounted in a dim and leafy hollow, and they unsaddled their horses and put them to graze. And the knights lay under the sheltering branches of the trees and fell asleep.

When it was midnight Merlin awakened them quietly. "Make ready quickly," he said. "Your chance is coming. Royns has stolen from his camp with only a bodyguard to pay a midnight visit of love to Lady de Vance."

From cover of the trees they saw horsemen coming.

"Which is Royns?" Balin asked.

"The tall one in the middle," Merlin said. "Hold back until they come abreast."

And when the cavalcade was passing in the starlit dark, the brothers charged out from their concealment and struck Royns from his saddle, and they turned on his startled men, striking right and left with their swords, and some went down and the rest turned tail and fled.

Then the brothers returned to the felled Royns to kill him, but he yielded and asked mercy. "Brave knights, do not murder me," he said. "My life is valuable to you and my death worth nothing."

"That is true," the brothers said, and they raised up the wounded Royns and helped him to his horse. And when they looked for Merlin he was gone, for he by his magic arts had flown ahead to Camelot. And he told Arthur that his worst enemy, Lord Royns, was overthrown and captured.

"By whom?" the king demanded.

"By two knights who wish your friendship and your grace more than anything in the world. They will be here in the morning and you will see who they are," Merlin said and he would not speak further.

Very early the two brothers brought their wounded prisoner, Royns, to the gates of Camelot and delivered him into the safekeeping of the warders and they rode away into the dawning day.

When it was reported, King Arthur went to his wounded enemy and he said, "Sir, you are a welcome sight to me. By what adventure have you come?"

"By a bitter adventure, my lord."

"Who took you?" the king asked.

"One who is called the Knight with the Two Swords and

his brother. They overturned me and swept away my body-guard."

Merlin broke in, "Now I can tell you, sir. It was that Balin who drew the cursed sword and his brother, Balan. Two better knights you will never find. The pity is that their fate is closing in and they have not long to live."

"He has put me in debt to him," said the king. "And I do not deserve kindness from Balin."

"He will do much more for you than this, my lord," said Merlin. "But I bring you news. You must prepare your knights for battle. Tomorrow before noon the forces of Royns's brother Nero will attack you. You have much to do now and I will leave you."

Then King Arthur mustered his knights quickly and rode toward the castle Terrabil. Nero was ready for him in the field with forces that outnumbered those of the king. Nero led the vanguard and he waited only for the arrival of King Lot with his army. But he waited in vain, for Merlin had gone to King Lot and held him enthralled with tales of wonder and of prophecy, while Arthur launched his attack on Nero. Sir Kay fought so well that day that the memory of his deeds has lived forever. And Sir Hervis de Revel of the line of Sir Thomas Malory distinguished himself as did Sir Tobinus Streat de Montroy. Into the battle Sir Balin and his brother raged so fiercely that it was said of them that they were either angels from heaven or devils from hell, depending on which side you held. And Arthur in the vanguard saw the brothers' actions and praised them above all his knights. And the king's forces prevailed and drove the enemy from the field and destroyed Nero's power.

A messenger rode to King Lot and reported the battle lost and Nero killed while Lot had listened to Merlin's tales. King Lot said, "I have been bewitched by this Merlin. If I had been there Arthur could not have won the day. This magician has fooled me and held me like a child listening to stories."

Merlin said, "I know that today one king must die, and much as I regret it, I would rather it were you than King Arthur," and Merlin vanished in the air.

Then King Lot gathered his leaders. "What should I do?" he asked. "Is it better to sue for peace or to fight? If Nero is defeated, half our army is gone."

A knight said, "King Arthur's men are weary with battle and their horses exhausted, while we are fresh. If we attack him now we have the advantage."

"If you all agree, we will fight," said King Lot. "I hope that you will do as well as I will try to do."

Then King Lot galloped to the field and charged Arthur's men, but they held firm and did not give ground.

King Lot, out of shame for his failure, held the forefront of his knights and fought like a devil raging, for he hated Arthur above all men. Once he had been the king's friend wedded to Arthur's half-sister. But when Arthur in ignorance seduced his friend's wife and got her with the child Mordred, King Lot's loyalty turned to hatred and he strove desperately to overcome his once friend.

As Merlin had foretold, Sir Pellinore, who once overthrew Arthur at the Fountain in the Forest, had become the king's loyal friend and fought in the first line of his knights. Sir Pellinore forced his horse through the press around King Lot and aimed a great swinging sword stroke at him. The blade glanced off and killed Lot's horse, and as he went down Pellinore struck him on the helm and drove him to the ground.

When King Lot's men saw him fallen, they gave up the fight and tried to flee, and many were taken and more were killed in fight.

When the bodies of the dead were gathered together, twelve great lords were found who had died serving Nero and King Lot. These were carried to St. Stephen's Church in Camelot for burial, while the lesser knights were interred nearby under a huge stone.

King Arthur buried Lot in a rich tomb separately, but the twelve great lords he placed together and raised a triumphal monument over them. Merlin by his arts made figures of the twelve lords in gilded copper and brass, in attitudes of defeat, and each figure held a candle which burned night and day. Above these effigies, Merlin placed a statue of King Arthur with a drawn sword held over his enemies' heads. And Merlin prophesied that the candles would burn until Arthur's death and at that moment would go out; and he made other prophecies that day of things to come.

Soon after this, Arthur, wearied with campaigns and governing, and sick of the dark, deep-walled rooms of castles, ordered his pavilion set up in a green meadow outside the walls where he might rest and recover his strength in the quiet and the sweet air. He laid himself down on a camp bed to sleep, but he had not closed his eyes when he heard a horse approaching and saw a knight riding near who spoke words of complaint and sorrow to himself.

As he passed the pavilion, the king called out to him, saying, "Come to me, good knight, and tell me the reason for your sadness."

The knight answered, "What good could that do? You cannot help me." And he rode on toward the castle of Meliot.

Then the king tried to sleep again but his curiosity had risen to keep him awake, and as he pondered, Sir Balin rode near, and when he saw King Arthur he dismounted and saluted his lord.

"You are always welcome," said the king. "But particularly now. A short time ago a knight went past and he was crying out in sorrow, and he would not answer when I asked the cause. If you wish to serve me, ride after this knight and bring him to me whether he wishes to come or not, for I am curious."

"I will bring him to you, my lord," Sir Balin said, "or else he will be more sad than he is."

And Balin mounted and cantered after the knight, and after a time he found him sitting under a tree with a damsel beside him. Sir Balin said, "Sir Knight, you come with me to King Arthur and tell him the cause of your sorrow."

"That I will not do," said the knight. "I would be in great danger if I did and you would gain nothing."

"Please come with me, sir," said Balin. "If you refuse I must fight you and I don't want to."

"I have told you my life is in danger. Will you promise to protect me?"

"I will protect you or die in the attempt," said Balin. And with that the knight mounted his horse and they rode away, leaving the damsel under the tree. As they came to King Arthur's tent, they heard the sound of a charging war horse but saw nothing, and suddenly the knight was hurled from his saddle by an invisible force, and he lay dying on the ground with a great spear through his body. And he gasped, "That was my danger – a knight named Garlon who has the art of invisibility. I was under your protection and you have failed me. Take my horse. He is better than yours. And go back to the damsel – she will lead you to my enemy and perhaps you may avenge me."

Balin cried, "On my honor and my knighthood I will. I swear it before God."

And with that the knight, Sir Harleus le Berbeus, died, and Balin pulled the truncheon of the spear from his body and rode sadly away, for he was grieved that he had not protected the knight as he had promised, and he understood at last why Arthur had been enraged at the death of the Lady of the Lake under his protection. And Balin felt a darkness of misfortune hanging over him. He found the damsel in the forest and gave her the truncheon of the spear that had killed her lover, and she carried it always, as a sign and a remembrance. She led Sir Balin on the quest he had accepted from the dying knight.

In the forest they came upon a knight fresh from hunting, who, seeing Balin's sorrow-clouded face, asked the reason for his pain and Balin curtly answered that he did not wish to speak of it.

The knight resented the discourtesy, saying, "If I were armed against men instead of stags, you would answer me."

Balin answered wearily, "I have no reason not to tell you," and he recounted his strange and fatal history. The knight was so moved by the tale that he begged leave to join him in the quest of vengeance. His name was Sir Peryne de Monte Belyarde, and he went to his house nearby and armed himself and joined them on their way. And as they rode past a little lonely hermitage and chapel in the forest, there came again the sound of charging hoofs and Sir Peryne fell with a spear through his body.

"Your story was true," he said. "The invisible enemy has slain me. You are a man fated to cause the destruction of your loved friends." And Sir Peryne died of his wounds.

Balin said in sorrow, "My enemy is something I cannot see. How can I challenge the invisible?"

Then the hermit helped him to carry the dead into the chapel and they buried him in pity and honor.

And afterward Balin and the damsel rode on until they came to a castle with strong defenses. Balin crossed the draw-bridge and entered first, and as he did the portcullis rattled down and held him prisoner, with the damsel outside, where many men attacked her with knives to kill her. Then Balin ran up to the top of the wall and he leaped into the moat far below, and the water broke his fall and saved him from injury. He crawled from the moat and drew his sword, but the attackers drew away and told him that they only followed the custom of the castle. They explained that the lady of the castle had long suffered a dreadful wasting sickness and the only cure for it was a silver dish of blood from the virgin daughter of a king and so it was their custom to take blood from every damsel who passed that way.

Balin said, "I am sure she will give you some of her blood, but you need not kill her to get it." Then he helped to lance her vein and they caught it in a silver dish, but it did not cure the lady wherefore it was thought that the damsel did not fulfill one or the other or both of the requirements. But because of the offering they were made welcome and given good cheer, and they rested for the night and in the morning took their way again. Four days they continued without adventure, and at last lodged in the house of a gentleman. And as they sat at their supper, they heard moans of pain from a chamber nearby and Balin asked about it.

"I will tell you about it," the gentleman said. "Recently at a jousting I rode against the brother of King Pelham. Twice I struck him from his horse and he was angry and threatened revenge against someone near to me. Then he made himself invisible and wounded my son, whom you hear crying out in pain. He will not be well until I have killed that evil knight and taken his blood."

"I know him well, but I have never seen him," Balin said. "He has killed two of my knights in the same way, and I would rather meet him in combat than have all the gold in the realm."

"I will tell you how to meet him," said the host. "His brother, King Pelham, has proclaimed a great feast within twenty days. And no knight may attend unless he brings his wife or his mistress. The king's brother, Garlon, is sure to be there."

"Then I will be there also," Balin said.

And in the morning the three started their journey and they rode for fifteen days until they came to Pelham's country, and they came to his castle on the day the feast began, and they stabled their horses and went to the great hall, but Balin's host was refused because he had brought neither wife nor paramour. But Balin was welcomed and taken to a chamber where he unarmed and bathed himself and servants brought him a rich robe to wear to the feasting. But then they asked him to leave his sword with his armor; Balin refused. He said, "In my country a knight must keep his sword with him always. If I cannot take it, I may not feast." Reluctantly they let him take his weapon, and he went into the great hall and sat among the knights, with his lady beside him.

Then Balin asked, "Is there a knight in this court named Garlon, brother of the king?"

"There he is now," said a man nearby. "Look, he is the one with the dark skin. He is a strange man and he has killed many knights because he has the secret of invisibility."

Balin stared at Garlon and considered what he should do, and he thought, "If I kill him now, I will not be able to escape, but if I do not I may never see him again, because he will not be visible."

Garlon had noticed Balin staring at him and it angered him. He rose from his place and came to Balin and slapped him in the face with the back of his hand and said, "I do not like you staring at me. Eat your meat, or do anything else you came to do."

"I will do what I came to do," Balin said and he drew his sword and cut off Garlon's head. Then he said to his lady, "Give me the truncheon that killed your love," and he took it from her and drove it through Garlon's body, crying, "You killed a good knight with that. Now it sticks in you," and he called to his friend outside the hall, "Here is blood enough to cure your son."

The assembled knights had sat astonished, but now they leaped to their feet to set on Balin. King Pelham stood up from the high table, saying, "You have killed my brother. You must die."

And Balin taunted him, "Very well – do it yourself if you are brave enough."

"You are right," Pelham said. "Stand back, you knights. I will kill him myself for my brother's sake."

Pelham took a huge battle ax from the wall and advanced and aimed a blow and Balin parried with his sword, but the heavy ax broke his sword in two so that he was weaponless. Then Balin ran from the hall with Pelham following. He went from chamber to chamber looking for a weapon, but he could not find one and always he could hear King Pelham following.

At last Balin came to a chamber and saw a wonder. The room was hung with cloth of gold figured with mystic holy symbols and a bed was curtained with marvelous curtains. On the bed under a cover woven of golden thread lay the perfect body of an ancient and venerable man, while on a golden table beside the bed there stood a strangely wrought spear, a haft of wood, a lean iron shank, and a small, pointed head.

Balin heard Pelham's pursuing steps and he seized the spear and drove it into the side of his enemy. And at that moment an earthquake rumbled and the walls of the castle cracked outward and the roof fell in and Balin and King Pelham rolled in the tumbling rubble to the ground and they lay unconscious, pinned under stones and pieces of timber. Inside the castle most of the gathered knights were killed by the falling roof.

After a time Merlin appeared and cleared the stones from Balin and brought him to his senses. And he brought him a horse and told him to leave the country as quickly as he could.

But Balin said, "Where is my damsel?"

"She lies dead under the fallen castle," Merlin said.

"What caused this ruin?" Balin asked.

"You have fallen on a mystery," Merlin said. "Not long after Jesus Christ was crucified, Joseph, a merchant of Arimathea who gave our Lord his sepulcher, came sailing to this land bringing the sacred cup of the Last Supper filled with the holy blood and also that spear with which Longinus the Roman pierced the side of Jesus on the Cross. And Joseph brought these holy things to the Island of Glass in Avalon and there he built a church, the first in all this land. That was Joseph's body on the bed and that Longinus's spear, and with it you wounded Pelham, Joseph's descendant, and it was the dolorous stroke I spoke of long ago. And because you have done this, a blight of sickness and hunger and despair will spread over the land."

Balin cried, "It is not fair. It is not just."

"Misfortune is not fair, fate is not just, but they exist just the same," said Merlin, and he bade Balin farewell. "For," he said, "we will not meet again in this world."

Then Balin rode away through the blighted land and he saw people dead and dying on every side, and the living cried after him, "Balin, you are the cause of this destruction. You will be punished for it." And Balin in anguish pushed his horse to leave the destroyed country. He rode eight days, fleeing from the evil, and he was glad when he passed out of the blighted land and into a fair, untroubled forest. His spirit awakened and threw off his gloomy garments. Above the tops of the trees in a fair valley he saw the battlements of a slender tower and turned his horse toward it. Beside the tower a great horse was tied to a tree and on the ground a handsome, well-made knight sat mourning aloud to himself.

And because he had given death and suffering to so many, Balin wished to make amends. He said to the knight, "God save you. Why are you sad? Tell me and I will try my best to help you."

The knight said, "Telling you would give me more pain that I have already."

Then Balin walked a little apart and looked at the tethered horse and its equipment, and he heard the knight say, "Oh, my lady, why have you broken your promise to meet me here at noon. You gave me my sword, a deadly gift, for I may kill myself with it for love of you." And the knight drew his shining sword from its sheath.

Then Balin moved quickly and grasped his wrist.

"Let me go or I will kill you," cried the knight.

"There is no good in that. I know now about your lady and I promise to bring her to you if you will tell me where she is."

"Who are you?" the knight demanded.

"Sir Balin."

"I know your fame," said the knight. "You are the Knight with the Two Swords, and you are said to be one of the bravest of knights."

"What is your name?"

"I am Sir Garnish of the Mountain. I am a poor man's son, but because I served well in battle, Duke Harmel took me under his protection and knighted me and gave me lands. It is his daughter I love and I thought she loved me."

"How far away is she?" Balin asked.

"Only six miles."

"Then why do you sit here mourning? Let us go to her and find the reason for her failure."

Then they rode together until they came to a well-built castle with high walls and a moat. And Balin said, "Remain here and wait for me. I will go into the castle and try to find her."

Balin went into the castle and found no one about. He searched through the halls and the rooms and at last came to a lady's chamber, but her bed was empty. He looked from her window to a lovely little garden within the walls and on the grass under a laurel tree he saw the lady and a knight lying on a green silken cloth, and they had fallen asleep in a close embrace, their heads on a pillow of grass and sweet herbs. The lady was fair but her lover was an ugly man, hairy and heavy and uncouth.

Then Balin went quietly out through chambers and halls and at the castle gate he told Sir Garnish what he had seen and led him softly to the garden. And when the knight saw his lady in the arms of another, his heart drummed with passion and his veins burst and blood streamed from his nose and mouth. In his blinding rage he drew his sword and cut off the heads of the sleeping lovers. And suddenly the rage was gone and he was sick and weak. And he blamed Balin bitterly, saying, "You have brought sorrow to me on sorrow. If you had not brought me here, I would not have known."

Balin replied angrily, "Was it not better to know her for what she was and so be cured of loving her? I only did what I would want done for me."

"You have doubled my pain," Sir Garnish said. "You have caused me to kill what I loved most in the world and I cannot live," and suddenly he plunged his own bloody sword through his heart and fell dead beside the headless lovers.

The castle was quiet, and Balin knew that if he were found there he would be charged with murdering all three. He went quickly out of the castle and rode away among the forest trees and the thick darkness of his fate was on him and he felt the curtains of his life closing in on him so that he seemed to be riding in a mist of hopelessness.

After a time he came to a stone cross in the path and on it in letters of gold was written, LET NO KNIGHT RIDE ALONE ON THIS WAY. An old and white-haired man approached him as he read the words and he said, "Sir Balin, this is the boundary of your life. Turn back and you may save yourself." And the old man vanished.

Then Balin heard a hunting horn blowing the call that announces the death of a stag. And Balin said somberly, "That death call is for me. I am the quarry and I am not dead yet."

And suddenly a crowd of people clustered around him, a hundred lovely ladies and many knights in rich and glinting armor, and they welcomed him sweetly and petted and soothed him and led him to a castle nearby where they unarmed him and gave him a rich soft robe and led him to sit in the great hall where there was music and dancing and gaiety and brittle joy.

And when Balin was comforted the Lady of the Castle came to him and said, "Sir Knight with the Two Swords, it is the custom here that any passing stranger must joust with a knight who guards an island nearby."

Balin said, "It is an unhappy custom to force a knight to joust whether he wants to or not."

"It is only one knight. Is the great Balin afraid of one knight?"

"I don't think I am afraid, my lady," Balin said. "But a man who has traveled far can be weary and his horse worn out. My body is weary but my heart is fresh." And he said hopelessly, "If I must, I must, and I would be glad to find here my death and rest and peace."

Then a knight who stood nearby said, "I have looked at your armor. Your shield is small and the handles are loose. Take my shield. It is large and well made." And when Balin protested, the knight insisted, saying, "I beg you to take it for your safety."

Then Balin wearily armed himself and the knight brought his new and well-painted shield and forced it on him, and Balin was too weary and confused to argue, and he thought how his squire had said he was a headstrong knight and therein lay his trouble, and so he accepted the shield and mounted and rode slowly to a lake in which there was a small island so near to the castle that it was overlooked by the battlements. And ladies and knights were gathered on the walls to see the combat.

A boat big enough for horse and man was waiting at the waterside and Balin entered it and was rowed to the island, where a damsel stood waiting for him, and she said, "Sir Balin, why have you left your shield with your own device?"

"I don't know why," said Balin. "I am ground down with misfortune and my judgment all askew. I am sorry I ever came to this place, but since I am here I may as well go on. I would be ashamed to turn back. No. I will accept what comes to me, my death or my life."

Then from long habit in the field he rested his weapons and tightened the girth of his saddle. Then he mounted and said a prayer for himself and closed the visor of his helmet and rode toward a little habitation on the island, and the knights and ladies watched him from the tower.

Then a knight in red armor and red horse trappings rode toward him. It was Sir Balan, and when he saw that his opponent wore two swords, he thought it was his brother, but when he saw the device on the shield, he knew it could not be.

In dreadful silence the two knights couched their spears and crashed together, and both spears struck true and did not shatter, and both knights were flung to the ground and lay stunned. Balin was sorely bruised by the fall and his body ached with weariness. And Balan was the first to recover. He rose to his feet and came toward Balin and Balin staggered up to face him.

Balan aimed the first stroke but Balin raised his shield and warded it, and striking underneath he pierced helmet, and he struck again with that unhappy sword and staggered Balan, and then they drew apart and fought warily, cutting and parrying until they were breathless.

Balin looked up at the towers and saw the ladies in bright dresses looking down on them, and closed with his opponent again. Then both drew new strength from battle rage and they slashed and cut ferociously and blades chopped through armor and blood poured from each one. A moment they rested and then returned to the deadly fight, each trying to kill quickly before their strength bled away; each cut mortal wounds in the body of the other until Balan staggered away and lay down, too weak to raise his hand.

Then Balin, leaning on his sword, said, "Who are you? I have never found anywhere a knight who could stand up to me."

And the fallen man said, "My name is Balan, and I am a brother of the famous knight Sir Balin."

When Balin heard this his head whirled and he fainted and fell to the ground. And when he came to his senses he crawled on hands and knees and took off Balan's helmet and saw his face so cut to pieces and covered with blood that he did not know that face. And Balin laid his head on his brother's breast and wept, and he cried, "Oh, my brother, my dear brother. I have killed you and you have wounded me to death."

Balin said weakly, "I saw the two swords, but your shield had a device unknown to me."

"It was a knight of that castle who made me take his shield because he knew you would have recognized mine. If I could live I would destroy that castle and its evil customs."

"I wish that might be done," Balan said. "They made me fight here on the island, and when I killed the defender they forced me to be the champion and would not let me go. If you should live, my brother, they would keep you here to fight for their pleasure, and you could not escape over the water."

Then the boat brought the Lady of the Castle and her retainers to the island, and the brothers begged her to bury them together. "We came out of one womb," they said, "and we go to one grave."

And the lady promised that it would be done.

"Now send for a priest," Balin said. "We want the sacrament and to receive the blessed body of our Lord Jesus Christ." And it was done, and Balin said, "Write on our tomb how through ill fortune two brothers killed each other so that passing knights may pray for us."

Then Balan died, but Balin's life lingered with him till midnight, and in the darkness the brothers were buried together.

In the morning Merlin appeared and by his arts he raised a tomb over the brothers and on it in letters of gold he wrote their story.

And then Merlin prophesied many things that were to come: how Lancelot would come, and Galahad. And he fore-told tragic matters: how Lancelot would kill his best friend Gawain.

And after Merlin had done many strange prophetic things, he went to King Arthur and told him the story of the brothers, and the king was saddened. "In all the world," he said, "I never knew two such knights."

THE WINNING OF A SWORD

Howard Pyle

We now move even further into legend. Where the Arthurian Mythos – a phrase I use to distinguish it from the rather more historically based but still essentially legendary Arthur – comes into its own is with the introduction of the sword Excalibur. Without that, and without the Holy Grail, which we will come to later, the legend wouldn't be much more than the story of a heroic though rather bloodthirsty bunch of knights under their powerful leader, who at length fall out with each other over the love of Guinevere and the desire for the kingdom. With Excalibur a more mystical element enters. Here is a sword which Arthur receives from the strange Lady of the Lake and which makes him invincible. Moreover the scabbard is more powerful than the sword and makes him invulnerable.

The sword was there from the start of the legend. Geoffrey of Monmouth refers to Caliburn (from the Latin chalybs meaning steel), though in his story there is nothing magical about the sword. As the legend developed Excalibur became associated with the sword-in-the-stone, but subsequently Excalibur became a special gift to Arthur alone, one that, at his death, he had to return to the owner. Here is Howard Pyle's version of how Arthur gains Excalibur.

I

Now it fell upon a certain pleasant time in the Springtide season
that King Arthur and his Court were making a royal progression
through that part of Britain which lieth close to the Forests of the
Usk. At that time the weather was exceedingly warm, and so the
King and Court made pause within the forest under the trees in
the cool and pleasant shade that the place afforded, and there
the King rested for a while upon a couch of rushes spread with
scarlet cloth.

And the knights then present at that Court were, Sir Gawaine,
and Sir Ewaine, and Sir Kay, and Sir Pellias, and Sir Bedevere,
and Sir Caradoc, and Sir Geraint, and Sir Bodwin of Britain and
Sir Constantine of Cornwall, and Sir Brandiles and Sir Mador de
la Porte, and there was not to be found anywhere in the world a
company of such noble and exalted knights as these.

Now as the King lay drowsing and as these worthies sat holding
cheerful converse together at that place, there came, of a sudden,
a considerable bustle and stir upon the outskirts of the Court, and
presently there appeared a very sad and woful sight. For there came
thither-ward a knight, sore wounded, and upheld upon his horse by
a golden-haired page, clad in an apparel of white and azure. And,
likewise, the knight's apparel and the trappings of his horse were
of white and azure, and upon his shield he bore the emblazonment
of a single lily flower of silver upon a ground of pure azure.

But the knight was in a very woeful plight. For his face was as
pale as wax and hung down upon his breast. And his eyes were
glazed and saw naught that passed around him, and his fair apparel
of white and blue was all red with the blood of life that ran from
a great wound in his side. And, as they came upon their way, the
young page lamented in such wise that it wrung the heart for to
hear him.

Now, as these approached, King Arthur aroused cried out, "Alas!
what doleful spectacle is that which I behold? Now hasten, ye my
lords, and bring succor to yonder knight; and do thou, Sir Kay, go
quickly and bring that fair young page hither that we may presently
hear from his lips what mishap hath befallen his lord."

So certain of those knights hastened at the King's bidding
and gave all succor to the wounded knight, and conveyed
him to King Arthur's own pavilion, which had been pitched
at a little distance. And when he had come there the King's
chirurgeon presently attended upon him – albeit his wounds

were of such a sort he might not hope to live for a very long while.

Meantime, Sir Kay brought that fair young page before the King, where he sat, and the King thought that he had hardly ever seen a more beautiful countenance. And the King said, "I prithee tell me, Sir Page, who is thy master, and how came he in such a sad and pitiable condition as that which we have just now beheld."

"That will I so, Lord," said the youth. "Know that my master is entitled Sir Myles of the White Fountain, and that he cometh from the country north of where we are and at a considerable distance from this. In that country he is the Lord of seven castles and several noble estates, wherefore, as thou mayst see, he is of considerable consequence. A fortnight ago (being doubtless moved thereunto by the lustiness of the Springtime), he set forth with only me for his esquire, for he had a mind to seek adventure in such manner as beseemed a good knight who would be errant. And we had several adventures, and in all of them my lord was entirely successful; for he overcame six knights at various places and sent them all to his castle for to attest his valor unto his lady.

"At last, this morning, coming to a certain place situated at a considerable distance from this, we came upon a fair castle of the forest, which stood in a valley surrounded by open spaces of level lawn, bedight with many flowers of divers sorts. There we beheld three fair damsels who tossed a golden ball from one to another, and the damsels were clad all in flame-colored satin, and their hair was of the color of gold. And as we drew nigh to them they stinted their play, and she who was the chief of those damsels called out to my lord, demanding of him whither he went and what was his errand.

"To her my lord made answer that he was errant and in search of adventure, and upon this, the three damsels laughed, and she who had first spoken said, 'An thou art in search of adventure, Sir Knight, happily I may be able to help thee to one that shall satisfy thee to thy heart's content.'

"Unto this my master made reply 'I prithee, fair damsel, tell me what that adventure may be so that I may presently assay it.'

"Thereupon this lady bade my master to take a certain path, and to follow the same for the distance of a league or a little more, and that he would then come to a bridge of stone that crossed a violent stream, and she assured him that there he might find adventure enough for to satisfy any man.

"So my master and I wended thitherward as that damoiselle had directed, and, by and by, we came unto the bridge whereof she had spoken. And, lo! beyond the bridge was a lonesome castle with a tall straight tower, and before the castle was a wide and level lawn of well-trimmed grass. And immediately beyond the bridge was an apple-tree hung over with a multitude of shields. And midway upon the bridge was a single shield, entirely of black; and beside it hung a hammer of brass; and beneath the shield was written these words in letters of red:

> Whoso Smiteth This Shield
> Doeth So at his Peril.

"Now, my master, Sir Myles, when he read those words went straightway to that shield and, seizing the hammer that hung beside it, he smote upon it a blow so that it rang like thunder.

"Thereupon, as in answer, the portcullis of the castle was let fall, and there immediately came forth a knight, clad all from head to foot in sable armor. And his apparel and the trappings of his horse and all the appointments thereof were likewise entirely of sable.

"Now when that Sable Knight perceived my master he came riding swiftly across the meadow and so to the other end of the bridge. And when he had come there he drew rein and saluted my master and cried out, 'Sir Knight, I demand of thee why thou didst smite that shield. Now let me tell thee, because of thy boldness, I shall take away from thee thine own shield, and shall hang it upon yonder apple-tree, where thou beholdest all those other shields to be hanging.' Unto this my master made reply. 'That thou shalt not do unless thou mayst overcome me, as knight to knight.' And thereupon, immediately, he dressed his shield and put himself into array for an assault at arms.

"So my master and this Sable Knight, having made themselves ready for that encounter, presently drave together with might and main. And they met in the middle of the course, where my master's spear burst into splinters. But the spear of the Sable Knight held and it pierced through Sir Myles, his shield, and it penetrated his side, so that both he and his horse were overthrown violently into the dust; he being wounded so grievously that he could not arise again from the ground whereon he lay.

"Then the Sable Knight took my master's shield and hung it up in the branches of the apple-tree where the other shields were hanging, and, thereupon, without paying further heed to my master, or inquiring as to his hurt, he rode away into his castle again, whereof the portcullis was immediately closed behind him.

"So, after that he had gone, I got my master to his horse with great labor, and straightway took him thence, not knowing where I might find harborage for him, until I came to this place. And that, my lord King, is the true story of how my master came by that mortal hurt which he hath suffered."

"Ha! By the glory of Paradise!" cried King Arthur, "I do consider it great shame that in my Kingdom and so near to my Court strangers should be so discourteously treated as Sir Myles hath been served. For it is certainly a discourtesy for to leave a fallen knight upon the ground, without tarrying to inquire as to his hurt how grievous it may be. And still more discourteous is it for to take away the shield of a fallen knight who hath done good battle."

And so did all the knights of the King's Court exclaim against the discourtesy of that Sable Knight.

Then there came forth a certain esquire attendant upon the King's person, by name Griflet, who was much beloved by his Royal Master, and he kneeled before the King and cried out in a loud voice: "I crave a boon of thee, my lord King! and do beseech thee that thou wilt grant it unto me!"

Then King Arthur uplifted his countenance upon the youth as he knelt before him and he said, "Ask, Griflet, and thy boon shall be granted unto thee."

Thereupon Griflet said, "It is this that I would ask – I crave that thou wilt make me straightway knight, and that thou wilt let me go forth and endeavor to punish this unkindly knight, by overthrowing him, and so redeeming those shields which he hath hung upon that apple-tree."

Then was King Arthur much troubled in his spirit, for Griflet was as yet only an esquire and altogether untried in arms. So he said, "Behold, thou art yet too young to have to do with so potent a knight as this sable champion must be, who has thus overthrown so many knights without himself suffering any mishap. I prithee, dear Griflet, consider and ask some other boon."

But young Griflet only cried the more, "A boon! A boon! and thou hast granted it unto me."

Thereupon King Arthur said, "Thou shalt have thy boon, though my heart much misgiveth me that thou wilt suffer great ill and misfortune from this adventure."

So that night Griflet kept watch upon his armor in a chapel of the forest, and, in the morning, having received the Sacrament, he was created a knight by the hand of King Arthur – and it was not possible for any knight to have greater honor than that. Then King Arthur fastened the golden spurs to Sir Griflet's heels with his own hand.

So Griflet was made a knight, and having mounted his charger, he rode straightway upon his adventure, much rejoicing and singing for pure pleasure.

And it was at this time that Sir Myles died of his hurt, for it is often so that death and misfortune befall some, whiles others laugh and sing for hope and joy, as though such grievous things as sorrow and death could never happen in the world wherein they live.

Now that afternoon King Arthur sat waiting with great anxiety for word of that young knight, but there was no word until toward evening, when there came hurrying to him certain of his attendants, proclaiming that Sir Griflet was returning, but without his shield, and in such guise that it seemed as though a great misfortune had befallen him. And straightway thereafter came Sir Griflet himself, sustained upon his horse on the one hand by Sir Constantine and upon the other by Sir Brandiles. And, lo! Sir Griflet's head hung down upon his breast, and his fair new armor was all broken and stained with blood and dust. And so woful was he of appearance that King Arthur's heart was contracted with sorrow to behold that young knight in so pitiable a condition.

So, at King Arthur's bidding, they conducted Sir Griflet to the Royal Pavilion, and there they laid him down upon a soft couch. Then the King's chirurgeon searched his wounds and found that the head of a spear and a part of the shaft thereof were still piercing Sir Griflet's side, so that he was in most woful and grievous pain.

And when King Arthur beheld in what a parlous state Sir Griflet lay he cried out, "Alas! my dear young knight, what hath happened thee to bring thee unto such a woful condition as this which I behold?"

Then Sir Griflet, speaking in a very weak voice, told King Arthur how he had fared. And he said that he had proceeded through the forest, until he had discovered the three beautiful damsels whereof the page of Sir Myles had spoken. And he said that these damsels had directed him as to the manner in which he should pursue his adventure. And he said that he had found the bridge whereon hung the shield and the brazen mall, and that he had there beheld the apple-tree hung full of shields; and he said that he smote the shield of the Sable Knight with the brazen mall, and that the Sable Knight had thereupon come riding out against him. And he said that this knight did not appear of a mind to fight with him; instead, he cried out to him with a great deal of nobleness that he was too young and too untried in arms to have to do with a seasoned knight; wherefore he advised Sir Griflet to withdraw him from that adventure ere it was too late. But, notwithstanding this advice, Sir Griflet would not withdraw but declared that he would certainly have to do with that other knight in sable. Now at the very first onset Sir Griflet's spear had burst into pieces, but the spear of the Sable Knight had held and had pierced through Sir Griflet's shield and into his side, causing him this grievous wound whereof he suffered. And Sir Griflet said that the Sable Knight had then, most courteously, uplifted him upon his horse again (albeit he had kept Sir Griflet's shield and had hung it upon the tree with those others that hung there) and had then directed him upon his way, so that he had made shift to ride thither, though with great pain and dole.

Then was King Arthur very wode and greatly disturbed in his mind, for indeed he loved Sir Griflet exceedingly well. Wherefore he declared that he himself would now go forth for to punish that Sable Knight, and for to humble him with his own hand. And, though the knights of his Court strove to dissuade him from that adventure, yet he declared that he with his own hand would accomplish that proud knight's humiliation, and that he would undertake the adventure, with God His Grace, upon the very next day.

And so disturbed was he that he could scarce eat his food that evening for vexation, nor would he go to his couch to sleep, but, having inquired very narrowly of Sir Griflet where he might find that valley of flowers and those three damsels, he spent the night in walking up and down his pavilion, awaiting for the dawning of the day.

Now, as soon as the birds first began to chirp and the east to brighten with the coming of the daylight, King Arthur summoned his two esquires, and, having with their aid donned his armor and mounted a milk-white war-horse, he presently took his departure upon that adventure which he had determined upon.

And, indeed it is a very pleasant thing for to ride forth in the dawning of a Springtime day. For then the little birds do sing their sweetest song, all joining in one joyous medley, whereof one may scarce tell one note from another, so multitudinous is that pretty roundelay; then do the growing things of the earth smell the sweetest in the freshness of the early daytime – the fair flowers, the shrubs, and the blossoms upon the trees; then doth the dew bespangle all the sward as with an incredible multitude of jewels of various colors;

then is all the world sweet and clean and new, as though it had been fresh created for him who came to roam abroad so early in the morning.

So King Arthur's heart expanded with great joy, and he chanted a quaint song as he rode through the forest upon the quest of that knightly adventure.

So, about noon-tide, he came to that part of the forest lands whereof he had heard those several times before. For of a sudden, he discovered before him a wide and gently sloping valley, a-down which ran a stream as bright as silver. And, lo! the valley was strewn all over with an infinite multitude of fair and fragrant flowers of divers sorts. And in the midst of the valley there stood a comely castle, with tall red roofs and many bright windows, so that it seemed to King Arthur that it was a very fine castle indeed. And upon a smooth green lawn he perceived those three damoiselles clad in flame-colored satin of whom the page of Sir Myles and Sir Griflet had spoken. And they played at ball with a golden ball, and the hair of each was of the hue of gold, and it seemed to King Arthur, as he drew nigh, that they were the most beautiful damoiselles that he had ever beheld in all of his life.

Now as King Arthur came unto them the three ceased tossing the ball, and she who was the fairest of all damoiselles demanded of him whither he went and upon what errand he was bound.

Then King Arthur made reply: "Ha! fair lady! whither should a belted knight ride upon such a day as this, and upon what business, other than the search of adventure such as beseemeth a knight of a proper strength of heart and frame who would be errant?"

Then the three damoiselles smiled upon the King, for he was exceedingly comely of face and they liked him very well. "Alas, Sir Knight!" said she who had before spoken, "I prithee be in no such haste to undertake a dangerous adventure, but rather tarry with us for a day or two or three, for to feast and make merry with us. For surely good cheer doth greatly enlarge the heart, and we would fain enjoy the company of so gallant a knight as thou appearest to be. Yonder castle is ours and all this gay valley is ours, and those who have visited it are pleased, because of its joyousness, to call it the Valley of Delight. So tarry with us for a little and be not in such haste to go forward."

"Nay," said King Arthur," I may not tarry with ye, fair ladies, for I am bent upon an adventure of which ye may wot right well, when I tell ye that I seek that Sable Knight, who hath overcome so many other knights and hath taken away their shields. So I do pray ye of your grace for to tell me where I may find him."

"Grace of Heaven!" cried she who spake for the others, "this is certainly a sorry adventure which ye seek, Sir Knight! For already, in these two days, have two knights assayed with that knight, and both have fallen into great pain and disregard. Ne'theless, an thou wilt undertake this peril, yet shalt thou not go until thou hast eaten and refreshed thyself." So saying, she lifted a little ivory whistle that hung from her neck by a chain of gold, and blew upon it very shrilly.

In answer to this summons there came forth from the castle three fair young pages, clad all in flame-colored raiment, bearing among them a silver table covered with a white napkin. And after them came five other pages of the same appearance, bearing flagons of white wine and red, dried fruits and comfits and manchets of white fair bread.

Then King Arthur descended from his war-horse with great gladness, for he was both hungry and athirst, and, seating himself at the table with the damsels beside him, he ate with great enjoyment, discoursing pleasantly the while with those fair ladies, who listened to him with great cheerfulness of spirit. Yet he told them not who he was, though they greatly marvelled who might be the noble warrior who had come thus into that place.

So, having satisfied his hunger and his thirst, King Arthur mounted his steed again, and the three damsels conducted him across the valley a little way – he riding upon his horse and they walking beside him. So, by and by, he perceived where was a dark pathway that led into the farther side of the forest land; and when he had come thither the lady who had addressed him before said to him, "Yonder is the way that thou must take an thou wouldst enter upon this adventure. So fare thee well, and may good hap go with thee, for, certes, thou art the Knight most pleasant of address who hath come hitherward for this long time."

Thereupon King Arthur, having saluted those ladies right courteously, rode away with very great joy of that pleasant adventure through which he had thus passed.

Now when King Arthur had gone some ways he came, by and by, to a certain place where charcoal burners plied their trade. For here were many mounds of earth, all a-smoke with the smouldering logs within, whilst all the air was filled with the smell of the dampened fires.

As the King approached this spot, he presently beheld that

something was toward that was sadly amiss. For, in the open clearing, he beheld three sooty fellows with long knives in their hands, who pursued one old man, whose beard was as white as snow. And he beheld that the reverend old man, who was clad richly in black, and whose horse stood at a little distance, was running hither and thither, as though to escape from those wicked men, and he appeared to be very hard pressed and in great danger of his life.

"Pardee!" quoth the young King to himself, "here, certes, is one in sore need of succor." Whereupon he cried out in a great voice, "Hold, villains! What would you be at!" and therewith set spurs to his horse and dropped his spear into rest and drove down upon them with a noise like to thunder for loudness.

But when the three wicked fellows beheld the armed Knight thus thundering down upon them, they straightway dropped their knives and, with loud outcries of fear, ran away hither and thither until they had escaped into the thickets of the forest, where one upon a horse might not hope to pursue them.

Whereupon, having driven away those wicked fellows, King Arthur rode up to him whom he had succored, thinking to offer him condolence. And behold! when he had come nigh to him, he perceived that the old man was the Enchanter Merlin. Yet whence he had so suddenly come, who had only a little while before been at the King's Court at Carleon, and what he did in that place, the King could in no wise understand. Wherefore he bespoke the Enchanter in this wise, "Ha! Merlin, it seemeth to me that I have saved thy life. For, surely, thou hadst not escaped from the hands of those wicked men had I not happened to come hitherward at this time."

"Dost thou think so, Lord?" said Merlin. "Now let me tell thee that I did maybe appear to be in danger, yet I might have saved myself very easily had I been of a mind to do so. But, as thou sawst me in this seeming peril, so may thou know that a real peril, far greater than this, lieth before thee, and there will be no errant knight to succor thee from it. Wherefore, I pray thee, Lord, for to take me with thee upon this adventure that thou art set upon, for I do tell thee that thou shalt certainly suffer great dole and pain therein."

"Merlin," said King Arthur, "even an I were to face my death, yet would I not turn back from this adventure. But touching the advice thou givest me, meseems it will be very well to take thee with me if such peril lieth before me as thou sayest."

And Merlin said, "Yea, it would be very well for thee to do so."

So Merlin mounted upon his palfrey, and King Arthur and he betook their way from that place in pursuit of that adventure which the King had undertaken to perform.

II

So King Arthur and Merlin rode together through the forest for a considerable while, until they perceived that they must be approaching nigh to the place where dwelt the Sable Knight whom the King sought so diligently. For the forest, which had till then been altogether a wilderness, very deep and mossy, began to show an aspect more thin and open, as though a dwelling-place of mankind was close at hand.

And, after a little, they beheld before them a violent stream of water, that rushed through a dark and dismal glen. And, likewise, they perceived that across this stream of water there was a bridge of stone, and that upon the other side of the bridge there was a smooth and level lawn of green grass, whereon Knights-contestants might joust very well. And beyond this lawn they beheld a tall and forbidding castle, with smooth walls and a straight tower; and this castle was built upon the rocks so that it appeared to be altogether a part of the stone. So they wist that this must be the castle whereof the page and Sir Griflet had spoken.

For, midway upon the bridge, they beheld that there hung a sable shield and a brass mall exactly as the page and Sir Griflet had said; and that upon the farther side of the stream was an apple-tree, amid the leaves of which hung a very great many shields of various devices, exactly as those two had reported: and they beheld that some of those shields were clean and fair, and that some were foul and stained with blood, and that some were smooth and unbroken, and that some were cleft as though by battle of knight with knight. And all those shields were the shields of different knights whom the Sable Knight, who dwelt within the castle, had overthrown in combat with his own hand.

"Splendor of Paradise!" quoth King Arthur, "that must, indeed, be a right valiant knight who, with his own single strength, hath overthrown and cast down so many other knights. For, indeed, Merlin, there must be an hundred shields hanging in yonder tree!"

Unto this Merlin made reply, "And thou, Lord, mayst be very happy an thy shield, too, hangeth not there ere the sun goeth down this even-tide."

"That," said King Arthur, with a very steadfast countenance, "shall be as God willeth. For, certes, I have a greater mind than ever for to try my power against yonder knight. For, consider, what especial honor would fall to me should I overcome so valiant a warrior as this same Sable Champion appeareth to be, seeing that he hath been victorious over so many other good knights."

Thereupon, having so spoken his mind, King Arthur immediately pushed forward his horse and so, coming upon the bridge, he clearly read that challenge writ in letters of red beneath the shield:

> Whoso Smiteth This Shield
> Doeth So At his Peril.

Upon reading these words, the King seized the brazen mall, and smote that shield so violent a blow that the sound thereof echoed back from the smooth walls of the castle, and from the rocks whereon it stood, and from the skirts of the forest around about, as though twelve other shields had been struck in those several places.

And in answer to that sound, the portcullis of the castle was immediately let fall, and there issued forth a knight, very huge of frame, and clad all in sable armor. And, likewise, all of his apparel and all the trappings of his horse were entirely of sable, so that he presented a most grim and forbidding aspect. And this Sable Knight came across that level meadow of smooth grass with a very stately and honorable gait; for neither did he ride in haste, nor did he ride slowly, but with great pride and haughtiness of mien, as became a champion who, haply, had never yet been overcome in battle. So, reaching the bridge-head, he drew rein and saluted King Arthur with great dignity, and also right haughtily. "Ha! Sir Knight!" quoth he, "why didst thou, having read those words yonder inscribed, smite upon my shield? Now I do tell thee that, for thy discourtesy, I shall presently take thy shield away from thee, and shall hang it up upon yonder apple-tree where thou beholdest all those other shields to be hanging. Wherefore, either deliver thou thy shield unto me without more ado or else prepare for to defend it with thy person – in the which event thou shalt certainly suffer great pain and discomfort to thy body."

"Gramercy for the choice thou grantest me," said King Arthur. "But as for taking away my shield – I do believe that that shall be as Heaven willeth, and not as thou willest. Know, thou unkind knight, that I have come hither for no other purpose than to do battle with thee and so to endeavor for to redeem with my person all those shields that hang yonder upon that apple-tree. So make thou ready straightway that I may have to do with thee, maybe to thy great disadvantage."

"That will I so," replied the Sable Knight. And thereupon he turned his horse's head and, riding back a certain distance across the level lawn, he took stand in such place as appeared to him to be convenient. And so did King Arthur ride forth also upon that lawn, and take his station as seemed to him to be convenient.

Then each knight dressed his spear and his shield for the encounter, and, having thus made ready for the assault, each shouted to his war-horse and drave his spurs deep into its flank.

Then those two noble steeds rushed forth like lightning, coursing across the ground with such violent speed that the earth trembled and shook beneath them, an it were by cause of an earthquake. So those two knights met fairly in the midst of the centre of the field, crashing together like a thunderbolt. And so violently did they smite the one against the other that the spears burst into splinters, even unto the guard and the truncheon thereof, and the horses of the riders staggered back from the onset, so that only because of the extraordinary address of the knights-rider did they recover from falling before that shock of meeting.

But, with great spirit, these two knights uplifted each his horse with his own spirit, and so completed his course in safety.

And indeed King Arthur was very much amazed that he had not overthrown his opponent, for, at that time, as aforesaid, he was considered to be the very best knight and the one best approved in deeds of arms that lived in all of Britain. Wherefore he marvelled at the power and the address of that knight against whom he had driven, that he had not been overthrown by the greatness of the blow that had been delivered against his defences. So, when they met again in the midst of the field, King Arthur gave that knight greeting, and bespoke him with great courtesy, addressing him in this wise: "Sir Knight, I know not who thou art, but I do pledge my knightly word that thou art the most potent knight that ever I have met in all of my life. Now I do bid thee get down straightway from thy horse, and let us two fight this battle with sword and upon foot, for it were pity to let it end in this way."

"Not so," quoth the Sable Knight – "not so, nor until one of us twain be overthrown will I so contest this battle upon foot."

And upon this he shouted, "Ho! Ho!" in a very loud voice, and straightway thereupon the gateway of the castle opened and there came running forth two tall esquires clad all in black, pied with crimson. And each of these esquires bare in his hand a great spear of ash-wood, new and well-seasoned, and never yet strained in battle.

So King Arthur chose one of these spears and the Sable Knight took the other, and thereupon each returned to that station wherefrom he had before essayed the encounter.

Then once again each knight rushed his steed to the assault, and once again did each smite so fairly in the midst of the defence of the other that the spears were splintered, so that only the guard and the truncheon thereof remained in the grasp of the knight who held it.

Then, as before, King Arthur would have fought the battle out with swords and upon foot, but again the Sable Knight would not have it so, but called aloud upon those within the castle, whereupon there immediately came forth two other esquires with fresh, new spears of ash-wood. So each knight again took him a spear, and having armed himself therewith, chose each his station upon that fair, level lawn of grass.

And now, for the third time, having thus prepared themselves thereof assault, those two excellent knights hurled themselves together in furious assault. And now, as twice before, did King Arthur strike the Sable Knight so fairly in the centre of his defence that the spear which he held was burst into splinters. But this time, the spear of the Sable Knight did not so break in that manner, but held; and so violent was the blow that he delivered upon King Arthur's shield that he pierced through the centre of it. Then the girths of the King's saddle burst apart by that great, powerful blow, and both he and his steed were cast violently backward. So King Arthur might have been overcast, had he not voided his saddle with extraordinary skill and knightly address, wherefore, though his horse was overthrown, he himself still held his footing and did not fall into the dust. Ne'theless, so violent was the blow that he received that, for a little space, he was altogether bereft of his senses so that everything whirled around before his eyes.

But when his sight returned to him he was filled with an anger so vehement that it appeared to him as though all the blood in his heart rushed into his brains so that he saw naught but red, as of blood, before his eyes. And when this also had passed he perceived the Sable Knight that he sat his horse at no great distance. Then immediately King Arthur ran to him and catching the bridle-rein of his horse, he cried out aloud unto that Sable Knight with great violence: "Come down, thou black knight! and fight me upon foot and with thy sword."

"That will I not do," said the Sable Knight, "for, lo! I have overthrown thee. Wherefore deliver thou to me thy shield, that I may hang it upon yonder apple-tree, and go thy way as others have done before thee."

"That will I not!" cried King Arthur, with exceeding passion, "neither will I yield myself nor go hence until either thou or I have altogether conquered the other." Thereupon he thrust the horse of the Sable Knight backward by the bridle-rein so vehemently, that the other was constrained to void his saddle to save himself from being overthrown upon the ground.

And now each knight was as entirely furious as the other, wherefore, each drew his sword and dressed his shield, and thereupon rushed together like two wild bulls in battle. They foined, they smote, they traced, they parried, they struck again and again, and the sound of their blows, crashing and clashing the one upon the other, filled the entire surrounding space with an extraordinary uproar. Nor may any man altogether conceive of the entire fury of that encounter, for, because of the violence of the blows which the one delivered upon the other, whole cantels of armor were hewn from their bodies and many deep and grievous wounds were given and received, so that the armor of each was altogether stained with red because of the blood that flowed down upon it.

At last King Arthur, waxing, as it were, entirely mad, struck so fierce a blow that no armor could have withstood that stroke had it fallen fairly upon it. But it befell with that stroke that his sword broke at the hilt and the blade thereof flew into three several pieces into the air. Yet was the stroke so wonderfully fierce that the Sable Knight groaned, and staggered, and ran about in a circle as though he had gone blind and knew not whither to direct his steps.

But presently he recovered himself again, and perceiving King Arthur standing near by, and not knowing that his enemy had now no sword for to defend himself withal, he cast aside his shield and took his own sword into both hands, and therewith smote so dolorous a stroke that he clave through King Arthur's shield and through his helmet and even to the bone of his brain-pan.

Then King Arthur thought that he had received his death-wound, for his brains swam like water, his thighs trembled exceedingly, and he sank down to his knees, whilst the blood and sweat, commingled together in the darkness of his helmet, flowed down into his eyes in a lather and blinded him. Thereupon, seeing him thus grievously hurt, the Sable Knight called upon him with great vehemence for to yield himself and to surrender his shield, because he was now too sorely wounded for to fight any more.

But King Arthur would not yield himself, but catching the other by the sword-belt, he lifted himself to his feet. Then, being in a manner recovered from his amazement, he embraced the other with both arms, and placing his knee behind the thigh of the Sable Knight, he cast him backward down upon the ground so violently that the sound of the fall was astounding to hear. And with that fall the Sable Knight was, awhile, entirely bereft of consciousness. Then King Arthur straightway unlaced the helm of the Sable Knight and so beheld his face, and he knew him in spite of the blood that still ran down his own countenance in great quantities, and he knew that knight was King Pellinore, aforenamed in this history, who had twice warred against King Arthur. (It hath already been said how King Arthur had driven that other king from the habitations of men and into the forests, so that now he dwelt in this poor gloomy castle whence he waged war against all the knights who came unto that place.)

Now when King Arthur beheld whom it was against whom he had done battle, he cried out aloud, "Ha! Pellinore, is it then thou? Now yield thee to me, for thou art entirely at my mercy." And upon this he drew his misericordia and set the point thereof at King Pellinore's throat.

But by now King Pellinore had greatly recovered from his fall, and perceiving that the blood was flowing down in great measure from out his enemy's helmet, he wist that that other must have been very sorely wounded by the blow which he had just now received. Wherefore he catched King Arthur's wrist in his hand and directed the point of the dagger away from his own throat so that no great danger threatened therefrom.

And, indeed, what with his sore wound and with the loss of blood, King Arthur was now fallen exceedingly sick and faint, so that it appeared to him that he was nigh to death. Accordingly, it was with no very great ado that King Pellinore suddenly heaved himself up from the ground and so overthrew his enemy that King Arthur was now underneath his knees.

And by this King Pellinore was exceedingly mad with the fury of the sore battle he had fought. For he was so enraged that his eyes were all beshot with blood like those of a wild boar, and a froth, like the champings of a wild boar, stood in the beard about his lips. Wherefore he wrenched the dagger out of his enemy's hand, and immediately began to unlace his helm, with intent to slay him where he lay. But at this moment Merlin came in great haste, crying out, "Stay! stay! Sir Pellinore; what would you be at? Stay your sacrilegious hand! For he who lieth beneath you is none other than Arthur, King of all this realm!"

At this King Pellinore was astonished beyond measure. And for a little he was silent, and then after a while he cried out in a very voice, "Say you so, old man? Then verily your words have doomed this man unto death. For no one in all this world hath ever suffered such ill and such wrongs as I have suffered at his hands. For, lo! he hath taken from me power, and kingship, and honors, and estates, and hath left me only this gloomy, dismal castle of the forest as an abiding-place. Wherefore, seeing that he is thus in my power, he shall now presently die; if for no other reason than because if I now let him go free, he will certainly revenge himself when he shall have recovered from all the ill he hath suffered at my hands."

Then Merlin said, "Not so! He shall not die at thy hands, for I, myself, shall save him." Whereupon he uplifted his staff and smote King Pellinore across the shoulders. Then immediately King Pellinore fell down and lay upon the ground on his face like one who had suddenly gone dead.

Upon this, King Arthur uplifted himself upon his elbow and beheld his enemy lying there as though dead, and he cried out, "Ha! Merlin! what is this that thou hast done? I am very sorry, for I do perceive that thou, by thy arts of magic, hath slain one of the best knights in all the world."

"Not so, my lord King!" said Merlin; "for, in sooth, I tell thee that thou art far nigher to thy death than he. For he is but in sleep and will soon awaken; but thou art in such a case that it would take only a very little for to cause thee to die."

And indeed King Arthur was exceeding sick, even to the heart, with the sore wound he had received, so that it was only with much ado that Merlin could help him up upon his horse. Having done the which and having hung the King's shield upon the horn of his saddle, Merlin straightway conveyed the wounded man thence across the bridge, and, leading the horse by the bridle, so took him away into the forest.

Now I must tell you that there was in that part of the forest a certain hermit so holy that the wild birds of the woodland would come and rest upon his hand whiles he read his breviary; and so sanctified was he in gentleness that the wild does would come even to the door of his hermitage, and there stand whilst he milked them for his refreshment. And this hermit dwelt in that part of the forest so remote from the habitations of man that when he rang the bell for matins or for vespers, there was hardly ever anyone to hear the sound thereof excepting the wild creatures that dwelt thereabout. Yet, ne'theless, to this remote and lonely place royal folk and others of high degree would sometimes come, as though on a pilgrimage, because of the hermit's exceeding saintliness.

So Merlin conveyed King Arthur unto this sanctuary, and, having reached that place, he and the hermit lifted the wounded man down from his saddle – the hermit giving many words of pity and sorrow – and together they conveyed him into the holy man's cell. There they laid him upon a couch of moss and unlaced his armor and searched his wounds and bathed them with pure water and dressed his hurts, for that hermit was a very skilful leech. So for all that day and part of the next, King Arthur lay upon the hermit's pallet like one about to die; for he beheld all things about him as though through thin water, and the breath hung upon his lips and fluttered, and he could not even lift his head from the pallet because of the weakness that lay upon him.

Now upon the afternoon of the second day there fell a great noise and tumult in that part of the forest. For it happened that the Lady Guinevere of Cameliard, together with her Court, both of ladies and of knights, had come upon a pilgrimage to that holy man, the fame of whose saintliness had reached even unto the place where she dwelt. For that lady had a favorite page who was very sick of a fever, and she trusted that the holy man might give her some charm or amulet by the virtue of which he might haply be cured. Wherefore she had come to that place with her entire Court so that all that part of the forest was made gay with fine raiment and the silence thereof was made merry with the sound of talk and laughter and the singing of songs and the chattering of many voices and the neighing of horses. And the Lady Guinevere rode in the midst of her damsels and her Court, and her beauty outshone the beauty of her damsels as the splendor of the morning star outshines that of all the lesser stars that surround it. For then and afterward she was held by all the Courts of Chivalry to be the most beautiful lady in the world.

Now when the Lady Guinevere had come to that place, she perceived the milk-white war-horse of King Arthur where it stood cropping the green grass of the open glade nigh to the hermitage. And likewise she perceived Merlin, where he stood beside the door of the cell. So of him she demanded whose was that noble war-horse that stood browsing upon the grass at that lonely place, and who was it that lay within that cell. And unto her Merlin made answer, "Lady, he who lieth within is a knight, very sorely wounded, so that he is sick nigh unto death!"

"Pity of Heaven!" cried the Lady Guinevere. "What a sad thing is this that thou tellest me! Now I do beseech thee to lead me presently unto that knight that I may behold him. For I have in my Court a very skilful leech, who is well used to the cure of hurts such as knights receive in battle."

So Merlin brought the lady into the cell, and there she beheld King Arthur where he lay stretched upon the pallet. And she wist not who he was. Yet it appeared to her that in all her life she had not beheld so noble appearing a knight as he who lay sorely wounded in that lonely place. And King Arthur cast his looks upward to where she stood beside his bed of pain, surrounded by her maidens, and in the great weakness that lay upon him he wist not whether she whom he beheld was a mortal lady or whether she was not rather some tall straight angel who had descended from one of the Lordly Courts of Paradise for to visit him in his pain and distresses. And the Lady Guinevere was filled with a great pity at beholding King Arthur's sorrowful estate. Wherefore she called to her that skilful leech who was with her Court. And she bade him bring a certain alabaster box of exceedingly precious balsam. And she commanded him for to search that knight's wounds and to anoint them with the balsam, so that he might be healed of his hurts with all despatch.

So that wise and skilful leech did according to the Lady Guinevere's commands, and immediately King Arthur felt entire ease of all his aches and great content of spirit. And when the Lady and her Court had departed, he found himself much uplifted in heart, and three days thereafter he was entirely healed and was as well and strong and lusty as ever he had been in all of his life.

And this was the first time that King Arthur ever beheld that beautiful lady, the Lady Guinevere of Cameliard, and from that time forth he never forgot her, but she was almost always present in his thoughts. Wherefore, when he was recovered he said thus to himself: "I will forget that I am a king and I will cherish the thought of this lady and will serve her faithfully as a good knight may serve his chosen dame."

III

Now, as soon as King Arthur had, by means of that extraordinary balsam, been thus healed of those grievous wounds which he had received in his battle with King Pellinore, he found himself to be moved by a most vehement desire to meet his enemy again for to try issue of battle with him once more, and so recover the credit which he had lost in that combat. Now, upon the morning of the fourth day, being entirely cured, and having broken his fast, he walked for refreshment beside the skirts of the forest, listening the while to the cheerful sound of the wood-birds singing their matins, all with might and main. And Merlin walked beside him, and King Arthur spake his mind to Merlin concerning his intent to engage once more in knightly contest with King Pellinore. And he said, "Merlin, it doth vex me very sorely for to have come off so ill in my late encounter with King Pellinore. Certes, he is the very best knight in all the world whom I have ever yet encountered. Ne'theless, it might have fared differently with me had I not broken my sword, and so left myself altogether defenceless in that respect. Howsoever that may be, I am of a mind for to assay this adventure once more, and so will I do as immediately as may be."

Thereunto Merlin made reply, "Thou art, assuredly, a very brave man to have so much appetite for battle, seeing how nigh thou camest unto thy death not even four days ago. Yet how mayst thou hope to undertake this adventure without due preparation? For, lo! thou hast no sword, nor hast thou a spear, nor hast thou even thy misericordia for to do battle withal. How then mayst thou hope for to assay this adventure?"

And King Arthur said, "That I know not, nevertheless I will presently seek for some weapon as soon as may be. For, even an I have no better weapon than an oaken cudgel, yet would I assay this battle again with so poor a tool as that."

"Ha! Lord," said Merlin, "I do perceive that thou art altogether fixed in thy purpose for to renew this quarrel. Wherefore, I will not seek to stay thee therefrom, but will do all that in me lies for to aid thee in thy desires. Now to this end I must tell thee that in one part of this forest (which is, indeed, a very strange place) there is a certain woodland sometimes called Arroy, and other times called the Forest of Adventure. For no knight ever entereth therein but some adventure befalleth him. And close to Arroy is a land of enchantment which has several times been seen. And that is a very wonderful land, for there is in it a wide and considerable lake, which is also of enchantment.

And in the centre of that lake there hath for some time been seen the appearance as of a woman's arm – exceedingly beautiful and clad in white samite, and the hand of this arm holdeth a sword of such exceeding excellence and beauty that no eye hath ever beheld its like. And the name of this sword is Excalibur – it being so named by those who have beheld it because of its marvellous brightness and beauty. For it hath come to pass that several knights have already seen that sword and have endeavored to obtain it for their own, but, heretofore, no one hath been able to touch it, and many have lost their lives in that adventure. For when any man draweth near unto it, either he sinks into the lake, or else the arm disappeareth entirely, or else it is withdrawn beneath the lake; wherefore no man hath ever been able to obtain the possession of that sword. Now I am able to conduct thee unto that Lake of Enchantment, and there thou mayst see Excalibur with thine own eyes. Then when thou hast seen him thou mayst, haply, have the desire to obtain him; which, an thou art able to do, thou wilt have a sword very fitted for to do battle with."

"Merlin," quoth the King, "this is a very strange thing which thou tellest me. Now I am desirous beyond measure for to attempt to obtain this sword for mine own, wherefore I do beseech thee to lead me with all despatch to this enchanted lake whereof thou tellest me." And Merlin said, "I will do so."

So that morning King Arthur and Merlin took leave of that holy hermit (the King having kneeled in the grass to receive his benediction), and so, departing from that place, they entered the deeper forest once more, betaking their way to that part which was known as Arroy.

And after awhile they came to Arroy, and it was about noon-tide. And when they had entered into those woodlands they came to a certain little open place, and in that place they beheld a white doe with a golden collar about its neck. And King Arthur said, "Look, Merlin, yonder is a wonderful sight." And Merlin said, "Let us follow that doe." And upon this the doe turned and they followed it. And by and by in following it they came to an opening in the trees where was a little lawn of sweet soft grass. Here they beheld a bower and before the bower was a table spread with a fair snow-white cloth, and set with refreshments of white bread, wine, and meats of several sorts. And at the door of this bower there stood a page, clad all in green, and his hair was as black as ebony, and his eyes as black as jet and exceeding bright. And when this page beheld King Arthur and Merlin, he gave them greeting, and welcomed the King very pleasantly saying, "Ha! King Arthur, thou art welcome to this place. Now I prithee dismount and refresh thyself before going farther."

Then was King Arthur a-doubt as to whether there might not be some enchantment in this for to work him an ill, for he was astonished that that page in the deep forest should know him so well. But Merlin bade him have good cheer, and he said, "Indeed, Lord, thou mayst freely partake of that refreshment which, I may tell thee, was prepared especially for thee. Moreover in this thou mayst foretell a very happy issue unto this adventure."

So King Arthur sat down to the table with great comfort of heart (for he was an hungered) and that page and another like unto him ministered unto his needs, serving him all the food upon silver plates, and all the wine in golden goblets as he was used to being served in his own court – only that those things were much more cunningly wrought and fashioned, and were more beautiful than the table furniture of the King's court.

Then, after he had eaten his fill and had washed his hands from a silver basin which the first page offered to him, and had wiped his hands upon a fine linen napkin which the other page brought unto him, and after Merlin had also refreshed himself, they went their way, greatly rejoicing at this pleasant adventure, which, it seemed to the King, could not but betoken a very good issue to his undertaking.

Now about the middle of the afternoon King Arthur and Merlin came, of a sudden, out from the forest and upon a fair and level plain, bedight all over with such a number of flowers that no man could conceive of their quantity nor of the beauty thereof.

And this was a very wonderful land, for, lo! all the air appeared as it were to be as of gold – so bright was it and so singularly radiant. And here and there upon that plain were sundry trees all in blossom; and the fragrance of the blossoms was so sweet that the King had never smelt any fragrance like to it. And in the branches of those trees were a multitude of birds of many colors, and the melody of their singing ravished the heart of the hearer. And midway in the plain was a lake of water as bright as silver, and all around the borders of the lake were incredible numbers of lilies and of daffodils. Yet, although this place was so exceedingly fair, there was, nevertheless, nowhere about it a single sign of human life of any sort, but it appeared altogether as lonely as the hollow sky upon a day of summer. So, because of all the marvellous beauty of this place, and because of its strangeness and its entire solitude, King Arthur perceived that he must have come into a land of powerful enchantment where, happily, dwelt a fairy of very exalted quality; wherefore his spirit was enwrapped in a manner of fear, as he pushed his great milk-white war-horse through that long fair grass, all bedight with flowers, and he wist not what strange things were about to befall him.

So when he had come unto the margin of the lake he beheld there the miracle that Merlin had told him of aforetime. For, lo! in the midst of the expanse of water there was the appearance of a fair and beautiful arm, as of a woman, clad all in white samite. And the arm was encircled with several bracelets of wrought gold; and the hand held a sword of marvellous workmanship aloft in the air above the surface of the water; and neither the arm nor the sword moved so much as a hair's-breadth, but were motionless like to a carven image upon the surface of the lake. And, behold! the sun of that strange land shone down upon the hilt of the sword, and it was of pure gold beset with jewels of several sorts, so that the hilt of the sword and the bracelets that encircled the arm glistered in the midst of the lake like to some singular star of exceeding splendor. And King Arthur sat upon his war-horse and gazed from a distance at the arm and the sword, and he greatly marvelled thereat; yet he wist not how he might come at that sword, for the lake was wonderfully wide and deep, wherefore he knew not how he might come thereunto for to make it his own. And as he sat pondering this thing within himself, he was suddenly aware of a strange lady, who approached him through those tall flowers that bloomed along the margin of the lake. And when he perceived her coming toward him he quickly dismounted from his war-horse and he went forward for to meet her with the bridle-rein over his arm. And when he had come nigh to her, he perceived that she was extraordinarily beautiful, and that her face was like wax for clearness, and that her eyes were perfectly black, and that they were as bright and glistening as though they were two jewels set in ivory. And he perceived that her hair was like silk and as black as it was possible to be, and so long that it reached unto the ground as she walked. And the lady was clad all in green – only that a fine cord of crimson and gold was interwoven into the plaits of her hair. And around her neck there hung a very beautiful necklace of several strands of opal stones and emeralds, set in cunningly wrought gold; and around her wrists were bracelets of the like sort – of opal stones and emeralds set into gold. So when King Arthur beheld her wonderful appearance, that it was like to an ivory statue of exceeding beauty clad all in green, he

immediately kneeled before her in the midst of all those flowers
as he said, "Lady, I do certainly perceive that thou art no mortal
damoiselle, but that thou art Fay. Also that this place, because of
its extraordinary beauty, can be no other than some land of Faerie
into which I have entered."

And the Lady replied, "King Arthur, thou sayest soothly, for
I am indeed Faerie. Moreover, I may tell thee that my name is
Nymue, and that I am the chiefest of those Ladies of the Lake
of whom thou mayst have heard people speak. Also thou art to
know that what thou beholdest yonder as a wide lake is, in truth,
a plain like unto this, all bedight with flowers. And likewise thou
art to know that in the midst of that plain there standeth a castle
of white marble and of ultramarine illuminated with gold. But, lest
mortal eyes should behold our dwelling-place, my sisters and I have
caused it to be that this appearance as of a lake should extend all
over that castle so that it is entirely hidden from sight. Nor may
any mortal man cross that lake, saving in one way – otherwise he
shall certainly perish therein."

"Lady," said King Arthur, "that which thou tellest me causes me
to wonder a very great deal. And, indeed, I am afraid that in coming
hitherward I have been doing amiss for to intrude upon the solitude
of your dwelling-place."

"Nay, not so, King Arthur," said the Lady of the Lake, "for, in
truth, thou art very welcome hereunto. Moreover, I may tell thee
that I have a greater friendliness for thee and those noble knights of
thy court than thou canst easily wot of. But I do beseech thee of thy
courtesy for to tell me what it is that brings thee to our land?"

"Lady," quoth the King, "I will tell thee the entire truth. I fought
of late a battle with a certain sable knight, in the which I was sorely
and grievously wounded, and wherein I burst my spear and snapped
my sword and lost even my misericordia, so that I had not a single
thing left me by way of a weapon. In this extremity Merlin, here,
told me of Excalibur, and of how he is continually upheld by an
arm in the midst of this magical lake. So I came hither and, behold,
I find it even as he hath said. Now, Lady, an it be possible, I would
fain achieve that excellent sword, that, by means of it I might fight
my battle to its entire end."

"Ha! my lord King," said the Lady of the Lake, "that sword is
no easy thing for to achieve, and, moreover, I may tell thee that
several knights have lost their lives by attempting that which thou
hast a mind to do. For, in sooth, no man may win yonder sword
unless he be without fear and without reproach."

"Alas, Lady!" quoth King Arthur, "that is indeed a sad saying for me. For, though I may not lack in knightly courage, yet, in truth, there be many things wherewith I do reproach myself withal. Ne'theless, I would fain attempt this thing, even an it be to my great endangerment. Wherefore, I prithee tell me how I may best undertake this adventure."

"King Arthur," said the Lady of the Lake, "I will do what I say to aid thee in thy wishes in this matter." Whereupon she lifted a single emerald that hung by a small chain of gold at her girdle and, lo! the emerald was cunningly carved into the form of a whistle. And she set the whistle to her lips and blew upon it very shrilly. Then straightway there appeared upon the water, a great way off, a certain thing that shone very brightly. And this drew near with great speed, and as it came nigh, behold! it was a boat all of carven brass. And the prow of the boat was carved into the form of a head of a beautiful woman, and upon either side were wings like the wings of a swan. And the boat moved upon the water like a swan – very swiftly – so that long lines, like to silver threads, stretched far away behind, across the face of the water, which otherwise was like unto glass for smoothness. And when the brazen boat had reached the bank it rested there and moved no more.

Then the Lady of the Lake bade King Arthur to enter the boat, and so he entered it. And immediately he had done so, the boat moved away from the bank as swiftly as it had come thither. And Merlin and the Lady of the Lake stood upon the margin of the water, and gazed after King Arthur and the brazen boat.

And King Arthur beheld that the boat floated swiftly across the lake to where was the arm uplifting the sword, and that the arm and the sword moved not but remained where they were.

Then King Arthur reached forth and took the sword in his hand, and immediately the arm disappeared beneath the water, and King Arthur held the sword and the scabbard thereof and the belt thereof in his hand and, lo! they were his own.

Then verily his heart swelled with joy an it would burst within his bosom, for Excalibur was an hundred times more beautiful than he had thought possible. Wherefore his heart was nigh breaking for pure joy at having obtained that magic sword.

Then the brazen boat bore him very quickly back to the land again and he stepped ashore where stood the Lady of the Lake and Merlin. And when he stood upon the shore, he gave the Lady great thanks beyond measure for all that she had done for to aid him in his great undertaking; and she gave him cheerful and pleasing words in reply.

Then King Arthur saluted the lady, as became him, and, having mounted his war-horse, and Merlin having mounted his palfrey, they rode away thence upon their business – the King's heart still greatly expanded with pure delight at having for his own that beautiful sword – the most beautiful and the most famous sword in all the world.

That night King Arthur and Merlin abided with the holy hermit at the forest sanctuary, and when the next morning had come (the King having bathed himself in the ice-cold forest fountain, and being exceedingly refreshed thereby) they took their departure, offering thanks to that saintly man for the harborage he had given them.

Anon, about noon-tide, they reached the valley of the Sable Knight, and there were all things appointed exactly as when King Arthur had been there before: to wit, that gloomy castle, the lawn of smooth grass, the apple-tree covered over with shields, and the bridge whereon hung that single shield of sable.

"Now, Merlin," quoth King Arthur, "I do this time most strictly forbid thee for to interfere in this quarrel. Nor shalt thou, under pain of my displeasure, exert any of thy arts of magic in my behalf. So hearken thou to what I say, and heed it with all possible diligence."

Thereupon, straightway, the King rode forth upon the bridge and, seizing the brazen mall, he smote upon the sable shield with all his might and main. Immediately the portcullis of the castle was let fall as afore told, and, in the same manner as that other time, the Sable Knight rode forth therefrom, already bedight and equipped for the encounter. So he came to the bridge-head and there King Arthur spake to him in this wise: "Sir Pellinore, we do now know one another entirely well, and each doth judge that he hath cause of quarrel with the other: thou, that I, for mine own reasons as seemed to me to be fit, have taken away from thee thy kingly estate, and have driven thee into this forest solitude: I, that thou has set thyself up here for to do injury and affront to knights and lords and other people of this kingdom of mine. Wherefore, seeing that I am here as an errant Knight, I do challenge thee for to fight with me, man to man, until either thou or I have conquered the other."

Unto this speech King Pellinore bowed his head in obedience, and thereupon he wheeled his horse, and, riding to some little distance, took his place where he had afore stood. And King Arthur also rode to some little distance, and took his station where he had afore stood. At the same time there came forth from the castle one of those tall pages clad all in sable, pied with crimson, and gave to King Arthur a good, stout spear of ash-wood, well seasoned and untried in battle; and when the two Knights were duly prepared, they shouted and drave their horses together, the one smiting the other so fairly in the midst of his defences that the spears shivered in the hand of each, bursting all into small splinters as they had aforetime done.

Then each of these two knights immediately voided his horse with great skill and address, and drew each his sword. And thereupon they fell to at a combat, so furious and so violent, that two wild bulls upon the mountains could not have engaged in a more desperate encounter.

But now, having Excalibur for to aid him in his battle, King Arthur soon overcame his enemy. For he gave him several wounds and yet received none himself, nor did he shed a single drop of blood in all that fight, though his enemy's armor was in a little while all stained with crimson. And at last King Arthur delivered so vehement a stroke that King Pellinore was entirely benumbed thereby, wherefore his sword and his shield fell down from their defence, his thighs trembled beneath him and he sank unto his knees upon the ground, Then he called upon King Arthur to have mercy, saying, "Spare my life and I will yield myself unto thee."

And King Arthur said, "I will spare thee and I will do more than that. For now that thou hast yielded thyself unto me, lo! I will restore unto thee thy power and estate. For I bear no ill-will toward thee, Pellinore, ne'theless, I can brook no rebels against my power in this realm. For, as God judges me, I do declare that I hold singly in my sight the good of the people of my kingdom. Wherefore, he who is against me is also against them, and he who is against them is also against me. But now that thou hast acknowledged me I will take thee into my favor. Only as a pledge of thy good faith toward me in the future, I shall require it of thee that thou shalt send me as hostage of thy good-will, thy two eldest sons, to wit: Sir Aglaval and Sir Lamorack. Thy young son, Dornar, thou mayest keep with thee for thy comfort."

So those two young knights above mentioned came to the Court of King Arthur, and they became very famous knights, and by and by were made fellows in great honor of the Round Table.

And King Arthur and King Pellinore went together into the castle of King Pellinore, and there King Pellinore's wounds were dressed and he was made comfortable. That night King Arthur abode in the castle of King Pellinore, and when the next morning had come, he and Merlin returned unto the Court of the King, where it awaited him in the forest at that place where he had established it.

Now King Arthur took very great pleasure unto himself as he and Merlin rode together in return through that forest; for it was the leafiest time of all the year, what time the woodlands decked themselves in their best apparel of clear, bright green. Each bosky dell and dingle was full of the perfume of the thickets, and in every tangled depth the small bird sang with all his might and main, and as though he would burst his little throat with the melody of his singing. And the ground beneath the horses' feet was so soft with fragrant moss that the ear could not hear any sound of hoof-beats upon the earth. And the bright yellow sunlight came down through the leaves so that all the ground was scattered over with a great multitude of trembling circles as of pure yellow gold. And, anon, that sunlight would fall down upon the armed knight as he rode, so that every little while his armor appeared to catch fire with a great glory, shining like a sudden bright star amid the dark shadows of the woodland.

So it was that King Arthur took great joy in that forest land, for he was without ache or pain of any sort and his heart was very greatly elated with the wonderfulness of the success of that adventure into which he had entered. For in that adventure he had not only won a very bitter enemy into a friend who should be of great usefulness and satisfaction to him, but likewise, he had obtained for himself a sword, the like of which the world had never before beheld. And whenever he would think of that singularly splendid sword which now hung by his side, and whenever he remembered that land of Faëry into which he had wandered, and of that which had befallen fallen him therein, his heart would become so greatly elated with pure joyousness that he hardly knew how to contain himself because of the great delight that filled his entire bosom.

And, indeed, I know of no greater good that I could wish for you in all of your life than to have you enjoy such happiness as cometh to one when he hath done his best endeavor and hath succeeded with great entirety in his undertaking. For then all the world appears to be filled as with a bright shining light, and the body seemeth to become so elated that the feet are uplifted from heaviness and touch the earth very lightly because of the lightness of the spirit within. Wherefore, it is, that if I could have it in my power to give you the very best that the world hath to give, I would wish that you might win your battle as King Arthur won his battle at that time, and that you might ride homeward in such triumph and joyousness as filled him that day, and that the sunlight might shine around you as it shone around him, and that the breezes might blow and that all the little birds might sing with might and main as they sang for him, and that your heart also might sing its song of rejoicing in the pleasantness of the world in which you live.

Now as they rode thus through the forest together, Merlin said to the King: "Lord, which wouldst thou rather have, Excalibur, or the sheath that holds him?" To which King Arthur replied, "Ten thousand times would I rather have Excalibur than his sheath." "In that thou art wrong, my Lord," said Merlin, "for let me tell thee, that though Excalibur is of so great a temper that he may cut in twain either a feather or a bar of iron, yet is his sheath of such a sort that he who wears it can suffer no wound in battle, neither may he lose a single drop of blood. In witness whereof, thou mayst remember that, in thy late battle with King Pellinore, thou didst suffer no wound, neither didst thou lose any blood."

Then King Arthur directed a countenance of great displeasure upon his companion and he said, "Now, Merlin, I do declare that thou hast taken from me the entire glory of that battle which I have lately fought. For what credit may there be to any knight who fights his enemy by means of enchantment such as thou tellest me of? And, indeed, I am minded to take this glorious sword back to that magic lake and to cast it therein where it belongeth; for I believe that a knight should fight by means of his own strength, and not by means of magic."

"My Lord," said Merlin, "assuredly thou art entirely right in what thou holdest. But thou must bear in mind that thou art not as an ordinary errant knight, but that thou art a King, and that thy life belongeth not unto thee, but unto thy people. Accordingly thou hast no right to imperil it, but shouldst do all that lieth in thy power for to preserve it. Wherefore thou shouldst keep that sword so that it may safeguard thy life."

Then King Arthur meditated that saying for a long while in silence; and when he spake it was in this wise: "Merlin, thou art right in what thou sayest, and, for the sake of my people, I will keep both Excalibur for to fight for them, and likewise his sheath for to preserve my life for their sake. Ne'theless, I will never use him again saving in serious battle." And King Arthur held to that saying, so that thereafter he did no battle in sport excepting with lance and a-horseback.

King Arthur kept Excalibur as the chiefest treasure of all his possessions. For he said to himself, "Such a sword as this is fit for a king above other kings and a lord above other lords. Now, as God hath seen fit for to intrust that sword into my keeping in so marvellous a manner as fell about, so must He mean that I am to be His servant for to do unusual things. Wherefore I will treasure this noble weapon not more for its excellent worth than because it shall be unto me as a sign of those great things that God, in His mercy, hath evidently ordained for me to perform for to do Him service."

So King Arthur had made for Excalibur a strong chest or coffer, bound around with many bands of wrought iron, studded all over with great nails of iron, and locked with three great padlocks. In this strong-box he kept Excalibur lying upon a cushion of crimson silk and wrapped in swathings of fine linen, and very few people ever beheld the sword in its glory excepting when it shone like a sudden flame in the uproar of battle.

For when the time came for King Arthur to defend his realm or his subjects from their enemies, then he would take out the sword, and fasten it upon the side of his body; and when he did so he was like unto a hero of God girt with a blade of shining lightning. Yea; at such times Excalibur shone with so terrible a brightness that the very sight thereof would shake the spirits of every wrong-doer with such great fear that he would, in a manner, suffer the pangs of death ere ever the edge of the blade had touched his flesh.

So King Arthur treasured Excalibur and the sword remained with him for all of his life, wherefore the name of Arthur and of Excalibur are one. So, I believe that that sword is the most famous of any that ever was seen or heard tell of in all the Courts of Chivalry.

THE TREASON
OF MORGAN LE FAY

George Cox

The following story introduces us to two of the most important women in Arthur's life – his wife Guinevere and his sister or half-sister Morgan le Fay. Both ultimately contribute to Arthur's downfall: Guinevere through her adultery with Lancelot, and Morgan who, in at least one of the legends, was the cause of Arthur's seduction and thus the birth of his nemesis Mordred. The origins of both characters are interesting. It is quite likely that Guinevere was a real person, named Gwenhwyfar, which means "fair and beautiful" – in fact the name was probably symbolic of purity, a state of spiritual perfection with which the legend and its association with the Holy Grail becomes obsessed. She was probably a Pictish princess, and in the world of the Picts, the authority of kingship passed through the female line not the male. Thus a king had to be the son of a Pictish princess. By marrying Guinevere, Arthur established the right of his sons over the Pictish kingdom. However, Pictish princesses were notably promiscuous since many princes demanded children by them, and this was probably the origin of Guinevere's adultery, not only with Lancelot, but with others in the legend, in particular Lanval and Mordred. Morgan is more a creature of legend and was probably originally a fairy-figure (hence "le Fay") who was humanized as the legend evolved into a wicked sister. At one point in this transition Morgan was depicted as the head of a sisterhood who had healing powers and, as we shall see elsewhere in this book, that image still lingers and remains one of the most powerful images at the end, when Morgan and two of her sisters take Arthur to Avalon.

The following extract comes from Popular Romances of the
Middle Ages *(1871) by George Cox (1827–1902). Cox was
fascinated with ancient history and legend. He wrote the very
popular* Tales from Greek Mythology *(1861) as well as a* History
of Greece *(1874), which in its day was regarded as definitive. He
was one of the first to seriously study the Arthurian Mythos and
place it in the context of other legends and folk tales.*

1. The Wedding of Arthur and Guenevere

Now the king took counsel with Merlin, because his barons would
have him take a wife; and Merlin asked, "Is there any on whom thy
love is set?" "Yes," said the king, "I love Guenevere, the daughter
of King Leodegrance who has in his house the Round Table which
he had from my father Uther." "In truth," answered Merlin, "the
maiden for her beauty is right well-fitted to be a queen: but if ye
loved her not so well as ye do, I might find another who should
please thee not less, for Guenevere can not be a wholesome wife
for thee, and she will bring great sorrow to thee and to thy realm.
But when a man's heart is set, it may not easily be turned aside."
"That is true," said the king: and straightway he sent messengers
to King Leodegrance to ask for his daughter, and Leodegrance
rejoiced at the tidings. "I would yield him rich lands with my
child," he said, "but Arthur has lands enough. Yet will I send
him a gift that shall please him more, for I will give him the Round
Table which Uther Pendragon gave me, and to which there were
a hundred knights and fifty. Of these fifty have been slain in my
days, but the hundred shall go with Guenevere." So they set out,
and by water and land came royally to London, where the king
joyously welcomed his bride and the hundred knights, and bade
Merlin spy out fifty more knights throughout the land, who might
be worthy to sit at that table: but only twenty-eight could Merlin
find. Then the Bishop of Canterbury came and blessed the seats
for the eight-and-twenty knights, who did homage to the king.
And when they were gone, Merlin found in every seat letters of
gold that told the names of the knights who had sat therein. But
two seats were void.

Then came young Gawaine and besought the king to make him a knight on the day in which he should wed Guenevere; and the king said that so it should be, because he was his sister's son. And after him, riding upon a lean mare, came a poor man who brought with him a fair youth; and he also besought Arthur that the youth might be made a knight. "Thou askest me a great thing," said Arthur. "Who art thou? and does this prayer come of thee or of thy son?" "I am Aries the cowherd," answered the man, "and I desire not this of myself. Nay, to say truth, I have thirteen sons, who will ever do that which I bid them: but this one will spend his time only in folly and delights only in battles and to see knights." Then the king bent his eyes on the youth, who was named Tor, and he saw that he was both brave and fair; and he bade that the other sons of the cowherd should be brought. But all these were shapen like the poor man, and none was in any wise like Tor. Then the youth knelt and besought the king to make him a knight of the Round Table. "A knight I will make you," said Arthur, "and hereafter thou shalt be also of the Round Table, if thou art found worthy." Then turning to Merlin, he said, "Will Tor be a good knight?" "Of a truth, he will," answered Merlin, "for he is no son of the cowherd. His father is King Pellinore."

When on the morrow King Pellinore came to the court, the king brought Sir Tor before him and told him that he was his son; and Sir Pellinore embraced him joyfully. Then the king asked Merlin why two places were void in the seats: and Merlin said, "No man shall sit in those places, but they that are of most worship: and on the Perilous Seat there is but one man on the earth who shall be found worthy to sit. If any who are not worthy dare to sit on it, he shall be destroyed." Then taking Pellinore by the hand, he put him next the two seats and the Seat Perilous, and said, "This is your place, for of all that are here you are the most worthy to sit in it." When Sir Gawaine heard these words, he was moved with envy, that the man who had slain his father, the King of Orkney, should be thus honoured; and he would have slain him straightway, but his brother Gaheris besought him not to trouble the high feast by so doing. "Let us wait till we have him out of the court:" and Gawaine said, "I will."

When now the marriage day was come, the king wedded Guenevere at Camelot in the Church of St. Stephen; and afterwards there was great feasting, and Arthur gave charge to Sir Gawaine and Gaheris his brother, to Sir Tor and his father Sir Pellinore, who went forth, and each did great deeds before they came back to the king. With Sir Pellinore came a lady, whom he had rescued, named Nimue; and as they journeyed to Camelot, and were resting under the shadow of thick trees, two knights met, as they rode by, and one asked the other what tidings there might be from Camelot; and the other told him of the fellowship of Arthur's table, and said, "We cannot break it up; and well nigh all the world holdeth with Arthur, for there is the flower of chivalry. Wherefore with these tidings I ride to the north." "Nay," said the other, "there is no need. I have a remedy with me; for I bear a poison to a friend who is right nigh to Arthur, and with it he will poison the king." So they went each on his way, and Sir Pellinore told all that he had seen and heard when he came to the king at Camelot, with the lady whom he had rescued.

But when Merlin set eyes on the damsel, he was besotted with her, and would let her have no rest, but always she must be with him. And she spake him fair till she had learned of him all manner of things that she sought to know. Yet the old man knew what should befall him, and he told the king that yet a little while, and he should go down into the earth alive, and he warned Arthur to keep well the sword and the scabbard, for these would be stolen by a woman whom he most trusted. "Nay," said the king, "but if thou knowest what shall befall thee, why dost thou not prevent that mishap by thy craft?" "It may not be," said Merlin; and presently the damsel went away, and Merlin followed whithersoever she went; but she had made him swear to do no inchantment upon her, if he would have her love. So he went with her over the sea to the land of Benwick, where Merlin spake with Elaine, King Ban's wife, and there he saw young Lancelot; and Elaine mourned greatly for the fierce war which Claudas made against Ban. "Heed it not," said Merlin, "for before twenty years are gone, this child shall revenge you on King Claudas, and he shall be the man of most worship in the world." "Shall I indeed," asked Elaine, "live to see my son a man of so great a prowess?" "Yea, indeed thou shalt see it," answered Merlin, "and live many years after." Soon after this, the maiden departed, and Merlin went with her till they came into Cornwall; but the damsel was weary of him, and afraid because he was a devil's son, and so it came to pass that when Merlin showed her a marvellous rock, beneath which there were great inchantments, she besought him to go under the stone and show her the marvels that were there; but when he was beneath it, she so wrought that he never came forth again; and she left him and went her way.

2. The Treason of Morgan Le Fay

ABOUT this time, as Arthur rode to Camelot, the tidings came that the King of Denmark, with five other kings, was ravaging the land of the north. "Alas!" said Arthur, "when have I had one month's rest since I became king of the land?" Nevertheless, he would not tarry an hour, although his lords were wroth because he set out thus hastily. So he hastened away with Guenevere the queen (for he said that he should be the hardier if she were with him), and came into a forest beside Humber; and a knight, when he heard that Arthur was come, warned the five kings to make haste and do battle with him, for the longer they tarried they would be ever the weaker, and Arthur stronger. And the five kings hearkened to his words, and fell on Arthur in the night; but though they killed many, and there was for some while a great tumult, yet Arthur and his knights, Sir Kay, Sir Gawaine, and Sir Griflet, slew the five kings. In the morning, when their people knew that they were dead, they were struck with such fear that they fell from their horses, and Arthur and his men came upon them, and slew them to the number of thirty thousand, so that well nigh no man escaped alive; but on Arthur's side were slain only two hundred, with eight knights of the Round Table. And Arthur raised a fair church and minster on the battle-field, and called it the Abbey of Good Adventure.

Then the king took counsel with Sir Pellinore about the knights who should be chosen for the Round Table in place of those who had been slain; and Pellinore gave counsel to choose Uriens, the husband of Morgan le Fay, the king's sister, and Galagars, and Hervise, and the King of the Lake, and with these four younger knights, of whom there were Gawaine, Griflet, and Kay; and for the fourth he bade Arthur choose between Tor and Bagdemagus. And Arthur choose Tor, because he said little and did much; and Bagdemagus went away sore displeased, and swore never to come back till he should be worthy to be chosen for the Round Table. As he rode with his squire he found a branch of an holy herb which was the sign of the Sangreal, and no man of evil life could ever find it. Then he came to the rock beneath which lay Merlin, making great dole; but when he would have helped him, Merlin bade him not to spend his strength for naught, for only she could help him who had put him there. So Bagdemagus went his way, and after doing many great deeds he came back and was chosen a knight of the Round Table.

Now Arthur, with many of his knights, went hunting and chased a hart till they left their people far behind them, and at last their horses fell dead. "Let us go on on foot," said Uriens; and at last they came up with the hart, and they saw also a great water, and on it a ship which came straight towards them, and landed on the sands. But when they looked into it they found no earthly creature therein, and they wondered for the beauty of the ship, which was hung all over with cloth of silk. And now it was dark night, when suddenly there burst forth a great light, and twelve damsels came forth, and welcomed Arthur by his name, and led him with Uriens and Accolon of Gaul, who were with him, to a table laden with wine and costly things, and then brought them each into a fair chamber that they might rest. But in the morning Uriens found himself in Camelot with Morgan le Fay, his wife, and King Arthur found himself in a dark prison, in which he heard the moaning of many who were shut up with him. Then the king asked them how they came there, and they told him that they had all been entrapped on their way by an evil knight, named Damas, who kept back part of his heritage from his brother Sir Ontzlake, whom men loved as much as they hated Damas; but because Ontzlake was the better knight, Damas was afraid to fight with him, and sought to get a champion, but none would take spear in hand for so evil a man; and so it came to pass that they abode in the weary prison till eighteen had died. Presently there came a damsel who asked Arthur if he would fight for Damas. "Yea, I will do so," he said, "for it is better to fight with a knight than to die in a dungeon – but only if all here be set free." Then the maiden said that so it should be, and that a horse and armour should be brought for the king. And the king said to the maiden, "Surely I have seen thee in the court of Arthur;" and she said, "Nay; for I am the daughter of the lord of this castle." But she spake falsely, for she was one of the damsels of Morgan le Fay. So was it sworn between them that Damas should set all the knights free, and that Arthur should do battle for him to the death.

Thus had it fared with Arthur. But when Accolon awoke, he found himself by a dark well-side, and from that fountain through a silver pipe the water ran in a marble basin; and Accolon said, "God help King Arthur, for these women have betrayed us." And even as he spake there came a dwarf who brought him greetings from Morgan le Fay, and bade him be of good heart. "In the morning," he said, "thou shalt fight with a knight at the hour of prime, and here is Excalibur, Arthur's sword, and the scabbard. Wherefore rise up and do battle without mercy, as ye love her." So he sware to do as he was bidden for the love of Morgan le Fay; and presently a

knight and a lady, with six squires, led him to the house of Sir
Ontzlake: and a messenger came from Damas to say that he had
found a knight to fight for him, and to challenge Ontzlake to the
battle. But Ontzlake was sorely wounded, and besought Accolon
to take his cause in hand, and thus it came to pass that Accolon
fought with the king's sword against the king whom he loved, for
he knew not who it was who fought for Sir Damas. Long and
terrible was the fight, for the false sword which Morgan le Fay
had given to Arthur hit not like Excalibur, and the blood streamed
from the king's body because the scabbard which he wore was not
the scabbard of Excalibur, and thus as the strife went on Arthur grew
weaker, while Accolon waxed stronger. But Arthur would not yield,
not even when his sword broke at the cross and fell into the grass
while the pommel remained in his hands. Then Accolon stood over
the king and bade him yield himself, for he was greatly loth to slay
him; but Arthur said, "I have sworn to fight to the death, and I lose
not good name because I lose my weapon." So when Accolon came
against him once more, Arthur struck him with the pommel a blow
so heavy that he reeled three strides backward. But the Lady of the
Lake was looking on, and it was a grief to her that such a knight as
Arthur should be slain. So at the next stroke she caused Excalibur
to fly from the hand of Accolon, and Arthur leaping forth seized it
in his hand, and said, "Too long hast thou been from me, and much
harm hast thou wrought me." Then looking at Accolon he spied the
scabbard of his own sword, and with a quick rush he seized it and
threw it far away from them both. "Now," said Arthur to Accolon,
"thou shalt die;" and he dealt him a blow that the blood rushed
from him in a torrent. "Slay me if thou wilt," said Accolon, "but
I have sworn not to yield me in this fight. Yet thou art the best
knight that ever I have seen, and well I know that God is with
you." "Tell me, then, who thou art," said Arthur; and he answered,
"I am Accolon of Gaul, of King Arthur's court." "Nay, but I am
Arthur," said the king, in great fear because of the inchantments
of Morgan le Fay; "tell me now, how camest thou by the sword
and the scabbard?" Then Accolon told him how the dwarf had
brought them from Morgan le Fay, but that he knew not against
whom he was using them in this fight; and he besought the king's
pardon. Then said Arthur, "Thee I can forgive; but upon my sister I
will take such vengeance that all Christendom shall ring with it, for I
have worshipped her more than all my kin, and trusted her more than
mine own wife." Then Arthur told the keepers of the field that there
would have been no battle between them if each had known who the

other was; and Accolon said, "This knight with whom I have fought, to my great sorrow, is the man of most manhood and worship in the world, for he is our liege lord, King Arthur." Then the people, falling on their knees, prayed for mercy. "Mercy ye shall have," said Arthur; "and this is my judgment betwixt the two brethren. For thee, Sir Damas, I learn that thou art but a worthless knight, and full of villainy; thou shalt give to thy brother the whole manor to hold of thee; also thou shalt swear no more to harm knights who may be journeying on their way, and thou shalt give back to those knights who have been set free from thy dungeon all the harness of which thou hast robbed them; and if any come to me to say thou hast not done this, thou shalt die. Thee, Sir Ontzlake, I bid to my court, for thou art a brave knight, and an upright man." Moreover, Arthur told Ontzlake how the battle between himself and Accolon had been brought about, and Ontzlake marvelled that any man or woman could be found to work treason against Arthur; and the king said, "I shall soon reward them by the grace of God." But the king needed rest after the fight, and they brought him to a fair abbey where in four days Sir Accolon died, for he had lost so much blood that he could not live. Then said Arthur, "Bear his body to my sister, Morgan le Fay, and say that I send it to her as a gift, and that I have my sword and its scabbard." So they bare the body of Accolon to Camelot.

But meantime Morgan le Fay made sure that Arthur had died, and she bade one of her maidens fetch her husband's sword, for now would she slay him. In vain the damsel besought her not to do so; and she went to Sir Uwaine and said, "Rise up, for thy mother is about to slay thy father, and I go to fetch the sword." Presently, as Morgan le Fay stood by the bedside with the sword in her hands, Sir Uwaine seized her and said, "Ah, fiend, what wilt thou do? Men say that a devil was Merlin's father, and I may say that a devil is my mother." Then Morgan cried for mercy and besought him not to discover her; and Uwaine made her swear that she would not do the like in time to come.

At last the tidings came that it was Accolon who had died, and that Arthur had again his sword and his scabbard, and the heart of Morgan almost burst with her grief. But because she would not have it known, she suffered not her face to betray her sorrow; and because she knew that if she tarried till Arthur came back no ransom should save her life, she besought Queen Guenevere for leave to ride into the country; and on the morrow she hastened to the abbey where Arthur lay sleeping, and lighting off her horse went straight into the chamber, where she found Arthur asleep and Excalibur naked in his right hand. So, grieving terribly that she might not take the sword without awaking him, she took the scabbard, and went her way. When Arthur awoke and saw that his scabbard was gone, he charged his knights with having watched him falsely; but they said, "We durst not withstand your sister's bidding." Then Arthur bid Sir Ontzlake arm and ride with him in all haste, and they hastened after Morgan, until they saw her speeding from them as fast as her horse could bear her. When at last she knew that there was no hope of escape, she swore that her brother should never have the scabbard, and taking it from her girdle she hurled it into a lake hard by, and it sunk forthwith, for it was heavy with gold and precious stones. Then riding on she came to a valley where there were many large stones, and because she saw that Arthur would soon overtake her, she turned herself and those who were with her into stones, so that when they came up, the king could not discern between his sister and her men. So he rode back to the abbey whence he had come; and when he was gone, Morgan turned herself and her men into their former likeness, and as she went on, she rescued, from a knight who was going to drown him, a cousin of Accolon named Manassen, and she bade him go tell Arthur that she had rescued him not for the love of the king but for love of Accolon, and that she feared nothing so long as she could change herself and those who were with her into stones, for she could do greater things than these when the time should come.

Not long had Manassen reached Camelot when there came a damsel, bearing the richest mantle that ever was seen, set full of precious stones, and she said, "Your sister sends this mantle that you may take this gift from her, and if in aught she had done you wrong, she will amend it." But the Lady of the Lake warned him in secret, "Take heed that the garment come not nigh thee or any of thy knights, until thou hast made the bringer of it put it on." Then said the king to the maiden, "I would see upon you this raiment which ye have brought," and when the damsel said that it was not seemly for her to wear a king's garment, Arthur made them put it on her, and she was burnt to coals. But the king turned to Sir Uriens and said, "I know not what these treasons may mean. Thee I can scarcely suspect, for Accolon confessed to me that Morgan would destroy thee as well as me; for Uwaine I hold suspected, and I bid thee send him from my court." Then said Gawaine, "He who banishes my cousin banishes me;" so the two departed, and Gaheris said, "We have lost two good knights for the love of one."

As they went upon their way Uwaine and Gawaine came to a tower in a valley, where twelve maidens with two knights went to and fro near a tree on which hung a white shield, and they spit at the shield and threw mire on it as they passed: and they asked the maidens why they did so, they said, "It is the shield of Sir Marhaus who hates all ladies." "It may be that he has cause," said Gawaine; and presently came Marhaus himself, and the two knights of the tower hastened to do battle with him, but they were both slain; and after this Marhaus jousted with Gawaine and Uwaine. The fight was long and fierce, for so it was that from nine of the clock till noontide Gawaine waxed stronger and stronger; but when it was past noon and drew toward evensong, Sir Gawaine's strength waned, and Sir Marhaus grew bigger and bigger; and at last Marhaus said, "It were a pity to do you hurt, for you are passing feeble." So they took off their helmets and kissed each other, and swore to love henceforth as brethren: and they went together to the home of Sir Marhaus, with whom Gawaine and Uwaine tarried seven days till their wounds were well healed. Then Marhaus guided them to the forest of Alroy, in which by a fair stream of water they saw three damsels sitting. The eldest had a garland of gold upon her head, and her hair was white under her garland, for she had seen threescore winters or more. The second had on her head a circlet of gold, and she was thirty winters old. The third, whose head was crowned with flowers, had seen only fifteen summers. "Wherefore sit ye by the fountain?" asked the knight, and the maidens answered, "We sit here watching for errant knights, that we may teach them strange adventures: and if ye be men who seek adventures, each one of you must choose one of us, and we will lead you to three highways, and then each of you shall choose his way and his damsel shall go with him; and when twelve months have passed, ye must meet here again; and to this ye must plight your troth." "It is well said," they answered; and Sir Uwaine said, "I am the youngest and the weakest, therefore will I have the eldest damsel, for she has seen much and can help me best when I have need." Then said Sir Marhaus, "I will have the second damsel, for she falls best to me." "I thank you," said Sir Gawaine, "for ye have left me the youngest and fairest, and she only it is whom I would have." When they came to the parting of the roads, they kissed and went each his way – Sir Uwaine to the west, Sir Marhaus to the south, and Sir Gawaine to the north.

Now, when he had gone some way, Gawaine came to a lawn, and near a cross which stood there, there came by the fairest knight that they had ever seen: but he was mourning as one in great grief. Then there followed ten knights who threw their spears at the sorrowful knight, but he unhorsed them all, and afterwards suffered them to bind him and to treat him shamefully. "Why go you not to his help?" said the damsel to Gawaine. "I would do so," he answered, "but it seems he will have no help." But now three knights came and challenged Gawaine to joust with them: and while they were jousting, another knight came to the damsel and asked why she abode with him who had brought her thither. "I find it not in my heart," she said, "to abide with him any longer, for he helps not those who need his aid;" and she departed with the stranger. When the jousting was ended, Gawaine asked who the sorrowful knight might be; and they told him that his name was Sir Pelleas, and that he loved the lady Ettard, who would not listen to his suit and even drove him from her with evil words, although in a great jousting he had won the right to crown the fairest lady, and had placed the circlet upon her brow. But so was Pelleas smitten by love for Ettard, that he suffered her knights to bind him after he had conquered them in fighting, in hopes that he might thus be brought into her sight; but he hoped in vain. Then said Gawaine, "I will go and help him, and he shall see the lady of his love." So on the next day he made an oath with Pelleas that he would win the damsel for him, and when he came to the house of Ettard, he told her that he was a knight who had slain Sir Pelleas. At this Ettard was so full of joy that she welcomed Gawaine and made him good cheer, until he forgot the word he had plighted to Pelleas, and wooed the maiden for himself. When Pelleas knew that Gawaine was forsworn, he took horse, for he could tarry no longer for pure sorrow; and he went his way and laid him down upon his bed to die. But the Lady of the Lake whom Merlin had loved came and looked on him as he slept, and she said, "So fair a knight shall not die;" and in two hours she came back with the lady Ettard, and threw such an inchantment upon her that Ettard loved Pelleas now as much as she had hated him in time past. But when Pelleas woke and saw her standing near, he hated her with all his soul. "Begone, traitress," he said, "and never come near me more." So Ettard went away and died of sorrow, and the Lady of the Lake led Pelleas into her own land, and they loved together while they lived.

But Marhaus with the maiden of thirty winters' age did better things, for he came first to the house of a duke who received him churlishly, and when he knew who he was, said that on the morrow he must fight with himself and his six sons, because Gawaine had slain his seven sons and now was the time for vengeance, and Marhaus must fight alone with seven against him. So on the morrow they fought, and Marhaus was so mighty that he overthrew them all, and made them swear never more to be foes to King Arthur or his knights. Then Marhaus went on with his damsel, and at a great tourney he won a rich circlet of gold worth a thousand besants, and afterwards slew a terrible giant who ravaged the lands of Earl Fergus, and delivered many ladies and knights out of the giant's dungeon. There he got great riches, so that he was never poor all the days of his life, and so went on his way with the maiden to the trysting-place.

Likewise with the damsel of sixty winters' age, Sir Uwaine bore himself as a good knight, for he avenged the Lady of the Rock against those who had robbed her of her heritage, and restored to her all her lands; and Sir Uwaine dwelt with the lady for nearly half a year, to be healed of the grievous wounds which he had received when he did battle on her behalf. Then as the year came round, he hastened with the maiden to the trysting-place: and all met there, as they had agreed; but the damsel that Gawaine had could say little good of him.

Deeds of the Round Table

THE WINNING OF OLWEN

Lady Charlotte Guest

Although the Arthurian legend as we popularly understand it came via Malory from the French romancers, we should not forget that Arthur was himself Celtic and that he was remembered equally in the Celtic legends, particularly in those known collectively as The Mabinogion. *Although that cycle of stories as presented to us today is much bigger than the original set of tales which came from the medieval manuscripts,* The White Book of Rhydderch *and* The Red Book of Hergest, *both extant in the fourteenth century. The first person to render these stories into modern English and present them as a unified whole was Lady Charlotte Guest (1812–95), daughter of the ninth earl of Lindsay. She spent over ten years on her studies and translation, which eventually appeared in 1849. They include five Arthurian stories, "Kilwch and Olwen", which is presented here, "The Dream of Rhonabwy", "The Lady of the Fountain", which I included in* The Pendragon Chronicles *and which has a variant version in the story "The Knight of the Lion" later in this volume, "Peredur, the son of Evrawc" and "Geraint the son of Erbin", a version of which appeared as "The Hedge of Mist" in* Chronicles of the Round Table.

Kilydd the son of Prince Kelyddon desired a wife as a helpmate, and the wife that he chose was Goleuddydd, the daughter of Prince Anlawdd. And after their union, the people put up prayers that they might have an heir. And they had a son through the prayers of the people. From the time of her pregnancy Goleuddydd became wild, and wandered about, without habitation; but when her delivery was at hand, her reason came back to her. Then she went to a mountain where there was a swineherd, keeping a herd of swine. And through fear of the swine the queen was delivered. And the swineherd took the boy, and brought him to the palace; and he was christened, and they called him Kilhwch, because he had been found in a swine's burrow. Nevertheless the boy was of gentle lineage, and cousin unto Arthur; and they put him out to nurse.

After this the boy's mother, Goleuddydd, the daughter of Prince Anlawdd, fell sick. Then she called her husband unto her, and said to him, "Of this sickness I shall die, and thou wilt take another wife. Now wives are the gift of the Lord, but it would be wrong for thee to harm thy son. Therefore I charge thee that thou take not a wife until thou see a briar with two blossoms upon my grave." And this he promised her. Then she besought him to dress her grave every year, that nothing might grow thereon. So the queen died. Now the king sent an attendant every morning to see if anything were growing upon the grave. And at the end of the seventh year the master neglected that which he had promised to the queen.

One day the king went to hunt, and he rode to the place of burial to see the grave, and to know if it were time that he should take a wife; and the king saw the briar. And when he saw it, the king took counsel where he should find a wife. Said one of his counsellors, "I know a wife that will suit thee well, and she is the wife of King Doged." And they resolved to go to seek her; and they slew the king, and brought away his wife and one daughter that she had along with her. And they conquered the king's lands.

On a certain day, as the lady walked abroad, she came to the house of an old crone that dwelt in the town, and that had no tooth in her head. And the queen said to her, "Old woman, tell me that which I shall ask thee, for the love of Heaven. Where are the children of the man who has carried me away by violence?" Said the crone, "He has not children." Said the queen, "Woe is me, that I should have come to one who is childless!" Then said the hag, "Thou needest not lament on account of that, for there is a prediction he shall have an heir by thee, and by none other. Moreover, be not sorrowful, for he has one son."

The lady returned home with joy; and she asked her consort, "Wherefore hast thou concealed thy children from me?" The king said, "I will do so no longer." And he sent messengers for his son, and he was brought to the Court. His stepmother said unto him, "It were well for thee to have a wife, and I have a daughter who is sought of every man of renown in the world." "I am not yet of an age to wed," answered the youth. Then said she unto him, "I declare to thee, that it is thy destiny not to be suited with a wife until thou obtain Olwen, the daughter of Yspaddaden Penkawr." And the youth blushed, and the love of the maiden diffused itself through all his frame, although he had never seen her. And his father inquired of him, "What has come over thee, my son, and what aileth thee?" "My stepmother has declared to me that I shall never have a wife until I obtain Olwen, the daughter of Yspaddaden Penkawr." "That will be easy for thee," answered his father. "Arthur is thy cousin. Go, therefore, unto Arthur, to cut thy hair, and ask this of him as a boon."

And the youth pricked forth upon a steed with head dappled grey, of four winters old, firm of limb, with shell-formed hoofs, having a bridle of linked gold on his head, and upon him a saddle of costly gold. And in the youth's hand were two spears of silver, sharp, well-tempered, headed with steel, three ells in length, of an edge to wound the wind, and cause blood to flow, and swifter than the fall of the dewdrop from the blade of reed-grass upon the earth when the dew of June is at the heaviest. A gold-hilted sword was upon his thigh, the blade of which was of gold, bearing a cross of inlaid gold of the hue of the lightning of heaven: his war-horn was of ivory. Before him were two brindled white-breasted greyhounds, having strong collars of rubies about their necks, reaching from the shoulder to the ear. And the one that was on the left side bounded across to the right side, and the one on the right to the left, and like two sea-swallows sported around him. And his courser cast up four sods with his four hoofs, like four swallows in the air, about his head, now above, now below. About him was a four-cornered cloth of purple, and an apple of gold was at each corner, and every one of the apples was of the value of an hundred kine. And there was precious gold of the value of three hundred kine upon his shoes, and upon his stirrups, from his knee to the tip of his toe. And the blade of grass bent not beneath him, so light was his courser's tread as he journeyed towards the gate of Arthur's Palace.

Spoke the youth, "Is there a porter?" "There is; and if thou holdest not thy peace, small will be thy welcome. I am Arthur's porter every first day of January. And during every other part of the year but this, the office is filled by Huandaw, and Gogigwc, and Llaeskenym, and Pennpingyon, who goes upon his head to save his feet, neither towards the sky nor towards the earth, but like a rolling stone upon the floor of the court." "Open the portal." "I will not open it." "Wherefore not?" "The knife is in the meat, and the drink is in the horn, and there is revelry in Arthur's Hall, and none may enter therein but the son of a king of a privileged country, or a craftsman bringing his craft. But there will be refreshment for thy dogs, and for thy horses; and for thee there will be collops cooked and peppered, and luscious wine and mirthful songs, and food for fifty men shall be brought unto thee in the guest chamber, where the stranger and the sons of other countries eat, who come not unto the precincts of the Palace of Arthur. Thou wilt fare no worse there than thou wouldest with Arthur in the Court. A lady shall smooth thy couch, and shall lull thee with songs; and early to-morrow morning, when the gate is open for the multitude that come hither to-day, for thee shall it be opened first, and thou mayest sit in the place that thou shalt choose in Arthur's Hall, from the upper end to the lower." Said the youth, "That will I not do. If thou openest the gate, it is well. If thou dost not open it, I will bring disgrace upon thy Lord, and evil report upon thee. And I will set up three shouts at this very gate, than which none were ever more deadly, from the top of Pengwaed in Cornwall to the bottom of Dinsol, in the North, and to Esgair Oervel, in Ireland. And all the women in this Palace that are pregnant shall lose their offspring; and such as are not pregnant, their hearts shall be turned by illness, so that they shall never bear children from this day forward." "What clamour soever thou mayest make," said Glewlwyd Gavaelvawr, "against the laws of Arthur's Palace shalt thou not enter therein, until I first go and speak with Arthur."

Then Glewlwyd went into the Hall. And Arthur said to him, "Hast thou news from the gate?" – "Half of my life is past, and half of thine. I was heretofore in Kaer Se and Asse, in Sach and Salach, in Lotor and Fotor; and I have been heretofore in India the Great and India the Lesser; and I was in the battle of Dau Ynyr, when the twelve hostages were brought from Llychlyn. And I have also been in Europe, and in Africa, and in the islands of Corsica, and in Caer Brythwch, and Brythach, and Verthach; and I was present when formerly thou didst slay the family of Clis the son of Merin, and when thou didst slay Mil Du the son of Ducum, and when thou didst conquer Greece in the East. And I have been in Caer Oeth and Annoeth, and in Caer Nevenhyr; nine supreme sovereigns, handsome men, saw we there, but never did I behold a man of equal dignity with him who is now at the door of the portal." Then said Arthur, "If walking thou didst enter in here, return thou running. And every one that beholds the light, and every one that opens and shuts the eye, let them shew him respect, and serve him, some with gold-mounted drinking-horns, others with collops cooked and peppered, until food and drink can be prepared for him. It is unbecoming to keep such a man as thou sayest he is, in the wind and the rain." Said Kai, "By the hand of my friend, if thou wouldest follow my counsel, thou wouldest not break through the laws of the Court because of him." "Not so, blessed Kai. It is an honour to us to be resorted to, and the greater our courtesy the greater will be our renown, and our fame, and our glory."

And Glewlwyd came to the gate, and opened the gate before him; and although all dismounted upon the horse-block at the gate, yet did he not dismount, but rode in upon his charger. Then said Kilhwch, "Greeting be unto thee, Sovereign Ruler of this Island; and be this greeting no less unto the lowest than unto the highest, and be it equally unto thy guests, and thy warriors, and thy chieftains – let all partake of it as completely as thyself. And complete be thy favour, and thy fame, and thy glory, throughout all this Island." "Greeting unto thee also," said Arthur; "sit thou between two of my warriors, and thou shalt have minstrels before thee, and thou shalt enjoy the privileges of a king born to a throne, as long as thou remainest here. And when I dispense my presents to the visitors and strangers in this Court, they shall be in thy hand at my commencing." Said the youth, "I came not here to consume meat and drink; but if I obtain the boon that I seek, I will requite it thee, and extol thee; and if I have it not, I will bear forth thy dispraise to the four quarters of the world, as far as thy renown has extended." Then said Arthur, "Since thou wilt not remain here, chieftain, thou shalt receive the boon whatsoever thy tongue may name, as far as the wind dries, and the rain moistens, and the sun revolves, and the sea encircles, and the earth extends; save only my ship; and my mantle; and Caledvwlch, my sword; and Rhongomyant, my lance; and Wynebgwrthucher, my shield; and Carnwenhau, my dagger; and Gwenhwyvar, my wife. By the truth of Heaven, thou shalt have it cheerfully, name what thou wilt." "I would that thou bless my hair." "That shall be granted thee."

And Arthur took a golden comb, and scissors, whereof the loops were of silver, and he combed his hair. And Arthur inquired of him who he was. "For my heart warms unto thee, and I know that thou art come of my blood. Tell me, therefore, who thou art." "I will tell thee," said the youth. "I am Kilhwch, the son of Kilydd, the son of Prince Kelyddon, by Goleuddydd, my mother, the daughter of Prince Anlawdd." "That is true," said Arthur; "thou art my cousin. Whatsoever boon thou mayest ask, thou shalt receive, be it what it may that thy tongue shall name." "Pledge the truth of Heaven and the faith of thy kingdom thereof." "I pledge it thee, gladly." "I crave of thee then, that thou obtain for me Olwen, the daughter of Yspaddaden Penkawr; and this boon I likewise seek at the hands of thy warriors. I seek it from Kai, and Bedwyr, and Greidawl Galldonyd, and Gwythyr the son of Greidawl, and Greid the son of Eri, and Kynddelig Kyvarwydd, and Tathal Twyll Goleu, and Maelwys the son of Baeddan, and Crychwr the son of Nes, and Cubert the son of Daere, and Percos the son of Poch, and Lluber Beuthach, and Corvil Bervach, and Gwynn the son of Nudd, and Edeyrn the son of Nudd, and Gadwy the son of Geraint, and Prince Fflewddur Fflam, and Ruawn Pebyr the son of Dorath, and Bradwen the son of Moren Mynawc, and Moren Mynawc himself, and Dalldav the son of Kimin Côv, and the son of Alun Dyved, and the son of Saidi, and the son of Gwryon, and Uchtryd Ardywad Kad, and Kynwas Curvagyl, and Gwrhyr Gwarthegvras, and Isperyr Ewingath, and Gallcoyt Govynynat, and Duach, and Grathach, and Nerthach, the sons of Gwawrddur Kyrvach (these men came forth from the confines of hell), and Kilydd Canhastyr, and Canastyr Kanllaw, and Cors Cant-Ewin, and Esgeir Gulhwch Govynkawn, and Drustwrn Hayarn, and Glewlwyd Gavaelvawr, and Lloch Llaw-wynnyawc, and Aunwas Adeiniawc, and Sinnoch the son of Seithved, and Gwennwynwyn the son of Naw, and Bedyw the son of Seithved, and Gobrwy the son of Echel Vorddwyttwll, and Echel Vorddwyttwll himself, and Mael the son of Roycol, and Dadweir Dallpenn, and Garwyli the son of Gwythawc Gwyr, and Gwythawc Gwyr himself, and Gormant the son of Ricca, and Menw the son of Teirgwaedd, and Digon the son of Alar, and Selyf the son of Smoit, and Gusg the son of Atheu, and Nerth the son of Kedarn, and Drudwas the son of Tryffin, and Twrch the son of Perif, and Twrch the son of Annwas, and Iona king of France, and Sel the son of Selgi, and Teregud the son of Iaen, and Sulyen the son of Iaen, and Bradwen the son of Iaen, and Moren the son of Iaen, and Siawn the son of Iaen, and Cradawc the son of Iaen. (They were men of Caerdathal, of Arthur's kindred on his father's side.) Dirmyg the son of Kaw, and Justic the son of Kaw, and Etmic the son of Kaw, and Anghawd the son of Kaw, and Ovan the son of Kaw, and Kelin the son of Kaw, and Connyn the son of Kaw, and Mabsant the son of Kaw, and Gwyngad the son of Kaw, and Llwybyr the son of Kaw, and Coth the son of Kaw, and Meilic the son of Kaw, and Kynwas the son of Kaw, and Ardwyad the son of Kaw, and Ergyryad the son of Kaw, and Neb the son of Kaw, and Gilda the son of Kaw, and Calcas the son of Kaw, and Hueil the son of Kaw (he never yet made a request at the hand of any Lord). And Samson Vinsych, and Taliesin the chief of the bards, and Manawyddan the son of Llyr, and Llary the son of Prince Kasnar, and Ysperni the son of Fflergant king of Armorica, and Saranhon the son of Glythwyr, and Llawr Eilerw, and Annyanniawc the son of Menw the son of Teirgwaedd, and Gwynn the son of Nwyvre, and Fflam the son of Nwyvre, and Geraint the son of Erbin, and Ermid the son of Erbin, and Dyvel the son of Erbin, and Gwynn the son of Ermid, and Kyndrwyn the son of Ermid, and Hyveidd Unllenn, and Eiddon Vawr Vrydic, and Reidwn Arwy, and Gormant the son of Ricca (Arthur's brother by his mother's side; the Penhynev of Cornwall was his father), and Llawnrodded Varvawc, and Nodawl Varyf Twrch, and Berth the son of Kado, and Rheidwn the son of Beli, and Iscovan Hael, and Iscawin the son of Panon, and Morvran the son of Tegid (no one struck him in the battle of Camlan by reason of his ugliness; all thought he was an auxiliary devil. Hair had he upon him like the hair of a stag). And Sandde Bryd Angel (no one touched him with a spear in the battle of Camlan because of his beauty; all thought he was a ministering angel). And Kynwyl Sant (the third man that escaped from the battle of Camlan, and he was the last who parted from Arthur on Hengroen his horse). And Uchtryd the son of Erim, and Eus the son of Erim, and Henwas Adeinawg the son of Erim, and Henbedestyr the son of Erim, and Sgilti Yscawndroed the son of Erim. (Unto these three men belonged these three qualities, – With Henbedestyr there was not any one who could keep pace, either on horseback or on foot; with Henwas Adeinawg, no four-footed beast could run the distance of an acre, much less could it go beyond it; and as to Sgilti Yscawndroed, when he intended to go upon a message for his Lord, he never sought to find a path, but knowing whither he was to go, if his way lay through a wood he went along the tops of the trees. During his whole life, a blade of reed grass bent not beneath his feet, much less did one ever break, so lightly did he tread.) Teithi Hên the son of Gwynhan (his dominions were swallowed up by the sea, and he himself hardly escaped, and he came to Arthur; and his knife had this peculiarity, that from the time that he came there no haft would ever remain upon it, and owing to this a sickness came over him, and he pined away during the remainder of his life, and of this he died). And Carneddyr the son of Govynyon Hên, and Gwenwynwyn the son of Nav Gyssevin, Arthur's champion, and Llysgadrudd Emys, and Gwrbothu Hên (uncles unto Arthur were they, his mother's brothers). Kulvanawyd the son of Goryon, and Llenlleawg Wyddel from the headland of Ganion, and Dyvynwal Moel, and Dunard king of the North, Teirnon Twryf Bliant, and Tegvan Gloff, and Tegyr Talgellawg, Gwrdinal the son of Ebrei, and Morgant Hael, Gwystyl the son of Rhun the son of Nwython, and Llwyddeu the son of Nwython, and Gwydre the son of Llwyddeu (Gwenabwy the daughter of [Kaw] was his mother, Hueil his uncle stabbed him, and hatred was between Hueil and Arthur because of the wound). Drem the son of Dremidyd (when the gnat arose in the morning with the sun, he could see it from Gelli Wic in Cornwall, as far off as Pen Blathaon in North Britain). And Eidyol the son of Ner, and Glwyddyn Saer (who constructed Ehangwen, Arthur's Hall). Kynyr Keinvarvawc (when he was told he had a son born he said to his wife, 'Damsel, if thy son be mine, his heart will be always cold, and there will be no warmth in his hands; and he will have another peculiarity, if he is my son he will always be stubborn; and he will have another peculiarity, when he carries a burden, whether it be large or small, no one will be able to see it, either before him or at his back; and he will have another peculiarity, no one will be able to resist fire and water so well as he will; and he will have another peculiarity, there will never be a servant or an officer equal to him'). Henwas, and Henwyneb (an old companion to Arthur). Gwallgoyc (another; when he came to a town, though there were three hundred houses in it, if he wanted anything, he would not let sleep come to the eyes of any one whilst he remained there). Berwyn the son of Gerenhir, and Paris king of France, and Osla Gyllellvawr (who bore a short broad dagger. When Arthur and his hosts came before a torrent, they would seek for a narrow place where they might pass the water, and would lay the sheathed dagger across the torrent, and it would form a bridge sufficient for the armies of the three Islands of Britain, and of the three islands adjacent, with their spoil). Gwyddawg the son of Menestyr (who slew Kai, and whom Arthur slew, together with his brothers, to revenge Kai). Garanwyn the son of Kai, and Amren the son of Bedwyr, and Ely Amyr, and Rheu Rhwyd Dyrys, and Rhun Rhudwern, and Eli, and Trachmyr (Arthur's chief huntsmen). And Llwyddeu the son of Kelcoed, and Hunabwy the son of Gwryon, and Gwynn Godyvron, and Gweir Datharwenniddawg, and Gweir the son of Cadell the son of Talaryant, and Gweir Gwrhyd Ennwir, and Gweir Paladyr Hir (the uncles of Arthur, the brothers of his mother). The sons of Llwch Llawwynnyawg (from beyond the raging sea). Llenlleawg Wyddel, and Ardderchawg Prydain. Cas the son of Saidi, Gwrvan Gwallt Avwyn, and Gwyllennhin the king of France, and Gwittart the son of Oedd king of Ireland, Garselit Wyddel, Panawr Pen Bagad, and Ffleudor the son of Nav, Gwynnhyvar mayor of Cornwall and Devon (the ninth man that rallied the battle of Camlan). Keli and Kueli, and Gilla Coes Hydd (he would clear three hundred acres at one bound: the chief leaper of Ireland was he). Sol, and Gwadyn Ossol, and Gwadyn Odyeith. (Sol could stand all day upon one foot. Gwadyn Ossol, if he stood upon the top of the highest mountain in the world, it would become a level plain under his feet. Gwadyn Odyeith, the soles of his feet emitted sparks of fire when they struck upon things hard, like the heated mass when drawn out of the forge. He cleared the way for Arthur when he came to any stoppage.) Hirerwm and Hiratrwm. (The day they went on a visit three Cantrevs provided for their entertainment, and they feasted until noon and drank until night, when they went to sleep. And then they devoured the heads of the vermin through hunger, as if they had never eaten anything. When they made a visit they left neither the fat nor the lean, neither the hot nor the cold, the sour nor the sweet, the fresh nor the salt, the boiled nor the raw.) Huarwar the son of Aflawn (who asked Arthur such a boon as would satisfy him. It was the third great plague of Cornwall when he received it. None could get a smile from him but when he was satisfied). Gware Gwallt Euryn. The two cubs of Gast Rhymi, Gwyddrud and Gwyddneu Astrus. Sugyn the son of Sugnedydd (who would suck up the sea on which were three hundred ships so as to leave nothing but a dry strand. He was broad-chested). Rhacymwri, the attendant of Arthur (whatever barn he was shown, were there the produce of thirty ploughs within it, he would strike it with an iron flail until the rafters, the beams, and the boards were no better than the small oats in the mow upon the floor of the barn). Dygyflwng and Anoeth Veidawg. And Hir Eiddyl, and Hir Amreu (they were two attendants of Arthur). And Gwevyl the son of Gwestad (on the day that he was sad, he would let one of his lips drop below his waist, while he turned up the other like a cap upon his head). Uchtryd Varyf Draws (who spread his red untrimmed beard over the eight-and-forty rafters which were in Arthur's Hall). Elidyr Gyvarwydd. Yskyrdav and Yscudydd (two attendants of Gwenhwyvar were they. Their feet were swift as their thoughts when bearing a message). Brys the son of Bryssethach (from the Hill of the Black Fernbrake in North Britain). And Grudlwyn Gorr.

Bwlch, and Kyfwlch, and Sefwlch, the sons of Cleddyf Kyfwlch, the grandsons of Cleddyf Difwlch. (Their three shields were three gleaming glitterers; their three spears were three pointed piercers; their three swords were three grinding gashers; Glas, Glessic, and Gleisad. Their three dogs, Call, Cuall, and Cavall. Their three horses, Hwyrdyddwd, and Drwgdyddwd, and Llwyrdyddwg. Their three wives, Och, and Garym, and Diaspad. Their three grandchildren, Lluched, and Neved, and Eissiwed. Their three daughters, Drwg, and Gwaeth, and Gwaethav Oll. Their three handmaids, Eheubryd the daughter of Kyfwlch, Gorascwrn the daughter of Nerth, Ewaedan the daughter of Kynvelyn Keudawd Pwyll the half-man.) Dwnn Diessic Unbenn, Eiladyr the son of Pen Llarcau, Kynedyr Wyllt the son of Hettwn Talaryant, Sawyl Ben Uchel, Gwalchmai the son of Gwyar, Gwalhaved the son of Gwyar, Gwrhyr Gwastawd Ieithoedd (to whom all tongues were known), and Kethcrwm the Priest. Clust the son of Clustveinad (though he were buried seven cubits beneath the earth, he would hear the ant fifty miles off rise from her nest in the morning). Medyr the son of Methredydd (from Gelli Wic he could, in a twinkling, shoot the wren through the two legs upon Esgeir Oervel in Ireland). Gwiawn Llygad Cath (who could cut a haw from the eye of the gnat without hurting him). Ol the son of Olwydd (seven years before he was born his father's swine were carried off, and when he grew up a man he tracked the swine, and brought them back in seven herds). Bedwini the Bishop (who blessed Arthur's meat and drink). For the sake of the golden-chained daughters of this island. For the sake of Gwenhwyvar its chief lady, and Gwennhwyach her sister, and Rathtyeu the only daughter of Clemenhill, and Rhelemon the daughter of Kai, and Tannwen the daughter of Gweir Datharweniddawg. Gwenn Alarch the daughter of Kynwyl Canbwch. Eurneid the daughter of Clydno Eiddin. Eneuawc the daughter of Bedwyr. Enrydreg the daughter of Tudvathar. Gwennwledyr the daughter of Gwaledyr Kyrvach. Erddudnid the daughter of Tryffin. Eurolwen the daughter of Gwdolwyn Gorr. Teleri the daughter of Peul. Indeg the daughter of Garwy Hir. Morvudd the daughter of Urien Rheged. Gwenllian Deg the majestic maiden. Creiddylad the daughter of Lludd Llaw Ereint. (She was the most splendid maiden in the three Islands of the mighty, and in the three Islands adjacent, and for her Gwythyr the son of Greidawl and Gwynn the son of Nudd fight every first of May until the day of doom.) Ellylw the daughter of Neol Kynn-Crog (she lived three ages). Essyllt Vinwen and Essyllt Vingul." And all these did Kilhwch the son of Kilydd adjure to obtain his boon.

Then said Arthur, "Oh! chieftain, I have never heard of the maiden of whom thou speakest, nor of her kindred, but I will gladly send messengers in search of her. Give me time to seek her." And the youth said, "I will willingly grant from this night to that at the end of the year to do so." Then Arthur sent messengers to every land within his dominions to seek for the maiden; and at the end of the year Arthur's messengers returned without having gained any knowledge or intelligence concerning Olwen more than on the first day. Then said Kilhwch, "Every one has received his boon, and I yet lack mine. I will depart and bear away thy honour with me." Then said Kai, "Rash chieftain! dost thou reproach Arthur? Go with us, and we will not part until thou dost either confess that the maiden exists not in the world, or until we obtain her." Thereupon Kai rose up. Kai had this peculiarity, that his breath lasted nine nights and nine days under water, and he could exist nine nights and nine days without sleep. A wound from Kai's sword no physician could heal. Very subtle was Kai. When it pleased him he could render himself as tall as the highest tree in the forest. And he had another peculiarity, – so great was the heat of his nature, that, when it rained hardest, whatever he carried remained dry for a handbreadth above and a handbreadth below his hand; and when his companions were coldest, it was to them as fuel with which to light their fire.

And Arthur called Bedwyr, who never shrank from any enterprise upon which Kai was bound. None was equal to him in swiftness throughout this island except Arthur and Drych Ail Kibddar. And although he was one-handed, three warriors could not shed blood faster than he on the field of battle. Another property he had; his lance would produce a wound equal to those of nine opposing lances.

And Arthur called to Kynddelig the Guide, "Go thou upon this expedition with the chieftain." For as good a guide was he in a land which he had never seen as he was in his own.

He called Gwrhyr Gwalstawt Ieithoedd, because he knew all tongues.

He called Gwalchmai the son of Gwyar, because he never returned home without achieving the adventure of which he went in quest. He was the best of footmen and the best of knights. He was nephew to Arthur, the son of his sister, and his cousin.

And Arthur called Menw the son of Teirgwaedd, in order that if they went into a savage country, he might cast a charm and an illusion over them, so that none might see them whilst they could see every one.

They journeyed until they came to a vast open plain, wherein they saw a great castle, which was the fairest of the castles of the world. And they journeyed that day until the evening, and when they thought they were nigh to the castle, they were no nearer to it than they had been in the morning. And the second and the third day they journeyed, and even then scarcely could they reach so far. And when they came before the castle, they beheld a vast flock of sheep, which was boundless and without an end. And upon the top of a mound there was a herdsman, keeping the sheep. And a rug made of skins was upon him; and by his side was a shaggy mastiff, larger than a steed nine winters old. Never had he lost even a lamb from his flock, much less a large sheep. He let no occasion ever pass without doing some hurt and harm. All the dead trees and bushes in the plain he burnt with his breath down to the very ground.

Then said Kai, "Gwrhyr Gwalstawt Ieithoedd, go thou and salute yonder man." "Kai," said he, "I engaged not to go further than thou thyself." "Let us go then together," answered Kai. Said Menw the son of Teirgwaedd, "Fear not to go thither, for I will cast a spell upon the dog, so that he shall injure no one." And they went up to the mound whereon the herdsman was, and they said to him, "How dost thou fare, O herdsman?" "No less fair be it to you than to me." "Truly, art thou the chief?" "There is no hurt to injure me but my own."[1] "Whose are the sheep that thou dost keep, and to whom does yonder castle belong?" "Stupid are ye, truly! Through the whole world is it known that this is the castle of Yspaddaden Penkawr." "And who art thou?" "I am called Custennin the son of Dyfnedig, and my brother Yspaddaden Penkawr oppressed me because of my possessions. And ye also, who are ye?" "We are an embassy from Arthur, come to seek Olwen the daughter of Yspaddaden Penkawr." "Oh men! the mercy of Heaven be upon you, do not that for all the world. None who ever came hither on this quest has returned alive." And the herdsman rose up. And as he arose, Kilhwch gave unto him a ring of gold. And he sought to put on the ring, but it was too small for him, so he placed it in the finger of his glove. And he went home, and gave the glove to his spouse to keep. And she took the ring from the glove when it was given her, and she said, "Whence came this ring, for thou art not wont to have good fortune?" "I went," said he, "to the sea to seek for fish, and lo, I saw a corpse borne by the waves. And a fairer corpse than it did I never behold. And from its finger did

---

[1] This dialogue consists of a series of repartees with a play upon words, which it is impossible to follow in the translation.

I take this ring." "O man! does the sea permit its dead to wear jewels? Show me then this body." "Oh wife, him to whom this ring belonged thou shalt see here in the evening." "And who is he?" asked the woman. "Kilhwch the son of Kilydd, the son of Prince Kelyddon, by Goleuddydd the daughter of Prince Anlawdd, his mother, who is come to seek Olwen as his wife." And when she heard that, her feelings were divided between the joy that she had that her nephew, the son of her sister, was coming to her, and sorrow because she had never known any one depart alive who had come on that quest.

And they went forward to the gate of Custennin the herdsman's dwelling. And when she heard their footsteps approaching, she ran out with joy to meet them. And Kai snatched a billet out of the pile. And when she met them she sought to throw her arms about their necks. And Kai placed the log between her two hands, and she squeezed it so that it became a twisted coil. "Oh woman," said Kai, "if thou hadst squeezed me thus, none could ever again have set their affections on me. Evil love were this." They entered into the house, and were served; and soon after they all went forth to amuse themselves. Then the woman opened a stone chest that was before the chimney-corner, and out of it arose a youth with yellow curling hair. Said Gwrhyr, "It is a pity to hide this youth. I know that it is not his own crime that is thus visited upon him." "This is but a remnant," said the woman. "Three-and-twenty of my sons has Yspaddaden Penkawr slain, and I have no more hope of this one than of the others." Then said Kai, "Let him come and be a companion with me, and he shall not be slain unless I also am slain with him." And they ate. And the woman asked them, "Upon what errand come you here?" "We come to seek Olwen for this youth." Then said the woman, "In the name of Heaven, since no one from the castle hath yet seen you, return again whence you came." "Heaven is our witness, that we will not return until we have seen the maiden." Said Kai, "Does she ever come hither, so that she may be seen?" "She comes here every Saturday to wash her head, and in the vessel where she washes, she leaves all her rings, and she never either comes herself or sends any messengers to fetch them." "Will she come here if she is sent to?" "Heaven knows that I will not destroy my soul, nor will I betray those that trust me; unless you will pledge me your faith that you will not harm her, I will not send to her." "We pledge it," said they. So a message was sent, and she came.

The maiden was clothed in a robe of flame-coloured silk, and about her neck was a collar of ruddy gold, on which were precious emeralds and rubies. More yellow was her head than the flower of the broom, and her skin was whiter than the foam of the wave, and fairer were her hands and her fingers than the blossoms of the wood anemone amidst the spray of the meadow fountain. The eye of the trained hawk, the glance of the three-mewed falcon was not brighter than hers. Her bosom was more snowy than the breast of the white swan, her cheek was redder than the reddest roses. Whoso beheld her was filled with her love. Four white trefoils sprung up wherever she trod. And therefore was she called Olwen.

She entered the house, and sat beside Kilhwch upon the foremost bench; and as soon as he saw her he knew her. And Kilhwch said unto her, "Ah! maiden, thou art she whom I have loved; come away with me, lest they speak evil of thee and of me. Many a day have I loved thee." "I cannot do this, for I have pledged my faith to my father not to go without his counsel, for his life will last only until the time of my espousals. Whatever is, must be. But I will give thee advice if thou wilt take it. Go, ask me of my father, and that which he shall require of thee, grant it, and thou wilt obtain me; but if thou deny him anything, thou wilt not obtain me, and it will be well for thee if thou escape with thy life." "I promise all this, if occasion offer," said he.

She returned to her chamber, and they all rose up and followed her to the castle. And they slew the nine porters that were at the nine gates in silence. And they slew the nine watch-dogs without one of them barking. And they went forward to the hall.

"The greeting of Heaven and of man be unto thee, Yspaddaden Penkawr," said they. "And you, wherefore come you?" "We come to ask thy daughter Olwen, for Kilhwch the son of Kilydd, the son of Prince Kelyddon." "Where are my pages and my servants? Raise up the forks beneath my two eyebrows which have fallen over my eyes, that I may see the fashion of my son-in-law." And they did so. "Come hither tomorrow, and you shall have an answer."

They rose to go forth, and Yspaddaden Penkawr seized one of the three poisoned darts that lay beside him, and threw it after them. And Bedwyr caught it, and flung it, and pierced Yspaddaden Penkawr grievously with it through the knee. Then he said, "A cursed ungentle son-in-law, truly. I shall ever walk the worse for his rudeness, and shall ever be without a cure. This poisoned iron pains me like the bite of a gadfly. Cursed be the smith who forged it, and the anvil whereon it was wrought! So sharp is it!"

That night also they took up their abode in the house of Custennin the herdsman. The next day with the dawn they arrayed themselves in haste and proceeded to the castle, and entered the hall, and they said, "Yspaddaden Penkawr, give us thy daughter in consideration of her dower and her maiden fee, which we will pay to thee and to her two kinswomen likewise. And unless thou wilt do so, thou shalt meet with thy death on her account." Then he said, "Her four great-grandmothers, and her four great-grandsires are yet alive, it is needful that I take counsel of them." "Be it so," answered they, "we will go to meat." As they rose up, he took the second dart that was beside him, and cast it after them. And Menw the son of Gwaedd caught it, and flung it back at him, and wounded him in the centre of the breast, so that it came out at the small of his back. "A cursed ungentle son-in-law, truly," said he, "the hard iron pains me like the bite of a horse-leech. Cursed be the hearth whereon it was heated, and the smith who formed it! So sharp is it! Henceforth, whenever I go up a hill, I shall have a scant in my breath, and a pain in my chest, and I shall often loathe my food." And they went to meat.

And the third day they returned to the palace. And Yspaddaden Penkawr said to them, "Shoot not at me again unless you desire death. Where are my attendants? Lift up the forks of my eyebrows which have fallen over my eyeballs, that I may see the fashion of my son-in-law." Then they arose, and, as they did so, Yspaddaden Penkawr took the third poisoned dart and cast it at them. And Kilhwch caught it and threw it vigorously, and wounded him through the eyeball, so that the dart came out at the back of his head. "A cursed ungentle son-in-law, truly! As long as I remain alive, my eyesight will be the worse. Whenever I go against the wind, my eyes will water; and per-adventure my head will burn, and I shall have a giddiness every new moon. Cursed be the fire in which it was forged. Like the bite of a mad dog is the stroke of this poisoned iron." And they went to meat.

And the next day they came again to the palace, and they said, "Shoot not at us any more, unless thou desirest such hurt, and harm, and torture as thou now hast, and even more." "Give me thy daughter, and if thou wilt not give her, thou shalt receive thy death because of her." "Where is he that seeks my daughter? Come hither where I may see thee." And they placed him a chair face to face with him.

Said Yspaddaden Penkawr, "Is it thou that seekest my daughter?" "It is I," answered Kilhwch. "I must have thy pledge that thou wilt not do towards me otherwise than is just, and when I have gotten that which I shall name, my daughter thou shalt have." "I promise thee that willingly," said Kilhwch, "name what thou wilt." "I will do so," said he.

"Seest thou yonder vast hill?" "I see it." "I require that it be rooted up, and that the grubbings be burned for manure on the face of the land, and that it be ploughed and sown in one day, and in one day that the grain ripen. And of that wheat I intend to make food and liquor fit for the wedding of thee and my daughter. And all this I require done in one day."

"It will be easy for me to compass this, although thou mayest think that it will not be easy."

"Though this be easy for thee, there is yet that which will not be so. No husbandman can till or prepare this land, so wild is it, except Amaethon the son of Don, and he will not come with thee by his own free will, and thou wilt not be able to compel him."

"It will be easy for me to compass this, although thou mayest think that it will not be easy."

"Though thou get this, there is yet that which thou wilt not get. Govannon the son of Don to come to the headland to rid the iron, he will do no work of his own good will except for a lawful king, and thou wilt not be able to compel him."

"It will be easy for me to compass this."

"Though thou get this, there is yet that which thou wilt not get; the two dun oxen of Gwlwlyd, both yoked together, to plough the wild land yonder stoutly. He will not give them of his own free will, and thou wilt not be able to compel him."

"It will be easy for me to compass this."

"Though thou get this, there is yet that which thou wilt not get; the yellow and the brindled bull yoked together do I require."

"It will be easy for me to compass this."

"Though thou get this, there is yet that which thou wilt not get; the two horned oxen, one of which is beyond, and the other this side of the peaked mountain, yoked together in the same plough. And these are Nynniaw and Peibaw whom God turned into oxen on account of their sins."

"It will be easy for me to compass this."

"Though thou get this, there is yet that which thou wilt not get. Seest thou yonder red tilled ground?"

"I see it."

"When first I met the mother of this maiden, nine bushels of flax were sown therein, and none has yet sprung up, neither white nor black; and I have the measure by me still. I require to have the flax to sow in the new land yonder, that when it grows up it may make a white wimple for my daughter's head, on the day of thy wedding."

"It will be easy for me to compass this, although thou mayest think that it will not be easy."

"Though thou get this, there is yet that which thou wilt not get. Honey that is nine times sweeter than the honey of the virgin swarm, without scum and bees, do I require to make bragget for the feast."

"It will be easy for me to compass this, although thou mayest think that it will not be easy."

"The vessel of Llwyr the son of Llwyryon, which is of the utmost value. There is no other vessel in the world that can hold this drink. Of his free will thou wilt not get it, and thou canst not compel him."

"It will be easy for me to compass this, although thou mayest think that it will not be easy."

"Though thou get this, there is yet that which thou wilt not get. The basket of Gwyddneu Garanhir, if the whole world should come together, thrice nine men at a time, the meat that each of them desired would be found within it. I require to eat therefrom on the night that my daughter becomes thy bride. He will give it to no one of his own free will, and thou canst not compel him."

"It will be easy for me to compass this, although thou mayest think that it will not be easy."

"Though thou get this, there is yet that which thou wilt not get. The horn of Gwlgawd Gododin to serve us with liquor that night. He will not give it of his own free will, and thou wilt not be able to compel him."

"It will be easy for me to compass this, although thou mayest think that it will not be easy."

"Though thou get this, there is yet that which thou wilt not get. The harp of Teirtu to play to us that night. When a man desires that it should play, it does so of itself, and when he desires that it should cease, it ceases. And this he will not give of his own free will, and thou wilt not be able to compel him."

"It will be easy for me to compass this, although thou mayest think that it will not be easy."

"Though thou get this, there is yet that which thou wilt not get. The cauldron of Diwrnach Wyddel, the steward of Odgar the son of Aedd, king of Ireland, to boil the meat for thy marriage feast."

"It will be easy for me to compass this, although thou mayest think that it will not be easy."

"Though thou get this, there is yet that which thou wilt not get. It is needful for me to wash my head, and shave my beard, and I require the tusk of Yskithyrwyn Penbaedd to shave myself withal, neither shall I profit by its use if it be not plucked alive out of his head."

"It will be easy for me to compass this, although thou mayest think that it will not be easy."

"Though thou get this, there is yet that which thou wilt not get. There is no one in the world that can pluck it out of his head except Odgar the son of Aedd, king of Ireland."

"It will be easy for me to compass this."

"Though thou get this, there is yet that which thou wilt not get. I will not trust any one to keep the tusk except Gado of North Britain. Now the threescore Cantrevs of North Britain are under his sway, and of his own free will he will not come out of his kingdom, and thou wilt not be able to compel him."

"It will be easy for me to compass this, although thou mayest think that it will not be easy."

"Though thou get this, there is yet that which thou wilt not get. I must spread out my hair in order to shave it, and it will never be spread out unless I have the blood of the jet-black sorceress, the daughter of the pure white sorceress, from Pen Nant Govid, on the confines of Hell."

"It will be easy for me to compass this, although thou mayest think that it will not be easy."

"Though thou get this, there is yet that which thou wilt not get. I will not have the blood unless I have it warm, and no vessels will keep warm the liquid that is put therein except the bottles of Gwyddolwyd Gorr, which preserve the heat of the liquor that is put into them in the east, until they arrive at the west. And he will not give them of his own free will, and thou wilt not be able to compel him."

"It will be easy for me to compass this, although thou mayest think that it will not be easy."

"Though thou get this, there is yet that which thou wilt not get. Some will desire fresh milk, and it will not be possible to have fresh milk for all, unless we have the bottles of Rhinnon Rhin Barnawd, wherein no liquor ever turns sour. And he will not give them of his own free will, and thou wilt not be able to compel him."

"It will be easy for me to compass this, although thou mayest think that it will not be easy."

"Though thou get this, there is yet that which thou wilt not get. Throughout the world there is not a comb or scissors with which I can arrange my hair, on account of its rankness, except the comb and scissors that are between the two ears of Twrch Trwyth, the son of Prince Tared. He will not give them of his own free will, and thou wilt not be able to compel him."

"It will be easy for me to compass this, although thou mayest think that it will not be easy."

"Though thou get this, there is yet that which thou wilt not get. It will not be possible to hunt Twrch Trwyth without Drudwyn the whelp of Greid, the son of Eri."

"It will be easy for me to compass this, although thou mayest think that it will not be easy."

"Though thou get this, there is yet that which thou wilt not get. Throughout the world there is not a leash that can hold him, except the leash of Cwrs Cant Ewin."

"It will be easy for me to compass this, although thou mayest think that it will not be easy."

"Though thou get this, there is yet that which thou wilt not get. Throughout the world there is no collar that will hold the leash except the collar of Canhastyr Canllaw."

"It will be easy for me to compass this, although thou mayest think that it will not be easy."

"Though thou get this, there is yet that which thou wilt not get. The chain of Kilydd Canhastyr to fasten the collar to the leash."

"It will be easy for me to compass this, although thou mayest think that it will not be easy."

"Though thou get this, there is yet that which thou wilt not get. Throughout the world there is not a huntsman who can hunt with this dog, except Mabon the son of Modron. He was taken from his mother when three nights old, and it is not known where he now is, nor whether he is living or dead."

"It will be easy for me to compass this, although thou mayest think that it will not be easy."

"Though thou get this, there is yet that which thou wilt not get. Gwynn Mygdwn, the horse of Gweddw, that is as swift as the wave, to carry Mabon the son of Modron to hunt the boar Trwyth. He will not give him of his own free will, and thou wilt not be able to compel him."

"It will be easy for me to compass this, although thou mayest think that it will not be easy."

"Though thou get this, there is yet that which thou wilt not get. Thou wilt not get Mabon, for it is not known where he is, unless thou find Eidoel, his kinsman in blood, the son of Aer. For it would be useless to seek for him. He is his cousin."

"It will be easy for me to compass this, although thou mayest think that it will not be easy."

"Though thou get this, there is yet that which thou wilt not get.

Garselit the Gwyddelian is the chief huntsman of Ireland; the Twrch Trwyth can never be hunted without him."

"It will be easy for me to compass this, although thou mayest think that it will not be easy."

"Though thou get this, there is yet that which thou wilt not get. A leash made from the beard of Dillus Varvawc, for that is the only one that can hold those two cubs. And the leash will be of no avail unless it be plucked from his beard while he is alive, and twitched out with wooden tweezers. While he lives he will not suffer this to be done to him, and the leash will be of no use should he be dead, because it will be brittle."

"It will be easy for me to compass this, although thou mayest think that it will not be easy."

"Though thou get this, there is yet that which thou wilt not get. Throughout the world there is no huntsman that can hold those two whelps except Kynedyr Wyllt, the son of Hettwn Glafyrawc; he is nine times more wild than the wildest beast upon the mountains. Him wilt thou never get, neither wilt thou ever get my daughter."

"It will be easy for me to compass this, although thou mayest think that it will not be easy."

"Though thou get this, there is yet that which thou wilt not get. It is not possible to hunt the boar Trwyth without Gwynn the son of Nudd, whom God has placed over the brood of devils in Annwvyn, lest they should destroy the present race. He will never be spared thence."

"It will be easy for me to compass this, although thou mayest think that it will not be easy."

"Though thou get this, there is yet that which thou wilt not get. There is not a horse in the world that can carry Gwynn to hunt the Twrch Trwyth, except Du, the horse of Mor of Oerveddawg."

"It will be easy for me to compass this, although thou mayest think that it will not be easy."

"Though thou get this, there is yet that which thou wilt not get. Until Gilennhin the king of France shall come, the Twrch Trwyth cannot be hunted. It will be unseemly for him to leave his kingdom for thy sake, and he will never come hither."

"It will be easy for me to compass this, although thou mayest think that it will not be easy."

"Though thou get this, there is yet that which thou wilt not get. The Twrch Trwyth can never be hunted without the son of Alun Dyved; he is well skilled in letting loose the dogs."

"It will be easy for me to compass this, although thou mayest think that it will not be easy."

"Though thou get this, there is yet that which thou wilt not get. The Twrch Trwyth cannot be hunted unless thou get Aned and Aethlem. They are as swift as the gale of wind, and they were never let loose upon a beast that they did not kill him."

"It will be easy for me to compass this, although thou mayest think that it will not be easy."

"Though thou get this, there is yet that which thou wilt not get; Arthur and his companions to hunt the Twrch Trwyth. He is a mighty man, and he will not come for thee, neither wilt thou be able to compel him."

"It will be easy for me to compass this, although thou mayest think that it will not be easy."

"Though thou get this, there is yet that which thou wilt not get. The Twrch Trwyth cannot be hunted unless thou get Bwlch, and Kyfwlch [and Sefwlch], the grandsons of Cleddyf Difwlch. Their three shields are three gleaming glitterers. Their three spears are three pointed piercers. Their three swords are three griding gashers, Glas, Glessic, and Clersag. Their three dogs, Call, Cuall, and Cavall. Their three horses, Hwyrdydwg, and Drwgdydwg, and Llwyrdydwg. Their three wives, Och, and Garam, and Diaspad. Their three grandchildren, Lluched, and Vyned, and Eissiwed. Their three daughters, Drwg, and Gwaeth, and Gwaethav Oll. Their three handmaids [Eheubryd, the daughter of Kyfwlch; Gorasgwrn, the daughter of Nerth; and Gwaedan, the daughter of Kynvelyn]. These three men shall sound the horn, and all the others shall shout, so that all will think that the sky is falling to the earth."

"It will be easy for me to compass this, although thou mayest think that it will not be easy."

"Though thou get this, there is yet that which thou wilt not get. The sword of Gwrnach the Giant; he will never be slain except therewith. Of his own free will he will not give it, either for a price or as a gift, and thou wilt never be able to compel him."

"It will be easy for me to compass this, although thou mayest think that it will not be easy."

"Though thou get this, there is yet that which thou wilt not get. Difficulties shalt thou meet with, and nights without sleep, in seeking this, and if thou obtain it not, neither shalt thou obtain my daughter."

"Horses shall I have, and chivalry; and my lord and kinsman Arthur will obtain for me all these things. And I shall gain thy daughter, and thou shalt lose thy life."

"Go forward. And thou shalt not be chargeable for food or

raiment for my daughter while thou art seeking these things; and when thou hast compassed all these marvels, thou shalt have my daughter for thy wife."

All that day they journeyed until the evening, and then they beheld a vast castle, which was the largest in the world. And lo, a black man, huger than three of the men of this world, came out from the castle. And they spoke unto him, "Whence comest thou, O man?" "From the castle which you see yonder." "Whose castle is that?" asked they. "Stupid are ye truly, O men. There is no one in the world that does not know to whom this castle belongs. It is the castle of Gwrnach the Giant." "What treatment is there for guests and strangers that alight in that castle?" "Oh! Chieftain, Heaven protect thee. No guest ever returned thence alive, and no one may enter therein unless he brings with him his craft."

Then they proceeded towards the gate. Said Gwrhyr Gwalstawt Ieithoedd, "Is there a porter?" "There is. And thou, if thy tongue be not mute in thy head, wherefore dost thou call?" "Open the gate." "I will not open it." "Wherefore wilt thou not?" "The knife is in the meat, and the drink is in the horn, and there is revelry in the hall of Gwrnach the Giant, and except for a craftsman who brings his craft, the gate will not be opened to-night." "Verily, porter," then said Kai, "my craft bring I with me." "What is thy craft?" "The best burnisher of swords am I in the world." "I will go and tell this unto Gwrnach the Giant, and I will bring thee an answer."

So the porter went in, and Gwrnach said to him, "Hast thou any news from the gate?" "I have. There is a party at the door of the gate who desire to come in." "Didst thou inquire of them if they possessed any art?" "I did inquire," said he, "and one told me that he was well skilled in the burnishing of swords." "We have need of him then. For some time have I sought for some one to polish my sword, and could find no one. Let this man enter, since he brings with him his craft." The porter thereupon returned and opened the gate. And Kai went in by himself, and he saluted Gwrnach the Giant. And a chair was placed for him opposite to Gwrnach. And Gwrnach said to him, "Oh man! is it true that is reported of thee, that thou knowest how to burnish swords?" "I know full well how to do so," answered Kai. Then was the sword of Gwrnach brought to him. And Kai took a blue whetstone from under his arm, and asked him whether he would have it burnished white or blue. "Do with it as it seems good to thee, and as thou wouldest if it were thine own." Then Kai polished one half of the blade and put it in his hand. "Will this please thee?" asked he.

"I would rather than all that is in my dominions that the whole of it were like unto this. It is a marvel to me that such a man as thou should be without a companion." "Oh! noble sir, I have a companion, albeit he is not skilled in this art." "Who may he be?" "Let the porter go forth, and I will tell him whereby he may know him. The head of his lance will leave its shaft, and draw blood from the wind, and will descend upon its shaft again." Then the gate was opened, and Bedwyr entered. And Kai said, "Bedwyr is very skilful, although he knows not this art."

And there was much discourse among those who were without, because that Kai and Bedwyr had gone in. And a young man who was with them, the only son of Custennin the herdsman, got in also. And he caused all his companions to keep close to him as he passed the three wards, and until he came into the midst of the castle. And his companions said unto the son of Custennin, "Thou hast done this! Thou art the best of all men." And thenceforth he was called Goreu, the son of Custennin. Then they dispersed to their lodgings, that they might slay those who lodged therein, unknown to the Giant.

The sword was now polished, and Kai gave it unto the hand of Gwrnach the Giant, to see if he were pleased with his work. And the Giant said, "The work is good, I am content therewith." Said Kai, "It is thy scabbard that hath rusted thy sword, give it to me that I may take out the wooden sides of it and put in new ones." And he took the scabbard from him, and the sword in the other hand. And he came and stood over against the Giant, as if he would have put the sword into the scabbard; and with it he struck at the head of the Giant, and cut off his head at one blow. Then they despoiled the castle, and took from it what goods and jewels they would. And again on the same day, at the beginning of the year, they came to Arthur's Court, bearing with them the sword of Gwrnach the Giant.

Now, when they told Arthur how they had sped, Arthur said, "Which of these marvels will it be best for us to seek first?" "It will be best," said they, "to seek Mabon the son of Modron; and he will not be found unless we first find Eidoel the son of Aer, his kinsman." Then Arthur rose up, and the warriors of the Islands of Britain with him, to seek for Eidoel; and they proceeded until they came before the Castle of Glivi, where Eidoel was imprisoned. Glivi stood on the summit of his castle, and he said, "Arthur, what requirest thou of me, since nothing remains to me in this fortress, and I have neither joy nor pleasure in it; neither wheat nor oats?

Seek not therefore to do me harm." Said Arthur, "Not to injure thee came I hither, but to seek for the prisoner that is with thee." "I will give thee my prisoner, though I had not thought to give him up to any one; and therewith shalt thou have my support and my aid."

His followers said unto Arthur, "Lord, go thou home, thou canst not proceed with thy host in quest of such small adventures as these." Then said Arthur, "It were well for thee, Gwrhyr Gwalstawt Ieithoedd, to go upon this quest, for thou knowest all languages, and art familiar with those of the birds and the beasts. Thou, Eidoel, oughtest likewise to go with my men in search of thy cousin. And as for you, Kai and Bedwyr, I have hope of whatever adventure ye are in quest of, that ye will achieve it. Achieve ye this adventure for me."

They went forward until they came to the Ousel of Cilgwri. And Gwrhyr adjured her for the sake of Heaven, saying, "Tell me if thou knowest aught of Mabon the son of Modron, who was taken when three nights old from between his mother and the wall." And the Ousel answered, "When I first came here, there was a smith's anvil in this place, and I was then a young bird; and from that time no work has been done upon it, save the pecking of my beak every evening, and now there is not so much as the size of a nut remaining thereof; yet the vengeance of Heaven be upon me, if during all that time I have ever heard of the man for whom you inquire. Nevertheless I will do that which is right, and that which it is fitting that I should do for an embassy from Arthur. There is a race of animals who were formed before me, and I will be your guide to them."

So they proceeded to the place where was the Stag of Redynvre. "Stag of Redynvre, behold we are come to thee, an embassy from Arthur, for we have not heard of any animal older than thou. Say, knowest thou aught of Mabon the son of Modron, who was taken from his mother when three nights old?" The Stag said, "When first I came hither, there was a plain all around me, without any trees save one oak sapling, which grew up to be an oak with an hundred branches. And that oak has since perished, so that now nothing remains of it but the withered stump; and from that day to this I have been here, yet have I never heard of the man for whom you inquire. Nevertheless, being an embassy from Arthur, I will be your guide to the place where there is an animal which was formed before I was."

So they proceeded to the place where was the Owl of Cwm

Cawlwyd. "Owl of Cwm Cawlwyd, here is an embassy from Arthur; knowest thou aught of Mabon the son of Modron, who was taken after three nights from his mother?" "If I knew I would tell you. When first I came hither, the wide valley you see was a wooded glen. And a race of men came and rooted it up. And there grew there a second wood; and this wood is the third. My wings, are they not withered stumps? Yet all this time, even until to-day, I have never heard of the man for whom you inquire. Nevertheless, I will be the guide of Arthur's embassy until you come to the place where is the oldest animal in this world, and the one that has travelled most, the Eagle of Gwern Abwy."

Gwrhyr said, "Eagle of Gwern Abwy, we have come to thee an embassy from Arthur, to ask thee if thou knowest aught of Mabon the son of Modron, who was taken from his mother when he was three nights old." The Eagle said, "I have been here for a great space of time, and when I first came hither there was a rock here, from the top of which I pecked at the stars every evening; and now it is not so much as a span high. From that day to this I have been here, and I have never heard of the man for whom you inquire, except once when I went in search of food as far as Llyn Llyw. And when I came there, I struck my talons into a salmon, thinking he would serve me as food for a long time. But he drew me into the deep, and I was scarcely able to escape from him. After that I went with my whole kindred to attack him, and to try to destroy him, but he sent messengers, and made peace with me; and came and besought me to take fifty fish spears out of his back. Unless he know something of him whom you seek, I cannot tell who may. However, I will guide you to the place where he is."

So they went thither; and the Eagle said, "Salmon of Llyn Llyw, I have come to thee with an embassy from Arthur, to ask thee if thou knowest aught concerning Mabon the son of Modron, who was taken away at three nights old from his mother." "As much as I know I will tell thee. With every tide I go along the river upwards, until I come near to the walls of Gloucester, and there have I found such wrong as I never found elsewhere; and to the end that ye may give credence thereto, let one of you go thither upon each of my two shoulders." So Kai and Gwrhyr Gwalstawt Ieithoedd went upon the two shoulders of the salmon, and they proceeded until they came unto the wall of the prison, and they heard a great wailing and lamenting from the dungeon. Said Gwrhyr, "Who is it that laments in this house of stone?" "Alas, there is reason enough for whoever is here to lament. It is Mabon the son of Modron who is here imprisoned; and no imprisonment was ever so grievous as mine, neither that of Llud Llaw Ereint, nor that of Greid the son of Eri." "Hast thou hope of being released for gold or for silver, or for any gifts of wealth, or through battle and fighting?" "By fighting will whatever I may gain be obtained."

Then they went thence, and returned to Arthur, and they told him where Mabon the son of Modron was imprisoned. And Arthur summoned the warriors of the Island, and they journeyed as far as Gloucester, to the place where Mabon was in prison. Kai and Bedwyr went upon the shoulders of the fish, whilst the warriors of Arthur attacked the castle. And Kai broke through the wall into the dungeon, and brought away the prisoner upon his back, whilst the fight was going on between the warriors. And Arthur returned home, and Mabon with him at liberty.

Said Arthur, "Which of the marvels will it be best for us now to seek first?" "It will be best to seek for the two cubs of Gast Rhymhi." "Is it known," asked Arthur, "where she is?" "She is in Aber Deu Cleddyf," said one. Then Arthur went to the house of Tringad, in Aber Cleddyf, and he inquired of him whether he had heard of her there. "In what form may she be?" "She is in the form of a she-wolf," said he; "and with her there are two cubs." "She has often slain my herds, and she is there below in a cave in Aber Cleddyf."

So Arthur went in his ship Prydwen by sea, and the others went by land, to hunt her. And they surrounded her and her two cubs, and God did change them again for Arthur into their own form. And the host of Arthur dispersed themselves into parties of one and two.

On a certain day, as Gwythyr the son of Greidawl was walking over a mountain, he heard a wailing and a grievous cry. And when he heard it, he sprang forward, and went towards it. And when he came there, he drew his sword, and smote off an ant-hill close to the earth, whereby it escaped being burned in the fire. And the ants said to him, "Receive from us the blessing of Heaven, and that which no man can give we will give thee." Then they fetched the nine bushels of flax-seed which Yspaddaden Penkawr had required of Kilhwch, and they brought the full measure without lacking any, except one flax-seed, and that the lame pismire brought in before night.

As Kai and Bedwyr sat on a beacon carn on the summit of Plinlimmon, in the highest wind that ever was in the world, they looked around them, and saw a great smoke towards the south, afar off, which did not bend with the wind. Then said Kai, "By the hand of my friend, behold, yonder is the fire of a robber!" Then they hastened towards the smoke, and they came so near to it, that they could see Dillus Varvawc scorching a wild boar. "Behold, yonder is the greatest robber that ever fled from Arthur," said Bedwyr unto Kai. "Dost thou know him?" "I do know him," answered Kai, "he is Dillus Varvawc, and no leash in the world will be able to hold Drudwyn, the cub of Greid the son of Eri, save a leash made from the beard of him thou seest yonder. And even that will be useless, unless his beard be plucked alive with wooden tweezers; for if dead, it will be brittle." "What thinkest thou that we should do concerning this?" said Bedwyr. "Let us suffer him," said Kai, "to eat as much as he will of the meat, and after that he will fall asleep." And during that time they employed themselves in making the wooden tweezers. And when Kai knew certainly that he was asleep, he made a pit under his feet, the largest in the world, and he struck him a violent blow, and squeezed him into the pit. And there they twitched out his beard completely with the wooden tweezers; and after that they slew him altogether.

And from thence they both went to Gelli Wic, in Cornwall, and took the leash made of Dillus Varvawc's beard with them, and they gave it into Arthur's hand. Then Arthur composed this Englyn –

Kai made a leash
Of Dillus son of Eurei's beard.
Were he alive, thy death he'd be.

And thereupon Kai was wroth, so that the warriors of the Island could scarcely make peace between Kai and Arthur. And thenceforth, neither in Arthur's troubles, nor for the slaying of his men, would Kai come forward to his aid for ever after.

Said Arthur, "Which of the marvels is it best for us now to seek?" "It is best for us to seek Drudwyn, the cub of Greid the son of Eri."

A little while before this, Creiddylad the daughter of Lludd Llaw Ereint, and Gwythyr the son of Greidawl, were betrothed. And before she had become his bride, Gwyn ap Nudd came and carried her away by force; and Gwythyr the son of Greidawl gathered his host together, and went to fight with Gwyn ap Nudd. But Gwyn overcame him, and captured Greid the son of Eri, and Glinneu the son of Taran, and Gwrgwst Ledlwm and Dynvarth his son. And he captured Penn the son of Nethawg, and Nwython, and Kyledyr Wyllt his son. And they slew Nwython, and took out his heart, and

constrained Kyledyr to eat the heart of his father. And therefrom
Kyledyr became mad. When Arthur heard of this, he went to the
North, and summoned Gwyn ap Nudd before him, and set free the
nobles whom he had put in prison, and made peace between Gwyn
ap Nudd and Gwythyr the son of Griedawl. And this was the peace
that was made: that the maiden should remain in her father's house,
without advantage to either of them, and that Gwyn ap Nudd and
Gwythyr the son of Greidawl should fight for her every first of
May, from thenceforth until the day of doom, and that whichever
of them should then be conqueror should have the maiden.

And when Arthur had thus reconciled these chieftains, he obtained
Mygdwn, Gweddw's horse, and the leash of Cwrs Cant Ewin.

And after that Arthur went into Armorica, and with him Mabon
the son of Mellt, and Gware Gwallt Euryn, to seek the two dogs of
Glythmyr Ledewic. And when he had got them, he went to the West
of Ireland, in search of Gwrgi Severi; and Odgar the son of Aedd
king of Ireland went with him. And thence went Arthur into the
North, and captured Kyledyr Wyllt; and he went after Yskithyrwyn
Penbaedd. And Mabon the son of Mellt came with the two dogs of
Glythmyr Ledewic in his hand, and Drudwyn, the cub of Greid the
son of Eri. And Arthur went himself to the chase, leading his own
dog Cavall. And Kaw, of North Britain, mounted Arthur's mare
Llamrei, and was first in the attack. Then Kaw, of North Britain,
wielded a mighty axe, and absolutely daring he came valiantly up
to the boar, and clave his head in twain. And Kaw took away the
tusk. Now the boar was not slain by the dogs that Yspaddaden
had mentioned, but by Cavall, Arthur's own dog.

And after Yskithyrwyn Penbaedd was killed, Arthur and his host
departed to Gelli Wic in Cornwall. And thence he sent Menw the
son of Teirgwaedd to see if the precious things were between the
two ears of Twrch Trwyth, since it were useless to encounter him
if they were not there. Albeit it was certain where he was, for he
had laid waste the third part of Ireland. And Menw went to seek
for him, and he met with him in Ireland, in Esgeir Oervel. And
Menw took the form of a bird; and he descended upon the top of
his lair, and strove to snatch away one of the precious things from
him, but he carried away nothing but one of his bristles. And the
boar rose up angrily and shook himself so that some of his venom
fell upon Menw, and he was never well from that day forward.

After this Arthur sent an embassy to Odgar, the son of Aedd
king of Ireland, to ask for the cauldron of Diwrnach Wyddel, his
purveyor. And Odgar commanded him to give it. But Diwrnach

said, "Heaven is my witness, if it would avail him anything even to look at it, he should not do so." And the embassy of Arthur returned from Ireland with this denial. And Arthur set forward with a small retinue, and entered into Prydwen, his ship, and went over to Ireland. And they proceeded into the house of Diwrnach Wyddel. And the hosts of Odgar saw their strength. When they had eaten and drunk as much as they desired, Arthur demanded to have the cauldron. And he answered, "If I would have given it to any one, I would have given it at the word of Odgar king of Ireland."

When he had given them this denial, Bedwyr arose and seized hold of the cauldron, and placed it upon the back of Hygwyd, Arthur's servant, who was brother, by the mother's side, to Arthur's servant, Cachamwri. His office was always to carry Arthur's cauldron, and to place fire under it. And Llenlleawg Wyddel seized Caledvwlch, and brandished it. And they slew Diwrnach Wyddel and his company. Then came the Irish and fought with them. And when he had put them to flight, Arthur with his men went forward to the ship, carrying away the cauldron full of Irish money. And he disembarked at the house of Llwydden the son of Kelcoed, at Porth Kerddin in Dyved. And there is the measure of the cauldron.

Then Arthur summoned unto him all the warriors that were in the three Islands of Britain, and in the three Islands adjacent, and all that were in France and in Armorica, in Normandy and in the Summer Country, and all that were chosen footmen and valiant horsemen. And with all these he went into Ireland. And in Ireland there was great fear and terror concerning him. And when Arthur had landed in the country, there came unto him the saints of Ireland and besought his protection. And he granted his protection unto them, and they gave him their blessing. Then the men of Ireland came unto Arthur, and brought him provisions. And Arthur went as far as Esgeir Oervel in Ireland, to the place where the Boar Trwyth was with his seven young pigs. And the dogs were let loose upon him from all sides. That day until evening the Irish fought with him, nevertheless he laid waste the fifth part of Ireland. And on the day following the household of Arthur fought with him, and they were worsted by him, and got no advantage. And the third day Arthur himself encountered him, and he fought with him nine nights and nine days without so much as killing even one little pig. The warriors inquired of Arthur what was the origin of that swine; and he told them that he was once a king, and that God had transformed him into a swine for his sins.

Then Arthur sent Gwrhyr Gwalstawt Ieithoedd, to endeavour to speak with him. And Gwrhyr assumed the form of a bird, and alighted upon the top of the lair, where he was with the seven young pigs. And Gwrhyr Gwalstawt Ieithoedd asked him, "By him who turned you into this form, if you can speak, let some one of you, I beseech you, come and talk with Arthur." Grugyn Gwrych Ereint made answer to him. (Now his bristles were like silver wire, and whether he went through the wood or through the plain, he was to be traced by the glittering of his bristles.) And this was the answer that Grugyn made: "By him who turned us into this form, we will not do so, and we will not speak with Arthur. That we have been transformed thus is enough for us to suffer, without your coming here to fight with us." "I will tell you. Arthur comes but to fight for the comb, and the razor, and the scissors which are between the two ears of Twrch Trwyth." Said Grugyn, "Except he first take his life, he will never have those precious things. And tomorrow morning we will rise up hence, and we will go into Arthur's country, and there will we do all the mischief that we can."

So they set forth through the sea towards Wales. And Arthur and his hosts, and his horses and his dogs, entered Prydwen, that they might encounter them without delay. Twrch Trwyth landed in Porth Cleis in Dyved, and Arthur came to Mynyw. The next day it was told to Arthur that they had gone by, and he overtook them as they were killing the cattle of Kynnwas Kwrr y Vagyl, having slain all that were at Aber Gleddyf, of man and beast, before the coming of Arthur.

Now when Arthur approached, Twrch Trwyth went on as far as Preseleu, and Arthur and his hosts followed him thither, and Arthur sent men to hunt him; Eli and Trachmyr, leading Drudwyn the whelp of Greid the son of Eri, and Gwarthegyd the son of Kaw, in another quarter, with the two dogs of Glythmyr Ledewic, and Bedwyr leading Cavall, Arthur's own dog. And all the warriors ranged themselves around the Nyver. And there came there the three sons of Cleddyf Divwlch, men who had gained much fame at the slaying of Yskithyrwyn Penbaedd; and they went on from Glyn Nyver, and came to Cwm Kerwyn.

And there Twrch Trwyth made a stand, and slew four of Arthur's champions, Gwarthegyd the son of Kaw, and Tarawc of Allt Clwyd, and Rheidwn the son of Eli Atver, and Iscovan Hael. And after he had slain these men, he made a second stand in the same place. And there he slew Gwydre the son of Arthur, and Garselit Wyddel, and Glew the son of Ysgawd, and Iscawyn the son of Panon; and there he himself was wounded.

And the next morning before it was day, some of the men came up with him. And he slew Huandaw, and Gogigwr, and Penpingon, three attendants upon Glewlwyd Gavaelvawr, so that Heaven knows he had not an attendant remaining, excepting only Llaesgevyn, a man from whom no one ever derived any good. And together with these he slew many of the men of that country, and Gwlydyn Saer, Arthur's chief Architect.

Then Arthur overtook him at Pelumyawc, and there he slew Madawc the son of Teithyon, and Gwyn the son of Tringad, the son of Neved, and Eiryawn Penllorau. Thence he went to Aberteivi, where he made another stand, and where he slew Kyflas the son of Kynan, and Gwilenhin king of France. Then he went as far as Glyn Ystu, and there the men and the dogs lost him.

Then Arthur summoned unto him Gwyn ab Nudd, and he asked him if he knew aught of Twrch Trwyth. And he said that he did not.

And all the huntsmen went to hunt the swine as far as Dyffryn Llychwr. And Grugyn Gwallt Ereint and Llwydawg Govynnyad closed with them and killed all the huntsmen, so that there escaped but one man only. And Arthur and his hosts came to the place where Grugyn and Llwydawg were. And there he let loose the whole of the dogs upon them, and with the shout and barking that was set up, Twrch Trwyth came to their assistance.

And from the time that they came across the Irish sea, Arthur had never got sight of him until then. So he set men and dogs upon him, and thereupon he started off and went to Mynydd Amanw. And there one of his young pigs was killed. Then they set upon him life for life, and Twrch Llawin was slain, and then there was slain another of the swine, Gwys was his name. After that he went on to Dyffryn Amanw, and there Banw and Bennwig were killed. Of all his pigs there went with him alive from that place none save Grugyn Gwalt Ereint and Llwydawg Govynnyad.

Thence he went on to Llwch Ewin, and Arthur overtook him there, and he made a stand. And there he slew Echel Forddwytwll, and Garwyli the son of Gwyddawg Gwyr, and many men and dogs likewise. And thence they went to Llwch Tawy. Grugyn Gwrych Ereint parted from them there, and went to Din Tywi. And thence he proceeded to Ceredigiawn, and Eli and Trachmyr with him, and a multitude likewise. Then he came to Garth Gregyn, and there Llwydawg Govynnyad fought in the midst of them, and slew

Rhudvyw Rhys and many others with him. Then Llwydawg went thence to Ystrad Yw, and there the men of Armorica met him, and there he slew Hirpeissawg the king of Armorica, and Llygatrudd Emys, and Gwrbothu, Arthur's uncles, his mother's brothers, and there was he himself slain.

Twrch Trwyth went from there to between Tawy and Euyas, and Arthur summoned all Cornwall and Devon unto him, to the estuary of the Severn, and he said to the warriors of this Island, "Twrch Trwyth has slain many of my men, but, by the valour of warriors, while I live he shall not go into Cornwall. And I will not follow him any longer, but I will oppose him life to life. Do ye as ye will." And he resolved that he would send a body of knights, with the dogs of the Island, as far as Euyas, who should return thence to the Severn, and that tried warriors should traverse the Island, and force him into the Severn. And Mabon the son of Modron came up with him at the Severn, upon Gwynn Mygdwn, the horse of Gweddw, and Goreu the son of Custennin, and Menw the son of Teirgwaedd; this was betwixt Llyn Lliwan and Aber Gwy. And Arthur fell upon him together with the champions of Britain. And Osla Kyllellvawr drew near, and Manawyddan the son of Llyr, and Kacmwri the servant of Arthur, and Gwyngelli, and they seized hold of him, catching him first by his feet, and plunged him in the Severn, so that it overwhelmed him. On the one side, Mabon the son of Modron spurred his steed and snatched his razor from him, and Kyledyr Wyllt came up with him on the other side, upon another steed, in the Severn, and took from him the scissors. But before they could obtain the comb, he had regained the ground with his feet, and from the moment that he reached the shore, neither dog, nor man, nor horse could overtake him until he came to Cornwall. If they had had trouble in getting the jewels from him, much more had they in seeking to save the two men from being drowned. Kacmwri, as they drew him forth, was dragged by two millstones into the deep. And as Osla Kyllellvawr was running after the boar, his knife had dropped out of the sheath, and he had lost it, and after that, the sheath became full of water, and its weight drew him down into the deep, as they were drawing him forth.

Then Arthur and his hosts proceeded until they overtook the boar in Cornwall, and the trouble which they had met with before was mere play to what they encountered in seeking the comb. But from one difficulty to another, the comb was at length obtained. And then he was hunted from Cornwall, and driven straight forward into the deep sea. And thenceforth it was never known whither he went;

and Aned and Aethlem with him. Then went Arthur to Gelli Wic, in Cornwall, to anoint himself, and to rest from his fatigues. Said Arthur, "Is there any one of the marvels yet unobtained?" Said one of his men, "There is – the blood of the witch Orddu, the daughter of the witch Orwen, of Pen Nant Govid, on the confines of Hell." Arthur set forth towards the North, and came to the place where was the witch's cave. And Gwyn ab Nudd, and Gwythyr the son of Greidawl, counselled him to send Kacmwri, and Hygwyd his brother, to fight with the witch. And as they entered the cave, the witch seized upon them, and she caught Hygwyd by the hair of his head, and threw him on the floor beneath her. And Kacmwri caught her by the hair of her head, and dragged her to the earth from off Hygwyd, but she turned again upon them both, and drove them both out with kicks and with cuffs.

And Arthur was wroth at seeing his two attendants almost slain, and he sought to enter the cave; but Gwyn and Gwythyr said unto him, "It would not be fitting or seemly for us to see thee squabbling with a hag. Let Hiramreu and Hireidil go to the cave." So they went. But if great was the trouble of the first two that went, much greater was that of these two. And Heaven knows that not one of the four could move from the spot, until they placed them all upon Llamrei, Arthur's mare. And then Arthur rushed to the door of the cave, and at the door he struck at the witch, with Carnwennan his dagger, and clove her in twain, so that she fell in two parts. And Kaw, of North Britain, took the blood of the witch and kept it.

Then Kilhwch set forward, and Goreu the son of Custennin with him, and as many as wished ill to Yspaddaden Penkawr. And they took the marvels with them to his court. And Kaw of North Britain came and shaved his beard, skin, and flesh clean off to the very bone from ear to ear. "Art thou shaved, man?" said Kilhwch. "I am shaved," answered he. "Is thy daughter mine now?" "She is thine," said he, "but therefore needest thou not thank me, but Arthur who hath accomplished this for thee. By my free will thou shouldest never have had her, for with her I lose my life." Then Goreu the son of Custennin seized him by the hair of his head, and dragged him after him to the keep, and cut off his head and placed it on a stake on the citadel. Then they took possession of his castle, and of his treasures.

And that night Olwen became Kilhwch's bride, and she continued to be his wife as long as she lived. And the hosts of Arthur dispersed themselves, each man to his own country. And thus did Kilhwch obtain Olwen, the daughter of Yspaddaden Penkawr.

THE TEMPTATION OF LAUNCELOT

Peter Valentine Timlett

The most famous of Arthur's knights is Lancelot though he was a late addition to the Mythos. He first appears in Le Chevalier de la charette *(c. 1177) or* The Knight of the Cart *by Chrétien de Troyes, the great French writer whose works were essentially the origins of the Arthurian Mythos. Lancelot is a very complex character. He is not simply the dashing hero we have come to imagine. He was, according to the more popular versions of the legend, an abandoned child, found and raised by the Lady of the Lake, and who is obsessed with purity and with his own failure to meet his high ideals. His own fall from grace with his adulterous affair with Guinevere is almost a fulfilment of his own fate, despite the fact that he attempts to redeem himself and go on the Grail Quest. It is not Lancelot, but his own son Galahad, who becomes regarded as the purest knight of all.*

Early in the Lancelot legend he is put to the test by Morgan le Fay. It is a little known episode that is given the full treatment here by Peter Valentine Timlett (b. 1934) the author of The Seedbearers *trilogy and of an unpublished novel about Merlin.*

Merlin returned to Camelot a few days after the Feast of Pentecost, though from where the king did not know, Dyfed probably, and further north to the hill fort at Carrock Fell and beyond to Carlisle, a favourite route of his. Merlin was always reticent as to where he was going and where he had been. Arthur received him immediately, and when the kitchen scullion had brought a wheaten loaf and meats – and a small goblet of fermented drink made from apples – Arthur said: "I expected to see you for the celebrations."

The archmage hacked off a piece of bread and set about breaking his fast, and the king waited patiently. "Feasting and jousting are not to my taste," he said finally, wiping his lips, "as you well know, nor do I enjoy seeing knights of honour sprawled about in drunken stupors."

Arthur shrugged. "It takes time to change a man's ways."

"True, but it shouldn't. An attitude can change in a moment; all it takes is a recognition of the truth." Merlin sighed, for it was an old argument between them; change came about so *slowly*, too slowly. He was no longer a young man and all the signs indicated that he would not live long enough to see the whole of his dream come true. "So, what's been happening here while I've been away?" he said, changing the subject.

The king smiled wryly. "Not a great deal. Many of the knights left immediately after Pentecost, and since then the court ladies have been doing what court ladies always do, gossiping and doing their utmost to shred each other's reputations."

Merlin grunted. "They do that whether the knights are here or not." He glanced at the king. "And your dreams?" he said softly. "I asked you to remember and recount your dreams."

Seeing Merlin eat was making the king feel hungry again, and he reached forward and hacked off a piece of meat for himself. Merlin spoke often about dreams, of the need to understand and even control the images – they are symbols of what is happening in your inner life, he had said often, but to Arthur they were merely haphazard scenes that made no sense to him. He shrugged. "I don't seem to dream very much at all, except for last night."

"Last night?"

Arthur laughed in an embarrassed way. "A very vivid but in truth a very silly dream. Twelve ambassadors arrived here at Camelot from Lucius, the Roman Emperor, to demand a tribute as was the custom during the Roman occupation of Britain. In my dream not only did we refuse the tribute but I raised a vast army comprising the knights and men-at-arms of fifteen realms, including Sir Launcelot, son of King Ban of Benwick, and drove the Roman horde out of

France and Lombardy back to their own country. We then followed them to Rome and crushed their power forever and I was anointed Emperor of Rome by the Pope himself."

Merlin laughed. "A curious dream indeed since Rome itself was pillaged by the Vandals over a century ago."

"And Launcelot?"

Merlin nodded thoughtfully. "Yes, now that is curious. Perhaps it is a herald. Certainly the time is right for he must be a young man now and probably already knighted, and I know that both King Ban and Queen Elayne would be anxious for their son to come to Camelot."

Coincidence or prophecy, none could say, but within a fortnight of Arthur's dream excited pages rushed through the passageways and corridors to all parts of the castle. "A great knight has come!" they cried. "As tall as a tree!"

In an upstairs chamber Arthur's hound burst to its feet baying furiously. "Quiet," the king growled, and as the page tumbled through the door he said: "Sweet Jesu, boy, have you not been taught to tread gently!"

"Yes sire, yes, but a great knight has come – Sir Launcelot of Benwick – seeking audience with you, my liege." The words tumbled from his young lips as a torrent down a mountainside. "And he is as tall as a steeple, with hair as yellow as corn, and he is as handsome as any knight I have ever seen! And the ladies are all of a-flutter already."

"So I should imagine," said Arthur drily. He had not the heart to chastise the boy further, for he was fond of the lad. "Very well, tell the seneschal to see to his comfort. I will receive him in the great hall at noon."

As the boy sped out, Merlin appeared in the doorway. "So, events begin to move with a firmer tread."

"So it would seem," said Arthur.

By noon all the knights and ladies in residence had assembled in the great hall. Arthur came in with Gwynevere, and the queen's eyebrows rose a trifle. "So many ladies," she murmured.

"And so early in the day," smiled Arthur. "He must indeed be handsome." He beckoned a page. "Very well, ask the seneschal to bring our guest in."

When the newcomer was announced and came striding down the hall Gwynevere's hand flew to her bosom for she felt sure that her heart had missed a beat. Oh yes, in truth he was handsome indeed, tall and broad-shouldered and yet slim and narrow-hipped, and the manner in which he bowed and knelt before Arthur showed a grace of movement not common amongst warrior-knights. She did not hear the precise words he used in his greeting, for his voice was as warm as honey, grave and courteous, and she heard only the timbre and melody of it.

He was being presented to her now, murmuring the words, his lips briefly touching her hand, and she felt her knees go weak and her body tremble as though she was but a blushing girl.

"Sir Launcelot has come bearing gifts and a message of lasting friendship from his father," Arthur was saying.

"Then he is doubly welcome," she murmured, recovering herself, "King Ban was always a true friend to Arthur and to this court."

"Yes, yes," said Arthur warmly, "and this court would be honoured if you would join our company of knights."

"The honour would be mine, sire," the young man said gravely, "for the Knights of the Round Table are already renowned for their courage and chivalry."

The formalities over, the company crowded forward, the ladies elbowing each other in a quite unseemly manner in order to flutter their eyelashes and curtsey to this gallant High Prince of Benwick, but through it all Launcelot was unfailingly courteous to all, favouring neither one nor the other, bowing and smiling with equal warmth to all, greeting the knights respectfully, brushing his lips no more lingeringly over one fair maidenly hand than any other.

Kay and Gawain stood aloof from the throng, standing together at the far end of the great hall. "Well," said Kay sourly, "his mother has taught him courtly manners, I'll say that for him."

"But can he fight?" said Gawain, acknowledged by all to be the most doughty knight of all.

"He's a big lad," said Kay.

Sir Gawain snorted dismissively. "All the more will it hurt when he hits the ground."

Bedivere emerged from the crowd and came towards them. "He has a hard hand," he said, without preamble, "but he is yet too young to be any battle-wise knight."

"We'll see," said Gawain firmly.

Other knights too, perhaps from jealousy, were also quick to discuss amongst themselves that so handsome a youth would not present any serious challenge, but Launcelot quickly disposed of that false notion, for in the weeks that followed he fought at tournament with almost every knight at Camelot and defeated them all without even being unhorsed.

Such prowess from a new arrival could have caused a stirring of animosity against him but his never-failing good manners dispersed such feelings even before they arose. The only criticism that could be levied against him was that he seemed curiously unhumorous for so young a man, never laughing or joking as did the other young knights, but his courtesy and gravity of manner were so genuine, so openly honest, that most were soon convinced of the true nobility of his character.

However, while accepting the genuineness of his noble bearing and good manners, there were some who still entertained doubts. "Too good to be true," said Gawain sourly on more than one occasion, and others echoed that uncharitable view. "He must have a weakness somewhere and sooner or later it will be revealed."

"Is that a tinge of jealousy?" said Aggravayne, his brother.

"I am envious, as indeed are we all," said Gawain, "but not jealous. Already I feel that I could follow a man like Launcelot to the ends of the earth, but I say again that no man is that perfect."

As far as Launcelot was concerned Merlin agreed with the general sentiment, his much vaunted nobility of soul did not seem to sit comfortably within the character of the man himself. The boy was as tense and tight as a drawn bowstring. Such tension yearns for release. But he did not agree with the concept that no man could be perfect. When the time came the successful completion of the Quest of the Holy Grail would indeed require such perfection, or near it.

At the end of three months Sir Launcelot was made a Knight of Honour and there was a gasp of astonishment from the assembly when it was seen that his name appeared at the seat immediately to the right of the Siege Perelous, one of the very special seats, though many had expected that it would appear at Perelous itself. As King Pellinore said later: "If a knight as noble as Launcelot is not deemed worthy enough to occupy the Siege Perelous, then what god-like creature is yet to appear in our midst?"

In response to this honour Sir Launcelot left Camelot to seek adventure, "and so prove myself worthy of the special favour shown to me," and for the next year tales of incredible valour were heard at Camelot of his exploits such that Arthur said on more than one occasion: "Surely this must be the greatest knight of all time."

"Be careful of your praise, my liege," murmured Gwynevere. "Already every lady at court is in love with him."

"And how could any woman prevent herself from loving such a man," he said, but he did not notice the quickening of her breath or the deepening of her colour. "It is fortunate that his character is beyond reproach otherwise every husband at Camelot would be a cuckold."

Before Launcelot returned to Camelot the tally of his victories had reached a total of forty-eight knights defeated, and a further three killed. No other knight at Camelot could boast of anywhere near so fine a record; indeed six Knights of the Round Table owed him their lives, for when Launcelot killed the treacherous Sir Tarquine he found amongst the sixty-four prisoners that he released the somewhat sheepish faces of Marhaus, Kay, Ector, Lyonel, Gaheris, and even Gawain who shrugged philosophically and said that despite the ignominy of it he much preferred to be rescued by Launcelot than to rot in Tarquine's dungeons.

But there was one tale that did not reach Camelot, nor did Launcelot speak of it on his return. Merlin discovered the tale through other sources but he was the only one ever to know of it, apart from the four priestesses involved.

Being wearied from battle and hard riding Launcelot chose one evening to camp by a stream and fell immediately into a sleep of exhaustion. Unknown to him the stream was one of the borders of the country of Gore and by ill chance one of the guards spotted him and informed his mistress, Queen Morgan Le Fay. So important was the news that she came herself, crossed the bridge, and peered at him through the willows that lined the river, the last few rays of the westering sun lighting his face as though for her benefit. For some moments she stared at him and then nodded in deep satisfaction. It was indeed the famous Sir Launcelot.

"Wait here," she commanded quietly, and then treading softly she moved forward to where Launcelot's horse stood tethered to a tree. "Shhhh," she whispered soothingly, "peace to you." The horse snuffled briefly and shook its mane, moving restlessly in the gathering gloom beneath the trees. "Shhh, all is well," and coming up to him she patted his neck and blew in his nostrils, and the horse grew quiet. She then moved silently to the sleeping Launcelot and bent over him. Slowly she took a vial of pale blue glass from her gown pocket and removed the stopper. Then, without causing him to waken, she lightly placed a tiny drop of a most potent drug onto his lips and within moments he was safely unconscious rather than merely asleep. Satisfied, she summoned the guards and ordered them to carry the knight on his shield across the bridge to the castle, and there she installed him in an elegant and sumptuous chamber high in the north tower, but one with a heavy oak door that could be barred.

Staying with Morgan le Fay for the rituals of the Summer Solstice in three days time were three senior priestesses of the faith, the queens of North Galys, Estelonde, and the Outer Isles, all of whose husbands were opposed to Arthur, and like Morgan le Fay herself, all three were strikingly handsome women. Few men, however, could boast of having known their favours, for each having achieved the right to wear the garter, they had long abandoned such trivial dalliances, though each had no compunction in practising the art when required by special ritual.

"He is handsome, true enough," said Estelonde as all four stood round the bed looking down at the unconscious Launcelot.

"And courageous," said North Galys.

The queen of the Outer Isles pursed her lips thoughtfully. "And of noble character, I hear, a knight who sits at the Round Table immediately to the right of Siege Perelous, a source of inspiration to all."

Morgan Le Fay waved them to silence. "Merlin's dream of the Holy Grail is a worthy enough ambition but you all know the danger as well as I. Like any priest, he makes of himself a vessel to hold the power that he invokes, and if ought goes wrong then the flow of power will shatter the vessel, causing a type of insanity that creates a schism between the soul and the personality. The power involved in an invocation of the Round Table of Glory and the Holy Grail is colossal – and those invoking the power would not be doing so for themselves alone. If I know Merlin he will attempt to use the Knights of the Round Table as being representative of the entire British race, perhaps even of the whole of humanity – he is certainly vain enough for that – and if he fails the schism will probably cause a gigantic abyss between the Group Soul and the Group Mind of the race. Such a failure could bring in a dark age that could last for centuries. It might even permanently prevent the Holy Grail from ever being able to manifest in earth. It is too early, far too early. The irresponsible old fool may cause untold damage to the spiritual life of the race."

"But what can we do?"

"In the long term, sow the seeds of corruption amongst Arthur's knights to prevent any contact between the symbol and the inner reality. Bring about the death of Arthur, or get rid of Merlin, or both. I tell you that I, Morgan Le Fay, would risk the very annihilation of my soul to prevent the Grail from being drawn into the earth sphere.

Utter chaos and devastation in the spiritual life of the realm would be the inevitable result. There is nothing I would not do to prevent that possibility, no matter how dangerous, how distasteful, and no matter how seemingly immoral. If I thought it would help I would kill him here and now with my own hands."

"It is tempting though," said North Galys.

"No, it would simply make a martyr of him." Her eyes darkened. "His value to Merlin and to the Grail lies in his noble character and therefore we must seek to corrupt that character so that he sets a quite different example."

"How?" said Estelonde.

"Rumour has it," said Morgan Le Fay, "that he will have nothing to do with women. He has apparently said that he will not marry for fear that domestic responsibility will interfere with his knightly duties, and that he will not take a paramour because he believes that a true knight is neither adulterous nor lecherous."

"No bad principle of honour," said Outer Isles. "Few knights espouse such a code."

"And fewer still who keep it," said Estelonde drily.

"True," said Morgan Le Fay, "and so it should not be difficult to influence Launcelot to betray that code." She turned to Estelonde. "Tomorrow when he wakes I want you to seduce him."

Estelonde looked doubtful. "He has met with many ladies younger and more fair than I."

"But not with your experience as a priestess."

Launcelot did not wake until late morning, and when he did he rushed to the door but found it locked, and when he strode to the embrasure and saw how high he was, his heart sank. It was not until then did he realise that he was dressed only in a thin bed-robe that barely reached his knees, with nothing beneath, nor did his frantic eye see any clothing in the chamber at all, nor his sword and scabbard, nor any of his armour. Taking a deep breath, and vowing to wreak vengeance on his captor, he sat himself grimly down to wait.

It was nearer noon before he heard the key, and he burst angrily to his feet, but instead of a knight or manservant as he had expected, a handsome woman entered, followed by a serving maid who bore a lidded wooden bowl, two small platters, and an earthen jug on a beaten silver salver. "Ah, awake at last," said the woman.

He backed away, embarrassed. "Who are you?" he managed to say.

"I am Estelonde, Queen Estelonde." She came towards him,

smiling warmly, her eyes liquid honey, her body undulating prettily beneath the thin blue robe that she wore, and from the way her body moved he knew that like himself she wore nothing beneath.

"And what is this place?" he said hoarsely. He snatched his eyes away, but they kept returning of their own volition. "Is this your lord's castle?"

She spoke to the serving-maid who put the salver on a low table, and then dragged the table so that it lay alongside the bed. The girl then curtsied to Launcelot, and as she leant forward in the curtsey her simple gown gaped open, and his eyes leapt hungrily to the soft shadows of her bosom, and at that moment the girl looked up and winked at him saucily and then leaped away laughing merrily, casting a coquettish glance back at him.

"A saucy wench," said Estelonde when the girl had gone. "I can send her to you later, if that is your wish."

"That will not be necessary," he said stiffly.

She sat on the side of the bed and lifted the lid of the bowl. "Hmmm, smells good. Come," she said, patting the bed beside her, "come and eat."

"I am not hungry."

"Nonsense, of course you are. Look at you, man, you're as thin as a wand of hazel. I don't suppose you've eaten properly since you left Camelot." She picked up one of the platters and ladled a generous portion of meat stew on to it. "Come, even princes of Benwick have to eat." She looked up at him and saw the suspicion in his eyes. She stirred the stew, mixing it thoroughly, and then took a spoonful herself. "It is not drugged, I assure you. Hmmm, that's rather nice," and she took the other platter and served a portion for herself.

Launcelot hesitated. He had not eaten since dawn the previous day, and sparsely even then. He sidled towards the table and snatched up a platter and spoon and withdrew to the embrasure to eat. "Where is this place? Whose castle is this?"

She sighed inwardly. The man was being tiresome. But he was not indifferent to her, she was sure of that. "This," she said shortly, "is Castle Charyot."

He stopped eating abruptly. "The sorceress?" he whispered.

She was beginning to be irritated by him. This prince, this too handsome son of Benwick was little more than a callow prig. "If by that you mean Queen Morgan le Fay, then yes, this is her castle."

He flung the platter down. "Then sweet Jesu, preserve me this day," he cried.

She rose haughtily. "You are in no danger from us," she said, but could scarce keep the anger from her voice.

"There are more of you?"

She sighed with exasperation. "Including Morgan herself, there are four of us gathered here for the ritual of the Summer Solstice which will take place in two days time, and we are *not* sorceresses. We are senior priestesses of the Elder Faith and owe our allegiance to the Lady of the Lake. Even as you are named for the Lake, so then are we." She raised her robe high above her knees, and there upon her left thigh was the garter. "And there is the symbol of my office."

"I care not for the signs and sygils of thy evil ways," he cried. "Get thee gone from here!"

She shook her head. What Gwynevere saw in this fool she could not begin to imagine. She dropped the hem of her gown. "Eat alone, then," she growled, "it's all you're good for!" and she turned and swept from the chamber with as much dignity as any rejected woman could muster.

Later, pacing Morgan le Fay's private chamber, she ended her tale of failure: ". . . but he was interested, of that I am sure. That hot and smoky expression in his eyes did not spring from any pious cause."

"Hmm, he seems to have affected you as much as you did him," said Morgan. "Calm yourself, priestess," and the other two smiled knowingly. "It is against nature for a man to deny the forces that constitute his very being, it but creates a dam within himself behind which the waters of his passion pile up with ever increasing pressure."

"Well, his dam wouldn't break for me," said Estelonde irritably.

"Perhaps," said North Galys, "perhaps we should be more bold." They all looked at her. "A woman invites only in subtle ways," she went on hastily, "by the modest lowering of her eyes, the hint of warmth in her voice, the posture that flatters her body, the blush, the glance full of passion – but it is left to the man to make the actual advance, the physical move, the touch, the clasping of hands, the arm about her waist – the kiss." She paused, and then added softly: "Perhaps we should be far more bold than that."

"What have you in mind?" said Morgan le Fay.

"Well, I was thinking that perhaps . . ."

For hour upon hour Launcelot lay upon the bed, his eyes tight shut, his arms rigid by his sides, his fists clenched. The Christian monks spoke of the flesh being weak. Oh no, they were grievously in error. The flesh wasn't weak at all, the flesh was strong, overpoweringly strong, and could only be held at bay by the exercise of indominant will.

He remembered as if it were but yesterday, in his twelfth year, the young serving-maid in a little-used corridor of his father's castle in Benwick, murmuring gentle words to him, taking his hand and guiding it beneath her gown, remembered the exquisite thrill that had coursed through his body, and remembered too how her hand, tentatively at first, unsure of its welcome, and then more boldly, had touched him, caressed him and explored until his very limbs had shaken as if with palsy.

But strong though the memory was, stronger still was the scene carved into his very soul of his father's red-faced fury when he had come across them quite by accident, there in the corridor, their clothing in such disarray that no denial was possible. He remembered his father sending him sprawling with one mighty slap across his face, and then driving him, as a swineherd would drive a pig, through the corridors and up the flight of steps, past servants and knights agape with shock, to the king's private chamber, and there had beaten him so severely that three days were to pass before he could creep painfully from his bed. And throughout that thrashing his father had roared and raged the creed demanded of a Prince of Benwick.

"I do not care what licentious practice is permitted in other castles," he had raged, "but here in Benwick you shall keep yourself unsullied as befitting the Christian knight that you will become. In future, each morning at dawn, and at evensong, you shall pray with the good monks to keep you pure for the holy task that God has decreed for you!" and then had bellowed for the servants to carry away the bloodied and unconscious body of his only son.

In the days that followed his mother had tried to comfort him, not knowing what his transgression had been, for her lord would say nothing, but what boy can speak to his mother of such things, his mother who in his eyes was as pure and good as Holy Mary herself.

And every day, whenever the Benwick flag flew proudly from the turret battlements to tell the world that the king was in residence, every day his father would lecture him on the duties required of a Christian knight.

"But above all, my son, put the wild things of the flesh aside, for they are not for you. In purity shall you be armoured, the flesh of woman and the flesh of man, unless bound together in the eyes of God in holy matrimony, are as an abomination that shall plunge you into the realm of the Dark One."

And over and over again, day after day, week after week, year in and year out, up to and even on the day he had set forth from Benwick bound for Camelot, every day his father had pounded the lesson into his skull. "Thou canst not partake of the flesh and remain a pure and noble knight – and should you weaken you shall disgrace thyself in the eyes of your king, your father, and in the eyes of God – and should that dreadful day ever dawn thou shalt of that moment cease to be any son of mine!"

He had tried. No mortal man or woman knew of his struggle, only God in his compassion knew of his many failures and had wept for him. For he was a Prince of Benwick, tall and handsome, mighty with the sword, and women by the scores, maids and matrons alike, were his for the taking. Again and again he would strive to resist, holding his body's passion down with ferocious will, but again and again he would weaken, and the dam would burst and he would wallow in the pleasures of the flesh as would a drunken sot among his flagons of ale, and after each transgression he would mortify his soul with endless prayer that did little save build up the pressure behind the dam for the next breach.

Setting forth for Britain he had hoped that their cold and gloomy climate had produced women cold of passion, but it was not to be. A woman's flesh was no different in Britain than it had been in France, and the women themselves no less eager to sample the charms of his young manhood – and then there was Gwynevere.

Oh dear God, was there to be no end to his torment!

The key grated in the lock, and for a moment he froze, still locked in his memories, but then he sprang from the bed, his thin robe flapping, but it was no sorceress who entered, but an old man white of hair and infirm of tread, bearing a salver of food. "Send for thy mistress," Launcelot commanded, but the old man made no reply but put the salver down on the table. "Send for thy mistress, I say!" he said more forcibly, but the old man, seeing his lips move, pointed at his own ears and shook his head, and opened his mouth wide and pointed to its tongueless depths. Deaf and dumb, the ideal servant.

The old man stirred the food and took a spoonful into his own mouth and swallowed it and then looked at Launcelot questioningly. Launcelot nodded wearily. The taster, of course. The old man withdrew and not until the door had closed and had been re-locked did Launcelot think that if he had been more alert he could have sprung past the old man to freedom.

He glanced at the embrasure and saw that the sun was setting already. All day he had lain, fretting with his memories, but then he shrugged and took up the platter and began to eat. He was safe enough here, for he would not submit even if it meant his death. The temptations of ordinary women, even of queens and high-born ladies, were hard to resist, but there was far more evil in the embrace of a sorceress than just passion.

He woke just as the first rays of the new-born sun came creeping into the chamber. It was going to be a warm day, for already the bed was too hot for comfort. He yawned and stretched his arms and then froze, for as he moved another form beside him also stirred, and there, snuggled into him, was a woman, a handsome, sleepy-eyed, moist-warm woman – and quite unclothed. Her arm slid about him languidly. "Again, my lover," she murmured.

He sprang from the bed, dismayed to find himself as unclothed as she, but nowhere could he see his robe. "Who by all the powers of darkness are you?!" he spat out.

North Galys raised herself up on one elbow and smiled. "Not a very gallant question, Sir Launcelot, considering how passionately you have embraced me throughout the night hours."

For a moment he was taken aback, but his mind knew the state of his flesh, and he knew that she lied. In a strange way it was comforting to know that even a sorceress could make an error, and it calmed him as perhaps nothing else could – and even made him grimly smile. "Do you not think, madam, that I would know if my body has loved or not."

It was an error of judgment, and she knew it, and knew also that Morgan le Fay would not be pleased. "True," she sighed, "but I had hoped that you would find me comely enough." She plucked back the bed coverings. "You do find me comely, do you not, young knight."

Launcelot shook his head and smiled, and there was pity in his eyes, and in a strange way even some compassion, aye even for the likes of her, sorceress though she was. In truth it was sad, for a lewd woman's body was as a sword for her, and if that failed what other weapon had she in her struggle.

North Galys saw the pity and was enraged by it. She sprang from the bed and snatched up her gown and dressed herself furiously.

"May your flesh rot in the next whore you plunge!" she said viciously and swept haughtily from the chamber.

A little later the old man returned bringing with him Launcelot's own clothing, freshly washed and dried, and he dressed himself triumphantly, for he knew in his heart that he had all but won.

Below, in a chamber off the great hall, the four priestesses were gathered to review the situation. "Perhaps you yourself should try," said Estelonde. It would ease her chagrin if the High Priestess herself also failed.

Morgan Le Fay shook her head. "No, if he will not succumb to any of you then he is hardly likely to leap into my arms."

"I have been a priestess all my life, since a young girl," said North Galys, "and never have I been so humiliated."

"Then learn from it," said Morgan le Fay unfeelingly. "Lessons learnt from failure are oft more rewarding than those learnt from success."

"He knows he's in Charyot," said Outer Isles, "he knows we are of the Elder Faith, sorceresses he calls us, and thus doubly, trebly will he resist any approach we make."

The High Priestess sighed. "Yes, quite possibly, but I still believe that his weakness is a woman's charm, though perhaps not ours." She smiled sardonically. "But there is one woman in Britain whom he cannot classify as an enemy; a woman whom he would find it difficult to deny." She rose and headed for the door. "We will have to let him go, but not before I have planted a seed whose growing tendrils may yet in the future crack the dam of his resolve."

When she entered the chamber that served as his prison Launcelot was standing at the embrasure, and he turned and stared at her in contempt. "Yet another lewd sorceress," he said scornfully. "Will you also offer to fling off your gown and welcome me to your arms?"

"Not I," said Morgan Le Fay cheerfully. "As High Priestess my mating is symbolic rather than actual, but not so with the others. We are not Christian but are of the Elder Faith as you well know. It is the custom of our priestesses at each of the four quarterlies to lie with a priest, or layman if no priest is available, to celebrate the male and female aspects of deity. The intentions of the ladies who came to you were ritual in nature, not lewd." She told the lie beautifully and could see that he half accepted it already. "It is they who are angry, for by our custom your refusal was an insult to our faith."

"I have heard of these things," he admitted, "and although I intended no insult I still hold these practices to be lewd."

She shrugged as though the matter was of no importance. "To each their own belief, and to each their own way of worshipping the One. Anyway, I did not think that you would take part in our rites, for all Britain knows that Gwynevere holds you for her own."

"That is a lie," he said angrily. "Were I free I would take pleasure in proving against any who would champion you that Queen Gwynevere is the noblest lady in the land."

She raised her eyebrows. "Perhaps she is, who knows, but any lady no matter how noble is also a woman." She looked at him with a deliberate half smile upon her lips. "You may not know it yet, or believe it, my bold young knight, but I can tell you of my own sure knowledge that our noble queen trembles at the knee with passion every time she sees you. Her every dream and almost her every waking thought is of you, Sir Launcelot, and now that I have seen you I cannot bring myself to blame her."

"You lie," he shouted. "No such thought has entered her head."

"It has, and frequently, I assure you," and taking a chance she went on: "and what is more that very same thought has entered your head also – do you deny it?" Too late to protest, his eyes and colour betrayed his acknowledgment, and he bit his lip and kept silent. "Yes, I thought so," she smiled, "though why you should be ashamed of it is beyond me, it is after all a very human reaction." He made as if to speak but she waved him to silence. "But it is none of my business and perhaps a little discourteous of me even to mention it."

"All I want from you, sorceress," he said bitterly, "is my freedom."

"But you are not a prisoner here. You may leave whenever you wish."

He stared at her suspiciously. "If that is true then I will leave now, tonight. I would rather spend the night in the wild than remain a moment longer within these walls."

"Certainly, I will have your horse brought from the stable immediately," and she turned to go. "But I have to say that it is a pity that your reputed noble character does not seem to have taught you even the rudiments of social courtesy," and she swept from the chamber leaving the door ajar behind her.

Within minutes Sir Launcelot was cantering across the lowered drawbridge, watched from a turret embrasure by the four priestesses, the fire in his loins raging more fiercely than ever, unsatisfied, demanding.

"Fare you well, noble knight," murmured Morgan Le Fay. "It may be that Gwynevere will have cause to thank me yet, though she may never know it."

SIR GAWAIN AND THE GREEN KNIGHT

Rosemary Sutcliff

Gawain is another of Arthur's most famous knights, and one who features in many stories as the central character. He was associated with the Arthurian stories long before Lancelot, and originally was portrayed as a mighty hero. The later French romancers and Malory depicted him as a darker character with a big attitude problem. You'll see this variation in his character in different stories in this collection, as he appears in many of them. He is central to two. The best known is Sir Gawain and the Green Knight *which is regarded as the finest of all medieval Arthurian romances. It was written sometime in the mid-fourteenth century, though it drew upon much earlier sources. Alas its author is not known. It has been the subject of many interpretations and translations, not least that by J.R.R. Tolkien, the author of* Lord of the Rings, *in an edition for Oxford University Press in 1967. The version printed here is by Rosemary Sutcliff (1920–92) one of the best historical novelists for children, whose books, especially* The Eagle of the Ninth *(1954), did much to bring Roman Britain to life. Her major Arthurian novel is* Sword at Sunset *(1964) where she portrayed Arthur in a more legitimate historical setting. She also retold the legends in the trilogy* The Sword and the Circle *(1981),* The Light Beyond the Forest *(1980) and* The Road to Camlann *(1981).*

Of all the knights who had their places at King Arthur's Round Table, Sir Gawain seemed always to be the one who had something strange about him. Gawain of the flaming red hair, and the temper that flamed to match it, as swift as fire to spring up and as dangerous, but as swift to sink again. He was of the Old People, the Dark People, but then so was Gaheris, and Agravane their younger brother who by now had also joined the court. So was his cousin Uwaine, and so was Arthur himself on his mother's side. It was more than that. Strange stories were told about Gawain; the country folk said that his strength waxed and waned with the sun. So it was fitting that one of the strangest adventures ever to befall the knights of the Round Table should come to him.

On the Christmas that Sir Lancelot was still away upon his own quest, Arthur held his court at Camelot, for the time had not yet come when he kept his Christmases at Carlisle. Yuletide went by with many festivities, and it came to New Year's Eve. Now Christmas was chiefly a matter for the Church, but New Year's Eve was for banqueting and merrymaking, and so when dusk came, the whole court gathered to their feasting in the Great Hall; the knights of the Round Table each in their places; the lesser knights and the squires at the side boards. Even the Queen and her ladies had come to join the feast and look on from under their silken canopy at the upper end of the Hall, for there would be dancing after the banquet was done. Already the serving squires were bringing in the great chargers of goose and venison, and swans and ships and towering castles made of almonds and honey. The wine glowed red in crystal goblets and the Hall leapt with torchlight and lilted with the music of the harper who sat at the Queen's feet.

The boar's head was brought in, wreathed in scented bay leaves and heralded by trumpets and carried high on the shoulders of four pages. But just as it was set on the table, the great doors of the Hall flew open, and a gust of wind burst in, making the torches stream sideways and the flames of the huge log fires crouch down upon the hearths. And a little snow eddied in on the dark wings of the wind.

The harper fell silent between note and note. The voices of the revelling company fell away, as every face turned towards the door and the night beyond. And a great silence took the Hall, where the cheerful sounds of merrymaking had been.

And into the silence came the clang and bell-clash of horse's hooves upon the frostbound courtyard stones, and out of the darkness into the torchlight and firelight that steadied and leapt as though in greeting, rode a great man, almost a giant, upon a warhorse that was of a fitting size to carry him.

At sight of him a long gasp ran through the Hall, for he was the strangest sight that any man there had ever seen, mighty of limb and goodly of face and holding himself in the saddle like a king, wearing no armour but clad from head to heel in the fierce fine green that is the colour of the Lordly Ones and not of mortal men. His jerkin and hose under his thick-furred cloak were all of green, and green was the jewelled belt that circled his waist. His saddle was of fine green leather enriched with gold, so were his horse's trappings which chimed like little bells as the great beast moved. Spurs of greenish gold sparked the heels of his boots that were the colour of moss under ancient oak trees. Even his thick crest of hair and his curling beard were of the same hue, and the great horse beneath him green from proud crest to sweeping tail, its mane fantastically braided and knotted up with golden threads. In one hand he carried a huge axe of green steel inlaid with the same strange greeny-gold; and high in the other a young holly tree thick with berries that sparked like crimson jewels in the torchlight. But save for the holly berries of Christmas, all else, even the sparks that his horse's hooves struck from the stone pavement as he rode up the Hall, was green; blazing and fiery green; the living green of spring-time itself.

When he came halfway up the Hall, he reined in, and flung down the holly tree upon the floor, and sat looking about him on all sides. And it seemed to everyone there, from the King himself to the youngest page, that the golden-green eyes, like the eyes of some proud and mighty forest beast, had looked for a moment directly and deeply into his own.

Then he cried out in a voice that boomed from wall to wall and hung under the roof and brought a startled spider down out of the rafters, "Where is the lord of this Hall, for I would speak with him and with no other!"

After the thunder of his voice, for three heartbeats of time all men sat as though stunned, and there was no sound save the whispering of the flames upon the hearths. Then Arthur said, "I am the lord of this Hall, and I bid you right welcome to it. Now pray you dismount, and while my stable squires tend to your horse, come and feast among us, this last night of the Old Year."

"Nay, that I will not," said the stranger. "I have not come to feast with you; nor have I come in war. That, you may see by my lack of armour, and by the green branch that I bear. But word of the valour of your knights has reached me in my own place; and for a while and a while I have been minded to put it to the test."

"Why, then," said Arthur, "I doubt not that you will find enough and to spare among my knights willing and eager to joust with you if that is your desire."

"That is as may be," said the Green Knight, "but for the most part I see here only beardless bairns who I could fell with one flick of a bramble spray! Nay, it is a valour-test of another kind that I bring here for a Yuletide sport. Let any man here stand forth as champion against me, and he may take from my hand this axe which has no equal in the world for weight and keenness, and with it strike me one blow. Only he must strike the blow in the place of my choosing. And he must swear to yield me the right to strike the return blow in the same place, if I am yet able, a year and a day from now."

And again there was silence in the Hall; and the knights looked at each other and away again, and here one drew a quick breath, and there one licked his lower lip. But none dared to take up the challenge of the beautiful and terrible stranger.

Then the Green Knight laughed, long and loud and mocking. "Not one of you? Is this indeed King Arthur's Hall? And you who feast here but dare not take up a simple challenge, are you indeed the knights of his Round Table? The flower of chivalry? Nay, let you go hang your heads in shame, I see I have had a bootless journey!"

Arthur sprang to his feet, though well he knew that it was not for the High King to take up such a challenge, and flung his shout of defiance in the stranger's face. "Yes! One! Off your horse now, give me your axe and make ready for the blow!"

But almost in the same instant, Sir Gawain also was on his feet. "My lord the King, noble uncle, I claim this adventure, for still I carry with me the shame of the lady's death whose head I cut off, and I have yet to prove my worthiness to sit at the Round Table!"

He seldom called Arthur "uncle", for they were almost the same age, and so when he did, it was as a jest between them. And now the familiar jest cut through the King's rage and reached him, and he knew that what Sir Gawain said was true. And so he drew a deep breath and unclenched his hands, and said, "Dear my nephew, the adventure is yours."

Then as Sir Gawain left his place and strode into the centre of the Hall, the Green Knight swung down from his horse, and so they came together. "It is good that I have found a champion to meet me in Arthur's Hall," said the Green Knight. "By what name are you called?"

"I am Gawain, son of Lot, King of Orkney, and nephew to my liege lord King Arthur. By what name do men call you?"

"Men call me the Knight of the Green Chapel, in my own North Country," said the stranger. "Swear now to the bargain between us; that you will strike the one blow in the place of my choosing, the one blow only. And that in a year and a day you will submit yourself to my blow, the one blow only, in return."

"I swear by my knighthood," said Gawain.

"Take the axe, and be ready to strike as I bid you."

Gawain took the mighty and terrible axe in his hand, and stood swinging it a little, feeling its weight and balance; and the Green Knight knelt down on the floor, and stooping, drew his long flame-green hair forward over the top of his head to lay bare his neck.

For a moment all things in the Hall seemed to cease, and Gawain stood as though turned to stone.

"In the place of my choice," said the Green Knight. "Strike now."

And life moved on again, and Gawain in a kind of fury swung up the great axe with a battle yell, and putting every last ounce of strength that he possessed into the blow, brought it crashing down.

The blade sheared through flesh and bone and set the sparks spurting from the pavement as though from an anvil; and the Green Knight's head sprang from his shoulders and went rolling along the floor almost to the Queen's feet.

There rose a horrified gasp, and while all men looked to see the huge body topple forward, the Green Knight shook his shoulders a little, and got to his feet, and walked after his head. He caught it up and, holding it by the hair, remounted his horse that stood quietly waiting for him. Holding his head high, he turned the face to Sir Gawain, and said, "See that you keep your oath, and come to me a year and a day from now."

"How shall I find you?" asked Gawain, white to the lips.

"Seek me through Wales and into the Forest of Wirrel; and if you bring your courage with you, you shall surely find me before noon of the appointed day."

And he wheeled his horse and touched his spurred heel to its flank, and was away out into the darkness and the eddying snow, his head still swinging by its long hair from his hand. And they heard the beat of his horse's hooves drumming away into the winter's night.

Behind him he left great silence in the Hall, and it was a while before the harper drew his hand across the bright strings again, and men returned to their laughter and feasting.

The snow melted and the buds began to swell along the wood shores. And at Eastertide Sir Lancelot returned from his questing, as has been told. The cuckoo came, the foxgloves stood proudly along the woodland ways and then were gone; and in farms and manors up and down the land the harvest was gathered in; and it was the time of blackberries and turning bracken once again. And at Michaelmas it was time for Sir Gawain to set forth upon his terrible quest.

King Arthur held his court at Caerleon that Michaelmas; and there gathered Sir Gaheris and Sir Agravane, and Lancelot and Lional and his brother Bors who was new-come from Less Britain to join him, Sir Uwaine and Sir Bedivere, King Bagdemagus and Sir Lamorack and Sir Gryflet le Fise de Dieu and many more. And their hearts were sore within them so that there was no joy nor savour to the feasting, for the sake of Sir Gawain, who was riding away from them and would surely never come riding back.

And Sir Gawain with his squire's help armed himself and belted on his sword, and mounted Gringolet his great roan horse, and set out.

For many days he rode through the ancient border country of Wales until he came to the wild dark mountain lands of North Wales; and he rode by steep valleys and roaring waters and mountain-clinging forests. And many times he was attacked by wild animals and wilder men and must fight for his life, knowing all the while that death must be waiting for him at the end of his quest. Autumn had turned to winter when he reached the end of the mountain country, and came down by Clwyd to the Holy Head near to Saint Winifred's Well on the shore of the broad and grey-shining Dee. He forded the river mouth at low tide, and barely winning clear of the sands and saltings before the tide came racing in again, he came to the black and ancient forest-fleece of the Wirrel.

And as he rode, whenever he came up with a forester or a wandering friar or an old woman gathering sticks, and whenever he found shelter at night in a swineherd's bothie or a charcoal-burner's hut (those were the nights he counted himself lucky; on other nights he slept huddled in his cloak under a pile of dead bracken or in the root-hollow of a tree brought down by the storms of some past winter), he asked for tidings of the Green Knight of the Green Chapel, but no one could tell him what he needed to know.

And the time was growing short . . .

On Christmas Eve, weary man on weary horse mired to the belly from the forest ways, he came out from among ancient trees that seemed to reach their twisted lichen-hung branches across his way as though to seize him and draw him into themselves, and saw before him open meadowland set about with fine tamed trees, a willow-fringed stream winding through; and beyond the stream, the land rising gently, crowned by a castle that was both strong and beautiful in the last light of the winter's day.

Now God be thanked, thought Sir Gawain, and he gently pulled Gringolet's twitching ear. There will be food and shelter to spare in this place and they will not refuse us welcome upon this night of all the year. And he forded the stream and rode up to the castle gate and beat upon the timbers with the pommel of his sword.

The gate opened almost at once, and the porter appeared in the entrance.

"Good fellow," said Sir Gawain, "pray you tell your master that a knight of King Arthur's court rides this way upon a quest; and begs shelter for himself and his horse."

"My master, the lord of this castle, has a welcome for all comers, especially any who come on this night of all the year," said the porter, standing aside, and Gawain rode through into the outer court of the castle. Squires came hurrying to take Gringolet to the stables, while others led Gawain himself through the inner court and then into the castle Hall, where the lord of the castle himself stood before a roaring fire with three great wolfhounds lying all about his feet, their bellies to the warmth.

He was a big man, broad across the shoulders and running just a trace to fat; his face weather-beaten, kindly and open, his mane of hair as red as Gawain's own; and as his guest entered the room, he thrust the wolfhounds aside and came striding to meet him with hands outstretched.

"Welcome, knight-at-arms, my home is your home, and all that I have is yours for as long as it pleases you to bide here."

"My thanks, noble sir," Gawain said, his heart warming to the man in instant friendship. "God be good to you, for the goodness of your hospitality."

And they clapped each other upon the shoulders as though they were old friends indeed.

The squires led Gawain to the guest chamber high in the keep, where they helped him to unarm, and brought him a robe of thick russet wool lined with the softest dappled lynx fur; then they escorted him back to the Hall, where another chair had been set for him opposite the lord of the castle; and one of the hounds came with proudly swinging tail and laid its chin on his knee.

Meanwhile the squires and pages were setting up the table boards and spreading them with fine white linen; and bringing in the food and setting ready the wine jugs. And the soft warm hunger-water ran into Sir Gawain's mouth at the sight and smell of the dishes; and the warmth of the fire and the heavy furred robe seeped through his chilled and weary body, and he was very well content.

When supper was over, the lord of the castle said, "Come, Sir Gawain, for you have not yet seen my lady, and she will be eager to greet you."

And they went together, by the stairway behind the Hall, to the Private Chamber; a fair chamber whose walls were painted green and scattered with small golden stars; and the lady of the castle sat beside the fire with a little silky lapdog on her knee, and her maidens all about her. And Gawain thought when she smiled at him that she was the fairest lady he had ever seen; fairer even than Queen Guenever. She made him sweetly welcome, while her maidens brought a chessboard with men of silver and crystal, for her lord and his guest to play; and the evening passed as happily as any that Gawain had ever known, so that for a little while he was almost able to forget the dark quest on which he rode.

And when the time came for sleep, the squires took him back, making a candle-lit procession of it, to the guest chamber, and left him with a goblet of spiced wine beside the bed.

Four days passed, with all the singing and feasting and rejoicing that goes with Christmas time; and always the lady of the castle stayed close to Gawain and talked to him and smiled upon him and attended to him in all things.

But on the evening of the fourth day Gawain knew that he must stay no longer from his quest. When he told the knight and the lady of this, they grieved, and would have had him stay longer. But Gawain held to his purpose. "I have stayed too long already, happy in your company, and my quest calls me. I must meet the Knight of the Green Chapel by noon of New Year's Day; and as yet I do not even know where this Green Chapel may be."

Then the lord of the castle laughed, and slapped his great hand upon his broad knee. "That makes good hearing indeed; for the Green Chapel I know well; it is not two hours' easy ride from here! Bide with us then until the morning of New Year's Day, and then one of my squires shall guide you to the place, and have you there before the sun stands at noon."

"Then gladly will I bide here," Sir Gawain said, "and warm me with your kindness, and do in all things as you will." (For he thought, if these be the last three days of my life, it were sweet that I should spend them among friends.)

"So then, we have three good days to spend," said the lord of the castle, "and I shall spend them as always I spend the three last days of the Old Year, hunting in the forest. But you, who have ridden so far and hard, and have, I doubt not, some great ordeal to face at the Green Chapel, shall abide here and take your ease, and keep the company of my lady who ever complains of her loneliness when I leave her to follow the boar or the red deer. And in the evenings we will make merry together."

"That will I do most willingly," said Gawain.

The lord's eyes flickered with laughter in his weather-beaten face. "And since this is the time for games and jests, and I have a fantastic mood on me, let us make a covenant together – that each evening I will give you whatever I have gained in my day's hunting; and you shall give me in exchange whatever you have gained here in my castle. This exchange let us swear to, for better or worse, however it may turn out."

"That is a fine covenant, and gladly will I swear to it," said Gawain; and they struck hands like men sealing a bargain.

Next day the lord of the castle summoned his companions and his hounds and rode away to hunt the red deer through the forests of Wirrel and Delamare. But Gawain lay abed, with a most unusual drowsiness upon him, for he was not used to late lying. And presently the lady of the castle came, stepping lightly, and sat down on the edge of the bed, as blithe as a linnet on a hawthorn spray, and began to tease him. And by little and little, from teasing she slipped into love-talk, and spoke sweet words as though half in jest. And Gawain took them as though they were all in jest, and turned them aside lightly and courteously as though they played some kind of game. And at last the lady rose to go. "God save you for a pleasant hour," she said. "But I find it hard to believe that you are Sir Gawain, as you claim to be."

"Why so?" asked Sir Gawain, startled.

And she laughed. "Would Sir Gawain ever have tarried so long with a damosel and never once asked for a kiss?"

"Faith, lady, I feared to displease you," said Sir Gawain, "but since it seems that you give me leave, I do indeed beg you most humbly for a kiss."

So the lady took his face between her hands, and kissed him most sweetly, and went her way. And Gawain called for the chamber squires, for he would get up.

At evening, the lord of the castle came home with the carcass of a fine red deer slung across the back of a hunting pony. And he bade his huntsmen lay it before Gawain, who had come to meet him in the courtyard. "See, now, here is the fruit of my hunting, which I give to you according to our bargain."

"I accept the gift with all thanks," said Gawain, "and bid you to sup with me, though in your own Hall, tomorrow, when it is cooked. And now in return I give to you the thing that I won here in the castle this day." And he set his hands on his host's shoulders and kissed him, once.

"So; that was a fine gift, and much do I thank you for it," said the lord of the castle. "Yet gladly would I know who gave you that kiss."

"Nay," said Sir Gawain, "that was no part of the bargain."

And presently they sat down to supper in great good fellowship.

Next morning the lord of the castle sent for his boar hounds and rode hunting again. And again Gawain lay in his bed with the sweet unaccountable drowsiness upon him, until again the lady of the castle came and sat down on the edge of the bed, with the little dog pattering after, to cuddle in the floor-folds of her gown. And again she fell to teasing him softly, playing with words and trying to coax words of love from him in return. But Sir Gawain continued to turn them all aside, lightly and with courtesy that held no unkindness nor rebuff; and at last she left him, though this time with two kisses instead of yesterday's one.

That evening, the lord of the castle returned home at dusk, and his huntsmen laid at Gawain's feet the grizzly carcass of a boar. "Here, guest of mine, I bring you the spoils of my day's hunting."

"I accept the spoils of your hunting," Gawain said, "and bid you to sup with me again tomorrow night."

"And what have you to give me in return?"

"These, that I have come by since you rode out this morning," said Gawain; and putting his hands on the other's shoulders, he gave him two kisses. "This, and no more, I have gained, and now I give them to you."

And together, with the rest of the castle knights, they supped royally on the red deer that had been Gawain's gift of the night before. And the lady, coming in with her maidens, smiled at Gawain and sent him sweet dark glances that he pretended not to see.

That night, Sir Gawain thought that for other reasons beside his quest it would be better if he rode on his way next morning. But when he said so to his host, the big man said, "Nay, but why?"

"Tomorrow will be the last day of the year; and by noon of the next day, I must be at my meeting-place with the Green Knight."

"Have I not sworn on my knightly honour that the place is but two hours' ride from here, and you shall come there long before noon on the appointed day? And there is yet one day of our bargain still to run."

So the next morning, the morning of New Year's Eve, the lord of the castle called for his huntsmen and his hounds and rode away into the dark forest, while Sir Gawain still lay sleeping, tangled in troubled dreams of his meeting with the Green Knight that was now so cruelly near.

He woke to find thin winter sunshine streaming into the chamber, and the lady of the castle bending over him. When she saw that he was awake, she gave him one kiss, lingering a little, then stood back, looking down at him, laughing still, but a little sadly under the laughter. "But one little kiss," she said, "does your heart freeze in the winter? Or have you a damosel waiting for you at court?"

"No damosel," Sir Gawain said gently, "and my heart is still mine to give; but lady, fairest and sweetest lady, I may not give it to you, for your lord and the lord of this castle is my host. If I were to love the wife, that would be to shame my knightly vows."

"But my lord rides hunting and will not be home till dusk, no one will ever know, not even he, and so he will feel no hurt. Can we not love in this one day, that all my life may be sweeter remembering that Gawain of Orkney once held me in his arms?"

Gawain shook his head. "The wrong would be none the less because no one knew of it. No, lady, it cannot be."

For a long while she besought him, but he turned her pleas aside; and at last she sighed as one admitting defeat, and kissed him again, and said, "Sir Gawain, you must be the truest to your vows of all knights living. So – I will plague you no more. But give me something of yours to remember you by; that I may cherish it, and it may comfort me a little in my sorrow."

"Alas," said Sir Gawain, "I have nothing to give, for I travel light upon this quest."

"Then will I give you something of mine. Take this green girdle and wear it for my sake."

"Lady, I cannot be your knight and wear your favour."

"Such a little thing," said the lady, "and you need not wear it openly as my favour, but hidden where no man shall see, and only I shall know of it. Pray you take it, for you ride into sore danger, that I know; and there is magic woven into it, that while you wear it you shall bear a charmed life. Only keep it hid, and tell not my lord of it."

And with his meeting with the terrible Green Knight so close, the temptation was too great, and Gawain took the girdle of gold-worked green ribbons and knotted it round his neck under his shirt.

And the lady kissed him for the third time, and went her way.

That evening at dusk, the lord of the castle returned from his hunting bearing with him nothing but one fox-skin swinging from his hand.

"Alas! I have had scurvy hunting," he said when Gawain met him in the courtyard, "and this is all that I have to give you on the last of your three days."

"Then it seems that my winnings have been better than yours. For I have this to give you," said Gawain, and setting his hands on his host's shoulders he gave him three kisses.

Then with great jest and merriment, their arms across each other's shoulders, they went back into the Great Hall where supper was made ready, and feasted on the boar which the knight of the castle had brought home from his hunting the day before.

But Gawain spoke no word of the green ribbons lying round his neck under his shirt and his borrowed robe.

On New Year's Morning, Sir Gawain arose early, having slept but little, and called for the squires to arm him – keeping the green ribbons well hidden beneath the neck-band of his shirt the while. They brought him food; dark crusty bread and cold pig-meat, a cup of wine, and a platter of last summer's little withered yellow apples; but there was small wish for food in him; he drank some wine and ate one of the apples, and that was all. Then he went down into the courtyard, where the stable squires had brought out Gringolet looking sleek and well-fed.

Gringolet whinnied with pleasure at sight of his master, and Gawain fondled him a moment, then sprang into the saddle. "Fare you well; the sun and the moon on your threshold," he said to the lord of the castle, who had come down to take leave of him. Of the lady, there was no sign. "If I might, I would do aught in my power to reward you for your kindness. But I think that I shall not see the rising of another sun."

And he rode out through the gates that had been flung wide, with the squire who was to guide him riding hard behind; out over the causeway and away through the grey light of a low sullen dawn, with sleet spitting down the wind. By forest and mire and dreary wasteland they went, until they came to the lip of a broad valley between steep rocky slopes, and reining in, sat looking down, and saw the whole valley full of swirling mist.

"Sir," said the squire, "I have brought you as far as I may. Down yonder under the mist is the Green Chapel you seek; and down there the Green Knight will be waiting, as always he waits to fight with and slay all who would pass him by. None who come into combat with him may escape living. Oh, sir, do not go down there! None shall ever know; I will not betray you, that I swear as I hope for knighthood myself one day."

"My thanks," said Gawain; "but my honour's lost and my knighthood shamed if I turn away now from my tryst. God knows how to save his servants if he wills it so."

"Then your death is on your own hands," said the squire. "Follow the cliff path yonder and it will bring you down into the deep-most heart of the valley; a stream runs down the valley, and the Green Chapel stands upon the opposite bank. I bid you farewell, Sir Gawain, for I dare come with you no further."

So Sir Gawain gentled his horse into the cliff path, and held on down, the rocks rising sheer on his right hand and dropping sheer into the mist on the other; and out of the mist came the sound of rushing water, rising to meet him. At last he came as it were down through the mist into the clear air below it, and reached the valley floor, and saw a deep narrow stream swirling its way in a tumble of white water among rocks and the roots of lichen-hung alder trees. But he could make out no sign of any chapel, until after a while of looking about him he saw a short way upstream and on the far side a low green mound covered with alder and hazel scrub; and as he rode doubtfully towards it, he heard above the rush and tumble of the water, a sound as of a scythe on a whetstone coming up from somewhere deep within the heart of it.

This must be the Green Chapel, he thought, and green it is indeed; and no Christian chapel but some secret place of the Hollow Hills. And within it the Green Knight is making keen his weapon that must surely be the death of me this day.

But he set his horse to ford the stream at a place where it broadened and ran for a few yards shallow over a gravel bed, and came out close below the green mound; and there he dismounted and hitched Gringolet's bridle to an alder branch. And standing in the strange grey light scarfed with mist, he called, "Sir Knight of the Green Chapel, I am here as I vowed, to keep our New Year tryst."

"Wait until I have done sharpening my axe," came the great booming voice he remembered, echoing from the cavernous heart of the mound. "I shall not be long. And then you shall have the greeting that I promised you."

And Gringolet pricked his ears and tossed his head and showed the whites of his eyes; but Gawain stood unmoving, and waited on.

And in a while the sound of scythe on whetstone ceased, and out from a patch of darkness beneath the hazel branches came the Green Knight, just as he had been when he rode into Arthur's Hall a year and a day gone by, beautiful and terrible, and swinging lightly in his hand a long axe with a blade of green steel that looked sharp enough to draw blood from the wind.

"Now welcome, Sir Gawain!" he cried. "Three times welcome to so brave a knight! Now off with your helmet and make ready for the stroke I owe you for the one you dealt me in Arthur's Hall a year ago last night."

Gawain unloosed and pulled off his helmet, and thrust back the chain-mail coif from his neck. And taking a last look at the wintry world about him, he knelt and bent his head forward for the blow. "Strike, then," he said.

The Green Knight swung up his great axe, and as he brought it sweeping down, Gawain heard the whistle of it, as the crouching bird must hear the wing-rush of the stooping hawk. And despite himself, he flinched back and ducked out from under the blow.

The Green Knight stood leaning on the long handle of his axe, and grinned at him, the grin of some wild thing out of the forest. "Can this indeed be Gawain of the bold heart? When it was you that swung the axe, I never flinched from *your* blow."

"Your pardon. My courage lacks the knowledge that I can set my head back on my shoulders when you have done with it," said Gawain with a flare of grim laughter. "But I will not shrink again. Come now, and strike quickly."

"That I will," said the Green Knight, and again he swung up the fearsome blade and again he brought it whistling down. But this time Gawain remained as still as though he had been one of the rocks of the stream-side. And the axe-blade missed his neck by the width of a grass-blade, and dug deep into the mossy turf beside him.

"Strike!" shouted Gawain. "It was no part of our bargain that you should play with me thus!"

"Why, nor it was," agreed the Green Knight, "and now your head out a little further . . ."

And for the third time he swung up his axe, and swung it singing around his head, and brought it down. And this time Gawain felt a sting like a gad-fly on the side of his neck, and a small trickle of blood running down inside his coif, and the axe stood quivering in the turf beside him.

Then Gawain sprang from his knees and leapt clear, drawing his sword as he did so. "Now I have borne the blow and you have drawn the red blood, and if you strike again, I am free of my vow and may defend myself!"

The Green Knight stood leaning on his axe and laughing a little; and suddenly Gawain saw that though his garments were still green, they were but the garments in which a man rides hunting, and he was not the Green Knight at all, but his kindly host of the past week. And then he saw that he was both.

"Gawain, Gawain," said the knight, "you have indeed borne the blow, and I am in no mind to strike again. Indeed, had I been so minded, your head would have lain at my feet the first time I raised my axe."

"Why, then, this game of three blows?" Gawain asked, breathing quickly.

"The first two blows that touched you not, these were for your promise truly kept, for the one kiss and the two kisses my wife gave to you while I rode hunting, and that you rendered up to me when I rode home at evening. The third blow that drew blood was for your promise broken, when you gave me her three kisses but not the green ribbons from her waist." He saw the look on the young knight's face, and his great smile broadened. "Oh, I know all that passed between you. It was at my will that she tempted you, and had you yielded to her tempting, and dishonoured your knighthood and my house, then indeed you would now be lying headless at my feet. As for the green girdle, you took and hid it but for love of your life. You are young, and he must be a sad man indeed who does not a little love the life God gave him. So now that I have drawn blood for it, I forgive you the girdle."

Gawain pulled the green ribbon girdle from its hiding-place and held it out to him. "I am ashamed, none the less. I am unworthy of my place at the Round Table."

"Nay," said his host the Green Knight, with booming kindness. "You are only young with the life running hot in you. And did I not say that you are forgiven? There will be few knights at the Round

Table with a better right to sit there than you. Keep the green girdle in remembrance of this adventure; and come back with me to my castle, that we may end the Twelve Days of Christmas in joy."

But Gawain, though he put the green ribbons round his neck again, would not stay. "I must away back to my liege lord," he said. "But before I go, pray you tell me, noble sir, who you are, and how you came to be both lord of the castle where I have been made welcome and happy this week past, and the terrible Green Knight, who dies not when his head is struck from his shoulders?"

"My name is Sir Birtilack," said the other. "I was minded to test for myself the courage of Arthur's champions of the Round Table, having heard much of the High King's court, even here in my northern wilderness. For the rest – question not the ways of magic."

So they parted as dear friends who have known each other a lifetime. And Gawain rode back through the Forest of Wirrel and the wild border country of Wales, until he came again to Arthur's court, and his own place that he had fully earned among the foremost of the brotherhood of the Round Table.

THE QUEST OF
THE SARACEN BEAST

Theodore Goodridge Roberts

One of the pleasures I have had in editing my Arthurian anthologies is in rediscovering the work of Theodore Goodridge Roberts (1877–1953). Roberts was a Canadian author who wrote several novels set in Newfoundland and Labrador and who established a minor reputation as a poet. Early in his long career he wrote several popular historical novels including The Red Feathers *(1907) and* The Cavalier of Virginia *(1910), but his later stories featuring the Arthurian court wit Sir Dinadan and published in the American magazine* Blue Book *were never published in book form and are very difficult to obtain. The following story appeared in the November 1950 issue and has not been reprinted until now.*

Attracted by groans and fretful cries, Sir Dinadan turned aside into the greenwood shade and discovered an elderly knight recumbent among ferns and pillowed on moss, whereat he dismounted and made courteous inquiry concerning the cause of the stranger's position and lamentations.

"Cause enough, the Lord knows!" the stranger exclaimed, sitting up and clapping a mailed hand to his helmeted head. "Here was I within but spear's-length of the beast – within prodding distance for the first time in twenty years – when down on his knees went my horse with such violence that I departed the saddle by the way of his ears. Then he galloped away and left me grassed."

"What beast was that, sir?" asked Dinadan.

"The Saracen Beast, young sir," the other replied, speaking less excitedly now and fingering his gray mustache through his open visor. "That monster famous in song and story, that has been the quest of good knights these hundred years and more. There was King Gort – then Sir Cockrum, a mighty champion – then Duke Ironsides, who perished in it and was found a skeleton at the foot of a cliff. Then Duke Peveral followed it till he contracted rheumatics and bequeathed it to me, Sir Nigel of the Tower and his favorite nephew, God help me, twenty weary years ago. And now, alas, a mare's son fails me and I sit here unhorsed!"

"Sir, I would horse you and speed you on your quest right cheerily but for my lack of a second mount," Dinadan assured him. "As it is, Sir Nigel – with my second horse back at Camelot, and a somewhat pressing errand of my own – I fear me I can offer Your Honor no more than a lift to the nearest farmhouse or inn."

The elderly knight looked surprised and asked: "Why did you leave it behind you?"

Dinadan looked embarrassed, and replied, somewhat stumblingly: "He is not quite a warhorse, really – more of a sturdy hackney, sir. And, to speak frankly, I left him at Camelot in hock for my armorer's and my tailor's bills. And my man Kedge along with him! Both of them in hock – to be quite frank with you, sir."

"D'ye tell me so!" chuckled Sir Nigel. "As short of cash as long of spur, what! How come, young sir?"

Dinadan admitted it with a smile at once whimsical and rueful, and then explained his position briefly, thus: "I am the third son of a northern baron whose mountainy domain produces larch and heather and whortleberries in abundance, but little else, and whose tenants pay their rents with smoked venison and usquebaugh. Upon leaving home I paged, and later squired, a stout and generous knight, hight Sir Gyles; and a year since, King Arthur dubbed me knight for a small deed connected with the whiskers of treasonous King Rience of North Wales."

At that, Sir Nigel rose and embraced the younger knight with a clanging of breastplates.

"I've heard of that doughty deed!" he cried. "It was well done, by my halidom! It is an honor to meet the hero that razored the villainous visage of that braggart."

"Nay, no hero!" protested Dinadan, in modest confusion. "Only a fumbling beginner, sir – but at your service."

"At my service, d'ye say? Then do I bequeath to you, here and now, the high quest of the Saracen Beast, even as my lamented uncle bequeathed it to me twenty weary years ago. It is all yours, my worthy and trusty Sir Dinadan. So mount now, and follow the Saracen Beast through thick and thin, even as it has been followed by the mighty King Gort, Sir Cockrum, Duke Ironsides and Duke Peveral, not to mention myself. Up and after it, noble youth!"

His embarrassment and confusion vastly increased by the bequest and the old knight's rising vehemence, Sir Dinadan was fairly flabbergasted.

"Gramercy, gramercy!" he stammered. "But who am I – full young and untried – to follow those illustrious princes and noble questers? And were I worthy even, I'd think shame to leave Your Honor alone and unhorsed in this forest."

"You are too modest, my boy," said Sir Nigel. "As for my position at the moment, think nothing of it. It will mend. I have a squire and grooms and spare horses somewhere back along the way, who frequently lose touch but always catch up to me sooner or later. So mount and spur now, I pray you!"

"But, sir, I am in no manner prepared or provisioned for this high adventure," poor Dinadan protested. "I was but riding at random in the hope of meeting some knight-errant less secure in the saddle than myself, and thereby obtaining the means – his arms and harness and horse – of recovering my chestnut hackney and my man Kedge. In fact, sir, I am operating on a shoestring, and at the moment, in greater need of quick money than of glory."

"You shall have both, my boy," said Sir Nigel. "I'll be in Camelot tomorrow, and shall release your man and hackney, and make generous provision for them, without delay, as I am a true knight. As for quick money, here are five silver crowns to enrich your pouch. And here is one of the two flasks I always carry on my sword-belt. As for victuals for today and tomorrow, my runaway charger carries two saddlebags stuffed with the very best, to which you are welcome. You have but to follow in his tracks to overtake him, or more likely, to meet him on his way back; for it is his habit, upon such occasions, to turn about and retrace his steps when he realizes I am not still on his back. In either case, snatch the saddlebags."

He pushed Dinadan gently yet strongly toward the latter's charger, and even boosted him into the saddle.

"Now I shall rest easy, my noble young friend, in the knowledge that I have relayed this high quest into such worthy and capable hands as your own," he added.

So, feeling that further protest would sound discourteous and ungrateful, Dinadan rode off on the quest of the Beast. He followed the trail of the runaway horse without difficulty, and had gone only a mile before sounds of movement in the leafy obscurity before him caused him to draw rein. The disturbance increased swiftly; and a large black horse, saddled and accoutered, burst suddenly into view and came galloping straight at him. A collision was narrowly avoided by quick footwork on the part of his dapple-gray: and in the moment of the black's passing, Dinadan made a long arm and snatched the coupled saddlebags. He went forward again, keeping to the double track of the runaway's going and coming with hardly a check, until he reached a patch of moist ground whereon Sir Nigel's horse had snubbed to a stop and reversed himself. It was all as easy to read as inked words on parchment.

"Now I shall have only the tracks of the Beast itself to guide me," Dinadan muttered.

Looking down from his high saddle, he saw nothing traceable leading onward from the gouges of iron-shod hooves. So he dismounted and peered closer, and still failed to find anything to his purpose.

"But what am I looking for?" he asked himself. "What do I know of this Saracen Beast and the kind of tracks it makes?"

He sat down on a convenient tussock of fern, and racked his brains. He had heard of the Saracen Beast before his meeting with Sir Nigel, but always incidentally and never with his full attention. Now he ransacked his memory for particulars concerning that high and exclusive quest and its exclusive object, neither of which had ever made a very strong appeal to the popular taste, evidently. He removed his helmet and gauntlets and clasped his bare head in bare hands. When and what had he first heard of it?

Hah, he had it! He was a mere toddler when a wandering bard had sung of it, and many more marvels, in his ancestral hall. The bard had called it the Saracen Beast. By his telling, it had been brought to Britain by a great traveler in a remote age, and had escaped from its cage and into impenetrable mountainy forests. He had clutched his nurse's skirts at the bard's description of that monster, and he shivered slightly even now at the memory. How had it gone?

"The head and neck of a great serpent, the body of an Afric

leopard but twice as great and long, and the legs and hooves of a hart, and a noise in its belly as of thirty couples of hounds questing." That was it. But between the episode of the bard and the meeting with good Sir Nigel, he had heard, or harkened to, only such talk of the Saracen Beast as had given him the impression that its pursuit offered little of knightly fame and even less of monetary reward. But now he, Dinadan, was pledged to it and embarked upon it, so there was nothing for him to do about it but his honest best.

Dinadan sighed, arose from the ferny tussock, hung his casque on the saddle and renewed his search afoot for the trail of the Saracen Beast. His tall dapple-gray Garry followed him with a polite show of interest.

He was rewarded sooner than he had expected.

"What's this!" he cried, staring at a cloven hoof-print in a patch of mud. "This is it – or the track of a royal hart of ten points, anyway."

He advanced again, scrutinizing the ground and finding further prints of cleft hooves in moist spots every here and there; and Garry followed close snuffling inquiringly at his shoulder. So they soon came to a spring of clear water under a bank of flowering May thorn and bramble; and by the depth of the hoof-prints in the soft margin thereof, Dinadan knew that his quarry had drunk its fill here. Now the sun was behind the westward forest and the leafy twilight was dimming; so Dinadan decided to pass the night beside the spring. He unbitted and unsaddled Garry, who straightway sank his muzzle to the water. He followed the horse's example, though the weight of his armor all but bogged him down. After extricating himself from the mud, he unarmed from neck to heels – a difficult task lacking squirish help. Then, after a swig at the flask which Sir Nigel had given him, he opened one of the saddlebags that he had snatched from the runaway's saddle-bow. Here was superior fare, in truth! Here was a tart of jam and rich pastry which he shared, bite and bite about, with nuzzling Garry. Here was a pigeon pie, of which the horse got only the pastry. They went fifty-fifty on the currant buns, but the knight had all of the roast chicken, and the charger all of a large barley loaf.

Dinadan slept soundly on fern and moss, but was early awake and astir. For breakfast, he and Garry shared what remained in the first saddlebag. Then (after a pull on the flask) he saddled and bitted Garry; but instead of rearming himself, he resumed the belt only, with his sword and a dagger convenient on his left hip and his wallet and Sir Nigel's flask to balance them. He placed all the rest

– helmet, the back- and breast-plates, shoulder pieces, thigh pieces, greaves and the rest – upon and about the great saddle. But he slung his shield at his own back and shouldered his war-spear. So he resumed the quest of the strange Saracen Beast on his own feet, with the tall horse and all his protective harness clanking after. Though he went lightly now, he still went slowly, searching for big cloven hoof-prints. The ground became higher and dryer and the prints so few and so far between that he just about lost interest in them before the morning was half gone. He sat down on a mossy boulder to reflect and to moisten his throat.

"This is too bad," he told his horse. "In twenty-four hours I have lost that which Sir Nigel kept tag of for twenty years – unless the venerable knight was exaggerating. Or so it seems. But we'll take another scout around, of course: but I must confess that I don't see much of a future for you and me in this high quest of the Saracen Beast. It sounded impractical to me – a trifle too high and wide – when I first heard of it. But we'll do our best, of course – for another day, at least. We owe that much to generous Sir Nigel."

So the search for cloven hoof-prints was resumed.

"What's that?" exclaimed Dinadan. But he was not looking at the ground. His head was up; and so was Garry's.

"Hark! Hounds in full cry! The Beast with the noise as of questing hounds in its belly! Nay – it's real hounds – and they have brought the Beast to bay!"

He leaped forward and ran hard and straight toward the clamor, with the gear-encumbered charger clanging after him. Now he heard the halloos of men mingled with the fierce outcry of hounds. He went through thick and thin, and soon burst from cover into a small glade and the scene of action. Here was the Beast . . . Nay, this was no monster, but a noble stag of ten points doing battle for its dear life against hopeless odds; the center of a milling ring of fangs and steel. It still struck with horns and hooves, but with failing force. There was froth on its muzzle now, and blood on neck and breast and flanks, and the great eyes were dimming. Dinadan saw plainly enough that this was not the Saracen Beast, but only a great hart of ten points overmatched and about to die and therefore no concern of his; but a sudden furious madness of indignation and pity seized him, and he dashed into the meêlée with a defiant yell and buffeting hands and feet. Hounds and two fellows in wool and leather slunk or jumped out of reach of his arms and legs, but a third huntsman turned upon him and threatened him with a boar-spear.

But only for a moment. Before the fellow could deliver even a jab,

Dinadan enveloped him like a whirlwind, snatched the short spear and clipped him over the nob with its butt-end. Now a menacing but inarticulate roar caused our hero to look to his left; and he beheld a large person in a tunic of green silk coming at him on a tall horse. A personage, evidently, by the quality of his tunic, the curly feather and gold brooch in his green cap and the arrogance of his voice.

Still roaring, this personage dismounted within a pace of Dinadan and threatened him with the butcher's knife with which he obviously intended to deliver the coup de grâce to the enfeebled stag. Dinadan, waggling the boar-spear in a calculating manner, warned him to make less noise and more sense, or he too would be laid flat with a broken head. At that, the other ceased his inarticulate bellowing suddenly and was silent for long enough to flap his mouth open and shut half a dozen times. Then in a controlled but dangerous voice Green Tunic demanded:

"Who are you, knave?"

To this Dinadan returned, in a voice that matched the questioner's: "Who wants to know, churl?"

At that, the two huntsmen who had jumped aside from Dinadan's first onset struck at him from the rear, only to have their blows nullified by the long shield on his back. He turned upon them and struck with the clubbed spear, thus presenting the shield to a vicious slash of their master's knife. He turned again, quick as a trout, dropped the borrowed boar-spear, drew his sword and sent Green Tunic stumbling back beyond the sweep of it.

"Fool, I am Sir Gregstone, lord of all this barony!" cried Green Tunic. "Put up that sword!"

Dinadan cried: "I am Sir Dinadan of the Quest of the Saracen Beast!" And he sent the two varlets leaping backward with a circular sweep of his long sword.

"The Saracen Beast, say you?" exclaimed Sir Gregstone, with a change for the better of both voice and countenance. "Just so. An exalted quest, truly, sir – ah – I didn't catch the name, sir."

"Dinadan."

"Dinadan. Quite. And what, then, of old Sir Nigel of the Tower?"

"He handed over to me, after twenty years of it, and went to Camelot."

"Just so. A fine old gentleman. But may I make so bold as to ask why you charged into this entirely private hunt of my own hart in my own forest, kicking my hounds and breaking the heads of my huntsmen?"

"I mistook your quarry for my own – your stag for the Beast – by the tracks of its cloven hooves," lied Dinadan.

"He's stole away an' got clean off, Lord," grumbled one of the spearmen.

Of the other spearmen, one still lay supine with a cracked nob, and one nursed a broken shoulder.

"My mistake, Sir Gregstone," lied Dinadan, feigning regret.

"Let it pass," said Gregstone, but with a wry grimace. "A head of ten points, by my halidom! I've never seen a greater. But let it pass. And put up your sword, I pray you, Sir Dinadan, and come home to dinner."

"Gramercy," accepted our hero, who even at this stage of his career seldom refused an invitation to dine or sup.

The grumbling spearman knelt beside the fellow on the ground and tried to rouse him, but without success. Dinadan joined them, unhooked Sir Nigel's flask from his belt and unstopped it, raised the unconscious churl's head and shoulders and tilted the flask to the parted lips. After three swallows, the sturdy fellow was up on his feet and staggering happily. Then Dinadan examined the other casualty's shoulder, advised him to see a doctor and administered two swigs from the flask . . .

They came to Sir Gregstone's residence shortly after high noon. It stood, or rather squatted, in a fair meadow, and was girt by a wide moat like a paunchy champion by his sword-belt. It consisted of structures of two or more periods, some of hewn timber and some of masonry, with a square tower in their midst. Its appearance was substantial and commodious rather than elegant.

"Like its lord's," thought Dinadan, with a glance at Sir Gregstone.

They were no more than across the drawbridge when loud halloos in their rear caused Dinadan to halt and turn. He saw a knight armed cap-à-pie riding hard toward them on a red horse.

"Who is that?" he asked. "And what does he want?"

"Pay him no heed!" cried Gregstone. "He is but a crackpot. An' dinner is waiting," he added urgently.

"Nay, he bawls your name and dubs you coward," protested Dinadan. "He dares you to arm and come out to him. Are you deaf?"

"I hear him, as I've heard him, almost daily, this past month and more, the devil take him! Come in to dinner, or 'twill be burnt to cinders."

"But he calls you coward an' knave and a disgrace to your golden spurs. He calls you glutton and tyrant."

"He's mad. Heed him not. He'll come no nearer than the bridge Ignore him and come in to dinner, and he'll return to his pitch in the forest."

"But all he asks is to run a tilt with you – but in villainous language, I admit. Why not arm yourself and oblige him – and have done with his clamor? I'll be glad to squire you."

"No, no! Not now, anyway! After dinner, maybe. I'll explain it all after dinner."

Sir Gregstone pushed and pulled Sir Dinadan into the great hall, and grooms followed with the horses; and while Dinadan was being nudged and plucked toward a table set beneath a canopy on a dais, the horses were led the whole length of the hall and out by a back door.

The two knights dined by themselves, but with service enough for a company of ten; and there was just as much too much of victuals and drink as of service. In truth, there was too much of everything except conversation, of which there was nothing for a long time. Dinadan was a good trencherman, but he could not hold a candle to his host in this respect, nor could he match him in the cup-and-can branch of gourmandry. At last, however, Sir Gregstone wiped his lips and fingers on a corner of the tablecloth of damask, sat back in his chair, hiccuped and closed his eyes.

"Now what about the knight on the red horse?" asked our hero, prodding him with an elbow.

Gregstone moved his fat lips, but nothing came of it. Dinadan prodded again and harder, and repeated the question louder. The fat lips this time emitted a thick whisper:

"It'll keep. Forty winks. No hurry."

Dinadan swore impatiently. Though he had plied knife and fingers and cup and horn with his customary heartiness, he was not sleepy, and his curiosity was as lively as ever. So he drew back his elbow for a third and yet sharper prod.

"Hold it!" someone exclaimed at his shoulder.

He held it, and turned his head and saw an elderly gentleman in a robe of black velvet standing behind him.

"I beg your pardon, young sir, but you'll gain nothing by nudging him," continued Black Robe, in a hurried and conciliatory voice. "His ribs are too well larded. He'll sleep for hours yet. But permit me to reply for him, sir. I know the answers as well as he does."

He introduced himself as Clark Andrew, one-time tutor to Sir Gregstone and for many years now seneschal of the great house and steward of the wide domain. At Dinadan's suggestion, he took a seat and helped himself to wine. He had already dined – "before the sirloin was done too hard for my waggly tender teeth," he explained. He dismissed the servants with a gesture.

"And now, young sir, what would you know?"

"Why your Sir Gregstone ignores the challenge and insults of the knight on the red horse, venerable sir."

"Quite. I myself would ask that question if I did not know my bully lord and friend as I do. Should you repeat it to Sir Gregstone three hours from now, when he wakes from his postprandial nap, he will tell you that he ignores challenges and insults because he lacks suitable harness in which to accept the former and resent the latter. Mere sophistry, young sir – though 'tis true that of his two suits of armor, which were made for his father, one is now too small for him and the other still too large."

"D'ye tell me he lacks the price of a new suit of mail?"

"Not at all, young sir. God forbid! He could have a suit of the best Spanish made to his measure every sennight of his life, had he a mind to; but like his father before him, he is a better patron to cooks and tailors than to armorers. He is no jouster; nor was Sir Guff. He has neither the seat nor the spirit for exchanges of thrusts and cuts with equally armed cavaliers; nor had his sire. Harts and hinds are more to his taste as antagonists – but only after they have been properly winded and worried by hounds and huntsmen. And so it was with Sir Guff, who took his first and only tumble in a passage of arms as a young man and harnessed to match his slimness, and who had no further ado with body armor until, when as big around as a hogshead, he ordered a new suit of mail for a purely ceremonious occasion. And so it is that Sir Gregstone, a true son of his father, can excuse himself from combat on the plea that he has nothing to wear."

"Hah! So he is truly the lily-livered, chicken-hearted knave that the knight on the red horse names him."

"Near enough, young sir. And yet not altogether a knave. Not an out-an'-out villain for a ballad, so to speak. There's good as well as bad in him – as in most of us. He's not vengeful, for one thing. Take your own case, for instance, young sir. I have heard from the huntsmen how you came crashing in when he was about to dispatch that great hart of many tines – one of the greatest ever seen in these parts, so they say – and cuffed and kicked hounds and huntsmen and threatened Sir Gregstone with your sword, to the end that the stag escaped with his life. And yet you sit here as safe as if you were in your own house; and you might lie here just as safely, asleep as awake. If you come to any harm here, young sir, it will be from emulating your host's prowess at this table. In other words, all will be aboveboard. Hah-hah! Not bad, wot?"

"Very good, sir. You have a pretty wit. But I must tell you that I'd be in a poor state of health right now if his hunting-knife had not been turned by the shield on my back."

"D'ye tell me that he struck at you?"

"Yes – and it was when my back was turned."

"Even so, young sir, it was a surprising show of spirit on his part. But don't let it worry you. He must have quite forgotten his true nature in the chagrin and excitement of the moment. He lacks both spirit and energy, as well as inclination, to strike at you again from behind or before. Consider his behavior in the case of the forward knight on the red horse. All Sir Gregstone does in retaliation to that gentleman's challenges and insults, which have been of almost daily recurrence for the past month, is ignore them and him."

At that, Dinadan sneered: "Because he's afraid to fight!"

"There's no denying it, young sir," agreed the seneschal. "Sir Gregstone, like Sir Guff before him, is averse to combat – to the exchanging of blows, that's to say. In the matter of thrusts and cuts, he holds that it is more blessed to give than to receive. Yes indeed. But his case is not as simple as you make it sound, my dear sir. If he were of a vengeful nature, or treacherously inclined, he would have rid himself of the pestiferous attentions of that knight weeks ago, by sending archers and pikemen out at him in broad day or a cutthroat after dark; for the vociferous challenger invites disaster every hour, open to arrows and mass attack daily, and lying asleep and unarmed every night in the same dell. And Sir Gregstone has only to say the word, and the murderous deed is done, for he is a generous master. But he has not said it; nor will he say it, for 'tis not in his nature, but turns deaf ears to the clamor and does not let it spoil his dinner."

"It sounds like madness to me," said Dinadan scornfully. "Madness and foolery! They both sound crazy, and worse, to me. Gregstone is an arrant coward, by your own telling, and a loathly glutton to boot, despite the one redeeming feature you claim for him. And his challenger must be utterly mad. Who is he? And what is he challenging about? What does he want of your guzzling coward?"

The seneschal scratched his bearded chin and a hairy ear, and drained and refilled his cup, before answering.

"He calls himself Sir Kelter," he said, and paused for a sip. "But what he wants," he continued slowly, as if weighing every word, "I am not prepared to say, as I have not the honor – questionable, maybe – of his confidence. I fully agree with you, however, that he must be mad: but there are so many varieties of madness in the knightage – in its junior circles especially – that I'll not venture an opinion on the exact nature and degree of his affliction."

"Maybe he is just spoiling for a fight?" suggested our hero hopefully.

"He is in a pugnacious mood, unquestionably," the other agreed.

"Maybe he would like a go at me?" Dinadan resumed. "Just a friendly bicker – or whatever he wants. Blunt spears or sharp ones, I'd leave him the choice."

The seneschal wagged his venerable pow and said: "I don't think he would like it, young sir."

"Not like it! Why not? I am a knight of King Arthur's own dubbing – hight Sir Dinadan – and good enough for my years. Not as good as many and yet better than some – both ahorse and afoot!"

"I don't question your quality, Sir Dinadan. Nor your prowess, sir. On the contrary. To be frank with you, bully knight, I have observed you closely; and not only that, I have visited your great charger and examined your fine harness; and I doubt if Sir Kelter would welcome your worship as a substitute for Sir Gregstone. And after all, his ire appears to be very particularly aroused by the person of Sir Gregstone."

"That may be; but if he is half as fierce as he sounds, he'll not refuse a fight simply for lack of a quarrel."

After a long minute of deep thought and another cup of mead, the old man said: "In my opinion, it is a bang at Sir Gregstone that he wants, rather than a fight. But if you, sir, are serious in your suggestion of meeting him in combat, you have only to go forth on Gregstone's charger and with Gregstone's green shield dressed before you."

Dinadan didn't half like the idea of doing battle on a strange horse and sporting his craven host's shield, but he felt such an urge for action that he accepted it. So he and the seneschal retired to the stables, leaving Sir Gregstone snoring in his chair.

With his companion's help, Dinadan was soon in his suit of superior and tested mail, the price of which had been several times more than he could afford. Then, after a brief visit to Garry's stall, for the purpose of embracing and apologizing to his puzzled dapple-gray, he went forth on a strange horse and behind a strange shield with the intention of amending the manners of a strange knight.

When Dinadan issued upon the meadow beyond the drawbridge, Sir Kelter was hovering at the forest's edge some two hundred yards away. At a blast on a horn blown by the venerable seneschal, Kelter wheeled, gave vent to a long-drawn whoop beginning on a note of incredulity and rising swiftly to a hoot of derision and an exultant shout, then laid his spear and launched to the attack. Whereupon our hero laid his spear and dressed the green shield and knocked spurred heels on the bulging flanks of his mount.

"Get going!" he urged. "Action front!"

But the horse only tossed his great head in protest and sank his great hooves deeper in the sod.

"What sort of warhorse are you?" Dinadan enquired, with appropriate epithets.

But breath and heels alike were wasted, for the animal was no sort of warhorse at all, but the biggest and laziest plowhorse within five leagues in every direction. In the meantime, Sir Kelter and the red charger came on, hard and straight.

"So be it, fool!" muttered Sir Dinadan. "Let them do the running – the devil take you! What happens when an irresistible force meets with an immovable object? We'll soon know!"

A number of things happened practically all at once. Sir Kelter's wavering point – he was only a third-rater after all, despite his noise – went wide in the last critical split second; but Sir Dinadan's held true. So Kelter sailed backward from his saddle on the point of our hero's bending lance – but with his breastplate no more than dented behind the pierced shield – and came to earth violently on the back of his neck. Then the collision! The forces of motion and immobility involved were so great that both horses fell down; and though the plowhorse dropped where he stood, without giving back an inch, the vibrations of the shock flung Dinadan from the saddle to the ground, where a hoof of one or the other of the stunned steeds clipped him on his helmeted head.

Upon regaining consciousness, Dinadan did not open his eyes at once, but tried to collect his wits; and while so stilly yet laboriously and painfully employed (for his head felt terrible), he heard a voice close at hand. It was the voice of Sir Gregstone; and though it was reduced to a wheezy whisper, he recognized it.

"But use your brains, I beg you!" wheezed Sir Gregstone with urgency. "This is the better match on every count, as I've explained a dozen times already. Must I go all over it again? So be it! He is by far the better jouster – since you set such store by the silly arts and mad antics of chivalry. Though handicapped by a mount that refused to budge, he hit your vociferous Kelter straight and hard and grassed him like a carp. That he was unhorsed by the collision, and so got his head trod on, was no fault of his. It might have happened to King Arthur, or to that master of romantic tomfoolery Sir Launcelot du Lake, under like circumstances.

"Kelter can take no credit for it, that's certain, for the spill was due entirely to his mount's stupidity, and the knockout was purely accidental, no matter which horse stepped on him. Instead of pouting, you should be thanking your stars for the quality of his helmet. Use your wits, child! With such a helmet as that, and every other item of his harness of matching quality – and consider that dapple-gray charger too – this Dinadan is as well turned out as any earl. So quit your sulking, and make the most of this opportunity."

A peevish feminine voice protested: "But you yourself named him for a fool, Papa, when you said that only the feeble-minded or utterly mad ever undertook that quest."

"True for you," wheezed Sir Gregstone. "I said that, and I repeat it. King Gort, Sir Cockrum, Duke Iron-sides, Duke Peveral and Sir Nigel – each and every one of those questers of the Saracen Beast was either as mad as a March hare dancing in the moonshine, or as simple as the village idiot: for if such a beast ever existed – which I doubt – it was dispatched even before old King Gort's time, or it would have fallen since to one of those eager questers, who were all good men of their hands, whatever can't be said for their heads. Nay, the Questing or Saracen Beast is not, and never was, anything more than an obsession bred of an old-wife's tale or a poet's fable. It exists and survives only in the imaginations of its succeeding pursuers, each of whom must needs be mad, or at least chuckleheaded, or he would have nothing to pursue. And so the fabulous quest has been passed on from madman to madman – but whether by accident or design I don't know.

"But this I do know, child. It has always moved on an exalted plane. From King Gort to Sir Nigel, every quester of the Beast has been of high blood and exalted possessions. And do you think for a moment that old Sir Nigel of the Tower would pass it on just to any come-by-chance hedge-running knight-errant? Don't be silly. I promise you that this young knight is a rich earl's son and heir at the very least, and more likely a duke's. So bestir yourself now that you have him at your mercy, while he is doubly a crackpot, so to speak; for you'll never have another chance – not with that nasty temper you got from your poor lamented mother – to make so fine a marriage. And if this young knight lacks something of intelligence, he will make the happier husband: the happier for himself as for you. I am sure that my own marriage would have been happier for all concerned had I been less generously endowed with intelligence and sensibility."

"Not to mention gluttony and cowardice, dear Papa," jeered the lady.

Breathing in angry snorts, Sir Gregstone exclaimed: "Your mother's own daughter! But harky to me, hussy! If you let this Godsend slip through your fingers, and continue to encourage that insolent pesky knave who calls himself Sir Kelter but is more likely a runaway scullion than a born cavalier, I shall lose my well-known sense of Christian forbearance entirely, and Black Tim or Sticker Mike will slit his villainous gullet."

Then there was silence; and after minutes of it, Sir Dinadan ventured to lift one eyelid just far enough for a peek. He was in a small chamber dimly lit by a smoky candle. *So I have been out for hours*, he thought. He saw that which twitched his venturesome eye wide open. It was a lady. She stood just beyond the candle, looking down at the smoking wick. He regained control of his eyelid. She snuffed the candle, waited till it burned clearly, then took it up and moved toward him. She stood close beside the narrow bed he was on, and gazed down at him with eyes as green and hard as emeralds. *God help me!* he thought, watching through screening lashes and trying to breathe like an innocent sleeper. She continued to gaze down at him, stooping a little. Her hair was like spun gold; her cheeks and brow were like eglantines and Easter lilies, and her small mouth was like a ruby. And now her green gaze took on a considering, musing softness.

"Maybe he really means it," she murmured. "And he may be right, for once. And to spare dear Kelt a slit gullet – why not? With a noble simpleton for a husband and my darling still alive and kissing – why not? A respectable son-in-law for Papa, and freedom for me. I'll do it!"

She stooped lower and touched her lips to his. He twitched

sharply. She straightened up slowly, with a gratified smile on her ruby mouth (having mistaken his twitch for reaction to her kiss instead of to a drip of hot tallow on his ear), murmured, "Till tomorrow, my poor fool," replaced the candle on the table and left the room.

Dinadan opened both eyes, then sat up cautiously and held his sore head in both hands, trying to steady it. After a little while, he recovered a piece of his armor from the floor and tried to put it on, but with such excess of anxious haste and lack of strength and direction that he accomplished nothing in ten minutes of frantic effort; and he was still fumbling futilely when discovered by the seneschal.

"What now, young sir?" asked the seneschal.

"Not so loud!" begged Dinadan. "Shut that door – for God's sake! An' lend a hand, I pray you, good Master Andrew. This cursed breastplate!"

"Nay, that's the backplate! What gives?"

"I'm leaving. No place for me. Must be gone before morning."

"What's your hurry?"

"That lady. I – she – God save me from such a fate!"

"Hah! I get it. Permit me to squire you, young sir."

The old seneschal had Dinadan ready for the road before the candle needed a second snuffing, then led him down and out to the stables by back stairs and passages, saddled Garry for him and gave him a leg-up, then led horse and rider away by a muddy lane and over the moat by the rear drawbridge. After thanking the seneschal warmly and promising to send a handsome acknowledgment as soon as he was in the money again, Dinadan expressed sportsmanly regret at thus condemning young Sir Kelter to a slit gullet.

"Though I'd personally prefer a slit gullet to marriage with that lady," he added.

'Tastes differ," chuckled the other. "But don't worry. Sir Gregstone's bark is worse than his bite."

So Dinadan rode back to Camelot: and that was the end of the illusionary quest of the fabulous Saracen Beast. Years later, he heard that Sir Kelter, who had lived to marry that lady and to cut his own throat, had been the secret and ambitious son of that crafty and ambitious seneschal.

SIR MARROK THE WOLF

Allen French

Another of the lesser-known Arthurian characters was Sir Marrok whose main notoriety was that he was transformed into a wolf for seven years. This legend seems to owe its origin to one of the ballads or lays composed in the late twelfth century by Marie de France, a poet who spent some time at the court of Henry II and Eleanor of Aquitaine. Her lay Bisclavret is about a werewolf but is not Arthurian. A later poet whose name is now lost recast this as part of the Arthurian legend in Melion (c.1200) and this became further integrated into the legend over the years with the knight's name being transformed to Marrok. The story was retold in its most complete form in the novel Sir Marrok (1902) by the American author Allen French (1870–1946). This book falls conveniently into two halves. The first tells of Marrok's early life at the court of Uther Pendragon and how he establishes his own castle in the forest of Bedegraine (now called Sherwood) before setting off to join Arthur's army in his war against Rome. While he is away all manner of betrayals happen at his castle and his wife Irma spreads the rumour that he is dead and that she is now in charge. The second half of the novel deals with what happens when Marrok returns from the wars and the consequences of his discovery of his wife's betrayal. That part of the novel is reprinted here complete for the first time in nearly a hundred years.

I

A little train, much smaller than that which had left Bedegraine, rode toward the north. Its leader, spurring out before the others, reached first the ridge which gave prospect over all Sir Marrok's land, and paused to look upon Bedegraine. Green was the land, as always, like a very Eden, and the dark mass of the forest, which once had held robbers, seemed to the knight as a home. He hastened down into the valley.

But as he passed along the road his countenance overclouded and his heart grew heavy. Gone were the waving fields of grain, the acres of prosperous crops. Again were the fields green with the luxuriance of weeds, and hosts of sapling oaks and beeches invaded lands which the peasants once had plowed. Changed indeed were the neat and smiling villages. The houses were squalid, the streets dirty and overgrown. And the human beings were again different from what they had been. At his coming the knight saw people look, then hide from sight; nor would they come at his call. The warrior bowed his head.

"Woe is me!" he cried. "War hath swept over Bedegraine!"

Then he spurred faster, anxious for sight of the castle. "My son!" he thought. But presently he cried: "God be praised!" Serene and strong, the castle lifted its rugged head above the trees. When he had it in full view he knew no harm had come to it. "At least," he thought, "that hath been spared. But oh, my poor people!"

It was evening; the castle drawbridge was raised. The knight blew his horn, and a warder looked over the battlement. "What aileth you all?" cried the knight. "Hath no news of peace come to Bedegraine? Let down the bridge."

"Who are you," asked the churl, "that you speak so high?"

"Go to the lady," answered the knight. "Tell her that Sir Marrok hath returned."

The warder laughed. "Go to!" he cried. "Sir Marrok is dead."

"Send for the lady," said the knight, again. "Tell her that one who calls himself Sir Marrok is at the gate."

The warder would have laughed again, but from the knight spoke dignity and authority. "If it should be true," he muttered, "then are we all sped! – I go," he said, and went.

The knight waited. "They have supposed me dead! But what of that? My poor people! Fire and sword hath swept my fields."

And yet that desolation in Bedegraine came not from the torch and ax of a pillaging army. The wicked, careless woman within the castle had caused it all, with over-great tithes, with seizure of cattle, and with exaction of severe labor.

At last upon its hinges creaked the bridge, and the chains rattled. The bridge sank, the portcullis rose, the great gate opened, and the knight rode forward. The courtyard was bright with torches; the archers stood about, each with a flaming knot. In their midst stood the Lady Irma, with white face.

The knight drew rein and looked about him. The lady he saw, Agatha he saw. The rest were strangers all. "My lady," he said, "gladly I see you again. Agatha, too. But where are Bennet and Father John, and where is my little son?"

"Marrok," said the lady, "it is you in sooth?"

"It is I," said the knight. "But where is Walter?"

"Nay," answered Irma, "would you disturb him in his slumbers? And Father John and Bennet are in the village. But rest thou here. Hast thou no word for me?"

Then Marrok kissed the lady's hand, and spoke to Agatha, and began to inquire of the castle servants. For Hugh he knew not, but he missed Christopher and Ronald and a dozen others of those he had left behind. But the lady interrupted, and ordered the servants to unarm him. They hastened to remove his helmet and his armor; they bore away his sword, and led the steed to the stable. And Marrok gladly gave up his arms, and wrapped himself in the rich mantle which Agatha brought. Anon the lady ordered food. With much talk and laughter she led him to the table in the hall.

But a thought was heavy on Marrok's mind, and he broke into her talk. "My Lady Irma, my heart was sad as I rode hither. For I perceived clearly that war hath visited my lands and spoiled my vassals of prosperity. Tell me, I pray you, when it happened, and who were killed, and how many are left. And who hath wrought all this ruin? Was it the army of a distant prince, or has a bad neighbor come to us here? It seems to me as if it were the latter, else is the thing recent, for the folk yet fear a stranger. And were ye besieged in the castle?"

But she hung upon his arm, and smiled, and said: "Nay, my lord; of these things ask not to-night. To-morrow will be time for sorrowful tidings. But now let me go and with my skill brew thee a drink that will cure thy fatigue, and make thee glad to be once more in thine own castle." Then she kissed his hand, and slipped away, laughing back over her shoulder, so that Marrok was pleased, and with a smile sat in the hall, watching the servants spread a table, and waiting her return.

The lady went quickly to her chamber, and shut herself in. To that little inner chamber she went where were her strange tapestries, her books, and her vials. And there hung a little cabinet on the wall, made almost in the manner of a shrine; yet it bore no holy signs. The lady took three candles and lighted them, and they burned with strange flames, one red, and one green, and one blue; and she set all of them before the shrine. Then she took wax, and softened it over a brazier; with deft fingers she kneaded it, and made of it a figure. A wolf she made, so small as to stand upon the hand, and she set the figure within the little cabinet. Then she took her vials, and quickly compounded a drink, mixing it in a golden chalice. And all the time she said strange words for spells and charms.

When this was done she left the room, and gave orders that the servants should leave their work and all go into the servants' hall. Agatha she sent to see that the gate of the castle, and the drawbridge, stood free. Alone she entered the hall, and kneeling before Marrok, offered him the golden chalice, that he might drink.

He took it, and pledged her. "May thy wishes prosper," he said.

"May thy wish come true," she answered, and she watched him keenly.

He sipped the wine, and smiled at the lady. "A noble taste!" he cried.

"Drink it all!" she said.

Then he drank the drink, glad at heart. But as he took the chalice from his mouth, smiling and about to speak, lo! words would not come! And a strange change came over him. For gray hair sprang on his hands and face, and his face became a snout, and his arms and legs were as those of an animal. The chalice fell to the ground. Then the Lady Irma struck at him with her hand, and laughed, and cried: "Down, beast!"

Then Marrok fell upon all fours, and behold, he was a wolf, long and lank and gray. The lady, with delight, pointed him to a mirror. There with horror he saw himself. Then she cried: "Out!"

Amazed, he fled from the hall, down the stairs, over the drawbridge, and out into the night. In deadly fear he sought the forest, and hid in its depths. And though his men came home, and his people watched and waited long, Marrok came not again, and none knew what had befallen him.

II

Truly it seems sometimes that injustice and cruelty triumph in the world, and innocence and right are trampled. And now, when the Lady Irma and her minions carried it with a high hand in the castle, and Marrok, in wolfish shape, cowered in the forest, did it especially so seem.

Never, indeed, had more terrible fate come to a man while living. It is hard to die; but there is life after death, with reward for virtue. And it is hard to be sick and imprisoned; yet is one still a man. But Marrok was very beast indeed, with a beast's form, yet with a man's heart.

Sad and pitiful were his feelings. Deep in the wood he hid himself, and with shame and dread avoided the sight of all living things. Even the birds that sang in the branches caused him to start, and as for the deer that fled at his coming, their fear could not be greater than his. For weeks he lay close, living on the scantiest of food, and grew thin with starvation and hatred of himself.

What was there left him in the world? Only as a wolf to hunt food in the wood, miserably to live as a beast in the forest, hated of men. And he cried to God from the depths of his heart: "Kill me and let this life finish!" But no such merciful end was sent.

Long time he lay thus hidden, himself as in a stupor at the calamity that had befallen him. And yet the nature of Marrok was not the nature of a selfish man, and this could not last forever. So finally, when he had learned to find food for himself, and had gained a little strength, his true nature came to him. He said to himself: "Let me view the place that I have loved, and understand what has happened to this my land." And he began to come forth from his coverts. First of all he viewed the forest.

Already he knew the unhappy truth that wolves had come again to Bedegraine. He had heard their distant calling, and had listened to the cry of the pack as it swept near his hiding, chasing the deer for food. Now he spied upon them, counting their numbers. There were many packs, large and small. And it seemed to Marrok that the wolves were as many as when first he came to Bedegraine.

He found little dwellings that had sprung up within the forest here and there, and he wondered who lived in them. One day he lingered near a hut that stood by a marsh not far from the edge of the forest, for he wished to find out who dwelt there. The door was tightly shut, yet at dusk it opened, and there came out an old woman, attended by a black cat. She was called the Witch of the

Marsh, whom the peasants greatly feared. Marrok feared her too, for all in those days thought that witches had great power; and in dismay he crept farther away into the forest. And he learned that the other little huts in the forest held other such creatures, men or women, and one, the man most powerful of them all, lived among the fallen stones of the Druids' Ring. So many seemed these workers of evil that Marrok was greatly cast down. Then he yearned to look upon men, even though they should see and slay him. He would steal to the edge of the forest and look out upon their homes. Sometimes he would creep close to the castle, and lie long in wait, hoping for a sight of his son. But though he saw the lady and her retainers, richly clad and making merry, he saw never the boy Walter, nor Bennet, nor Father John. And sometimes Marrok would look upon the villages; but all he saw was the poverty of his vassals. No longer sent they into the forest rich herds of swine to feed upon acorns. Many swine had been killed by the wolves, and the others were kept close within pens at the farms. And only in little hidden patches did the peasants till the soil, as long ago they did; for the lady sometimes sent her archers and seized the greater part of all they had. And the peasants, Marrok saw, were fearful of what might happen to them any day – death or the loss of all their possessions; and they were thin as their own cattle.

Yet one day Marrok heard voices of men talking in the forest, and looking from his thicket, he saw a dozen going boldly, men strong of body and well fed. They were not archers from the castle, though they went armed, but were like men of the lower class. And Marrok was glad at the thought that some of his peasants were prosperous. He followed after them as they went.

They went to the edge of the old Roman road, and waited within the bushes, as if for some one to come. But when he sought to creep up close to hear their speech and comfort himself with the sound, one of them saw him, and Marrok ran away. Only on the next day did he return to see if, on the place where they had been, they had left anything which, as once belonging to man, he could look upon with pleasure. Alas, he saw too much!

For by the roadside men lay dead upon the ground, and horses and mules strayed masterless, and chests lay strewn, open and plundered. And Marrok knew that the men had been robbers.

Then his heart almost burst within him, and he cried: "Woe is me! Bedegraine is again but a savage place, and all the work of my life is made nothing!"

III

When Marrok had learned all these things, he struggled with despair; but always he said to himself: "Despair is not made for man." And something in his heart said to him: "Wait and trust." But he saw nothing that he could do. Yet even to better his people a little he longed for the opportunity. And the opportunity came.

One day he lay upon a height. Bedegraine lay before him like the green ocean, the wind moving the leaves like waves. In one place he could see the towers of his own castle, and in another a village, and in another the open land and wooden house of old Sir Simon, once his friend.

And as Marrok watched, behold, he saw new proof that evil reigned. For he saw fighting before the house of Sir Simon, and the servants of the old knight driven within pell-mell. And men-at-arms, with archers on their horses' croups, came rushing up to enter with the others, but the gate was shut in their faces. Yet in a twinkling the archers sprang from the horses, and ringed themselves about the house, ready to shoot at those within. And Marrok was greatly astonished, for he recognized the banner that was borne by one of the men-at-arms.

"Those," he thought, "are the men of Sir Morcar!"

They were indeed the men of Sir Morcar who had attacked Sir Simon's house. And the reason was that Agnes, the daughter of Sir Simon, was betrothed, and was about to marry Sir Roger. There goes with this a story of treachery unpleasant to relate: how Sir Morcar, by advice of the Lady Irma, pretended such gladness at the happiness of the maiden that Sir Simon forgot his caution. Then Sir Morcar, hoping to seize the maiden, set his men in an ambushment, and attacked Sir Simon by sudden force. Sir Simon closed the gates in time, but the end was not far off.

For Marrok, as he watched, saw arrows tipped with fire fly to the roof of the house, and marked the besiegers battering at the door. Before long the gate was falling from its hinges, and the ancient grange was burning brightly at all its four corners. Marrok cried to himself: "They must flee!" Then suddenly those within came rushing out, in the attempt to save their lives by flight.

Marrok saw women in the midst of a valiant little band. On horseback they pushed their way, and made for the wood. Nobly the men fought, and their leader, who from his vigor scarcely seemed to be the old knight, was opening a way through the opponents. Some one struck at him with a mace, and cracked the helmet that he wore, so that it broke in two parts and fell to the ground. Then Marrok saw the white hair of the old knight. But Sir Simon was dismayed no whit, and fought on as before. Yet another by guile got behind him, and struck him on the head with a sword, and the old knight fell from his horse. There he died, who had been kind master to his people and good friend to Sir Marrok, and ever a doer of the right since he was a boy. And Marrok groaned, for the blow that killed the old knight seemed to pierce himself. Moreover, he saw no hope for the others. Yet, after all, they burst their way through the ring of Sir Morcar's men, and made for the forest.

Then suddenly the distant panorama became flight and pursuit along the forest road. A girl, as it seemed, was ahead on her steed, and Marrok saw her golden hair. A young man, who was but a stripling, followed her close, ever turning in his saddle, ready to strike at those behind. Men-at-arms came thundering after, with the knight Sir Morcar at their head, eager to reach the fugitives. And thus they disappeared within the screen of leaves.

Marrok rushed from his place and plunged into the wood.

Now it was Agnes, the daughter of Sir Simon, who led the flight, and her brother who defended her. Their escape was sure if only their horses could endure; and on that road they might speed a long way, then by cross-roads and bridle-paths reach the castle of Sir Roger. And her brother bade Agnes not fear. Yet she knew by the laboring breath of her horse that the poor beast was wounded and could not run far. In fact, when they were scarce a mile within the forest, the horse stopped and stood trembling, ready to sink. The pursuers shouted and spurred the faster. Her brother cried: "Into the woods!" and turning, rode to meet his fate. Right at Sir Morcar he rode, hoping he might slay the knight. But Sir Morcar, rising in his stirrups, struck terribly with his ax, and dashed the boy from the saddle.

Agnes waited till she saw her brother fall, then sprang to the ground and slipped into the covert. Where the bushes were thick she ran, as she had hidden a hundred times when playing with her companions; yet a far different chase was this. Behind her she heard shouts, and men crashing in the bushes. Carefully she saved herself, and ran, not with speed but with caution, seeking always to keep hidden, while still the noises sounded behind her. Then pattering on the leaves came steps at her very side, and she thought: "I am caught!" She looked, and it was a wolf that was running with her.

But she feared him less than the men. Nay, he was welcome to her; for she dreaded Morcar, and would rather be slain by the wolf. She ran on, and the wolf kept at her side, nor offered to molest her. But at last she stopped breathless, and sat on a stone, for she was spent. She looked at the long and terrible fangs of the beast, and thought: "Now let me die!" Yet the wolf looked at her not at all, but placed himself before her, listening to the sounds of her pursuers. And they two were in a thicket, very small and close.

Men beat the forest to right and left, and to her every sound was a torture. But only one man came where they lurked, pushing his way into the thicket. Then he died with the wolf at his throat, and, as the Lay saith, he was the first man that Marrok the wolf killed. Of that short, silent struggle no sound was heard by the other men, and at last the maiden, gaining breath and with it courage, said to the wolf as if to a friend: "I can go on." And he, understanding her, led her away. Deeper and deeper they went among the trees, until no sounds came from behind. Safe, the maiden fell on her knees, and wept and prayed.

There, as they delayed, night fell, and Marrok watched her troubled sleep. He heard a human voice again, and from her broken words learned her story. "Nay, father," she cried earnestly, "not Morcar – Roger do I love. Him only can I wed." Then words of thanks, as to the kindness of a father; and then, waking to the forest night, she clung eagerly to her preserver, wet his fur with her tears, and, lying close, slept again, only to wake once more, crying: "Mercy, Morcar! Spare my father!" Then she lay long awake, moaning: "Roger – Roger! Oh, how shall I find him?"

And Marrok, once more appealed to, once more trusted, trembled with joy at the touch of her arms, the moisture of her tears. And, understanding the story, he knew what to do.

Now at this point in the Lay are given two tales, the one entitled "The Adventure of Marrok and the Lady Agnes with the Robbers," and the other entitled "How Marrok Gat the Lady Safely from the Wolves." The first tells how six robbers, coming upon Marrok and the lady as they journeyed, took the lady and kept her until night; but in the dark Marrok came and stole her away, and slew four of the robbers who followed. And the other relates a tale of the wolves of Bedegraine, how some would have eaten the Lady Agnes, but others would have kept her among them to rule over them, as it has been said that wolves sometimes do. But Marrok rescued her from this danger also. These are the two tales which the Lay gives here. But learned men dispute over them, many being inclined to believe that they are additions by later writers, and not a part of the true Lay. Indeed, parts of the stories seem not true; therefore they are not given here in all their length, but only mentioned. Then the Lay turns to speak of Sir Roger of the Rock.

On the third morning after the burning of the house of Sir Simon, Sir Roger went forth early into the wood, wishing, in the happiness of his heart, to see the coming of bright day and to hear the birds sing. And no news whatever had come to him of the sad hap to Sir Simon, but the knight was merry at the thought of his coming marriage. He wandered on the turf under the trees, and made himself a song and a tune thereto. The tune to the song is lost; but the words, say the wise men, are older than the Lay, being taken from the Chronicle. And the song reads thus:

> "My Lady Agnes, fair and bright,
> Happy I who am your knight;
> Happy that to-morrow morn
> I shall no more be alone;
> For to-day I ride to marry
> My lady fair
> With golden hair,
> And shall no longer tarry."

Thus ever smiling to himself, and at times singing, Sir Roger went farther into the wood, until he was nearly a mile from his castle. Thinking upon his lady, and how fair and sweet she was, he went farther than he meant. But at last he remembered the hour, and that soon he must ride to the house of Sir Simon, and there take the Lady Agnes to wife. So he turned himself about and started to return.

But there, right there under an oak-tree, lay a lady, young, it seemed, and perhaps fair, but he could not see her face. At her side couched a wolf, the largest ever seen, grim and terrible of aspect, but fast asleep. Sir Roger thought: "The beast hath slain the lady!" But on looking, lo! her breast was moving gently, and she also slept. Sir Roger stood marveling.

At last he thought: "I must slay the wolf and save the lady." With all quietness he drew his sword and stole upon the beast, meaning to strike. The eyes of the wolf opened, and he rose to his feet, and Sir Roger was astonished at his size. But seeing the lady move, he said to himself, "Haste!" and gripped his sword for the attack. Then he heard a voice cry, "Roger!" It sounded as the voice of his love. In truth, the lady who had been sleeping stepped between him and the wolf, and it was Agnes, his betrothed.

Then doubly he feared for her life, and cried: "Agnes, beware the wolf at your back!" He sought to pass her, and struck eagerly at the beast. But the lady caught his arm, and the wolf, turning away, vanished among the trees of the forest.

"Oh, Roger," said Agnes, in tears, "now is he gone! My life hath he saved; leagues hath he led me in the forest, even, when I was tired, bearing me upon his back." And she told him her story. Then Sir Roger joined her in searching for the wolf; but he was indeed gone.

Now as to the revenge which Sir Roger took upon Sir Morcar that may be read later in this book. But Marrok went away rejoicing. Once more he had been of use in the world. And since he had defended Agnes against the men of Morcar, at last he knew his power, and knew how he should use it.

IV

Many were the wolves of Bedegraine, and fierce. They hunted in great packs, and to them day and night were the same, for none opposed them. That Marrok, alone, should war upon them, seemed madness.

But one day, where more than twenty wolves lay sodden, gorged upon two does and their fawns, Marrok walked into their midst. Slowly, with anger at the intrusion, but with no alarm, they straggled to their feet and faced him. One by one he measured them with his eye. He was longest of limb, deepest of chest, firmest of muscle; but he knew that he could do little against twenty, without his human brain. The plan of his brain was ready.

He singled the leader as the wolf who growled quickest and loudest of all. Now animals have no speech, and no words could pass. But signs are much, defiance is easy of expression, and the cool, slow stare of the intruder enraged the leader-wolf. He challenged first, then sprang, – and in an instant lay with broken back.

Marrok moved slowly from the circle, contemptuous. Another of the pack leaped at him, to be flung bleeding. Then the whole, recovering from their amazement, hurled themselves blindly on his footsteps, and followed him furiously into the bushes as he began his easy run. In the long chase that then commenced, again and again the fugitive turned, and the first pursuer, from a single snap of iron jaws, gasped out his life amid the leaves. From the pursuit but ten returned.

So began Marrok's hunting. On the second day the terrible wolf sought out the remnant of the pack, attacked, fled, and killed the pursuers singly, till at the last three in their turn fled before him, and but one escaped. Confident, Marrok sought the survivor in the very center of the pack in which it had found refuge, killed it there, and then the leader also of this new band. That night he lay down wounded; but six more wolves were dead, and the shuddering rumor of his deeds passed through the forest. Two months more, and a pack of thirty fled at sight of him.

Then gradually he herded them northward, from side to side ranging the forest and sweeping it clear. He was not as other wolves, and nothing could deceive him. Here a band of six, there a pack of a dozen, broke back to their old haunts. He hunted them down, every one, and again commenced his northward drive. Each time, when their panic left them and the wolves sought to return, he appeared among them, however numerous, and slew without mercy. Neither spared he himself. Gaunt, haggard, sore from wounds, stiff from hard fights, tired from long running, his hunt began each morning at dawn, rested only at dark, and ceased not day after day. At last, and for good, the wolves fled across the open lands to the forests far beyond. Forever it was known among them: no wolf might live in Bedegraine.

The year came round again, and Bedegraine was free of wolves. Yet Marrok, scarred and weary, might not rest. The second pest of his lands must go. He had marked each house of warlock or witch, and had watched their actions. Necromancers might they not be; he could not tell; but this they were: spies for Irma, revealing to her the hidden stores of the peasants. The beldame who was called "the old Witch of the Marsh" was the most active of all. To her abode he went. Within, she crooned a spell.

Listening, Marrok cowered. The sounds in the air seemed from the invisible wings of spirits, whose powers might blight him where he stood. Yet with all his force he pushed at the door.

The Witch of the Marsh saw a wolf on the threshold, and forgot her spells. Her herbs fell from her hands into the fire, and flamed out; she retired into the corner. The white fangs of the wolf showed as in a smile. "She fears me," thought Marrok, and advanced. He seized a brand from the hearth.

The witch screamed. "Out!" she cried. "Imp of Satan – beast

of the pit – out! Will ye fire my house? Out!" Feebly she threw at him a dish.

"If I am of Satan," thought Marrok, "why should she fear me? She throws but a dish. I had feared spells. Is a witch, then, not able to harm me?"

But he paused not to puzzle; instead, he thrust the brand into a heap of tow in the corner. Barely did the Witch of the Marsh escape with her life from the destruction of the hut. Marrok left her wailing in the night.

That night three other huts went up in flames. The next night others followed. Only the warlock of the Druids' Ring, who lived among the fallen stones of the ancient altar, could retire into his house and defy fire. Marrok scratched at the stone slab that made the door, but could not seize to lift it. Then he pushed at a tottering stone that stood near, until it fell across the slab. Imprisoned for days, the warlock at length dug his way out, then fled far from Bedegraine.

But his fellows gathered at the castle and begged protection of the Lady Irma. "We have served you," they said with quavering voices and shaking hands. "Do thou now help us."

The lady in her silken robes looked at the witches and warlocks dressed in rags. Long hair and matted beards, lean bodies and shrunk limbs – she sneered at them.

"Get ye hence," she said. "Out of my castle!"

They fell on their knees. "We are all of the same source," they cried. "The great should help the small." Their shrill cries smote upon the lady's ear.

"You offend me," she answered. "Get ye forth! Ho, archers, drive them hence!"

As the archers whipped them away, Agatha plucked the lady's sleeve. "Truly," she said, "we are as much witches as are they. And they have served us."

"But can do so no longer."

"But this wolf of which they speak?"

"Believe you such a tale? The forest wolves are hungry and bold. The witches have been frightened; that is all."

So the witches were driven forth, and wandered up and down the roads, sleeping in the ditches, till at last, in other regions, they found new homes.

And yet – their story of the wolf! Irma could not forget it.

Outside, in the forest, Marrok hesitated before beginning his next task. To fight men! But one day he met a robber alone in the wood.

The man laughed. "A royal wolf!" he cried. "Standeth at gaze! Sith he runs not, I must e'en have his skin." And he began to string his bow.

The distance was short between them; the man had no sword. Marrok saw his chance, and on his third task made a beginning there and then.

V

Irma sat in the hall, and her vassals paid their tithes. The peasants, one by one, brought in their produce and laid it, sighing, at her feet. Servants bore it away to the store-rooms, after the lady with keen eyes had measured each man's share.

To none she gave praise, to none thanks. Glad were they to step aside without an order to bring more. But when all was finished, she commanded them to stand before her again.

"Knaves," she cried, "your produce is still bad. What oats are these? What fruit? What meat? Lean meats and musty grain have ye brought now for the fourth year. For the last time I say it, bring better, or ye leave your farms!"

With the cold hand of fear on their hearts they went away. Then from where he stood within a bay she beckoned forward one who had been waiting – a strong man, fierce of face.

"Peter," she said, "thou also hast come. Little hast thou brought of late. How much bringest thou now?"

"My lady," he said, and he bowed low even as the peasants. "Here is the tale of my tribute: forty golden crowns, and two hundred of silver; seventy yards of silken cloth, ninety of woolen, a hundred ten of linen bleached, and a packet of fine lace."

A smile came upon the lady's face – a smile at which her archers were uneasy and the man before her quailed.

"Peter," she said, "Peter the Robber! Thou hidest in my woods, thou robbest travelers on my lands. Half thy gains are mine. I laugh at the trifles you bring. Seek you to deceive me?"

"Lady," said the surly robber, "I bring you fair half – nay, more. For misfortune has come among us. My men are frightened; they will scarcely forth to rob even a rich train. One hardly dares go forty yards from another for fear of the wolf. Even I, lady–"

The lady bent forward. "The wolf, sayst thou?" She waved her hand to her archers. "Clear the hall!"

The hall was cleared. Irma, Agatha, Peter, alone remained. "Now," said the lady, "speak plainly. If thou liest, 't is at peril of thy head. A wolf, thou saidst?"

"Ay," said the robber, "a wolf. My lady, 't is two months now since my men began to fail me, going out to hunt, returning not. Three, then six, were missed. Then we came on one lying dead. A beast had slain him as with one leap. More men were missed; we found more bodies. Then, one day, – I saw it with my own eyes, – as my best man walked not the length of this hall away from us, a wolf rose out of a thicket and killed him on the instant."

"Nay!" said the lady.

"We were all there," cried Peter. "Forty of us within a javelin's cast. Since then more men are lost. He follows, attacks even openly. The men fear. I fear – I myself."

"A single wolf?"

"One wolf alone. Lady, there has been war among the wolves. Many have died. Now see we none except this wolf."

"He is large?"

"The largest of any."

"And strong?"

"Can break a man's neck. And cunning as a cat."

"And so," said the lady, "ye fear him as old women fear the tale of a witch! Call ye yourselves men?"

"Men are we," said Peter, stoutly. "Naught human do we fear. But, my lady, listen. This fortnight past, heard we news of the coming of a train of wealthy merchants through from the south. Them had we seized, we all were rich. I laid my men in ambush on the road; the trap was sure. I heard the distant bells on the mules coming along the road, when sudden fell a panic among our men. My lady, 't was the wolf!"

"Ay!" cried Irma, angrily.

"Hear me, my lady," cried Peter. "He slew the farthest quietly; three were dead before the rest were ware. Then sprang he right among us."

"And you fled?"

"Ay, quickly, and he on our heels. 'T was twenty minutes before we drew together against him."

"And the merchants?"

"Passed through scatheless."

The lady rose and stamped her foot. "Peter," she said, "ye may speak sooth. But go. Bring me the skin of the wolf!"

"My lady!" cried he.

"Go; come not again without it."

"He is a werewolf!" gasped Peter. "We cannot slay him." But he went.

Then Agatha and the lady looked at each other long without speaking, and in the faces of both was alarm.

VI

There was a man in Bedegraine named Andred, and he was of those who came to the land after Marrok's first coming, to settle there. He had been to the great war with the knight, following him even to Italy; and returning after him, found him gone. And though Andred was a hardy man and a good worker, he was discontented since his lord was gone and matters were in such a state, and he thought of moving away from Bedegraine to the southward, to live on the lands of some other lord. For he, being experienced and adventurous, was different from the men of Bedegraine, who, like most in those days, abided where they were born, nor lived in new places all the days of their lives. Now Andred began to speak with his friends of his desires.

But they said: "Here are Bennet and Father John living among us now, and our lot is better than before."

He answered: "Ay; but it is the life of a dog, and I will go."

Then they said: "But your wife is sick and cannot travel."

"Yes," said Andred; "but when she is well shall I go. Come you with me."

They answered: "The lady would prevent."

But he replied: "Then let us go out by families, not together; and in the night, so that we shall not be seen."

Yet they were unwilling, since in that ancient time was strong in a man the love for the place where he was born, and other places seemed strange and barbarous, even beside Bedegraine. And for a long time Andred's wife remained sick, so that he could not move her.

It came to a day when the robbers issued from the wood and descended upon the village of Bedegraine for mere pastime. And all the peasants barred their doors. But the robbers went to the house of Andred, whom they knew, and called to him: "Thou Andred, come out and fight with us, and we will spare thy barn. Or give thyself up to us, and we will spare thy house also. And if ye shoot with arrows upon us from loopholes, then will we fire both thy house and thy barn."

Now Andred was a bold man, and for himself even desperate. He had built him a house with loopholes, and was a good archer, and could have done the robbers much mischief, dying gladly at the end, being weary of life. But he could not doom his sick wife to death, nor his children. And so he agreed with the robbers, that they should leave the village unpillaged, but he should give himself up. So he did, and the robbers took him away into the forest.

They kept him with them three days, and always they tried, in one way or another, to make him one of them. But he was stanch, and said always: "Ye are wicked, and wicked will I be never, so long as I draw breath." So at last they were weary of him, and one day, being cruel from much drinking of wine, they set him away to die, horribly and alone.

For they took him into the forest far from their stronghold, and tied him to a tree. They put food before him on the ground to tantalize him, and saying to him, "Now, be good, Andred, so long as ye draw breath," they left him.

Two days and two nights he remained there, with the cords cutting him deeply, and feeling himself ever growing weaker from hunger. And he thought of his children and wife – who was to support them; and of this as a reward for a life of right living. But he said then: "Soon shall I be with my lord Sir Marrok in heaven!" Anon he fell into a fever, and forgot where he was, but thought he was again at the wars, fighting at his lord's side. And he shouted with all his force, so that the woods rang with the war-cry of Sir Marrok. And then, as he stopped for breath, he saw a great gray wolf looking at him, close at hand.

All Andred's fever fled away, and he gazed at the wolf, but not with fear. For he thought: "Now Heaven be praised! I shall die quickly. Come," he called to the beast. "Come and kill me!" And the wolf came.

And the beast came close, and reared up, putting its paws on Andred's shoulders. It looked into the man's eyes, and its own eyes seemed as those of a man, kindly. Then it laid its cheek against Andred's own, as a dog caresses a friend. But then it dropped again on all its four feet, and in a trice set Andred free from all the cords that bound him.

So weak was Andred that he fell at once to the ground; and so far gone was he that he lay a long time in a faint. When he came to himself the wolf was at a little distance, watching. Andred said: "The beast doth not intend harm to me"; and so thinking, he ate of the food which the robbers had left. Then, after resting, his strength came back, and he rose and walked toward his home, the wolf following. And Andred met no robbers, nor feared he any, since God, who had saved him thus from death, surely meant that he should live. When he came to the edge of the forest, he looked behind, and the wolf was gone. But Andred walked joyfully to his home.

They welcomed him as one from the dead, and he told his story. Then they called Father John, and Andred must tell the story all over again. Then said the friar: "Let us go to the church and there thank God for this strange deliverance." So they did as he said.

And when the service was finished, and Father John had left the chancel, he said to Andred at the church door: "Now, Andred, what wilt thou do? Wilt thou leave Bedegraine as thou designedst?"

Andred answered: "Nay; for light has been given to me, and I understand. My life is saved that I may stay here and work among my friends until such time as men in Bedegraine shall be as kind as are the brutes."

So Andred remained in his house, and went much with Bennet and Father John, learning from them how to uphold the courage of the people; and though his wife shortly after became well, he removed not from Bedegraine.

Now this was the first that the peasants learned of the great gray wolf.

VII

A peasant in Bedegraine had a son named Blaise, whom the people regarded as simple; yet he was only a dreamer, being still a lad. He was fond of the pipe and flute, and often made himself verses. Also from Father John he had learned to read, and secretly was ambitious to be a clerkly man. Yet to his father he was of little service beyond tending the swine, because of his abstraction.

Now the father of Blaise had been a notable breeder of swine, and once had owned the greatest herd in all Bedegraine. Therefore he lost many of them when the wolves came, and more by the seizures of the Lady Irma, so that at last he had but a dozen, which he kept in a strong inclosure on the edge of the forest, where few were likely to pass and see it. And while he himself worked in the fields each day, he set the lad Blaise to watch the swine. And there the boy piped to himself all day long, being happy with the beasts and the open air.

But Blaise had pity for the poor swine, since for all their rooting they found but little food, and were very thin. Sometimes he would gather for them fresh weeds, which they ate eagerly; yet some of the weeds were poisonous, so that his father forbade him. And as time went on the swine grew thinner, so that some of the young ones died.

One evening at his supper, Blaise, being downcast over their losses, asked of his father: "What is the food which the swine best like, and which is best for them?"

His father sighed and said: "In the good days when Sir Marrok was still with us, fed we the swine in the forest; but then you were very young. The beasts ate the acorns and beech-nuts, and were fat on them, and their flesh was wonderful. No food could be better for swine."

Now he did not forbid his son to take the swine to the woods, for he had no thought that the boy would be so careless, since all in Bedegraine dreaded the forest as a deadly thing. But Blaise had a love for the great trees, and their soft, cool depths, and the birds that sang in the branches. Especially he longed to hear the birds, for it seemed to him that the birds of the forest sang sweeter than the birds of the open, and he used to think: "From their songs could I make me prettier tunes to my pipe." Moreover, two more of the young pigs died, so that the pity of the lad increased.

Now one morning the pigs all gathered together before Blaise where he sat piping, and seemed to complain to him, asking for food. It cut him to the heart, and he went away to the forest, a little way into its depths, where he looked upon the many nuts that had fallen from the latest wind, and saw that, besides the nuts, there was fine rooting among the herbs of the forest. Then he said to himself: "My father has not forbidden me. I will bring the swine hither, and at evening bring them home again by means of the horn." So he went back to the inclosure, and opened a way out of it, calling the swine. They all ran out, and the oldest of them led the others directly toward the forest. Blaise went after, and for a long time watched them as they rooted with delight for the herbs, or ate the nuts. Then he sat himself down with his pipe at the foot of the tree, and played until near nightfall.

But when he tried to gather the swine together to follow him home, they would not come. Only the oldest had any recollection of the meaning of the sound of the horn, and Blaise could not herd the young ones with them. Moreover, even the old swine were unruly, preferring the warm night and the fine fodder to the barren inclosure. And Blaise was almost in despair, for they avoided him when he tried to catch them. He thought: "I must call my father to help me." But he knew his father would be already weary, and he began to fear the task would be very difficult, to herd the swine.

Nevertheless, when he was about to give up, he saw, as he thought, a great dog come out from among the trees and begin to collect the swine together. A very great dog it seemed to be, and once a fighter, for it bore the scars of many wounds. But like a sheep-dog it herded the swine, and the swine feared it, running quickly back to the farm. Blaise followed, and the dog at a little distance; then, when Blaise called the beast, it came to him and suffered itself to be caressed. Yet it would not follow the lad to the farm, staying within the forest. So Blaise secured the swine, and went to his supper.

And he thought to himself: "Now what shall I do? Shall I tell my father of what I have done, or shall I keep it as a surprise, showing him the swine when all are fat?" Then he decided to do the latter, thinking it would be a great pleasure to his father.

Two weeks thereafter there came a day when the father needed his son greatly at the field-work, so he went for Blaise to the inclosure. But he found there neither the lad nor the swine. In great alarm, he studied the signs on the ground, and found the opening where the swine had gone out. He feared robbers, but the path to the forest was already well worn, and there were no other human footmarks than those of the boy. Then he understood that Blaise had done this before, for lately the lad had laughed much to himself when at the house. He followed on the track of the lad, until he heard him piping. Then he saw him sitting at the foot of a tree.

But there was a great marvel, for a wolf couched beside the boy. The father hid quickly, thinking what he should do; for if he showed himself he feared that the wolf would harm the boy. "The beast is charmed by the music," thought the father. "I have heard tales of such happenings. But if the music stops he will be savage." Then he stole quietly away to get help.

By hap he met in the fields Andred; and he called: "Andred, get thy bow and come quickly, for Blaise is in danger in the forest." Then Andred got his bow, and the two men went hastily together, till they came to the spot where they saw, from a thicket, Blaise still piping, and the wolf lying quietly at his side. The father of Blaise whispered: "Lay an arrow on thy bow, and shoot."

But Andred did nothing, so that the father whispered again, "Make haste! See you not that the wolf is charmed?"

But Andred answered: "That is my wolf, which saved me. I cannot shoot him."

Then Blaise's father was in great fear, and he knew not what to do. But it was now late of the afternoon, the hour when the swine must be brought home. And the two men in the bushes saw the lad Blaise lay aside his pipe, and put his hand on the head of the wolf, as if thanking him for his company. Then Blaise blew his horn, and the swine came running, and Blaise began to lead them toward the farm. And, to their great wonder, the two men saw how the wolf walked behind, herding along the young pigs who were wilful and wished to stray.

Then the men, stealing along from bush to bush to observe the marvel, were seen by the wolf. He did not run, but looked at them a moment, then walked into the bushes. And Blaise, seeing that the wolf no longer followed, looked about, and also perceived his father.

"So, father," he cried, "you have found my secret! But you have sent my dog away."

They told him it was not a dog, but a wolf, and they were greatly alarmed for him. And the father, in much relief, scolded his on roundly, which is the manner of many fathers.

Yet Blaise said: "If that was a wolf, yet has he never done me harm. For two weeks have I led the swine into the forest, and he has been with me every day." Because the lad always spoke the truth, they believed him; and he showed his father how fat the swine had grown.

But Marrok, who was the wolf, went away into the forest with a heavy heart. For the youth, innocent and fearless as he was, had been a great comfort, while his piping was a solace. And Marrok had taken no thought that he, a knight, herded swine, but had done all that humbly, as one who helps men. But now he believed that the swine and the boy would come never again to the forest, since the men had seen him – Marrok the wolf.

But when all this tale was told to Father John, he thought upon it deeply; and he asked the father of Blaise: "Will you send your son again into the forest with your swine?"

The peasant answered: "No!"

"Methinks," said the friar, "it would be a good thing to send the boy again. For perhaps this is a sign that better things are coming to

Bedegraine; and surely this is the only way to save the remainder of our swine, which are dying on every hand."

But the peasant declared again he would not send his son into the forest. Yet this was talked over among them all, and Andred cried that he was not afraid to risk either himself or his swine, and Bennet was consulted, and finally the end was this: Andred, armed with his bow, took into the forest his own swine, three miserable beasts, and no harm came to them, but they began to grow strong. And other peasants sent their swine, and Blaise went again, till at last he had all the swine of the village with him to take out at morning and bring back at night, for the swine learned to come at call. And sometimes the wolf was seen, and sometimes not; but no harm came either to the swine or to the swineherd.

And Blaise, when he grew up, became, as he desired, a clerkly man, so that people no longer called him simple. And when he was old, and Marrok and Father John were both dead, then Blaise read in the Chronicle of Sir Marrok, and understood all that he had seen in his youth. And it is said that he wrote the Lay, which may well be true.

VIII

There was a monk named Norris, a true man, who lived in the abbey of Bedegraine. And he was a thorn in the side of Richard the prior, by reason of his stubbornness. For Anselm the abbot ever grew weaker, and he was as wax in the hands of Richard, who did in the abbey as he pleased. Now the ways of Richard were as the ways of the world, and what with eating rich foods and drinking fine wines, and with merrymaking, he led an easy life. And shrewdly he endeavored to corrupt the monks to luxury, relaxing all discipline, so that there was a party of them who aped his ways. Then would Richard have entirely succeeded but for the monk Norris.

Norris was a stanch man, and he loved the old ways. Not stern was he or harsh, but unyielding toward every evil influence. And he was stiff-necked before the prior, even openly teaching that his ways were wrong, so that those of the monks who were inclined to the good kept heart, and observed the fast-days and the hours of prayer, even though it was a diminished company which assembled for early matins. For Norris, whenever it was his turn, caused the early bell to be rung; and on other days he waked betimes and roused the brothers, and by his word and his example he kept a little remnant of the monks who yearned for the old times. And Richard suffered this only because he was not sure of his position, biding his time until Anselm was too dull to take notice of events, or until he was dead.

Now there came a day when Anselm lay sick with a little fever, and must lie in his bed every day. So he was removed from the knowledge of things. Then Richard went down to the refectory to the midday meal, nursing wrath against Norris. And the monks sat at the long table, with Richard at the head; and the meal was served – a long meal and well cooked, which should delight the heart of any good liver. But to Richard it was as if he were eating poison.

For it was the habit, as the brothers ate, that one of them should read aloud from a pulpit placed in the wall at the side of the hall, so that all could hear clearly. On this day it was the turn of Norris to read, and he read of the captivity of the Israelites, how they were grievously oppressed. And Norris chose the passages skilfully, showing how they bore their sufferings like men, and bided their time, and in the end were freed. And every one there, from Richard the prior to the newest brother, knew that Norris meant them to understand that he likened the captivity of Israel to the oppression in Bedegraine, and that he was counseling them all to patience, promising that in the end they should be delivered. And all stole glances at Richard, who fumed as he sat at the table's head, and could not eat his food.

But Richard was thinking of revenge, for he believed the time had come. Then he commanded that a certain basket be brought and placed by his chair, and when the meal was finished, Richard called Norris. The monk stood before him.

"Norris," said Richard, "thou art called the best gatherer of herbs among us."

Now this was true, for Norris was a good gardener, growing herbs for medicine; and of the herbs which grew wild he was the best in knowledge, being familiar with the places where they grew. So he bowed, but wondered at the praise, for he saw evil in the prior's eye.

"Our Father Anselm," said Richard, "lieth sick; and the leech declares that he must have much of the herb called feverset. Now we have great quantity, but it is dried, and the leech must have fresh. Also he needeth the whole of this basket full. Therefore go thou, Norris, for the sake of our dear father the abbot, and fill this basket as soon as thou canst."

Then Norris looked at the basket, and he understood the design of the prior. For the herb feverset grew only in the forest, under the great beeches. Also the herb was small and grew sparsely, but the basket was large, and it would take hours to fill the basket, so that the monk would have to spend the night in the forest, amid its dangers, for it was already afternoon. But the request was cunningly worded, and no brother could refuse to go for the sake of his abbot. So Norris took the basket and said he would go, and prepared to go at once.

Then, as he laced on heavier sandals, the monks who depended on him came to him and asked him what would become of him, for he might meet the robbers; but he only said: "God will sustain me." And they said he might meet wolves; yet he said again: "God will sustain me." Then he went, and they took leave of him as a man that goes to his death; but Richard and those who held with him were glad at heart.

Then Norris walked a half-mile in the fields, and entered the forest. He went far under the trees before he found any of the herb, and for a long time he found little. But he searched diligently, with his eyes on the ground, and after hours he had filled his basket half. Then he came to a place where the herb grew plentifully, and he worked quickly, for the light was going, until his basket was full. But then the light was almost gone, and when he looked about him he knew that in the diligence of his search he had lost his direction, and there was no moon, and the leaves hid the stars, so that he could not make out where lay the southeast, where the abbey should be. So he knew that he must stay there for the night, and, besides, it was ill walking on the uneven ground, for he might fall and break a limb. But the dusk of the forest closed in on him, and he said to himself: "Norris, art thou afraid?"

He knew that he was afraid, for he was but a monk, and had lived ever since he was a child either in towns or in walled monasteries, well guarded. In the things of the spirit he was fearless, but bodily dangers he had never met, and there were terrors in the silent forest which were strange to him. But he called to mind those saints who had lived in deserts and waste places, encountering beasts, and they had been saved. Then he struggled with his fears, saying that he was with God, and he knelt and prayed, and lay down and slept peacefully, like a trusting child.

But of a sudden he awoke in the night, for he heard a sound. And it was all strange about him: the whispering of the trees, and the thick darkness, and nothing to touch when he put out his hand. Yet there was a sound like the moving of feet, and then Norris, looking, saw close at hand two spots of light, greenish – the eyes of a beast.

So fresh was he waked from sleep, and so dreadful was the sight of the eyes, that Norris lost himself in fear. He leaped up and rushed madly away, without knowledge of what he was doing. Yet he struck no tree, which might have stunned him, and better if he had; and the beast which ran after him failed of its clutch on his gown, which would have saved him. Then, as he ran, his feet met nothing, and he fell down with a cry into the darkness, and fell upon something, and fell off again, and struck again hard, and knew nothing until the sun was high.

But at noon on the next day, behold, there was Norris on a little ledge, with another ledge above him, and above that the level of the forest. And in falling he had struck the first ledge, and stopped on the second, which was lucky, for below was a wide quarry, whence had been taken the stone for three castles and for the abbey, and it was a great fall, so that no man could have lived, since beneath were jagged points of rock. And above was first the other ledge, and then the forest level, as said before; and there, walking up and down, was a huge wolf, looking down at Norris.

"Truly, crazed was I," said Norris to himself, for he was not hurt and his courage was better, "to have run from the beast last night. Better to have been eaten. For I cannot throw myself down, since it is a sin for a man to kill himself. And I cannot climb up, for the ledge is too high to reach; besides, there waits the wolf to eat me. So I must stay here and starve to death."

So he looked off across the broad quarry, and saw the green woods beyond, and he sighed for his father's home in the south. Then he looked at the wolf above, and the beast was restless, seeming to prepare to leap down.

"Now a fool art thou, beast," said Norris. "For thou canst eat me, but how wilt thou get up again?"

But the wolf leaped down to the ledge above, which was broad; then he crouched for the leap to the ledge below, which was narrow and short. Anon he leaped, and Norris, with the spirit of a man, seized him by the shoulders as he alighted, and strove to hurl him into the quarry. But the wolf stood like the very rock, and looked up into the face of the monk, and Norris desisted.

"Now slay me, beast," he said, "and of a truth, I forgive thee my death."

But the wolf rubbed against the man, and then placed himself against the wall of rock, looking up at the ledge above. Norris was astonished. And the wolf rubbed again upon him, and put himself against the rock once more. And Norris, knowing nothing of the ways of beasts, thought that the wolf played with him, as the cat does with a mouse.

But suddenly, as the monk stood withdrawn from the wolf as far as he could go on the ledge, he saw what he could do. With the energy of hope, he strode quickly to the wolf, and placed a foot on his back, and leaped for the ledge above. He threw his arms across the edge, and caught his hands in a crevice, and pulled himself up, fearing the while to feel the grip of the beast upon him to pull him down. But when he stood in safety and looked down, the wolf looked up at him without motion, seeming to wait.

"A stupid beast!" thought Norris. And he turned and climbed to the ground above, for the distance was not great. Then he looked at the wolf and said good-by, and turned to go.

But the beast sent after him such a cry that the monk's heart was troubled, even though he continued to go away. And when he found his basket of herbs he stood awhile, listening for the wolf to cry again. Once again the wolf cried, and the call sounded human with reproach and despair. Then the heart of Norris was greatly touched, and he said: "Though the beast kill me, I will not leave him there to starve." And he went back to the quarry.

Then the wolf was pleased to see him, and Norris, leaping down to the first ledge, took from his waist the cord that tied his gown. One end he held in his hand, and one end he threw down to the wolf, who seized it. Then Norris drew the rope up, the wolf helping with his claws against the rock; and it was hard work for the monk, for the beast was heavy. But he gained the ledge, and the wolf rubbed against Norris as if it were a dog.

"Now," cried Norris, in surprise, "I believe the beast meant to save me, from the first!"

Then they clambered to the other ledge, which was easy for them both, and again the wolf rubbed against the monk, seeming to thank him. But the monk, who had no more fear, caressed the head of the beast, saying as if it had spoken: "Nay, for rather should I thank thee." Then together, the wolf guiding the monk, they went through the forest, and they came out upon the fields at the point where Norris had left them, nearest the abbey.

The wolf would come only a short way into the fields, but returned again to the forest; yet some monks who were working in a garden-patch saw him. And Richard the prior bit his lip when

Norris returned again, for he thought to have been rid of him. Also the abbot got well of his fever. But Norris told to the monks, whether bad or good, the story of the wolf – telling it to the good monks to hearten them, and to the bad to shame them from their ways.

Then was told throughout Bedegraine the stories that are here written: the story of Andred, and the story of Blaise, and the story of the monk Norris. Upon these stories the peasants greatly heartened themselves; and the monks, learning what had happened elsewhere, began to doubt of evil and to hope of good. The peasants worked the harder to improve their farms, and everywhere they spoke of the noble wolf of the forest. And so Marrok began to work good among his people.

IX

The Lady Irma, by every charm at her command, tried to bewitch Marrok again, to his harm. But it was in vain that she made incantations and recited spells, for the wolf was not to be reached by such means. Then at last she sent a message to Morgan le Fay, asking: "What shall I do? This man whom I have made a wolf troubles me, and I would have him killed."

Morgan sent this answer: "Except some one slay him outright by a weapon, by two means only can you work him harm. Gain sight of him, and before he flees pronounce the third word of the fourth spell which is on the ninth page of the Book. Then will he fall in sleep, and you can slay him. Or pluck three hairs from his back, three living hairs, and burn them in the three candles, one hair to the red candle, and one to the green, and one to the blue. Then shall you melt the little wolf of wax, and the man's strength shall depart from him as the image melts; and when it is all melted, then will he die. And all this shall you do by the aid of the spell which is in the fourth note on the seventh page of the Book." This book was the Great Book of Necromancy, and only Merlin and Morgan le Fay had perfect copies of the book. And Irma had only a copy of the book which went to the twelfth page, but for these purposes that was enough. So she had great hopes.

And she rode out from the castle, along the border of the forest, with her men blowing horns, and all making noises so that the wolf should come. At every moment she was ready to say the word which should throw Marrok into sleep. Three days did she this, but saw the wolf never. Then Hugh, who was a good hunter, looked within the forest, and said to the lady: "See, the wolf has been watching us all these three days, for here are his tracks in plenty."

Irma was angry, for she thought: "He knows too much to let me see him, fearing spells. Show me," she said to Hugh, "where he has been."

Then Hugh showed her one place where the beast had been lying, watching them comfortably. And Irma stamped with anger at his cunning. But when she looked closer she saw a single hair from the wolf's body among the briers where he had been. "Show me more!" she commanded of Hugh.

Hugh showed her more, and Irma, searching carefully, found two more hairs. With these she hastened to the castle, and went to the little inner chamber, and lighted the three candles, and got out the book. Then she burned the three hairs, one in each candle, reciting the spell, and prepared to melt the little waxen wolf.

And then she turned white, for she remembered that the letter of Morgan le Fay had said "three living hairs," but these hairs had been dead hairs. She put the little waxen wolf away again carefully, all the time shaking with fright. For if the image were destroyed without this spell, then would Marrok become a man again.

"Now since the wolf will never come into my sight, who," she said, "will pluck me three living hairs from his back?"

Though she tried, she could find no one, and nothing served to bring Marrok to harm. But one day she heard of a man who was a great trapper of beasts, and she sent for him to come to her.

This man was Wat, the son of Wat, who lived on the lands of another lord, beyond Bedegraine. He lived always in forests, gaining his living from the flesh and skins of the beasts he trapped. And he knew the ways of all forest-beasts, trapping them with great skill. Because the lady promised him much money, he came to her in her castle, and she spoke with him in private.

"It is a small matter, lady," he said, "this trapping of a wolf. You shall have his skin in a week."

"Then I will make you rich," she said. "But he is no common beast."

"Had he the skill of a man," said Wat, "yet should I catch him."

"Listen," said the lady. "It needs not even to trap him. Bring me three hairs plucked by your own hand from his back, and I will pay you the same money."

"It were safer to trap him," quoth Wat. And he went out into the forest to begin.

Now Wat was a clever man, and, for all his boasting, a thoughtful one. Soon he discovered that he had no usual task, for the week went by, and all his traps were sprung, and he saw where the wolf, unseen, had followed him and spied on all that he was doing. Then Wat, seeing that this would not do, tried a trick. He went out of the forest, and walked a long way on the plain, and, entering the forest again at a different point, put all his skill into another trap. Then he went away into the fields once more, and waited overnight.

Now Marrok, thinking that the man had gone, was searching for food, and came upon a glade in the forest where it seemed to him there was something that had not been there before. Yet it looked natural, as if it had grown there. And Marrok, not being sure, went to the thing that seemed a little thicket, for he knew that a rabbit was there, from the smell.

Then he saw how the little trees seemed to have grown almost in a circle, very closely set, but with an opening at one side. Looking in, he saw the body of a rabbit, but the tiny beast was dead. Now Marrok never ate food but what he himself had killed, yet he wished to know how the rabbit came there. He put his head in at the opening, and was about to touch the rabbit, when he saw it was fixed on a piece of a twig, small and stiff. Then he took his head quickly out, and studied the thicket again. Greater craft had he never seen.

"Nearly had he caught me!" thought Marrok.

He went around behind the semicircle of little trees, and put in his paw, and pulled at the little twig. Behold, a great leaning log fell with a crash, and other logs upon it, and had Marrok been at the mouth of the trap, they would have broken his back.

Then Marrok sat down and thought. For he had avoided pitfalls and snares and nooses, and bows set so that arrows should shoot him as he walked in a path; and now he had avoided this trap. But he saw that the man would catch him in the end.

"Now," said Marrok, "will I set a trap for him." And he began to dig under the fallen log with his paws, scattering the dirt far away.

On the next day came Wat again to the place, and when he peered at it cautiously from a distance, he gave a shout of satisfaction. For the wolf lay under the fallen log. Then Wat ran to him. He saw as he came near that the wolf was stretched out stiff, as if he had been dead for some hours. So the man went to him, without thought of caution.

Then the wolf rose up from under the log, and sprang upon the man, and threw him to the ground and stood over him. Wat was helpless. He looked up into the wolf's eyes as the beast looked down at him. But they were not the glaring eyes of an angry wolf, such as Wat had seen many times; they were rather like those of a man, sad and reproachful, as if saying: "And you would even slay me!" Then for a full minute the two looked at each other.

But then the wolf released the man, and went away without looking back, going with great dignity, so that Wat was awed, as if he saw a king among beasts. He lay where he was until the wolf had disappeared in the forest, and not until then did he think of seizing his bow.

And then, as he rose and felt of himself, to see if he were really still alive, he felt hairs upon his hands. He looked, and they were hairs of the wolf, seven hairs, for Wat had clutched at the beast's shoulders. And he cried to himself with joy: "I shall earn the money, after all!" So he started to return to the castle, carrying the hairs.

As he went he thought, and he thought in this wise. First it was: "That was near death for me!" And then it was: "But the wolf let me go." And then it was: "Shall I doom the good beast to death?" For he saw that the lady must have some witch's purpose against the wolf.

Then Wat, who was a true man, cast the hairs of the wolf upon the ground, and he went away out of the forest at a point distant from the castle, going to his own place. When he was almost at the borders of Bedegraine he met a peasant, and said to the man (being bold because he was within sight of his home, as men often are): "Tell thy lady I will not serve her, because I think she is a witch." Now the peasant delivered not the message, being afraid of the anger of the lady. But Wat went away, and would never go to Bedegraine again.

So the lady failed in this plan.

X

It was believed in Bedegraine that the son of Sir Simon was dead, but in truth he lay in the dungeons of Sir Morcar, grievously wounded. And he lay there for more than a year, until his wound had healed; but the youth himself was wasting away for lack of good food and the use of his limbs. Very miserably he lay, until he thought to try to escape. Then hope came to him, which is the best gift that is given to man, as all nations agree, from the Greeks to our own.

And this poor prisoner, when he found a piece of iron which had been a spear-point, took such comfort in hope that it was meat and drink to him, and he began with much labor to dig his way out. It needs not be told how he loosened stones in his cell, and pierced through the wall of the castle, and swam the moat, and escaped to the forest. But he was seen, and word was sent to Irma, and she sent a command to the robbers in the forest that they should look everywhere for the son of Sir Simon, and bring him again.

But the forest was so great that for a long time they found him not. And he lived but poorly on the berries and herbs that he found, and, being weak, made his way slowly across the forest on the way to the castle of Sir Roger. And he missed his way, going too far to the north, where the forest was broader, so that he thought that he should never come out. Then one day as he walked he saw a great wolf lie in his path.

Now there was no help in running, for the wolf could outrun him. And there was no hope in fighting, for the lad had no weapon, since he had lost his piece of iron. So he essayed to pass by. But the wolf arose and went with him, and the youth allowed him to walk at his side. He looked down at the neck of the gaunt beast, and thought: "Could I strangle him?" But no man, even though of great strength, with his hands alone could master that wolf.

As he went it seemed to the youth that the wolf was trying to turn him more to the south. He said to himself: "The beast will bring me to his den without the trouble of carrying me." And he laughed at his own plight, having no more hope of life; yet he went with the wolf, because there was naught else to do.

But before he had gone a mile he heard voices in the bushes. Then the wolf took him by the garment and tried to bring him hastily in another direction. But the youth preferred even robbers to the beast, and tore himself away and ran toward the sound, shouting. He met six men, who drew bows on the wolf, so that it ran away. But when the young man tried to thank the men for his deliverance, they laughed at him, telling him that he would best have stayed with the wolf, for they would bring him again to Sir Morcar. But first they took him where was Peter, with others of the band.

Peter looked upon the prisoner evilly. "Here," he said, "is the son of the man who injured us much, and we are to be paid for him, whether he be dead or alive." He said no more, but what he said was with intent, for he knew that Sir Morcar preferred the youth dead, but feared to kill him.

"Tie him to a tree," he continued. "We will talk about this." So they tied him to a tree, and sat down to consult, and the son of Simon heard every word that was said, whether he should live or die; and the wolf, listening in the bushes, heard also.

But Marrok saw not what he could do, since the robbers all were armed, and many always went with drawn swords or knives, because he had killed so many of them by surprise. And he could help the young man not at all by dying with him, while his own life was valuable to the peasants. Sadly Marrok went away a little space, but lingered near, waiting to hear them begin upon the killing of the youth.

Then as he lay he heard a sound, which was the merriest that had been heard in Bedegraine for many a long year. It seemed to Marrok that it was the noise of a pack of hounds in full cry, many hounds on the track of a stag, following eagerly, and for a moment he listened with delight. But then he asked himself: "Who hunts in Bedegraine, and what doth he hunt?" Then he saw something coming amid the trees, and he cowered close.

For he saw a beast, the strangest that ever man saw, whether in field or wood. Its head was shaped like a serpent's head, and it had the neck of a serpent. But its body was like a leopard's in shape, and in color it was like a leopard, being spotted. And its haunches were like those of a lion. But its feet were like a stag's, and it was of great speed, for it came quickly. And out of its body (but the books say not by what means) came the cry as of dogs, as it were thirty couple of hounds questing or baying on a chase. And Marrok knew it for the beast Glatisant, which was called the Questing-Beast.

Anon it came near, ever making the marvelous noise, so that the robbers stopped their discussion to listen. Then it paused near Marrok, and when it paused the noise ceased, and it looked the way it had been coming, seeming to harken. Anon it ran on, and the questing began again, and was heard after the beast had departed, coming down the wind.

But Marrok leaped from his hiding, and ran back on the track of the beast, thinking: "The beast looked behind. Perhaps Pellinore followeth. Then there may be help."

For in those days, whenever there was peace on his marches, King Pellinore left his castle and followed after the Questing-Beast for the sake of adventure. And of Pellinore need I write here no praise, for he was the hardiest knight of his generation, and it may be doubted if his own son Sir Lamorak, or Launcelot, or Tristram, the three greatest knights of later days, surpassed him, who now were still but young men. But, to quit talking and go to telling, before long

Marrok saw a knight pricking after the Questing-Beast, and knew that it was King Pellinore.

Then Marrok hid in a thicket until the horse was close, when he leaped out. The horse reared, and strove mightily to throw his rider; but Pellinore kept his seat by fine force, until the girths broke. Then the knight dismounted adroitly, and, holding the beast by the bridle, strove to calm it, having no fear of the wolf. But Marrok leaped again, and bit at the bridle and severed it, both the reins, so that the horse was free and ran away. And Pellinore was there alone with the wolf.

"Now a plague on thee, beast!" said Pellinore, still having no fear, for he was all in armor. "And you chase not my horse, but stay with me? Now what?" For he perceived here an adventure.

Now Pellinore, as is written, followed the Questing-Beast not entirely with hope of catching it, since the beast was so swift. But he followed for the adventures which came to him, since in that quest he had many strange haps, and joyed in them, whether to fight or to see new things. So Pellinore looked at the wolf which had not acted like a wolf, and he asked: "What wouldst thou?"

Then the wolf, as with understanding, ran a little way and stood looking back for the knight to follow. So Pellinore drew his sword, saying, "I will take the adventure." He followed the wolf, and the beast led him to the glade where the son of Sir Simon was bound, and the robbers were ready to slay him. And to make a long story short, Pellinore, walking quietly with little clashing of his armor, was among the robbers before they were aware, and struck to right hand and to left, slaying four. The robbers fled nimbly, having no iron armor, so that the knight could not follow; but Marrok was on their heels, chasing them away. Then when Marrok returned, leaving the robbers still fleeing, having drawn together in a band, he found that Pellinore had cut the bonds of the youth.

The youth begged the knight to go with him to Sir Roger's castle, for there should he be thanked properly and given good cheer.

"Nay," answered Pellinore, "for the direction is wrong, and I must find my horse to follow my quest. Yet yonder stands in the bushes the wolf who is your true deliverer. Go thou with him." And he told how the wolf had led him.

"Now," said the son of Sir Simon, "this is a true wonder, and I will trust myself to the beast. But tell me thy name, that I may be grateful to thee."

"Nay," said Pellinore; "grateful can you be without knowledge of my name, and when on this quest tell I my name to none."

Then said the youth: "At least show me thy face, that I may remember it."

So Pellinore showed his face, and the youth looked upon it; and it is a pretty story how, in another year, the son of Sir Simon knew his deliverer again, when they both were in the court of King Arthur. Yet until then it was not known who had saved him. Then the two parted and went their ways, the youth with the wolf, and Pellinore after his horse.

Now the Lay says that Pellinore, following the tracks of his steed, came to a strong castle, and saw how the beast had been met by a man who led it within. Then he blew his horn for the castle to open, and he was admitted to the courtyard, where he saw a lady.

"Lady," said he, "you have my horse."

"A horse I have," answered the lady, "which may be thine. And you shall have him again. But if you are a knighterrant ye shall first do me a service, which is all I shall require of thee."

But Pellinore was not pleased that she should ask of him a service before ever she had offered him rest and food, which always should be the first thought of a lady. So he asked: "What is thy service?"

"It is to kill a wolf in this forest," said she.

He remembered the wolf he had met, and looked keenly into her face. Now Pellinore was a man of wisdom, of good judgment as regarded persons, since he had ruled long over many people. And never but once made he mistake in his life, yet that mistake was grievous. For he trusted where he had done great service, and met ingratitude, even as had Marrok; yet his misfortune was greater than Marrok's, since it brought death. But that story is to be read in another book. King Pellinore looked long at the Lady Irma, and he saw that she was evil.

"Lady," quoth he, "no service will I do you, but give you me my horse."

"Now," she cried, "your horse shall you not have, but you shall abide here." She signed to her men, and the portcullis fell, so that Pellinore was shut within the castle. Yet he cared no whit.

"Lady," said he, "loath am I to threaten a woman, but I take no force. And I warrant you I am hard to deal with, so that however great be the number of your men, this castle is mine an I list. But give me my horse, and I depart without harm."

The lady looked upon his armor, and saw how it had stood great strokes, for he had fought much. And arrows could not pierce that steel. She thought: "Better to let him go than to lose some of my men; for he is great in size, and bears his armor as if it were silken clothes." So then she said: "Take thy horse, uncourtly knight, and depart."

So he took his horse and mounted him, without saddle or bridle as the beast was, and when the portcullis was raised he guided the horse by the pressure of his knees out of the castle. And in the village he got saddle and reins, and paid the men well, giving the first gold that Bedegraine had seen for many a year. Then he rode again into the forest, and found the track of the Questing-Beast, and followed it far away from Bedegraine.

But Marrok led the son of Sir Simon to the castle of Sir Roger, where the youth was welcomed heartily. And Sir Roger and the Lady Agnes went quickly into the forest to call the wolf, who had departed; but, though he heard them, he would not come, since in the forest was his task. Then the news went around the country; and when Irma and Morcar heard that the son of Sir Simon had escaped, they were furious, but the peasants of Sir Simon were joyful. And all began to take hope of the good day which it seemed soon must come.

XI

There came to the Lady Irma the news that the peasants were more prosperous. She set about to find the reason.

In fact, the peasants were fatter and more content. Now their dependence, as in the days of Marrok, was their swine and their crops.

"Truly, madam," said Hugh, "in hunting I have seen larger herds of the villains' swine, and the men are beginning to cut down the saplings that were springing in their fallow land."

"Send out," quoth the lady, "and catch me a peasant."

Presently one was brought in, trembling properly at a horse's tail, a rope around his neck.

"Hark ye, villain," said the lady. "Tell me of thy fellows. How is it that ye have more swine?"

"Lady," answered the fellow, in fear, "there are fewer wolves in the forest."

"What," she asked, "hath that to do with thy swine?"

"Two years agone," he said, "I had but two. Last year but three young swine grew up. But this year I have raised in safety two great litters – sixteen in all."

"And that is because there are few wolves?"

"Ay. For this twelvemonth, lady, have I seen not one, save the great gray wolf that doth no harm."

"Go," said the lady. "See that thou bringest, within the week, six of thy young porkers, killed and dressed."

The peasant went, wringing his hands. The lady caught others, and learned more things. There were surely no wolves to do harm. Peter the Robber said so also. The peasants even dared to pasture their milch-cows, most valuable of their belongings, on the fine herbage that grew at the edge of the forest.

"Thus the cows are growing fat, and give more milk, and the calves are stronger," said Peter. "The peasants are becoming sturdier, with more milk and meat. This also have I learned, lady: 't is Bennet and Father John that have set the peasants at saving their old lands. This spring and summer at least a hundred of the old acres are again under the plow."

"And the great gray wolf?" asked the lady, looking into Peter's eyes.

Peter became confused. "The wolf – my lady – we have killed him not yet."

"So," sneered Irma; "my valiant robbers are afeard!"

"My lady," he cried, "surely it is no beast. The wolf is human. We dare go about only by threes. With two it is not safe. The wolf killeth one, and escapes before the other can raise his bow."

"Not an arrow in him yet?"

"Not one."

"Nay," cried the lady, in anger, "but I see ye are all cowards. Hark ye. Hunt him the more! Follow him! Track him! Give him no sleep!"

"But he is swifter than a horse," muttered Peter. "He leaveth no trail, and none know his lair."

"Find it," said the lady. "Begone, and act. And you," quoth she, turning to Hugh, "take archers and go to the village. Rout me that old villain Bennet from his daughter's house, where he liveth now these seven year. Take Father John from his manse by the church. Too long have these men comforted and counseled the peasants. Bid them leave my lands. Proclaim it death for any to harbor them. They work against me secretly. I will be rid of them."

And so that evening, while within Bedegraine Peter and his men again laid their heads together to catch the gray wolf, in the village women wept, and children wailed, and men knitted brows and clenched their fists. For Father John and Bennet were driven away, and had no place to go except into the forest.

They found the house of the warlock of the Druids' Ring, and made it habitable for themselves. On the heathen stones Father John hourly offered prayer. But old Bennet, though he hunted long, brought in no food.

"There is game in plenty," he grumbled. It was the third day, and both were faint with hunger. "But I cannot shoot as I used. This arm, that I injured in saving the Lady Irma from the bear, permits me not to draw the bow."

"It is well," said Father John. "The Lord, who fed his prophet by his ravens, will feed us also. Let us ask him for help."

But there, as he turned to the altar, stood a great gray wolf and looked at them.

Bennet put hand to knife.

"Stir not," said the priest. " 'T is the wolf of which the peasants tell. He will not harm us." And he knelt. But as Father John prayed, Bennet watched the wolf.

"O Lord," he said, "whose land this is, we pray thee, take us in thy care. And first, we pray thee, send Marrok, our beloved master, to rule over us again."

At these words the wolf trembled.

"Or, if this cannot be, bring us the boy Walter, to take his father's place, and grow into a man, and rule over us. Yet, since we have not seen him from that day when he was driven forth, a child, bound upon a horse's back, here into the wintry forest – grant us, if he be dead, to find his bones, that we may give them Christian burial."

At this the wolf dropped his head, and great tears rolled from his eyes and fell upon the sod.

"But if we ask too much," said Father John, "stretch forth at least thy hand over these poor people, and lift them up. Give again swine and cattle, crops and fruit. And soften the heart of the lady of the castle, that her cruelties may cease."

The wolf gritted his teeth, his bristles rose, and he looked so fierce that the priest almost feared to proceed. With a weaker voice he concluded:

"And send food, we pray thee, to us thy two servants, who starve here helpless."

"Thank Heaven," cried Bennet, "the wolf is gone."

He had indeed vanished in the bushes. But at the end of half an hour the thicket cracked, and lo, there was the wolf again, and over his back was a fresh-killed fawn. This he dropped before the friar.

"Praised be the Lord," cried Father John, "who hath sent us a helper! Make fire, Bennet, and cook the meat."

"If only the beast spring not upon my back," grumbled Bennet. And he made the fire, ever ready to clap his hand upon his weapon. But the wolf lay and watched, and when the crisp meat was done he drew near, as if himself ready to eat.

"Mayhap he will partake," said the priest, and he laid a collop before the wolf. "Look; he eateth, and daintily, unlike an animal."

"He seemeth to like cooked food," whispered Bennet – which was true.

Then daily the wolf brought food to the two men, and they lived in comfort. But also he searched the forest from end to end and from side to side; yet never found he, whether in thicket or in grove, bones of horse or boy.

XII

The peasants of Bedegraine continued to prosper. The fame of the gray wolf spread. In irritation the lady oppressed the peasants more, and systematized the hunt for the wolf; but to no purpose.

For the swine and cattle multiplied, and the crops grew plentiful. And when men beat the forest for the wolf, he was not to be found. When packs of hounds were brought and put upon his trail, he fled from them, and, turning, killed the first pursuer, till many were slain – which has been the method of one against many since the time of the Horatii. So, when the lady could find no more hounds, she ceased hunting in this manner.

But the news came to her ears that the wolf abode with Bennet and Father John, and fed them daily; also that the sanctity of the priest became multiplied in the eyes of the peasants, and they reverenced him greatly. Then the lady laid a plan to catch the wolf. Yet, when the men of Peter's band closed in one morn around the Druids' Ring, the wolf slipped out through a gap in their line and, turning on their backs, slew three.

Now, in the abbey of Bedegraine, the godliness of Father John had long since made him friends, and he had been a great help to Norris and those other monks who had striven to keep to the old ways of godliness. Moreover, when they knew that he abode in the forest with the wolf, they took still more of courage. Surely this friar was a saintly man, upon whom showed the special favor of God; and were he, not Anselm, abbot of the monastery, then would all things be well. Though they saw not how this thing could come about, they resolved to imitate Father John, and to wait, and watch, and pray.

One day came to the Lady Irma a monk in haste. "My lady, the abbot lies at the point of death, and the prior is far away."

"What matters that to me?"

"This: that the lesser monks are murmuring. Unless the prior can be brought back before the abbot dies, they will make Father John abbot, and then —"

And then farewell many good things! That was the monk's thought. But the lady saw further. She frowned. "Send for Peter the Robber!"

Peter came, with sword and bow and dagger, and a hunted light in his eyes.

"Nay, Peter," quoth the lady; "thou lookest strange."

"Strange I feel, and strange feel we all, not knowing whom the wolf will take next."

"A pest on him!" cried the lady, and wished it true. "But, Peter," said the lady, "here is a letter, which take thou to the Prior Richard. Three days ago went he to the west. Seek him out and bring him back."

"Nay," said Peter. "Give me a horse. Afoot will I not travel without my fellows."

The lady commanded to give him a horse, and Peter rode forth into Bedegraine and took the forest road. His horse was fresh and fleet, he was well armed. Wayside flowers bloomed along the ancient turfy road, and the great trees of the forest were calm. Bright shone the sun, yet Peter's mood was dark and fearsome. He scanned the forest on either hand, and urged his horse that he might quickly pass the three leagues of the forest. And though he was so high on his horse, he rode with knife in hand, to defend his life.

But nothing showed among the trees except the dun deer. And though the bright sun, the warm air, the beauties of the forest, were nothing to Peter, he was a stout carl, and at last gained heart. When but a league of the road was left, he slipped his knife into its sheath. "Ho!" he said, "I meet not the gray wolf to-day."

Then as he rode he hummed a catch, to prove his courage. And he sat easier on his horse, cocked his bonnet, and thought of his reward, for the lady had promised many crowns. But out of a thicket shot suddenly the great gray wolf, and sprang on the horse's croup.

Peter screamed, felt for his knife, and struck with his spurs. The wolf seized him by the neck from behind; rearing, the horse flung them both to the ground. The wolf leaped up, but Peter lay still. His neck was broken.

Then the wolf, pawing and nuzzling, drew the letter out of Peter's doublet, for he knew that not without purpose did Peter ride on horseback. He broke the seal and spread the letter out, and stood with wrinkled forehead, scanning the lines. Then he took the parchment in his mouth and sped away among the trees.

He came to where Father John and Bennet had celebrated their daily mass. At the priest's feet he laid the letter. The priest read the screed:

TO PRIOR RICHARD: Why wanderest thou in the west? Anselm the abbot lieth on his death-bed, and the monks murmur. If thou returnest not in haste, not thou will be abbot, but the hedge-priest, Father John, who with his werewolf mightily impresseth all here in Bedegraine. And if that happeneth thou wilt not even be prior. Return, therefore, and guard thy interests and mine. This by the hands of Peter the Robber, from thy lady IRMA.

Then Father John arose, and took his staff and scrip, and said: "I go to the abbey. Bennet, lead thou me by the straightest way."

But Bennet cried: "The way lies past the castle!"

Then Father John, with ready wit, turned to the wolf and said: "O noble wolf, much hast thou done for this land. Canst thou now not lead us quickly to the abbey?"

The wolf, at such a pace that the priest and Bennet might follow, led them through the forest. By devious ways he brought them, until at last, when they left the shelter of the trees, the abbey towers were close in front. Bennet thundered at the gate and demanded admittance.

"But who are ye?" asked the warder. "Our abbot lieth dying, and we are all in fear."

"I am Father John," said the priest, "and I come to shrive the abbot."

When that was heard within the abbey, monks came running. The gate was opened, and Bennet and the father went in. But Marrok watched outside, and would not enter.

On his bed lay Anselm the abbot, sick to death. Had Prior Richard been there, no thought of repentance would have stirred the abbot's mind. But lying in his cell alone, thinking of his past life, fear came to him, for he knew he had been remiss in many things. He had heard of Father John, and he welcomed him. And Father John, standing by the bed, confessed the abbot, and shrived him. Then the abbot commanded the monks to come to the door of his cell. As they stood in the passage outside, he commanded them that they should immediately make Father John abbot in his place. Then he begged for their prayers, and died.

Anon in full chapter – all being there but the Prior Richard and the monk that had gone to the lady – they elected Father John abbot, and installed him in the abbot's chair. And they made Norris prior, but cast Richard out from the brotherhood. When this was done, the new abbot went to the gate, and the wolf started out of the edge of the forest, where he had watched.

"O wolf," said Father John, "now am I abbot, thanks to thee. Come now within these walls, and spend at rest the remainder of thy days."

But the wolf, having heard this news, went away. He returned to Bedegraine, knowing that Peter's men, so soon as they found the body, would be in confusion. They were so already. Fright had fallen on them. By twos and threes they fled away, nor stopped for their treasure. And the wolf was content to scare away those that would have sought refuge in the castle. None did he slay, for he was weary of killing.

Thus was Bedegraine cleared of outlaws, and we hear of no more until the time of Robin Hood; but in his time Bedegraine was called Sherwood.

When the Lady Irma heard the news, she laughed bitterly, and hid her chagrin with scornful words. Nevertheless she knew that two of the props of her strength were gone.

And Bennet, stoutly refusing to be made priest, dwelt in the abbey and became overseer of the lands. Soon as he might, he began to train the peasants to arms, meaning some day to take revenge on the lady. Had she known of it she would have laughed, for in the castle she felt secure.

XIII

Now let us understand that time passed by, and many things happened in the land of Britain. For there came into fame the young knights: first, Pellinore's son Sir Lamorak, and then Sir

Launcelot, and finally Sir Tristram, of whom this chapter tells. Sir Tristram was of Lyonesse; and he was nephew of Mark, King of Cornwall. And he was a gentle, joyous knight, and loved singing and harping; also he was the greatest hunter that had ever lived, and he invented all the terms of the chase, and all blasts and horn-blowing: these Sir Tristram made. And once Marrok had known Tristram and befriended him, as an older knight befriends a younger; and they two had sworn never to fight each other.

And it came into the fifth year that Marrok was a wolf, while ever the lady sought to destroy him. But her spells were vain, and he still lived in the forest, while year by year the peasants grew more prosperous and the land was richer. But the lady hated the thrift of the peasants, and more and more she feared the wolf. Night and day she planned how to be rid of him. Then one day seemed promised her her heart's desire.

A knight came riding to the castle. He was tall and fair, with flowing locks and open, cheerful face. A squire and two servants attended him, with horses and dogs. Six dogs there were, great hounds for the chase, and with them two little bratchets. On his shield the knight bore the arms of Cornwall.

The lady met him in the court and bade him welcome. The servants she sent to the servants' hall; the knight she led to her own table, where she charmed him with her hospitality and her conversation. At last she asked him his name – "if you are under no vow to conceal it," she said, for to that all knights were much given.

"Lady," he said, "my name is Sir Tristram of Lyonesse."

"Nay," she cried, "and is it true? See I in my hall the noble Tristram, greatest of the knights of Britain?"

"My lady," he said, "there are better knights than I. Launcelot, and Sir Lamorak –"

"Forgive me, sir," she said. "Your modesty is beyond praise, but also your worth. Known are you everywhere for a noble knight, and a sweet singer, and the greatest of all hunters. Known is your fight against Sir Marhaus of Ireland, and your many valiant deeds."

And she flattered him to his face, but so sweetly that Sir Tristram was pleased. Then she persuaded him to sing, and sat as rapt in delight, but really she was thinking deeply. When he had finished, she sighed.

"Lady," he asked, "why sigh you?"

"Ah, Sir Tristram," she answered, "thy harping and singing were so sweet that I had forgotten my troubles. When you finished I remembered them again. Therefore did I sigh."

"Truly, lady," he responded, "if you have troubles, tell them to me; for the heart becomes lighter by confidence."

Irma had put Gertrude into a deep sleep in her chamber, and she now sent Agatha to busy the squire and Hugh with pleasant chat. Then, knowing she could speak freely, she began her tale to Sir Tristram.

"Saw ye," she said, "my lands as ye rode hither? What thinkest thou of them?"

" 'T is a rich land," he said, "with prosperous and happy peasants. Lady, to them thou art a benefactress."

Irma sighed. "Truly I seek to be to them as was my dead lord" (but she mentioned not Marrok's name); "and my peasants have been happy. But lately has come a plague into my land that is beginning to waste our substance."

"What is it?" he asked. For Tristram was a noble knight, and, as Irma meant, he started at the hope of adventure.

"These five years," she said, "hath there lived a wolf in my forest. He killeth swine and cattle; he seizeth children; and now hath it come to such a pass that two must work always in the field together, for one man dares not work alone."

Then Tristram laughed a mighty laugh. "Lady, is that all? Ere to-morrow's sun is set, lay I this wolf dead."

"How?" she asked. "With thy dogs?"

"With my dogs and my fleet steed, and my hunting-spear."

"But the wolf is strong, and pulls down one by one the dogs that pursue him."

"Yet will he not pull down my hounds; and if he should, he will not escape my bratchets."

The lady's eyes sparkled. "Oh, Sir Tristram, if thou deliverest this land, my people will bless thee, and I more than they. A great pest and unbearable has this wolf become."

"Lady," he said, "fear not. But now let me to rest, for I have traveled far. And in the morning will I hunt the wolf."

The lady gave orders that the knight should be conducted to his chamber, and that his squire and men should be well served. And she and Agatha and Hugh rejoiced together, since Tristram was such a mighty hunter.

In the morning Tristram mounted his steed at the castle gate; and Gouvervail his squire mounted his, and Hugh, who would go too, mounted his. The dogs were loosed, eager for the chase, and all moved into the forest. Before long the lady, listening, heard Sir Tristram's horn, and knew that they had found the scent.

But Marrok, couched in the forest, heard the horn, and groaned. "That," said he, "is the horn of Sir Tristram." For since no one in the world could blow the horn so well as the knight of Lyonesse, Marrok knew the blast. And he groaned again, for he believed his end had come.

But he ran a good race, doing as he had done before. For the great hounds of Sir Tristram, the fleetest and the strongest in all Britain, one by one he slew. The swiftest first, the slowest last, one by one they lay dead. And Marrok thought for one instant: "Perhaps now I am free."

Then he heard the baying of the bratchets, which so long as the hounds bayed were silent, but now gave tongue. And he knew that against bratchets he could do nothing, for they were small dogs and slight, quick to turn and dodge, and he could never take them. He stood a moment in despair, and they came upon him among the trees, and waited and barked. Then Marrok saw the fair-haired knight coming upon his white horse, and turned and ran.

Minstrel and gleeman chanted of that chase for full four hundred years. Northward first fled Marrok, through the forest, till he reached its border. Then he turned west, and through the roughest country he led his pursuers. Then he ran south, then east, till the fair towers of Sir Roger of the Rock shone upon his sight. For a moment he was minded to flee there for protection. But the bratchets and the knight came upon him, – all else were left behind, – and Marrok fled south once more.

Then in despair he was minded to stay in the bushes and wait the knight, and attack him. For ever, whether through swamp or thicket, or over knoll, or among rocks, Sir Tristram followed close. But Marrok could not slay his friend, and he ran on. His heart grew heavy in his breast, his lungs and mouth were dry, and his legs weary. Then he said at last: "I will die among my people."

He turned toward the village of Bedegraine, and with his last strength fled thither. One bratchet fell and died, but the other and Sir Tristram followed on. And Marrok, almost spent, reached the village, ran into a yard, stood, and panted. The last bratchet, at the entrance, fell, and the horse stopped for weariness. But Sir Tristram leaped to the ground, his short spear in his hand, and walked up to Marrok.

Marrok looked him in the eye and thought: "Better die from friend's hand than from foe's." He budged not, but waited for the blow. And Sir Tristram admired him, and said: " 'T is pity, brave wolf, but thy end hath come at last."

He raised his spear. But a little flitting figure came in between, and behold, there was a child by the side of the wolf! She threw her arms about his neck, and covered him with her body. And looking over her shoulder with sparkling eyes, she cried to the knight: "Thou shalt not slay him!"

"Stand aside!" cried Sir Tristram. "Child, he will kill thee!" And he sought to find place for a blow. But he might not hurl his weapon without striking the child, and as he hesitated, the men of the house came running, and with scythes and pitchforks confronted Sir Tristram. "Sir Knight," cried they all in one voice, "hold thy hand!"

Sir Tristram stood in amazement. "This," he cried, "is the wolf ye all hate!"

"But we love him!" they answered.

"He killeth your swine and cattle."

"Nay," they protested. "Since he came to the land our kine feed in peace."

"But he beareth away children!"

The oldest man stood out before the others, and spoke: "Sir Knight, listen. Last winter was a snow-storm, great and terrible. And the child that thou seest here was bewildered in the storm, and though we sought for hours, we might not find her, and the cold and snow drove us within doors to save our own lives. While we waited and lamented, we heard a scratching at the door. We opened, and there was the child in the drift at the door, and this wolf stood a little way off. In the snow were no other marks than his. He had brought her home on his back."

"Is this truth?" queried Sir Tristram, greatly puzzled. "The lady said –"

"Oh, the lady!" cried they all. And Sir Tristram heard things that astonished him.

At last he mounted again his wearied steed, and gave gold to the peasants so that they should bury his bratchet. And while the wolf, soul-weary and yet glad, made his way to the wood, Sir Tristram took the road to the castle. As he went he met his squire and men; but Hugh, fearing to remain in the forest, had returned to the castle. Tristram rode thither.

From the castle battlement the Lady Irma spoke to Tristram; but reading much in his face, she kept the gate barred.

"How now, Sir Tristram?" she asked as if eagerly. "Is the wolf slain?"

"Lady," he answered, "the wolf hath escaped."

"Alas!" she responded, "my peasants will lament."

"Out upon thee, traitress!" cried Sir Tristram, fiercely. "Deceiver art thou truly, and oppressor of thy people. Would thou wert a man!"

She laughed without words.

He turned his horse's head away. "Lady," he said, "I shall tell of thy deeds among knights."

But the lady still laughed serenely. Tristram was not of Arthur's court, and none but Arthur did she fear.

XIV

There came a day when the archers of the lady, riding out into the villages, were attacked by the peasants, and driven back within the castle. So now had come the time when the lady had cause for thought, and to her counsels she called Morcar, who long had chafed in his castle at the loss of Agnes and the escape of her brother. He came in haste, for he hoped that now something would be done, since for some time Irma had repressed his eagerness, saying that they must wait.

"Now," he asked, "seest thou not that I was right, since ever the other party waxeth stronger?"

Then they had words unpleasing to them both, for both were heated and somewhat fearsome. But at last the lady composed herself and said: "Now talk we sensibly, else is no good done. And you and I must depend on each other, or we both fall." So Morcar was appeased and said no more reproaches.

"I have considered our strength and theirs," said the lady. "Twenty men-at-arms have I, with my hundred archers. Thirty horsemen have you, and sixty bowmen. And only a score of men-at-arms hath Roger."

"But the peasants?" asked Morcar. "They are archers all."

"If we sit in quiet," answered the lady, "then will Roger train the people to arms, and overcome us. But if we strike quickly, we can overthrow him."

"I am ready," said Morcar, gloomily.

Then they consulted long, calling Hugh for his opinion; and when they separated they went to the armories of their castles, and chose new arms, and repaired the old, and fed the horses well, and made all preparations for action. And Roger in his castle, with the son of Sir Simon, was making himself strong; but he was not ready against the scheme of those others. And so passed the time for ten days, until a night came when the moon was bright and full.

Upon that night all were sleeping in the village over which Sir Roger ruled, and in the castle itself there was but one man to watch. And Sir Roger lay asleep in his chamber, with the casement open, for it was a summer night. Right so it seemed that into his dream came the howling of a wolf, and he writhed long as he slept, oppressed by the noise, before he waked. And then he heard that it was the howling of a wolf indeed; and there was but one wolf in all Bedegraine, so Sir Roger started from his bed. Anon came rapping at his door the warder, who said: "Sir, the wolf howleth without in the fields, and will not be appeased."

"I will attend him," said Sir Roger.

Then in haste he threw a robe upon him, and went out upon the battlements. There he saw how the wolf ran to and fro in the fields, crying now toward the village and now toward the castle, and his great form was clearly to be seen. Anon Roger descended and stood above the castle gate; and the wolf saw him, and came to the farther side of the moat, and stood and bayed at him.

"Now," quoth Roger, "there is mischief toward." He gave orders that the castle be lighted and all the men armed, and quickly it was done. And Roger saw also how there were lights appearing in the village. But he went down to the courtyard and opened the gate, and lowered the draw, and went and stood by the side of the wolf, who ceased his crying.

"Now, good wolf," said Roger, without fear, "what is it that thou wishest of me? Shall I go with you and succor some one?"

But the beast made no sign.

"Then is it danger to me?" asked the knight.

Anon the wolf turned himself and looked toward the forest, that rose blackly at a little distance, and he seemed to listen, and then to whine, and then to listen again.

"So," said Sir Roger, "they come against me. Well, I thank thee for the warning. I will prepare."

Then the wolf ran off into the fields toward the village, and presently the knight heard him crying among the houses, as if he were saying: "Haste ye, and arm!" But the knight went again into the castle, and sent out men to watch, and armed every one, even the boys. Before long were the peasants coming to the castle with such arms as they had, bringing their families to shelter, for the wolf had alarmed them all. Sir Roger took them in and gave orders that all lights be put out, and that all should be silent, for he had made a plan. And still no word came from those who were sent out to watch. Then the knight led men out into the fields, and himself arranged them in hiding in the ditches. Then when all this was done came a watcher in haste, to say that there were noises and movements in the forest.

Now, while so much was being done at the castle of Sir Roger, through the wood were coming men on horseback and on foot, and the moonlight, falling through the leaves, glinted on their arms. Their leaders were Morcar and Hugh, and the men marched silently, save for the noise of their feet and the rattle of their arms, so that at a little distance they could not be heard. They reached the border of the forest, and halted while the leaders looked upon the plain. There lay the hamlet of Sir Roger, but there were no lights in it; and there rose the castle, dark and silent, so that all was as they had hoped. And the men began to issue from the forest.

Now, though they marched eagerly to surprise the castle, and made somewhat more noise, they roused no answering sound. They left the village on the right, and went by a bypath till they came near the castle. And behold, no watcher walked upon its battlements, and the drawbridge was down, the portcullis was raised, and the gate yawned wide. Then the men hurried, their leaders before them, till they were at the moat. There the men-at-arms dismounted quickly, and with stealthy steps, wondering but triumphant, they went in a body across the bridge, and entered the courtyard. But all was still within the court, and Morcar and Hugh began searching for the doors that led to the passages of the castle. They found them, but found them barred.

Then, as they hesitated, not knowing how to force the doors, but all talking in whispers in the silent court, where the walls towered high above, and the moon shed its light down among them, there came upon the air, from a distance, the long howl of the wolf. Those outside were startled, and those within listened. Anon upon the battlement rose a figure, drawing a bow; the bow twanged sweetly in the night, and in the courtyard a man was stricken by the arrow.

At the signal the walls were swarming with men, and the battle-cry of Sir Roger rose. Then buzzed arrows down among the men within the court, and rattled upon the armor of those outside. A commotion began, for Morcar and Hugh saw that they were trapped, and they shouted: "Back!" Then all struggled for the gateway, fearing that the gates would be closed on them. The portcullis rushed in its grooves, striking down men, and the chains creaked as the drawbridge began to rise.

And only the hap that the portcullis fell upon those men saved any of the others. For it did not reach the ground, and men wriggled under it to get away. The weight on the bridge was too great for it to be lifted far, and the chains broke, and back it fell. Across it some men reached safety, and got their horses and mounted, and among them were Morcar and Hugh. But twenty men were either killed in the courtyard, or else yielded themselves prisoners. Then Sir Roger and his men charged out across the bridge as the others fled, and from ditches and behind hedges archers rose and shot at the men of Hugh and Morcar. Had not a cloud come to obscure the moon, few would have got away; but in the darkness some reached the forest, and gathered themselves together, and made their way quickly to safety.

But thus it was that the forces of Sir Roger, and the forces of Irma and Morcar, were made equal.

Then Sir Roger, in great ease and lightness of heart, sent to the abbey the news, and begged that Father John and all the monks of the abbey should give thanks for the good fortune. And from that day he began on the lands of Morcar a serious war, harrying his farms and catching his men, so that when autumn came Morcar began to fear. For Roger knew the roads of the forest, and his men were mounted on swift horses, and they came, and struck, and went again, before ever Sir Morcar could strike in return. And Morcar saw that soon he would lose all his men by such means, and, because Roger had seized his harvests, food was short in the castle, not sufficient for the winter.

Then he went to Irma and complained, begging her to help him. Now Irma had not been disturbed by Roger, for between them had not yet been open war, and there was no proof that any of the men slain in Roger's castle had been Irma's men. So Roger left her lands unharried, for he said: "One enemy is enough at a time, and when I have finished Morcar then will I treat with the lady, and demand that she yield her lands." So Irma, for the present secure, felt little disturbed at Morcar's complaints. As for helping him, she said that half of her men were gone, which was true, so that she could give no help. And she scolded that Morcar and Hugh had been so easily trapped, saying that, had she been there, that foolishness would not have been committed. But she told Morcar what he could do to kill Roger, and another plan was formed, in which craft should take the place of force.

Then Morcar sent a message to Roger, with these words: "It seems that in our quarrel many men are slain, and yet the real matter concerns only thee and me. Therefore I challenge thee to fight me singly, to save good men's lives, an thou darest to meet me." And he set a day, and named a place in the forest where they should meet, which was an open space and grassy, where men might have good room. And Morcar would come alone, without any men; also should Roger come alone, without any men; and they two would fight it out between them.

Roger answered that he would come, and he stilled the fears of his wife, and on the day armed himself and rode to the forest alone, bidding all that, as they loved honor, they should stay away. "And if I come not at nightfall," said he, "ye shall send for my body." So he rode confidently into the forest, and met Morcar.

Now Morcar was heavy and tall, mighty of blow but slow of movement. And Roger was well-knit, and of medium height, and quick in his actions. So it promised to be an even fight between them. But, ere they commenced, the wolf walked out of the bushes, and lay down as if to watch.

"Now," cried Morcar, in alarm, "thou hast brought that beast to aid thee, and he will spring upon my horse."

"Nay," said Roger; "I knew naught of his coming, and, moreover, I have no power over him. Yet I will request him to go away, for he seems almost human." And courteously he asked the beast to go away, not thinking it would understand. To his surprise, it rose and went into the bushes.

"But how know I," cried Morcar, again, "that it comes not again, when I am busy with thee?" But this he said with cunning, and looked into the bushes at a certain spot. And with satisfaction he saw that the bushes moved, but with fear he heard the cry of the wolf.

Thereupon a struggle began in the thicket, and men's voices sounded choking, and a man with the wolf on his back came plunging into the open, and fell and died. Then Roger looked, and saw that it was one of Morcar's men, a desperate fellow well known in Bedegraine. And he looked farther, and saw that another man lay dead in the bushes, and they both had borne bows and arrows wherewith to slay his horse.

"Now, thou liar!" cried Roger, fiercely, to Sir Morcar, "here and now payest thou for the treachery which thou wouldst have executed!"

And the Lay says that they fought there for a half-hour, and seldom was seen such a fight. For Morcar was no coward, and he was desperate, yet Roger was furious. And they laid on strongly, neither sparing himself, so that both received wounds. And all the time the wolf watched that fight, and joyed to watch it, for he foresaw the outcome. Slain lay Morcar at the end, and the wolf, crying as with triumph, went away into the forest.

And thus Irma lost her last outward help; yet she sat secure in the castle, with her archers and her men-at-arms, and she laughed at Sir Roger when he demanded that she yield her fief. But the son of Sir Simon was put in the castle of Morcar, and he ruled over the lands of Morcar, and over his own lands. Then in the two castles and the monastery they consulted much together, and Bennet sometimes stole at night to the castle of the lady, looking to see how strict guard was kept, and whether in any place the walls of the castle were weak.

XV

Gertrude, the daughter of Irma, grew tall and beautiful. She lived in the castle like a flower in a moss-grown wall, and lighted it by her presence. Therefore it came naturally that Hugh, the captain of the archers, wished her for his wife.

Hugh was stout of body and bold of deed, cruel and hateful. He served the Lady Irma in her own spirit, and she trusted him. He called himself knight, but he was none, nor yet a gentleman born. So for a while the lady denied him the hand of Gertrude, putting him off from time to time.

But one day Hugh came to her and said: "My lady, what wish ye most in the world?"

She answered: "The death of the wolf."

"Lady Irma," he asked, "if I slay the wolf, wilt thou give me thy daughter Gertrude to wife?"

The lady thought, but not long. She answered: "I will."

Hugh said with joy: "Make ready the bridal dress, for the wolf dieth soon."

Now Hugh had learned that Marrok slept at the Druids' Ring, in the hut of the warlock, where Father John and Bennet once lived. Loving the Lady Gertrude greatly, he dared a deed. "I will go alone," he thought, "and seek him out. If I wear my shirt of mail, he cannot harm me."

He put on beneath his doublet a fine shirt of chain mail, and armed his horse as if for a tourney. In the bright morning he rode out from the castle, and went to the Druids' Ring. There Marrok lay sleeping, but he waked at the tramp of the horse. When Hugh appeared among the great stones, the wolf stood looking at him. Hugh cast a javelin, and missed. Then Marrok, hearing the chink of chain mail, and seeing it was useless to attack, turned limping, and slipped away into the forest. "He is lame!" cried Hugh, in delight, and gave chase. The horse with his heavy burden could go but slowly among the trees. But the wolf seemed wounded and sore, and Hugh kept him in sight. He urged his horse with the spurs, and rode eagerly. "Nay," he cried, "the wolf is mine!"

But go as he might, Hugh could not gain until he came out upon a great ledge which overhung the quarry where once the monk Norris had near lost his life. Below, fifty feet, were jagged stones. But the ledge was broad and mossy, and the wolf seemed so near, limping in front, that Hugh gave a shout and beat the horse with the flat of his sword. "I have him!" he cried. "I have him!" And the horse, lumbering into full speed, lessened the distance between them.

Then the wolf, just as the horse was close behind, and Hugh leaned forward to strike, leaped nimbly to one side. His lameness vanished. For one instant he waited, until the horse was quite abreast. Then he sprang under the horse's body, avoiding the blow of the sword, and caught the steed by his farther forefoot. Quickly he wrenched backward, and the steed, tripped as with a noose, plunged and fell at the edge of the crag. But Hugh was hurled into the depths.

The steed, in great fear, scrambled to his feet and fled headlong. The wolf stood listening. From below he heard a mighty crash. Then was silence.

That very day, soon after noon, Agatha wandered into the mead to watch for Hugh. She picked crocuses, and at the edge of the wood waited long, to wish him joy of his success. Then she spied flowers in the forest, earliest snowdrops, and went into the wood to pick them.

She heard a sound behind her, and turned. Almost she fainted from fright, for there stood the wolf, gray and great. He advanced upon her slowly. "Marrok!" she cried, and fell on her knees for mercy.

Still he advanced, and she gained strength from despair. She sprang up and rushed away, ever deeper into the forest. Behind her trotted the wolf, and at each glimpse of him she ran faster. He kept between her and the castle, and she had no chance to return, but went always farther from safety. When she had gone a mile, she came upon the forest road.

There at the edge of the trees was a horse, in the panoply of war, cropping the turf. And Agatha ran to him in hope. He let her seize the bridle and mount. " 'T is Hugh's horse. Hugh must be dead," she thought. "But I shall escape." She headed the horse to the north, and urged him to start.

Then into the road came the wolf, and the horse started indeed. Snorting with fear, he ran, and the wolf for a little way followed. Then Agatha, looking back, saw that he fell farther behind. At last he stopped, satisfied, for he knew she would not return. In truth, she rode eagerly, far away, into the country of the north. Never was she seen again in Bedegraine.

XVI

Hugh and Agatha came no more, and a new life began for the Lady Irma – a lonely, irksome life.

She was shut in and companionless. Her one-time friends were gone, for Sir Roger had slain Sir Morcar, and Father John ruled in the abbey. No longer might she ride thither for merrymaking. And in the castle were none but her serving-maids, her archers, and her daughter Gertrude.

Between Gertrude and her mother was no affection, but only tyranny and suspicion. The mother kept the daughter close, watched her, checked her, and commanded her. Therefore she received not love, but patient service. Also there was no heartiness, for Gertrude could not but dislike her mother's ways. She sat silent in her presence, and Irma complained angrily of her sullenness. Yet it was not sullenness – merely timidity and repression, for Gertrude was sweet and gentle.

Thus Irma, bored and wrathful, chafed in her castle. And a constant cause for irritation there was, that the peasants refused her all supplies, but beat off her archers when they were sent for tithes. The lady might not send to the abbey, neither could she longer depend upon traveling merchants. For the road from the south ran through the village, and the peasants warned all travelers away, lest they should pay heavy toll. Sir Roger stopped the eastern road, and the son of Sir Simon the western. The wolf himself guarded, day and night, the road from the north.

It was fortunate for Irma that Marrok had built the castle as a very granary, holding food for five years' siege. The great chambers had always been kept full, and there was store of gold and wine. So the lady lived secure; but she bit her fingers in impatience, and vowed vengeance on all. When a luckless trader chanced into her clutches she fleeced him. If she caught a peasant she made him a slave. And when knights fell into her hands she held them long time for ransom. She feared nothing, and laughed away the forebodings that sometimes came, telling her the end was drawing near.

One day there rode through the forest a young knight coming from the north. Strong and handsome he was, brown-haired and blue-eyed. It was in May. He hung his helmet on his saddle-bow, and looked about in the beautiful wood. The birds sang sweetly among the trees, the sky was blue, the turf was green, and the first daisies, Chaucer's darling flowers, nodded by the wayside. His heart laughed and his eyes danced. Another knight would have caroled gaily, but the young man was silent by nature, and he said no word.

He came to a cross-road, and behold! across the southern road lay a great wolf, gray and shaggy and scarred. The horse shrank with fear, but the knight urged him on. There lay his way. Then the wolf rose and fawned on the young man, as if to turn him to the right or left. But the knight, greatly wondering, kept the horse's head to the southern way, and would not turn.

Then the wolf stood in the path and growled. But the young man had no fear. He raised his spear and threatened. The wolf, crying as with a human voice, vanished in the forest, and his cry sounded often as the knight pursued his way, coming now from the right, now from the left. But the sound ceased when the knight came to a great mead, in the midst of which stood a castle.

Perhaps the crying of the wolf, perhaps the whispers of the forest, had called strange voices to the young knight's heart, speaking to him of the past. As he drew rein at the edge of the wood, it was more than the mere beauty of the scene that made the castle seem to him familiar, even kindly. "Mayhap," he said, "my search is ended." With childish memories stirring, and hope rising fast, he gave no heed to the last call of the wolf, that seemed to say: "Back! back!" He rode forward to the castle.

It was near nightfall, and the knight blew his horn at the castle gate. He was admitted. A lady, beautiful and gracious, met him in the court. "Welcome, fair knight," she cried. "Dismount and unarm thyself, and come to the feast. I am the Lady Irma of Castle Bedegraine, and thou art welcome."

The knight, with slow, grave smile, answered with few words: "Lady, thou art kind." He dismounted.

The archers took his arms and armor, a groom his horse. The lady led him to a great hall, where the young man paused and looked about. "Nay, my lady," he said, with brightening face; "were it not for these hangings and yonder great banner, I should think I had ended my search. I pray thee, under the banner is there not a shield carved in stone, and thereon a lion couchant?"

Now under the banner was the shield indeed, the arms of Marrok, which the lady had covered with the banner. Yet she answered: "Nay, there is no carving there." And her heart leaped in her breast, for she knew from his slow speech, and from his question, that the knight was Walter, Marrok's son.

Now Gertrude had come into the hall, and stood at her mother's back; but Irma did not see her. And Walter, looking at the banner, sighed, and said: "Almost it seems the same hall. Lady, I seek my birthplace, the home of my father, whence years agone I was cruelly driven. The castle's name I know not, nor my father's; but I remember the hall with the carved shield, and I should know my own little chamber."

Then Gertrude caught her breath, and they both saw her. But while Walter, in the midst of disappointment, looked on her with a sudden strange delight, thinking her the most beautiful girl he had ever seen, Irma was frightened and angry. She cast on Gertrude the old glance of command, and the daughter, shuddering, knew that she must obey her mother, even to the words she spoke.

"Gertrude," asked Irma, "thou art not well?"

"Nay, mother."

"Then go to thy chamber." And Gertrude, struggling to stay, to speak, went from the hall.

Irma turned to Walter. "Sir Knight," she said, "I pray thee forgive my daughter's intrusion. She is ill-mannered. But for yourself, prithee wait here a little space. I will bring a spiced drink for welcome, and will order for thee fresh robes." She left the young man wondering at the vision he had seen, and sought her secret chamber.

At its door was Gertrude, who marked the look on her mother's face, and fell at her feet. "Mother," she cried, "what go you to do?"

"Gertrude," said Irma, "I bade you go to your chamber."

"Mother," cried Gertrude, "I cannot. The young man is Walter. What wilt thou do to him?"

Irma strove to fix her with a glance, but she failed. Gertrude, summoning her will, threw off Irma's power, even at this late time. "I will go," she said, "to warn him."

And she turned away.

But Irma seized her suddenly by the arms. By force she drew

Gertrude to her chamber, thrust her in, and locked the door. "Now," she said, as she heard Gertrude's cries, "do thy worst."

Gertrude leaned from the window, and there, far below in the dusk, on the edge of the moat, she saw the figure of a man. "Ho!" she cried, "who is there?"

"My Lady Gertrude," answered a cautious voice, "is it thou? I am old Bennet."

"Bennet," cried Gertrude, "fly for help! Here within is Walter, Marrok's son. He knoweth my mother not, and I fear for his life!"

But though she saw Bennet hasten toward the village, she despaired. The village was a half-mile thence, and it would take time to gather men.

Meanwhile Irma went to the secret chamber, and shut herself in. She took wax, and warmed it at the brazier, and as she warmed it she thought. Should she make Walter a cat, or a dog, or a snake? Remembering the unexpected deeds of the wolf, she thought any of these too dangerous. So when the wax was warmed she modeled with it swiftly the figure of an owl – the small brown horned owl. She put the figure on the little shrine on the wall, and lit before it three candles, one red, one blue, and one green. "There," quoth she, "let him hoot in the forest, and catch mice!"

Then she took her vials and compounded a drink, and all the while she muttered charms and spells. And bearing the drink in her golden chalice, she left the room and went down to the banqueting-hall.

Now without, in the forest, the wolf mourned for the young man. Seven years had he lived in Bedegraine, but never had he felt so drawn toward human being as by this stranger knight. A great sadness came upon him, and he wandered, striving to throw it off. But instead it grew upon him, and he could think upon nothing but the young man lying dead. And Marrok remembered all that had happened since he became a wolf: how he had saved Agnes and Andred and Norris, and had warned Sir Roger and again saved him from treachery, and how he had led Pellinore to the rescue of the son of Sir Simon. But now he saw no rescue, here where his heart was most deeply set, so that he was willing to give his own life for the young man's. For now all Bedegraine was prosperous, and Marrok had done all that, as a wolf, he could do, and he saw the end of his usefulness on earth. Then suddenly, as he pondered, wishing to give his life for the young knight's, he saw a way. And he ventured all.

He went to a knoll in the wood, grown all about with low, thick junipers and cedars; he crept into the thicket, and came to an iron door among rocks. And that was the door which he had made on the advice of Merlin.

Then Marrok pushed upon a hidden lever, and the door swung inward. He entered, and shut the door, and went forward in darkness. The passage led straight, then curved, and Marrok came upon a wall. He found a spring, and pushed, and the heavy stones moved aside.

This time he was on a stair, up which he clambered. Again he came on the solid stone, but again it moved at his touch on a spring, and let him pass. And there he was in a little chamber, lit by a lamp. There were hangings on the walls, books on shelves, and vials within cupboards. In one place hung a suit of armor – his own. And upon the wall was a little shrine, and a waxen figure of an owl thereon, and three candles, one red, one blue, and one green, burning before it.

Then he understood everything; and hastily rearing, he reached at the shrine with clumsy forefoot, meaning to destroy the figure of the owl. The figure fell to the floor at his touch, and, rolling away, hid under the hangings. The wax was still warm and tough, and it did not break. But from within the shrine, as it swayed upon the wall, fell out another figure, and broke in two upon the stone flags of the floor. And it was the figure of a wolf.

Then Marrok, standing there upright, felt a change come over him. The fur vanished from his body, his paws became hands and feet, and his limbs were those of a man. Behold, he was himself again, clothed in the robes he wore when he became a wolf!

He knew the change, and uttered a great cry of joy. But pausing not, he seized from the wall his sword, and casting down the scabbard, hastened from the room. Down the stone stair he hurried, till he came to the banqueting-hall, and stood at the door.

Within were Irma and the stranger knight, and she was playing with him, as a cat. Marrok heard her words. "Thou art Walter, son of Marrok, and thy father's castle is not far from here. Pledge me in this wine, and I will tell thee where to find him."

The young knight, with sparkling eyes, took the chalice from her hand. "Lady," he said, "a thousand times I thank thee for this news. I pledge thee."

But Marrok strode forward from the door, and cried: "Drink not!" And Walter, seeing a man with drawn sword, put down the wine hastily upon the table, and seized his dagger.

Then Marrok turned to Irma, and cried in triumph, "Traitress, thou hast failed!" He raised his sword to strike the cup to the floor.

But she, thinking he meant to slay her, snatched quickly at the chalice, and drained the drink to the dregs. Then she looked the knight in the face, and dropped the chalice. "Marrok! Marrok!" Those were her last words. For she changed quickly into a little owl, circled upward, found an open window, and flew hooting into the night.

Marrok turned to his son, dropped his sword, and held out his arms. "Walter," he cried, "she was a sorceress. But I am Marrok, thine own father!"

Long was their embrace and loving, and then they sat and told each other many things. But after a while they heard a great commotion in the castle, and each seized his sword, fearing the servants of Irma.

Yet it was Bennet that they heard, who had come with help. For while the old squire mustered men in the village, but all too slowly, there had ridden up Sir Roger of the Rock, and Father John, each with retainers. All together hastened to the castle, and forced the gate. Bennet sent the peasants to the servants' hall to surprise the archers. Great and complete was the vengeance that the peasants took. But Bennet himself, and Sir Roger, and Father John, with the men-at-arms, arms, rushed to the banquet-hall, and it was they who burst in the door upon Sir Marrok and his son.

Joyous was the greeting, and deep was the delight of all. Gertrude they brought from her chamber. She hung upon Sir Marrok's neck, and Walter was delighted at the sight. And the peasants, thronging into the hall, fell upon their knees and gave thanks at the sight of their lord.

Of Irma, who had become an owl, nothing more was heard; yet an owl she remained, for that waxen image had slipped away into a crevice in the stone floor of the little chamber, and was lost. But Walter, the son of Marrok, married Gertrude, the daughter of Irma, some six months from that day. And all the land of Bedegraine was happy, except that the peasants lamented that they saw the great gray wolf no more; for after the return of Marrok the wolf was never again seen. And Marrok told no one that he had been the wolf, except Walter and Gertrude and Father John. And Father John, growing old, wrote all this in the Chronicle, whence Blaise wrote the Lay which minstrels sang, from which was written the story that is printed here.

THE MARRIAGE OF SIR GAWAYNE

Maude Ebbutt

Here is the second story featuring Sir Gawain, or Gawayne as Maude Ebbutt preferred to call him. This episode, sometimes known as "Sir Gawain and the Loathly Lady" shows Gawain at his most chivalrous, and is perhaps the most typical of all Arthurian stories as we have come to imagine them. I know little about Maude Ebbutt who was evidently a student of Celtic history at the turn of the century. This story comes from her study Hero Myths and Legends of the British People *(1910).*

One year the noble King Arthur was keeping his Christmas at Carlisle with great pomp and state. By his side sat his lovely Queen Guenever, the brightest and most beauteous bride that a king ever wedded, and about him were gathered the Knights of the Round Table. Never had a king assembled so goodly a company of valiant warriors as now sat in due order at the Round Table in the great hall of Carlisle Castle, and King Arthur's heart was filled with pride as he looked on his heroes. There sat Sir Lancelot, not yet the betrayer of his lord's honour and happiness, with Sir Bors and Sir Banier, there Sir Bedivere, loyal to King Arthur till death, there surely Sir Kay, the churlish steward of the King's household, and King Arthur's nephews, the young and gallant Sir Gareth, the gentle and courteous Sir Gawayne, and the false, gloomy Sir

Mordred, who wrought King Arthur's overthrow. The knights and ladies were ranged in their fitting degrees and ranks, the servants and pages waited and carved and filled the golden goblets, and the minstrels sang to their harps lays of heroes of the olden time.

Yet in the midst of all this splendour the king was ill at ease, for he was a warlike knight and longed for some new adventure, and of late none had been known. Arthur sat moodily among his knights and drained the wine-cup in silence, and Queen Guenever, gazing at her husband, durst not interrupt his gloomy thoughts. At last the king raised his head, and, striking the table with his hand, exclaimed fiercely: "Are all my knights sluggards or cowards, that none of them goes forth to seek adventures? You are better fitted to feast well in hall than fight well in field. Is my fame so greatly decayed that no man cares to ask for my help or my support against evildoers? I vow here, by the boar's head and by Our Lady, that I will not rise from this table till some adventure be undertaken." "Sire, your loyal knights have gathered round you to keep the holy Yuletide in your court," replied Sir Lancelot; and Sir Gawayne said: "Fair uncle, we are not cowards, but few evildoers dare to show themselves under your rule; hence it is that we seem idle. But see yonder! By my faith, now cometh an adventure."

Even as Sir Gawayne spoke a fair damsel rode into the hall, with flying hair and disordered dress, and, dismounting from her steed, knelt down sobbing at Arthur's feet. She cried aloud, so that all heard her: "A boon, a boon, King Arthur! I beg a boon of you!" "What is your request?" said the king, for the maiden was in great distress, and her tears filled his heart with pity. "What would you have of me?" "I cry for vengeance on a churlish knight, who has separated my love from me." "Tell your story quickly," said King Arthur; and all the knights listened while the lady spoke.

"I was betrothed to a gallant knight," she said, "whom I loved dearly, and we were entirely happy until yesterday. Then as we rode out together planning our marriage we came, through the moorland ways, unnoticing, to a fair lake, Tarn Wathelan, where stood a great castle, with streamers flying, and banners waving in the wind. It seemed a strong and goodly place, but alas! it stood on magic ground, and within the enchanted circle of its shadow an evil spell fell on every knight who set foot therein. As my love and I looked idly at the mighty keep a horrible and churlish warrior, twice the size of mortal man, rushed forth in complete armour; grim and fierce-looking he was, armed with a huge club, and sternly he bade my knight leave me to him and go his way alone. Then my love drew his sword to defend me, but the evil spell had robbed him of all strength, and he could do nought against the giant's club; his sword fell from his feeble hand, and the churlish knight, seizing him, caused him to be flung into a dungeon. He then returned and sorely ill-treated me, though I prayed for mercy in the name of chivalry and of Mary Mother. At last, when he set me free and bade me go, I said I would come to King Arthur's court and beg a champion of might to avenge me, perhaps even the king himself. But the giant only laughed aloud. 'Tell the foolish king,' quoth he, 'that here I stay his coming, and that no fear of him shall stop my working my will on all who come. Many knights have I in prison, some of them King Arthur's own true men; wherefore bid him fight with me, if he will win them back.' Thus, laughing and jeering loudly at you, King Arthur, the churlish knight returned to his castle, and I rode to Carlisle as fast as I could."

When the lady had ended her sorrowful tale all present were greatly moved with indignation and pity, but King Arthur felt the insult most deeply. He sprang to his feet in great wrath, and cried aloud: "I vow by my knighthood, and by the Holy Rood, that I will go forth to find that proud giant, and will never leave him till I have overcome him." The knights applauded their lord's vow, but Queen Guenever looked doubtfully at the king, for she had noticed the damsel's mention of magic, and she feared some evil adventure for her husband. The damsel stayed in Carlisle that night, and in the morning, after he had heard Mass, and bidden farewell to his wife, King Arthur rode away. It was a lonely journey to Tarn Wathelan, but the country was very beautiful, though wild and rugged, and the king soon saw the little lake gleaming clear and cold below him, while the enchanted castle towered up above the water, with banners flaunting defiantly in the wind.

The king drew his sword Excalibur and blew a loud note on his bugle. Thrice his challenge note resounded, but brought no reply, and then he cried aloud: "Come forth, proud knight! King Arthur is here to punish you for your misdeeds! Come forth and fight bravely. If you are afraid, then come forth and yield yourself my thrall."

The churlish giant darted out at the summons, brandishing his massive club, and rushed straight at King Arthur. The spell of the enchanted ground seized the king at that moment, and his hand sank down. Down fell his good sword Excalibur, down fell his shield, and he found himself ignominiously helpless in the presence of his enemy.

Now the giant cried aloud: "Yield or fight, King Arthur; which will you do? If you fight I shall conquer you, for you have no power to resist me; you will be my prisoner, with no hope of ransom, will lose your land and spend your life in my dungeon with many other brave knights. If you yield I will hold you to ransom, but you must swear to accept the terms I shall offer."

"What are they," asked King Arthur. The giant replied: "You must swear solemnly, by the Holy Rood, that you will return here on New Year's Day and bring me a true answer to the question, 'What thing is it that all women most desire?' If you fail to bring the right answer your ransom is not paid, and you are yet my prisoner. Do you accept my terms?" The king had no alternative: so long as he stood on the enchanted ground his courage was overborne by the spell and he could only hold up his hand and swear by the Sacred Cross and by Our Lady that he would return, with such answers as he could obtain, on New Year's Day.

Ashamed and humiliated, the king rode away, but not back to Carlisle – he would not return home till he had fulfilled his task; so he rode east and west and north and south, and asked every woman and maid he met the question the churlish knight had put to him. "What is it all women most desire?" he asked, and all gave him different replies: some said riches, some splendour, some pomp and state; others declared that fine attire was women's chief delight, yet others voted for mirth or flattery; some declared that a handsome lover was the cherished wish of every woman's heart; and among them all the king grew quite bewildered. He wrote down all the answers he received, and sealed them with his own seal, to give to the churlish knight when he returned to the Castle of Tarn Wathelan; but in his own heart King Arthur felt that the true answer had not yet been given to him. He was sad as he turned and rode towards the giant's home on New Year's Day, for he feared to lose his liberty and lands, and the lonely journey seemed much more dreary than it had before, when he rode out from Carlisle so full of hope and courage and self-confidence.

Arthur was riding mournfully through a lonely forest when he heard a woman's voice greeting him: "God save you, King Arthur! God save and keep you!" and he turned at once to see the person who thus addressed him. He saw no one at all on his right hand, but as he turned to the other side he perceived a woman's form clothed in brilliant scarlet; the figure was seated between a holly-tree and an oak, and the berries of the former were not more vivid than her dress, and the brown leaves of the latter not more brown and wrinkled than her cheeks. At first sight King Arthur thought he must be bewitched – no such nightmare of a human face had ever seemed to him possible. Her nose was crooked and bent hideously to one side, while her chin seemed to bend to the opposite side of her face; her one eye was set deep under her beetling brow, and her mouth was nought but a gaping slit. Round this awful countenance hung snaky locks of ragged grey hair, and she was deadly pale, with a bleared and dimmed blue eye. The king nearly swooned when he saw this hideous sight, and was so amazed that he did not answer her salutation. The loathly lady seemed angered by the insult: "Now Christ save you, King Arthur! Who are you to refuse to answer my greeting and take no heed of me? Little of courtesy have you and your knights in your fine court in Carlisle if you cannot return a lady's greeting. Yet, Sir King, proud as you are, it may be that I can help you, loathly though I be; but I will do nought for one who will not be courteous to me."

King Arthur was ashamed of his lack of courtesy, and tempted by the hint that here was a woman who could help him. "Forgive me, lady," said he; "I was sorely troubled in mind, and thus, and not for want of courtesy, did I miss your greeting. You say that you can perhaps help me; if you would do this, lady, and teach me how to pay my ransom, I will grant anything you ask as a reward." The deformed lady said: "Swear to me, by Holy Rood, and by Mary Mother, that you will grant me whatever boon I ask, and I will help you to the secret. Yes, Sir King, I know by secret means that you seek the answer to the question, 'What is it all women most desire?' Many women have given you many replies, but I alone, by my magic power, can give you the right answer. This secret I will tell you, and in truth it will pay your ransom, when you have sworn to keep faith with me." "Indeed, O grim lady, the oath I will take gladly," said King Arthur; and when he had sworn it, with uplifted hand, the lady told him the secret, and he vowed with great bursts of laughter that this was indeed the right answer.

When the king had thoroughly realized the wisdom of the answer he rode on to the Castle of Tarn Wathelan, and blew his bugle three times. As it was New Year's Day, the churlish knight was ready for him, and rushed forth, club in hand, ready to do battle. "Sir Knight," said the king, "I bring here writings containing answers to your question; they are replies that many women have given, and should be right; these I bring in ransom for my life and lands." The churlish knight took the writings and read them one by one, and each one he flung aside, till all had been read; then he said to the king: "You must yield yourself and your lands to me, King Arthur, and rest my prisoner; for though these answers be many and wise, not one is the true reply to my question; your ransom is not paid, and your life and all you have is forfeit to me." "Alas! Sir Knight," quoth the king, "stay your hand, and let me speak once more before I yield to you; it is not much to grant to one who risks life and kingdom and all. Give me leave to try one more reply." To this the giant assented, and King Arthur continued: "This morning as I rode through the forest I beheld a lady sitting, clad in scarlet, between an oak and a holly-tree; she says, 'All women will have their own way, and this is their chief desire.' Now confess that I have brought the true answer to your question, and that I am free, and have paid the ransom for my life and lands."

The giant waxed furious with rage, and shouted: "A curse upon that lady who told you this! It must have been my sister, for none but she knew the answer. Tell me, was she ugly and deformed?" When King Arthur replied that she was a loathly lady, the giant broke out: "I vow to heaven that if I can once catch her I will burn her alive; for she has cheated me of being King of Britain. Go your ways, Arthur; you have not ransomed yourself, but the ransom is paid and you are free."

Gladly the king rode back to the forest where the loathly lady awaited him, and stopped to greet her. "I am free now, lady, thanks to you! What boon do you ask in reward for your help? I have promised to grant it you, whatever it may be." "This is my boon, King Arthur, that you will bring some young and courteous knight from your court in Carlisle to marry me, and he must be brave and handsome too. You have sworn to fulfil my request, and you cannot break your word." These last words were spoken as the king shook his head and seemed on the point of refusing a request so unreasonable; but at this reminder he only hung his head and rode slowly away, while the unlovely lady watched him with a look of mingled pain and glee.

On the second day of the new year King Arthur came home to Carlisle. Wearily he rode along and dismounted at the castle, and wearily he went into his hall, where sat Queen Guenever. She had been very anxious during her husband's absence, for she dreaded magic arts, but she greeted him gladly and said: "Welcome, my dear lord and king, welcome home again! What anxiety I have endured for you! But now you are here all is well. What news do you bring, my liege? Is the churlish knight conquered? Where have you had him hanged, and where is his head? Placed on a spike above some

town-gate? Tell me your tidings, and we will rejoice together." King
Arthur only sighed heavily as he replied: "Alas! I have boasted too
much; the churlish knight was a giant who has conquered me, and
set me free on conditions." "My lord, tell me how this has chanced."
"His castle is an enchanted one, standing on enchanted ground, and
surrounded with a circle of magic spells which sap the bravery from
a warrior's mind and the strength from his arm. When I came on
his land and felt the power of his mighty charms, I was unable to
resist him, but fell into his power, and had to yield myself to him.
He released me on condition that I would fulfil one thing which he
bade me accomplish, and this I was enabled to do by the help of
a loathly lady; but that help was dearly bought, and I cannot pay
the price myself."

By this time Sir Gawayne, the king's favourite nephew, had
entered the hall, and greeted his uncle warmly; then, with a few
rapid questions, he learnt the king's news, and saw that he was
in some distress. "What have you paid the loathly lady for her
secret, uncle?" he asked. "Alas! I have paid her nothing; but I
promised to grant her any boon she asked, and she has asked a
thing impossible." "What is it?" asked Sir Gawayne. "Since you
have promised it, the promise must needs be kept. Can I help you
to perform your vow?" "Yes, you can, fair nephew Gawayne, but
I will never ask you to do a thing so terrible," said King Arthur. "I
am ready to do it, uncle, were it to wed the loathly lady herself."
"That is what she asks, that a fair young knight should marry her.
But she is too hideous and deformed; no man could make her his
wife." "If that is all your grief," replied Sir Gawayne, "things shall
soon be settled; I will wed this ill-favoured dame, and will be your
ransom." "You know not what you offer," answered the king. "I
never saw so deformed a being. Her speech is well enough, but
her face is terrible, with crooked nose and chin, and she has only
one eye." "She must be an ill-favoured maiden; but I heed it not,"
said Sir Gawayne gallantly, "so that I can save you from trouble
and care." "Thanks, dear Gawayne, thanks a thousand times! Now
through your devotion I can keep my word. To-morrow we must
fetch your bride from her lonely lodging in the greenwood; but we
will feign some pretext for the journey. I will summon a hunting
party, with horse and hound and gallant riders, and none shall
know that we go to bring home so ugly a bride." "Gramercy,
uncle," said Sir Gawayne. "Till to-morrow I am a free man."

The next day King Arthur summoned all the court to go hunting
in the greenwood close to Tarn Wathelan; but he did not lead the

chase near the castle: the remembrance of his defeat and shame was too strong for him to wish to see the place again. They roused a noble stag and chased him far into the forest, where they lost him amid close thickets of holly and yew interspersed with oak corpses and hazel bushes – bare were the hazels, and brown and withered the clinging oak leaves, but the holly looked cheery, with its fresh green leaves and scarlet berries. Though the chase had been fruitless, the train of knights laughed and talked gaily as they rode back through the forest, and the gayest of all was Sir Gawayne; he rode wildly down the forest drives, so recklessly that he drew level with Sir Kay, the churlish steward, who always preferred to ride alone. Sir Lancelot, Sir Stephen, Sir Banier, and Sir Bors all looked wonderingly at the reckless youth; but his younger brother, Gareth, was troubled, for he knew all was not well with Gawayne, and Sir Tristram, buried in his love for Isolde, noticed nothing, but rode heedlessly, wrapped in sad musings.

Suddenly Sir Kay reined up his steed, amazed; his eye had caught the gleam of scarlet under the trees, and as he looked he became aware of a woman, clad in a dress of finest scarlet, sitting between a holly-tree and an oak. "Good greeting to you, Sir Kay," said the lady, but the steward was too much amazed to answer. Such a face as that of the lady he had never even imagined, and he took no notice of her salutation. By this time the rest of the knights had joined him, and they all halted, looking in astonishment on the misshapen face of the poor creature before them. It seemed terrible that a woman's figure should be surmounted by such hideous features, and most of the knights were silent for pity's sake; but the steward soon recovered from his amazement, and his rude nature began to show itself. The king had not yet appeared, and Sir Kay began to jeer aloud. "Now which of you would fain woo yon fair lady?" he asked. "It takes a brave man, for methinks he will stand in fear of any kiss he may get, it must needs be such an awesome thing. But yet I know not; any man who would kiss this beauteous damsel may well miss the way to her mouth, and his fate is not quite so dreadful after all. Come, who will win a lovely bride!" Just then King Arthur rode up, and at sight of him Sir Kay was silent; but the loathly lady hid her face in her hands, and wept that he should pour such scorn upon her.

Sir Gawayne was touched with compassion for this uncomely woman alone among these gallant and handsome knights, a woman so helpless and ill-favoured, and he said: "Peace, churl Kay, the lady cannot help herself; and you are not so noble and courteous that you have the right to jeer at any maiden; such deeds do not become a knight of Arthur's Round Table. Besides, one of us knights here must wed this unfortunate lady." "Wed her?" shouted Kay. "Gawayne, you are mad!" "It is true, is it not, my liege?" asked Sir Gawayne, turning to the king; and Arthur reluctantly gave token of assent, saying, "I promised her not long since, for the help she gave me in a great distress, that I would grant her any boon she craved, and she asked for a young and noble knight to be her husband. My royal word is given, and I will keep it; therefore have I brought you here to meet her." Sir Kay burst out with, "What? Ask me perchance to wed this foul quean? I'll none of her. Where'er I get my wife from, were it from the fiend himself, this hideous hag shall never be mine." "Peace, Sir Kay," sternly said the king; "you shall not abuse this poor lady as well as refuse her. Mend your speech, or you shall be knight of mine no longer." Then he turned to the others and said: "Who will wed this lady and help me to keep my royal pledge? You must not all refuse, for my promise is given, and for a little ugliness and deformity you shall not make me break my plighted word of honour." As he spoke he watched them keenly, to see who would prove sufficiently devoted, but the knights all began to excuse themselves and to depart. They called their hounds, spurred their steeds, and pretended to search for the track of the lost stag again; but before they went Sir Gawayne cried aloud: "Friends, cease your strife and debate, for I will wed this lady myself. Lady, will you have me for your husband?" Thus saying, he dismounted and knelt before her.

The poor lady had at first no words to tell her gratitude to Sir Gawayne, but when she had recovered a little she spoke: "Alas ! Sir Gawayne, I fear you do but jest. Will you wed with one so ugly and deformed as I? What sort of wife should I be for a knight so gay and gallant, so fair and comely as the king's own nephew? What will Queen Guenever and the ladies of the Court say when you return to Carlisle bringing with you such a bride? You will be shamed, and all through me." Then she wept bitterly, and her weeping made her seem even more hideous; but King Arthur, who was watching the scene, said: "Lady, I would fain see that knight or dame who dares mock at my nephew's bride. I will take order that no such unknightly discourtesy is shown in my court," and he glared angrily at Sir Kay and the others who had stayed, seeing that Sir Gawayne was prepared to sacrifice himself and therefore they were safe. The lady raised her head and looked keenly at Sir Gawayne, who took her hand, saying: "Lady, I will be a true and loyal husband to you if you will have me; and I shall know how to guard my wife from insult. Come, lady, and my uncle will announce the betrothal." Now the lady seemed to believe that Sir Gawayne was in earnest, and she sprang to her feet, saying: "Thanks to you! A thousand thanks, Sir Gawayne, and blessings on your head! You shall never rue this wedding, and the courtesy you have shown. Wend we now to Carlisle."

A horse with a side-saddle had been brought for Sir Gawayne's bride, but when the lady moved it became evident that she was lame and halted in her walk, and there was a slight hunch on her shoulders. Both of these deformities showed little when she was seated, but as she moved the knights looked at one another, shrugged their shoulders and pitied Sir Gawayne, whose courtesy had bound him for life to so deformed a wife. Then the whole train rode away together, the bride between King Arthur and her betrothed, and all the knights whispering and sneering behind them. Great was the excitement in Carlisle to see that ugly dame, and greater still the bewilderment in the court when they were told that this loathly lady was Sir Gawayne's bride.

Only Queen Guenever understood, and she showed all courtesy to the deformed bride, and stood by her as her lady-of-honour when the wedding took place that evening, while King Arthur was groomsman to his nephew. When the long banquet was over, and bride and bridegroom no longer need sit side by side, the tables were cleared and the hall was prepared for a dance, and then men thought that Sir Gawayne would be free for a time to talk with his friends; but he refused. "Bride and bridegroom must tread the first dance together, if she wishes it," quoth he, and offered his lady his hand for the dance. "I thank you, sweet husband," said the grim lady as she took it and moved forward to open the dance with him; and through the long and stately measure that followed, so perfect was his dignity, and the courtesy and grace with which he danced, that no man dreamt of smiling as the deformed lady moved clumsily through the figures of the dance.

At last the long evening was over, the last measure danced, the last wine-cup drained, the bride escorted to her chamber, the lights out, the guests separated in their rooms, and Gawayne was free to think of what he had done, and to consider how he had ruined his whole hope of happiness. He thought of his uncle's favour, of the poor lady's gratitude, of the blessing she had invoked upon him, and he determined to be gentle with her, though he could never love her as his wife. He entered the bride-chamber with the feeling of a man who has made up his mind to endure, and did not even look towards his bride, who sat awaiting him beside the fire. Choosing a chair, he sat down and looked sadly into the glowing embers and spoke no word.

"Have you no word for me, husband? Can you not even give me a glance?" asked the lady, and Sir Gawayne turned his eyes to her where she sat; and then he sprang up in amazement, for there sat no loathly lady, no ugly and deformed being, but a maiden young and lovely, with black eyes and long curls of dark hair, with beautiful face and tall and graceful figure. "Who are you, maiden?" asked Sir Gawayne; and the fair one replied: "I am your wife, whom you found between the oak and the holly-tree, and whom you wedded this night."

"But how has this marvel come to pass?" asked he, wondering, for the fair maiden was so lovely that he marvelled that he had not known her beauty even under that hideous disguise. "It is an enchantment to which I am in bondage," said she. "I am not yet entirely free from it, but now for a time I may appear to you as I really am. Is my lord content with his loving bride?" asked she, with a little smile, as she rose and stood before him. "Content!" he said, as he clasped her in his arms. "I would not change my dear lady for the fairest dame in Arthur's court, not though she were Queen Guenever herself. I am the happiest knight that lives, for I thought to save my uncle and help a hapless lady, and I have won my own happiness thereby. Truly I shall never rue the day when I wedded you, dear heart." Long they sat and talked together, and then Sir Gawayne grew weary, and would fain have slept, but his lady said: "Husband, now a heavy choice awaits you. I am under the spell of an evil witch, who has given me my own face and form for half the day, and the hideous appearance in which you first saw me for the other half. Choose now whether you will have me fair by day and ugly by night, or hideous by day and beauteous by night. The choice is your own."

Sir Gawayne was no longer oppressed with sleep; the choice before him was too difficult. If the lady remained hideous by day he would have to endure the taunts of his fellows; if by night, he would be unhappy himself. If the lady were fair by day other men might woo her, and he himself would have no love for her; if she were fair to him alone, his love would make her look ridiculous before the court and the king. Nevertheless, acting on the spur of the moment, he spoke: "Oh, be fair to me only – be your old self by day, and let me have my beauteous wife to myself alone." "Alas!

is that your choice?" she asked. "I only must be ugly when all are beautiful, I must be despised when all other ladies are admired; I am as fair as they, but I must seem foul to all men. Is this your love, Sir Gawayne?" and she turned from him and wept. Sir Gawayne was filled with pity and remorse when he heard her lament, and began to realize that he was studying his own pleasure rather than his lady's feelings, and his courtesy and gentleness again won the upper hand. "Dear love, if you would rather that men should see you fair, I will choose that, though to me you will be always as you are now. Be fair before others and deformed to me alone, and men shall never know that the enchantment is not wholly removed."

Now the lady looked pleased for a moment, and then said gravely: "Have you thought of the danger to which a young and lovely lady is exposed in the court? There are many false knights who would woo a fair dame, though her husband were the king's favourite nephew; and who can tell? – one of them might please me more than you. Sure I am that many will be sorry they refused to wed me when they see me to-morrow morn. You must risk my beauty under the guard of my virtue and wisdom, if you have me young and fair." She looked merrily at Sir Gawayne as she spoke; but he considered seriously for a time, and then said: "Nay, dear love, I will leave the matter to you and your own wisdom, for you are wiser in this matter than I. I remit this wholly unto you, to decide according to your will. I will rest content with whatsoever you resolve."

Now the fair lady clapped her hands lightly, and said: "Blessings on you, dear Gawayne, my own dear lord and husband! Now you have released me from the spell completely, and I shall always be as I am now, fair and young, till old age shall change my beauty as he doth that of all mortals. My father was a great duke of high renown who had but one son and one daughter, both of us dearly beloved, and both of goodly appearance. When I had come to an age to be married my father determined to take a new wife, and he wedded a witch-lady. She resolved to rid herself of his two children, and cast a spell upon us both, whereby I was transformed from a fair lady into the hideous monster whom you wedded, and my gallant young brother into the churlish giant who dwells at Tarn Wathelan. She condemned me to keep that awful shape until I married a young and courtly knight who would grant me all my will. You have done all this for me, and I shall be always your fond and faithful wife. My brother too is set free from the spell, and he will become again one of the truest and most gentle knights alive, though none can excel my own true knight, Sir Gawayne."

The next morning the knight and his bride descended to the great hall, where many knights and ladies awaited them, the former thinking scornfully of the hideous hag whom Gawayne had wedded, the latter pitying so young and gallant a knight, tied to a lady so ugly. But both scorn and pity vanished when all saw the bride. "Who is this fair dame?" asked Sir Kay. "Where have you left your ancient bride?" asked another, and all awaited the answer in great bewilderment. "This is the lady to whom I was wedded yester evening," replied Sir Gawayne. "She was under an evil enchantment, which has vanished now that she has come under the power of a husband, and henceforth my fair wife will be one of the most beauteous ladies of King Arthur's court. Further, my lord King Arthur, this fair lady has assured me that the churlish knight of Tarn Wathelan, her brother, was also under a spell, which is now broken, and he will be once more a courteous and gallant knight, and the ground on which his fortress stands will have henceforth no magic power to quell the courage of any knight alive. Dear liege and uncle, when I wedded yesterday the loathly lady I thought only of your happiness, and in that way I have won my own lifelong bliss."

King Arthur's joy at his nephew's fair hap was great, for he had grieved sorely over Gawayne's miserable fate, and Queen Guenever welcomed the fair maiden as warmly as she had the loathly lady, and the wedding feast was renewed with greater magnificence, as a fitting end to the Christmas festivities.

THE CARLE OF CARLISLE

Ron Tiner

Gawain features in another anonymous fourteenth century ballad romance, Syre Gawene and the Carle of Carlyle, *a tale which seems to have some connection with* Gawain and the Green Knight, *especially in the beheading motif. The original ballad was subsequently adapted as* The Carle of Carlile *in the sixteenth century by another forgotten poet. Both of these tales were incomplete and the episode is not widely known. It is sometimes referred to as* Carl of Carlisle, *as if the hero's name is Carl but, as the original title shows, it is about a lowly-born carl. The legend has been retold here by Ron Tiner (b. 1940) a comic-book artist with a penchant for fantasy illustration, and the co-author of* The Encyclopedia of Fantasy and Science Fiction Art Techniques *(1996).*

A dying sun reddened the winter sky as the lonely figure of Corlac the pedlar trudged wearily northwards. The rough, stony highway, bordered with leafless scrub and ragged woodland, stretched ahead of him, its surface criss-crossed with lengthening tree shadows.

The heavy box of wares strapped to his back was chafing the skin from his spine and the freezing cold bit into his meagre flesh. He slowed his pace a little and hoisted the box to ease his aching shoulders, then stopped to scan the bleak terrain on either side of the road for any sign of life. His spirits were sinking lower with the setting sun.

For a young man in the prime of his life, he cut a pathetic figure. His russet cloak was patchily faded, with tattered edges. His scarlet doublet was holed at the elbows, its front liberally besmeared with greasy foodstains. His brown leather trousers, little more than knee length, bore stains of another sort.

He swung the box to the ground and started to massage the tired muscles of his thighs as he contemplated the unattractive prospect of spending another night under the stars. It would be punctuated as always with the frequent need to rise and urinate. The landlord at the inn in the small town, four miles away over the hill behind him had been generous with his watery brew, and Corlac's weakness of bladder had made a couple of stops necessary already. Now he began unlacing his magenta codpiece – far too flamboyantly decorated to comply with the dictates of good taste – to answer nature's call once again. All his life he had borne this tiresome and embarrassing affliction.

He stood in the middle of the road, trying to ignore the biting cold, as the watery sounds broke the stillness. Above him, skeletal branches groped at the cold, still air. Black with impending night, the shadows crept across patches of tangled boscage and up the sinewy stems of cankerous, twisted trees. He shuddered.

The landlord's generosity had extended to an offer of a bed, which a more honest trader than Corlac would have accepted with alacrity, but knowledge of the unfortunate side-effects of some of the medicines and pills he had sold to regular customers of the place moved him to decline the offer, and to determine to be many miles away before morning.

Suddenly, through the bony branches, he saw the glint of a distant light. He quickly laced up and, lifting the box onto one shoulder, left the road to wade noisily into the brittle undergrowth beneath the trees. Gnarled boughs snagged at his cloak and thorny shrubs scratched his legs but he kept the pale glimmer in view and headed unerringly towards it.

The ground began to slope gently downwards, and eventually he found himself approaching a small lake, in the middle of which was an island, where the dark bulk of a great, stone castle loomed out of the gathering dusk. A paved causeway led from the forested shore, out over the water. Mounting this, he set off at a more confident pace.

Although the flags sagged and sloped at odd angles, the going was easier now; it was less noisy, too, and in the utter stillness of the forest behind him, he began to imagine some formless horror marshaling its forces. He tried to walk more quickly, but missed his footing in the deepening gloom and slipped on a sloping surface, to fall heavily to his knees.

He swore through clenched teeth. The sound of it split the freezing silence, and he looked nervously about as he rubbed his bruises. The black surface of the lake was utterly still. The darkness itself seemed to be closing in on him, threatening incalculable abominations. He rose and hobbled onto the wooden bridge that gave access to the island.

At last, he reached the foot of a ruined flight of steps, with its cracked and broken slabs slewed out of alignment and the tendrils of an unearthly climbing plant grasping octopuslike at the scattered pieces. Beyond it, the vast structure loomed, black and forbidding against the rapidly darkening sky, its eaves and cornices groaning with grotesque, weatherbeaten gargoyles.

Picking his way up the treacherous stair, he gained the massive portals and tugged at the bellrope, sending sonorous echoes moaning along endless corridors and up cavernous stairwells within.

Deep inside the bowels of the castle, the doleful sound died slowly away and the dark silence closed in again.

High above his head, a fierce mythical beast, carved from the stone of the building's very fabric, jutted from the wall, pocked and mutilated by the elements. Its blind granite eyes glared an impotent challenge to the world. On its jaw, a stalactite had started to grow like a ridiculous, calcite goatee, and upon this, a drop of icy water began to form. It glistened briefly, then dropped down, down through the accumulating darkness to land with a smack at Corlac's feet.

Muted sounds reached him of bolts being drawn and chains clinking. He stepped back and waited, tapping his foot rapidly as he ran through his mind the line of patter he would utilize. He would launch straight into his usual routine, he decided; a barrage of charm and enthusiasm to disarm and intrigue. That would be the right approach.

The huge door creaked ajar and the emaciated visage of an old man was thrust out. The top of his head was narrow and bald. The great, beaklike nose was hooked and gnarled like old bleached timber. Long, greasy locks hung like soft corkscrews over his hunched shoulders and down his back.

"Good evening, sir. Corlac the travelling merchant at your service. This could well be the luckiest day of your life, if I may say so. I bring with me today, sir, from exotic locations all over the civilised world, pills and medicines, elixirs and potions of an efficacy hitherto unknown in this kingdom. You look like a wise man, sir, if I may say so, able to recognise a remarkable opportunity if fate should chance to cast one in your path. And fate has seen fit to do just that today, sir."

The words tumbled out in a voluble stream. He had rehearsed and refined them in a thousand taverns and feasting halls over the preceding decade and a half of wanderings. He hardly listened to himself as he watched their effect and calculated how to make the best advantage of the situation. If he could inveigle his way beyond the door, the chances were good that he could stay the night and even get a breakfast before leaving in the morning.

"A discerning man such as your good self, sir, will know that such opportunities are rare in these parts, but I come to your door today sir, carrying in this specially constructed box, aromatic juices from the mysterious orient, sir; potent concoctions from the halls of the world's most learned alchemists; pills and medicines efficacious in the treatment of all the little ailments and malfunctions the human body is heir to, sir."

The few rotting stumps that remained anchored in the old man's jaws were clamped firmly together as his thin lips stretched in a travesty of a smile and his eyes glittered.

"I see you smile, sir, and well you might, if I may say so. Today is, sir, a fortunate one for you, sir. The stars portend a happy turning of the tide of events in your favour, sir. You may see my appearance at your door as the beginning of a brighter future for you, sir; a future in which all life's little ailments and irritations are eradicated."

He prattled on, but was disconcerted to perceive that his intended victim was evidently not listening to him. He just stared and smiled his gap-toothed smile, muttering:

"Just what I want! Just what I want! Ha ha!"

He grabbed Corlac by the front of his doublet with a horny hand.

"Bring him inside! Ha ha! Bring him in!"

The antique voice rose to a cackle as he pulled the pedlar over the threshold and kicked the door shut. They stood in a great, echoing hall, while the air about them reverberated with the booming sound of the closing door. Corlac's patter hardly faltered.

"And a beautiful domicile it is, if I may say so, sir. One of the finest I have seen in a lifetime of travels far and wide, through many strange and wonderful lands. You are evidently a man of taste and discernment, sir, I can see that, and I have in my specially constructed box here items of unique interest to one such as your good self, sir."

Still the ancient appraised him with an eager smile.

"Just what I need! Just when I need it! It's an omen!"

"Indeed it is, sir! An omen, sir. You said it! Took the words right out of my . . ."

"Give him a drink first. Drink . . ."

"Well thank you, sir! I call that most hospitable. You're a member of the quality class, sir. I knew that as soon as I clapped eyes . . . I mean . . . soon as you opened your door to me, sir. A real gentleman, I thought. Shows in every feature, if I may say so."

Clutching his sleeve, the scrawny figure scuttled across the hall and into a huge, vaulted study, dragging Corlac with him.

"Sit down, boy. I'll get you a goblet. Sit there, by the fire."

Corlac sat in the big, wooden armchair and stopped talking to survey his surroundings. The room was full of books; great leatherbound tomes, stacked in unsteady piles all round the walls, reaching at least three times the height of a man, so that the topmost volumes were lost in the gloom above. Smaller piles were stacked in front of them: little books in horizontal rows, on top of great, bulky grimoires with tattered spines and ragged edges. Bookmarks hung out of them like alien tongues with tattoos upon them. Metal studs and clasps glinted in the firelight and a smell of old leather pervaded the air. In front of the books was a scattering of odd scientific instruments: an astrolabe, a telescope of some kind and a great number of smaller objects he could not recognise. Among these, there were also a number of small cages, containing what appeared to be live rodents.

In one corner was a curtained alcove, and beside it hung a huge diagrammatic representation of a human body, its limbs and organs labelled with signs of the zodiac.

The old man shuffled over to him with a goblet of dark liquor. He was wearing a pair of grimy slippers which scuffed across the flagstones.

"Drink it down, boy," he said. "All of it."

He stood over him, rubbing his hands together in a greedy fashion as he surveyed Corlac's youthful frame.

"You're not a buck virgin, by any chance, are you, boy?" he asked.

"Um, well, not exactly, I'm afraid, sir. I've tried to keep myself pure, of course, resisting temptations of every variety . . ." The dark liquid in the goblet was remarkably good; it had a full-bodied, musky flavour. He opted to concentrate on that.

"No matter! It's not vital."

His host scuttled away to bring a flagon, from which he topped up the goblet to overflowing.

Corlac took several more long draughts of the dusky fluid and felt a welcome heat begin to course through his veins, sending warmth to the ends of his fingers and toes. He started to speak again but the dry, cracked voice cut across him.

"It is fortuitous that you should come to my door at this time. I find myself in need of a young man of your calibre just now. You will exactly suit my purpose."

"Prepared to turn my hand to anything for the right remuneration, sir," Corlac assured him. "What would you be needing, I wonder? I can read, sir. So I could help you organise that nice big pile of books you've got there. Or perhaps you're the victim of a painful ailment or condition. I carry a unique range of remedies for . . ."

But the old man paid no attention.

"Drink up. Drink up, boy," he said, approaching with the flagon once more and filling the goblet to its brim.

"Well, thank you, Sir. Right hospitable of you. If you could just leave that container beside me, I could . . ."

"I am Sarabana. No doubt you have heard of me."

"Well, sir, no. I'm afraid not. I'm a stranger in these parts, sir. Only here briefly as I pass through, bringing relief to suffering humanity. If you'd care to take a look at my unrivalled selection of . . ." He reached for his box.

"No need of that. I have potions here you've never even dreamed of, boy. But they are of no importance beside the main trend of my work."

Placing the flagon on the floor at his guest's feet, Sarabana went and sat on the other side of the fire. Leaning his elbows on the arms of his chair, and placing his fingertips together, he looked across at the pedlar and pursed his thin lips.

Corlac swigged more of the dark brew. He felt warm and relaxed.

"For many years," Sarabana continued, "I have sought, through necromancy, to determine the hidden truths of the netherworld. My researches have given me the key to that abode of demons and you, young sir, shall help me to gain mastery of it."

"Mmmm, certainly," Corlac slurred. For this nice man he would do almost anything. Unsteadily he refilled his goblet.

"This very night, you shall assist me to harvest the fruits of my labours."

A rat in one of the small cages on the floor, made a scuffling noise. The timbre of the old man's voice, which had at first had much in common with that of a complaining crow, seemed to be mellowing and becoming almost melodic to Corlac's increasingly inebriate mind. The internal warmth generated by the liquor had reached the tips of his ears. He glowed with goodwill towards this benevolent old gentleman. What a stroke of luck: a warm bed and a hearty breakfast were now a strong possibility, and he might even be able to slip something valuable into his pocket before leaving. Sarabana was still speaking.

". . . for I am the most powerful sorcerer in existence, and tonight you shall have the honour to act as an instrument in my greatest experiment. Tonight, I shall summon the beasts of Belial and force them to do my bidding!" His voice was taking on a fanatical pitch.

"No prol-bem . . . p-proddle-bem," Corlac assured him confidently.

The aged figure leapt to his feet and went over to the curtained alcove in the corner. He held the edge of the drapes and turned with a dramatic gesture.

"Behind this curtain lies the secret that will guarantee for me power beyond the dreams of the greatest magicians in the world." In his excitement, his voice rose to a demented scream. "Brought into reality from the dusty pages of myth! Men said it could not be done, but I, Sarabana, have created it!"

He flung the curtains aside.

"Behold . . . The mandrake vine!"

In a small patch of earth was revealed a tangle of strange plants, with stems like the naked, misshapen bodies of emaciated men and women, their limbs extruded into long, waving tentacles, intertwining and slowly writhing in the air. There was a sound like the distant screaming of souls in torment.

Corlac shuddered with horror. The goblet dropped from his grasp, ringing like a bell as it hit the flagstones and danced across the floor to crash against the bars of one of the small cages. He forced himself to his feet, but his legs were unsteady. His knees clunked bruisingly together and he fell down on all fours.

Sarabana continued in fanatical tones:

"By delving into the thaumaturgic lore of countless centuries ago, I discovered how it could best be used."

He grabbed the huge chart which showed a ludicrously mispro-
portioned diagram of the human body, with scorpions, lions, goats
and bulls attached to various parts.

"With the mandrake vine I can secure your body to the positive
signs shown on this astral chart, and you shall be the mortal bait
with which I will entice the denizens of hell to appear."

Keeping the old man in view, Corlac tried once more to stand
up. As he swayed to his feet, Sarabana came towards him.

"And this will be merely the beginning," he ranted. "With the
beasts in my power, I can invoke the favour of Astaroth, and then
Orias, and finally control the Legions of Bileth!"

He grabbed Corlac by the ears and shook him.

"With you and the vine, I can defy the powers of darkness and
win immortality!"

Corlac wrenched himself away and turned to run. But his legs
were useless. He fell headlong and his skull hit the stone floor with
a smack. A bilious fog of pain and nausea enveloped him.

Corlac might have been unconscious for hours or even days. He
came to slowly, to find himself in a smoky atmosphere, with
his limbs strangely paralyzed. He struggled to move them, but
gradually the realisation dawned on him that he was shackled.
He became aware that he was naked and tied to a diagonal cross,
propped upright in the centre of a vast hall. Around him, chalked
on the floor, was an enormous circle, divided into segments, each
segment having a zodiac sign marked in it, along with myriad other
symbols and hieroglyphics. Tied to various parts of his anatomy
were lengths of the strange vine, still writhing feebly. The outer
end of each tendril was pegged securely to a chalk-drawn symbol
at the edge of the circle.

His arms were tied to the twins of Gemini, his neck to the bull
of Taurus. His thighs were attached to the centaur of Sagittarius,
his feet to the fishes of Pisces. Most painful of all, his testicles
were encircled by a whiplike vine which tethered him to the sign
of Scorpio.

And his bladder was full to bursting point.

Around the outer circle stood four grotesquely moulded braziers,
in which burned some kind of incense which sent an aromatic smoke
curling and spiralling up into the darkness above.

In a clear area of the circle, away from the entangling vines, stood
Sarabana, dressed in a long robe of red silk, profusely decorated with
strange runes. He held an ornate sword aloft as he intoned ritualistic

incantations. On and on he droned, using words and sounds that held no meaning for the trembling pedlar.

At last he stopped, and holding the sword aloft in both hands, he shouted at the top of his voice:

"Spirits of Lucifer, monarch of burning hell, hear us!"

The hall was filled with a dreadful moaning sound and, in the darkness beyond the smoking braziers, obscure movements could be discerned.

"Take heed, ye devils! For there is one at your threshold who is great with wisdom and knowledge concerning your vasty deep domains; learned in the laws which govern your coming up and your going down."

The mournful sounds increased in intensity. Accompanying the doleful moaning and wailing, agonised howls and screams of despair echoed about the hall. Sarabana's high-pitched voice screamed above the cacophony:

"Within this circle are the characters of signs and erring stars by which the spirits are enforced to rise."

The shifting shapes in the darkness became more unruly.

"Anchored to them by the mystic mandrake vine is a tender morsel of humanity, whose chaste and virtuous flesh I hereby promise to you. While he remains thus secured ye may not have him, for the vine has untold powers."

Dismal sobs and roars shook the air.

"Pay obeisance to me and I shall unloose him and cast him among you, for I am Sarabana, master of the mystic sciences and doyen of the arts of sorcery. Therefore let the beasts of Belial appear and ascend to do us service.

"I do now command this in the mighty names of *Zasa Natas Zazatanada!*"

As the wizard uttered the terrible formula to open the gates of hell, wraithlike forms began to appear within the smoke of the braziers. A terrifying caterwauling filled the room. The writhing forms separated themselves from the smoke in a confusion of groping limbs, decaying flesh oozing and dripping from their bones. More and more of them spewed forth, each more grotesque and terrifying than the last, until a deformed and ghastly horde was cavorting tormentedly about the circle.

Trembling with revulsion and fear, Corlac lost control and the contents of his bladder gushed out in a steady stream.

"Dance, ye minions!" yelled Sarabana, exultantly. "Entertain your new master!"

The appalling creatures howled and squirmed about the circle, unable to cross its chalked circumference, their fetid bodies convulsed in agony and frustration, plunging and groping wildly.

Meanwhile, the evidence of Corlac's incontinence formed a meandering river and began making its slow way across the floor, towards the chalk lines.

The monstrous horde continued its wild tumultation. Rotting bodies, displaying every kind of sickening deformity, seethed in a frantic mass of gesticulating limbs.

"Sing, my creatures! Dance!" Sarabana's crazed falsetto could hardly be heard above the chaos.

"Grovel before me, you cringing filth!" he screamed.

He waved his arms exultantly, like a demented conductor of music. The insane commotion around him roistered on.

Unnoticed, the pale yellow liquid reached the edge of the protecting circle and paused as it met the thick belt of chalk. Dissolving the soft, white particles, it ate into the magician's fragile defensive line and then, bursting through, the caustic tide spread out in a wide arc.

Immediately, the shambling, capering beasts howled in mad triumph and scrambled through the widening gap, scampering eagerly towards Sarabana. The first to reach him tore off limbs and bit off chunks of flesh, uttering dreadful shrieks of victory. His screams of pain were lost in the cacophonous din.

The hellborn creatures ignored Corlac, avoiding all contact with the vines. They scurried past him carrying bloody pieces of the sorcerer, which they alternately waved aloft and attempted to devour. The raucous pandemonium continued as they fought among themselves for the last vestiges of Sarabana's body.

Finally, they scuttled away and leapt back into the billowing pillars of smoke. Now, all that could be heard was the scratching, scrabbling, frantic sounds of their departure.

Soon, the hellish apparitions were gone. A ragged red stain was all that remained to mark the place where the mage had stood. The smoke from the braziers resumed its lazy, upward spiral. Silence fell.

Corlac hung on his cross, paralyzed with fear. For a long, long time, nothing stirred.

Eventually, he realised he was still alive, though cold to the very marrow of his bones. The lengths of mandrake vine that held him to the cross, which had earlier seemed like living tendrils, now sagged limp and dead from his limbs and, by pulling and twisting his right hand, managed at last to wrench it free, although he tore the skin off his knuckles in doing so. Exhausted as he was, another hour had passed before he finally succeeded in liberating himself completely and then, on trembling legs, he stumbled out of the ruins of the circle and past the still smoking braziers. Placing his feet carefully he made his feeble way across the gore-spattered floor to one end of the great hall, where a staircase led upwards. Slowly, he climbed to the top, and shuffled along a corridor, passing rooms and alcoves fearfully. He walked like an old man, bent and shivering with cold, hugging himself and hunching his shoulders in a vain attempt to conserve what little warmth he could.

He came finally to the part of the castle he knew. In the book-lined room, the fire burned still. He found a long, woollen robe and went to sit, still shivering, close to the flames.

For many hours he sat, numb with shock, unable to collect his thoughts. The great piles of books loomed over him. The firelight flickered on their brown leather bindings, glinted on their dull metal clasps.

He began to look about him. The realization dawned upon him that this castle now lacked an owner. The massive building and all it contained could be his.

He went over to a table, on which lay one of the largest volumes, along with a heavy candlestick and an inkstand. He opened the book and read the title:

SPELLES AND MEASURES BY WHICH YE MAGE MAYE PERFORME WONDROUSE FEATES

He turned the pages at random, making little attempt to read, until one particularly apposite page heading caught his attention:

Howe ye Weaknesse of Bladder maye be Cured: now here was something that could be useful!

But then he hesitated. A weak bladder could prove an advantage sometimes. He decided to give the matter further consideration some other time.

It was not until several weeks later that Corlac returned to peruse again the large, bound volume of spells in the book-lined study. During this period, he had embarked upon a methodical exploration of his new home.

The castle's previous occupant had evidently spent most of his time in the study, for it was here that the finest furnishings were, and curtained off at one end, there was a large and very comfortable bed covered with animal skins. Just inside the great door through which Corlac had first entered, was a well with a serviceable windlass and

bucket, and on either side of the study, were store rooms, one of
which was evidently the buttery, in which were kept food, drink
and kindling. In the other, he found a vast collection of bottles
and jars and sacks containing all manner of strange ointments,
oils, potions and mysterious concoctions. These were all labelled
with unfamiliar names and symbols and he decided that he would
do well to leave them alone. There was also gold. Hoards of it in
big, iron-bound chests.

In a cupboard, he had found a stock of candles, each between
three and four feet long and four inches in diameter. He held them
against his shoulders like a halberdier on a route march, so that
the white columns rested next to his ears, casting a pool of light
around him from above the back of his head. On one occasion, he
actually set light to his hair in this way, but his main problem had
been the gobbets of wax which fell onto the stone floors behind
him. These formed a trail of splashes, upon which he invariably
trod on his return trip, slipping up and bruising his skinny rump
time and time again.

At first, he had approached every bend in a corridor, every arched
alcove and iron-studded door, with trepidation, expecting at any
moment to encounter a lost and straying remnant of the fiendish
horde that Sarabana had conjured up. But, as time passed and he
investigated more and more of the cavernous building, it became
evident that such dangers were unlikely. The rather less daunting
fear that he might meet some other resident of the place also proved
unfounded; the wizard, it seemed, had lived entirely alone.

It was also evident that the door by which Corlac had first
gained access to the antique pile was a modification to its original
plan, excavated through the ten-foot thick wall – with the aid of
something resembling a thunderbolt, if the blackened and melted
edges of the stones was anything to judge by – to allow the wizard
convenient access to the lake shore on that side.

On the other side of the keep, which constituted a banqueting
hall, living quarters and numerous other rooms of various sizes,
with the vast cellar beneath, in which the fateful ceremony had
been conducted, there was an extensive tiltyard, surrounded by
a curtain wall with defensive turrets. At the far end of this was
a massive gatehouse and a drawbridge that looked as though it
had not been used for a century or more. Ivy covered most of the
stonework but, all in all, it was a very commodious and desirable
piece of real estate, thank you very much.

The only other living thing in the place – the caged rats Corlac had seen in the study on that first night had died of starvation – was a gigantic warhorse, standing fully eighteen hands at the shoulder, which was housed in a stable block to one side of the yard. Its fierce eye and fearsome hooves, along with its aggressive ill-temper, kept him from approaching it, but its glossy, well-groomed black coat showed evidence of regular care in the recent past.

There were weapons in the stables too: lances, sword and shield, and a magnificent suit of armour, all polished and gleaming in the semi-darkness. His dreams of personal aggrandisement were crushed by the perception that they had clearly been crafted for a man considerably bigger and stronger than he.

In those few weeks, however, Corlac's slight figure had filled out considerably. The copious store of food in the buttery included bread, honey, cheese, and fruit and vegetables of every kind. And a barrel of very acceptable beer, along with another of red wine. Having no culinary skills he freshened the long loaves of bread by the simple expedient of soaking one of them in water each day and then placing it on a spit over the fire. He even tried fishing in the lake and caught a carp large enough to keep him full for two days.

But he soon became bored.

And sexually frustrated.

He dreamed of returning to the village inn he had visited before arriving at Sarabana's door, riding the great black stallion that snorted and kicked for hours every night in the stable. In his imagination he cut an impressive figure as he lifted the landlord's pretty daughter onto the pillion and cantered off into the sunset for an endless night of sweating passion.

This was what brought him back to the book of spells. He had searched in vain for a book on horse control, and now sat with a generous goblet of beer beside him, idly turning these king-size pages.

Howe ye Powre of Speatche maye be Givvn to Dumme Cretures.
He considered this for a moment but, remembering the look in the beast's eye, quaked at the thought of what it might want to say to him and quickly turned over.

Howe ye Mage maye Harness Lightenynge and Thunder.
He glumly turned more pages.

Howe a Golem maye be Created from Commonne Erthe.
Howe ye Mage maye Growe Featheres and Flie.
Nothing about controlling horses.

He went off to the primitive latrine to relieve himself, and came back determined to relocate the spell for the relief of incontinence. But the first page that he read on his return bore the heading: *Howe ye Mage maye Increese his Strengthe Tenfolde and Becumme Irresistabelle to Womenne.*

He had turned the page before the meaning of this had fully penetrated. Of course! He turned back. Why had it not occurred to him to seek out such a spell? Wizards must do this sort of thing all the time. He read on avidly, his old problem forgotten.

"*To wreake this powerfulle change, the whiche muste be performyd under ye nyte starres, ye mage muste firste concocte ye magickalle unguent callyd Catamalque. This Catamalque muste be kepyt pure at alle tymes and is made in this wyse:*"

There followed a long list of ingredients, many of which he had seen on the labels of jars in the wizard's storeroom. He read carefully through the instructions several times, then set about making preparations to perform the weird ceremony. He carried the spellbook with him into the storeroom and, scrupulously checking and rechecking each label, he selected jars and bottles of many different sizes and colours and placed them in a long row for convenient access. He was encouraged to find that every constituent of the miraculous concoction was, indeed, available to him from this single source. He studied every aspect of the mystic ritual with meticulous care.

Within two days he had dug a pit in the castle yard and carefully cut into the earth beside it a circle, containing a five-pointed star with strange runes and occult names in precise positions inside it. At each point of the pentagram, outlandish names were scored clearly into the ground: Eligor, Zepar, Saleos, Gomory and Dantalian.

He began to pour the mysterious ingredients into the pit as the sun set in a cloudless sky. Darkness fell and he worked on under the stars for hour after hour into the night, tossing aside each empty vessel and reaching for the next until every muscle in his tired body ached with the exertion. Late in the night, he poured out the contents of the last container, an enormous earthenware jar. He flung it away from him and stretched his aching back. The surface of the viscous, milky fluid heaved gently, reflecting the starlight.

He placed Sarabana's aged grimoire in the centre of the circle, stripped off his clothes and stood beside it with his back to the pool. With legs astride and arms akimbo, he began reading the incantation.

"Salom arepo lemel opera molas," he intoned. The echo of

his voice sounded embarrassed as it came feebly back from the surrounding walls.

"I, Corlac of Polsloe, do call, exorcise, conjure and invoke the services of the spirits named on this pentacle, to aid me at my pleasure and behest. I conjure in the mighty names of the giants Gog and Magog that the animus of the spirit Zepar do appear in this place without tarrying, without noise, deformity or murmuring, and cause me to become strong and irresistible to women. Come hither and accomplish my will and desire to be handsome and virile and hung like a stallion.

"Eme, lemel, olemelo. Arepo lemel opera. Salom arepo lemel opera molas."

Suddenly, there appeared in front of him a giant warrior dressed in red. His features were red, too, and his crimson eyes glowed with a brilliant fire. He smote Corlac a terrific blow in the chest and sent him sprawling backwards with an enormous splash into the bath of catamalque. With a squawk of panic, Corlac sank beneath the surface and blacked out.

He came slowly to his senses.

He was lying on his back and the brightness of approaching day was creeping across the sky above him as the sun rose over the horizon. The catamalque had all gone.

He became aware of an unaccustomed vitality within his belly and gradually a new muscular tension spread into his limbs. A stupendous surge of raw power began to flood through him. He got to his knees in the centre of the now dry pit, and threw his arms wide. With his fists clenched, he let out a roar of exultation to the heavens, then jumped to his feet and ran round the yard shouting his new found strength aloud. It reverberated back energetically from the ivy-covered walls.

The neighing and kicking of the great black stallion came to his ears. He rushed into the stable, flinging back the doors with a crash. The horse, sensing the unfamiliar brute force seething inside him, stood looking at him uncertainly. Corlac leapt onto its back and rode it forcefully out into the night, yelling and howling with delight. Round and round the yard they sped, kicking up great sods as they charged on in a wave of unbounded energy that man and beast now shared.

They galloped up the castle steps and along the corridor to the banqueting hall. The clash of iron-shod hooves on the stone floor was deafening in the confined space. He rode the animal round the hall and into the book-lined study. Swinging his leg over its neck, he dropped to the floor and gave it a hearty smack on the rump that sent it careering off again through the hall and away outside. Panting from the exertion, Corlac stood listening as the resounding echoes of its departing footfalls died away. He looked about the room. Lit now only by firelight, the tall piles of books loomed over him. He caught sight of his reflected image in a polished brass shield beside the now empty curtained alcove that had once nurtured the dreadful mandrake vine. He lit a candle and regarded his new self. The changes in his appearance were subtle ones. His chin was a little more firmly shaped. His cheekbones were a shade more prominent, his hair thicker and more lustrous. His eyes shone with an energetic fire and the musculature of his body had gained definition.

He began to sing a filthy ditty and to dance a jig that quickly developed into a raucous exhibition of lusty vigour. He threw himself about, barging his shoulder against the leathern walls and rebounding away to fall to the floor, laughing exuberantly.

Unnoticed, the clumsy stacks teetered.

Drunk with exultation, Corlac continued his dancing and singing. But, high above his head, a fateful sequence of events had been set in motion. Bulky volumes of ancient science swayed gently atop huge illuminated demonolatories. Ungodly tracts and songbooks, nestling in horizontal lines, shifted infinitesimally. A *Principia Discordia* of Melaclipse the younger scuffed quietly against a *Pseudomonarchia Demonum* of Abdul Alhazred and knocked askew an *Apocalypse* of Magius.

For the first time in many decades, there was movement among the books.

A tiny lexicon of necromancy, that had rested undisturbed on the sloping back cover of a mouldering grimoire for more than half a century, slid slowly down the incline, bulldozing a little pile of dust before it. It bumped into *The Book of Eibon*, which in turn fell against the *Necronomicon* and nudged *Magapolisomancy*. A landslide was beginning like the slowly increasing rumble of an earthquake.

Far below, the nude figure of Corlac whooped and cavorted, oblivious to the ominous sounds.

The towering piles of books sagged against one another and tipped inexorably forward. The first to fall was a hefty bound text on astrology. It bounced on his head, knocking him to the floor as its spine split with a loud crack and its pages slewed out in a wide arc. It was quickly followed by an increasing shower of leatherbound tomes. The shower became a storm and the storm an avalanche as missals, grimoires, folios and massive unholy books crashed downwards. Dust obscured the scene in great grey clouds. Corlac was buried under layer upon layer of learned writings as the crashing, tumbling bombardment continued to rain down on him.

Gradually, the bruising downpour ceased. The dust settled. The noise died to a murmur that wafted back and forth in the castle's cavernous depths. The room was quiet, and was lit now by a shaft of sunlight through a high window that had been hidden by the books.

Suddenly, with a roar of laughter, Corlac burst upwards like a whale coming up for breath, scattering the topmost books in all directions. He extricated himself from the great mound of leather and parchment and was about to begin his capers again when he stopped and stared in astonishment.

High above the floor, in the stone wall that had been hidden by the books, he could discern the pale shape of a woman. She appeared to be trapped inside a thick block of greenish glass.

He improvised a ladder of the biggest books and climbed up to look more closely. There, within a rectangle of glass set in the wall, was a naked young woman. Her black tresses and the black triangle of her pubic hair stood out in stark contrast to the deathly white of her flesh. Absolutely immobile, her pleading eyes and open mouth communicated a mute appeal against her imprisonment. Her hands, with fingers spread wide, were reaching out in supplication.

Corlac tried to communicate with the young woman by calling out and signalling through the thick glass, but was unable to discern whether she was dead, or alive and in some magically induced trance. Nor could he be sure if she was encased in a solid block of glass or whether he was seeing her through a substantial transparent barrier. He held up a candle and peered in. Had it not been for the jet black of her hair, she might have been merely a remarkably skilful, white marble sculpture. Her lips, her eyes, the inside of her lovely open mouth, every other inch of her was the colour of virgin snow. He rapped on the glass but she showed no sign of life. She remained utterly still in that pitiful imploring stance.

He jumped down and went to the fire where an iron poker leant against the hearth. Clambering up again to his unsteady perch, he began scraping at the stones around the glass. There was no doubt that, at some time in the past, great heat had been applied to them which had almost fused the blocks together. But his newly acquired physical strength slowly prevailed and eventually he was able to get a finger hold on the edges of the glass.

Fifteen feet above the floor as he was, his position was precarious. He braced his feet against the wall and heaved. There was a deep rasping sound as it shifted against its granite setting. He heaved again, straining with all his might. A two foot thick block of glass slid free from the wall, and Corlac took it with him as he plummeted down onto his back on the jumbled bed of books.

Jolted but still miraculously unhurt, he lay there awed by the transformation that now took place within the rectangular niche that had been revealed. The girl staggered against the side of her tiny prison and fell to her knees, almost falling headlong out of the opening in the process. As she peered down at the sprawled naked figure of Corlac, still holding the glass block, colour began to spread over her body. Her eyes gradually turned from deathly white to a deep orange-brown. Her lips and the large circular areas around her nipples became a warm pink and her flesh took on an almost golden hue as it was suffused with warmth and life.

They gazed at one another in silence. The young woman bent forward and placed her small hands on the lip of the precipitous drop, her eyes wide and her mouth forming a small "O" of surprise. Spread-eagled as he was, Corlac was aware that the sight of her ample breasts with their large areolae was causing his penis to shift and stiffen.

He was tempted to wag it at her with a bawdy compliment on the size of her bosom but, with remarkable sensitivity, judged this inappropriate and forbore. It was she who broke the silence.

"Thou hast rescued me." Her voice had a melodic sweetness which was subtly enhanced by the slight echo in that lofty room. He made a modest dismissive gesture.

"Oh, you're welcome, lady. Glad to be of service."

With uncharacteristic delicacy, he tried to cover his rising manhood with the great block of glass he still held in his hands, unaware that it had the effect of magnifying it to enormous proportions from the lady's point of view.

"I should like to come down," she said.

"Ah! Yes, right." He put aside the glass and scrambled up the makeshift staircase. He lifted her without effort; she seemed almost weightless in his newly fortified arms. He brought her to the floor and they stood facing each other, smiling. She discreetly avoided looking directly at his evident state of arousal, but allowed a pink flush to warm her cheeks in its honour.

"Though I perceive that thou art but a lowborn carle, yet the comeliness of thy face and form speak strongly to my heart. What is thy name?"

He drew breath to launch into his old introductory patter, but only said quietly:

"Corlac."

"I owe thee my whole life, Corlac the carle."

"You're welcome," said Corlac again. "Who . . .?"

"I am Mariana," she said in a soft, trembling voice.

"How long . . . ?" This strange naked encounter seemed to have robbed Corlac of his usual loquacity.

"I know not how long I have been incarcerated up there." The question evidently caused her some distress, for her voice was tinged with fear, and Corlac reached out to comfort her. With his hands gently touching her shoulders, they stood silently regarding each other. "Does Vortigern still wear the crown of England?" she asked.

"Vortigern? He's been dead eighty years or more!" Corlac replied in astonishment.

She stared at him with terror in her eyes. Corlac stared back, his heart thumping.

"You knew the world before my father was born!" he said.

"Yet have I lived in it only twenty years," she responded in a frightened voice. "Did . . . did Vortigern die as Ambrosius Merlin predicted?"

"They say he was burned to death in his tower by the sons of Constantine."

"So! It all came to pass, then. And what became of Merlin? Doth he still live?"

"We don't hear much of Merlin these days. They do say that, in his old age he allowed the witch, Vivian, to enthrall him and imprison him under the earth. Uther Pendragon held the crown by his aid, and now great Arthur is king of all England."

He ran his hands softly up and down her arms as she stood wide-eyed before him, silently fighting down her panic. Then he draped Sarabana's woollen cloak around her and drew her tenderly to him. Cradling her head on his chest, he caressed and comforted her.

The gentle physical contact gradually quietened her fear. He brought bread, honey, fruit and wine and they sat close together on the bed, eating and talking quietly. He told her the startling sequence of events that had brought him into possession of the castle and heard how, so long ago now, Mariana had refused to submit to the advances of the wizard after he had used his powers to kill her husband and take possession of their castle. Not interested enough to use enchantment to get her, he had simply sealed her up as an ornamental addition to the decor.

As they talked in soft voices, a comfortable intimacy slowly developed. In the shaft of warm sunshine that came through the window to fall upon their naked bodies, tiny dustmotes hovered. Gradually a tense sexual electricity began to charge the air between them.

Their lips brushed together, then kissed. They sank down into the furs, arms and legs embracing and caressing as time and place faded and were forgotten. As he entered her and was engulfed in the warm, moist sweetness of her body, he was filled with a tremendous sense of elation.

Their two bodies writhed and interlinked and writhed again in a rhythmic, ever changing pattern. Their limbs alternately held and caressed each other, overcome by surging waves of intense emotion.

Many hours of frenzied, passionate lovemaking, interspersed with quiet periods of soft conversation, left Corlac lying on his back with the girl, Mariana, sleeping peacefully beside him.

He left her there to go and sluice himself in cold water from the well. He poured an icy bucketful over himself, but it seemed to burn him and he quickly dried himself off again.

Thinking no more of this, he returned to bed to lie ruminating upon the astonishing series of events that, in a few short weeks, had transformed him from a scrawny, penurious pedlar to this happy state of having everything he could ever have wished for.

But he had just received a sign that his destiny was about to take another fateful turn.

In the idyllic weeks that followed, Mariana became increasingly certain that she was pregnant. The deep contentment that ensued from this development overcame her horror regarding the terrifying length of time she had spent frozen in the wall.

But as the weeks stretched into months, and her glowingly healthy body swelled with new life, as she introduced into the castle homely feminine comforts such as carpets and furnishings, and she brought in dozens of servant families that filled the place with a lively, bustling community, Corlac became more and more certain that something had gone wrong in the magical spell he had used on himself.

The painful effects of water on his body increased in severity. He searched through the great mass of ruined books, trying to find Sarabana's book of spells. When he finally located it, he read again the awful words:

"*This catamalque muste be kepyt pure at alle tymes . . .*" and the conviction grew that he might have inadvertently piddled in the magic liquor and contaminated it.

He began to get bigger. At first his height had increased by no more than an inch or so, but as week succeeded week, he passed six feet and grew nearer to seven. The touch of water on his skin became more and more painful so that he started to avoid it altogether.

He was seven feet tall when his daughter was born and he had taken to scraping the dirt from his limbs, being now quite unable to wash. His skin became coarser and began to show signs of cracks and fissures. His fingers looked like substantial sticks of wood and the skin all over his body began to resemble the bark of a tree.

And dirt and grime clung to him.

He searched the spellbook for a solution, but what he found offered him little comfort, and he felt he could expect no happy outcome to his predicament:

"*Ye mage maye be releasyd from this powerfulle spelle in only one wyse, and it is this. Ye mage shalle fynde a knyght of noble birthe that cannot be defeatyd in battaille and shalle gyve him leeve to lie with ye womanne that is closeste to his hearte. Whenne this is accomplishyd, that noble knyght must smyte off ye head of ye mage, at whyche tyme, ye mage shalle be releasyd and shall be as before.*"

They christened their daughter Eleanor, and as she grew up, Corlac's heart swelled with love for the child. Uniting as she did, her mother's beauty and the vulnerable delicacy of childhood, she became the object of unselfish emotions which he could never have conceived of before.

But his increasingly frightful appearance caused many of the servant families to refuse to stay at the castle. Rumours of his humble origins were whispered among the surrounding villages with the result that he became known as "the carle" and the island on which he lived as Carleisle.

Year by year, he grew more hideous, yet Mariana continued to show towards him the same gentleness she had expressed on their first meeting. Often, he would observe the sorrow in her eyes when she looked at him, as though she could still glimpse the man he once was, within the body of this gruesome giant, and it gave him hope

In a ceaseless effort to reverse the enchantment, he issued a challenge for any noble knight to come and try to defeat him in mortal combat. Many came over the years, but the spell which held him imprisoned in that dreadful body was a powerful one, and he defeated them all.

Meanwhile little Eleanor grew into beautiful womanhood. Corlac, unable now to get near her, so grotesque and repulsive had he become, watched over her with a breaking heart.

One evening in early autumn, as the few remaining servants prepared the table for the evening meal, the gatekeeper entered the hall to announce the arrival of three men at the castle gate.

Many years had passed since the weaving of the spell, and Corlac was now a terrifying sight. He had grown to a prodigious size, and sat with his back against the wall, the upper regions of his gross and repulsive body looming up into the semi-darkness under the roof. Up there in the gloom, his face, such as it still was, was almost lost in a wilderness of coarse hair and beard. His clothing consisted of swathes of tapestry, bound about his limbs and torso like bandages. His hands rested upon the arms of his enormous throne; their fingers resembled old wooden stakes, weathered and cracked. A sizeable spear was leaning against his thigh, and at his belt, hung a massive sword.

He sat as still as stone.

The gatekeeper dropped to his knees in the doorway, not daring to look at him. His affrighted voice quavered up into the vast emptiness of the hall. Corlac's response sounded like the deep, sonorous growl of distant thunder.

"Who are they?"

"Two noble knights of the Round Table and a bishop, my lord," the timid utterance seemed to hang apologetically in the air.

"Let them be welcome."

The first to enter was a brawny middle-aged man of above average height. He blanched at the awesome sight of Corlac, lurking in the gloomy shadows at the end of the hall like an ancient oak. The retainer began to announce him in apprehensive tones.

"The Lord Kaye, knight of the Round . . ."

With an obvious effort, Sir Kaye regained his swaggering

composure and buffeted the wretch aside. He fell to the floor and stayed there.

"We are noble knights of the court of King Arthur. Tell your servants to bring your finest meat and drink; though what kind of muck you eat in these parts I dread to imagine."

The giant lifted his spear, and swung it with remarkable speed to hit his visitor a blow on the legs that sent him hurtling across the hall.

"While you are a guest in my house, you will keep a civil tongue in your head."

Kaye staggered to his feet and pointed an impotent threatening finger.

"I shall make you pay dearly for that one day," he shouted. "You would not have dared to do it if you weren't surrounded by your men." He avoided looking at the pathetic retinue that cringed about the table.

In response, Corlac neither moved nor spoke. This stupid braggart could be killed later, along with his two companions. He had long ago given up hope of encountering any human individual who could fulfil the criteria necessary to enable the enchantment to be lifted.

From his position on the floor, the gatekeeper announced:

"The Lord Bodwyne, Bishop of the holy church of Jesus Christ our saviour."

The plump, rosy cheeks and corpulent figure of the clergyman attested eloquently to the many years of good living he had enjoyed as a result of his profession. On seeing the welcome that Kaye had received, he decided to remain discreetly near the doorway.

Then the last of three walked in. He was a young man of above average height, but not heavily built. Showing no sign of surprise at the sight which confronted him, he bowed as he was introduced.

"The Lord Gawaine, knight of the Round Table."

"Carle of Carleisle," said Gawaine with practised civility, "We have become lost in our hunting and would ask a share of your board and a shelter for the night."

Corlac placed his hands on his knees and leaned forward. His baleful eyes glittered with interest. There was something about this young man that seemed unassailable: he recognized in him the rare quality of total fearlessness. Was it just possible that here was a knight who could not be defeated? He stood and the sound of his movement was reminiscent of the creaking of the branches of a great tree. Flakes and crumbs of dirt fell from him.

He hefted the spear in his hand, and with sudden dreadful ferocity, flung it at Gawaine.

The young man jumped aside and it sank point-deep in the door of the buttery. Gawaine ran across to tear it free. In doing so he had to place his foot against the door and work it up and down to loosen it. Corlac roared forth a rumbling travesty of a laugh and bellowed:

"Go on, boy! Bury that spear in the middle of my face."

Gawaine ran three steps forward and threw it with all his strength, but the giant avoided it with ease. It hit the wall with a ringing crash which reverberated deafeningly around the hall and sent out a shower of sparks briefly lighting up the dreadful face. The bone-shuddering sound of Corlac's mirth echoed round the hall.

"Bring food and wine. And call my wife to make music for our guests."

A quiet and somewhat uneasy feast began which grew more relaxed as the fine red wine began to have its effect on their spirits. Mariana played on a harp and sang love songs and ballads of long ago, and Eleanor, their daughter, sat beside Gawaine. Shyly at first, but more animatedly as their talk grew more intimate, the two conversed together, ignoring the rest of the company.

They all became merry, but not one of them noticed the meaningful glances that Corlac exchanged from time to time with his beautiful wife. Still less did they see the look of deep sorrow in her eyes as she glanced at him and quietly left the hall late in the evening, taking her daughter with her.

Not long after this, the combined effects of a long day's hunting and a full belly saw Kaye snoring loudly at one end of the table and the fat cleric drowsing off in his chair. Gawaine rose to his feet and addressed Corlac with the same unaffected courtesy as before.

"May God reward you for your generosity, Carle of Carleisle. I should like to lie down on that straw over there for the remainder of the night, if you will allow me."

With a heavy heart, Corlac now rose from his throne. The dreadful inevitability of the next step in the arcane ritual had prevented him from participating in the evening's merriment. His movements were surprisingly fluid, in spite of the creaking and groaning of his joints, as he walked forward and bent down to take Gawaine by the hand. Within the sonorous rumble of his voice was a note of despair.

"Come," he said, simply.

He led the young man to his wife's bed and pulled wide the

sheets. Through the window, a full moon shone its silver light on Mariana's naked body.

"Noble knight, you will do me a service far greater than you could ever know, if you will, as I stand by, lie with this lady and kiss her." The tear that started down his face burned like a descending trickle of fire. He stepped back in the darkness to witness his humiliation. Mariana lay on her back, looking up at him sadly.

Gawaine took off his clothes and lay on the bed.

Gritting his great teeth in anguish, Corlac watched as the two pale bodies moved closer. The gentle sound of kissing seemed to cut like a rusty dagger into his belly. In the cold moonlight he saw Gawaine becoming aroused and caressing his wife's lovely breasts. She lay still on her back, looking up at him.

Suddenly, Corlac raised his sword and let out an almighty roar.

"No-oooooooo!" The doleful, agonized protest echoed mournfully through the castle. As the couple parted in horror at the sound, he thrust the shining blade vertically down between their two bodies, almost severing Gawaine from his manhood.

Corlac swept him up and carried him by one arm and one leg, away down the corridor to his daughter's bedchamber.

She sat up with a startled cry as they entered.

"Eleanor, my dearest daughter," he said, his deep, ponderous voice softened with emotion. But words failed him. How could he tell her of the incredible revelation that had just occurred to him?

"Be soft for this young man," he said. "Sleep now both of you with my blessing." And he left them alone.

Would every father understand the turmoil of emotion in which Corlac returned to his nightly place on the great throne in the hall? Trapped as he was in this grotesque giant's body, his contact with the world outside himself seemed somehow tenuous and distant, but his inner world of emotion seemed to envelop him completely. Did he love his wife now less than he loved his daughter? No, she was the source of all his longing. But while she was yet so young, so vulnerable, so recently a child, Eleanor was closest to his heart.

The following morning, he returned to the bedchamber and led them both out into the courtyard, where everyone was assembled.

"Today," he said, "you will see something to wonder at. Perhaps it will be a marvel so great that you can not now imagine it. Perhaps it will be merely the end of a mortal tragedy."

He turned to Gawaine and held out his sword.

"Take this and strike off my head."

"Are you so weary of living this mortal life in that dreadful shape?"

"Yes," said Corlac, "I am. Strike." And he lay down on his belly.

Gawaine raised the sword high and brought the blade down with all his strength on the giant's neck.

There was no blood. The head was lopped off like the hollow bough of a dead tree. Immediately, the rest of the body began to fall apart as Corlac the pedlar stood up and climbed out of the ruined hulk. The onlookers gaped at the astounding spectacle. Mariana stepped forward and threw a cloak around his shoulders and led him away into the castle. The assembled company broke into a noisy chatter. The timid doorkeeper began to dance a jig. Middle-aged women fainted away. Many just sat down and tried to recover their composure.

That evening a magnificent feast was prepared. Corlac, having sat for several hours in a bath, with servants running back and forth bringing warm water, which his wife poured over him in an almost continuous stream, was now wearing rich, clean clothing for the first time in many years. But later, as he and Mariana sat, quietly regarding the scene, he found it necessary to make his apologies and leave the hall to go and relieve himself. His old ailment was back.

Returning later wearing new breeches, he sought out Bishop Bodwyne.

"I have heard it said that some of you men of the cloth learn the sciences of healing and medicine. Do you have knowledge of these sciences?"

"I do," replied the bishop.

"Ah, good," said Corlac. "I wonder if you could help me. I've got this embarrassing little problem . . ."

SIR LANVAL

A. R. Hope Moncrieff

Ascott Robert Hope Moncrieff (1846–1927) – what a wonderful name – was better known under his alias Ascott R. Hope, which he used on dozens of boys' books from 1865 to his death. Moncrieff was an Edinburgh schoolmaster, who turned to full-time writing in 1868. Apart from his boys' fiction he was an expert on American history. He was also entranced by medieval legend and romance. He brought the fruits of those studies together in a volume Romance and Legend of Chivalry *(1913) which contained both a study of the development of medieval romance and a collection of legends which Moncrieff had revised for publication. The story of Sir Lanval came from the twelfth century lays of Marie de France, where he seems to have been the prototype of Sir Lancelot.*

At King Arthur's court was a knight of foreign birth, by name Sir Lanval, who, even among that famed brotherhood of the Round Table, excelled in knightly graces and virtues. Sir Lancelot, Sir Percival, Sir Gawayne, the bravest of his companions in battle and the wisest in council, knew well the worth of this stranger, and were proud to call him friend; and, when his name was spoken, the bitter Sir Kay himself forbore to sneer. By the poor, as well as by his own attendants, he was much beloved, for his kindness and generosity were unbounded, and he gave freely to all in need, so that his purse would have been always empty but for the rich rewards which the king was wont to bestow on those who served him faithfully.

Thus all went well with him till Arthur wedded the false and fair Guinevere. Henceforth Lanval had one enemy at the court, and that an all-powerful one. Once the new queen had loved this knight, but when she found her love unreturned, it changed to bitter hatred, and she set her mind on working his ruin.

It is an old tale, how the greatest heroes have shown themselves weak to the wiles of a woman. The noble Arthur too easily listened to and too blindly confided in his unworthy wife. She soon took occasion to poison his mind by false charges against Lanval, so that the king began to look coldly on his good knight; nor was it long before Lanval felt the ill effects of this disfavour. When, after a successful war, distribution was made of honours and rewards, he alone found himself passed over, though none had less deserved to be thus slighted.

Right well knew he to whom he owed such neglect, but he was too loyal to let any word pass his lips that might assail the name of his master's queen. Patiently he bore himself under the king's displeasure, and made no complaint of the troubles which soon came upon him. His liberality had always kept him poor, and now that the just recompense of his services was withheld, he found himself falling into arrant want. No longer could he indulge his disposition by feeding the hungry and clothing the naked. It began to be a question with him how he might maintain himself and his household.

He lodged in the house of a burgher, who, now that he was without money, seemed to grudge him entertainment. Pride drove him to conceal his poverty, and he was fain to keep his chamber day and night. He could no more appear at tournaments in gallant array; his friends ceased to invite him to feasts; he could not even go to church for want of decent clothes. One by one, he had parted with his servants, his chargers, his equipments, till at last there was nothing left him but an old baggage horse, a torn saddle, and a rusty bridle. For three days he had not tasted meat or drink. Having come to this, he saw nothing for it but to leave the court of Arthur, and seek his fortune elsewhere.

So one day, while his brother knights were holding high festival at the castle, he mounted his sorry steed, and rode forth in such a plight that the people he met hooted and laughed as he urged on the stumbling beast, dreading to be seen by any who had known him in the days of his prosperity. Having thus stealthily left the town, he hid himself in the nearest wood, then rode through it till he came to a rich plain, across which ran a clear sparkling river. Here the unfortunate knight dismounted, to let his horse feed at will, and, wrapping himself in his tattered cloak, lay down beneath the wide branches of an oak that overshadowed the stream.

But now, when he would have given himself up to his sorrowful thoughts, he raised his eyes for a moment from the ground, and was aware of two damsels advancing towards him on the shady bank. As they drew near, and he stood up to salute them, he saw that they were strangely fair and richly attired. The one bore a gold basin, the other a silk napkin, with which they came to Lanval and offered to serve him, saying:

"Speed thee, Sir Knight! Our lady greets thee, and prays thee, if it be thy will, to speak with her."

"Lead me whither ye please," answered Lanval courteously. "Whichever way ye go, there I gladly follow, for never saw I fairer damsels."

"Nay, but you have yet to see our mistress," said they, smiling, and forthwith led him to a blooming meadow, where was set a magnificent pavilion covered with rich hangings and ornaments of gold and dazzling jewels, such as no queen on earth could call her own.

Within, all was alike costly and bright, but Sir Lanval had eyes only for the mistress of the place, a lady pure as the lilies of May and sweet as the roses of June, with hair shining like threads of gold, and eyes of enchanting radiance. At the first glance this marvellous beauty made all charms he had ever beheld or dreamed of seem as naught. And when she rose to give him friendly welcome, the knight felt that his heart had already gone into slavery after his eyes; he could love no other woman in the world, now that he had once seen this image of perfect loveliness.

"Gentle sir," she began in tones that thrilled him with delight, "think not that you are a stranger to me. I have long seen your worth, and now I have sent for you to ask if you may deem me worthy of your love."

"Oh, lady, command me in all things!" faltered the knight, scarce able to believe his senses. "What more might man hope than to serve such a peerless dame? But I am poor – friendless – despised."

"I know all," said the lady. "But so you will freely and truly give me your heart, I can make you richer than any emperor, for I have wealth at will, and nothing shall be wanting to him who is my knight."

For answer, Sir Lanval could only throw himself speechless at her feet. Need she ask if he loved her? She gave him her hand and made him sit down by her side, all ragged and rusty as he was; then short time served for his misery to be lost in a happiness too great for words.

The two damsels now appeared, covering a table with exquisite viands, of which neither the half-starved knight nor his fair hostess cared to eat. Long and lovingly they held converse together, and the hours flew by like minutes. Fain would Lanval have lingered in that charmed spot for ever, if the lady herself had not bid him return to Arthur's court, where she promised he should have means of putting to shame all who had scorned him.

At parting she gave him noble gifts – a suit of white armour such as the most cunning smith might have been proud to claim for his handiwork; a curiously worked purse which, she told him, he would always find full of gold, let him spend as he pleased; and, best of all, the assurance that he should see her again.

"One thing only I require of you," was her last word, "that you take heed not to boast of my love. Call me when and where you please, so it be in some secret place, and I will come; but you must never speak of me to mortal ears, on pain of seeing me no more on earth."

Sir Lanval kissed her hand, and vowed by his knighthood that her wishes should be obeyed. Then they took tender leave, promising each other that it was not for long.

Without, a gallant white charger was awaiting the knight, and bore him like the wind to his lodging in the town. There sumptuous furniture and apparel now abounded where he had left bareness and signs of poverty. At the door he was met by a retinue of servants, well provided with new liveries and everything needful for a wealthy household. Astonished, he perceived that he had to do with a queen of fairyland. And when he opened her purse, he found that it verily held an endless supply of gold. The more he took out, the less it ever seemed to be empty.

Lanval rejoiced that he was now able to place no stint on his open-handedness. He hastened to search out all who might be in want or distress, and abundantly relieved them. He feasted the poor; he gave alms to pilgrims; he ransomed prisoners; he became the bountiful patron of minstrels; he heaped rich gifts on his friends and rewards on his followers. Once more his name was everywhere spoken with gratitude and affection, and he held his head high among his fellows at the court. The white armour that had been given him was enchanted against every weapon; so, mounted on his matchless courser, he still overthrew all comers in tourney or battle. But his greatest joy was in seeing his fairy princess; for as often as he repaired to a solitary spot, and called upon her, she would appear, to bestow on him a wealth of bright glances and sweet words that could have made the most wretched of men forget his woes.

One alone grudged the young knight's good fortune. This was the queen, who had brought him to such a point of poverty that he might be fain to sue humbly for her favour. She was sore at heart to see him more and more generous and beloved; and she cast about for new means of venting her ill will upon him.

On the feast of St. John the knights and ladies had gathered to sport and dance in a meadow, whither came also the queen with her maidens. And when she saw that Sir Lanval joined not in the diversions of the others but walked apart, thinking ever of his mistress, she turned aside to him and spoke scornfully, saying that he was not fit to be in the king's service, since he loved no woman, and no woman found him worthy of her love. At this the knight's pride took fire; forgetting the command that had been laid upon him, as well as the reverence due to the queen, he cried:

"Nay, madam; for know that I am beloved by the most beautiful lady in the world!"

"Who dares speak to my face of one more fair than me?" exclaimed the queen with kindling eyes.

"Aye, the least of her maidens is fairer than you," answered Lanval hotly; but, as he spoke, his spotless white armour turned black as coal, and he remembered with dismay how the fairy had bid him tell of her to no mortal ears.

And these words filled up the cup of Guinevere's hatred. Furiously she broke away from him and hurried to her chamber, where she shut herself, weeping for shame and rage, till Arthur returned from hunting; then she presented herself before him with red eyes and dishevelled hair, making loud complaint of the insult she had received that day, and demanding that a heavy punishment should be dealt out to the presumptuous knight who had so set at naught his duty and her charms. And other false and shameful things she laid to his charge, trying to provoke her husband's utmost vengeance. Nor was Arthur unmoved by the dishonour done to his queen. Wrathfully he bid four of his sergeants seek out Sir Lanval, and bring him to answer for what he had said.

Little did Lanval heed this displeasure; a heavier misfortune had fallen upon him, beside which the king's displeasure seemed but a light matter. When Guinevere left him, what would he not have given to recall his rash words? But nothing had he now to give. No sooner had he disobeyed the commands of his mistress than all her gifts melted away like snow. His magic purse was empty; he found his lodging bare as before; his servants had disappeared. He hurried to the wood where they had been wont to meet, and loudly and often called upon the fairy, but only the echoes mocked him. She came not; the charm was broken, and his love was lost for ever.

Bitterly he reproached himself and cursed his folly, but little could this avail him now. Beating his breast and tearing his hair, he fell on the ground as in a swoon, and thus Arthur's officers found him.

"Thou traitor," said the king, when Lanval was brought bound into his presence, "how hast thou stained thy loyalty! What boasts be these that thy mistress is fairer than my queen? Speak and justify thyself, if thou wouldst not be hanged like a thief."

But Sir Lanval's eye quailed not, as he bent before the king and spoke: "My lord, so have I said, and what I have said is true, though I should die for it."

"Now, falsely hast thou spoken, and sorely shalt rue it!" vowed the king, and named twelve lords who should be sworn to sit in judgment on the accused knight.

All were sorry for him, and the noblest champions of the Round Table came forward to offer themselves as sureties that he should appear before the court on the day of trial. But Lanval heeded little what might now be his fate. If he could no longer live in the love of his lady, he could at least expiate his fault by death for her sake.

The day came, and the judges assembled. Some few of them, wishing to make court to the queen, were for condemning the poor knight forthwith; but the most part, knowing her falseness, thought it pity that such a brave man should thus be lost, and were willing to find cause for acquitting him, or at least for changing his sentence from death to banishment. And one of the oldest of the lords spoke thus, careless of Guinevere's frowns.

"Sir Lanval is arraigned because he has boasted his lady to be fairer than the queen. It is right that we have knowledge of the crime, and, therefore, let him be required to bring this lady here that so we may judge whether or no he has spoken truth."

To this all readily agreed; but Sir Lanval shook his head, knowing that he could not call his lady there, or even speak her name; and men murmured that he must die the death.

But as the judges still deliberated, there came to the castle two damsels robed in rich samite, and riding upon royally caparisoned mules. Dismounting before the king, they let him know how a great princess was approaching, who desired him to receive her. Arthur declared that their mistress should have all courteous entertainment, ordering certain of his knights to attend upon the damsels. Then he bid the trial proceed, for the queen was urgent to have that proud traitor condemned without more ado.

The lords were at last about to give sentence when a great cry was heard without, announcing the arrival of the mistress of the two damsels. Clad in a wondrous robe of silver sheen, over which was a purple mantle bordered with ermine, and crowned with a circlet of gold and gems, she rode upon a milk-white steed, the housings of which were worth an earldom. On her wrist sat a falcon that marked her high birth, and behind her ran two gallant greyhounds of the purest breed. All in the town, old and young, gentle and simple, had come forth to see her pass, and now, as she entered the hall of the castle, the whole assembly rose to do her honour. Every eye could not but gaze upon her, for such a wonder of beauty and loveliness had never before been seen in Arthur's land. And well Sir Lanval knew her.

"O lady, I forget all my troubles since I have seen thee once again!" he cried, stretching his hands towards her; but she answered him not a word, and passed proudly on to where the king waited to greet her. Then she mounted the dais on which sat Guinevere among her maidens, whose beauty grew pale before hers, as the moon and stars before the sun. Standing beside the queen and throwing off her mantle, this marvellous stranger turned herself to address the judges.

"Sirs, ye do wrong to this good knight, and may well see that he is unjustly accused. I loved him; he hath called me; I am here. Judge for yourselves which of us two be the fairer."

With one voice all exclaimed that she was fairer than any lady upon earth. It was in vain for Guinevere to frown and weep; the king himself exclaimed that she was no peer of this unknown dame. Lanval had but spoken the truth.

So amidst loud acclamations the knight was justified and let go free. But little recked he, since his love, taking leave of none present, after throwing one scornful glance upon the false queen, had strode from the dais and was already remounting her steed at the gate of the castle, without a word or a look for him.

"Oh, have pity on me!" he cried in vain. "Why give me my life when, without thee, it were more bitter than death?"

Still she answered him not, nor so much as turned her head, but rode away with her attendant damsels. Sir Lanval's horse stood by the castle gate. In despair he leaped upon its back and spurred wildly after her, none staying him.

By field and forest he followed her, ever crying piteously and beseeching her to speak to him if it were but one word. But in silence she rode swiftly on, till she reached the river bank on which they had first met. There she dismounted and plunged into the deep and rapid stream. The knight, all in mail as he was, did the same, stretching out his arms and trying to seize and hold her. Deeper and deeper she made her way into the water, and on he pressed after her, though the current was strong, and he had much ado to keep his footing. Still deaf to his entreaties, she disappeared below the surface; whereon Lanval, throwing himself forward with a last effort to snatch at her shining robe, was carried away, sank, lost sight and hearing, and gave himself up for dead.

But as the waters closed round his helpless form the lady turned and caught him and bore him with her. And when he came to himself he was lying on a flowery bank, his love bending over him, while, with a radiant smile, she told him that he was forgiven, and that they never more should be parted.

Never again was Sir Lanval seen by mortal eyes. But men tell how, with his bride, he dwells for ever in fairyland. His gallant steed – so the story goes – has ever since roamed riderless through the country. Often has it been seen by peasants and travellers, but it will suffer itself to be approached by none. Every year, on the day when it lost its master, it still comes to the river bank and stands long, neighing loudly and tearing up the ground with its hoofs by the place where Sir Lanval disappeared.

SIR PERCIVALE OF WALES

Roger Lancelyn Green

Roger Lancelyn Green (1918–87) was long a friend of the fantasy field. He compiled several anthologies of fantasy and supernatural fiction, wrote a number of studies of authors of fantasy fiction, and penned a few fantasies himself, most notably From the World's End *(1948). But he is most likely to be remembered for his retellings of myths and legends which covered* The Adventures of Robin Hood, The Tale of Troy *and, of course,* King Arthur and His Knights of the Round Table *(1953). Green spared no research in his background to King Arthur and his volume drew not only on Malory but on many of the lesser known medieval romances and ballads. For the following story he used a Middle English poem as his source plus incidents from the French* Conte du Graal.

In the wild forests of Wales there lived once a boy called Percivale, with his mother. Never another living soul did he meet for the first fifteen years of his life, nor did he learn anything of the ways of men and women in the world. But Percivale grew strong and hardy in the wild wood, of deadly aim with the dart, and simple of heart, honest and upright.

Now, one day as he wandered alone, discontented suddenly and longing for he knew not what, a sound fell upon his ears – not the voice of any bird, nor the music of wind or water, yet music it was, of a kind that set his heart leaping, he knew not why. He paused listening in a leafy glade, and as he waited there five knights came riding towards him, their armour jingling and the bridles of their horses ringing like silver bells.

"Greetings, fair youth!" cried the first knight, reining in his steed and smiling down at Percivale. "Nay, look not so stricken with wonder: surely you have seen our like before?"

"Indeed not," said Percivale. "And, truth to tell, I know not what you are, unless you be angels straight out of Heaven, such as those of whom my mother teaches me. Come tell me, noble sirs, do you not serve the King of Heaven?"

"Him do we serve indeed," said the knight, crossing himself reverently. "And so also do all men who live truly in this the realm of Logres. But on earth we serve His appointed Emperor – the noble King Arthur, at whose Round Table we sit. It is he who made us knights – for that is all we are: and you too he will make a knight if you but prove yourself worthy of that great honour."

"How may I do that?" asked Percivale.

"Come to King Arthur at Caerleon," answered the knight. "Tell him that I sent you thither – I, Sir Launcelot of the Lake who, under King Arthur, rule this land of Pant, which is also called North Wales. Then he will set you such deeds to do, such quests to accomplish, as we of his Court follow after all our days: and, if you prove worthy, he will make you a knight. But not in great deeds of arms lies the true worth of knighthood – rather in the heart of the doer of such deeds: if he be pure and humble, doing all things to the glory of God and to bring that glory and that peace throughout all our holy kingdom of Logres."

Then Sir Launcelot bowed his head to Percivale, and rode on his way, followed by the four other knights, leaving him wrapped in wonder – but with a great longing and a great humility stirring dimly within him.

"Mother! cried Percivale excitedly as he came striding up the path to the little cave where they lived. "Mother, oh mother – I have indeed met with wonders this day! They said they were not angels, but knights – yet to me they seemed fairer than all the hosts of Heaven! And one of them – the leader – Sir Launcelot was his name – said that I too could be a knight . . . Mother, I shall set out to-morrow morning and seek for King Arthur who dwells in Caerleon!"

Then Percivale's mother sighed deeply, and she wept for a little while, knowing that the appointed time had come when she must lose her son. Indeed, at first she tried to persuade Percivale to remain with her in the peace and safety of the forest, telling him of the dangers and sufferings that a knight must undergo. But all that she said only made Percivale the more eager to set out on his quest; and at length she bowed her head quietly and gave him his way.

Early on the following morning Percivale clad himself in his simple garments of skins, took a long sharp dart in his hand, and prepared to bid his mother good-bye.

"Go bravely forward, my son," she said as she kissed and blessed him. "Your father was the bravest and best of knights: be worthy of him and of me. And if you live all your days in honour and purity, you too shall be numbered among the chosen few whose names will live for ever among the true knights of Logres . . . Go on your way now, and remember that if dame or damsel ask your aid, give it freely and before all else, seeking no reward. Yet you may kiss the maiden who is willing, but take no more than a kiss, unless it be a ring – but be that only when you place your own ring upon her finger. Beware in whose company you travel on your quest, and see to it that only worthy men come near to your heart: but above all, pray to God each day that He may be with you in all your deeds – and pass not by church nor chapel without pausing awhile in His honour."

Very gravely Percivale kissed his mother good-bye, and set out through the forest, walking swiftly, yet with his head bowed as he thought of the solemn things which she had said to him. But in a little while the spring came back into his step and he went on his way singing joyfully and tossing his long dart up into the air until the keen blade flashed like silver in the sunlight as he caught it and whirled it up again and again.

The shadows were falling in long black folds between the trees and the sun drew near to the western hills when Percivale came suddenly to an open glade in the forest where the daisies clustered the green grass like snowflakes, and saw a pavilion of silk pitched beside a tinkling stream.

"Be this church or chapel," thought Percivale, "it is wondrous fair – and I will go into it!"

Stepping softly over the threshold, he passed into the shadowy bower, and there stood in wonder looking down upon a damsel who lay sleeping on a couch of rich silk and samite, with one arm stretched out, more white than the coverlet and her hair lighting up the pillowlike sun shine. Very gently Percivale bent down over her and took from her finger the one ring that she wore – a plain gold band set with a single red ruby: in its place he put his own gold ring from which shone one white diamond, and the maiden's ring he set on his own finger. Then, still without waking her, he kissed her gently on the lips and stole once more from the tent, his heart singing with a new wonder and a new longing.

Deep into the forest went Percivale, slept, when darkness fell, among the roots of a great oak tree, and with the first light was on his way again, striding through the wood until he came to the wide road which led to Caerleon.

At noon he reached the city gates, passed them without stopping, and in time found himself within the very castle.

King Arthur with many of his knights sat feasting there that day, for the time was Easter and they had ceased from their labours for a little while. Percivale stood by the door, marvelling at all he saw and envying even the serving-men who waited upon the King and his company.

And suddenly as he stood there unobserved, all eyes turned towards the door as a great man in golden-red armour strode unannounced into the hall. Now at that moment Sir Kay was standing beside the King holding in his hands the golden goblet from which it was Arthur's custom to pledge all his company ere the cup was passed round from hand to hand that each might drink to him and to the glory of the realm of Logres.

"Stay, you pack of wine-bibbing hinds!" roared the great red stranger. "Here is one better than all of you!" And with that he snatched the goblet from Sir Kay, drained it at a draught, and, with a great roar of laughter, strode from the hall with it still in his hand, leapt upon his horse and galloped swiftly away.

"Now, by my faith!" cried King Arthur springing to his feet, "this insult shall not go unpunished. Who will bring me back my cup?"

Then every knight rose as one man and cried: "Let this quest be mine!"

"Not so," said King Arthur, motioning them to sit once more. "Yonder red braggart is not worthy to fall at a knight's hands. Let some humble squire follow and overthrow him – one who seeks to be made a knight. Such a one who returns to my Court wearing the Red Knight's armour and carrying my golden goblet, will I knight forthwith!"

Then Percivale sprang forward from his place by the doorway and stood in the midst, clad as he was in the skins of wild goats and with the long dart held in his hand.

"King Arthur!" he cried, "I'll fetch your cup! I want some armour, and that golden suit will do me very well!"

"Bah!" exclaimed Sir Kay rudely. "What can this miserable goat-herd do against so great a knight?"

"Who are you, fair sir?" asked King Arthur, courteous as always to all men.

"My name is Percivale," was the answer. "I do not know who my father was, for I never saw him nor heard my mother speak of him. But she has brought me up in the forests of Wales – and I come now to ask you to make me a knight!"

"Make you a knight, indeed!" scoffed Sir Kay. "Go and tend sheep on the mountains before yonder ram in the golden armour makes you run away in terror!"

"A knight shall you be," said King Arthur, "if you bring back my cup and return wearing the armour of the robber who has taken it. Lo now, this quest is yours! Follow it only and no other!"

"I have no horse," said Percivale.

"One shall be ready for you at the door," answered Arthur. "Eat now swiftly, and get you gone . . . But you need arms and weapons . . ."

"I have my dart," interrupted Percivale. "As for armour, I'll wait until I can put on that golden suit which you all saw not long ago!"

When he had eaten Percivale rose to go: but as he passed down the hall, a damsel stood before him and cried aloud: "The King of Heaven bless you, Sir Percivale, the best of knights!"

"Be silent, witless wench!" cried Sir Kay angrily, and he struck the damsel across the face.

"Beware of me when I return in my golden armour!" said Percivale looking scornfully at Sir Kay. "That unknightly stroke will I revenge with a blow that you will not lightly forget!"

Then he hastened from the hall, sprang upon the waiting horse, and rode away into the forest.

Percivale went much faster than the Red Knight so that before sunset he overtook him as he rode quietly up a mountain path towards a lone grey tower outlined against the pale pink of the clouds.

"Turn, thief!" shouted Percivale as soon as he was near enough. "Turn and defend yourself!"

A little way behind him three of King Arthur's knights reined in their horses to watch: they had followed all the way from Caerleon to see what should befall but not even now did Percivale know that they were there.

"Ha!" cried the Red Knight, wheeling his steed. "What insolent boy are you? And why do you bid me stand?"

"I come from King Arthur," answered Percivale. "Give me back the golden goblet which you stole this day at his feast! Moreover, you must go yourself to the Court and do homage there – but first of all you must yield to me and give me that fine suit of armour which you wear so proudly!"

"And if I do not?" asked the Red Knight, speaking quietly but his eyes flashing with fury like the lightning in the quiet sky before a mighty storm.

"Why then I will kill you – and help myself to cup and armour!" exclaimed Percivale.

"Insolent child!" roared the Red Knight in a voice of thunder. "You have asked for death – now take it!"

With that he set his spear in rest and came down the hillside like a mighty avalanche, expecting to transfix his enemy as if he were a butterfly on a pin. But Percivale leapt suddenly from his horse so that the spear passed harmlessly over its head, and stood in the middle of the path, shouting taunts:

"You great coward!" he jeered. "First you try to spear an unarmed man, and then you run away down the hillside!"

With horrible oaths the Red Knight wheeled his horse once more and came charging up the path, his spear aimed at Percivale. But this time Percivale drew back his dart and threw it suddenly – so suddenly that it sped like a flash of light over the Red Knight's shield and caught him in the throat just above the rim of his armour, so that he fell backwards from his horse and lay there dead.

Percivale knelt down triumphantly beside his fallen foe and drew out King Arthur's golden cup from the wallet at his waist. But when he tried to loosen the golden armour from the body he found himself defeated: for he did not know how it was fastened on, and thought indeed that it was all made in one piece.

After many vain attempts to pull the Red Knight through the gorget or neck-piece of the armour, Percivale changed his tactics. Swiftly he gathered together a pile of dry wood, and was busily striking a flint from the road against the point of his dart when suddenly he heard the sound of a horse's hooves, and looking up saw an old man on horseback dressed in dark armour, whose helmet hung at his saddle-bow, and whose grey hair fell to his shoulders.

"Greetings, young sir," said the old knight smiling kindly upon Percivale. "What do you with this dead robber whom you have slain so valiantly?"

"Out of the iron burn the tree," said Percivale, quoting a

woodman's saying which his mother had taught him. "I want to get this man out of the armour and wear it myself."

The old knight's smile grew broader still, but he dismounted from his horse and showed Percivale how to unlace the armour and draw it off and on piece by piece.

"My name is Gonemans," said the knight presently, "and I dwell near by in an ancient manor-house. Come you thither with me, young sir, and I will teach you all things that you should know before you can become a worthy knight, for not alone by such a deed as this may you win to the true honour."

So Percivale went with Sir Gonemans and dwelt all that summer in his house, learning to fight with sword and spear, to wear his armour and sit his horse as a knight should. And he learnt also of the high order of knighthood which was so much more noble than the mere doing of mighty deeds: he learnt of right and wrong, of a knight's duty ever to defend the weak and punish the cruel and evil.

And at last he rode forth on his way once more, clad in shining armour, with a tall spear in his hand, after bidding a courteous farewell to Sir Gonemans. It was late autumn by now, and as he rode beneath the trees in the deep woods and forests the leaves gleamed red and gold like his armour which seemed almost to be part of the foliage and bracken through which he passed.

Many days rode Percivale in quest of adventure, and often as he went his eyes fell upon the ruby ring on his finger, and he thought more and more of the lovely damsel whom he had found sleeping in the pavilion.

At length on a dark, sombre evening when the clouds lowered threateningly above him, he came by a winding way among great bare rocks through a sad and desolate land, until suddenly he saw a dark castle in front of him.

The walls were shattered and overthrown, the towers were cracked down the sides as if by lightning: yet no weeds grew among the stones or even between the cobbles under the yawning gateway; and in the centre stood the great keep firm and solid in the midst of that desolation.

Beneath the sharp teeth of the portcullis rode Percivale, his horse's hooves ringing hollowly on the stone and on through dark arches and deserted courtyards until he came to the entrance of the great hall. Here he could see a light burning and so, having tied his horse to a ring in the wall, he walked up the steps and into a mighty room with a high roof of black beams. There was no one to be seen, and yet a fire burned merrily in the great fireplace, torches shone brightly from rings in the walls, and dinner was set at a table on the dais. Percivale walked slowly up the hall and stood looking about him: on a little table not far from the fire he saw laid out a set of great ivory chessmen, with a chair drawn up on one side as if ready for a game. While still wondering what all this might mean, Percivale sat down in the chair, and presently he reached out idly and moved a white pawn forward two squares on the board. At once a red pawn moved forward by itself: Percivale was alert in an instant, but all was quiet, there was not even the sound of any breath but his own. So he moved another piece, and immediately a red piece was moved also. Percivale moved again as if playing – and behold! the red pieces moved in turn, so cunningly that in a very few minutes he saw that he was checkmated.

Swiftly he re-arranged the pieces, and this time the red moved first and a second game was played, which Percivale lost also. A third time this happened, and Percivale rose in a sudden fury, drawing his sword to crush the pieces and hack the board.

But as he did so a damsel ran suddenly into the room: "Hold your hand, Sir knight!" she cried. "If you strike at these magic chesspieces a terrible evil will befall you!"

"Who are you, lady?" asked Percivale.

"I am Blanchefleur," she answered, and as she spoke she came forward into the light of the candles which stood near to the chess-table, and with a sudden gasp of wonder and joy Percivale knew her for the maiden in the pavilion. And even as he recognized her he saw his diamond ring shining on her finger.

He held out his hand to her, and saw her suddenly pause as she recognized her own ring which he still wore.

"Lady Blanchefleur," he said gently, "I have sought for you long. My name is Percivale – and I beg you to pardon me for the wrong I did you, meaning no wrong, when I took this ring from you as you slept, and took also one kiss from your lips."

"Percivale," she answered gently, "I have seen you only in dreams: each night you have come to me, wearing my ring, and have kissed me once on the lips – and my heart has gone out to you across the darkness . . . But in this magic castle I have waited for you: the time to speak of love is not yet. Come sit down to supper, for you shall see a more wondrous thing than yonder enchanted chess-board."

They took their places at the table: but there was no food nor wine upon it, nor did any man or woman come to wait upon them.

Yet Percivale sat silent, looking at Blanchefleur.

"Lady," he said at length, "all times are the true time for such a love as mine: lady, will you be my wife? I swear to you that no other in all the world shall come near me, nor shall my lips touch those of any save you alone."

Blanchefleur laid her hand in his with never a word, and as she touched him suddenly a roar of thunder shook the castle, the great door of the hall flew open, and a strange damsel, dressed and veiled in white, walked slowly into the hall, holding aloft a great goblet or grail covered in a cloth. A light shone from within the Grail, so bright that no man might look upon it: yet it was with another and a holy awe that Percivale sank to his knees and bowed his head in his hands.

A second veiled woman followed the first, bearing a golden platter, and a third followed her, carrying a spear with a point of white light from which dripped blood that vanished ere it touched the floor. As they passed up the hall and round the table where Percivale and Blanchefleur knelt, the whole room seemed to be filled with sweet scents as of roses and spices, and when the Procession of the Grail had passed down the hall once more and out of the door, which closed again behind them, there fell upon Percivale a peace of heart that passed all understanding, and a great joy.

"The Holy Grail draws near to Logres," said Blanchefleur. "Ask me no more concerning what you have seen, for the time has not yet come. One other must enter this castle and see it – and that is Sir Launcelot of the Lake. But, Percivale, you are more blessed than he: for through him shall come the ending of the glory of Logres, though in Logres there has so far been none so glorious as he, save only Gawain. Go you now to Camelot and wait for the coming of Galahad: on the day when he sits in the Siege Perilous you shall see the Holy Grail once more."

"Lady," said Percivale, rising to his feet, but standing with bowed head, "I would seek for it now! It seems to me that there is no quest in all the world so worthy."

"No quest indeed," answered Blanchefleur, "but not yet may you seek it. On the day when the glory of Logres is at its full, the Grail shall come to Camelot: then all shall seek, but only the most worthy shall find it."

"I would be one of those!" cried Percivale. "None but I shall achieve the Quest of the Grail!" And forgetting all else he ran down the hall, never heeding Blanchefleur's cry, leapt upon his horse and galloped away into the forest.

When morning came the madness seemed to leave him suddenly,

and turning round, he tried to ride back in search of Blanchefleur. But though he wandered for many, many days he could never again find any trace of the desolate land or of the mysterious Castle of Carbonek.

Sad and wretched, Percivale turned at length and rode towards Caerleon. It was winter by now and the snow lay thick on the high road as Percivale came out from the mountains and forests of Central Wales and drew near to the city. One night he slept at Tintern on the Wye, and early next day rode slowly and sadly down the valley by the bright river.

Suddenly as he went he saw a hawk swoop from above like a shining bolt of brown and strike a dove. For a moment the two birds fluttered together in mid-air, and then the hawk flew triumphant up once more bearing his victim in his claws. But from the dove's breast fell three drops of blood which lay and glistened in the white snow at Percivale's feet. As he looked he thought of the blood that fell from the spear at Castle Carbonek; he thought of the ruby ring on his finger; but most of all he thought of Blanchefleur, of her red lips, red as blood, and of her skin like the white snow.

As he sat there on his horse four knights came riding towards him: and these were Sir Kay, Sir Ywain, Sir Gawain and King Arthur himself.

"Ride forward now," said King Arthur to Sir Kay, "and ask yonder knight his name, whither he journeys and why he sits thus lost in thought."

"Ho, Sir knight!" shouted Kay as he drew near. "Tell me your name and business!"

But Percivale was lost so deeply in his thoughts that he neither saw or heard.

"Answer, if you be not a dumb man!" shouted Kay, and then, losing his temper somewhat, he struck at Percivale with his iron gauntlet.

Then Percivale sat upright on his horse, reined backwards a little way, set his spear in rest, and cried:

"No man shall strike me thus and go unpunished! Defend yourself, you cowardly, craven knight!"

Sir Kay drew back also, levelled his spear, and they galloped together with all their strength. Sir Kay's spear struck Percivale's shield and broke into pieces; but Percivale smote so hard and truly that he pierced Kay's shield, wounding him deeply in the side and hurling him to the ground.

Then he sat with his spear ready, in case one of the other knights should attack him.

"I will joust with all or any of you!" he cried, "I will defend my right to sit my horse by the roadside without having to suffer the blows and insults of such a shameful knight as this!"

"It is Percivale!" exclaimed Sir Gawain suddenly. "He who slew the Red Knight – whose armour now he wears! Truly he must have been lost in deep thought of love to sit as he did while Sir Kay struck him!"

"Ask him to speak with us, fair nephew," said King Arthur, and Gawain rode forward towards Percivale.

"Gentle sir," said he with all courtesy, "yonder is King Arthur, our sovereign lord, and he desires you to speak with him. As for Sir Kay, whom you have smitten down, well he deserves this punishment for his lack of knightly gentleness!"

When Percivale heard this he was glad.

"Then are both mine oaths fulfilled," he cried. "I have punished Sir Kay for the evil blow he gave the damsel on the day when I came first to Caerleon; and I come before King Arthur wearing the armour of the Red Knight whom I have slain and carrying in my wallet the golden goblet which was stolen from his board!"

Percivale rode forward, dismounted from his horse, and knelt before King Arthur.

"Lord King," he said, "make me a knight, I pray you. And here I swear to spend all my days in your service, striving to bring glory to the realm of Logres."

"Arise, Sir Percivale of Wales," said King Arthur. "Your place awaits you at the Round Table – between Sir Gawain and the Siege Perilous. In the days long past Merlin the good enchanter told me that you would come when the highest moment of the realm of Logres drew near."

Then Sir Percivale rode to Caerleon between King Arthur and Sir Gawain, while Sir Ywain followed after them, leading Sir Kay's horse while Sir Kay lay groaning across its saddle.

Many deeds did Sir Percivale after this, but there is no space to tell of his adventures with Rosette the Loathly Damsel, how he fought with the Knight of the Tomb who lived in a great cromlech on a mountain in Wales, how he overcame Partiniaus and Arides, King Margon and the Witch of the Waste City. But always he sought for the Lady Blanchefleur, always he was true to her alone: but he could not find her – until the years were accomplished, and he found his way once to the Castle of Carbonek not long after the Holy Grail came to Camelot.

JOHN, THE KNIGHT
OF THE LION

H. Shück

Earlier I mentioned the story "The Lady of the Fountain" from
The Mabinogion. *The following story has that same tale as its base,*
although it has passed through many transmutations. Chrétien de
Troyes used it for his romance Yvain: Le *chavelier au lion (c. 1177).*
It was later picked up by a Norwegian balladeer, possibly one Brother
Robert, who translated several Arthurian sagas around the year
1226. The original Norwegian version was lost but its translation
into Swedish survives. This happened at the request of the Norwegian
queen Euphemia in about 1303. It was that version that was saved by
Professor Shück, an authority on Swedish history and literature for
his volume Medieval Stories, *and which was translated into English*
by W.F. Harvey, Professor of English Literature at the University of
Malta, in 1902. The John of the title was Chrétien's Yvain or the
original Celtic Owain, who was a real king. Historically the son
of Urien of Rheged, a kingdom roughly equal to modern Cumbria,
he lived at the end of the sixth century. He was killed in the Battle
of Catraeth against the Angles of Northumbria in AD 595.

Many a long year ago there reigned a mighty king in England whose
name was Arthur. He was the finest warrior of his time, and kings'
sons, dukes, earls, and counts came from far and wide to his court

to gain instruction in courtesy and the practices of chivalry; but only the bravest were received, and these formed themselves into a league which, under the title of the Knights of the Round Table, became feared and famous throughout the whole world. A knight of the Round Table never shrank from any adventure however daring it might be, and had always to be prepared to take the field for the protection of the weak and persecuted. He had to be brave, generous, faithful and high-minded, and show tact and delicacy of feeling in his behaviour, and for these reasons membership of the Knights of the Round Table was regarded as the highest honour that a knight could attain.

Once upon a time King Arthur held his court at Caerleon, and the noblest knights in that country had foregathered there. The day began with a magnificent tournament, and at night the king gave a banquet in his castle, where the knights, who had now doffed their armour, led the dance with the fair ladies whom King Arthur's queen Guenevere had brought together. During the dancing the king sat on his throne, watching the dancers and listening to the songs which were sung as an accompaniment, but suddenly he was seized with an unaccountable sleepiness and had to withdraw to his chamber, where he was followed by his queen and a few attendants. His knights accompanied them, and remained outside the door, and soon they got into conversation about the adventures they had severally met with. There sat Segramore, Gavan, Kalegrevanz, John, and many knights far-renowned for bravery; but there was also with them a knight named Kay who was disliked by the rest for his sharp tongue and his spitefulness.

At length Kalegrevanz related an adventure with which he had recently met. He told it without any embellishments or any attempt to make it appear that his own share in it was more glorious than it actually was. When he had finished there arose a murmur among the rest, and the general opinion was that Kalegrevanz had only reaped shame and infamy in the incident he had related. Kay naturally pronounced this opinion more strongly and pitilessly than the others.

The queen, who was attracted to the spot by the murmuring, inquired what they were talking about, and when Kay in a few scoffing words had hinted at the thing, she upbraided him for his discourteous way of speaking, and went on to say:

"It almost seems to me, my dear Kay, as if it were an absolute necessity for you to speak ill of your friends. It is well they never pay you back in your own coin, for you have, I doubt not, some weak points, and would possibly not come off quite so well in the verdict of ungentle tongues. In any case, it is better not to turn others to ridicule, but to treat all with modesty and friendliness. Let me now hear the adventure of which Knight Kalegrevanz was speaking."

"I will not wrangle with Kay," said the latter. "Whatever I say he turns into ridicule against me, and, with my gracious queen's permission, I would much rather keep silence about the matter."

"Do not trouble yourself about Kay's revilings," answered the queen, "but tell us your adventure. I know you to be a noble knight, and am convinced that you have no cause to blush for any deed you have done."

"Although I should prefer not to speak of this matter again, yet I will comply with your wish and tell my adventure once more. I beg only that you will put the best construction on it.

"A short time ago," he began, "I clad myself in full armour and rode out from Karidol. On taking a turning to the right, I came to a narrow bridlepath which led me to a dark and dense grove, and after riding a whole day without halting, towards evening I perceived a strong castle surrounded by broad ramparts and approached by a drawbridge. On this bridge I met the lord of the castle, who had just returned home from hunting, and was still carrying a falcon on his hand. He greeted me in a friendly manner and said:

" 'I was fortunate to meet you. Pray alight from your horse and rest the night at my house. We will do all we can to make you comfortable.'

"I thanked him and sprang off my horse, and followed him into the hall, and there he again bade me welcome. Then he went to a table wrought of melted bell-metal, grasped the hammer that lay on the table and struck it in such a way that there was a sound like thunder all over the house. At this summons the knights and squires who were up in the tower hurried down at once to the drawbridge, welcomed me, and took my horse and led it to the stables. With them came the most lovely damsel I had ever beheld. She greeted me with modest dignity, took off my armour, and had some other raiment brought with which she arrayed me. The mantle she threw over me was of scarlet lined with ermine, and fastened round the neck by a clasp of gold set with precious stones. After this she conducted me to a grove where lilies and roses bloomed amid the trees, and there we enjoyed ourselves for some while, she and I alone, and gradually I utterly forgot all else in the world for her.

"I declared to her that my sole desire was to remain near her;

but just as I was on the point of making my meaning plainer, the owner of the castle came and bade us come into supper, which was now ready. It was as exquisite as everything else in that hospitable castle, and the amiability of my host made the dishes on the table even more delicious. He asked me to promise that I would again claim his hospitality when I returned from my journey, and this promise I was naturally not loth to make, and then I was ushered into my chamber.

"At the dawn of day I arose, thanked the people of the house for their hospitality, took my horse and rode away. After riding for a while I met a whole herd of wild beasts, lions, buffaloes, bears and panthers, which were fighting with each other amid an awful din; but with these creatures I noticed a shepherd whose appearance was even more appalling. He was blacker than a negro and uglier than any human being I had ever beheld. His head was bigger than a horse's, his nose was as crooked as a ram's horn; his hair was, in stiffness and roughness, like the thorns on a briar-bush; his lips were blue, and his chin hung down over his chest. His face was as hairy as a bearskin rug; his beard bristly and matted; his back adorned with a hump; his feet had claws like a griffin's, and were flat and misshaped. His clothes consisted of two ox hides, and he held a sledge hammer in his hands; serpents and lizards were crawling over him. When he saw me he ran up a hillock, and stared at me like an idiot, without uttering a word. After looking at him for a while, hesitating what I should do, I said:

" 'What kind of being are you? Are you an evil spirit or what?'

" 'I am what I am,' answered he, 'and no man has seen me better looking than I now appear to you.'

" 'Well, and what is your calling?'

" 'I tend the beasts which you see here.'

" 'Your answer seems to me strange. I do not think you can be minding the beasts that are roaming about the woods here, and they do not appear to me to be tied up.'

" 'They are as gentle as lambs. As soon as they hear my voice they come immediately; but should one of them prove refractory I merely seize him by the horns and throw him on the ground; then the others tremble, become tame, and run to me as if to plead for the forward ones. They obey me without a murmur, but I should not advise any one else to try the same thing, for it would not go well with him. But tell me, pray, what you yourself are.'

" 'I am a knight who has ridden out in quest of adventures. Tell me, therefore, if you know of any difficult enterprise that I might perform and so win renown.'

" 'Readily, if such be your pleasure. Not far from here there is a spring, the loveliest you could see. Yonder path leads to it, but I fear you will not return if you actually venture to approach the spring of which I am now going to tell you more. Rose bushes and trees rich in foliage hem it in, and they never lose their leaves even in winter. These trees extend their greenery so thickly over the spring that the rays of the sun can never reach it, and the water remains as chilly as ice. On a post hard by the spring there hangs a golden cup attached to a chain of such length that by means of it you can fetch water out of the well, and near the post there stands a chapel. Now, if you fill the cup with water from the spring, and throw it over the post a hurricane of such awful violence breaks out that all the beasts near – lions, bears, and birds tremble and flee before the rainfloods and hailstones that stream from the sky. Thunderbolts will whizz round you, and thunderclaps boom in your ears. If you escape unscathed you will be luckier than other knights that have ventured on the same quest.'

"After uttering these words he bade me farewell, and I rode along the way he had showed me to the spring. After riding for some time, I saw the loveliest grove I had ever beheld, and in it I discovered the spring as the shepherd had said. It was entirely hidden by foliage, so much so that hardly a drop of rain could trickle through it. I also noticed the precious cup and the post which was of emerald set with rubies. On dismounting from my horse I filled the cup with water, and poured the contents over the post, but instantly I regretted my daring act, for suddenly the sky grew overcast, and certain violent gusts of wind came and shook the trees. Then the inky clouds belched forth a pattering shower of hail, and the lightning began to flash, so that I feared that I must needs perish. I swooned away and fell like a corpse to the ground, and had not our Lord been specially gracious to me, I should, in good sooth, have been killed by the trees that the wind broke and uprooted.

"After I had lain unconscious for some time, I began to recover my senses, and now I heard the nightingales singing and trilling as before, and lifting up my eyes I again saw the sun shining, and at the sight I forgot the peril through which I had lately passed. I arose to my feet, and observed the grove, which again seemed like a paradise, but I had scarcely recovered from my swoon before I saw a knight in full armour come galloping towards me. When I perceived that he was alone and none were in his company I rushed to my horse, mounted the saddle, and hurried to meet him, glad at having at length come across some one with whom I might measure my strength. The knight who approached me was in a terrible fury. He cried out to me:

"Halt, you knave! For this you shall pay. Had you had grounds of complaint against me it would have been your duty to challenge me to single combat; but now you have insulted me out of sheer wantonness, and dearly you shall smart for it. You have destroyed a great part of my wood, and not even in my own castle can I rest in peace by reason of the hurricane which you, in your folly, have raised. I will give you something to remember this by, and that you won't forget in a hurry."

"After he had uttered this, he drove at me with his spear, but I caught the blow with my shield; however, I could not long contend against him, for his horse was as swift as a hind and his blows rained thick. Finally, my lance broke on meeting his helmet, and with a single blow he hurled me, there and then, off my horse. Then he took my charger from me, and rode right away without bestowing a glance at me. I have never yet come across a knight so stalwart.

"I lay for a long time on the ground utterly bewildered at my overthrow, but when I perceived that day and night were at odds, I got up, mangled in all my limbs, and approached the spring. I was now without a horse, and did not know what to do. In a shamefaced way I wandered through the wood back to the castle where I had, on the previous evening, been received with such hospitality, and I now stood once more blushing before the master of the castle. He received me, however, with the same cordiality as before, and even the other inmates of the castle – the maidens, knights, and squires – treated me quite in the same way, and showed me no lack of respect, but, on the contrary, congratulated me on having got off so easily, for hitherto no one who had striven with Red Vadoin – such was the name of the knight at the spring – had escaped with his life.

"Such then is my adventure. I have added nothing to it which could redound to my honour, and I have concealed nothing which might lessen the shame of my defeat."

"By the saints," said John, "I am ill pleased with you, my kinsman, for not having told me this adventure before, but, by God's help, I will avenge you or lose my life."

"John," exclaimed Kay, in his usual irritating way, "vaunts his bravery overmuch, but it seems to me that he has fetched his courage from the winebowl that he so industriously emptied this evening. He will sing another song when he has slept over the matter, for I'll warrant he will dream such horrible dreams about Red Vadoin that, when morning comes, he will have lost all desire of venturing on a bout with such a redoubtable antagonist."

The queen then chided Kay for his malice, and said:

"It almost seems as if your heart must have burst if you had forborne discharging your spleen; but shame on every evil tongue. We blush for you, and, as for you, sooner or later, this malice will occasion you misfortune."

"Noble queen," said John, "don't bandy words with Kay, for it is part of his nature to revile and flout, but when it comes to manly exploits he holds aloof. A gallant man is quick in action, but cautious in judging."

Kay was about to retort when the king, who had been disturbed by the wrangle, came out and asked what the brawl was about. The queen told him, in a few words, about Kalegrevanz's defeat, and ended by recommending his cause to the king. Then the king waxed mighty wroth, and swore a great oath that he would, within fourteen days, proceed with all his knights to the spring, and there avenge the insult which Red Vadoin had put on the Round Table.

When this was known all rejoiced at the thought of the adventures and frays that awaited them. John alone heard of this expedition with other feelings, for he had hoped to have avenged the wounded honour of his kinsman; so, in order to prevent the rest from robbing him of this opportunity, he resolved that very same night to betake himself immediately to the spring, without waiting for the others. He therefore hurried home to his squire, and bade him, straight-way saddle his charger. Then he strictly forbade his squire to reveal anything about his departure, especially before Kay, and, without wasting time in further talk, he mounted his steed and rode into the dark wood. Without other adventures than those Kalegrevanz had experienced in the course of his journey, he reached at length the wonderful spring, and there found everything as his friend had described.

He immediately grasped the drinking-cup, filled it with water, and dashed its contents over the post. That instant, just as Kalegrevanz had related, a furious hurricane, accompanied by thunderbolts and hailstones, arose, but John endured it without quaking. When the clouds dispersed and the sun again broke forth, he saw a knight dashing towards him at a furious pace. John was not loth to meet him, and they rushed at one another with such violence that their lances were splintered like glass, strong and heavy as they were. When Red Vadoin saw John sitting calmly in his saddle, he was beside himself with vexation, and shouted to him:

"Never before has the shame befallen me that one who has met my lance has not been forthwith hurled to the ground; but you shall not escape me."

Then they drew their swords and dashed against each other again. Blow followed blow with such violence that fire glinted from their helmets when the strokes told, their shields were shivered, and their coats of mail hacked to pieces; but neither would yield to the other. At last John dealt Vadoin a blow which cleft his helmet and reached his head, so that a stream of blood gushed down over his armour. When Vadoin received that crushing blow he collected his remaining strength, turned his horse, and fled back to his castle, closely pursued by John.

When those that were in the castle perceived this unwonted spectacle they let down the drawbridge and opened the gates to admit Vadoin; but John pursued him over the bridge, and pressed in through the small outer door immediately after him. There was a portcullis over this, which was let down as Vadoin rode through, and John very narrowly escaped being cut into pieces by the sharp iron of the gate. His horse was cloven in twain just behind the saddle, so that its hinder part fell outside the drawbridge, whilst the foremost part tumbled down in front of the portcullis. Even both John's spurs were cut off by the fall of the portcullis, and it was only by the gain of a second that the rider did not share his horse's fate. However, he fell down and Vadoin disappeared through the principal gateway, which was closed upon him at once, so that John now found himself shut in the little passage between the two gates. The situation he now found himself in was anything but agreeable. He was a prisoner in a strong castle, the master of which was his deadly enemy, and his valour could avail him little against the latter's numerous retainers. As he was vainly searching for the means of rescuing himself from this danger a maid came to him.

"Good knight," said she, "why tarry you still here? My master has just died of the wound you gave him; my mistress is beside herself with despair, and all the people in the castle are burning with eagerness to avenge his death; but know that, though you are hidden here, still you are not forgotten. They will be up on you directly."

"Ere they overcome me," he answered, "many lives will be lost, for they shall not take me captive without a struggle."

"Resistance against such superior force is of no avail, but you once stood by me, and so I will help you. Once I came wretched and abandoned to King Arthur's court, and it was you who took care of me. The courtesy and kindness you then showed me I will now try to requite."

With these words she pressed a golden ring into his hand and said:

"The stone in this ring is from India, and the man who wears the ring and closes his hand becomes that moment invisible. Employ it to extricate yourself from your peril, but let me have it back afterwards."

"God reward you, noble maiden, for this gift. I shall never forget your goodness."

"Let us now flee at once from here. Shut your hand so as to become invisible, and follow me, and I will conduct you to a hiding-place where you can be concealed till I can free you altogether."

Then he followed her across the vast courtyard, where all was bustle and confusion, by reason of Vadoin's death, to a little chamber, and there she showed him a bed on which he threw himself down and soon fell asleep, exhausted by all the struggles and hardships he had undergone.

Some hours afterwards the maid returned and brought him wine and food. John helped himself to the refreshments, and looked down through the window and saw how they were searching for him everywhere. Swords rattled and bows clanged as Vadoin's men rushed about to find the man who had slain their master.

First they hurried to the arch in which John had been shut, but they found to their astonishment that it was empty, though the locks were unbroken. John heard them talking among themselves and exhorting each other to make further search, "for," said they, "unless he is a bird and has wings he cannot have cleared the wall". Then they at once began to make a fresh search, and poked about in all the nooks and crannies in the castle. They even went into the room John was in, and almost touched him, but not a trace could they find of the vanished knight.

While they were engaged in searching, the body of the deceased lord of the castle was carried across the courtyard, accompanied by a crowd of women and squires uttering lamentations. At the head of them walked the dead lord's widow, a tall and beautiful woman, whose countenance, however, was disfigured by grief. She wept and lamented aloud, and, when her glance happened to fall on the bier, she shrieked wildly and fell to the ground in a swoon.

As soon as those about her had restored her to consciousness, a messenger was dispatched for priests and monks to say masses for the soul of the dead man, and then they all went in procession to the castle chapel, where the bier was laid on the ground, and the priests began to intone the service.

John had, without being perceived, contrived to mingle with the funeral party and entered the chapel with them; but, as he drew near the body, its wounds began to bleed afresh, and then every one was aware that the slayer was somewhere near the slain. The knights began therefore to search afresh, and the châtelaine burst out sobbing again.

"There is sorcery at work here," said she, "for the murderer is in the midst of us without our being able to see him. Alas, my God, I shall never be able to bear the sorrow of not even looking on him who wrought me such great affliction! He would never have slain my noble husband if he had not employed treachery, for no braver knight was ever born. No one dared to await his onset, much less engage him in battle, and even this man would have failed to win the fight had he not had recourse to sorcery."

With weeping and wailing they carried the body to the grave and buried it. Then masses were sung for his soul, and at last all departed; but when the burial was over the maid who had succoured John – her name was Luneta – went to the chamber in which she had hidden the knight, and to which he had withdrawn himself.

"Noble knight," said she, "you heard yourself how they were searching for you everywhere. Now, give thanks to God that they failed to find you."

"For my rescue I have, methinks, to thank God in the first place, and you too for having shown me such kindness. You have saved my life, and this service might be deemed sufficient, but I have still a boon to crave of you, and that is that I may see just once the noble lady who owns this castle."

"I will readily satisfy you in this request. You have only to cast a glance through this window to see what you desire. She is sitting in mourning weeds in the midst of the other dames."

When John looked at her, he found her again lamenting in their presence the hard lot that had befallen her, and marked how her gestures betrayed deeper and deeper despair, so that at last she swooned away again for grief. John's first impulse was to go up to her and crave her pardon and seek to console her, knowing that he himself was the cause of her despair, but Luneta held him back.

"Now you must obey me and not stir from your place here.

Should any one see you here, then your fate is sealed, for no one will show you mercy. Keep quiet where you are, and where you can observe without danger the course of events. I shall meanwhile tell you all that it is important for you to know, and my only fear is that my lady, or one of her attendants, may grow suspicious at my absence, and suspect that I am with you."

After she had said this she left the knight alone to his reflections. He now began to consider his position more calmly. He determined not to steal secretly from the castle without having revealed to some one that it was he who had defeated Red Vadoin, for he stood in fear of Kay's jeers if he was not in a position to prove that Vadoin had fallen by his sword and not by another's. On the other hand, his life would be in danger if any one discovered him in the castle.

Whilst engaged in these thoughts he again cast his eyes at the poor châtelaine who was now slowly recovering from her swoon, and when he saw her beauty he sighed and thought to himself:

"Would to God you were mine. Could I but gain your love I would willingly renounce all the honours in the world; but that can never come to pass, for I have done her so much wrong that she can never forgive me. I have slain him whom she loved best in this world, and she has every reason to hate me. Loving her is sheer madness, and I well know she would rather see me dead; but, nevertheless, I have heard a certain man who knew human nature assert that women's feelings often change, and perhaps even her hate may be turned to love. All things rest in God's hands, and He has power even over her heart. Possibly He may induce her to grant me pardon and love."

While he was thus musing, the lovely châtelaine arose and went, accompanied by her dames, into the castle. John gazed at her for a long time, and acknowledged to himself that it was not merely fear of Kay's gibes that kept him in the castle, but also love for Red Vadoin's widow. He knew he would rather die than flee from where she was.

After a while Luneta came back to him, and on perceiving his sadness she asked him what had occasioned it.

"When you come here," replied John, "I forget my sorrows altogether and wax as merry as of yore. Let us therefore not speak of them."

"Open your heart to me if there is aught that makes you sad. Possibly I may be of some help to you."

"Well, then, know that it is love for your mistress that makes me so downcast: I cannot live without her."

"I guessed that already, and will, to the best of my ability, advance your cause; but first you must ride away from the castle, where your life is every moment in jeopardy."

"In this respect I cannot obey you. I will not steal away from the castle secretly, but ride hence so that every one may see me."

"Do what seems good to you. I shall watch over your safety as well as I can, and now I am going to my mistress to endeavour to question her heart. I shall not tarry long ere I return to tell you what my impressions are."

Then she went to the châtelaine, whose name was Laudine, and, after falling on her knees before her and saluting her, she said:

"Noble lady, try and calm your bitter grief, and think of this: he whom you are now weeping for can never come back."

"Alas," answered Laudine, "I know full well I can never have him again, though I loved him with all my soul. Nothing remains to me but to weep till I die of weeping."

"Rather than that should be I hope that God may bestow on you another husband who shall be as good a knight as him you have lost. Even you yourself ought to admit that that would be best for you."

"You ought to blush to talk like that. *His* peer is not to be found in the whole world."

"Oh, yes," replied Luneta, "I know one who quite equals him. Please god he may be your husband."

"Now I really ought to be angry with you for saying that; the like of it I have never heard."

But Luneta held her ground bravely and proceeded to say:

"My noble lady, there is still another thing to be thought of, and that is, if King Arthur with all his troops and knights were to come here to lay your lands waste, who is there to defend them against him? Out of all your people I cannot find a knight capable of performing such a deed. They could not do it in a body even if they were to enlist us women to help them. No doubt they could ride to the spring, but as for protecting it, that they could not; so listen to my advice, and try and find some knight capable of protecting your land and yourself. Take him for your consort, and hold him dear, for both you and your country will be the gainers by it."

Laudine acknowledged to herself that Luneta not only spoke wisely, but to the point; yet she was not of a mind to let herself be persuaded quite so readily, but pretended to get very angry, and cried:

"Go your way, you silly wench. I do not fully understand your meaning; some hidden purpose lies, methinks, behind your words. Never will I follow your advice."

"Say not so, for I venture to prophesy that, in the end, you will do what I have said."

After saying this Luneta got up and departed, but Laudine sat where she was, engrossed in her thoughts.

"What knight can that be," thought she, "that Luneta alluded to? A brave and famous man must he be, forsooth."

Her curiosity was now aroused, and she could no longer restrain it, so she summoned Luneta again into her presence for the purpose of questioning her. The artful girl came and repeated her previous conversation.

"Away with dull care," she exclaimed. "What boots it your longing after one who is departed never to return? It is absurd, you know, to shorten your life in that way; besides, you are mistaken if you think that chivalry and honour died in this world with Red Vadoin. Marry, no; brave as he was, there are many braver knights than he to be found."

"Name me one, then," cried Laudine, "and if you can prove you have spoken the truth, I am ready to listen to you."

"That I will," answered Luneta, "but you must first promise me not to be angry if I happen to name one whom, perhaps, you have cause to hate."

Luneta, after she had extorted a solemn promise from Laudine, went on to say:

"As we are now sitting quite by ourselves, with no one to hear us, I will gladly reply to your question, and only hope you will bestow your love on the knight I am now going to tell you of; but first answer me one question. If two knights fight together, which do you deem the superior – he who is slain, or the one that slew the other?"

"Luneta, I think I suspect what you are driving at. With cunning words you are seeking to lead me astray."

"That I cannot admit. What I am saying is simply the truth, and that is that the knight who slew Vadoin was braver and stronger than he."

"You are mad to talk in the way you do. Never again let me hear any hint at such a thing, or you will forfeit my friendship for ever. How can you imagine I could bring myself to love the man who slew my husband?"

But Luneta was not a girl to be easily frightened by a few angry words. She remained, and began her speech once more, but with

greater caution, and thus, little by little, Laudine began to repent of
her impetuosity. What seemed to her at first an all but mad idea now
appeared, at any rate after what the artful Luneta had said, something
worth considering. She turned to the zealous girl and said:

"Pardon me the words that escaped me ere my wrath subsided,
and tell me more of this knight who seems to have grown so dear
to you. I would know of what lineage he is, and if he be my equal
in birth."

"You need harbour no misgivings on that score. A knight more
courteous or of gentler birth cannot be found than he."

"Tell me the name of the man whom you vaunt so highly."

"His name has often sounded in your ears, for he is known
everywhere where knightly sports are prized. He is called John."

"True it is that I have often heard speak of him," cried Laudine,
"and his bravery is not unknown to me, for no finer knight than
John, King John's son, is to be found if you search the wide world
over. Where is he, for I would fain speak with him?"

Luneta began to laugh at her eagerness, and when she found
she had gained a complete victory, she could not refrain from
making some little fun of her mistress. Then, assuming a serious
countenance, she said the knight was a long distance off from them,
and it would take him five days to reach the castle; but when she
noticed from the lady's dejected mien that the time seemed to her
to be too long, she added:

"A bird could not fly quicker, so long is the journey; but I have
a squire who is a fleeter messenger than the rest. Him I will send
to the knight, and try if the latter can come in three days hence
– quicker than that I do not think it could be done. Meanwhile
we will assemble all your knights and squires, and ask them the
question if there be one among them who would dare take it upon
himself to defend your land and castle against King Arthur when
he comes hither; and I tell you for certain beforehand that not a
single one would venture to take upon himself so hazardous a task.
If such be the case, then no one will wonder at your choosing for
yourself a consort that can defend your kingdom, especially when
he is so renowned a warrior as John, King John's son. This must
not appear to be your own proposal, but ask the advice of your
friends and kinsmen, and let them propose this expedient."

Laudine found this plan excellent, and, on the date fixed, she
summoned her council; but, ere that, Luneta went to John to impart
to him the intelligence which he was awaiting so impatiently. After
greeting him, she said:

"Now you can be happy, for everything has come about as you have wished. Soon, perhaps, the woman you love will be yours."

Then she gave him a detailed description of the conversation between Laudine and herself, and depicted the gradual awakening of her mistress' heart on being told that it was John, the famous Knight of the Round Table, who had defeated Red Vadoin; but she refrained from telling him that her lady had fully pardoned him, and was ready to take him for her husband, for that was a sudden shock which she wished to spare him as yet.

After Luneta had in this wise restored heart and interest in life to the knight, she had a bath prepared for him, brought out some precious raiment – a cloak, jerkin, and baldric – in which she attired him, in place of the damaged armour he had worn in the fight with Red Vadoin; and she herself combed his hair and made him so trim that she herself thought, when she had put the finishing touches on, that she had never seen a more handsome or stately knight.

Then she went to Laudine and said:

"The squire I sent after John has now returned. He has fulfilled his commission, and the knight is now here only awaiting your behests."

"Send him to me at once," said the châtelaine, "but take particular heed that none in the castle see him. For the present this must be a secret between us three."

Luneta did as her mistress bade her, and went to John; but even at the very last she could not refrain from teasing the love-sick knight.

"My lady," said she, "now knows that you are hiding here in the castle, and she is very angry with me for having deceived her so long; but I hope you will put me right with her again, and regain me her favour. You are to go to her now. Entertain no fears, but should things go awry and she take you captive, resign yourself submissively to that fate."

"Alas," replied John, "you know as well as I do that there is no one whose prisoner I would rather be than hers. For good or evil I yield myself up to her."

"I do not think," said Luneta laughing, "that this captivity is likely to bring any disgrace on you. But let us go at once."

They betook themselves forthwith to Laudine's room without being noticed by any one, and when the lady of the castle saw John's manly figure before her, she was so struck by his beauty that it was long before she was able to speak; even John was disconcerted at this interview, and did not quite know how to begin his speech. Luneta, on perceiving their embarrassment, could not repress a smile, and, turning to John, said:

"Noble knight, why are you so faint-hearted as not to venture on a yea or a nay? I presume you did not come here to be silent. Take heart and approach my mistress. I can now tell you to your face that she has granted you full pardon for Red Vadoin's death, that it was she herself who summoned you to tell you this, and that no one can be more welcome to her than you."

When John heard this he fell on his knee before the lovely châtelaine and said:

"Noble lady, I came here to give myself to you for weal or woe: my life is in your hands."

"I shall do you no hurt," answered Laudine. "I have already forgiven you everything."

"I know, unfortunately, that I have caused you a great sorrow, but I am ready to make all the reparation in my power. I will hold all my life at your service."

"You acknowledge, then, that you did me sore wrong when you killed my husband."

"Judge for yourself. He assailed me with all his might, and I am not used to brook defeat. I had no choice between killing or being killed, and every man defends his own life."

"You are right, and I cannot refuse you my pardon. I pardon you willingly, for all that I have heard of you is good. Sit here by my side, and tell me how it came about that you conceived such a passion for me as to love me beyond all other women."

"Can you ask that? As soon as I gazed on your beauty I felt that my life depended on your returning my love."

Laudine listened to his words with pleasure, but interrupted him after a while by asking this question:

"Tell me now on your honour as a knight if, in the event of King Arthur coming here to lay waste my land, would you venture to do battle with him in my defence?"

"That I swear to you on my honour as a knight."

When Laudine received this promise she plighted him her troth, and both swore that nothing but death should part them. Then they proceeded together to the hall, where all Laudine's knights and squires were assembled for the conference to which she had summoned them; and when they saw John they said among themselves that they had never beheld a more majestic knight.

"Just such another man we want for our lord. Our mistress

should take him for her husband, and that would be as great an honour to her as if she got the imperial crown in Rome."

Laudine bade them all be seated, and after they had sat down, the chamberlain called for silence and said:

"You know full well how great a loss we have lately suffered through the death of our lord Red Vadoin, and just now we are more than ever in need of a leader, for King Arthur has now armed himself to attack us with shield and sword in order to conquer our kingdom. He will be here within fourteen days, and then our future fate will hang in the balance. It seems to me necessary, on that account, that our lady should marry again and choose herself a husband who could protect her kingdom. No one shall be able to censure her for such a step, and we therefore hope that she will, for our sakes, agree to take it, though, possibly, out of love for Vadoin, she be reluctant to comply with our wish."

All agreed with this speech, and they besought her, on their knees, to choose a consort fit to direct the helm of her state and maintain its ancient renown. But the châtelaine feigned that this request was highly objectionable to her, and made them beseech her for a long time before she would say yes, but, nevertheless, she finally suffered herself to be prevailed on by their necessities, and said:

"As this matter is of such grave importance to you I will sacrifice my personal feelings to the common weal. This knight whom you here see" (pointing to John) "has long desired me for his spouse. He is both wise and courteous, in birth my peer, being a king's son, and pre-eminent in valour and might in war. I surrender to you the choice of my husband, and ask you, therefore, if you will accept him for your lord."

When they had all expressed their consent in a loud voice, she went on to say:

"Since this marriage is thus decreed, it seems to me foolish to long delay that which must some time or other take place, and my will, therefore, is that this wedding be celebrated at once."

All the knights waxed marvellously glad thereat, and thanked her warmly for having met their wishes with such exceeding readiness, and the marriage was at once celebrated with mirth and merriment. Minstrels from all directions flocked together to exhibit their skill, and returned home laden with rich gifts, and extolling the generosity of the bridegroom. Squires and maidens threaded the dance with each other, and the dance-songs chimed merrily in the vast banqueting-hall, but, outside, the more veteran knights contended in a grand tournament, and the clash of their arms was heard far and wide. John was now radiantly happy; he had gained for himself a kingdom and a bride, and the dead man was already forgotten. The new bridegroom was loved and honoured by all, and he marked that they greatly preferred him for their leader to Red Vadoin.

But the marriage mirth was soon to be troubled by the din of war. King Arthur had not forgotten to avenge the insult put on Kalegrevanz, but summoned all his knights, and marched to the land whose lord was now John. They reached the spring on Mid-summer-day, and there encamped. At the council which was opened at once, Kay was the first to speak; and, in accordance with his usual practice, he began to slander the absent John.

"I wonder," said he, "where John can now be lurking, seeing he came not hither with the rest of us. When the wine had mounted to his head he bragged valiantly, and swore that he would alone avenge his kinsman, contentious that we should leave him this honour; but it comes to pass that his courage seems to have vanished after he had considered the matter more closely. Well, yes, a man in his cups says much that he cannot afterwards perform, and this proves the truth of the saying, 'Big in words, little in deeds'."

"If John is not here," Gavian answered him, "there is some cause for his absence. Who knows what may have happened to him. After he rode from Caerleon much may have occurred to hinder him from reaching here; but one thing I *do* know is that John would never have spoken ill of a man absent, and so unable to defend himself; and we all know well enough that never yet has John kept aloof from a perilous venture out of fear."

"I will not bandy words with you," replied Kay, "but the truth of my words is sure to be established, and I venture, moreover, to assert that he fled from the palace like one distraught."

This wrangle ended, King Arthur approached the spring, took the cup, filled it with water, and poured the contents over the post. At once a pelting shower of rain came down, as on the previous occasion, followed by thunder and lightning. As soon as John perceived this from the castle, he put on his armour, and leapt on the best courser Red Vadoin had, and dug his spurs into its flanks, and galloped at full speed towards the well. When Kay caught sight of the strange knight he went into the king's presence and eagerly sought his permission to break the first lance with the defender of the spring, and as King Arthur did not refuse him this favour he hurriedly donned his armour and rode against John. The latter recognized his adversary at once, and his heart was filled with joy at having at length found an opportunity of punishing the man who had so long disparaged and flouted him. He grasped his lance with a lusty grip, and struck it into Kay's breast with such force that both horse and knight rolled over, and each wallowed in the mire. Kay experienced no sympathy as he lay there helpless and beaten.

"God help you," said they all. "You, who used to gibe at every one else, have now got a lesson that you will not forget. Lie where you are, a laughing-stock to all."

He got on his feet at last in a shamefaced sort of way, but he did not dare to return to the camp and expose himself to the jeers of the rest. John took no further notice of him, but led his horse by the bridle, and rode with it to the tent without any one recognizing him. When he reached it he exclaimed:

"Although, by the law of battle, this horse belongs to me, yet I will not carry it off, for I do not wish to appropriate to myself anything that belongs to King Arthur or his knights, so take the steed, and treat him well, while I pursue my journey."

When King Arthur heard this he said:

"Who are you who speak such words as these? I do not remember having seen your badge before."

"My lord," replied the unknown knight, "perhaps you will know when I tell you my name. I am called John."

Great was the rejoicing now, and all hastened to bid John welcome. After they had partly got over their surprise, King Arthur bade him explain the mystery, and tell what had taken place since the night he quitted Caerleon. John then recounted all his adventures, the victory over Vadoin, whereby he gained a kingdom and a wife, and ended by inviting King Arthur and all his suite to his castle. The king expressed his thanks, and John rode home to inform his wife that the dreaded enemy was now coming as a welcome guest, and had promised to stay in their castle for eight days. When Laudine heard this news she rejoiced exceedingly, and at once gave orders for receiving the king in the most sumptuous fashion.

On the following morning King Arthur sallied forth from his camp, and was greeted first by a troop of knights and squires, who came out to meet him with drums and music. When these saw the king they alighted from their horses, and bade him, in their mistress' name, welcome to the castle. Immediately afterwards he was met by another company composed of minstrels and musicians, who played their instruments in his honour. The castle itself was adorned with precious cloth of gold and costly stuffs which swayed from every nook and corner, even the walls were hung with mats of various colours. The mistress of the castle, followed by a bodyguard of knights, met the strangers at the drawbridge, in order to accompany them to their quarters, and soon her retinue mingled with King Arthur's.

The eight days were taken up with chivalrous exercises, hunting, and sport, and when they were over King Arthur resolved to take his departure. He had John summoned secretly to his presence, and ordered him to come with him, and even his kinsman Gavian advised him to accompany them.

"It ill-beseems you," said he, "to lie idle henceforward in this castle and let all the honour you have won fade away; neither is it honourable to your bride. As a knight it is your bounden duty to fare from court to court where joust and tournament are held, and break a lance in her honour. And is it not far more noble to hazard life and lands in her honour than to lie at home like a woman? You shall never lack a trusty comrade-in-arms, for in sunshine and in rain I will follow you, so that only death shall part us. Do not think I say this because I grudge you and your spouse the happiness you enjoy in mutual love, or that I would lure you to forget her, but that both she and you may gain the highest renown by following my counsel and again setting out in quest of adventures."

John, who was rent between his wish to stay with Laudine and his desire to resume the life to which the knights of the Round Table were accustomed, answered that he would follow his comrades-in-arms, provided his wife gave her consent thereto. He went to her at once and said:

"I venture to approach you with a petition. You are my wife, and as such it is within your rights to grant or refuse it. Let me once more for a season go forth in quest of adventures, for I am loth to hear it said that I laid aside all chivalrous exercises on the very day I won myself a bride."

His wife could not rightly understand his wishing to abandon her so soon, but she gave in to his wish, and granted him leave to go.

"But," she added, "I give you this permission only on one condition – you must return before the lapse of a year; if not you will have lost my love for ever, and I should then look on you as a recreant knight."

When John heard these strong words he grew exceedingly rueful, and sighed:

"God forbid that I should not come back to you as speedily as I can, but none can provide against accidents, and mayhap sickness or captivity may hinder me from returning within the year."

"Harbour no fears of dangers such as those," answered she, placing a ring on his finger. "So long as you wear this ring and think of me sickness shall not reach you, nor shall any man take you captive; but guard it well, for it is a miraculous ring which I can bestow only on him who is dearest to me of all the world. Now God be with you."

John thanked her with many kisses for this precious gift and then they parted. John rode with King Arthur's company, pleased at finding himself once more among his brethren-in-arms, but at the same time melancholy, for his heart still tarried with the fair lady of the castle whom he had been constrained to give up.

Gavian and he soon parted from the others, and set out in quest of adventures.

In every tournament that was held they took their part and always came off conquerors, and, consequently, there was but one universal, unanimous opinion, and that was that no braver knights were to be found elsewhere. But, as time went on, months slipped away without John, in his eagerness for the fray, paying any heed to them, and soon the year was gone without his having remembered his promise. At the beginning of the new year King Arthur called all his knights together to a meeting, and thither went John and Gavian, who received much praise for the feats they had recently accomplished; but whilst they were sitting at the Round Table they saw a maiden come riding up to them. On reaching their tent she alighted from her horse, divested herself of her mantle, and courteously stepped into the presence of the assembled knights. John recognised her as one of his wife's maids, and then remembered with dismay his promise. The damsel greeted King Arthur and said:

"My mistress has sent me to you to give you and all your knights her greeting; but for John I have a special message. I declare him, in my lady's name, to be a liar and a recreant knight that has broken the word he gave a woman. Despite his promise, he has not returned to her within the year, and so she declares through me that he has forfeited her love, and she will never more look with favour on him. The ring she gave him at parting she now demands back, for he is no longer worthy of wearing that symbol of her troth."

While she was speaking John sat mute and motionless without replying, and it seemed as if her words had deprived him of his senses; but the damsel hurriedly walked up to him, pulled the ring off his finger without his even making an effort to resist her.

"Blush, false knight!" exclaimed she, "and never dare show yourself among men of gentle breeding or where manly deeds are done. May you be dead to all as you are to my mistress. And now farewell, King Arthur. God shield you and your knights."

Then she rode away, but John remained as it were unconscious, only brooding over the shame that had befallen him. At length he rushed wildly from the table, and ran off without uttering a word. Madness instantly clouded his brain so that he tore his clothes to pieces, and he scourged himself with thorns and twigs. People tried to stop him and lead him back, but he ran away and sped towards the woods, and so all traces of him were soon lost. After running for a good while he saw a man hunting in the wood, and assailed him, and snatched the bow and arrow from him, and disappeared before the hunter could recover from his amazement.

Without regaining the use of his reason, he lived for some time amid the woods and fells, where he wandered about without shelter or any sort of clothing wherewith to cover his nakedness. Thanks to the bow, he was not without food, for he brought down by his arrows the wild creatures of the wood. He ate his food raw, for he no longer understood the use of fire; he had no bread, and took no notice of the herbs in the wood.

One day, in the course of his wanderings, he came to a hut in the wood, where a poor hermit dwelt. When the hermit saw the naked and almost black man he became dreadfully frightened and thought the latter had come to rob him, so he called to him out of the window:

"Of my own free will I will readily give you all I possess, but there is nothing here save water and coarse bread. I have nothing else to live upon. You may have that and welcome."

Through the little window-hole he handed him all the bread there was in the hut, and John sat down and ate up ravenously every bit, as if it had been the most dainty food. After he had finished he got up and ran again to the woods, but though he had long been weak in intellect, nevertheless he preserved a sense of gratitude. He carried to the hermit the first beast he shot, and laid it down before his cottage by way of repayment for the bread the hermit had given him. The good hermit, who was touched by this silent gratitude, sold the animal and bought with the money meat and wine which, on the following day, when John returned, he handed to the latter through the window. This was repeated day after day, for John came daily to the hermit with some bird or beast he had shot, and the hermit boiled or baked the meat for him, as well as gave him bread and wine for the parts of the animals he had sold.

One day, as John lay sleeping under a lime tree in the wood, there came a bevy of ladies riding past him, to wit, a châtelaine of the name of Murina and three of her handmaids. On their remarking the queer black figure, one of the handmaids was moved by curiosity, and stepped off her palfrey to observe the strange object. His skin had become black through the savage nature of the life he had been leading, and his face was hidden by a long matted beard. Well, the more closely she scrutinized his features the more familiar they seemed to her to be, and at last she noticed a scar on his forehead, and then recognised the unhappy knight, for John had received this scar in a tourney that had been held in Murina's castle. She was seized with sorrow and amazement at seeing the ghastly state to which he had been reduced, and hurriedly remounted her horse and rode back to her mistress.

"My lady," cried she, "the man who lies there is the bravest knight that ever splintered a lance: it is John, King John's son. I cannot conceive what has happened to him, but it is clear that some great misfortune has overtaken him, and he has lost the use of his reason. God grant that he may be again the man he was when last I saw him, for, in good sooth, he would avenge all the wrongs that Arlan the earl has committed against you."

"If he would only remain there long enough for me to ride home," answered her mistress, "I think I have a remedy which will make him hale and hearty again. My godmother, the fairy Morgana, has given me a salve which possesses the marvellous virtue of being able to drive madness from the brain, and this salve I will blithely give him." After saying this the lady of the castle rode home as fast as she could, opened her coffer, and took from it a box which she delivered to the damsel who had first caught sight of John. She not only gave her the box of ointment but also a store of rich garments with which John might array himself, as well as two splendid coursers, one for her, and the other for the knight. She then told her to ride back fast to the luckless wight to release him from his misery.

The damsel, on returning to the lime tree, found John still asleep, so she alighted from her horse, stepped up to him cautiously, not without some trepidation, for she knew, of course, that he had not the use of his reason. Then she rubbed him with ointment from the crown of his head to the soles of his feet, laid the raiment beside him, and concealed herself right in the wood, so that he should not suspect, when he woke up, the part she had played in his recovery. After a while the sun began to shine through the leaves, and warmed the wonderful ointment, and, as this penetrated his body, reason slowly returned to John. Then he awoke and looked about him in amazement, without any recollection of the long season during which he had been wandering about the wood, like one bereft of his senses. He was seized with shame at discovering his nakedness, and at once hastened to don the handsome suit of raiment that lay beside him on the grass. Directly he had done this he looked round to discover some human being who might tell him where he was, and help him to find his way out of the wood. When the damsel perceived from her hiding-place that he was completely cured, she resolved to conceal herself no longer, but walked towards him, without letting him suspect that she had been there. When he saw her he rejoiced exceedingly, and called out to her:

"Noble damsel, tell me where I am, and help me out of here".

But when she affected not to notice him he repeated his request, and begged her fervently not to abandon him. She stopped her palfrey and asked him courteously what he wanted. He replied that he could not tell her how miserable and forlorn he felt, and ended his speech by asking her if she would lend him the horse she was leading.

"I will let you have it willingly, provided you will bear me company."

"Where do you live, then?"

"In a castle that lies not very far from here."

"With your leave I will gladly escort you. I know not how I shall repay your kindness. Is there no service I can render you?"

"Perhaps there is," replied she. "Only follow me, and it will not be long before I shall remind you of the offer you have made."

They rode away, and soon they reached Murina's castle, and there the châtelaine met and received him with marks of deep respect. She had a luxurious bath prepared for him, and her servants not only washed him, but clipped his long hair and shaved his matted beard. The châtelaine did all she could to make his stay at the castle as pleasant as possible, and all her dependants were only too ready to satisfy his lightest wishes. Thus the days passed by, and, little by little, he got back his health, his strength returned to him, and he began anew to long for the combat. He had not long to tarry ere such an opportunity came into his way.

I should mention that the châtelaine had an enemy named Arlan, the earl with whom she had a feud of long standing, and this fellow attacked her territory, laying it waste far and wide, even going so far as to burn the houses that lay immediately under the castle-hill. All the inmates of the castle donned their armour, knights and squires, and strove as to which of them should first be ready to confront the earl's people. John, who had now recovered his old lust of fighting, was the first to get his armour on, and galloped on his battle-steed out of the castle in advance of all the rest. The first knight he encountered was struck so violently by his spear that he fell to the ground never more to rise from it. Then John rode like a nettled lion into the very ranks of the foe, gripped with both his hands the hilt of his broad falchion, and hacked wildly about him so that his enemies fell round about him like corn before the sickle. The knights who were in his train were encouraged still further by his valour, and exhorted each other not to abandon so brave a leader. From the castle towers the châtelaine and her dames looked on the savage strife and recognized John's helmet in the midst of the hostile ranks. They marked how he hurled himself, like a hawk, down on his enemies and slew such as failed to yield themselves up at once. They thought they had never seen a braver knight before, and there was many a maiden who would fain have had such a warrior for her husband.

The enemy was just meditating flight when one of their bravest knights galloped up to John, and attacked him so valiantly that the tide of victory almost turned. With a single blow he cleft John's shield, and Murina's champion narrowly escaped being dangerously wounded; but he managed to snatch another shield from one of the enemy, and levelled his spear against the knight with such force that both horse and rider were overthrown. Then John waxed wroth and hacked away at the foe until his sword streamed with blood. Resistance was no longer to be thought of, and those who escaped his steel sought safety in flight. John, on perceiving this, put spurs into his horse and pursued them. He observed Arlan, the earl, amid the ranks of the fugitives, recognizing him by his arms, and then directed his onslaught against him, having sternly resolved not to let the earl escape, but to kill him or take him prisoner. The earl put his spurs into his jaded horse to try to escape, but both horse and rider were too much exhausted to get the start of John. At last he overtook the earl, and raised his sword over him, and as the latter was alone, his man having ridden away, he had no choice but to surrender.

"For God's sake," cried he, "leave me my life, and then you are welcome to hold my lands and castle as your own."

"It is possible that I may spare you; but it is not I who shall pronounce your doom, for I shall lead you to Lady Murina, and it rests with her to grant you mercy or withhold it."

Then John deprived him of his arms and carried him captive to the castle. When they came before the châtelaine, and John had delivered to her the captive earl, the latter fell on his knees before her and craved for mercy.

"I acknowledge," said he, "that I have wronged you, but I will offer you all the reparation that lies within my power, money and goods as much as you desire, and for what you suffer me to retain I will be your vassal."

When John had pleaded for the captive earl the Lady Murina agreed to pardon him for John's sake. The earl then rose up gladly and thanked his generous foe, but John advanced to the châtelaine, and asked her leave to go his way now the strife was over. Although she would have liked to keep him even longer with her, she said she could not hinder him from going, and thanked him with tears for the help he had afforded her.

John now rode from the castle the same way he had come. He was utterly alone, for his gloomy spirits caused him as much as possible to shun the society of his fellows. When he had journeyed a while he heard a terrible roaring in the thicket, and saw, on riding there, a serpent and a lion engaged in deadly strife with each other. The serpent had wound itself round the lion, and was holding it in such a tight embrace that it could not move. When John saw that the poor beast could not resist any longer, but would be choked, he was moved with compassion, jumped off his horse, and tied it up a good distance from the scene of combat, where the serpent's venom could not harm it. Then he held his shield in front of him and nimbly attacked the serpent. With the first blow he cut its head off, and the lion was then able to release itself from its adversary's fatal embrace. John next put himself on the defensive, thinking that the lion would now attack him, but when the lion saw the serpent lying dead, it walked up to John, laid itself at his feet, and tried to express its gratitude as best it could. John noticed a wound in the lion's neck – the result of the serpent's poisonous bite – and, in order to prevent the poison from spreading, he promptly cut off the flesh round the wound. It seemed as if the lion understood the service he had rendered it, for it made no resistance, but stretched its neck forward and glanced gratefully at its deliverer. When John rode away the lion followed him, and, showed, as well as an animal can express, that it meant to serve and follow him for the future; and so it did constantly. The lion followed him as faithfully as a dog, and this companionship caused him to be known everywhere by the name of the Knight of the Lion.

The faithful beast, determined to manifest its attachment in every way, ran before the rider into the wood, seized a buck, and hurried off to overtake him with it. The lion then laid down its prey in front of the horse, and when John did not stop, but pursued his journey, the lion would not delay to consume the animal, but ran along by the knight. When night came on, and John interrupted his ride, the lion seemed to understand that he was hungry, and rushed off at once amongst the trees to hunt for some game. It knocked over and killed the first stag it saw, threw it on its back, and hurried with it to John, who drew his hunting-knife and flayed the creature, giving the lion its entrails, liver, lungs and heart, and roasting the rest for himself. When he sat down to eat, the lion stretched itself at his feet, and refused to leave him. Even by night the faithful animal kept watch over his master when he laid himself down to sleep on his shield beside the camp fire.

When day dawned John rode on, and so they lived together for fourteen days, hunting and roaming about the wild wood, but on the evening of the fifteenth day they came to a spring, and when John saw it he recognized it as being the very same spring beside which he had done battle with Red Vadoin. All his sorrowful memories surged through his soul, shame and despair overwhelmed him once more with such violence that he fell to the ground unconscious. As he fell his sword slipped out of its sheath and wounded him in both shoulder and breast, so that blood poured forth from beneath his coat of mail. When the lion saw this it began to tremble with anxiety, and crept cautiously up to the fallen knight, grasped his sword with its teeth and carried it off some distance so that it should not further hurt him; then it laid itself at his feet and waited until he returned to life. On opening his eyes, John's first thought was of his broken promise to his wife, and then his despair began afresh.

"Why should I seek further to avoid my fate?" he sighed; "all my happiness in life is over, and sorrow alone is left to me. It is best, then, that I end my days. There is none to see me here, and I can kill myself without a soul knowing it. The only creature to mourn me would be this poor lion."

As he uttered these words he was standing near a chapel which had been built just beside the fountain. In this chapel there was a captive maid who, hearing his voice, interrupted her melancholy reflections and asked, in moving words, to have speech with him. John, much amazed, went to the chapel and asked who was in there.

"I am," answered the captive, "the most luckless being the sun shines upon."

"Do not say that," said John, "for my sorrow is many times greater than yours."

"You, indeed, are free, and your time is your own; you can ride whither you will; but I am sitting in captivity here on a false charge, and to-morrow they will burn me on a pyre."

"Tell me what they have charged you with, and why they have condemned you to such a painful death."

"Let God be my judge. If I be guilty may He never succour me in body or in soul. The chancellor and both his brothers accuse me of having betrayed my mistress, and on this false charge I am doomed to lose my life, unless I can find a knight willing to fight single-handed on behalf of my innocence against all my three slanderers."

"Then your misfortune is less than mine," said John, "for you can get help; but as for my grief, that no man can cure."

"Who do you suppose will be my champion? There are only two knights in the whole world in whom I dare hope. God grant I may find them."

"Let me hear who these are who would dare to fight against three knights at the same time."

"One is the knight Gavian and the other is John, King John's son. It is because of him that I am to die on the morrow."

"What is it you say?" shouted John. "It is because of him that you are accused? Well, then, know that he whom you are now addressing is John, King John's son, and by God's help I will set you free if it be that you are the girl who so generously helped me after I had slain Red Vadoin. You saved my life, and what you did for me then I will do for you now. But tell me what has happened since that luckless hour when I rode away from the castle."

"You remember that I helped you in your direst need, and you remember also that it was I who brought you and your lady together – and these things I do not regret. Afterwards you rode away with Knight Gavian, and the year went by without any tidings being heard of you. Then my mistress waxed wroth, and blamed me for having treacherously brought about this marriage. When the chancellor perceived that I had lost her favour, his old spite against me broke out; he began to slander me, and ended by charging me formally with treason towards my mistress. He bade me get a knight who would dare single-handed to vindicate my innocence against him and his two brothers; but if none would or could do this, the pyre awaited me. No one in the castle ventured to stand forth as my champion, and all in vain I made my supplication at other courts: not a soul would take up my cause. Then I rode to King Arthur at Caerleon, and inquired after Knight Gavian, but there I heard sad tidings. A knight had been there and carried the queen off by main force, and Gavian had been sent by the king to take vengeance on the ruffian, and bring back the stolen queen. I could find neither you nor Gavian, and I was forced, woe-begone as I was, to return hither. So, I am now sitting in captivity. To-day a priest prepared me for death, and to-morrow I must die, unless you will, of yourself, do battle single-handed with the three."

"Fear not," answered John, "to-morrow I shall come hither ere the judgment falls on you, and I will either save you or fall in the lists; but, whatever may happen, you must promise me that you will reveal my name to none: that must remain a secret 'twixt us twain."

"I would rather die than utter aught which you have bidden me keep secret; but, alas, they will perhaps kill you and then burn me."

"Say not so, for were they ten instead of three, I should vanquish them to-morrow. I shall now ride off to seek lodging for the night and bait for my horse, but do not fear my not appearing in the lists. God forbid that I should betray you, so, good-night, noble damsel, and rely on my word."

John remounted his horse and plunged into the wood, followed by his lion. Soon the trees began to grow less numerous, and he perceived a castle before him, the walls of which were strong and high, but the country round about was desolate and laid waste. Not a habitation appeared, and he failed to find even bait for his horse. Seeing this he rode straight to the castle, and when he reached it the drawbridge was lowered for him, and its lord and his men came out and received him with great courtesy. They asked him, however, to chain up the lion outside the gate, for they feared that it would otherwise do mischief, but John answered:

"That I cannot do, for he and I have promised never to be parted, and I myself will answer for us both; but have no fear, the lion shall not do any one harm."

They answered that he might do what seemed best to him, and then they went into the castle, and there John was welcomed by the dames and damsels, who met him with torches, and lighted him into the banqueting-hall. There they took off his armour and gave him other raiment, and then ushered him into supper. John could not, however, help noticing that their merriment at table was occasioned more by politeness to him than by cheerfulness of mind;

and when he heard his host heaving deep sighs, and saw him unable any longer to conceal his tears, John thought he ought to ask him the cause of his distress.

"Right gladly will I tell you," replied his host, "concerning the misfortune that has befallen me. Hard by there dwells a fierce giant of the name of Harpin, and he is moved by hatred towards me. He has laid waste my land; my manors and castles are burnt down, and now nothing remains to me of all my possessions save this castle, which has hitherto resisted his attacks, though he has come hither day after day. I had six sons – the bravest knights you could see – and this giant has succeeded in taking the whole six prisoners. Two of them he slew outside this castle. I witnessed the deed with my own eyes; and to-morrow he is coming back with two others to slay them in sight of us all. There is only one means of my escaping this, namely, the monster has demanded my only daughter, not to take her to wife himself, but to give her to the foulest and most scoundrelly scullion he has; and I would rather suffer death than an indignity such as this."

"It seems to me passing strange," said John, "that you have not informed King Arthur of this matter, for there are many at his court who would willingly help you, and do battle with this giant, however strong he be."

"I have done what I could and sought to find the brave Gavian, for my wife and he are sister and brother. However, as ill-luck would have it, he was not in Caerleon, but had ridden off in quest of the queen, who had been carried off. Had he been aware of what his sister has to suffer he would assuredly have been here long ere this."

"If I can do anything for you," said John, "you may count on me, and should the giant come here early to-morrow morning, ere I ride hence, I will do battle with him whatever the issue be, but I cannot tarry longer than daybreak, for I have promised to fight at midday on behalf of a captive maiden whose life depends on my being present, and that promise I must irrevocably keep."

The lord of the castle was beside himself with joy at this promise, and could not say enough to express his thanks; but, while he was talking, his wife and daughter came into the banqueting-hall, both with tear-stained faces, which they sought to conceal under their veils. On seeing them the lord of the castle cried out:

"Now, dry your tears, for God has sent us this noble knight to assuage all our grief."

When they heard this, and learnt that John had promised to fight the fierce Harpin, they grew exceeding glad and fell on their knees before him in thanksgiving; and when the daughter lifted her veil John beheld the loveliest face he had ever looked upon. He hastened to raise them up, and said:

"You ought not to go down on your knees before me, and you must put off your thanks until the morrow. What the issue of this fray will be, even supposing I can wait for it, no man can tell; but it is high time to sleep and recruit our strength for to-morrow's fight."

John, followed by his faithful lion, then proceeded to the bed-chamber assigned to him. Shortly before daybreak a priest knocked at his door and asked him if he would like to hear Mass. John expressed his thanks, clad himself hurriedly in his armour, and went down to the chapel to prepare himself by devotion and prayer for the perilous encounter which he would have to sustain that day. When Mass was over he went out into the courtyard to look for the giant. The sun had already risen, but not a glimpse of the giant was yet to be seen. After waiting a while, he turned to the lord of the castle and said:

"God knows how gladly I would stay with you, but my promise prevents me waiting any longer for your enemy; so, farewell, and may God retain you in His keeping."

He then took farewell of them at once, and as he was about to mount his horse the damsel fell on her knees before him, entreating him not to abandon them, and her parents offered him lands and gold if he would but stay, but he said:

"God forbid that I should sell my service. Never let Gavian or any other valiant knight hear that you made me such an offer."

"Then stay for Blessed Mary's sake," entreated the damsel in tears. "Stay for your friend Gavian's sake, and forget not that my mother is his sister."

John knew not quite what to answer them. It cut him to the heart to see the young girl's tears, but he could not break the oath he had sworn to Luneta, and he knew he could never survive the grief and shame which would befal him if she were to suffer death through his broken promise. In his perplexity he turned to the damsel and said:

"I leave this matter in God's hands, and, relying on His succour, I will bide yet awhile."

He had hardly uttered these words before he saw the giant rushing over the plain like a madman, and carrying on his shoulder a tremendous bar of steel, so heavy that ten men could hardly have managed to carry it. He had brought with him the two knights, both bound hand and foot. He had thrown each on a horse, and there they lay across the saddles, with their heads hanging down towards the ground. The horses themselves were wretched, half-starved jades, hardly able to go by themselves, and driven by a miserable dwarf, who lashed with his scourge not only them, but also the poor knights, whose clothes were torn to rags, and from whom blood was flowing in streams. When the giant reached the castle gate he lifted up his voice and ordered that the damsel should be given up to his scullion, otherwise they would have reason to repent it.

John then turned to the lord of the castle, who was bewailing his hard lot, and said:

"I have never heard of such an outrage before, but, with God's help, we will hinder him from getting your daughter into his power."

Then he called for his horse and arms, the drawbridge was let down, and he galloped over the plain towards the astonished giant.

"Who are you?" cried the latter, as he saw the knight; "who dare fight against me? They are no real friends of yours who urge you to such a foolhardy act."

"I have not come here to waste time in bandying words," answered John. "Your threats do not alarm me, and you shall see I have no intention of running away from you."

Having said this he dug his spurs into the horse's sides and rushed towards the giant. The giant wore for armour a thick bear's hide, but that was pierced by John's lance so that the blood gushed out in a stream. But he troubled himself little or nothing about the wound, but seized hold of his iron bar and aimed a blow at John which shattered his shield into splinters. John waxed mightly wroth, and swore that the giant should pay dearly for this, whereupon he grasped his sword with both hands and gave the giant such a tremendous cut across the forehead that a piece of flesh, the size of an ordinary man's head, dropped off at the blow. Harpin shrieked with pain and rushed blindly at his enemy. His steel bar glanced so close to John that the knight reeled in his saddle and looked, for an instant, as if he was about to fall to the ground; but the lion, as soon as it perceived the peril in which John stood, rushed up and took his share in the sport. The faithful beast hurled himself on the giant, tore his bear's skin to tatters, dug his claws into the monster's body, and tore and rent it till the flesh and muscles flew about. The giant managed, after some few minutes, to extricate himself; but it was in vain that he tried to reach the lion with his iron bar. It was too unwieldy and the lion far too nimble. In spite of all his blows, it knew how to avoid them, and at last the giant, in aiming a crushing blow at this enemy that constantly eluded his efforts to reach him, directed his weapon with such force that the bar fastened itself into the ground and there stuck. John then rushed forward and buried his sword right in the monster's body. The fight was now finished, and the giant tottered to the ground a dead man.

The people in the castle, who had trembled as they watched the varying fortunes of the fray, now hurried out when they saw the giant fall. Their joy at their deliverance from the monster knew no bounds, and the lord of the castle said to John:

"I do not know how I shall ever thank you enough for delivering us all. Unfortunately, I know I must not keep you longer with me, but I hope you will not be long before you came back, so that I may prove to you that you have helped no ungrateful man."

"Let us say nothing more on this score," replied John, "but only ask your sons to take the dwarf that was in the giant's retinue, and send him to Gavian as a gift from me."

"We will willingly do that," said they, "but if he asks us who has sent him, what are we to say?"

"Well, only say it was the Knight of the Lion, and that his friendship for Gavian induced him to fight this battle for his sister's sake; but naught further than this are you to tell him."

After saying this he waved his hand to them in farewell, and galloped at a furious pace to the enchanted spring.

The sun indicated that noon was already past when he reached the spot, and poor Luneta had already been brought from the chapel and conducted to the pyre. The faggots had been carried there, and only needed to be lighted, just as John came galloping up to order them to desist from their work. When the people saw the steel-clad knight galloping up at full speed they scampered away so as to escape the horse's hoofs, and a broad road was opened out between the rider and the pyre. John saw where Luneta lay. Her clothing consisted only of coarse linen, which hardly concealed her nakedness. When John arrived she had already made her confession and prepared herself for death. Around her stood a crowd of women lamenting and shedding tears. John shouted out that he had come to vindicate her innocence, and urged those who accused her to step forth and do battle with him, after which he approached the pyre, and sought to comfort her with some kindly words.

"My poor Luneta," said he, "tell me now who they are who have so shamefully belied you. I have come to vindicate you, and

I shall compel them to withdraw their charges or else perish in the attempt."

"God requite you, noble knight, for having come," answered Luneta. "Had you been but a few minutes later, I had been undone; but now I hope my sorrow will be turned to joy. My accusers are standing here close by the pyre, but I know that God will grant you the victory, as surely as I am innocent."

When the chancellor and his two brothers heard her say this, they bade her hold her peace.

"Do not put any faith in what she says," cried they to John. "You are bereft of your senses if you mean to risk your life for such a liar. Be wise and ride away; and venture not to fight one against three."

"I am not going to run away for your big words," answered John. "It is true enough that I have no friends or kinsmen here; but I put my trust in God and my good sword, and I shall not blench from you, though I am one and you are three. You must either withdraw your words or else maintain them sword in hand."

"Since you refuse to follow good advice, then let your death be on your own head. But before the combat begins be good enough to order your lion to quit the lists."

"Should the lion attack you then you must strive to protect yourselves as well as you can."

"We will not fight against both of you; either tie up your lion or ride off. In any case we will not begin the fray."

John made a sign to the lion to go away, and the sagacious beast went off at once and lay down at a distance. John fastened his helmet tighter on his head, seized a lance, and the fray began. The chancellor and his brothers immediately attacked the solitary knight with the greatest fury, but John carefully reserved his strength. When they rushed against him he avoided their attack by a clever movement, but they had hardly passed him before he turned his horse and made for the chancellor. He tilted against him with all his might, and caught him full in the chest with his lance, so that he was lifted out of his saddle and hurled to the ground, where he lay long in a swoon. When the brothers saw this they brought their horses close together, and rode against John. Dexterous as his movements were and doughty his blows, yet he found it difficult to defend himself against their furious attack, and, worse still, the chancellor, having recovered consciousness, and frantic at his overthrow, seized his arms and joined his brothers. There was now three of them again, and he felt that his strength was beginning to desert him in the unequal fight.

But the lion, when it saw the peril in which John stood, could no longer keep still; it rushed up and hurled itself on the chancellor, throwing him to the ground. With its powerful teeth the savage beast caught hold of the rings in his coat-of-mail, wrenched them apart one from another, and then dug its claws into his side, and butchered him instantly. John was now released from his most dangerous enemy, but the two others now attacked him the more fiercely, and he thought he had never before been so hard pressed. The lion, however, again came to his assistance by jumping up from the lacerated corpse of the chancellor, and rushing on both the brothers. They were not unprepared, but received the lion's onset so that it fell down before them sorely wounded. However, when John saw the faithful beast's fall, he was beside himself with rage, and fell on the two knights with such fury that they were constrained to give themselves up and declare themselves vanquished, in order to save their lives. But this did not avail them much, for when John pointed his sword at their breasts, and forced them to acknowledge that they had slandered poor Luneta out of nothing but malice, the multitude waxed so frantic that both her traducers were dragged to the pyre, instead of her, and there died the death they had devised for her.

Luneta's innocence was now established, and she descended from the pyre to thank her preserver, but, according to her promise, pretended that the knight was a stranger to her. No one else knew who he was, and not even his own wife suspected who the Knight of the Lion in reality was. She approached him, however, in a courteous manner, and invited him to accompany her to the castle to stay there until the lion's wounds should be healed. John bowed low in his saddle, and expressed his thanks without lifting his visor.

"God requite you for the honour you would show me, but I cannot enter any man's house, or find joy or gladness in life, until I have regained my wife's love which I forfeited through my own fault."

The châtelaine answered that she thought it strange for a woman not to love so brave a knight, and added that she did not suppose he had committed such a serious crime against his wife that it was beyond the reach of forgiveness.

"I must not reveal my crime: it is a secret between her and me."

"Tell me, noble knight," she went on to say, "is it only

you two who are aware of the way in which you displeased your wife?"

"Only we two. If any third party could suspect it, it is you."

"Now I do not understand you any longer. Tell me, then, your name that I may have some clue to solving your riddle."

"People call me the Knight of the Lion. I possess no other name."

"The name itself sounds strange to me, and I have never heard the Knight of the Lion spoken of."

"The reason of that is not far to seek. I am no renowned knight whose name has been on every man's tongue. If I had more often joined in the fray or assisted at tournaments doubtless you would have heard the name of the Knight of the Lion mentioned."

"Again I ask you to come with me to my castle."

"No, noble lady; I will not go thither until I am reconciled with my wife."

"Good-bye, then, and may God grant you, in all fulness, your desire for forgiveness."

"May your prayer be heard, and," added he in a whisper, "may you yourself be not more implacable than you would have the wife of the Knight of the Lion to be."

Then he remounted his horse and proceeded to the wood. Luneta, who had now regained her mistress' favour, followed him a part of the way, partly to thank him, and partly to question him further. To her expression of thanks he merely answered:

"Whatever may happen, I beg you not to betray my name."

"No one shall beguile it out of me."

"I have yet one petition to make to you. You have now regained your lady's heart, and you can talk with her as of yore. Keep me in your thoughts, and should you seem to have an opportunity of assuaging her anger against me, and effecting our reconciliation, do not utterly forget me."

"I have no higher wish than that," answered Luneta, "and be assured that I shall have you always in my thoughts."

Then they parted, and John returned to his sick lion, which now could hardly stand on its legs from loss of blood. He jumped off his horse and entered the wood to collect leaves and moss, and after a while he came back with an armful and laid them together on the shield and made a soft couch for the wounded creature. At last he hoisted the shield up on the horse's back, and there lay the lion while John walked beside the litter. About nightfall they reached the castle which John visited the first time he went to the enchanted spring, and was there received by all the inmates of the castle with their wonted hospitality. He thankfully accepted the master's invitation to stay until the lion's wounds were healed, and for this he had not long to wait, as both the master and his daughter were skilled in leechcraft, and soon the lion regained his former strength. Then John took leave of his hosts, and went forth in quest of adventures, seeking thereby to blot out his transgressions.

One evening, after he had been riding the whole day long and was very tired, he came to a strong castle that was called Torture Castle; and when those who kept watch on its towers saw John, they cried out to him:

"Go away. You have nothing to do here, where only a madman would seek shelter. Sorrow and despair alone make this their home. Hasten away from it as fast as you can."

"What do you mean?" answered John dumb-founded. "What have I done to you that you should receive me with such discourteous words?"

"Ride away at once. Evil will befall you if you venture to force yourself in."

At these words John grew angry, and rode right up to the gate, which he ordered the porter to open at once.

"I insist on entering," said he, "whatever fate be mine."

"Noble knight," answered the porter, "insist not on that. There is no honour to be won in this abode of woe. Ride away, and seek not to enter this castle."

As he was speaking a courteous old damsel came out and said:

"Be not angry, noble sir, at these harsh words, and, believe me, that all they have said to you has been said in a kindly spirit. It is their wont to receive all strangers with snubs and rudeness so as to warn them against entering this castle, for they know that no one who has found shelter here has had cause to rejoice at it. Now I have said my customary say, so hearken to my counsel and pursue your journey."

"The night is now far spent, and I prefer this shelter, however bad it be, to all other."

"Do as you will, but should you go hence with your life, thank God and His inexhaustible mercy."

"May He requite you for this friendly counsel, but my curiosity has now been roused, and even if it should cost me my life, I shall still not swerve from my purpose."

He called again to the porter and ordered him to open, and this time the latter no longer refused to obey; the gate was opened, the drawbridge let down, and John, followed by his lion, rode into the courtyard, which was extensive and almost as big as a plain. In the middle of this was an enclosure made of poles and brambles, and in it he saw three hundred women engaged in spinning gold and weaving it into ribbons. Notwithstanding all the precious things that lay strewn around them, they all seemed to be in deep despair, and had scarcely a whole thread on their bodies; their clothes were torn and patched, their cheeks sunken, and their complexions sallow from hunger and neglect. When they saw John they all began to weep grievously and betray the deepest despair. When John had watched this ghastly spectacle for a while he grew heavy of heart, and rode back to the gate to get away from this abode of misery; but the porter went up to him and said:

"I warned you beforehand, but you would not heed my advice, and now it is too late. A stranger may, I trow, gain admission herein, but no man who has once entered escapes."

"Good," answered John; "I am not thinking of slinking away, however inhospitable the place appears. But tell me, my friend, who these women are who sit here and spin, and who, methinks, are suffering such sore distress."

"You shall never get from me the key to the mystery. Find someone else to tell you what has happened."

John, fully convinced that he would learn nothing from the porter, turned his horse, and rode again into the great courtyard, and observed, in the enclosure itself, a little gate standing open. He dismounted from his horse, and after tying it up to a pole, went in, and, on approaching the unhappy women, said:

"God be with you both old and young, and may He turn your sorrow into joy".

"O, may He grant your prayer," answered an aged woman. "I believe you have come hither to learn who we are, and why we are tortured in this wise. Listen, then, to the story of our unhappy lot. Once upon a time there was a brave young king who ruled over the land whence we came. He was seldom at home, but journeyed into all countries in quest of adventures and to take part in tournaments and jousts. Once he came to this castle, and for that deed we are all paying the penalty now, and perhaps you, too, will have to suffer for his mad daring. Two fiends hold sway over this castle. Now, when our king had lain here a night, and was about to pursue his way on the morrow, these two fiends hindered him, and offered him the choice between fighting them both, or abandoning himself to their tender mercies. Our king was young – not quite twenty years old – and, brave as he was, he dared not engage the monsters in battle, so he had no choice but to yield himself captive. Then they put before him another choice, which was that they should either kill him or else, to regain his freedom, he was to send each of them a hundred and fifty damsels from the country wherein he was king; nor were they satisfied with that, but demanded that whenever one of them died he was to send another in her stead, so that the number should always be complete. This has been the state of things for many years past, and so it will continue until some one slays our tormentors and sets us free; but the man who can fight these fiends single-handed is not to be found, and so our sufferings will therefore, I believe, go on for ever. You yourself see how we are treated. We suffer hunger and thirst, and though we labour from morning till night, we do not get enough wages to sustain our bodies or clothe our nakedness; and we suffer not only from our own ill-fate, for often knights and squires come here to free us, but they have all, for our sakes, perished in the enterprise."

"Do not despair," replied John, "for I will release you if I can."

The night was now far spent, and John quitted the enclosure to find shelter for himself. Followed by his lion, he began strolling about the wide courtyard, and came at last to a building that was lighted up, and servants, hearing the tramp of the horse, came out and invited him to enter. They took his horse and led it to a stable, and ushered him into the hall. There he was received by an old knight and his daughter, who both bade him welcome. They all tried to serve him to the utmost of their power, but John could not be certain whether this hospitality was the outcome of kindness, or whether some mockery lay hidden under all the attention they were showing him. Meantime, however, he did not trouble to inquire about this, but betook himself, tired out as he was, to the bed-chamber that was assigned him, and soon fell asleep there. In the morning the old knight went up to him, and conducted him to a chapel where a priest said Mass for them. When this was over John wished to take leave of the old knight, but he laid hold of him saying:

"Dear friend, you may not go so soon, for there is a certain custom in this house – to wit, that every stranger who finds shelter for the night must, ere he depart, fight with two devils, unless he submits to yielding himself their prisoner."

"That was a curious custom for you to introduce into your house, and one that reflects scant honour on your hospitality."

"*My* house," exclaimed the old knight; "you are mistaken, young man. I have no longer any voice in this house wherein I too am a prisoner, although I am treated less harshly than the rest. Do not believe that it was I who introduced this savage custom, which is as scandalous to me as it is to you. I have no dearer wish than that you may overcome the two monsters and free all the prisoners in this castle. If you succeed in performing this achievement I will gladly give you my only daughter for your wife."

"I thank you for your kindly promise, but your daughter is too good for a poor knight-errant whose sole possessions are his sword and steed. Reserve her rather for some powerful emperor. I have no desire for so rare a reward."

Whilst he was speaking the two devils came rushing into the courtyard, each of them having in his hand a mighty club studded with spikes and formed of the entire stem of a tree. Their heads and feet were bare, but the rest of their bodies was protected by a strong coat of mail, and, for further defence, each of them had a shield. When the lion saw these horrid creatures it began to tremble like an aspen leaf, arched its back, and lashed the ground with its tail: the poor beast was both angry and frightened at the same time. When the two devils saw the lion they said to John:

"Drive your lion away, for we will have nothing to do with it."

"You seem frightened at the lion. I should be amused to see a fight between the lion and you two."

"Are you afraid to fight us by yourself that you must needs make use of that sort of help?"

"Do not imagine that. I am quite ready to shut the lion up if you will show me some place."

Then they showed him a place, and in it John shut up his lion, locked the door, and threw the key in the devils' faces to show them he was not afraid of them, and, immediately afterwards, vaulted into the saddle and rode against the two.

Before the fiends could put themselves into position to meet the knight's attack, John struck one of them with his spear and hurled him to the ground, so that he howled with agony; but the next minute the fiend was on his legs again, and now a hot fight began. Both their clubs whizzed all the time about John's ears, and blow succeeded blow with such rapidity that he could not ward them off himself, but was beaten about just as one beats a piece of meat. His shield broke into bits, and his helmet was dented just as if it had been made of leather. He cut about him with both hands, but that was of little use, and he felt that he had never been in a worse plight, feeling his strength getting exhausted, and his blows more and more beside the mark. For a second he thought it best to give up such a hopeless fight and acknowledge himself worsted, but just then he received help that he little expected.

The lion had witnessed this combat from its cage, and grew more and more restless as John was more furiously beset. It looked everywhere for some means of getting out, but the cage was shut, and the bars resisted the lion's efforts; but suddenly it caught sight of a little hole in the flooring, and this the faithful beast began to widen, and after that scratched up a passage through the ground, by means of which it was able to crawl out. It had hardly got into the open air before it threw itself, with a wild rush, on one of John's adversaries, dashed him to the ground, and laid its terrible paws on his breast. Now John took fresh courage, and when his remaining adversary was torn from his clutches by the lion's unexpected assault, John took advantage of this to give him a terrible slash, so that his head was cleft smartly from his trunk. The other of the two devils then began to howl to John for mercy, promising him at the same time lands and gold, on condition that he released him from the ravening beast that had dug its claws into his breast; but John answered that as this devil had, to his knowledge, never shown mercy to others, he, therefore, was undeserving of human compassion, and so left him for the lion to work its will on. It was not many minutes before it had torn him to pieces.

All who dwelt in the castle now came running out to congratulate John on the victory he had gained, and the porters craved his forgiveness for having treated him on the previous evening in such a discourteous manner. The old knight, too, came and congratulated him, adding that John had now honestly won his daughter and all the treasures that were to be found in the castle.

"Your daughter, old man, can never be my bride, for I already love another, of whose affection I am trying to make myself worthy, and, as to the treasures in the castle, I will not touch them, for I do not fight for gold. Keep them, then, and give them as a dowry to your daughter. But I desire you to set free all unhappy women that are held captive here, and send them back to their own country."

Although the old man could not conceal his disappointment at not getting the brave Knight of the Lion for his son-in-law, he, nevertheless, lost no time in carrying out his behest, and the poor women now approached with tears to thank their saviour. After he had given them seemly clothing they went merrily past him out of the castle in which they had spent so many melancholy years. After seeing them depart he vaulted into the saddle, waved farewell with his hand to the people of the castle, and rode away.

He then returned to King Arthur's court, where he was received with uncommon joy, inasmuch as they had given up all hope of seeing him again in the flesh; but his good friend Gavian, who had just succeeded in conducting back to the court King Arthur's stolen queen, rejoiced above the rest. To his astonishment he found that the mysterious Knight of the Lion, who had so nobly helped his sister, was none other than John, his good friend and brother-in-arms. Side by side they did many a doughty deed, but still John could not win back his joyousness of old days, for the thought of Laudine's cold indifference incessantly grieved him sorely.

At last he could bear the agony no longer, but resolved to go to her and crave her forgiveness. If she refused it he felt that he no longer had the strength to live. So early one morning, ere the sun was up, he started on his journey, without telling any one, and with no other company than that of his trusty lion. On reaching the enchanted spring he seized the cup once more, and poured the water in it over the post, and, as happened before, a raging hurricane broke forth, lightning flashes darted round him, and peals of thunder rattled.

When the people in the castle heard the roaring of the thunder and saw how the gusts of wind shook the battlements and towers, all trembled and bewailed aloud that the castle had been built on such a dangerous spot. It seemed to them a sorry fate to have to suffer insult because they could no longer protect the spring, or, failing that, be exposed to the violence of thunder, lightning and storm; for now that Red Vadoin was dead and John had gone away, there was no longer any one powerful enough to overcome all the knights errant who had a mind to mock them.

Then Luneta said to her mistress:

"Again some fellow has ventured to insult us, and it looks as if we must forfeit the honour we held for so many years of being guardians of the enchanted spring. It seems to me absolutely necessary for us to try to find some knight with the will and the courage to protect our land against such miscreants. It cuts me to the heart to think that this fellow may go his way unmolested because there is no one in our castle to punish his arrogance."

"Well, Luneta, as you are always rich in resources, you must hit on some expedient to help us out of our troubles, for I myself am at my wits' end to think of anything."

"You know I would do all in my power for you, but what can a poor girl like me do? You have such a number of clever counsellors. Ask them what their advice is; and, to tell the truth, I dare not venture to suggest any expedient, for, supposing it did not turn out according to your wishes, you would hold me responsible for it, and perhaps I should again forfeit your favour."

"Alas!" replied Laudine, "my counsellors are of no more avail than my knights, and they certainly cannot help me. My sole hope is centred in you."

"Very well, then, I have one piece of counsel to offer you. You remember the Knight of the Lion, who overcame single-handed the chancellor and both brothers. Before that he had slain the terrible giant Harpin, and a braver knight is not to be found. If we could but gain him for our champion, then our troubles would be over; but, as you remember, he refused to enter this castle until he had made his peace with his wife. Our fate, therefore, depends on this reconciliation being effected."

"My dear Luneta, make haste at once to find where this knight is and bring him hither. If he comes I promise to do all in my power to reconcile him and his wife."

"Before I go I want you to promise me solemnly that you will not be angry with me for what I am about to do on your behalf, be the issue what it may."

When Laudine said she would readily take the oath that Luneta demanded, the damsel produced a reliquary and a Mass-book, and bade her mistress swear on them, first, that she would never hold Luneta responsible if things went contrary to her wishes; secondly, that she should reconcile the Knight of the Lion and his wife, and make the latter forgive the knight all his marital transgressions. When Luneta had exacted the oath, she could not repress a furtive smile, and, in order that her mistress should not perceive it, she commanded her horse to be brought round immediately, vaulted into the saddle, and rode to the spring, and there met the Knight of the Lion, who greeted her blithely. It did not take her long to tell him what had occurred at the castle, and let him into the secret of the new ruse she had employed to overcome the châtelaine's pride. When John wished to thank her for the trusty help she had given him, she interrupted his thanks by saying:

"Let us not delay this reconciliation, but mount your steed and make for the castle."

"Does not my wife know who I really am?"

"Not a soul suspects that John and the Knight of the Lion are one and the same person."

When they reached the castle John went up to his wife and greeted her courteously. His visor was lowered over his face so that she could not recognize him, whereupon she welcomed him heartily; but Luneta said:

"Now, my lady, the time has come for you to show what you can do. You promised to procure him his wife's pardon, and you alone can do that."

"Noble knight," said Laudine, "be seated here beside me and tell me your story, and I will do all I can, in accordance with my oath, to soften your wife's hard heart."

"There is no good whatever in hiding the truth any longer from you," interrupted Luneta. "That hard-hearted creature is yourself, and the Knight of the Lion is your lawful husband John, the son of John, who has now suffered quite enough for his forgetfulness. All you have to do now is to keep your promise, and render him back the love you promised, and the pardon which you alone can grant."

When the haughty dame heard this she first fell into a violent rage with the artful Luneta for having fooled her in this manner, but, ere long, she felt grateful to her trusty friend for having constrained her to pronounce the words of pardon which had hung upon her lips, but had hitherto been kept back by pride. She thereupon offered John her hand, drew him to her bosom, saying that she would now grant him full pardon by reason of her oath, and with this pardon ends the story of John, the Knight of the Lion, who went forth no more in quest of adventures, but stayed in his castle, content with his spouse's love, without any desire to gain any other honour whatsoever.

THE ROMANCE OF
TRISTAN AND ISEULT

Hilaire Belloc

Like Yvain, or Owain, Tristan was also almost certainly a real historical character. He is most commonly associated with the figure called Drust named on an ancient Celtic pillar situated just outside Fowey in Cornwall, where he is identified as the son of King Cunomor, who ruled both Cornwall and Brittany in the middle of the sixth century. Drust fell in love with his future stepmother, the Iseult of the tales, thus incurring the wrath of his father. In most versions of the legend, Tristan was the nephew of Cunomor, or Mark as he is usually named. It is possible that Cunomor was a Pictish king. Certainly Drust was a common Pictish name, and in the Welsh version of the tale Mark's name is Tallwch, suggestive of Talorc, another common Pictish name. There were two instances when a king of the Picts called Talorc was succeeded by a nephew called Drust, the most likely being Talorg mac Mordileg and Drust mac Munait, who lived at the same time as Cunomor. Both of these kings were heavily involved in battles against the invading Angles of Northumbria and as likely against the remnant British tribes of northern Britain. It is entirely possible that Drust wished to marry the same Pictish princess as his father and that an enmity followed where Drust was banished. The historical record shows that he ruled for only a year after his uncle.

The name of Hilaire Belloc (1870–1953) does not come immediately to mind when thinking of Arthurian fiction. He was a very prolific writer, turning his hand to a wide variety of subjects – politics, history, philosophy, travel, as well as fiction and verse.

He is probably best remembered today for his Cautionary Tales for Children *(1907).* His book The Romance of Tristan and Iseult *(1913) was a fairly free translation of a French volume,* Le Roman de Tristan et Iseut *(1990) by Joseph Bédier (1864–1938), Professor of French Medieval Language and Literature. The primary text for the Tristan story comes from the lay of Marie de France called* Chevrefoil *written sometime before 1175. The story was further developed by Gottfried von Strassburg in* Tristan *(c. 1210) which formed the basis for Richard Wagner's opera* Tristan and Isolde *(1865).*

My lords, if you would hear a high tale of love and of death, here is that of Tristan and Queen Iseult; how to their full joy, but to their sorrow also, they loved each other, and how at last they died of that love together upon one day; she by him and he by her.

Long ago, when Mark was King over Cornwall, Rivalen, King of Lyonesse, heard that Mark's enemies waged war on him; so he crossed the sea to bring him aid; and so faithfully did he serve him with counsel and sword that Mark gave him his sister Blanchefleur, whom King Rivalen loved most marvellously.

He wedded her in Tintagel Minster, but hardly was she wed when the news came to him that his old enemy Duke Morgan had fallen on Lyonesse and was wasting town and field. Then Rivalen manned his ships in haste, and took Blanchefleur with him to his far land; but she was with child. He landed below his castle of Kanoël and gave the Queen in ward to his Marshal Rohalt, and after that set off to wage his war.

Blanchefleur waited for him continually, but he did not come home, till she learnt upon a day that Duke Morgan had killed him in foul ambush. She did not weep: she made no cry or lamentation, but her limbs failed her and grew weak, and her soul was filled with a strong desire to be rid of the flesh, and though Rohalt tried to soothe her she would not hear. Three days she awaited re-union with her lord, and on the fourth she brought forth a son; and taking him in her arms she said:

"Little son, I have longed a while to see you, and now I see you the fairest thing ever a woman bore. In sadness came I hither, in sadness did I bring forth, and in sadness has your first feast day gone. And as by sadness you came into the world, your name shall be called Tristan; that is the child of sadness."

After she had said these words she kissed him, and immediately when she had kissed him she died.

Rohalt, the keeper of faith, took the child, but already Duke Morgan's men besieged the Castle of Kanoël all round about. There is a wise saying: "Foolhardy was never hardy," and he was compelled to yield to Duke Morgan at his mercy: but for fear that Morgan might slay Rivalen's heir the Marshal hid him among his own sons.

When seven years were passed and the time had come to take the child from the women, Rohalt put Tristan under a good master, the Squire Gorvenal, and Gorvenal taught him in a few years the arts that go with barony. He taught him the use of lance and sword and 'scutcheon and bow, and how to cast stone quoits and to leap wide dykes also: and he taught him to hate every lie and felony and to keep his given word; and he taught him the various kinds of song and harp-playing, and the hunter's craft; and when the child rode among the young squires you would have said that he and his horse and his armour were all one thing. To see him so noble and so proud, broad in the shoulders, loyal, strong and right, all men glorified Rohalt in such a son. But Rohalt remembering Rivalen and Blanchefleur (of whose youth and grace all this was a resurrection) loved him indeed as a son, but in his heart revered him as his lord.

Now all his joy was snatched from him on a day when certain merchants of Norway, having lured Tristan to their ship, bore him off as a rich prize, though Tristan fought hard, as a young wolf struggles, caught in a gin. But it is a truth well proved, and every sailor knows it, that the sea will hardly bear a felon ship, and gives no aid to rapine. The sea rose and cast a dark storm round the ship and drove it eight days and eight nights at random, till the mariners caught through the mist a coast of awful cliffs and sea-ward rocks whereon the sea would have ground their hull to pieces: then they did penance, knowing that the anger of the sea came of the lad, whom they had stolen in an evil hour, and they vowed his deliverance and got ready a boat to put him, if it might be, ashore: then the wind and sea fell and the sky shone, and as the Norway ship grew small in the offing, a quiet tide cast Tristan and the boat upon a beach of sand.

Painfully he climbed the cliff and saw, beyond, a lonely rolling heath and a forest stretching out and endless. And he wept, remembering Gorvenal, his father, and the land of Lyonesse. Then the distant cry of a hunt, with horse and hound, came suddenly and lifted his heart, and a tall stag broke cover at the forest edge. The pack and the hunt streamed after it with a tumult of cries and winding horns, but just as the hounds were racing clustered at the haunch, the quarry turned to bay at a stone's throw from Tristan; a huntsman gave him the thrust, while all around the hunt had gathered and was winding the kill. But Tristan, seeing by the gesture of the huntsman that he made to cut the neck of the stag, cried out:

"My lord, what would you do? Is it fitting to cut up so noble a beast like any farm-yard hog? Is that the custom of this country?"

And the huntsman answered:

"Fair friend, what startles you? Why yes, first I take off the head of a stag, and then I cut it into four quarters and we carry it on our saddle bows to King Mark, our lord: So do we, and so since the days of the first huntsmen have done the Cornish men. If, however, you know of some nobler custom, teach it us: take this knife and we will learn it willingly."

Then Tristan kneeled and skinned the stag before he cut it up, and quartered it all in order leaving the crow-bone all whole, as is meet, and putting aside at the end the head, the haunch, the tongue and the great heart's vein; and the huntsmen and the kennel hinds stood over him with delight, and the Master Huntsman said:

"Friend, these are good ways. In what land learnt you them? Tell us your country and your name."

"Good lord, my name is Tristan, and I learnt these ways in my country of Lyonesse."

"Tristan," said the Master Huntsman, "God reward the father that brought you up so nobly; doubtless he is a baron, rich and strong."

Now Tristan knew both speech and silence, and he answered:

"No, lord; my father is a burgess. I left his home unbeknownst upon a ship that trafficked to a far place, for I wished to learn how men lived in foreign lands. But if you will accept me of the hunt I will follow you gladly and teach you other crafts of venery."

"Fair Tristan, I marvel there should be a land where a burgess's son can know what a knight's son knows not elsewhere, but come with us since you will it; and welcome: we will bring you to King Mark, our lord."

Tristan completed his task; to the dogs he gave the heart, the head, offal and ears; and he taught the hunt how the skinning and the ordering should be done. Then he thrust the pieces upon pikes and gave them to this huntsman and to that to carry, to one the snout to another the haunch to another the flank to another the chine; and he taught them how to ride by twos in rank according to the dignity of the pieces each might bear.

So they took the road and spoke together, till they came on a great castle and round it fields and orchards, and living waters and fish ponds and plough lands, and many ships were in its haven, for that castle stood above the sea. It was well fenced against all assault or engines of war, and its keep, which the giants had built long ago, was compact of great stones, like a chess board of vert and azure.

And when Tristan asked its name:

"Good liege," they said, "we call it Tintagel."

And Tristan cried:

"Tintagel! Blessed be thou of God, and blessed be they that dwell within thee."

(Therein, my lords, therein had Rivalen taken Blanchefleur to wife, though their son knew it not.)

When they came before the keep the horns brought the barons to the gates and King Mark himself. And when the Master Huntsman had told him all the story, and King Mark had marvelled at the good order of the cavalcade, and the cutting of the stag, and the high art of venery in all, yet most he wondered at the stranger boy, and still gazed at him, troubled and wondering whence came his tenderness, and his heart would answer him nothing; but, my lords, it was blood that spoke, and the love he had long since borne his sister Blanchefleur.

That evening, when the boards were cleared, a singer out of Wales, a master, came forward among the barons in Hall and sang a harper's song, and as this harper touched the strings of his harp, Tristan who sat at the King's feet, spoke thus to him:

"Oh master, that is the first of songs! The Bretons of old wove it once to chant the loves of Graëlent. And the melody is rare and rare are the words: master, your voice is subtle: harp us that well."

But when the Welshman had sung, he answered:

"Boy, what do you know of the craft of music? If the burgesses of Lyonesse teach their sons harp-play also, and rotes and viols too, rise, and take this harp and show your skill."

Then Tristan took the harp and sang so well that the barons softened as they heard, and King Mark marvelled at the harper from Lyonesse whither so long ago Rivalen had taken Blanchefleur away.

When the song ended, the King was silent a long space, but he said at last:

"Son, blessed be the master that taught thee, and blessed be thou of God: for God loves good singers. Their voices and the voice of the harp enter the souls of men and wake dear memories and cause them to forget many a mourning and many a sin. For our joy did you come to this roof, stay near us a long time, friend."

And Tristan answered:

"Very willingly will I serve you, sire, as your harper, your huntsman and your liege."

So did he, and for three years a mutual love grew up in their hearts. By day Tristan followed King Mark at pleas and in saddle; by night he slept in the royal room with the councillors and the peers, and if the King was sad he would harp to him to soothe his care. The barons also cherished him, and (as you shall learn) Dinas of Lidan, the seneschal, beyond all others. And more tenderly than the barons and than Dinas the King loved him. But Tristan could not forget, or Rohalt his father, or his master Gorvenal, or the land of Lyonesse.

My lords, a teller that would please, should not stretch his tale too long, and truly this tale is so various and so high that it needs no straining. Then let me shortly tell how Rohalt himself, after long wandering by sea and land, came into Cornwall, and found Tristan, and showing the King the carbuncle that once was Blanchefleur's, said:

"King Mark, here is your nephew Tristan, son of your sister Blanchefleur and of King Rivalen. Duke Morgan holds his land most wrongfully; it is time such land came back to its lord."

And Tristan (in a word) when his uncle had armed him knight, crossed the sea, and was hailed of his father's vassals, and killed Rivalen's slayer and was re-seized of his land.

Then remembering how King Mark could no longer live in joy without him, he summoned his council and his barons and said this:

"Lords of the Lyonesse, I have retaken this place and I have avenged King Rivalen by the help of God and of you. But two men Rohalt and King Mark of Cornwall nourished me, an orphan, and a wandering boy. So should I call them also fathers. Now a free man has two things thoroughly his own, his body and his land. To Rohalt then, here, I will release my land. Do you hold it, father, and your son shall hold it after you. But my body I give up to King Mark. I will leave this country, dear though it be, and in Cornwall

I will serve King Mark as my lord. Such is my judgment, but you, my lords of Lyonesse, are my lieges, and owe me counsel; if then, some one of you will counsel me another thing let him rise and speak."

But all the barons praised him, though they wept; and taking with him Gorvenal only, Tristan set sail for King Mark's land.

I

When Tristan came back to that land, King Mark and all his Barony were mourning; for the King of Ireland had manned a fleet to ravage Cornwall, should King Mark refuse, as he had refused these fifteen years, to pay a tribute his fathers had paid. Now that year this King had sent to Tintagel, to carry his summons, a giant knight; the Morholt, whose sister he had wed, and whom no man had yet been able to overcome: so King Mark had summoned all the barons of his land to Council, by letters sealed.

On the day assigned, when the barons were gathered in hall, and when the King had taken his throne, the Morholt said these things:

"King Mark, hear for the last time the summons of the King of Ireland, my lord. He arraigns you to pay at last that which you have owed so long, and because you have refused it too long already he bids you give over to me this day three hundred youths and three hundred maidens drawn by lot from among the Cornish folk. But if so be that any would prove by trial of combat that the King of Ireland receives this tribute without right, I will take up his wager. Which among you, my Cornish lords, will fight to redeem this land?"

The barons glanced at each other but all were silent.

Then Tristan knelt at the feet of King Mark and said:

"Lord King, by your leave I will do battle."

And in vain would King Mark have turned him from his purpose, thinking, how could even valour save so young a knight? But he threw down his gage to the Morholt, and the Morholt took up the gage.

On the appointed day he had himself clad for a great feat of arms in a hauberk and in a steel helm, and he entered a boat and drew to the islet of St. Samson's, where the knights were to fight each to each alone. Now the Morholt had hoisted to his mast a sail of rich purple, and coming fast to land, he moored his boat on the shore. But Tristan pushed off his own boat adrift with his feet, and said:

"One of us only will go hence alive. One boat will serve."

And each rousing the other to the fray they passed into the isle.

No man saw the sharp combat; but thrice the salt sea-breeze had wafted or seemed to waft a cry of fury to the land, when at last towards the hour of noon the purple sail showed far off; the Irish boat appeared from the island shore, and there rose a clamour of "the Morholt!" When suddenly, as the boat grew larger on the sight and topped a wave, they saw that Tristan stood on the prow holding a sword in his hand. He leapt ashore, and as the mothers kissed the steel upon his feet he cried to the Morholt's men:

"My lords of Ireland, the Morholt fought well. See here, my sword is broken and a splinter of it stands fast in his head. Take you that steel, my lords; it is the tribute of Cornwall."

Then he went up to Tintagel and as he went the people he had freed waved green boughs, and rich cloths were hung at the windows. But when Tristan reached the castle with joy, songs and joy-bells sounding about him, he drooped in the arms of King Mark, for the blood ran from his wounds.

The Morholt's men, they landed in Ireland quite cast down. For when ever he came back into Whitehaven the Morholt had been wont to take joy in the sight of his clan upon the shore, of the Queen his sister, and of his niece Iseult the Fair. Tenderly had they cherished him of old, and had he taken some wound, they healed him, for they were skilled in balms and potions. But now their magic was vain, for he lay dead and the splinter of the foreign brand yet stood in his skull till Iseult plucked it out and shut it in a chest.

From that day Iseult the Fair knew and hated the name of Tristan of Lyonesse.

But over in Tintagel Tristan languished, for there trickled a poisonous blood from his wound. The doctors found that the Morholt had thrust into him a poisoned barb, and as their potions and their theriac could never heal him they left him in God's hands. So hateful a stench came from his wound that all his dearest friends fled him, all save King Mark, Gorvenal and Dinas of Lidan. They always could stay near his couch because their love overcame their abhorrence. At last Tristan had himself carried into a boat apart on the shore; and lying facing the sea he awaited death, for he thought: "I must die; but it is good to see the sun and my heart is still high. I would like to try the sea that brings all chances . . . I would have the sea bear me far off alone, to what land no matter, so that it heal me of my wound."

He begged so long that King Mark accepted his desire. He bore him into a boat with neither sail nor oar, and Tristan wished that his harp only should be placed beside him: for sails he could not lift, nor oar ply, nor sword wield; and as a seaman on some long voyage casts to the sea a beloved companion dead, so Gorvenal pushed out to sea that boat where his dear son lay; and the sea drew him away.

For seven days and seven nights the sea so drew him; at times to charm his grief, he harped; and when at last the sea brought him near a shore where fishermen had left their port that night to fish far out, they heard as they rowed a sweet and strong and living tune that ran above the sea, and feathering their oars they listened immovable.

In the first whiteness of the dawn they saw the boat at large: she went at random and nothing seemed to live in her except the voice of the harp. But as they neared, the air grew weaker and died; and when they hailed her Tristan's hands had fallen lifeless on the strings though they still trembled. The fishermen took him in and bore him back to port, to their lady who was merciful and perhaps would heal him.

It was that same port of Whitehaven where the Morholt lay, and their lady was Iseult the Fair.

She alone, being skilled in philtres, could save Tristan, but she alone wished him dead. When Tristan knew himself again (for her art restored him) he knew himself to be in the land of peril. But he was yet strong to hold his own and found good crafty words. He told a tale of how he was a seer that had taken passage on a merchant ship and sailed to Spain to learn the art of reading all the stars, – of how pirates had boarded the ship and of how, though wounded, he had fled into that boat. He was believed, nor did any of the Morholt's men know his face again, so hardly had the poison used it. But when, after forty days, Iseult of the Golden Hair had all but healed him, when already his limbs had recovered and the grace of youth returned, he knew that he must escape, and he fled and after many dangers he came again before Mark the King.

II

My lords, there were in the court of King Mark four barons the basest of men, who hated Tristan with a hard hate, for his greatness and for the tender love the King bore him. And well I know their names: Andret, Guenelon, Gondoïne and Denoalen. They knew that the King had intent to grow old childless and to leave his land to Tristan; and their envy swelled and by lies they angered the chief men of Cornwall against Tristan. They said:

"There have been too many marvels in this man's life. It was marvels enough that he beat the Morholt, but by what sorcery did he try the sea alone at the point of death, or which of us, my lords, could voyage without mast or sail? They say that warlocks can. It was sure a warlock feat, and that is a warlock harp of his pours poison daily into the King's heart. See how he has bent that heart by power and chain of sorcery! He will be king yet, my lords, and you will hold your lands of a wizard."

They brought over the greater part of the barons and these pressed King Mark to take to wife some King's daughter who should give him an heir, or else they threatened to return each man into his keep and wage him war. But the King turned against them and swore in his heart that so long as his dear nephew lived no king's daughter should come to his bed. Then in his turn did Tristan (in his shame to be thought to serve for hire) threaten that if the King did not yield to his barons, he would himself go over sea to serve some great king. At this, King Mark made a term with his barons and gave them forty days to hear his decision.

On the appointed day he waited alone in his chamber and sadly mused: "Where shall I find a king's daughter so fair and yet so distant that I may feign to wish her my wife?"

Just then by his window that looked upon the sea two building swallows came in quarrelling together. Then, startled, they flew out, but had let fall from their beaks a woman's hair, long and fine, and shining like a beam of light.

King Mark took it, and called his barons and Tristan and said:

"To please you, lords, I will take a wife; but you must seek her whom I have chosen."

"Fair lord, we wish it all," they said, "and who may she be?"

"Why," said he, "she whose hair this is; nor will I take another."

"And whence, lord King, comes this Hair of Gold; who brought it and from what land?"

"It comes, my lords, from the Lady with the Hair of Gold, the swallows brought it me. They know from what country it came."

Then the barons saw themselves mocked and cheated, and they turned with sneers to Tristan, for they thought him to have counselled the trick. But Tristan, when he had looked on the Hair of Gold, remembered Iseult the Fair and smiled and said this:

"King Mark, can you not see that the doubts of these lords shame me? You have designed in vain. I will go seek the Lady with the Hair of Gold. The search is perilous: never the less, my uncle, I would once more put my body and my life into peril for you; and that your barons may know I love you loyally, I take this oath, to die on the adventure or to bring back to this castle of Tintagel the Queen with that fair hair."

He fitted out a great ship and loaded it with corn and wine, with honey and all manner of good things; he manned it with Gorvenal and a hundred young knights of high birth, chosen among the bravest, and he clothed them in coats of home-spun and in hair cloth so that they seemed merchants only: but under the deck he hid rich cloth of gold and scarlet as for a great king's messengers.

When the ship had taken the sea the helmsman asked him:

"Lord, to what land shall I steer?"

"Sir," said he, "steer for Ireland, straight for Whitehaven harbour."

At first Tristan made believe to the men of Whitehaven that his friends were merchants of England come peacefully to barter; but as these strange merchants passed the day in the useless games of draughts and chess, and seemed to know dice better than the bargain price of corn, Tristan feared discovery and knew not how to pursue his quest.

Now it chanced once upon the break of day that he heard a cry so terrible that one would have called it a demon's cry; nor had he ever heard a brute bellow in such wise, so awful and strange it seemed. He called a woman who passed by the harbour, and said:

"Tell me, lady, whence comes that voice I have heard, and hide me nothing."

"My lord," said she, "I will tell you truly. It is the roar of a dragon the most terrible and dauntless upon earth. Daily it leaves its den and stands at one of the gates of the city: Nor can any come out or go in till a maiden has been given up to it; and when it has her in its claws it devours her."

"Lady," said Tristan, "make no mock of me, but tell me straight: Can a man born of woman kill this thing?"

"Fair sir, and gentle," she said, "I cannot say; but this is sure: Twenty knights have tried and run the venture, because the King of Ireland has published it that he will give his daughter, Iseult the Fair, to whomsoever shall kill the beast; but it has devoured them all."

Tristan left the woman and returning to his ship armed himself in secret, and it was a fine sight to see so noble a charger and so good a knight come out from such a merchant-hull: but the haven was empty of folk, for the dawn had barely broken and none saw him as he rode to the gate. And hardly had he passed it, when he met suddenly five men at full gallop flying towards the town. Tristan seized one by his hair, as he passed, and dragged him over his mount's crupper and held him fast:

"God save you, my lord," said he, "and whence does the dragon come?" And when the other had shown him by what road, he let him go.

As the monster neared, he showed the head of a bear and red eyes like coals of fire and hairy tufted ears; lion's claws, a serpent's tail, and a griffin's body.

Tristan charged his horse at him so strongly that, though the beast's mane stood with fright yet he drove at the dragon: his lance struck its scales and shivered. Then Tristan drew his sword and struck at the dragon's head, but he did not so much as cut the hide. The beast felt the blow: with its claws he dragged at the shield and broke it from the arm; then, his breast unshielded, Tristan used the sword again and struck so strongly that the air rang all round about: but in vain, for he could not wound and meanwhile the dragon vomited from his nostrils two streams of loathsome flames, and Tristan's helm blackened like a cinder and his horse stumbled and fell down and died; but Tristan standing on his feet thrust his sword right into the beast's jaws, and split its heart in two.

Then he cut out the tongue and put it into his hose, but as the poison came against his flesh the hero fainted and fell in the high grass that bordered the marsh around.

Now the man he had stopped in flight was the Seneschal of Ireland and he desired Iseult the Fair: and though he was a coward, he had dared so far as to return with his companions secretly, and he found the dragon dead; so he cut off its head and bore it to the King, and claimed the great reward.

The King could credit his prowess but hardly, yet wished justice done and summoned his vassals to court, so that there, before the Barony assembled, the seneschal should furnish proof of his victory won.

When Iseult the Fair heard that she was to be given to this coward first she laughed long, and then she wailed. But on the morrow, doubting some trick, she took with her Perinis her squire and Brangien her maid, and all three rode unbeknownst towards the dragon's lair: and Iseult saw such a trail on the road as made her wonder – for the hoofs that made it had never been shod in her land. Then she came on the dragon, headless, and a dead horse beside him: nor was the horse harnessed in the fashion of Ireland. Some foreign man had slain the beast, but they knew not whether he still lived or no.

They sought him long, Iseult and Perinis and Brangien together, till at last Brangien saw the helm glittering in the marshy grass: and Tristan still breathed. Perinis put him on his horse and bore him secretly to the women's rooms. There Iseult told her mother the tale and left the hero with her, and as the Queen unharnessed him, the dragon's tongue fell from his boot of steel. Then, the Queen of Ireland revived him by the virtue of an herb and said:

"Stranger, I know you for the true slayer of the dragon: but our seneschal, a felon, cut off its head and claims my daughter Iseult for his wage; will you be ready two days hence to give him the lie in battle?"

"Queen," said he, "the time is short, but you, I think, can cure me in two days. Upon the dragon I conquered Iseult, and on the seneschal perhaps I shall reconquer her."

Then the Queen brewed him strong brews, and on the morrow Iseult the Fair got him ready a bath and anointed him with a balm her mother had conjured, and as he looked at her he thought, "So I have found the Queen of the Hair of Gold," and he smiled as he thought it. But Iseult, noting it, thought, "Why does he smile, or what have I neglected of the things due to a guest? He smiles to think I have forgotten to burnish his armour."

She went and drew the sword from its rich sheath, but when she saw the splinter gone and the gap in the edge she thought of the Morholt's head. She balanced a moment in doubt, then she went to where she kept the steel she had found in the skull and she put it to the sword, and it fitted so that the join was hardly seen.

She ran to where Tristan lay wounded, and with the sword above him she cried:

"You are that Tristan of the Lyonesse, who killed the Morholt, my mother's brother, and now you shall die in your turn."

Tristan strained to ward the blow, but he was too weak; his wit, however, stood firm in spite of evil and he said:

"So be it, let me die: but to save yourself long memories, listen awhile. King's daughter, my life is not only in your power but is yours of right. My life is yours because you have twice returned it me. Once, long ago: for I was the wounded harper whom you healed of the poison of the Morholt's shaft. Nor repent the healing: were not these wounds had in fair fight? Did I kill the Morholt by treason? Had he not defied me and was I not held to the defence of my body? And now this second time also you have saved me. It was for you I fought the beast . . .

"But let us leave these things. I would but show you how my life is your own. Then if you kill me of right for the glory of it, you may ponder for long years, praising yourself that you killed a wounded guest who had wagered his life in your gaining."

Iseult replied: "I hear strange words. Why should he that killed the Morholt seek me also, his niece? Doubtless because the Morholt came for a tribute of maidens from Cornwall, so you came to boast returning that you had brought back the maiden who was nearest to him, to Cornwall, a slave."

"King's daughter," said Tristan, "No . . . One day two swallows flew, and flew to Tintagel and bore one hair out of all your hairs of gold, and I thought they brought me good will and peace, so I came to find you over-seas. See here, amid the threads of gold upon my coat your hair is sown: the threads are tarnished, but your bright hair still shines."

Iseult put down the sword and taking up the Coat of Arms she saw upon it the Hair of Gold and was silent a long space, till she kissed him on the lips to prove peace, and she put rich garments over him.

On the day of the barons' assembly, Tristan sent Perinis privily to his ship to summon his companions that they should come to court adorned as befitted the envoys of a great king.

One by one the hundred knights passed into the hall where all the barons of Ireland stood, they entered in silence and sat all in rank together: on their scarlet and purple the gems gleamed.

When the King had taken his throne, the seneschal arose to prove by witness and by arms that he had slain the dragon and that so Iseult was won. Then Iseult bowed to her father and said:

"King, I have here a man who challenges your seneschal for lies and felony. Promise that you will pardon this man all his past deeds, who stands to prove that he and none other slew the dragon, and grant him forgiveness and your peace."

The King said, "I grant it." But Iseult said, "Father, first give me the kiss of peace and forgiveness, as a sign that you will give him the same."

Then she found Tristan and led him before the Barony. And as he came the hundred knights rose all together, and crossed their arms upon their breasts and bowed, so the Irish knew that he was their lord.

But among the Irish many knew him again and cried, "Tristan of Lyonesse that slew the Morholt!" They drew their swords and clamoured for death. But Iseult cried: "King, kiss this man upon the lips as your oath was," and the King kissed him, and the clamour fell.

Then Tristan showed the dragon's tongue and offered the seneschal battle, but the seneschal looked at his face and dared not.

Then Tristan said:

"My lords, you have said it, and it is truth: I killed the Morholt. But I crossed the sea to offer you a good blood-fine, to ransom that deed and get me quit of it.

"I put my body in peril of death and rid you of the beast and have so conquered Iseult the Fair, and having conquered her I will bear her away on my ship.

"But that these lands of Cornwall and Ireland may know no more hatred, but love only, learn that King Mark, my lord, will marry her. Here stand a hundred knights of high name, who all will swear with an oath upon the relics of the holy saints, that King Mark sends you by their embassy offer of peace and of brotherhood and goodwill; and that he would by your courtesy hold Iseult as his honoured wife, and that he would have all the men of Cornwall serve her as their Queen."

When the lords of Ireland heard this they acclaimed it, and the King also was content.

Then, since that treaty and alliance was to be made, the King her father took Iseult by the hand and asked of Tristan that he should take an oath; to wit that he would lead her loyally to his lord, and Tristan took that oath and swore it before the knights and the Barony of Ireland assembled. Then the King put Iseult's right hand into Tristan's right hand, and Tristan held it for a space in token of seizin for the King of Cornwall.

So, for the love of King Mark, did Tristan conquer the Queen of the Hair of Gold.

III

When the day of Iseult's livery to the Lords of Cornwall drew near, her mother gathered herbs and flowers and roots and steeped them in wine, and brewed a potion of might, and having done so, said apart to Brangien:

"Child, it is yours to go with Iseult to King Mark's country, for you love her with a faithful love. Take then this pitcher and remember well my words. Hide it so that no eye shall see nor no lip go near it: but when the wedding night has come and that moment in which the wedded are left alone, pour this essenced wine into a cup and offer it to King Mark and to Iseult his queen. Oh! Take all care, my child, that they alone shall taste this brew. For this is its power: they who drink of it together love each other with their every single sense and with their every thought, forever, in life and in death."

And Brangien promised the Queen that she would do her bidding.

On the bark that bore her to Tintagel Iseult the Fair was weeping as she remembered her own land, and mourning swelled her heart, and she said, "Who am I that I should leave you to follow unknown men, my mother and my land? Accursed be the sea that bears me, for rather would I lie dead on the earth where I was born than live out there, beyond . . ."

One day when the wind had fallen and the sails hung slack Tristan dropped anchor by an island and the hundred knights of Cornwall and the sailors, weary of the sea, landed all. Iseult alone remained aboard and a little serving maid, when Tristan came near the Queen to calm her sorrow. The sun was hot above them and they were a thirst and, as they called, the little maid looked about for drink for them and found that pitcher which the mother of Iseult had given into Brangien's keeping. And when she came on it, the child cried, "I have found you wine!" Now she had found not wine – but Passion and Joy most sharp, and Anguish without end, and Death.

The Queen drank deep of that draught and gave it to Tristan and he drank also long and emptied it all.

Brangien came in upon them; she saw them gazing at each other in silence as though ravished and apart; she saw before them the pitcher standing there; she snatched it up and cast it into the shuddering sea and cried aloud: "Cursed be the day I was born and cursed the day that first I trod this deck. Iseult, my friend, and Tristan, you, you have drunk death together."

And once more the bark ran free for Tintagel. But it seemed to Tristan as though an ardent briar, sharp-thorned but with flower most sweet smelling, drave roots into his blood and laced the lovely body of Iseult all round about it and bound it to his own and to his every thought and desire. And he thought, "Felons, that charged me with coveting King Mark's land, I have come lower by far, for it is not his land I covet. Fair uncle, who loved me orphaned ere ever you knew in me the blood of your sister Blanchefleur, you that wept as you bore me to that boat alone, why did you not drive out the boy that was to betray you? Ah! What thought was that! Iseult is yours and I am but your vassal; Iseult is yours and I am your son; Iseult is yours and may not love me."

But Iseult loved him, though she would have hated. She could not hate, for a tenderness more sharp than hatred tore her.

And Brangien watched them in anguish, suffering more cruelly because she alone knew the depth of evil done.

Two days she watched them, seeing them refuse all food or comfort and seeking each other as blind men seek, wretched apart and together more wretched still, for then they trembled each for the first avowal.

On the third day, as Tristan neared the tent on deck where Iseult sat, she saw him coming and she said to him, very humbly, "Come in, my lord."

"Queen," said Tristan, "why do you call me lord? Am I not your liege and vassal, to revere and serve and cherish you as my lady and Queen?"

But Iseult answered, "No, you know that you are my lord and my master, and I your slave. Ah, why did I not sharpen those wounds of the wounded singer, or let die that dragon-slayer in the grasses of the marsh? But then I did not know what now I know!"

"And what is it that you know, Iseult?"

She laid her arm upon Tristan's shoulder, the light of her eyes was drowned and her lips trembled.

"The love of you," she said. Whereat he put his lips to hers.

But as they thus tasted their first joy, Brangien, that watched them, stretched her arms and cried at their feet in tears:

"Stay and return if still you can . . . But oh! that path has no returning. For already Love and his strength drag you on and now henceforth forever never shall you know joy without pain again. The wine possesses you, the draught your mother gave me, the draught the King alone should have drunk with you: but that old Enemy has tricked us, all us three; friend Tristan, Iseult my friend, for that bad ward I kept take here my body and my life, for through me and in that cup you have drunk not love alone, but love and death together."

The lovers held each other; life and desire trembled through their youth, and Tristan said, "Well then, come Death."

And as evening fell, upon the bark that heeled and ran to King Mark's land, they gave themselves up utterly to love.

IV

As King Mark came down to greet Iseult upon the shore, Tristan took her hand and led her to the King and the King took seizin of her, taking her hand. He led her in great pomp to his castle of Tintagel, and as she came in hall amid the vassals her beauty shone so that the walls were lit as they are lit at dawn. Then King Mark blessed those swallows which, by happy courtesy, had brought the Hair of Gold, and Tristan also he blessed, and the hundred knights who, on that adventurous bark, had gone to find him joy of heart and of eyes; yet to him also that ship was to bring sting, torment and mourning.

And on the eighteenth day, having called his Barony together he took Iseult to wife. But on the wedding night, to save her friend, Brangien took her place in the darkness, for her remorse demanded even this from her; nor was the trick discovered.

Then Iseult lived as a queen, but lived in sadness. She had King Mark's tenderness and the barons' honour; the people also loved her; she passed her days amid the frescoes on the walls and floors all strewn with flowers; good jewels had she and purple cloth and tapestry of Hungary and Thessaly too, and songs of harpers, and curtains upon which were worked leopards and eagles and popinjays and all the beasts of sea and field. And her love too she had, love high and splendid, for as is the custom among great lords, Tristan could ever be near her. At his leisure and his dalliance, night and day: for he slept in the King's chamber as great lords do, among the lieges and the councillors. Yet still she feared; for though her love were secret and Tristan unsuspected (for who suspects a son?) Brangien knew. And Brangien seemed in the Queen's mind like a witness spying; for Brangien alone knew what manner of life she led, and held her at mercy so. And the Queen thought: Ah, if some day she should weary of serving as a slave the bed where once she passed for Queen . . . If Tristan should die from her betrayal! So fear maddened the Queen, but not in truth the fear of Brangien who was loyal; her own heart bred the fear.

Not Brangien who was faithful, not Brangien, but themselves had these lovers to fear, for hearts so stricken will lose their vigilance. Love pressed them hard, as thirst presses the dying stag to the stream;

love dropped upon them from high heaven, as a hawk slipped after long hunger falls right upon the bird. And love will not be hidden. Brangien indeed by her prudence saved them well, nor ever were the Queen and her lover unguarded. But in every hour and place every man could see Love terrible, that rode them, and could see in these lovers their every sense overflowing like new wine working in the vat.

The four felons at court who had hated Tristan of old for his prowess, watched the Queen; they had guessed that great love, and they burnt with envy and hatred and now a kind of evil joy. They planned to give news of their watching to the King, to see his tenderness turned to fury, Tristan thrust out or slain, and the Queen in torment; for though they feared Tristan their hatred mastered their fear; and, on a day, the four barons called King Mark to parley, and Andret said:

"Fair King, your heart will be troubled and we four also mourn; yet are we bound to tell you what we know. You have placed your trust in Tristan and Tristan would shame you. In vain we warned you. For the love of one man you have mocked ties of blood and all your Barony. Learn then that Tristan loves the Queen; it is truth proved and many a word is passing on it now."

The royal King shrank and answered:

"Coward! What thought was that? Indeed I have placed my trust in Tristan. And rightly, for on the day when the Morholt offered combat to you all, you hung your heads and were dumb, and you trembled before him; but Tristan dared him for the honour of this land, and took mortal wounds. Therefore do you hate him, and therefore do I cherish him beyond thee, Andret, and beyond any other; but what then have you seen or heard or known?"

"Naught, lord, save what your eyes could see or your ears hear. Look you and listen, Sire, if there is yet time."

And they left him to taste the poison.

Then King Mark watched the Queen and Tristan; but Brangien noting it warned them both and the King watched in vain, so that, soon wearying of an ignoble task, but knowing (alas!) that he could not kill his uneasy thought, he sent for Tristan and said:

"Tristan, leave this castle; and having left it, remain apart and do not think to return to it, and do not repass its moat or boundaries. Felons have charged you with an awful treason, but ask me nothing; I could not speak their words without shame to us both, and for your part seek you no word to appease. I have not believed them . . . had I done so . . . but their evil words have troubled all my soul and only by your absence can my disquiet be soothed. Go, doubtless I will soon recall you. Go, my son, you are still dear to me."

When the felons heard the news they said among themselves, "He is gone, the wizard; he is driven out. Surely he will cross the sea on far adventures to carry his traitor service to some distant King."

But Tristan had not strength to depart altogether; and when he had crossed the moats and boundaries of the Castle he knew he could go no further. He stayed in Tintagel town and lodged with Gorvenal in a burgess' house, and languished oh! more wounded than when in that past day the shaft of the Morholt had tainted his body.

In the close towers Iseult the Fair drooped also, but more wretched still. For it was hers all day long to feign laughter and all night long to conquer fever and despair. And all night as she lay by King Mark's side, fever still kept her waking, and she stared at darkness. She longed to fly to Tristan and she dreamt dreams of running to the gates and of finding there sharp scythes, traps of the felons, that cut her tender knees; and she dreamt of weakness and falling, and that her wounds had left her blood upon the ground. Now these lovers would have died, but Brangien succoured them. At peril of her life she found the house where Tristan lay. There Gorvenal opened to her very gladly, knowing what salvation she could bring.

So she found Tristan, and to save the lovers she taught him a device, nor was ever known a more subtle ruse of love.

Behind the castle of Tintagel was an orchard fenced around and wide and all closed in with stout and pointed stakes and numberless trees were there and fruit on them, birds and clusters of sweet grapes. And furthest from the castle, by the stakes of the pallisade, was a tall pine-tree, straight and with heavy branches spreading from its trunk. At its root a living spring welled calm into a marble round, then ran between two borders winding, throughout the orchard and so, on, till it flowed at last within the castle and through the women's rooms.

And every evening, by Brangien's counsel, Tristan cut him twigs and bark, leapt the sharp stakes and, having come beneath the pine, threw them into the clear spring; they floated light as foam down the stream to the women's rooms; and Iseult watched for their coming, and on those evenings she would wander out into the orchard and find her friend. Lithe and in fear would she come, watching at every step for what might lurk in the trees observing, foes or the felons whom she knew, till she spied Tristan; and the night and the branches of the pine protected them.

And so she said one night: "Oh, Tristan, I have heard that the castle is faëry and that twice a year it vanishes away. So is it vanished now and this is that enchanted orchard of which the harpers sing." And as she said it, the sentinels bugled dawn.

Iseult had refound her joy. Mark's thought of ill-ease grew faint; but the felons felt or knew which way lay truth, and they guessed that Tristan had met the Queen. Till at last Duke Andret (whom God shame) said to his peers:

"My lords, let us take counsel of Frocin the Dwarf; for he knows the seven arts, and magic and every kind of charm. He will teach us if he will the wiles of Iseult the Fair."

The little evil man drew signs for them and characters of sorcery; he cast the fortunes of the hour and then at last he said:

"Sirs, high good lords, this night shall you seize them both."

Then they led the little wizard to the King, and he said:

"Sire, bid your huntsmen leash the hounds and saddle the horses, proclaim a seven days' hunt in the forest and seven nights abroad therein, and hang me high if you do not hear this night what converse Tristan holds."

So did the King unwillingly; and at fall of night he left the hunt taking the dwarf in pillion, and entered the orchard, and the dwarf took him to the tall pine-tree, saying:

"Fair King, climb into these branches and take with you your arrows and your bow, for you may need them; and bide you still."

That night the moon shone clear. Hid in the branches the King saw his nephew leap the pallisades and throw his bark and twigs into the stream. But Tristan had bent over the round well to throw them and so doing had seen the image of the King. He could not stop the branches as they floated away, and there, yonder, in the women's rooms, Iseult was watching and would come.

She came, and Tristan watched her motionless. Above him in the tree he heard the click of the arrow when it fits the string.

She came, but with more prudence than her wont, thinking, "What has passed, that Tristan does not come to meet me? He has seen some foe."

Suddenly, by the clear moonshine, she also saw the King's shadow in the fount. She showed the wit of women well, she did not lift her eyes.

"Lord God," she said, low down, "grant I may be the first to speak."

"Tristan," she said, "what have you dared to do, calling me

hither at such an hour? Often have you called me – to beseech, you said. And Queen though I am, I know you won me that title – and I have come. What would you?"

"Queen, I would have you pray the King for me."

She was in tears and trembling, but Tristan praised God the Lord who had shown his friend her peril.

"Queen," he went on, "often and in vain have I summoned you; never would you come. Take pity; the King hates me and I know not why. Perhaps you know the cause and can charm his anger. For whom can he trust if not you, chaste Queen and courteous, Iseult?"

"Truly, Lord Tristan, you do not know he doubts us both. And I, to add to my shame, must acquaint you of it. Ah! but God knows if I lie, never went out my love to any man but he that first received me. And would you have me, at such a time, implore your pardon of the King? Why, did he know of my passage here to-night he would cast my ashes to the wind. My body trembles and I am afraid. I go, for I have waited too long."

In the branches the King smiled and had pity.

And as Iseult fled: "Queen," said Tristan, "in the Lord's name help me, for charity."

"Friend," she replied, "God aid you! The King wrongs you but the Lord God will be by you in whatever land you go."

So she went back to the women's rooms and told it to Brangien, who cried: "Iseult, God has worked a miracle for you, for He is compassionate and will not hurt the innocent in heart."

And when he had left the orchard, the King said smiling: "Fair nephew, that ride you planned is over now."

But in an open glade apart, Frocin, the Dwarf, read in the clear stars that the King now meant his death; he blackened with shame and fear and fled into Wales.

V

King Mark made peace with Tristan. Tristan returned to the castle as of old. Tristan slept in the King's chamber with his peers. He could come or go, the King thought no more of it.

Mark had pardoned the felons, and as the seneschal, Dinas of Lidan, found the dwarf wandering in a forest abandoned, he brought him home, and the King had pity and pardoned even him.

But his goodness did but feed the ire of the barons, who swore this oath: If the King kept Tristan in the land they would withdraw to their strongholds as for war, and they called the King to parley.

"Lord," said they, "Drive you Tristan forth. He loves the Queen as all who choose can see, but as for us we will bear it no longer."

And the King sighed, looking down in silence.

"King," they went on, "we will not bear it, for we know now that this is known to you and that yet you will not move. Parley you, and take counsel. As for us if you will not exile this man, your nephew, and drive him forth out of your land forever, we will withdraw within our Bailiwicks and take our neighbours also from your court: for we cannot endure his presence longer in this place. Such is your balance: choose."

"My lords," said he, "once I hearkened to the evil words you spoke of Tristan, yet was I wrong in the end. But you are my lieges and I would not lose the service of my men. Counsel me therefore, I charge you, you that owe me counsel. You know me for a man neither proud nor overstepping."

"Lord," said they, "call then Frocin hither. You mistrust him for that orchard night. Still, was it not he that read in the stars of the Queen's coming there and to the very pine-tree too? He is very wise, take counsel of him."

And he came, did that hunchback of Hell: the felons greeted him and he planned this evil.

"Sire," said he, "let your nephew ride hard to-morrow at dawn with a brief drawn up on parchment and well sealed with a seal: bid him ride to King Arthur at Carduel. Sire, he sleeps with the peers in your chamber; go you out when the first sleep falls on men, and if he love Iseult so madly, why, then I swear by God and by the laws of Rome, he will try to speak with her before he rides. But if he do so unknown to you or to me, then slay me. As for the trap, let me lay it, but do you say nothing of his ride to him until the time for sleep."

And when King Mark had agreed, this dwarf did a vile thing. He bought of a baker four farthings' worth of flour, and hid it in the turn of his coat. That night, when the King had supped and the men-at-arms lay down to sleep in hall, Tristan came to the King as custom was, and the King said:

"Fair nephew, do my will: ride tomorrow night to King Arthur at Carduel, and give him this brief, with my greeting, that he may open it: and stay you with him but one day."

And when Tristan said: "I will take it on the morrow."

The King added: "Aye, and before day dawn."

But, as the peers slept all round the King their lord, that night, a mad thought took Tristan that, before he rode, he knew not for how long, before dawn he would say a last word to the Queen. And there was a spear length in the darkness between them. Now the dwarf slept with the rest in the King's chamber, and when he thought that all slept he rose and scattered the flour silently in the spear length that lay between Tristan and the Queen; but Tristan watched and saw him, and said to himself:

"It is to mark my footsteps, but there shall be no marks to show."

At midnight, when all was dark in the room, no candle nor any lamp glimmering, the King went out silently by the door and with him the dwarf. Then Tristan rose in the darkness and judged the spear length and leapt the space between, for his farewell. But that day in the hunt a boar had wounded him in the leg, and in this effort the wound bled. He did not feel it or see it in the darkness, but the blood dripped upon the couches and the flour strewn between; and outside in the moonlight the dwarf read the heavens and knew what had been done and he cried:

"Enter, my King, and if you do not hold them, hang me high."

Then the King and the dwarf and the four felons ran in with lights and noise, and though Tristan had regained his place there was the blood for witness, and though Iseult feigned sleep, and Perinis too, who lay at Tristan's feet, yet there was the blood for witness. And the King looked in silence at the blood where it lay upon the bed and the boards and trampled into the flour.

And the four barons held Tristan down upon his bed and mocked the Queen also, promising her full justice; and they bared and showed the wound whence the blood flowed.

Then the King said:

"Tristan, now nothing longer holds. To-morrow you shall die."

And Tristan answered:

"Have mercy, Lord, in the name of God that suffered the Cross!"

But the felons called on the King to take vengeance, saying:

"Do justice, King: take vengeance."

And Tristan went on, "Have mercy, not on me – for why should I stand at dying? – Truly, but for you, I would have sold my honour high to cowards who, under your peace, have put hands on my body – but in homage to you I have yielded and you may do with me what you will. But, lord, remember the Queen!"

And as he knelt at the King's feet he still complained:

"Remember the Queen; for if any man of your household make so bold as to maintain the lie that I loved her unlawfully, I will stand up armed to him in a ring. Sire, in the name of God the Lord, have mercy on her."

Then the barons bound him with ropes, and the Queen also. But had Tristan known that trial by combat was to be denied him, certainly he would not have suffered it.

For he trusted in God and knew no man dared draw sword against him in the lists. And truly he did well to trust in God, for though the felons mocked him when he said he had loved loyally, yet I call you to witness, my lords who read this, and who know of the philtre drunk upon the high seas, and who understand whether his love were disloyalty indeed. For men see this and that outward thing, but God alone the heart, and in the heart alone is crime and the sole final judge is God. Therefore did He lay down the law that a man accused might uphold his cause by battle, and God himself fights for the innocent in such a combat.

Therefore did Tristan claim justice and the right of battle and therefore was he careful to fail in nothing of the homage he owed King Mark, his lord.

But had he known what was coming, he would have killed the felons.

VI

Dark was the night, and the news ran that Tristan and the Queen were held and that the King would kill them; and wealthy burgess, or common man, they wept and ran to the palace.

And the murmurs and the cries ran through the city, but such was the King's anger in his castle above that not the strongest nor the proudest baron dared move him.

Night ended and the day drew near. Mark, before dawn, rode out to the place where he held pleas and judgment. He ordered a ditch to be dug in the earth and knotty vine-shoots and thorns to be laid therein.

At the hour of Prime he had a ban cried through his land to gather the men of Cornwall; they came with a great noise and the King spoke them thus:

"My lords, I have made here a faggot of thorns for Tristan and the Queen; for they have fallen."

But they cried all, with tears:

"A sentence, lord, a sentence; an indictment and pleas; for killing without trial is shame and crime."

But Mark answered in his anger:

"Neither respite, nor delay, nor pleas, nor sentence. By God that made the world, if any dare petition me, he shall burn first!"

He ordered the fire to be lit, and Tristan to be called.

The flames rose, and all were silent before the flames, and the King waited.

The servants ran to the room where watch was kept on the two lovers; and they dragged Tristan out by his hands, though he wept for his honour; but as they dragged him off in such a shame, the Queen still called to him:

"Friend, if I die that you may live, that will be great joy."

Now, hear how full of pity is God and how He heard the lament and the prayers of the common folk, that day.

For as Tristan and his guards went down from the town to where the faggot burned, near the road upon a rock was a chantry, it stood at a cliff's edge steep and sheer, and it turned to the sea-breeze; in the apse of it were windows glazed. Then Tristan said to those with him:

"My lords, let me enter this chantry, to pray for a moment the mercy of God whom I have offended; my death is near. There is but one door to the place, my lords, and each of you has his sword drawn. So, you may well see that, when my prayer to God is done, I must come past you again: when I have prayed God, my lords, for the last time."

And one of the guards said: "Why, let him go in."

So they let him enter to pray. But he, once in, dashed through and leapt the altar rail and the altar too and forced a window of the apse, and leapt again over the cliff's edge. So might he die, but not of that shameful death before the people.

Now learn, my lords, how generous was God to him that day. The wind took Tristan's cloak and he fell upon a smooth rock at the cliff's foot, which to this day the men of Cornwall call "Tristan's leap."

His guards still waited for him at the chantry door, but vainly, for God was now his guard. And he ran, and the fine sand crunched under his feet, and far off he saw the faggot burning, and the smoke and the crackling flames; and fled.

Sword girt and bridle loose, Gorvenal had fled the city, lest the King burn him in his master's place: and he found Tristan on the shore.

"Master," said Tristan, "God has saved me, but oh! master, to what end? For without Iseult I may not and I will not live, and I rather had died of my fall. They will burn her for me, then I too will die for her."

"Lord," said Gorvenal, "take no counsel of anger. See here this thicket with a ditch dug round about it. Let us hide therein where the track passes near, and comers by it will tell us news; and, boy, if they burn Iseult, I swear by God, the Son of Mary, never to sleep under a roof again until she be avenged."

There was a poor man of the common folk that had seen Tristan's fall, and had seen him stumble and rise after, and he crept to Tintagel and to Iseult where she was bound, and said:

"Queen, weep no more. Your friend has fled safely."

"Then I thank God," said she, "and whether they bind or loose me, and whether they kill or spare me, I care but little now."

And though blood came at the cord-knots, so tightly had the traitors bound her, yet still she said, smiling:

"Did I weep for that when God has loosed my friend I should be little worth."

When the news came to the King that Tristan had leapt that leap and was lost he paled with anger, and bade his men bring forth Iseult.

They dragged her from the room, and she came before the crowd, held by her delicate hands, from which blood dropped, and the crowd called:

"Have pity on her – the loyal Queen and honoured! Surely they that gave her up brought mourning on us all – our curses on them!"

But the King's men dragged her to the thorn faggot as it blazed. She stood up before the flame, and the crowd cried its anger, and cursed the traitors and the King. None could see her without pity, unless he had a felon's heart: she was so tightly bound. The tears ran down her face and fell upon her grey gown where ran a little thread of gold, and a thread of gold was twined into her hair.

Just then there had come up a hundred lepers of the King's, deformed and broken, white horribly, and limping on their crutches. And they drew near the flame, and being evil, loved the sight. And their chief Ivan, the ugliest of them all, cried to the King in a quavering voice:

"O King, you would burn this woman in that flame, and it is sound justice, but too swift, for very soon the fire will fall, and her ashes will very soon be scattered by the high wind and her agony be done. Throw her rather to your lepers where she may drag out a life for ever asking death."

And the King answered:

"Yes; let her live that life, for it is better justice and more terrible. I can love those that gave me such a thought."

And the lepers answered:

"Throw her among us, and make her one of us. Never shall lady have known a worse end. And look," they said, "at our rags and our abominations. She has had pleasure in rich stuffs and furs, jewels and walls of marble, honour, good wines and joy, but when she sees your lepers always, King, and only them for ever, their couches and their huts, then indeed she will know the wrong she has done, and bitterly desire even that great flame of thorns."

And as the King heard them, he stood a long time without moving; then he ran to the Queen and seized her by the hand, and she cried:

"Burn me! rather burn me!"

But the King gave her up, and Ivan took her, and the hundred lepers pressed around, and to hear her cries all the crowd rose in pity. But Ivan had an evil gladness, and as he went he dragged her out of the borough bounds, with his hideous company.

Now they took that road where Tristan lay in hiding, and Gorvenal said to him:

"Son, here is your friend. Will you do naught?"

Then Tristan mounted the horse and spurred it out of the bush, and cried:

"Ivan, you have been at the Queen's side a moment, and too long. Now leave her if you would live."

But Ivan threw his cloak away and shouted:

"Your clubs, comrades, and your staves! Crutches in the air – for a fight is on!"

Then it was fine to see the lepers throwing their capes aside, and stirring their sick legs, and brandishing their crutches, some threatening: groaning all; but to strike them Tristan was too noble. There are singers who sing that Tristan killed Ivan, but it is a lie. Too much a knight was he to kill such things. Gorvenal indeed, snatching up an oak sapling, crashed it on Ivan's head till his blood ran down to his misshapen feet. Then Tristan took the Queen.

Henceforth near him she felt no further evil. He cut the cords that bound her arms so straightly, and he left the plain so that they plunged into the wood of Morois; and there in the thick wood Tristan was as sure as in a castle keep.

And as the sun fell they halted all three at the foot of a little hill: fear had wearied the Queen, and she leant her head upon his body and slept.

But in the morning, Gorvenal stole from a woodman his bow and two good arrows plumed and barbed, and gave them to Tristan, the great archer, and he shot him a fawn and killed it. Then Gorvenal gathered dry twigs, struck flint, and lit a great fire to cook the venison. And Tristan cut him branches and made a hut and garnished it with leaves. And Iseult slept upon the thick leaves there.

So, in the depths of the wild wood began for the lovers that savage life which yet they loved very soon.

VII

They wandered in the depths of the wild wood, restless and in haste like beasts that are hunted, nor did they often dare to return by night to the shelter of yesterday. They ate but the flesh of wild animals. Their faces sank and grew white, their clothes ragged, for the briars tore them. They loved each other and they did not know that they suffered.

One day, as they were wandering in these high woods that had never yet been felled or ordered, they came upon the hermitage of Ogrin.

The old man limped in the sunlight under a light growth of maples near his chapel: he leant upon his crutch, and cried:

"Lord Tristan, hear the great oath which the Cornish men have sworn. The King has published a ban in every parish: Whosoever may seize you shall receive a hundred marks of gold for his guerdon, and all the barons have sworn to give you up alive or dead. Do penance, Tristan! God pardons the sinner who turns to repentance."

"And of what should I repent, Ogrin, my lord? Or of what crime? You that sit in judgment upon us here, do you know what cup it was we drank upon the high sea? That good, great draught inebriates us both. I would rather beg my life long and live of roots and herbs with Iseult than, lacking her, be king of a wide kingdom."

"God aid you, Lord Tristan; for you have lost both this world and the next. A man that is traitor to his lord is worthy to be torn by horses and burnt upon the faggot, and wherever his ashes fall no grass shall grow and all tillage is waste, and the trees and the green things die. Lord Tristan, give back the Queen to the man who espoused her lawfully according to the laws of Rome."

"He gave her to his lepers. From these lepers I myself conquered her with my own hand; and henceforth she is altogether mine. She cannot pass from me nor I from her."

Ogrin sat down; but at his feet Iseult, her head upon the knees of that man of God, wept silently. The hermit told her and re-told her the words of his holy book, but still while she wept she shook her head, and refused the faith he offered.

"Ah me," said Ogrin then, "what comfort can one give the dead? Do penance, Tristan, for a man who lives in sin without repenting is a man quite dead."

"Oh no," said Tristan, "I live and I do no penance. We will go back into the high wood which comforts and wards us all round about. Come with me, Iseult, my friend."

Iseult rose up; they held each other's hands. They passed into the high grass and the underwood: the trees hid them with their branches. They disappeared beyond the curtain of the leaves.

The summer passed and the winter came: the two lovers lived, all hidden in the hollow of a rock, and on the frozen earth the cold crisped their couch with dead leaves. In the strength of their love neither one nor the other felt these mortal things. But when the open skies had come back with the springtime, they built a hut of green branches under the great trees. Tristan had known, ever since his childhood, that art by which a man may sing the song of birds in the woods, and at his fancy, he would call as call the thrush, the blackbird and the nightingale, and all winged things; and sometimes in reply very many birds would come on to the branches of his hut and sing their song full-throated in the new light.

The lovers had ceased to wander through the forest, for none of the barons ran the risk of their pursuit knowing well that Tristan would have hanged them to the branches of a tree. One day, however, one of the four traitors, Guenelon, whom God blast! drawn by the heat of the hunt, dared enter the Morois. And that morning, on the forest edge in a ravine, Gorvenal, having unsaddled his horse, had let him graze on the new grass, while far off in their hut Tristan held the Queen, and they slept. Then suddenly Gorvenal heard the cry of the pack; the hounds pursued a deer, which fell into that ravine. And far on the heath the hunter showed – and Gorvenal knew him for the man whom his master hated above all. Alone, with bloody spurs, and striking his horse's mane, he galloped on; but Gorvenal watched him from ambush: he came fast, he would return more slowly. He passed and Gorvenal leapt from his ambush and seized the rein and, suddenly, remembering all the wrong that man had done, hewed him to death and carried off his head in his hands. And when the hunters found the body, as they followed, they thought Tristan came after and they fled in fear of death, and thereafter no man hunted in that wood. And far off, in the hut upon their couch of leaves, slept Tristan and the Queen.

There came Gorvenal, noiseless, the dead man's head in his hands that he might lift his master's heart at his awakening. He hung it by its hair outside the hut, and the leaves garlanded it about. Tristan woke and saw it, half hidden in the leaves, and staring at him as he gazed, and he became afraid. But Gorvenal said: "Fear not, he is dead. I killed him with this sword."

Then Tristan was glad, and hence-forward from that day no one dared enter the wild wood, for terror guarded it and the lovers were lords of it all: and then it was that Tristan fashioned his bow "Failnaught" which struck home always, man or beast, whatever it aimed at.

My lords, upon a summer day, when mowing is, a little after Whitsuntide, as the birds sang dawn Tristan left his hut and girt his sword on him, and took his bow "Failnaught" and went off to hunt in the wood; but before evening, great evil was to fall on him, for no lovers ever loved so much or paid their love so dear.

When Tristan came back, broken by the heat, the Queen said: "Friend, where have you been?"

"Hunting a hart," he said, "that wearied me. I would lie down and sleep."

So she lay down, and he, and between them Tristan put his naked sword, and on the Queen's finger was that ring of gold with emeralds set therein, which Mark had given her on her bridal day; but her hand was so wasted that the ring hardly held. And no wind blew, and no leaves stirred, but through a crevice in the branches a sunbeam fell upon the face of Iseult, and it shone white like ice. Now a woodman found in the wood a place where the leaves were crushed, where the lovers had halted and slept, and he followed their track and found the hut, and saw them sleeping and fled off, fearing the terrible awakening of that lord. He fled to Tintagel, and going up the stairs of the palace, found the King as he held his pleas in hall amid the vassals assembled.

"Friend," said the King, "what came you hither to seek in haste and breathless, like a huntsman that has followed the dogs afoot? Have you some wrong to right, or has any man driven you?"

But the woodman took him aside and said low down:

"I have seen the Queen and Tristan, and I feared and fled."

"Where saw you them?"

"In a hut in Morois, they slept side by side. Come swiftly and take your vengeance."

"Go," said the King, "and await me at the forest edge where the red cross stands, and tell no man what you have seen. You shall have gold and silver at your will."

The King had saddled his horse and girt his sword and left the city alone, and as he rode alone he minded him of the night when he had seen Tristan under the great pine-tree, and Iseult with her clear face, and he thought:

"If I find them I will avenge this awful wrong."

At the foot of the red cross he came to the woodman and said: "Go first, and lead me straight and quickly."

The dark shade of the great trees wrapt them round, and as the King followed the spy he felt his sword, and trusted it for the great blows it had struck of old; and surely had Tristan wakened, one of the two had stayed there dead. Then the woodman said:

"King, we are near."

He held the stirrup, and tied the rein to a green apple-tree, and saw in a sunlit glade the hut with its flowers and leaves. Then the King cast his cloak with its fine buckle of gold and drew his sword from its sheath and said again in his heart that they or he should die. And he signed to the woodman to be gone.

He came alone into the hut, sword bare, and watched them as they lay: but he saw that they were apart, and he wondered because between them was the naked blade.

Then he said to himself: "My God, I may not kill them. For all the time they have lived together in this wood, these two lovers, yet is the sword here between them, and throughout Christendom men know that sign. Therefore I will not slay, for that would be treason and wrong, but I will do so that when they wake they may know that I found them here, asleep, and spared them and that God had pity on them both."

And still the sunbeam fell upon the white face of Iseult, and the King took his ermined gloves and put them up against the crevice whence it shone.

Then in her sleep a vision came to Iseult. She seemed to be in a great wood and two lions near her fought for her, and she gave a cry and woke, and the gloves fell upon her breast; and at the cry Tristan woke, and made to seize his sword, and saw by the golden hilt that it was the King's. And the Queen saw on her finger the King's ring, and she cried:

"O, my lord, the King has found us here!"

And Tristan said:

"He has taken my sword; he was alone, but he will return, and will burn us before the people. Let us fly."

So by great marches with Gorvenal alone they fled towards Wales.

VIII

After three days it happened that Tristan, in following a wounded deer far out into the wood, was caught by night-fall, and took to thinking thus under the dark wood alone:

"It was not fear that moved the King . . . he had my sword and I slept . . . and had he wished to slay, why did he leave me his own blade? . . . O, my father, my father, I know you now. There was pardon in your heart, and tenderness and pity . . . yet how was that, for who could forgive in this matter without shame? . . . It was not pardon, it was understanding; the faggot and the chantry leap and the leper ambush have shown him God upon our side. Also I think he remembered the boy who long ago harped at his feet, and my land of Lyonesse which I left for him; the Morholt's spear and blood shed in his honour. He remembered how I made no avowal, but claimed a trial at arms, and the high nature of his heart has made him understand what men around him cannot; never can he know of the spell, yet he doubts and hopes and knows I have told no lie, and would have me prove my cause. O, but to win at arms by God's aid for him, and to enter his peace and to put on mail for him again . . . but then he must take her back, and I must yield her . . . it would have been much better had he killed me in my sleep. For till now I was hunted and I could hate and forget; he had thrown Iseult to the lepers, she was no more his, but mine; and now by his compassion he has wakened my heart and regained the Queen. For Queen she was at his side, but in this wood she lives a slave, and I waste her youth; and for rooms all hung with silk she has this savage place, and a hut for her splendid walls, and I am the cause that she treads this ugly road. So now I cry to God the Lord, who is King of the World, and beg Him to give me strength to yield back Iseult to King Mark; for she is indeed his wife, wed according to the laws of Rome before all the Barony of his land."

And as he thought thus, he leant upon his bow, and all through the night considered his sorrow.

Within the hollow of thorns that was their resting-place Iseult the Fair awaited Tristan's return. The golden ring that King Mark had slipped there glistened on her finger in the moonlight, and she thought:

"He that put on this ring is not the man who threw me to his lepers in his wrath; he is rather that compassionate lord who, from the day I touched his shore, received me and protected And he loved Tristan once, but I came, and see what I have done! He should have lived in the King's palace; he should have ridden through King's and baron's fees, finding adventure; but through me he has forgotten his knighthood, and is hunted and exiled from the court, leading a random life . . ."

Just then she heard the feet of Tristan coming over the dead leaves and twigs. She came to meet him, as was her wont, to relieve him of his arms, and she took from him his bow, "Failnaught," and his arrows, and she unbuckled his sword-straps. And, "Friend," said he, "it is the King's sword. It should have slain, but it spared us."

Iseult took the sword, and kissed the hilt of gold, and Tristan saw her weeping.

"Friend," said he, "if I could make my peace with the King; if he would allow me to sustain in arms that neither by act nor word have I loved you with a wrongful love, any knight from the Marshes of Ely right away to Dureaume that would gainsay me, would find me armed in the ring. Then if the King would keep you and drive me out I would cross to the Lowlands or to Brittany with Gorvenal alone. But wherever I went and always, Queen, I should be yours; nor would I have spoken thus, Iseult, but for the wretchedness you bear so long for my sake in this desert land."

"Tristan," she said, "there is the hermit Ogrin. Let us return to him, and cry mercy to the King of Heaven."

They wakened Gorvenal; Iseult mounted the steed, and Tristan led it by the bridle, and all night long they went for the last time through the woods of their love, and they did not speak a word. By morning they came to the Hermitage, where Ogrin read at the threshold, and seeing them, called them tenderly:

"Friends," he cried, "see how Love drives you still to further wretchedness. Will you not do penance at last for your madness?"

"Lord Ogrin," said Tristan, "hear us. Help us to offer peace to the King, and I will yield him the Queen, and will myself go far away into Brittany or the Lowlands, and if some day the King suffer me, I will return and serve as I should."

And at the hermit's feet Iseult said in her turn:

"Nor will I live longer so, for though I will not say one word of penance for my love, which is there and remains forever, yet from now on I will be separate from him."

Then the hermit wept and praised God and cried: "High King, I praise Thy Name, for that Thou hast let me live so long as to give aid to these!"

And he gave them wise counsel, and took ink, and wrote a little writ offering the King what Tristan said.

That night Tristan took the road. Once more he saw the marble well and the tall pine-tree, and he came beneath the window where the King slept, and called him gently, and Mark awoke and whispered:

"Who are you that call me in the night at such an hour?"

"Lord, I am Tristan: I bring you a writ, and lay it here."

Then the King cried: "Nephew! nephew! for God's sake wait awhile," but Tristan had fled and joined his squire, and mounted rapidly. Gorvenal said to him:

"O, Tristan, you are mad to have come. Fly hard with me by the nearest road."

So they came back to the Hermitage, and there they found Ogrin at prayer, but Iseult weeping silently.

IX

Mark had awakened his chaplain and had given him the writ to read; the chaplain broke the seal, saluted in Tristan's name, and then, when he had cunningly made out the written words, told him what Tristan offered; and Mark heard without saying a word, but his heart was glad, for he still loved the Queen.

He summoned by name the choicest of his baronage, and when they were all assembled they were silent and the King spoke:

"My lords, here is a writ, just sent me. I am your King, and you my lieges. Hear what is offered me, and then counsel me, for you owe me counsel."

The chaplain rose, unfolded the writ, and said, upstanding:

"My lords, it is Tristan that first sends love and homage to the King and all his Barony, and he adds, 'O King, when I slew the dragon and conquered the King of Ireland's daughter it was to me they gave her. I was to ward her at will and I yielded her to you. Yet hardly had you wed her when felons made you accept their lies, and in your anger, fair uncle, my lord, you would have had us burnt without trial. But God took compassion on us; we prayed him and he saved the Queen, as justice was: and me also – though I leapt from a high rock, I was saved by the power of God. And since then what have I done blameworthy? The Queen was thrown to the lepers; I came to her succour and bore her away. Could I have done less for a woman, who all but died innocent through me? I fled through the woods. Nor could I have come down into the vale and yielded her, for there was a ban to take us dead or alive. But now, as then, I am ready, my lord, to sustain in arms against all comers that never had the Queen for me, nor I for her, a love dishonourable to you. Publish the lists, and if I cannot prove my right in arms, burn me before your men. But if I conquer and you take back Iseult, no baron of yours will serve you as will I; and if you will not have me, I will offer myself to the King of Galloway, or to him of the Lowlands, and you will hear of me never again. Take counsel, King, for if you will make no terms I will take back Iseult to Ireland, and she shall be Queen in her own land.'"

When the barons of Cornwall heard how Tristan offered battle, they said to the King:

"Sire, take back the Queen. They were madmen that belied her to you. But as for Tristan, let him go and war it in Galloway, or in the Lowlands. Bid him bring back Iseult on such a day and that soon."

Then the King called thrice clearly:

"Will any man rise in accusation against Tristan?"

And as none replied, he said to his chaplain:

"Write me a writ in haste. You have heard what you shall write. Iseult has suffered enough in her youth. And let the writ be hung upon the arm of the red cross before evening. Write speedily."

Towards midnight Tristan crossed the Heath of Sand, and found the writ, and bore it sealed to Ogrin; and the hermit read the letter; "How Mark consented by the counsel of his barons to take back Iseult, but not to keep Tristan for his liege. Rather let him cross the sea, when, on the third day hence, at the Ford of Chances, he had given back the Queen into King Mark's hands." Then Tristan said to the Queen:

"O, my God! I must lose you, friend! But it must be, since I can thus spare you what you suffer for my sake. But when we part for ever I will give you a pledge of mine to keep, and from whatever unknown land I reach I will send some messenger, and he will bring back word of you, and at your call I will come from far away."

Iseult said, sighing:

"Tristan, leave me your dog, Toothold, and every time I see him I will remember you, and will be less sad. And, friend, I have here a ring of green jasper. Take it for the love of me, and put it on your finger; then if anyone come saying he is from you, I will not trust him at all till he show me this ring, but once I have seen it, there is no power or royal ban that can prevent me from doing what you bid – wisdom or folly."

"Friend," he said, "here give I you Toothold."

"Friend," she replied, "take you this ring in reward."

And they kissed each other on the lips.

Now Ogrin, having left the lovers in the Hermitage, hobbled upon his crutch to the place called The Mount, and he bought ermine there and fur and cloth of silk and purple and scarlet, and a palfrey harnessed in gold that went softly, and the folk laughed to see him spending upon these the small moneys he had amassed so long; but the old man put the rich stuffs upon the palfrey and came back to Iseult.

And "Queen," said he, "take these gifts of mine that you may seem the finer on the day when you come to the Ford."

Meanwhile the King had had cried through Cornwall the news that on the third day he would make his peace with the Queen at the Ford, and knights and ladies came in a crowd to the gathering, for all loved the Queen and would see her, save the three felons that yet survived.

On the day chosen for the meeting, the field shone far with the rich tents of the barons, and suddenly Tristan and Iseult came out at the forest's edge, and caught sight of King Mark far off among his Barony:

"Friend," said Tristan, "there is the King, your lord – his knights and his men; they are coming towards us, and very soon we may not speak to each other again. By the God of Power I conjure you, if ever I send you a word, do you my bidding."

"Friend," said Iseult, "on the day that I see the ring, nor tower, nor wall, nor stronghold will let me from doing the will of my friend."

"Why then," he said, "Iseult, may God reward you."

Their horses went abreast and he drew her towards him with his arm.

"Friend," said Iseult, "hear my last prayer: you will leave this land, but wait some days; hide till you know how the King may treat me, whether in wrath or kindness, for I am afraid. Friend,

Orri the woodman will entertain you hidden. Go you by night to the abandoned cellar that you know and I will send Perinis there to say if anyone misuse me."

"Friend, none would dare. I will stay hidden with Orri, and if any misuse you let him fear me as the Enemy himself."

Now the two troops were near and they saluted, and the King rode a bowshot before his men and with him Dinas of Lidan; and when the barons had come up, Tristan, holding Iseult's palfrey by the bridle, bowed to the King and said:

"O King, I yield you here Iseult the Fair, and I summon you, before the men of your land, that I may defend myself in your court, for I have had no judgment. Let me have trial at arms, and if I am conquered, burn me, but if I conquer, keep me by you, or, if you will not, I will be off to some far country."

But no one took up Tristan's wager, and the King, taking Iseult's palfrey by the bridle, gave it to Dinas, and went apart to take counsel.

Dinas, in his joy, gave all honour and courtesy to the Queen, but when the felons saw her so fair and honoured as of old, they were stirred and rode to the King, and said:

"King, hear our counsel. That the Queen was slandered we admit, but if she and Tristan re-enter your court together, rumour will revive again. Rather let Tristan go apart awhile. Doubtless some day you may recall him."

And so Mark did, and ordered Tristan by his barons to go off without delay.

Then Tristan came near the Queen for his farewell, and as they looked at one another the Queen in shame of that assembly blushed, but the King pitied her, and spoke his nephew thus for the first time:

"You cannot leave in these rags; take then from my treasury gold and silver and white fur and grey, as much as you will."

"King," said Tristan, "neither a penny nor a link of mail. I will go as I can, and serve with high heart the mighty King in the Lowlands."

And he turned rein and went down towards the sea, but Iseult followed him with her eyes, and so long as he could yet be seen a long way off she did not turn.

Now at the news of the peace, men, women, and children, great and small, ran out of the town in a crowd to meet Iseult, and while they mourned Tristan's exile they rejoiced at the Queen's return.

And to the noise of bells, and over pavings strewn with branches, the King and his counts and princes made her escort, and the gates of the palace were thrown open that rich and poor might enter and eat and drink at will.

And Mark freed a hundred of his slaves, and armed a score of squires that day with hauberk and with sword.

But Tristan that night hid with Orri, as the Queen had counselled him.

X

Denoalen, Andret, and Gondoïn held themselves safe; Tristan was far over sea, far away in service of a distant king, and they beyond his power. Therefore, during a hunt one day, as the King rode apart in a glade where the pack would pass, and hearkening to the hounds, they all three rode towards him, and said:

"O King, we have somewhat to say. Once you condemned the Queen without judgment, and that was wrong; now you acquit her without judgment, and that is wrong. She is not quit by trial, and the barons of your land blame you both. Counsel her, then, to claim the ordeal in God's judgment, for since she is innocent, she may swear on the relics of the saints and hot iron will not hurt her. For so custom runs, and in this easy way are doubts dissolved."

But Mark answered:

"God strike you, my Cornish lords, how you hunt my shame! For you have I exiled my nephew, and now what would you now? Would you have me drive the Queen to Ireland too? What novel plaints have you to plead? Did not Tristan offer you battle in this matter? He offered battle to clear the Queen forever: he offered and you heard him all. Where then were your lances and your shields?"

"Sire," they said, "we have counselled you loyal counsel as lieges and to your honour; henceforward we hold our peace. Put aside your anger and give us your safe-guard."

But Mark stood up in the stirrup and cried:

"Out of my land, and out of my peace, all of you! Tristan I exiled for you, and now go you in turn, out of my land!"

But they answered:

"Sire, it is well. Our keeps are strong and fenced, and stand on rocks not easy for men to climb."

And they rode off without a salutation.

But the King (not tarrying for huntsman or for hound but straight away) spurred his horse to Tintagel; and as he sprang up the stairs the Queen heard the jangle of his spurs upon the stones.

She rose to meet him and took his sword as she was wont, and bowed before him, as it was also her wont to do; but Mark raised her, holding her hands; and when Iseult looked up she saw his noble face in just that wrath she had seen before the faggot fire.

She thought that Tristan was found, and her heart grew cold, and without a word she fell at the King's feet.

He took her in his arms and kissed her gently till she could speak again, and then he said:

"Friend, friend, what evil tries you?"

"Sire, I am afraid, for I have seen your anger."

"Yes, I was angered at the hunt."

"My lord, should one take so deeply the mischances of a game?"

Mark smiled and said:

"No, friend; no chance of hunting vexed me, but those three felons whom you know; and I have driven them forth from my land."

"Sire, what did they say, or dare to say of me?"

"What matter? I have driven them forth."

"Sire, all living have this right: to say the word they have conceived. And I would ask a question, but from whom shall I learn save from you? I am alone in a foreign land, and have no one else to defend me."

"They would have it that you should quit yourself by solemn oath and by the ordeal of iron, saying 'that God was a true judge, and that as the Queen was innocent, she herself should seek such judgment as would clear her for ever.' This was their clamour and their demand incessantly. But let us leave it. I tell you, I have driven them forth."

Iseult trembled, but looking straight at the King, she said:

"Sire, call them back; I will clear myself by oath. But I bargain this: that on the appointed day you call King Arthur and Lord Gawain, Girflet, Kay the Seneschal, and a hundred of his knights to ride to the Sandy Heath where your land marches with his, and a river flows between; for I will not swear before your barons alone, lest they should demand some new thing, and lest there should be no end to my trials. But if my warrantors, King Arthur and his knights, be there, the barons will not dare dispute the judgment."

But as the heralds rode to Carduel, Iseult sent to Tristan secretly her squire Perinis: and he ran through the underwood, avoiding paths, till he found the hut of Orri, the woodman, where Tristan for many days had awaited news. Perinis told him all: the ordeal, the place, and the time, and added:

"My lord, the Queen would have you on that day and place come dressed as a pilgrim, so that none may know you – unarmed, so that none may challenge – to the Sandy Heath. She must cross the river to the place appointed. Beyond it, where Arthur and his hundred knights will stand, be you also; for my lady fears the judgment, but she trusts in God."

Then Tristan answered:

"Go back, friend Perinis, return you to the Queen, and say that I will do her bidding."

And you must know that as Perinis went back to Tintagel he caught sight of that same woodman who had betrayed the lovers before, and the woodman, as he found him, had just dug a pitfall for wolves and for wild boars, and covered it with leafy branches to hide it, and as Perinis came near the woodman fled, but Perinis drove him, and caught him, and broke his staff and his head together, and pushed his body into the pitfall with his feet.

On the appointed day King Mark and Iseult, and the barons of Cornwall, stood by the river; and the knights of Arthur and all their host were arrayed beyond.

And just before them, sitting on the shore, was a poor pilgrim, wrapped in cloak and hood, who held his wooden platter and begged alms.

Now as the Cornish boats came to the shoal of the further bank, Iseult said to the knights:

"My lords, how shall I land without befouling my clothes in the river-mud? Fetch me a ferryman."

And one of the knights hailed the pilgrim, and said:

"Friend, truss your coat, and try the water; carry you the Queen to shore, unless you fear the burden."

But as he took the Queen in his arms she whispered to him:

"Friend."

And then she whispered to him, lower still:

"Stumble you upon the sand."

And as he touched shore, he stumbled, holding the Queen in his arms; and the squires and boatmen with their oars and boat-hooks drove the poor pilgrim away.

But the Queen said:

"Let him be; some great travail and journey has weakened him."

And she threw to the pilgrim a little clasp of gold.

Before the tent of King Arthur was spread a rich Nicean cloth upon the grass, and the holy relics were set on it, taken out of their covers and their shrines.

And round the holy relics on the sward stood a guard more than a king's guard, for Lord Gawain, Girflet, and Kay the Seneschal kept ward over them.

The Queen having prayed God, took off the jewels from her neck and hands, and gave them to the beggars around; she took off her purple mantle, and her overdress, and her shoes with their precious stones, and gave them also to the poor that loved her.

She kept upon her only the sleeveless tunic, and then with arms and feet quite bare she came between the two kings, and all around the barons watched her in silence, and some wept, for near the holy relics was a brazier burning.

And trembling a little she stretched her right hand towards the bones and said: "Kings of Logres and of Cornwall; my lords Gawain, and Kay, and Girflet, and all of you that are my warrantors, by these holy things and all the holy things of earth, I swear that no man has held me in his arms saving King Mark, my lord, and that poor pilgrim. King Mark, will that oath stand?"

"Yes, Queen," he said, "and God see to it."

"Amen," said Iseult, and then she went near the brazier, pale and stumbling, and all were silent. The iron was red, but she thrust her bare arms among the coals and seized it, and bearing it took nine steps.

Then, as she cast it from her, she stretched her arms out in a cross, with the palms of her hands wide open, and all men saw them fresh and clean and cold. Seeing that great sight the kings and the barons and the people stood for a moment silent, then they stirred together and they praised God loudly all around.

XI

When Tristan had come back to Orri's hut, and had loosened his heavy pilgrim's cape, he saw clearly in his heart that it was time to keep his oath to King Mark and to fly the land.

Three days yet he tarried, because he could not drag himself away from that earth, but on the fourth day he thanked the woodman, and said to Gorvenal:

"Master, the hour is come."

And he went into Wales, into the land of the great Duke Gilain, who was young, powerful, and frank in spirit, and welcomed him nobly as a God-sent guest.

And he did everything to give him honour and joy; but he found that neither adventure, nor feast could soothe what Tristan suffered.

One day, as he sat by the young Duke's side, his spirit weighed upon him, so that not knowing it he groaned, and the Duke, to soothe him, ordered into his private room a fairy thing, which pleased his eyes when he was sad and relieved his own heart; it was a dog, and the varlets brought it in to him, and they put it upon a table there. Now this dog was a fairy dog, and came from the Duke of Avalon; for a fairy had given it him as a love-gift, and no one can well describe its kind or beauty. And it bore at its neck, hung to a little chain of gold, a little bell; and that tinkled so gaily, and so clear and so soft, that as Tristan heard it, he was soothed, and his anguish melted away, and he forgot all that he had suffered for the Queen; for such was the virtue of the bell and such its property: that whosoever heard it, he lost all pain. And as Tristan stroked the little fairy thing, the dog that took away his sorrow, he saw how delicate it was and fine, and how it had soft hair like samite, and he thought how good a gift it would make for the Queen. But he dared not ask for it right out since he knew that the Duke loved this dog beyond everything in the world, and would yield it to no prayers, nor to wealth, nor to wile; so one day Tristan having made a plan in his mind said this:

"Lord, what would you give to the man who could rid your land of the hairy giant Urgan, that levies such a toll?"

"Truly, the victor might choose what he would, but none will dare."

Then said Tristan:

"Those are strange words, for good comes to no land save by risk and daring, and not for all the gold of Milan would I renounce my desire to find him in his wood and bring him down."

Then Tristan went out to find Urgan in his lair, and they fought hard and long, till courage conquered strength, and Tristan, having cut off the giant's hand, bore it back to the Duke.

And "Sire," said he, "since I may choose a reward according to your word, give me the little fairy dog. It was for that I conquered Urgan, and your promise stands."

"Friend," said the Duke, "take it, then, but in taking it you take away also all my joy."

Then Tristan took the little fairy dog and gave it in ward to a

Welsh harper, who was cunning and who bore it to Cornwall till he came to Tintagel, and having come there put it secretly into Brangien's hands, and the Queen was so pleased that she gave ten marks of gold to the harper, but she put it about that the Queen of Ireland, her mother, had sent the beast. And she had a goldsmith work a little kennel for him, all jewelled, and incrusted with gold and enamel inlaid; and wherever she went she carried the dog with her in memory of her friend, and as she watched it sadness and anguish and regrets melted out of her heart.

At first she did not guess the marvel, but thought her consolation was because the gift was Tristan's, till one day she found that it was fairy, and that it was the little bell that charmed her soul; then she thought: "What have I to do with comfort since he is sorrowing? He could have kept it too and have forgotten his sorrow; but with high courtesy he sent it to me to give me his joy and to take up his pain again. Friend, while you suffer, so long will I suffer also."

And she took the magic bell and shook it just a little, and then by the open window she threw it into the sea.

XII

Apart the lovers could neither live nor die, for it was life and death together; and Tristan fled his sorrow through seas and islands and many lands.

He fled his sorrow still by seas and islands, till at last he came back to his land of Lyonesse, and there Rohalt, the keeper of faith, welcomed him with happy tears and called him son. But he could not live in the peace of his own land, and he turned again and rode through kingdoms and through baronies, seeking adventure. From the Lyonesse to the Lowlands, from the Lowlands on to the Germanies; through the Germanies and into Spain. And many lords he served, and many deeds did, but for two years no news came to him out of Cornwall, nor friend, nor messenger. Then he thought that Iseult had forgotten.

Now it happened one day that, riding with Gorvenal alone, he came into the land of Brittany. They rode through a wasted plain of ruined walls and empty hamlets and burnt fields everywhere, and the earth deserted of men; and Tristan thought:

"I am weary, and my deeds profit me nothing; my lady is far off and I shall never see her again. Or why for two years has she made no sign, or why has she sent no messenger to find me as I wandered? But in Tintagel Mark honours her and she gives him joy, and that little fairy bell has done a thorough work; for little she remembers or cares for the joys and the mourning of old, little for me, as I wander in this desert place. I, too, will forget."

On the third day, at the hour of noon, Tristan and Gorvenal came near a hill where an old chantry stood and close by a hermitage also; and Tristan asked what wasted land that was, and the hermit answered:

"Lord, it is Breton land which Duke Hoël holds, and once it was rich in pasture and ploughland, but Count Riol of Nantes has wasted it. For you must know that this Count Riol was the Duke's vassal. And the Duke has a daughter, fair among all King's daughters, and Count Riol would have taken her to wife; but her father refused her to a vassal, and Count Riol would have carried her away by force. Many men have died in that quarrel."

And Tristan asked:

"Can the Duke wage his war?"

And the hermit answered:

"Hardly, my lord; yet his last keep of Carhaix holds out still, for the walls are strong, and strong is the heart of the Duke's son Kaherdin, a very good knight and bold; but the enemy surrounds them on every side and starves them. Very hardly do they hold their castle."

Then Tristan asked:

"How far is this keep of Carhaix?"

"Sir," said the hermit, "it is but two miles further on this way."

Then Tristan and Gorvenal lay down, for it was evening.

In the morning, when they had slept, and when the hermit had chanted, and had shared his black bread with them, Tristan thanked him and rode hard to Carhaix. And as he halted beneath the fast high walls, he saw a little company of men behind the battlements, and he asked if the Duke were there with his son Kaherdin. Now Hoël was among them; and when he cried "yes," Tristan called up to him and said:

"I am that Tristan, King of Lyonesse, and Mark of Cornwall is my uncle. I have heard that your vassals do you a wrong, and I have come to offer you my arms."

"Alas, lord Tristan, go you your way alone and God reward you, for here within we have no more food; no wheat, or meat, or any stores but only lentils and a little oats remaining."

But Tristan said:

"For two years I dwelt in a forest, eating nothing save roots and herbs; yet I found it a good life, so open you the door."

They welcomed him with honour, and Kaherdin showed him the wall and the dungeon keep with all their devices, and from the battlements he showed the plain where far away gleamed the tents of Duke Riol. And when they were down in the castle again he said to Tristan:

"Friend, let us go to the hall where my mother and sister sit."

So, holding each other's hands, they came into the women's room, where the mother and the daughter sat together weaving gold upon English cloth and singing a weaving song. They sang of Doette the fair who sits alone beneath the white-thorn, and round about her blows the wind. She waits for Doon, her friend, but he tarries long and does not come. This was the song they sang. And Tristan bowed to them, and they to him. Then Kaherdin, showing the work his mother did, said:

"See, friend Tristan, what a work-woman is here, and how marvellously she adorns stoles and chasubles for the poor minsters, and how my sister's hands run thread of gold upon this cloth. Of right, good sister, are you called, 'Iseult of the White Hands.' "

But Tristan, hearing her name, smiled and looked at her more gently.

And on the morrow, Tristan, Kaherdin, and twelve young knights left the castle and rode to a pinewood near the enemy's tents. And sprang from ambush and captured a waggon of Count Riol's food; and from that day, by escapade and ruse they would carry tents and convoys and kill off men, nor ever come back without some booty; so that Tristan and Kaherdin began to be brothers in arms, and kept faith and tenderness, as history tells. And as they came back from these rides, talking chivalry together, often did Kaherdin praise to his comrade his sister, Iseult of the White Hands, for her simplicity and beauty.

One day, as the dawn broke, a sentinel ran from the tower through the halls crying:

"Lords, you have slept too long; rise, for an assault is on."

And knights and burgesses armed, and ran to the walls, and saw helmets shining on the plain, and pennons streaming crimson, like flames, and all the host of Riol in its array. Then the Duke and Kaherdin deployed their horsemen before the gates, and from a bow-length off they stooped, and spurred and charged, and they put their lances down together and the arrows fell on them like April rain.

Now Tristan had armed himself among the last of those the sentinel had roused, and he laced his shoes of steel, and put on his mail, and his spurs of gold, his hauberk, and his helm over the gorget, and he mounted and spurred, with shield on breast, crying:

"Carhaix!"

And as he came, he saw Duke Riol charging, rein free, at Kaherdin, but Tristan came in between. So they met, Tristan and Duke Riol. And at the shock, Tristan's lance shivered, but Riol's lance struck Tristan's horse just where the breast-piece runs, and laid it on the field.

But Tristan, standing, drew his sword, his burnished sword, and said:

"Coward! Here is death ready for the man that strikes the horse before the rider."

But Riol answered:

"I think you have lied, my lord!"

And he charged him.

And as he passed, Tristan let fall his sword so heavily upon his helm that he carried away the crest and the nasal, but the sword slipped on the mailed shoulder, and glanced on the horse, and killed it, so that of force Duke Riol must slip the stirrup and leap and feel the ground. Then Riol too was on his feet, and they both fought hard in their broken mail, their 'scutcheons torn and their helmets loosened and lashing with their dented swords, till Tristan struck Riol just where the helmet buckles, and it yielded and the blow was struck so hard that the baron fell on hands and knees; but when he had risen again, Tristan struck him down once more with a blow that split the helm, and it split the headpiece too, and touched the skull; then Riol cried mercy and begged his life, and Tristan took his sword.

So he promised to enter Duke Hoël's keep and to swear homage again, and to restore what he had wasted; and by his order the battle ceased, and his host went off discomfited.

Now when the victors were returned Kaherdin said to his father:

"Sire, keep you Tristan. There is no better knight, and your land has need of such courage."

So when the Duke had taken counsel with his barons, he said to Tristan:

"Friend, I owe you my land, but I shall be quit with you if you will take my daughter, Iseult of the White Hands, who comes of kings and of queens, and of dukes before them in blood."

And Tristan answered:

"I will take her, Sire."

So the day was fixed, and the Duke came with his friends and Tristan with his, and before all, at the gate of the minster, Tristan wed Iseult of the White Hands, according to the Church's law.

But that same night, as Tristan's valets undressed him, it happened that in drawing his arm from the sleeve they drew off and let fall from his finger the ring of green jasper, the ring of Iseult the Fair. It sounded on the stones, and Tristan looked and saw it. Then his heart awoke and he knew that he had done wrong. For he remembered the day when Iseult the Fair had given him the ring. It was in that forest where, for his sake, she had led the hard life with him, and that night he saw again the hut in the wood of Morois, and he was bitter with himself that ever he had accused her of treason; for now it was he that had betrayed, and he was bitter with himself also in pity for this new wife and her simplicity and beauty. See how these two Iseults had met him in an evil hour, and to both had he broken faith!

Now Iseult of the White Hands said to him, hearing him sigh:

"Dear lord, have I hurt you in anything? Will you not speak me a single word?"

But Tristan answered: "Friend, do not be angry with me; for once in another land I fought a foul dragon and was near to death, and I thought of the Mother of God, and I made a vow to Her that, should I ever wed, I would spend the first holy nights of my wedding in prayer and in silence."

"Why," said Iseult, "that was a good vow."

And Tristan watched through the night.

XIII

Within her room at Tintagel, Iseult the Fair sighed for the sake of Tristan, and named him, her desire, of whom for two years she had had no word, whether he lived or no.

Within her room at Tintagel Iseult the Fair sat singing a song she had made. She sang of Guron taken and killed for his love, and how by guile the Count gave Guron's heart to her to eat, and of her woe. The Queen sang softly, catching the harp's tone; her hands were cunning and her song good; she sang low down and softly.

Then came in Kariado, a rich count from a far-off island, that had fared to Tintagel to offer the Queen his service, and had spoken of love to her, though she disdained his folly. He found Iseult as she sang, and laughed to her:

"Lady, how sad a song! as sad as the Osprey's; do they not say he sings for death? and your song means that to me; I die for you."

And Iseult said: "So let it be and may it mean so; for never come you here but to stir in me anger or mourning. Ever were you the screech owl or the Osprey that boded ill when you spoke of Tristan; what news bear you now?"

And Kariado answered:

"You are angered, I know not why, but who heeds your words? Let the Osprey bode me death; here is the evil news the screech owl brings. Lady Iseult, Tristan, your friend is lost to you. He has wed in a far land. So seek you other where, for he mocks your love. He has wed in great pomp Iseult of the White Hands, the King of Brittany's daughter."

And Kariado went off in anger, but Iseult bowed her head and broke into tears.

Now far from Iseult, Tristan languished, till on a day he must needs see her again. Far from her, death came surely; and he had rather die at once than day by day. And he desired some death, but that the Queen might know it was in finding her; then would death come easily.

So he left Carhaix secretly, telling no man, neither his kindred nor even Kaherdin, his brother in arms. He went in rags afoot (for no one marks the beggar on the high road) till he came to the shore of the sea.

He found in a haven a great ship ready, the sail was up and the anchor-chain short at the bow.

"God save you, my lords," he said, "and send you a good journey. To what land sail you now?"

"To Tintagel," they said.

Then he cried out:

"Oh, my lords! take me with you thither!"

And he went aboard, and a fair wind filled the sail, and she ran five days and nights for Cornwall, till, on the sixth day, they dropped anchor in Tintagel Haven. The castle stood above, fenced all around. There was but the one armed gate, and two knights watched it night and day. So Tristan went ashore and sat upon the beach, and a man told him that Mark was there and had just held his court.

"But where," said he, "is Iseult, the Queen, and her fair maid, Brangien?"

"In Tintagel too," said the other, "and I saw them lately; the Queen sad, as she always is."

At the hearing of the name, Tristan suffered, and he thought that neither by guile nor courage could he see that friend, for Mark would kill him.

And he thought, "Let him kill me and let me die for her, since every day I die. But you, Iseult, even if you knew me here, would you not drive me out?" And he thought, "I will try guile. I will seem mad, but with a madness that shall be great wisdom. And many shall think me a fool that have less wit than I."

Just then a fisherman passed in a rough cloak and cape, and Tristan seeing him, took him aside, and said:

"Friend, will you not change clothes?"

And as the fisherman found it a very good bargain, he said in answer:

"Yes, friend, gladly."

And he changed and ran off at once for fear of losing his gain. Then Tristan shaved his wonderful hair; he shaved it close to his head and left a cross all bald, and he rubbed his face with magic herbs distilled in his own country, and it changed in colour and skin so that none could know him, and he made him a club from a young tree torn from a hedge-row and hung it to his neck, and went bare-foot towards the castle.

The porter made sure that he had to do with a fool and said:

"Good morrow, fool, where have you been this long while?"

And he answered:

"At the Abbot of St. Michael's wedding, and he wed an abbess, large and veiled. And from the Alps to Mount St. Michael how they came, the priests and abbots, monks and regulars, all dancing on the green with croziers and with staves under the high trees' shade. But I left them all to come hither, for I serve at the King's board to-day."

Then the porter said:

"Come in, lord fool; the Hairy Urgan's son, I know, and like your father."

And when he was within the courts the serving men ran after him and cried:

"The fool! the fool!"

But he made play with them though they cast stones and struck him as they laughed, and in the midst of laughter and their cries, as the rout followed him, he came to that hall where, at the Queen's side, King Mark sat under his canopy.

And as he neared the door with his club at his neck, the King said:

"Here is a merry fellow, let him in."

And they brought him in, his club at his neck. And the King said:

"Friend, well come; what seek you here?"

"Iseult," said he, "whom I love so well; I bring my sister with me, Brunehild, the beautiful. Come, take her, you are weary of the Queen. Take you my sister and give me here Iseult, and I will hold her and serve you for her love."

The King said laughing:

"Fool, if I gave you the Queen, where would you take her, pray?"

"Oh! very high," he said, "between the clouds and heaven, into a fair chamber glazed. The beams of the sun shine through it, yet the winds do not trouble it at all. There would I bear the Queen into that crystal chamber of mine all compact of roses and the morning."

The King and his barons laughed and said:

"Here is a good fool at no loss for words."

But the fool as he sat at their feet gazed at Iseult most fixedly.

"Friend," said King Mark, "what warrant have you that the Queen would heed so foul a fool as you?"

"O! Sire," he answered gravely, "many deeds have I done for her, and my madness is from her alone."

"What is your name?" they said, and laughed.

"Tristan," said he, "that loved the Queen so well, and still till death will love her."

But at the name the Queen angered and weakened together, and said: "Get hence for an evil fool!"

But the fool, marking her anger, went on:

"Queen Iseult, do you mind the day, when, poisoned by the Morholt's spear, I took my harp to sea and fell upon your shore? Your mother healed me with strange drugs. Have you no memory, Queen?"

But Iseult answered:

"Out, fool, out! Your folly and you have passed the bounds!"

But the fool, still playing, pushed the barons out, crying:

"Out! madmen, out! Leave me to counsel with Iseult, since I come here for the love of her!"

And as the King laughed, Iseult blushed and said:

"King, drive me forth this fool!"

But the fool still laughed and cried:

"Queen, do you mind you of the dragon I slew in your land? I hid its tongue in my hose, and, burnt of its venom, I fell by the roadside. Ah! what a knight was I then, and it was you that succoured me."

Iseult replied:

"Silence! You wrong all knighthood by your words, for you are a fool from birth. Cursed be the seamen that brought you hither; rather should they have cast you into the sea!"

"Queen Iseult," he still said on, "do you mind you of your haste when you would have slain me with my own sword? And of the Hair of Gold? And of how I stood up to the seneschal?"

"Silence!" she said, "you drunkard. You were drunk last night, and so you dreamt these dreams."

"Drunk, and still so am I," said he, "but of such a draught that never can the influence fade. Queen Iseult, do you mind you of that hot and open day on the high seas? We thirsted and we drank together from the same cup, and since that day have I been drunk with an awful wine."

When the Queen heard these words which she alone could understand, she rose and would have gone.

But the King held her by her ermine cloak, and she sat down again.

And as the King had his fill of the fool he called for his falcons and went to hunt; and Iseult said to him:

"Sire, I am weak and sad; let me be go rest in my room; I am tired of these follies."

And she went to her room in thought and sat upon her bed and mourned, calling herself a slave and saying:

"Why was I born? Brangien, dear sister, life is so hard to me that death were better! There is a fool without, shaven criss-cross, and come in an evil hour, and he is warlock, for he knows in every part myself and my whole life; he knows what you and I and Tristan only know."

Then Brangien said: "It may be Tristan."

But – "No," said the Queen, "for he was the first of knights, but this fool is foul and made awry. Curse me his hour and the ship that brought him hither."

"My lady!" said Brangien, "soothe you. You curse over much these days. May be he comes from Tristan?"

"I cannot tell. I know him not. But go find him, friend, and see if you know him."

So Brangien went to the hall where the fool still sat alone. Tristan knew her and let fall his club and said:

"Brangien, dear Brangien, before God! have pity on me!"

"Foul fool," she answered, "what devil taught you my name?"

"Lady," he said, "I have known it long. By my head, that once was fair, if I am mad the blame is yours, for it was yours to watch over the wine we drank on the high seas. The cup was of silver and I held it to Iseult and she drank. Do you remember, lady?"

"No," she said, and as she trembled and left he called out: "Pity me!"

He followed and saw Iseult. He stretched out his arms, but in her shame, sweating agony she drew back, and Tristan angered and said:

"I have lived too long, for I have seen the day that Iseult will nothing of me. Iseult, how hard love dies! Iseult, a welling water that floods and runs large is a mighty thing; on the day that it fails it is nothing; so love that turns."

But she said:

"Brother, I look at you and doubt and tremble, and I know you not for Tristan."

"Queen Iseult, I am Tristan indeed that do love you; mind you for the last time of the dwarf, and of the flower, and of the blood I shed in my leap. Oh! and of that ring I took in kisses and in tears on the day we parted. I have kept that jasper ring and asked it counsel."

Then Iseult knew Tristan for what he was, and she said:

"Heart, you should have broken of sorrow not to have known the man who has suffered so much for you. Pardon, my master and my friend."

And her eyes darkened and she fell; but when the light returned she was held by him who kissed her eyes and her face.

So passed they three full days. But, on the third, two maids that watched them told the traitor Andret, and he put spies well-armed before the women's rooms. And when Tristan would enter they cried:

"Back, fool!"

But he brandished his club laughing, and said:

"What! May I not kiss the Queen who loves me and awaits me now?"

And they feared him for a mad fool, and he passed in through the door.

Then, being with the Queen for the last time, he held her in his arms and said:

"Friend, I must fly, for they are wondering. I must fly, and perhaps shall never see you more. My death is near, and far from you my death will come of desire."

"Oh friend," she said, "fold your arms round me close and strain me so that our hearts may break and our souls go free at last. Take me to that happy place of which you told me long ago. The fields whence none return, but where great singers sing their songs for ever. Take me now."

"I will take you to the Happy Palace of the living, Queen! The time is near. We have drunk all joy and sorrow. The time is near. When it is finished, if I call you, will you come, my friend?"

"Friend," said she, "call me and you know that I shall come."

"Friend," said he, "God send you His reward."

As he went out the spies would have held him; but he laughed aloud, and flourished his club, and cried:

"Peace, gentlemen, I go and will not stay. My lady sends me to prepare that shining house I vowed her, of crystal, and of rose shot through with morning."

And as they cursed and drave him, the fool went leaping on his way.

XIV

When he was come back to Brittany, to Carhaix, it happened that Tristan, riding to the aid of Kaherdin his brother in arms, fell into ambush and was wounded by a poisoned spear; and many doctors came, but none could cure him of the ill. And Tristan weakened and paled, and his bones showed.

Then he knew that his life was going, and that he must die, and he had a desire to see once more Iseult the Fair, but he could not seek her, for the sea would have killed him in his weakness, and how could Iseult come to him? And sad, and suffering the poison, he awaited death.

He called Kaherdin secretly to tell him his pain, for they loved each other with a loyal love; and as he would have no one in the room save Kaherdin, nor even in the neighbouring rooms, Iseult of the White Hands began to wonder. She was afraid and wished to hear, and she came back and listened at the wall by Tristan's bed; and as she listened one of her maids kept watch for her.

Now, within, Tristan had gathered up his strength, and had half risen, leaning against the wall, and Kaherdin wept beside him. They wept their good comradeship, broken so soon, and their friendship: then Tristan told Kaherdin of his love for that other Iseult, and of the sorrow of his life.

"Fair friend and gentle," said Tristan, "I am in a foreign land where I have neither friend nor cousin, save you; and you alone in this place have given me comfort. My life is going, and I wish to see once more Iseult the Fair. Ah, did I but know of a messenger who would go to her! For now I know that she will come to me. Kaherdin, my brother in arms, I beg it of your friendship; try this thing for me, and if you carry my word, I will become your liege, and I will cherish you beyond all other men."

And as Kaherdin saw Tristan broken down, his heart reproached him and he said:

"Fair comrade, do not weep; I will do what you desire, even if it were risk of death I would do it for you. Nor no distress nor anguish will let me from doing it according to my power. Give me the word you send, and I will make ready."

And Tristan answered:

"Thank you, friend; this is my prayer: take this ring, it is a sign between her and me; and when you come to her land pass yourself at court for a merchant, and show her silk and stuffs, but make so that she sees the ring, for then she will find some ruse by which to speak to you in secret. Then tell her that my heart salutes her; tell her that she alone can bring me comfort; tell her that if she does not come I shall die. Tell her to remember our past time, and our great sorrows, and all the joy there was in our loyal and tender love. And tell her to remember that draught we drank together on the high seas. For we drank our death together. Tell her to remember the oath I swore to serve a single love, for I have kept that oath."

But behind the wall, Iseult of the White Hands heard all these things; and Tristan continued:

"Hasten, my friend, and come back quickly, or you will not see me again. Take forty days for your term, but come back with Iseult the Fair. And tell your sister nothing, or tell her that you seek some doctor. Take my fine ship, and two sails with you, one white, one black. And as you return, if you bring Iseult, hoist the white sail; but if you bring her not, the black. Now I have nothing more to say, but God guide you and bring you back safe."

With the first fair wind Kaherdin took the open, weighed anchor and hoisted sail, and ran with a light air and broke the seas. They bore rich merchandise with them, dyed silks of rare colours, enamel of Touraine and wines of Poitou, for by this ruse Kaherdin thought to reach Iseult. Eight days and nights they ran full sail to Cornwall.

Now a woman's wrath is a fearful thing, and all men fear it, for according to her love, so will her vengeance be; and their love and their hate come quickly, but their hate lives longer than their love; and they will make play with love, but not with hate. So Iseult of the White Hands, who had heard every word, and who had so loved Tristan, waited her vengeance upon what she loved most in the world. But she hid it all; and when the doors were open again she came to Tristan's bed and served him with food as a lover should, and spoke him gently and kissed him on the lips, and asked him if Kaherdin would soon return with one to cure him . . . but all day long she thought upon her vengeance.

And Kaherdin sailed and sailed till he dropped anchor in the haven of Tintagel. He landed and took with him a cloth of rare dye and a cup well chiselled and worked, and made a present of them to King Mark, and courteously begged of him his peace and safeguard that he might traffick in his land; and the King gave him his peace before all the men of his palace.

Then Kaherdin offered the Queen a buckle of fine gold; and "Queen," said he, "the gold is good."

Then taking from his finger Tristan's ring, he put it side by side with the jewel and said:

"See, O Queen, the gold of the buckle is the finer gold; yet that ring also has its worth."

When Iseult saw what ring that was, her heart trembled and her colour changed, and fearing what might next be said she drew Kaherdin apart near a window, as if to see and bargain the better; and Kaherdin said to her, low down:

"Lady, Tristan is wounded of a poisoned spear and is about to die. He sends you word that you alone can bring him comfort, and recalls to you the great sorrows that you bore together. Keep you the ring – it is yours."

But Iseult answered, weakening:

"Friend, I will follow you; get ready your ship to-morrow at dawn."

And on the morrow at dawn they raised anchor, stepped mast, and hoisted sail, and happily the barque left land.

But at Carhaix Tristan lay and longed for Iseult's coming. Nothing now filled him any more, and if he lived it was only as awaiting her; and day by day he sent watchers to the shore to see if some ship came, and to learn the colour of her sail. There was no other thing left in his heart.

He had himself carried to the cliff of the Penmarks, where it overlooks the sea, and all the daylight long he gazed far off over the water.

Hear now a tale most sad and pitiful to all who love. Already was Iseult near; already the cliff of the Penmarks showed far away, and the ship ran heartily, when a storm wind rose on a sudden and grew, and struck the sail, and turned the ship all round about, and the sailors bore away and sore against their will they ran before the wind. The wind raged and big seas ran, and the air grew thick with darkness, and the ocean itself turned dark, and the rain drove in gusts. The yard snapped, and the sheet; they struck their sail, and ran with wind and water. In an evil hour they had forgotten to haul their pinnace aboard; it leapt in their wake, and a great sea broke it away.

Then Iseult cried out: "God does not will that I should live to see him, my love, once – even one time more. God wills my drowning in this sea. O, Tristan, had I spoken to you but once again, it is little I should have cared for a death come afterwards. But now, my love, I cannot come to you; for God so wills it, and that is the core of my grief."

And thus the Queen complained so long as the storm endured; but after five days it died down. Kaherdin hoisted the sail, the white sail, right up to the very masthead with great joy; the white sail, that Tristan might know its colour from afar: and already Kaherdin saw Britanny far off like a cloud. Hardly were these things seen and done when a calm came, and the sea lay even and untroubled. The sail bellied no longer, and the sailors held the ship now up, now down, the tide, beating backwards and forwards in vain. They saw the shore afar off, but the storm had carried their boat away and they could not land. On the third night Iseult dreamt this dream: that she held in her lap a boar's head which befouled her skirts with blood; then she knew that she would never see her lover again alive.

Tristan was now too weak to keep his watch from the cliff of the Penmarks, and for many long days, within walls, far from the shore, he had mourned for Iseult because she did not come. Dolorous and alone, he mourned and sighed in restlessness: he was near death from desire.

At last the wind freshened and the white sail showed. Then it was that Iseult of the White Hands took her vengeance.

She came to where Tristan lay, and she said:

"Friend, Kaherdin is here. I have seen his ship upon the sea. She comes up hardly – yet I know her; may he bring that which shall heal thee, friend."

And Tristan trembled and said:

"Beautiful friend, you are sure that the ship is his indeed? Then tell me what is the manner of the sail?"

"I saw it plain and well. They have shaken it out and hoisted it very high, for they have little wind. For its colour, why, it is black."

And Tristan turned him to the wall, and said:

"I cannot keep this life of mine any longer." He said three times: "Iseult, my friend." And in saying it the fourth time, he died.

Then throughout the house, the knights and the comrades of Tristan wept out loud, and they took him from his bed and laid him on a rich cloth, and they covered his body with a shroud. But at sea the wind had risen; it struck the sail fair and full and drove the ship to shore, and Iseult the Fair set foot upon the land. She heard loud mourning in the streets, and the tolling of bells in the minsters and the chapel towers; she asked the people the meaning of the knell and of their tears. An old man said to her:

"Lady, we suffer a great grief. Tristan, that was so loyal and so right, is dead. He was open to the poor; he ministered to the suffering. It is the chief evil that has ever fallen on this land."

But Iseult, hearing them, could not answer them a word. She went up to the palace, following the way, and her cloak was random and wild. The Bretons marvelled as she went; nor had they ever seen woman of such a beauty, and they said:

"Who is she, or whence does she come?"

Near Tristan, Iseult of the White Hands crouched, maddened at the evil she had done, and calling and lamenting over the dead man. The other Iseult came in and said to her:

"Lady, rise and let me come by him; I have more right to mourn him than have you – believe me. I loved him more."

And when she had turned to the east and prayed God, she moved the body a little and lay down by the dead man, beside her friend. She kissed his mouth and his face, and clasped him closely; and so gave up her soul, and died beside him of grief for her lover.

When King Mark heard of the death of these lovers, he crossed the sea and came into Brittany; and he had two coffins hewn, for Tristan and Iseult, one of chalcedony for Iseult, and one of beryl for Tristan. And he took their beloved bodies away with him upon his ship to Tintagel, and by a chantry to the left and right of the apse he had their tombs built round. But in one night there sprang from the tomb of Tristan a green and leafy briar, strong in its branches and in the scent of its flowers. It climbed the chantry and fell to root again by Iseult's tomb. Thrice did the peasants cut it down, but thrice it grew again as flowered and as strong. They told the marvel to King Mark, and he forbade them to cut the briar any more.

The good singers of old time, Beroul and Thomas of Built, Gilbert and Gottfried told this tale for lovers and none other, and, by my pen, they beg you for your prayers. They greet those who are cast down, and those in heart, those troubled and those filled with desire. May all herein find strength against inconstancy and despite and loss and pain and all the bitterness of loving.

The Final Days

THE DOG'S STORY

Eleanor Arnason

We now move into the final stages of the Arthurian Mythos, in which everything starts to fall apart. The first sign of this was the fate of Merlin. Originally Arthur's counsellor, Merlin fell in love with the enchantress Nimuë, a pawn of Morgan le Fay's, who eventually traps Merlin in either a cave, or under a stone or within a tree. Without him Arthur was bereft of wise counsel and his world starts to crumble.

The following story takes an original look at Merlin's fate. It is by Eleanor Arnason (b. 1942), an American writer, whose novels continue to test the borders of science fiction and fantasy and challenge established icons. Her books include The Sword Smith *(1978),* To the Resurrection Station *(1986) and* Daughter of the Bear King *(1987).*

The wizard Merlin, traveling on his monarch's business, came to a ford where a knight was raping a maiden. The rape had just begun, though it had apparently been preceded by a murder. A second man, most likely the girl's companion, lay on the ground nearby, bloody and unmoving. Three horses wandered loose. Merlin reined his own animal and considered the scene to make sure that his first impression was correct.

The girl had already lost her long embroidered belt. The knight held it in one hand, while his other arm assumed the belt's position around the girl's waist. This seemed clear enough to Merlin. It isn't easy to rape anyone while garbed in a knee-length mail shirt. Nor is it easy to pull such a garment off, while holding a struggling woman. Struggle the maiden did, screaming like a peacock, a creature that Merlin had seen – and heard – in King Arthur's menagerie. The knight was planning to tie the girl up, then undress the two of them at leisure.

By this time he had noticed Merlin. He gave the wizard a brief glance, returning to his contest with the girl. An old man on a palfrey could be no threat. After the girl was tied, maybe to the tree that shaded the ford and the two contestants, he'd be free to drive off Merlin or kill him; and then he'd be able to get back to his pleasure, if pleasure was the right word here.

Merlin, who'd been a sensualist in his youth, began to feel anger. This man dishonored all lovers of women and love. The old man straightened in his saddle and lifted a hand. "A cur you are," he cried. "A cur you shall be in the future!"

The knight turned as if jerked at the end of a rope. His armor fell in pieces around him; his clothing vanished; and for a moment he stood naked: a tall, fair, ruddy man with an erection. Then he dropped on all fours. A moment after that, he became a dog. In this form he glanced at the fragments of his mail and at the girl, who was trying to arrange her torn garments. He groaned; it was an oddly human sound to be coming from the dark lips and long curling tongue of a dog; then he ran away.

"You must be a magician," the girl said in the calm voice of one who had experienced too much.

"Evidently." Merlin dismounted and examined the man on the ground. Beyond any question he was dead.

Her brother, the girl told Merlin. They had been on a pilgrimage to a local shrine. On the way back, the false knight had attacked them. Their servants had fled. Her brother had fought and died. "And I was on the road to death when you arrived. What good fortune!"

Merlin kept quiet, knowing the events that occur around wizards are rarely accidental.

They loaded the dead man on Merlin's palfrey, which was not disturbed by blood, and the wizard coaxed the three loose horses, till they approached him, lowering their heads, letting him take their reins. Mounted once again, he and the girl went on.

The name of the false knight was Ewen. He was the younger son of a minor baron: a rough, healthy, violent lad, awkward around women. At the time he met Merlin, he was eighteen years old.

Now a dog, he ran through a forest, one of the many that grew in England in those days. If a person wanted to, he or she could travel the length of the king's realm and never leave the forest shadow, except briefly to cross a road or field. Outlaws used this green route, as did fairies and people grown tired of their obligations.

At first Ewen ran at full speed. Becoming tired, he trotted, then walked, pausing now and then to sniff at something that seemed interesting: a dead bat, folded among last year's fallen leaves, a badger's scat, the mark left by a male fox on a tree. Finally, exhausted, he settled in a patch of ferns and slept.

In the morning, he woke hungry and went looking for food. There was plenty, but he'd not hunted on four feet till now. The pungent aromas of the forest confused him. For some reason – who can understand the mind of a wizard, or the paths that magic follows? – the enchantment had not affected his vision. He still saw color as a human would. This was no help; it might even have been a hindrance. In any case, he couldn't see animals in hiding. When the animals leaped out of hiding, he chased but did not catch them, being unaccustomed to his new form, though it was a fine body: large, rangy, fierce of aspect and entirely white except for a pair of blood red ears. Looking in a pool of still water, he saw himself and fled, horrified.

After several days of hunger, he came to a farm. It was nothing much: a rough cottage, a couple of outbuildings that were little more than sheds, and a pen that held pigs.

There was food in the cottage and in the pen. Ewen could smell it, but the scent of people frightened him, and no one in his right mind would climb in a pen with pigs. They were (and are) fierce, strong animals, intelligent enough to know that humans mean them no good. If they can, they'll kill.

He waited till nightfall and slunk close. The pigs grunted angrily. The cottage door opened. Ewen slunk away.

In the morning he hunted again, caught an unwary rabbit and ate it, crunching the bones between powerful jaws. It wasn't enough. He returned to the farmstead.

This time he investigated the outbuildings. One smelled of grain and vegetables, things he'd liked when human, but which did not entice him now. The second hut smelled of meat. Saliva filled his mouth. His tongue lolled out and dripped. He nosed the door. Unfastened, it swung open. Even as a man, he hadn't been much for thinking. Now, as a hungry dog, he didn't think at all. Instead of considering the possibility of danger, he pushed inside. The night was moonless and the hut as black as pitch, but he could smell roast pig above him. Ewen leaped and caught nothing, then leaped a second time. On the third try, his teeth closed around a bone. He held on, off the ground and twisting in the darkness. The bone was one of many, fastened together and hung from the hut's low roof. They knocked against each other now and made a loud clattering noise, while Ewen swung below them like the clapper on a bell.

The hut's door closed. A bar came down with a bang. "There!" said the farmer. "He's a fine big dog. Someone must own him, a noble, if looks are anything. Or if not, a noble may buy him."

Merlin delivered the maiden to her father, along with the corpse of her brother. Then he rode on, leading the false knight's charger. For two days, he traveled along the forest's edge, coming at last to an isolated farm.

The farmer made him welcome. Although nobles often ignored or mistook the old man in plain dark clothing, peasants usually realized he was someone important and dangerous, maybe because they actually looked at him.

The farmer's wife prepared dinner. The farmer told Merlin about the dog he'd captured.

"Can I see him?" the wizard asked.

They went to the hut, and Merlin peered through a crack. It was mid-summer. The days were long. Rays of sunlight slanted through the hut, and Merlin had no trouble making out the white hound lying on the floor and gnawing bones.

"He's mine," said Merlin. "I'll pay you for your trouble."

The farmer praised his good fortune and Merlin's.

In the morning, Merlin went out to the hut and opened the door. Ewen raised his head. He'd eaten the few shreds of meat on the pig bones, then cracked the bones and licked out the marrow. Now he was bored and ready to leave.

"The man you killed has a father, who has sworn to hunt you down. He hasn't decided whether to kill you or tie you in his courtyard. It might be satisfying to have his boy's killer as a dog by his door. If I leave you here, he'll get you." Merlin tilted his head, considering. "Maybe I should have made you a wolf. You might have lasted longer in the wild. But you don't have a wolf's nature. Come on." The wizard beckoned. Ewen rose and followed.

In the histories, Camelot is a fine lofty city built of stone. In point of fact, it was made of low wood buildings, narrow dirt streets, yards with manure and midden heaps. The king's fort stood in the center of the town. *It* was stone, good Roman work from the days before the empire had abandoned Britain, though damaged by time, war, and neglect. Arthur was rebuilding. The gaps in the outer walls had been filled by rubble and logs bound with iron; inside the fort, scaffolding stood against most of the surviving buildings; and heaps of stone were piled next to the scaffolding, ready for use.

Merlin rode in the fortress gate, the captured charger following, the white hound running at his side. Before him, in the large front court, men practiced with swords. Among them was Arthur, a big handsome man just entering middle age. His hair was dark and curly, his face fair, his eyes grey. He was the love of Merlin's life, and both men knew it, though it was never mentioned. Their relationship was too complicated already.

Merlin dismounted stiffly. Arthur called a halt to the swordplay, and they embraced. Then the king asked about the new horse and the white dog that was trying to hide behind Merlin, afraid of all these people, especially the king.

"You know I have a way with animals. They'll follow if I tell them to."

"I know that you don't want to tell the story that lies in back of these new acquisitions. The dog is handsome, though a bit timid. Will you give him to me?"

"I'll give you the horse, but not the dog."

The king frowned, then laughed and accepted the horse.

"Not up to my weight, of course, but I'll find some poor young knight in need of a mount."

Merlin excused himself and went to his quarters, the white hound following. Servants brought him water and a brazier full of coals: the weather was cool, the wizard past his prime. He washed all over and put on a clean robe, then settled with a cup of wine, also brought by the king's servants.

"You're wondering why I refused to tell the king about you," Merlin said to the dog. "One can never tell about Arthur. He might insist that I turn you back into a man. He might want to kill you. I doubt that he'd want to have a former knight fighting over scraps of food in his feasting hall." The wizard snapped his fingers. The dog came near. He ran his hand over the white head and tugged gently at the blood red ears. "Keep close to me for the next few days, till I have a collar made. Gold, I think. You're a noble-looking animal, though as a man you were a failure. I'll have my name and emblem put on the collar. Few people will steal from a wizard, especially the king's wizard."

Ewen nosed the old man's hand, then licked the palm.

It was surprisingly easy to be a dog. Ewen had never been much of a talker. Now he didn't have to make the effort. Barks and snarls served for almost every purpose. When they failed, he bared his long sharp teeth. Even the king's dogs gave him room.

Human women had always baffled him. Now, he had no interest in them. It was female dogs that attracted him, and it was far easier to court a bitch in heat than any human woman he'd ever met. Whether high or low in rank, they always seemed to want something Ewen couldn't provide. What the bitches wanted Ewen had and gave willingly.

Arthur, laughing, said, "All the dogs in Camelot are going to be white," then added, "You wouldn't give me the dog, but I'll have his children."

When they were alone Merlin said, "Don't worry about fathering dogs. The king wants his bitches to bear white pups. They will, and the pups will grow up to be everything Arthur is hoping for. But they won't be your children."

Ewen, chewing on an ox bone, had not considered the problem. After all, he'd been a younger son. His children, if any, would not have mattered much, except to his wife. Let them be dogs and hunt for the king! But he was sterile, the wizard said, at least when he mated with dogs.

"I have changed your appearance, but not your essence. You are still as human as ever you were."

Ewen cracked the bone held between his front paws, extended his long, rough tongue and licked the marrow out.

He became famous: the big white dog with red ears and a gold collar who followed the king's wizard through Camelot, lay at Merlin's feet, ran beside his horse. He did not age in the ordinary fashion of dogs, as Arthur noticed.

"Nor do I," said Merlin. "Ewen is a wizard's dog, and he never leaves my side. Magic slows the passage of time, as you ought to have noticed."

This was a reference to the magic in the royal lineage. The king grimaced, not wanting to think about his family or about the family he had failed to produce – unlike Ewen, whose progeny filled the kennels of Camelot, Arthur believed. The queen was childless and increasingly restless.

By this time, Merlin had fallen into the habit of talking with his dog. Ewen had retained his original intelligence, which was considerable. His problem had never been stupidity, but rather greed, rashness and brutality. These were the traits that led him to attack the maiden at the ford and the pig bones in the storage hut. He understood most of what the old man told him, though not everything, of course. He could repeat nothing. Nor could he use what he learned for his own benefit or against his master: the perfect companion for a lonely wizard.

So began a strange double life. In daylight and in public, Ewen was an animal. At night, alone with Merlin, he was an audience for the great wizard's ideas, worries, reflections, speculations. Gradually, under Merlin's influence, he learned to think, but this process – thinking – had almost nothing to do with his daylight life. There he fought for scraps, mounted bitches, confronted other males, coursed the king's prey, followed at the heels of the king's wisest counselor. Thought belonged to the evening, when Merlin drank wine and tugged Ewen's blood red ears.

In his way, he grew to love the old man. In part, it was a dog's love. In part, it was the love of a man whose own father had been stupid as well as brutish. Strange, maybe, to look at the enchanter who'd made him a domestic animal and see, not an enemy, but a loved father or master. Such things do happen. The heart hath its reasons, which reason knoweth not, as Pascal tells us.

Sometimes, when they were traveling and had stopped for the night in a place distant from other people, Merlin would turn the hound back into a man. Magic *had* slowed time. He looked no more than twenty, fair and muscular. His hair had grown just a little. It fell over his shoulders, curly and shaggy, the color of wheat at midsummer. His eyes were summer blue. His beard was like a wheat field after harvest: blond stubble shining in the light of their evening fire.

In his youth and middle age, Merlin had been a lover of men as well as women. The church forbade this kind of love, of course; but the church also forbade witchcraft and wizardry. Being a scholar, Merlin knew that the basis for these injunctions was a script that also forbade the eating of shellfish. Yet he had seen Christian kings and prelates consume oysters with the zeal of pagan Romans, pausing only to give praise to God for the excellent food. He kept his counsel and did not abandon his inclinations.

In his old age, his passions diminished. Little remained except his love for Arthur, which had always been more familial than anything else. This was the baby Merlin had carried in his arms, the boy he'd watched over, the youth he'd made king. From the beginning,

Arthur's future had enveloped him like a cloak or veil of light, visible to Merlin and a few others. The babe in his hands had shone as if swaddled in moonbeams. The boy had seemed garbed in the pale, clear light of dawn. The young man had been like morning. The veil was still present, though dimmed by age and compromise. At night, when Arthur sat in his feasting hall, surrounded by retainers, Merlin saw glory flicker around the king. Duty and a sense of history transformed the wizard's love, as iron is changed by fire and water.

Ewen was different. Merlin looked at him, on those nights when the two of them camped alone. If the weather was cold enough, the boy would wrap himself in a blanket. Otherwise, he wore nothing except the gold dog collar engraved with Merlin's name. Whatever human modesty he might once have had was gone. He'd been a dog too long.

Merlin remembered lust, and that what was he felt now, stirring in his groin. The boy had no sexual interest in men.

Merlin could force him and be a rapist. He could seduce him using magic. In either case, he'd be a brute, acting from simple need without regard for reason, consequence or the dignity of his art.

No, the old man thought. Better to end his days a celibate.

Now and then, Ewen seemed briefly uncomfortable, as if he suspected what Merlin was thinking. Usually, he was at ease, though rarely talkative. Even in human form, he preferred to listen.

When Merlin wanted to travel in disguise, he gave the boy clothing, and Ewen became a servant or a young relative. At first, Merlin insisted that he not wear the collar. It was too rich and distinctive. But Ewen missed the weight. It was difficult being a man, he told the wizard. His clothes were binding and scratchy. Women were once again exciting.

"When I see one who seems in heat, I get an erection. But what can I do with it? I know you won't let me push the woman down and mount her. As for seduction, it requires skills I don't have and more time than I'm willing to put in. It isn't time I want to put in, in these situations.

"When men brush against me or give me an insulting stare, I want to growl and bite. I know I could leave marks on them, even with human teeth. But you have told me to be mannerly.

"Let me wear the collar. It reminds me that I'll be a dog again soon. I'll keep it hidden."

Merlin gave in, though with foreboding. The inevitable happened at a little roadside lodging place. A fastening came undone. The innkeeper saw gold gleaming at the boy's throat. That night, six men came to rob the travelers.

In his old age, Merlin slept fitfully, and the robbers made the mistake of waiting. By the time they crept down the hall, the wizard had passed through the deep sleep brought on by fatigue to a state close to waking. The noise they made was enough to rouse him entirely. He roused Ewen, who pulled a sword out of their baggage.

One of the robbers had a lantern made of horn. By its dim light, they saw a man emerge from the travelers' room, naked except for a wide gold collar, bare steel in his hand. The six robbers advanced, made confident by their numbers, their knives and their cudgels. A moment later, the lantern went out, dropped or tossed aside. This proved an advantage to Ewen, who knew he had no friends in the dark hall. He charged, swinging his sword. Deep growls came from his throat, interspersed with yelps and howls. It was the noise that settled the battle. The robbers, stumbling into one another in the darkness and striking out at random, became terrified. Surely this snarling creature was a madman or a demon. They turned and ran. Ewen followed.

Merlin picked up the horn lantern and relit it. Two men lay in the hall. One was dead, his head crushed by a cudgel blow. The other wept noisily, holding onto his belly. Blood welled between the robber's fingers. Merlin lifted his hands; the man did the same, as if in imitation. Now the wound was visible. It was deep. Intestines spilled out. A fatal wound, unless the wizard used his magic. Why bother? England was already well supplied with robbers and murderers. On the other hand, no living thing should suffer, if the suffering could be ended. Merlin gestured a second time. The man slept, his hands falling to his sides. The wound continued to bleed.

The other men were in the yard: one dead and two dying. The last robber, a lad of fifteen or so, had scrambled to the top of the manure heap and was slinging dung at Ewen, as the naked man climbed toward him, coated now in blood and excrement. The moon shone down on all of this. The noise was terrific: the dying men groaning and calling out to God, the boy screaming curses, Ewen howling.

"Heel!" called Merlin.

Ewen paused and shook his head as if to clear it, then climbed down to join his master.

"Who planned this?" Merlin asked the boy on the dung heap.

"My brother. The one who keeps the inn."

They searched for the innkeeper, but he was gone.

"When he comes back," said Merlin to the boy. "Tell him that he tried to rob Merlin the wizard, and that his comrades –"

"Our brothers," said the boy. "There were seven of us, and you have killed five."

"Tell him that his brothers were killed by my famous white hound, which I turned into a man for the night. If I ever hear anything about the two of you again, I'll send him back as a dog or a man or something worse than either; and I'll tell him to spare no one."

They cleaned up and left, going into the forest. Merlin guided them with the horn lantern, which shone more brightly than before. They stopped finally. Ewen gathered wood in the lantern's light: by this time it was a second moon, shining under the trees.

"That could lead them to us," Ewen said.

Merlin gestured. The lantern grew dim. Ewen built his fire in almost-darkness. When it was burning well, the lantern went out. The lad cared for their horses, while Merlin sat by the fire. His dark, lined faced looked weary.

At length, the young man joined him, pulling out the sword he'd used against the robbers and making sure that it was entirely clean. That done, he resheathed the weapon and unfastened the collar around his neck. "I'll miss it."

Merlin took the collar and put it away. "You did well tonight. It may be time for you to consider becoming a man."

"I was always good at doing harm," said Ewen. "In any case, it wasn't necessary. You were there. You could have turned them all into toads."

"Magic has more to do with form than substance," Merlin said after a moment. "If I had turned them into toads, they would have been extremely large toads. It's possible that their new shape and structure – the toad skeletons and muscles and organs – would not have been sufficient given their size, which would have been the size of men. They might have collapsed in on themselves and died of their own weight."

"Small loss," said Ewen.

"If this hadn't happened, you would have been dealing with mouths large enough to swallow you and long grasping tongues." The wizard paused again.

Ewen waited. He'd leaned back on his elbows and stretched his legs in front of him, comfortable in spite of the scratches and bruises he'd gotten in the fight. Tomorrow he'd feel all his injuries, as he knew. Tonight he felt tired and content.

"There is another possibility," the wizard said finally. "Magic likes to follow the rules of nature, to create things that are possible and have existed, if not now, then in the past. If I had tried to enchant the robbers in the way you have suggested, they might have turned into the ancient relatives of toads. Some of these animals were as large as men. Some were carnivores with heads like mastiffs and teeth that could put your teeth to shame."

"My dog teeth?" asked Ewen.

The wizard nodded. "The Flood, or some other catastrophe, destroyed these creatures. The world does not need to see them again."

"You are less powerful than I thought," Ewen said.

Merlin considered, then answered. "For the most part, magic has to do with seeing. I saw your canine nature at the ford. I saw Arthur's future while he was *in utero*."

Ewen knew some Latin by this time, as well as a little Arabic and Hebrew. He had no trouble understanding *in utero*.

"Doing is more difficult," the wizard added. "Though it can be done." He glanced up, smiling. "As you know."

In the morning, they continued, riding through the forest shadow. The road they followed was narrow and grey. Sunlight stippled it like the spots on a trout.

As Ewen had expected, he hurt all over. Conversation might be a distraction. He said, "I've been thinking of those animals, the ancestors of toads. How do you know about them? Are they in the Bible or Aristotle?"

His knowledge did not come from human texts, whether sacred or profane, Merlin said. Rather, he had learned it from the fairies. Humans knew those folk as students of magic, and so they were, but they studied nature with an equal zeal, and they were obsessed with the passage of time. "They have dug out the bones that are preserved in stone, and they know these are not the bones of giants, nor are they unusual mineral formations. Rather, they are the remains of animals, unlike any animal alive today."

Using magic, the fairy scholars had recreated these ancient animals. "Some are solid and alive," Merlin told Ewen. "The fairies keep them as pets or use them as the prey for their hunts. But most of the animals – especially the enormous ones – are illusory. A reptile the size of a feasting hall would be difficult to make, difficult to feed and possibly dangerous."

Ewen nodded his agreement.

Illusions, on the other hand, were safe, economical, and comparatively easy to make. The fairy scholars could study them, without having to cage or feed them. The fairies who were not scholars could take pleasure in their strangeness.

Ewen asked about the real animals in fairyland, the ones that could fight and had to be fed. Merlin described what he had seen on his visits to the Fair Realm: elephants covered with shaggy fur, pill bugs as big as his palm, a toothy creature with a sail on its back, a toothy creature that ran on two legs and gathered food with sharp-clawed hands.

The shaggy elephants had tusks that curved like hunting horns. The pill bugs had large eyes faceted like jewels. The sail creature was like a salamander, save that it was as big as a man and had a thick, leathery hide. The creature that ran on two legs could be compared to nothing.

The fairies had tried to train these bipeds, as they might have trained ostriches or humans; the creatures proved to be intractably wild. "Instead of being turned into a new kind of hunting dog, they became a new kind of quarry; and the fairies have bred dogs to course them and bring them down. The dogs are your size, when you are a hound, blue-grey in color with hanging jowls and long ears that are usually cropped. They are fearless, as they have to be. The bipeds have great curving claws on their feet, in addition to grasping hands and piercing teeth."

The Fair People were obsessed with all the aspects of time, Merlin told his companion. They studied the future as well as the past, though this area of study was full of challenge and obscurity. The future is always uncertain. Nonetheless, they had managed to create images of what the future might be like, and these also could be encountered in fairyland. "Though these illusions waver and shift and are rarely convincing." The wizard described groups of oddly dressed people, involved in activities that made little sense to him or the fairy scholars, and devices that seemed magical or perhaps like the devices made by ancient engineers such as Daedalus. Cities would appear in the distance, at times as bright as adamant, at other times dark and wreathed in smoke. If one approached the cities, they receded. They could never be reached, nor could travelers get close enough to see them clearly. Instead, the travelers were left with confused impressions – of puissance, valor, and confidence or poverty, sadness, and pain.

Ewen had small use for illusion or for the future. Better to concentrate on what was present and real. He glanced around. Large ferns lined the road, so green that they seemed to glow with their own light. Farther back, in the forest shadow, fungi dotted the trunks of trees. Ewen recognized a number of kinds and recited the names to himself, as a charm against unreality: Jew's Ear, Dryad's Saddle, Witch's Butter, Poor Man's Beef.

Some of the animals in fairyland sounded interesting: the real ones, not the illusions. Maybe some day his master would take him there. In dog form, he'd chase the bipeds.

That evening they came to a village, and Merlin bought liniment from the local witch, a tall handsome woman of more than fifty. She offered to put the liniment on. "I have the healing touch. But maybe you'd prefer to do this yourself, Merlin."

As much as possible, he did not touch the boy when he was human. In any case, this was a situation that required rubbing rather than magic. His own hands were stiff. He nodded his agreement to the witch's plan, and they entered her cottage: a single room, lit by a fire that flared up as they entered. Herbs hung from the rafters. Sealed pots stood along the walls. A pallet lay in one corner, and there were two three-legged stools. Merlin took one. The witch took the other. The boy settled in front of her on the dirt floor.

It was disturbing to watch the witch's dark strong fingers move over Ewen's back, the pale skin mottled with bruises. The lad's evident pleasure was also disturbing, how he leaned back against the hands, eyes closed and full lips faintly smiling. "Soon," Merlin told himself, "I am going to have an erection, and the witch will notice." It was the kind of thing that witches noticed. She might remember the old gossip about the wizard. It wasn't likely she'd disapprove. It was churchmen, not witches, who called sodomy a sin. But she was likely to make a joke, and then the boy would know for certain what went on in his master's mind.

Merlin excused himself and took a walk by the river. When he got back, the two of them were on the floor, naked and entangled. The boy was incorrigible! Merlin stepped forward, intending to grab Ewen by the scruff of the neck and pull him off the women.

"Get that look off your face," the witch said. "And take another walk. The boy is younger than I am, but old enough to know what he's doing. I used no charms. Both of us are willing."

He went back to the river. Swallows flew back and forth over the water like shuttles in a loom, though they wove nothing except the death of bugs and obedience to their own natures. Merlin waited till darkness, then returned to the cottage a second time.

They spent the night there. Twice Merlin woke to the sound of Ewen and the woman coupling. "Patience," he told himself. "You are old enough to have learned patience."

In the morning, the witch gave them food for their journey and a second jar of liniment. "You have a fine big penis," she said to Ewen. "And you're certainly willing to use it. But you lack skill. If your master ever lets you go, come to me. I'll teach you how to fuck properly."

Ewen blushed. The witch laughed.

Late in the morning, Merlin asked, "What would you have done if she'd been unwilling?"

"Have I learned restraint? Some, but probably not enough." Ewen paused to watch a woodpecker flash – black, white, and red – across the road. "It really is easier being a dog."

They traveled north. Rain fell, and the weather was unseasonably cool. Merlin's joints hurt. "We'll stay with lords this time, and I'll be the king's wizard."

Ewen, riding miserably through a misty rain, lifted his head. He'd be a dog again.

"You'll be a youth of good family, not yet a knight."

"*Why?*"

"I want you to practice being a man."

He said nothing in reply, knowing it was futile to argue with Merlin in weather like this.

"If you forget your manners and act doggishly – well, it's a long distance from the north to Camelot; and these northerners might not even notice."

The lords along the border made them welcome. These were rough men, who guarded King Arthur's realm against the incursions of bandits, infidels and Scots, as well as an occasional monster or dragon. Most were loyal in their way; all knew enough to treat the royal wizard with respect.

Ewen puzzled the lords. A promising lad, but past the age when most northern boys were knighted. He did not seem to be sickly or clerical. Everything in the south went at an odd pace, either too slowly or too quickly; and a lad in Merlin's care must be noble or even royal, though maybe not legitimate. They did not puzzle further. Instead, they loaned him armor and told their younger sons to treat him well.

By days, he practiced the arts of war or hunted on horseback, though he would sooner have run four-footed in the baying pack, as he told Merlin privately.

"Patience," said the wizard.

He killed a boar with a spear, on foot after his horse fell. The lord of that keep offered to make him a knight.

"Not yet," said Merlin. "I'm not satisfied with his manners."

"What use are manners to a soldier? D'you think dragons care about manners? Or Scots, for that matter?"

"I see things you do not," Merlin said firmly.

The lord grew quiet then.

At another keep, Ewen joined a war band going after thieves who had taken twenty head of the lord's best cattle. They got most of the cattle back, but all the thieves escaped.

When they returned, the lord held a feast, honoring the warriors who'd recovered his favorite cow, a great rough beast with wide horns. "A fountain of milk," said the lord with satisfaction. "And the daughters she's produced! She is a mother of queens!"

Ewen sat among his comrades from the war band, drinking as little as possible and trying to ignore the serving women. This had happened in other keeps. The women brushed against him. The men made sly remarks and gave him mocking names: Master Prudence, Master Silence, the Squire without Reproach.

Always before this, he'd managed to control himself. Tonight, he could feel the control slipping, though he wasn't certain why. The lord's lewd praise for his favorite cow and for the bull they'd recovered? The noisiness in the hall? Or his own weariness, after the long chase toward the Scottish border and over many weeks of self-restraint?

He knew what he wanted: to be a dog again, close to Merlin rather than separated by half the feasting hall. It had never been said aloud, but he knew this would be his reward, if he passed the test that Merlin had set him.

If he did not – Ewen shivered. Merlin might refuse to change him. He might remain as he was, awkward and uncomfortable. Worst of all, the wizard might cast him out to wander through England in human form.

The soldier next to him pushed a woman into his lap. She screamed and grabbed hold of Ewen. He wrapped one arm around her waist and with his other hand pushed up her skirt, knowing what he'd find – a wet furry hole like the witch's, though most likely wetter and furrier. The witch had been old. His penis was engorged. He would mount the woman here. Most likely, the men around him would cheer.

Merlin's hand gripped his shoulder. Merlin's voice said, "Down."

He shivered and withdrew his hand, pushed the girl away and stood. Merlin was sitting next to the lord, having never moved.

"You have a prick," said one of the other men. "We can see it. Why are you so unwilling to use it?"

"A promise," he said with difficulty. "To Merlin."

"Is he teaching you magic? Does that art require that you be celibate?"

"A hard art, if this is so," said a second man.

A third man said, "Nay, if this is so, then we must call magic a soft art, rather than a hard one, for it requires softness rather than hardness in those who practice it. Look at our squire now. His male member has diminished to nothing. If we believe him, this is the influence of magic and the wizard Merlin."

Oh God, thought Ewen, turned and left the hall. It was raining again. He stood in the muddy yard, face lifted to the dark sky, a howl forming in his throat. He pressed his lips together. The test was too difficult. He could not endure it. On the morrow, he'd go down on his knees to Merlin and beg for an end.

"No," the wizard said. "You will continue. You did well last night." He reached out a hand, the fingers stiff with age and the weather, and touched Ewen's golden hair. "Surely it is nobler to be what you are now."

"If you hadn't intervened, I would have treated that servant the way I tried to treat the maiden at the ford. How is this noble? These men along the border are animals and do not know it. I know what I am, Merlin. Let me be content."

"Winter draws near," the wizard said finally. "Arthur waits in Camelot. Be patient. Your test is almost over."

The northern foliage began to change. So did the weather, though too late to save most of the harvest. They rode south in sunlight, through drying fields.

"Something in the north has been troubling me," said Merlin. "A sense of darkness, a feeling of oppression. For that reason I stayed as long as I did, talking to the beldams and the local magicians, trying to discover the nature of the problem. I thought a dragon might be stirring or maybe a pestilence was beginning to spread, though most plagues come to us from France."

He stretched his aching shoulders, enjoying the sun's heat. "Maybe the problem was the weather. My vision was cloudy because it was a vision of clouds."

Ewen had pulled his shirt off and rode bare to the waist, his fair skin turning ruddy. Looking at him, Merlin realized how much the lad had changed in the time he'd spent free of enchantment. His adolescent ranginess was gone. Thick muscles covered his long tall frame. His hair, which had been ragged and unruly, was short and neatly trimmed. So was the beard he'd grown. So much in only a summer, the wizard thought.

When they got close to Camelot, they stopped with a farmer, an old friend of Merlin's. That evening, the wizard got out the gold collar. "Are you certain?"

"Yes."

The wizard felt perturbed and must have looked it. "You can't take me into Camelot like this," said Ewen. "How would you explain me? Arthur knows you have no noble ward, and he certainly knows I'm not a royal bastard; and if you think I want to listen to orders from Kay or insults from the rest of Arthur's knights – the royal hounds have better manners."

The farm was built in the ruins of an ancient Roman farm. There was a tiled pool that still held water. Ewen bathed carefully – he was always cleanly – dried himself, folded his clothes and packed them, then put on the collar. "Now."

Merlin gestured. Where the man had stood was a white hound, tail wagging, tongue lolling, a look of amusement in the hazel eyes.

Ewen's horse stayed with the farmer, who knew better than to ask questions about the vanished companion or the suddenly present dog. That afternoon, they were in Camelot. Arthur greeted Merlin with a hug and gave the hound a brisk rub over the head and shoulders. "How can I do less for the sire of my kennels?" Then he took his wizard off for a conference. The white hound followed.

They talked first about the harvest in the north, the lords there, the Scottish menace, then about other problems which concerned Arthur: rebellious barons, false knights, rival kings, and a dragon on the Welsh border.

Finally, Arthur got to his chief concern. "It's Guinevere. I know she pines for children."

"Pining" was not a word that Merlin would have used for the queen. She was a large, rosy, healthy woman with enough energy for ten or twenty children. Lacking these children – there were not even any royal bastards for her to gather and raise, except for Borre, who had a perfectly good and noble mother, unwilling to give her son up – Guinevere did her best to keep busy in other ways. Camelot was full of the hangings that she and her ladies embroidered: the deeds of Sir Hercules and King Alexander in the feasting hall, the deeds of the saints and prophets in the royal chapel, blooming gardens in the royal bower and the rooms used by royal and noble guests. This was in addition to all the everyday work a queen must do: managing the king's household, training his pages, greeting his guests of high and low degree – kings, nobles, prelates, bards, and jugglers. Guinevere was especially fond of the jugglers. She was a woman in love with activity.

When Arthur made royal progresses, she accompanied him.

"She stops to visit with every good wife famous for her herbal lore and every hermit famous for his piety," the king said. "It's obvious why. I have the most famous wizard in the kingdom in my employ. I ask again, is there nothing you can do?"

"In the first place, don't presume that you know your wife's mind. Women are not easy to understand. Even I, with my vision, make mistakes about them. In the second place, my liege, I am not a village witch dealing in potions and cures, though I have met one recently who seems excellent to me. You can send for her, if you like. If she's honest, she'll tell you that the problem does not lie with Guinevere."

The king's fair skin reddened slightly. "Are you certain?"

"I've told you there's magic in your line. Most likely, one of your ancestors was a fairy. They are slow to reproduce and rarely have more than a child or two. If this were not so, they'd fill the world, since they age slowly and are difficult to kill.

"Sometimes they take our children, raise them and mate with them, hoping to produce offspring who combine fairy magic and endurance with human fecundity. In general, the fairies tell me, these experiments do not achieve the hoped-for end. Most of the half-breed children lack magical ability and die young, being barely a hundred or a hundred and fifty, and they are only slightly more fertile than their fairy relatives."

Merlin paused. Arthur looked uncomfortable.

"It's possible you might have better luck with a fairy wife or with someone who, like you, has fairy blood. But I promise nothing."

The king shook his head. "I love Guinevere. Tell me where to find this witch."

She came to Camelot on a white mare, a fine new cloak over her shoulders. Arthur and Guinevere received her privately. Afterward, she sought out Merlin. He was in his quarters, reading the *Logic* of Aristotle, which a learned Jew of Cairo had translated into Latin and sent to the wizard in return for a book on fairy natural history. The white hound slept at his feet.

Merlin greeted the woman and poured wine for her, which she tasted before she spoke. "I could have said 'no' to the king, but not to that sweet lady. Where's your serving man? Has he left you?"

"No."

She laughed. "You've hidden him, for fear that I'll seduce him."

Merlin stirred the white dog with a foot. Ewen, who was dreaming of deer or possibly of bipeds, made a wuffing sound.

"What did you tell them?" Merlin asked the witch.

She tried the wine a second time, giving it so thorough an assay that Merlin had to refill her cup.

"I gave the queen a potion that will calm her. In my experience, women who fret have trouble breeding, especially if the thing they fret about is their infertility. Why this is, I don't know, though worry can disrupt the behavior of the body in many ways. Also, it's possible that the queen's activity – especially the traveling she does – is having an adverse effect on her female functions, though I have certainly known farm wives who worked as hard as any queen and bred like rabbits.

"I'm not happy with the number of shrines she visits. Or with the hermits. A pestilent lot! Full of vermin and bad advice! I told her to travel less, and if she must talk with religious folk, let them be seemly nuns and clerics who wash."

Merlin smiled and stirred the dog again. This time Ewen was silent.

"I told the king to wear loose clothing whenever possible. Monks and priests have no trouble fathering children. I have long suspected it's their clothing that makes them fertile."

"None of this will do any harm," said Merlin. "No good either, I fear."

"I could not say 'no' to the lady," the witch replied, finished her wine and rose to go. Merlin escorted her to the door of his quarters. She glanced up at him, her face flushed with wine. "I'm going to the kitchen to brew a tisane for Sir Kay. He suffers from headaches, he has told me. After that, I'll go to my room. I would like company, if your serving man is free and willing."

Merlin closed the door behind her, then walked back to his study. The white hound was up on all fours, ears lifted and tail wagging.

"Do you think you can behave in a seemly fashion, like a knight, instead of a cur?"

The tail-wagging grew more furious.

"Very well," the wizard said after a moment. "I imagine this woman can take care of herself, but you are to act as if she were the mildest and silliest of maidens. Do you understand?"

The dog wagged harder.

Laughing, Merlin changed him into a man. He dressed quickly, pulling clothing from one of Merlin's chests, then hurried through the palace, already dark in the early evening of autumn.

In dog-form he had explored every corridor; and he had no trouble finding the witch's lodging-place. (In any case, she had described the location to Merlin.) At the moment, it was empty, unlit and as black as pitch. But the witch's aroma was everywhere. He could smell it through all the other odors: the dry herbs in the bedclothes, the dry rushes on the floor, the dust in corners and – very faintly – a mold.

He undressed and realized, when he was done, that he was still wearing the hound's gold collar. No time to take it back to Merlin. He wanted to be in the room when the witch arrived. He unfastened the collar and hid it in the middle of his clothing, then settled on the bed, among blankets that smelled of herbs and the woman.

She took longer than he had expected, in his eagerness. At last, the door opened. The witch entered, carrying a lamp. In the dim glow cast by it, she took on the appearance of a young matron, blooming the way some women do after their first few children.

Ewen raised himself on an elbow. She glanced at him, her dark eyes shining, then laughed and blew out the light.

He listened to the sound of her undressing, then felt her settle on top of him, astride his hips. In this fashion they coupled the first time: the witch on top and riding like a knight in a tournament.

The second time was side by side. They were both less eager than the first time. Their coupling was slow, gentle, and affectionate. When they finished, Ewen fell asleep.

He woke to lamplight. The witch stood in the middle of her room, dressed in a plain white shift. In one of her hands was the lamp, now relit. Her other hand held his gold collar.

"How have I deserved this?" she said.

Puzzled, he did not answer.

"I am a woman of no great birth, never beautiful, no longer young – those being the only virtues a village woman may have, as I know. My skills are nothing much, compared to Merlin's art and science. Your master might well look down on me. But to play such a trick! To make me couple with his dog!"

Now Ewen understood the expression on her face. As quickly as possible, he explained he was a man. "Though I have spent most of my time as a dog in recent years. Still, I began my life in human form, and my birth was gentle."

"Why did Merlin turn you into a dog?"

Ewen flushed with shame, sat up and told the story of his life before he met the wizard.

The witch listened, frowning. When he finished, she said, "I'm glad that Merlin did not trick me into an act contrary to nature, which requires us to mate with our own kind. But it doesn't sound as if you're much of a man."

He flushed again and nodded.

"Though you were young and had a bad upbringing. That much is evident. Have you learned to do better?"

"I don't know."

She glanced at the collar and held it out. "Put it on."

He obeyed, then looked up. The witch wore a smile that combined affection with malice. "It certainly is a fine piece of jewelry, fit for a prince or king; and now that I know you're a man, I like how it looks on you." She set the lamp down, came over, bent and kissed him, one hand resting on his shoulder. Her fingers touched the collar. He could feel her caressing the gold links.

He pulled her down, pushing up the shift, which was made of wool, coarse and prickly. They coupled a third time, with less vigor than the first time, but more passion than the second, then slept tangled together.

At dawn, he returned to Merlin's quarters. The wizard had spent the night with Aristotle and was still up, a lamp burning next to him.

Ewen told him about the witch's discovery, then added, "I will never know enough to be a man."

"What makes you say that?" asked Merlin.

"Why was she disgusted by the collar, then enticed by it?"

"That's a question she will have to answer, though every witch and magician knows that things have many qualities that can be called accidental – or, if these qualities are not entirely accidental, then they are capable of variation, depending on context and use. The same herb may be a medicine or a poison. A knife can be used for surgery or murder. A gold collar on a man does not have the same meaning as a gold collar on a dog.

"Also –" The wizard closed his book. "Actions performed in knowledge and through choice are not the same as actions performed in ignorance, without decision. No one likes to be tricked."

Ewen frowned, not understanding much of this. Merlin told him to go to bed. When he woke again, midway through the morning, he was a hound.

The witch left, having promised Merlin that she would keep

Ewen's secret. "If you ever decide to let him remain a man, send him to me. He needs teaching, and not by men. This father of his seems to have almost ruined him, and I'm not certain about the education you have given him."

For a while after that, Guinevere took the witch's potion, and Arthur wore long robes, made by his wife and richly embroidered, so he looked (his knights said) as fine as a priest at mass.

But the potion made Guinevere languid and drowsy. She missed her energy. Kay the seneschal took Arthur aside and told him in full what the knights were saying.

"You can't keep the respect of rough fellows like these, if you dress like a priest or a lady. This isn't Constantinople or even Rome."

Arthur sighed and nodded.

"Just as well," Merlin said later to his white hound. "The queen was nodding off in the middle of banquets, and Arthur could not learn to manage his robes. He kept tripping over the hems."

Ewen listened, while chewing on his flank. Something itched in an infuriating fashion.

"Do you have fleas again?" Merlin asked, but didn't wait for an answer. "I've not told this to anyone, but the king is not fated to have a legitimate heir. I have seen this and also seen –" Merlin paused. "Harm will come to him from a child he fathers. I've been watching young Borre for years now. He seems a harmless lad. Maybe he'll turn malevolent as he ages, or maybe there is someone else I don't know about. My vision isn't as clear as it used to be. Time vanquishes everything."

Not you, thought Ewen.

The beginning of the end was ordinary: one of Arthur's fellow kings came to Camelot on a visit, bringing in his train a maiden, slim and comely with black eyes and hair. Her face was pale, except for a faint blush in the cheeks, as if wild roses – the kind that bloom along every road in spring – bloomed there. Her name was Nimue.

In the old story, it says that Merlin became "sotted," a word that means "foolish, stupid, drunk, or wasted." A sot is a dolt, a blockhead or a soaker: harsh words to use on a man so old, wise, and learned.

What happened was this: Nimue was interested in magic. While the king she followed spent time with Arthur, she sought out Arthur's ancient wizard, drawn by his wisdom and learning. Even his age was attractive, or so she explained to Merlin. Wisdom is not found in the young. Nor is true learning, which requires not only memorization, but also pondering and the testing of learned truths by experience.

Merlin, in his turn, was attracted by her interest in magic, as well as by her beauty. Ewen disliked her at once, though she fawned on him, rubbing his red ears and his snow-white neck and shoulders, praising him to his master. What a fine dog! How handsome and famous! He wanted to bite her.

How could Merlin, the wisest man in England, fail to see the calculating look in Nimue's dark eyes and fail to hear the falsity in her honey-sweet voice?

Maybe falsity is too harsh a word. Beyond any question Nimue was interested in magic and respected Merlin as a magician. But she had no interest in him as a man, as Ewen could tell by her odor and her expression, when Merlin turned away from her.

Merlin, on the other hand, was in love, as he had not been for years. That a woman so young and fair and graceful should be drawn to him! She was intelligent, as well, and knew something of magic already, enough to ask him good questions. She listened to his answers intently, her dark eyes fixed on him.

Ewen, at Merlin's feet, felt the fur on his back prickle and his upper lip lift. A growl was forming in his throat. He pushed his head down between his paws, trying to keep his hatred hidden, telling himself to be patient. The visiting king would not stay forever. When he left, he'd take the woman, and Merlin would recover.

So it went, through late spring and early summer, until the king – Nimue's host and Arthur's guest – made ready to return home. Merlin asked Nimue to stay in Camelot.

"The city is growing hot," she said in answer. "Soon it will be filled with flies and foul aromas. I will not remain in such a place. Nor should you, Lord Merlin. A man as venerable as you, a repository of so much knowledge, should guard himself against discomfort, which can lead to disease." She added that she had a villa in the country. "Which the ancient Romans built and my relatives restored to its former splendor and dignity. Come there with me."

That evening, at the end of yet another long feast and drinking bout in honor of Arthur's guest, Merlin walked back to his rooms. Ewen was beside him. The dog was uneasy, nudging his master and nipping at the old man's hand. When they were alone, Merlin changed him and said, "What is it?"

It had been months since Ewen had been a man. Something had happened. He no longer felt comfortable with nakedness. His human body seemed horribly bare. It was difficult to stand upright and face the wizard, who was frowning at him, obviously angry. Prescient as always, the old man knew he wasn't going to like what Ewen had to say. The youth thought of dropping back down on all fours, so his belly and genitals would be protected. Instead, he pulled a robe from one of Merlin's chests and put it on.

"Speak!" said the wizard.

Ewen tried, but he'd never been good at talking, and most of what he knew was canine, having to do with Nimue's scent and the tone of her voice, the way she moved, how her hands felt when she petted him or tugged his ears. The woman was selfish and dishonest. As wise as Merlin was, he was being tricked.

The wizard listened. His eyes – usually a soft faded blue, like cloth washed many times and laid out in the sun to dry – darkened, becoming the hard blue-grey color of steel. Ewen faltered and finally stopped.

"Do you think I'll listen to a dog about such matters? Or to a rapist? You have not learned much, have you, in all your years at Camelot? Not respect for women, nor courtesy, nor chivalry. My fault, I suppose. I should have kept you a man and sent you to the witch or to a monastery. What can a dog learn, except obedience and odors?"

Loyalty and love, Ewen thought. A dog can learn those as well. But he could not force his tongue to move and speak.

"I intend to go with Nimue," the wizard said. "If you wish, you can stay here. Arthur will take good care of you, though he will treat you like a dog, as I never have. Or you can go to the witch in human form. That might be best."

And leave the old man with Nimue, who stank of falsity? No. Ewen shook his head. "Take me with you."

Merlin pondered, saying finally, "If I do, you will have to remain a dog. I want no more conversations like this one."

Ewen agreed.

The three of them set out several days later, the wizard and maiden on palfreys, Ewen running beside them in dog form. The weather was pleasant, once they left the closeness of Camelot, and their journey ordinary. Because he traveled with a woman, Merlin stopped in the houses of noblemen and the hostels maintained by religious orders. In most of these places, Ewen stayed in the stables. Every morning, it seemed to him, Merlin looked happier and younger, though the wizard did not smell of satisfied lust. Nor did Nimue smell like a bitch who'd been mounted. Her odor remained the same as always: a combination of eau de rose and something Ewen could not put into words: self-containment, aloofness, an absence of sensuality so marked that it became a presence.

It was not lust that had transformed the wizard, but rather love and hope.

The villa, when they reached it, proved to be on an island in the middle of a lake and hidden by trees, so no one on the lake shore could tell the island was inhabited.

They left their horses and rowed across in a small boat. Ewen, at the prow, felt his fur go up. Something about this place was uncanny. Merlin, pulling the heavy oars, noticed nothing except his own strength – surprising in a man of his age – and a sense of happiness.

It was, in fact, a Roman villa, restored as if by magic, though a bit dusty at the moment. The floors were covered with mosaics and the walls with paintings: the deeds of Dame Venus, portrayed in the style of the ancients but with colors so fresh and bright that they could not be genuinely Roman. In one room, she rose from the ocean, as naked and lovely as a pearl. In another room, Prince Paris awarded her the golden apple. A third room showed her husband Vulcan exposing her adultery. The goddess lay with the war god Mars, the two of them imprisoned by a net, which Vulcan had made through magic and thrown over them, as they coupled. Mars grimaced, and rage was evident on Vulcan's face, but the lovely goddess remained tranquil, faintly smiling, as if none of this – her infidelity, her exposure, the trap that held her – mattered.

Nimue guided them through the villa, then out into the garden that surrounded it. If she had servants, they were careless. The garden had a half-wild look. Still, it was full of mid-summer flowers, roses especially. Sweet aromas filled the air.

Some of his old acuteness returned to Merlin. "This place is a wonder. Who are your relatives?"

Nimue smiled. "I have kin in fairyland."

She settled on a marble bench, and Merlin settled next to her, Ewen at his feet, panting a little in the midday heat. There, in the overgrown and aromatic garden, the maiden told her story. She was one of the fairy experiments, not an ordinary hybrid but the product of generations of interbreeding between fairies and the human children they stole. In the end, it had been decided that the experiment was a failure. Her line would not be continued.

"The fairies had no further use for me, and I did not wish to stay in their country. There is enough of them in me so I'm not especially affected by their enchantments. Pure humans are and rarely leave, if they have the chance to stay, though you have come and gone many times, as I have heard."

Merlin said, "Yes."

She picked a rose and turned it in her hands. "They would have let me stay. They recognize their obligation to me and the other hybrids. But I didn't want to be a poor relation, and I didn't want to grow old, while my cousins remained as fresh and blooming as this rose."

While she spoke, she tore at the rose, apparently without noticing what she was doing. When she glanced down finally, nothing remained in her hands except the stalk. Her lap was full of bright red petals. Nimue laughed and stood, brushing the petals off, then invited Merlin into the house.

They remained there for the rest of the summer, while Merlin taught Nimue about magic. She had little interest in the other things he knew: the logic of Aristotle, the philosophy of Plato, the medicine and mathematics he had learned as a young man, traveling in India and China. Now and then, she would permit the old man to speak of such things. Ewen listened, feeling more comfortable with human knowledge than with the spells that fascinated Nimue.

The house remained empty except for the three of them. Meals appeared out of the air. So did music, pipes and stringed instruments playing through the long summer evenings. The musicians were never visible, nor were the instruments they played.

Though the house was always a little dusty and slovenly, it never became dirty. It was being cleaned somehow, by someone, though never thoroughly. This was no surprise to Ewen. Merlin had told him years before that the stories humans told about the excellent work of spirits were untrue. "Some are quick, but also careless and slipshod. Others are so meticulous that they finish nothing. Their idea of what's important is not the same as ours. With the best will in the world – and they often lack good will – they can't do a job to our satisfaction."

The garden remained ragged, but never turned entirely wild. Sometimes, in the morning, they would find bouquets throughout the house, filling the rooms with sweet aromas. Merlin must be doing this, thought Ewen. The old man remained sotted. Now that they were alone, away from other people, his passion grew stronger and more obvious. He began to court Nimue as a lover would, praising her beauty, speaking of his own desire, creating illusions to amuse and entice her.

Some days, the mountains of China rose outside the villa, tall and strangely shaped. Mist floated among them. The sky above was pearly grey. Now and then, Ewen saw a flash of green or blue.

At first, he thought these were breaks in the clouds through which he could see the sunlit upper heavens. No, as Merlin explained to Nimue. The flashes of color were Chinese dragons. Unlike the local English dragons, who were compounded largely of earth and fire and liked living underground and causing trouble, the oriental dragons were creatures of air and water, who lived in the clouds as well as in lakes, rivers, and the Great Eastern Ocean. As a rule, they were beneficent, though powerful and very proud.

On other days, Ewen went out and found the meadows of fairyland. Animals grazed there such as he had never seen before: huge quadrupeds, their faces and necks covered with helmets made of bone and skin. Three horns – as straight and sharp as lances – protruded from each armored face.

He ran out among the animals, barking from pleasure. They, being illusions, ignored him. Still, it was pleasant to trot past gigantic leathery haunches and catch the gleam of a tiny eye, the pupil a vertical black line across an orange iris, or to sit and watch some massive cow or bull – he could not distinguish the sexes – shear grass with a great curving falcon-like beak.

Nimue was interested in the dragons, since they were magical. The quadrupeds were not, and she had seen them often before. "Make them vanish," she said to Merlin. The old man did.

She remained cool and aloof, interested in the wizard's skill, but not his body. Would any body have interested her? A handsome young knight? A fairy lord? The dog could not tell. She always smelled of distance and self-control.

Merlin's passion continued to grow, and his courtesy decreased. He began to stand close to Nimue and touch her as if by accident, his old withered hand brushing her arm or the fabric over her thigh. He spoke of his love, usually indirectly – hinting, making allusions, frowning, and heaving sighs.

She was growing angry. Ewen could see this and smell it. But she would not send the old man away. She was too curious, too anxious to have Merlin's power and knowledge.

So the summer ended: in dry heat and a conflict of wills. Now, instead of flowers, Ewen smelled dying vegetation, the old man's frustrated lust, the woman's anger and dislike, which she hid from Merlin, but could not hide from Ewen. A bad situation! Beyond any question the woman was dangerous. He needed to speak with Merlin, to issue a warning. But how could he? The old wizard had to change him. Ewen nosed and licked Merlin's hand, whined softly, stared beseechingly.

"No," the wizard said. "I told you, no further conversation. You came here as a dog. A dog you will remain."

He had reached the limit of his endurance. He could no longer bear the sight of Merlin fawning over the woman, all his dignity and wisdom forgotten, sharing his magical knowledge with Nimue, giving her with open hands the power that made him the greatest wizard alive. In the end, Ewen knew, she would turn on his master.

Very well. If he could not speak as a man, he would act as a dog.

One morning he came upon Nimue in the garden. The day was already hot. She stood by a rose bush, as languid and drooping as the plant's last blowzy flowers, which she gathered, bending slightly, her long white neck exposed. The two of them were alone; and as far as he could tell, the woman did not realize that he was in the garden. He attacked, going straight for her throat.

The moment he began to move, she whirled, flinging her basket of flowers aside and raising an arm. His teeth closed on tender flesh, but it was not the flesh of her throat. Nimue screamed.

A moment later Merlin was with them.

The old man said nothing. Nor did he lift a hand. But Ewen felt as if he'd been struck by a giant. He let go of Nimue, falling to the ground and cowering in the dust of the garden path. The other two ignored him. The woman stood absolutely straight, holding her arm, from which blood gushed. Her lips were pressed together. No sound emerged.

The wizard touched her gently. The flow of blood stopped; the wound closed; and there was no evidence of Ewen's crime, save the bright splotches of blood on Nimue's white gown.

"Is the dog mad?"

Merlin glanced at Ewen. "He has no disease, if that's what you are asking."

"Kill him," Nimue said.

For a moment, Ewen thought the wizard would do it. Then Merlin shook his head. "I've had the brute for a long time. I won't kill him, even now. But I will tie him up."

He snapped his fingers. Ewen rose and followed him to the back of the garden. An old stone hut stood there, a storage place for garden tools and pots. Merlin led him inside. Ewen stood shaking in darkness while the wizard rummaged and found an iron collar fastened to an iron chain.

His gold collar came off; the iron collar was fastened in its place.

"When I have time, when I'm not otherwise occupied, I will decide what to do with you," Merlin said. He left the hut, closing and locking the door. Ewen began to whine. The wizard rapped on the door. Ewen found that he could make no noise.

At first, he lunged at the end of the chain, trying to break it and reach the door. At the same time, he tried to bark and howl. Neither effort produced any result, except his throat became sore, and the iron collar rubbed his neck until it was raw.

Finally, he gave up and sat. What had happened? Had he really been trying to kill Nimue? He reflected on the question, while licking his chest and paws. Some of Nimue's blood had spurted onto him. It tasted of salt and magic. Yes. Murder had been the plan, though not a deeply considered plan, but rather the impulse of a moment. Still, he had failed another test of chivalry. After years at Camelot and in Merlin's care, he'd ended as he began: a bad dog imprisoned in a hut, waiting for who knew what kind of punishment.

Ewen lay down in the dark, staring at the hut's locked door. A whimper formed in his throat like a tic that wouldn't go away. He couldn't release it, though he opened his mouth and yawned and shook his head, trying to break the noise free.

Late in the afternoon, two dishes appeared in the hut: one of water, the other of meat. Ewen ate and drank, then went to sleep.

He remained in the hut all autumn. Every day food and drink appeared, and his waste products vanished. The hut never became filthy, though it always smelled of dirt and dog. The sores on his neck became scabby and itched. Bugs came into the hut and bit him. These wounds itched as well. No one visited except the bugs and, now and then, a field mouse. The mice were timid and quick. He never managed to catch one.

In the high corners of the hut were spiders. They spun webs, catching a few of the bugs that tormented Ewen, like angels helping the damned just a little. Enough light shone in through cracks in the door so he could see his benefactors: little round bodies glowing in the sunlight, with as many legs as angels had wings.

The punishment was just, Ewen concluded. He had failed as a man and a dog.

And what was going on with Merlin? How could such a man succumb to lust and folly? The old man had, though Ewen was reluctant to admit this. Still, the dog thought, nosing at the problem, if he knew nothing else – not honor, not chivalry, not courtesy – he could recognize the urge to mount a bitch.

If Merlin had wandered from the *via media* and lost himself in wilderness, what hope was left for lesser men? Who could live wisely, if the wise could not? The problem was an itch, almost as painful as his bites and sores. He worried it whenever he was unoccupied by bugs, mice, or spiders. No answer came to him.

One day the door opened. Nimue stood before him, rimmed with sunlight. She gestured, and he felt himself change, becoming a man. The iron collar remained around his neck.

Nimue looked him over. "I wondered what lay under your enchantment. You're certainly handsome enough. Why couldn't Merlin be satisfied with you?"

He tried to speak and couldn't. She gestured a second time.

"He wasn't a man who fell in love with men," said Ewen. "What's happened to him?"

"Of course he was a lover of men. Did you know nothing about him? And of women also, of course. He would not leave me alone, though I tried every way I could to hint him off."

Ewen went up on one knee. It seemed more decent than standing, naked as he was, and less humiliating than remaining on all fours. He leaned cautiously against the chain. It held. The collar cut into his neck. "Where is he?" His voice sounded rough.

"Under a stone. A big one, which ought to serve to hold him down, though he lifted it with a gesture. There was a treasure under the stone, which he wanted to show me. He was always trying to show me wonders, as if they could win me. As a teacher, yes. I wanted nothing more than to be his student. But his leman? No.

"He went into the pit beneath the stone, the stone hanging above him, held in midair by magic; and he opened the chests and jars that held the treasure, pulling out – oh, necklaces and bracelets made of gold, silver goblets with satyrs dancing on them, bowls engraved with nymphs and goddesses, and glass that had been transmuted by time, so it shone as many-colored as an opal. All the while he smiled at me from a face made of wrinkles.

"I knew the charm he used to raise the boulder and used it to bring the boulder down."

"He's dead then," said Ewen, his heart full of sorrow.

Nimue shook her head. "It's not easy to kill a man so powerful. He is trapped beneath the stone and tangled in the spells he set to guard the place. But most likely he's still alive and will remain so."

"This was a bad action," Ewen said. "Unkind, discourteous, ungrateful, and lacking in respect. He was your teacher, an old man and very wise."

"Don't talk to me of courtesy and kindness. He made you a dog and chained you in this hut; he was after me day and night to have sex with him. Was this courteous? Or kind? Did he respect my maidenhood or your manhood? Who knows what he might have done next – a man of such great power, no longer held in rein by reason?"

Ewen frowned, trying to puzzle out right and wrong. "I'm here as punishment, for trying to harm you and for other crimes."

"Is that so? I could ask what you've done. But it's not my concern. Nor does it interest me." Nimue turned as if to go.

"I'll die here, if you leave me chained."

She turned back. "Then you have an argument with Merlin. You don't believe you deserve what's happened to you."

"I'd prefer not to die, especially here and now. As to my deserts, I can't answer you. I don't think Merlin would have killed me or let me die."

She tilted her head, considering. He waited, still on one knee. Finally she snapped her fingers. The iron collar opened and fell away.

Ewen leaped to his feet, lunging at Nimue. He moved less quickly and gracefully that he had before his imprisonment. None the less he reached her.

As soon as he laid hands on her, she turned into a dragon of the western variety, as black as iron, rather than blue or green. Magic is mostly illusion, Ewen told himself and held on tightly. The dragon twisted its long serpentine neck, opened a mouth full of teeth like daggers and spat a gout of fire into his face.

He screamed with pain, but his grip did not loosen, though his face felt as if a mask of red hot metal had been fastened over it, which burned through skin and flesh to the bones of his skull.

The pain should have killed him or at least made him let go. It didn't. *Ergo*, it was illusion.

As soon as he decided this, the dragon became a fish as long as he was tall. It thrashed in his arms: cold, slimy and powerful. Better than a dragon, Ewen thought, though difficult to hold. He tightened his grip further. His face still hurt.

The fish became an eagle, which he gripped around the lower body. The creature beat him with broad strong wings. As the feathers brushed his face, he felt pieces of flesh fall away.

The bird lasted only briefly, turning into a spotted cat that screamed (a sound like the scream of an eagle) and bit Ewen in the neck. Blood, his own blood, ran into Ewen's lungs. He was drowning.

The cat became a troll with green skin and foul stinking breath. Ewen's arms were locked around the creature's torso. Its marks were free and beat his head and shoulders like a pair of hammers, wielded by two strong smiths. His face was almost gone by now, and blood filled his lungs, so he was no longer able to breathe. What an illusion! His old master was without equal, and Nimue had obviously been an exceptional student.

The troll became a slim young man, who stood quietly in Ewen's arms. The lad had all of Nimue's beauty, transformed so it (and he) was clearly masculine.

"Well," said the youth. "You are certainly brave, or else extremely stupid. I can't tell which. Why are you holding me?"

"I won't let you go till you promise to free Merlin," Ewen said. He looked down at the lad and thought, why should I trust him? This is still Nimue. "I won't let you go till Merlin is free."

The youth shook his head. "You're no danger to me. But if the old man were free and had the use of his powers, there's no place on Earth where I'd be safe."

"Then you are trapped, as he is trapped," said Ewen.

"Don't be ridiculous," said the youth and clicked his tongue.

Ewen's arms fell to his sides, heavy and powerless. His entire body seemed made of stone.

The youth stepped back, and Ewen could see him clearly for the first time. Dark curls fell around his shoulders. His straight young torso was garbed in fine mail; a sword with a jeweled hilt hung at his side; and his tall boots were made of a leather so thin and soft it must have come from fairyland or Constantinople. Ewen had never seen a knight or squire more comely or better dressed.

"Can you swim?" Nimue asked.

"Not well."

"I'll send the boat back for you. By the time this spell wears off, I'll be long gone. Don't bother to look for me or Merlin. You won't find either of us. If you get hungry, there are plants in the back of the garden. My kin brought them from a land in the distant west. Their fruit will give you both food and drink. Farewell." The lad turned and walked off, stepping lightly and whistling with right good cheer. Long after he'd vanished from sight, Ewen heard the whistle, still clear but growing gradually fainter, as if Nimue were departing into an unimaginably distant place. A trick of magic, Ewen thought, or a rare natural phenomenon.

Still it was disturbing to hear the high clear music recede farther and farther.

Late in the afternoon, he found himself able to move. He stretched cautiously, then felt his face. It seemed as always. There was no charred flesh, no burning mask. His throat was not torn open, though it certainly felt sore.

So much to the good. He went to the villa. The rooms were empty of furniture. Carpets of dust covered the mosaic floors. The frescoes looked old and faded, as if years had passed instead of weeks. He searched every corner, though without much hope. There was only dust and cobwebs. His gold collar was gone. So were the clothes that Nimue and Merlin had brought.

In the end, he realized that he was going to find nothing; and he was filthy and hungry. He went to the shore of the island. The boat was there, waiting for him, oars shipped. He waded in next to it and washed.

After he was done, he looked at his reflection. What his hands had told him was confirmed by vision. His face was the same as always. The damage done by Nimue had been illusory. Though he'd never been vain about his human body, Ewen felt relief.

He pulled the boat farther up on shore and returned to the garden. The plants described by Nimue were there: knee-high, bushy, laden with round red fruit that was obviously too heavy for the branches. Narrow stakes had been driven into the ground, and the branches fastened to them. In spite of this support, the plants drooped, so heavy was the load they bore. He picked a fruit. Sun-warmed, almost certainly ripe, it lay comfortably in his palm. Now that he looked closely, he could see it was not perfectly round, but rather flattened at top and bottom. Grooves ran down it, dividing the flesh – soft under the thin skin – into lobes. Of what did the fruit remind him? An undersized melon? A new kind of apple?

In truth, the fruit resembled nothing he had seen before.

Was it poisonous?

Nimue could have killed him easily, or left him chained in the hut to starve. She meant him no harm, apparently, though he had tried to kill her.

Ewen took a bite. The fruit was juicy with a flavor that combined sweetness and sharpness. Both food and drink, Nimue had said. He remembered her words as liquid ran down his chin. The fruit had seeds, too many to pick out, so he ate them, then licked his palm to get the last of the sweet, acidic juice.

He was a man again, with no clothing, no weapons, no money,

no master, no home. Merlin was under a stone, which stone he did not know; and he lacked the skill to free his master. Nimue had vanished. He doubted that he'd be able to find her. In addition – he counted over his problems, while his throat grew tight with grief – winter was not far off. The fairy fruit might survive cold and snow. He would not. If he stayed on the island, he'd freeze and maybe starve.

He sat a while longer in the dust, October sunlight pouring over him, the warm air full of the scent of the fairy bushes weeping for Merlin and himself. For the most part, his weeping was silent. Now and then he groaned. It was a harsh, human sound.

At last he ate another fruit, taking pleasure in the combination of sweetness and acidity, also in the way the liquid felt running down his raw throat. A thought had come to him, and he returned to the hut where he'd been a prisoner.

The two dishes that had provided food for him were empty. That magic had ended, as he might have expected. But the spirits who had taken everything from the house had not been told to clean here, or else they had forgotten, as minor spirits often did. The iron collar and chain still lay on the dirt floor, and the corners were full of piled up pots and tools. He even found a gardening smock, folded in an ancient battered basket.

He need not go into the world entirely empty-handed. The basket would serve to carry some of the fairy fruit. The smock might hold together, though the fabric was old and badly worn. If he took the tools, the scythe especially, he'd have a way to defend himself and to earn his keep. Adam, who was the father of all humans, had kept a garden; and many hermits and pious monks still did, some of them men of noble birth. According to Merlin, there had been kings in ancient times who took pleasure in such things; and monarchs in Asia still vied with one another to build and maintain gardens. Such an activity could not dishonor him. Surely it wasn't any worse than coursing game or catching rats in Arthur's stables, as he had done now and then, mostly for his own amusement, though also to help the stable boys.

Thinking this, he carried his discoveries out of the hut.

He'd find the witch. She knew more of magic and human behavior than he did. Maybe she'd be able to explain what had happened on the island. It must have a meaning, this test that he had failed and Merlin also, apparently. Maybe she would know a way to rescue Merlin. If not – he would not think so far ahead. The important thing was to go forward, remembering what his old master had taught him.

THE QUEST OF THE HOLY GRAIL

Andrew and Leonora Lang

As Arthur's world disintegrates so he comes to believe that it can only be saved by the discovery of the Holy Grail. The purity of the Holy Grail, which in Christian myth once held the blood of Christ, can only be discovered by the pure of heart, and would thus restore the land.

The full story of the Holy Grail is long and complicated. I covered it in detail in Chronicles of the Holy Grail, *but the complete story is retold here in abridgement. Although the following is usually attributed to Andrew Lang (1844–1912), because it features in his volume* The Book of Romance *(1902), Lang tells us in his preface that the story was in part an adaptation by his wife, Leonora, from the* High History of the Holy Graal *(1898) by Sebastian Evans (1830–1909), itself a rendition of the medieval texts. So from that you can pick-and-mix your authors.*

I

Now the King was minded to go on a pilgrimage, and he agreed with the Queen that he would set forth to seek the holy chapel of St. Augustine, which is in the White Forest, and may only be found by adventure. Much he wished to undertake the quest alone, but this the Queen would not suffer, and to do her pleasure he consented that a youth, tall and strong of limb, should ride with him as his squire. Chaus was the youth's name, and he was son to Gwain li Aoutres. "Lie within to-night," commanded the King, "and take heed that my horse be saddled at break of day, and my arms ready." "At your pleasure, Sir," answered the youth, whose heart rejoiced because he was going alone with the King.

As night came on, all the Knights quitted the hall, but Chaus the squire stayed where he was, and would not take off his clothes or his shoes, lest sleep should fall on him and he might not be ready when the King called him. So he sat himself down by the great fire, but in spite of his will sleep fell heavily on him, and he dreamed a strange dream.

In his dream it seemed that the King had ridden away to the quest, and had left his squire behind him, which filled the young man with fear. And in his dream he set the saddle and bridle on his horse, and fastened his spurs, and girt on his sword, and galloped out of the castle after the King. He rode on a long space, till he entered a thick forest, and there before him lay traces of the King's horse, and he followed till the marks of the hoofs ceased suddenly at some open ground and he thought that the King had alighted there. On the right stood a chapel, and about it was a graveyard, and in the graveyard many coffins, and in his dream it seemed as if the King had entered the chapel, so the young man entered also. But no man did he behold save a Knight that lay dead upon a bier in the midst of the chapel, covered with a pall of rich silk, and four tapers in golden candlesticks were burning round him. The squire marvelled to see the body lying there so lonely, with no one near it, and likewise that the King was nowhere to be seen. Then he took out one of the tall tapers, and hid the candlestick under his cloak, and rode away until he should find the King.

On his journey through the forest he was stopped by a man black and ill-favoured, holding a large knife in his hand.

"Ho! you that stand there, have you seen King Arthur?" asked the squire.

"No, but I have met you, and I am glad thereof, for you have under your cloak one of the candlesticks of gold that was placed in honour of the Knight who lies dead in the chapel. Give it to me, and I will carry it back; and if you do not this of your own will, I will make you."

"By my faith!" cried the squire, "I will never yield it to you!

Rather, will I carry it off and make a present of it to King Arthur."

"You will pay for it dearly," answered the man, "if you yield it not up forthwith."

To this the squire did not make answer, but dashed forward, thinking to pass him by; but the man thrust at him with his knife, and it entered his body up to the hilt. And when the squire dreamed this, he cried, "Help! help! for I am a dead man!"

As soon as the King and the Queen heard that cry they awoke from their sleep, and the Chamberlain said, "Sir, you must be moving, for it is day"; and the King rose and dressed himself, and put on his shoes. Then the cry came again: "Fetch me a priest, for I die!" and the King ran at great speed into the hall, while the Queen and the Chamberlain followed him with torches and candles. "What aileth you?" asked the King of his squire, and the squire told him of all that he had dreamed. "Ha," said the King, "is it, then, a dream?" "Yes, Sir," answered the squire, "but it is a right foul dream for me, for right foully it hath come true," and he lifted his left arm, and said, "Sir, look you here! Lo, here is the knife that was struck in my side up to the haft." After that, he drew forth the candlestick, and showed it to the King. "Sir, for this candlestick that I present to you was I wounded to the death!" The King took the candlestick in his hands and looked at it, and none so rich had he seen before, and he bade the Queen look also. "Sir," said the squire again, "draw not forth the knife out of my body till I be shriven of the priest." So the King commanded that a priest should be sent for, and when the squire had confessed his sins, the King drew the knife out of the body and the soul departed forthwith. Then the King grieved that the young man had come to his death in such strange wise, and ordered him a fair burial, and desired that the golden candlestick should be sent to the Church of Saint Paul in London, which at that time was newly built.

After this King Arthur would have none to go with him on his quest, and many strange adventures he achieved before he reached the chapel of St. Augustine, which was in the midst of the White Forest. There he alighted from his horse, and sought to enter, but though there was neither door nor bar he might not pass the threshold. But from without he heard wondrous voices singing, and saw a light shining brighter than any that he had seen before, and visions such as he scarcely dared to look upon. And he resolved greatly to amend his sins, and to bring peace and order into his kingdom. So he set forth, strengthened and comforted, and after divers more adventures returned to his Court.

II

It was on the eve of Pentecost that all the Knights of the Table Round met together at Camelot, and a great feast was made ready for them. And as they sat at supper they heard a loud noise, as of the crashing of thunder, and it seemed as if the roof would fall on them. Then, in the midst of the thunder, there entered a sunbeam, brighter by seven times than the brightest day, and its brightness was not of this world. The Knights held their peace, but every man looked at his neighbour, and his countenance shone fairer than ever it had done before. As they sat dumb, for their tongues felt as if they could speak nothing, there floated in the hall the Holy Graal, and over it a veil of white samite, so that none might see it nor who bare it. But sweet odours filled the place, and every Knight had set before him the food he loved best; and after that the Holy Vessel departed suddenly, they wist not where. When it had gone their tongues were loosened, and the King gave thanks for the wonders that they had been permitted to see. After that he had finished, Sir Gawaine stood up and vowed to depart the next morning in quest of the Holy Graal, and not to return until he had seen it. "But if after a year and a day I may not speed in my quest," said he, "I shall come again, for I shall know that the sight of it is not for me." And many of the Knights there sitting swore a like vow.

But King Arthur, when he heard this, was sore displeased. "Alas!" cried he unto Sir Gawaine, "you have undone me by your vow. For through you is broken up the fairest fellowship, and the truest of knighthood, that ever the world saw, and when they have once departed they shall meet no more at the Table Round, for many shall die in the quest. It grieves me sore, for I have loved them as well as my own life." So he spoke, and paused, and tears came into his eyes. "Ah, Gawaine, Gawaine! you have set me in great sorrow."

"Comfort yourself," said Sir Lancelot, "for we shall win for ourselves great honour, and much more than if we had died in any other wise, since die we must." But the King would not be comforted, and the Queen and all the Court were troubled also for the love which they had to these Knights. Then the Queen came to

Sir Galahad, who was sitting among those Knights though younger he was than any of them, and asked him whence he came, and of what country, and if he was son to Sir Lancelot. And King Arthur did him great honour, and he rested him in his own bed. And next morning the King and Queen went into the Minster, and the Knights followed them, dressed all in armour, save only their shields and their helmets. When the service was finished the King would know how many of the fellowship had sworn to undertake the quest of the Graal, and they were counted, and found to number a hundred and fifty. They bade farewell, and mounted their horses, and rode through the streets of Camelot, and there was weeping of both rich and poor, and the King could not speak for weeping. And at sunrise they all parted company with each other, and every Knight took the way he best liked.

III

Now Sir Galahad had as yet no shield, and he rode four days without meeting any adventure, till at last he came to a White Abbey, where he dismounted and asked if he might sleep there that night. The brethren received him with great reverence, and led him to a chamber, where he took off his armour, and then saw that he was in the presence of two Knights. "Sirs," said Sir Galahad, "what adventure brought you hither?" "Sir," replied they, "we heard that within this Abbey is a shield that no man may hang round his neck without being dead within three days, or some mischief befalling him. And if we fail in the adventure, you shall take it upon you." "Sirs," replied Sir Galahad, "I agree well thereto, for as yet I have no shield."

So on the morn they arose and heard Mass, and then a monk led them behind an altar where hung a shield white as snow, with a red cross in the middle of it. "Sirs," said the monk, "this shield cannot be hung round no Knight's neck, unless he be the worthiest Knight in the world, and therefore I counsel you to be well advised."

"Well," answered one of the Knights, whose name was King Bagdemagus, "I know truly that I am not the best Knight in the world, but yet shall I try to bear it," and he bare it out of the Abbey. Then he said to Sir Galahad, "I pray you abide here still, till you know how I shall speed," and he rode away, taking with him a squire to send tidings back to Sir Galahad.

After King Bagdemagus had ridden two miles he entered a fair valley, and there met him a goodly Knight seated on a white horse and clad in white armour. And they came together with their spears, and Sir Bagdemagus was borne from his horse, for the shield covered him not at all. Therewith the strange Knight alighted and took the white shield from him, and gave it to the squire, saying, "Bear this shield to the good Knight Sir Galahad that thou hast left in the Abbey, and greet him well from me."

"Sir," said the squire, "what is your name?"

"Take thou no heed of my name," answered the Knight, "for it is not for thee to know, nor for any earthly man."

"Now, fair Sir," said the squire, "tell me for what cause this shield may not be borne lest ill befalls him who bears it."

"Since you have asked me," answered the Knight, "know that no man shall bear this shield, save Sir Galahad only."

Then the squire turned to Bagdemagus, and asked him whether he were wounded or not. "Yes, truly," said he, "and I shall hardly escape from death"; and scarcely could he climb on to his horse's back when the squire brought it near him. But the squire led him to a monastery that lay in the valley, and there he was treated of his wounds, and after long lying came back to life. After the squire had given the Knight into the care of the monks, he rode back to the Abbey, bearing with him the shield. "Sir Galahad," said he, alighting before him, "the Knight that wounded Bagdemagus sends you greeting, and bids you bear this shield, which shall bring you many adventures."

"Now blessed be God and fortune," answered Sir Galahad, and called for his arms, and mounted his horse, hanging the shield about his neck. Then, followed by the squire, he set out. They rode straight to the hermitage, where they saw the White Knight who had sent the shield to Sir Galahad. The two Knights saluted each other courteously, and then the White Knight told Sir Galahad the story of the shield, and how it had been given into his charge. Afterwards they parted, and Sir Galahad and his squire returned unto the Abbey whence they came.

The monks made great joy at seeing Sir Galahad again, for they feared he was gone for ever; and as soon as he was alighted from his horse they brought him unto a tomb in the churchyard where there was night and day such a noise that any man who heard it should be driven nigh mad, or else lose his strength. "Sir," they said, "we deem it a fiend." Sir Galahad drew near, all armed save his helmet, and stood by the tomb. "Lift up the stone," said a monk, and Galahad lifted it, and a voice cried, "Come thou not nigh me, Sir Galahad, for thou shalt make me go again where I have been so long." But Galahad took no heed of him, and lifted the stone yet higher, and there rushed from the tomb a foul smoke, and in the midst of it leaped out the foulest figure that ever was seen in the likeness of a man. "Galahad," said the figure, "I see about thee so many angels that my power dare not touch thee." Then Galahad, stooping down, looked into the tomb, and he saw a body all armed lying there, with a sword by his side. "Fair brother," said Galahad, "let us remove this body, for he is not worthy to be in this churchyard, being a false Christian man."

This being done they all departed and returned unto the monastery, where they lay that night, and the next morning Sir Galahad knighted Melias his squire, as he had promised him aforetime. So Sir Galahad and Sir Melias departed thence, in quest of the Holy Graal, but they soon went their different ways and fell upon different adventures. In his first encounter Sir Melias was sore wounded, and Sir Galahad came to his help, and left him to an old monk who said that he would heal him of his wounds in the space of seven weeks, and that he was thus wounded because he had not come clean to the quest of the Graal, as Sir Galahad had done. Sir Galahad left him there, and rode on till he came to the Castle of Maidens, which he alone might enter who was free from sin. There he chased away the Knights who had seized the castle seven years agone, and restored all to the Duke's daughter, who owned it of right. Besides this he set free the maidens who were kept in prison, and summoned all those Knights in the country round who had held their lands of the Duke, bidding them do homage to his daughter. And in the morning one came to him and told him that as the seven Knights fled from the Castle of Maidens they fell upon the path of Sir Gawaine, Sir Gareth, and Sir Lewaine, who were seeking Sir Galahad, and they gave battle; and the seven Knights were slain by the three Knights. "It is well," said Galahad, and he took his armour and his horse and rode away.

So when Sir Galahad left the Castle of Maidens he rode till he came to a waste forest, and there he met with Sir Lancelot and Sir Percivale; but they knew him not, for he was now disguised. And they fought together, and the two Knights were smitten down out of the saddle. "God be with thee, thou best Knight in the world," cried a nun who dwelt in a hermitage close by; and she said it in a loud voice, so that Lancelot and Percivale might hear. But Sir Galahad feared that she would make known who he was, so he spurred his horse and struck deep into the forest before Sir Lancelot and Sir Percivale could mount again. They knew not which path he had taken, so Sir Percivale turned back to ask advice of the nun, and Sir Lancelot pressed forward.

IV

He halted when he came to a stone cross, which had by it a block of marble, while nigh at hand stood an old chapel. He tied his horse to a tree, and hung his shield on a branch, and looked into the chapel, for the door was waste and broken. And he saw there a fair altar covered with a silken cloth, and a candlestick which had six branches, all of shining silver. A great light streamed from it, and at this sight Sir Lancelot would fain have entered in, but he could not. So he turned back sorrowful and dismayed, and took the saddle and bridle off his horse, and let him pasture where he would, while he himself unlaced his helm, and ungirded his sword, and lay down to sleep upon his shield, at the foot of the cross.

As he lay there, half waking and half sleeping, he saw two white palfreys come by, drawing a litter, wherein lay a sick Knight. When they reached the cross they paused, and Sir Lancelot heard the Knight say, "O sweet Lord, when shall this sorrow leave me, and when shall the Holy Vessel come by me, through which I shall be blessed? For I have endured long, though my ill deeds were few." Thus he spoke, and Sir Lancelot heard it, and of a sudden the great candlestick stood before the cross, though no man had brought it. And with it was a table of silver and the Holy Vessel of the Graal, which Lancelot had seen aforetime. Then the Knight rose up, and on his hands and knees he approached the Holy Vessel, and prayed, and was made whole of his sickness. After that the Graal went back into the chapel, and the light and the candlestick also, and Sir Lancelot would fain have followed, but could not, so heavy was the weight of his sins upon him. And the sick Knight arose and kissed the cross, and saw Sir Lancelot lying at the foot with his eyes shut. "I marvel greatly at this sleeping Knight," he said to his squire, "that he had no power to wake when the Holy Vessel was brought hither." "I dare right well say," answered the squire, "that he dwelleth in some deadly sin, whereof he was never confessed." "By my faith," said the Knight, "he is unhappy, whoever he is, for he is of the fellowship of the Round Table, which have undertaken the quest of the Graal." "Sir," replied the squire, "you have all your arms here, save only your sword and your helm. Take therefore those of this strange Knight, who has just put them off." And the Knight did as his squire said, and took Sir Lancelot's horse also, for it was better than his own.

After they had gone Sir Lancelot waked up wholly, and thought of what he had seen, wondering if he were in a dream or not. Suddenly a voice spoke to him, and it said, "Sir Lancelot, more hard than is the stone, more bitter than is the wood, more naked and barren than is the leaf of the fig tree, art thou; therefore go from hence and withdraw thee from this holy place." When Sir Lancelot heard this, his heart was passing heavy, and he wept, cursing the day when he had been born. But his helm and sword had gone from the spot where he had lain them at the foot of the cross, and his horse was gone also. And he smote himself and cried, "My sin and my wickedness have done me this dishonour; for when I sought worldly adventures for worldly desires I ever achieved them and had the better in every place, and never was I discomfited in any quarrel, were it right or wrong. And now I take upon me the adventures of holy things, I see and understand that my old sin hinders me, so that I could not move nor speak when the Holy Graal passed by." Thus he sorrowed till it was day, and he heard the birds sing, and at that he felt comforted. And as his horse was gone also, he departed on foot with a heavy heart.

V

All this while Sir Percivale had pursued adventures of his own, and came nigh unto losing his life, but he was saved from his enemies by the good Knight, Sir Galahad, whom he did not know, although he was seeking him, for Sir Galahad now bore a red shield, and not a white one. And at last the foes fled deep into the forest, and Sir Galahad followed; but Sir Percivale had no horse and was forced to stay behind. Then his eyes were opened, and he knew it was Sir Galahad who had come to his help, and he sat down under a tree and grieved sore.

While he was sitting there a Knight passed by riding a black horse, and when he was out of sight a yeoman came pricking after as fast as he might, and, seeing Sir Percivale, asked if he had seen a Knight mounted on a black horse. "Yes, Sir, forsooth," answered Sir Percivale, "why do you want to know?" "Ah, Sir, that is my steed which he has taken from me, and wherever my lord shall find me, he is sure to slay me." "Well," said Sir Percivale, "thou seest that I am on foot, but had I a good horse I would soon come up with him." "Take my hackney," said the yeoman, "and do the best you can, and I shall follow you on foot to watch how you speed." So Sir Percivale rode as fast as he might, and at last he saw that Knight, and he hailed him. The Knight turned and set his spear against Sir Percivale, and smote the hackney in the breast, so that he fell dead to the earth, and Sir Percivale fell with him; then the Knight rode away. But Sir Percivale was mad with wrath, and cried to the Knight to return and fight with him on foot, and the Knight answered not and went on his way. When Sir Percivale saw that he would not turn, he threw himself on the ground, and cast away his helm and sword, and bemoaned himself for the most unhappy of all Knights; and there he abode the whole day, and, being faint and weary, slept till it was midnight. And at midnight he waked and saw before him a woman, who said to him right fiercely, "Sir Percivale, what doest thou here?" "Neither good nor great ill," answered he. "If thou wilt promise to do my will when I call upon you," said she, "I will lend you my own horse, and he shall bear thee whither thou shalt choose." This Sir Percivale promised gladly, and the woman went and returned with a black horse, so large and well-apparelled that Sir Percivale marvelled. But he mounted him gladly, and drove in his spurs, and within an hour and less the horse bare him four days' journey hence, and would have borne him into a rough water that roared, had not Sir Percivale pulled at his bridle. The Knight stood doubting, for the water made a great noise, and he feared lest his horse could not get through it. Still, wishing greatly to pass over, he made himself ready, and signed the sign of the cross upon his forehead.

At that the fiend which had taken the shape of a horse shook off Sir Percivale and dashed into the water, crying and making great sorrow; and it seemed to him that the water burned. Then Sir Percivale knew that it was not a horse but a fiend, which would have brought him to perdition, and he gave thanks and prayed all that night long. As soon as it was day he looked about him, and saw he was in a wild mountain, girt round with the sea and filled with wild beasts. Then he rose and went into a valley, and there he saw a young serpent bring a young lion by the neck, and after that there passed a great lion, crying and roaring after the serpent, and a fierce battle began between them. Sir Percivale thought to help the lion, as he was the more natural beast of the twain, and he drew his sword and set his shield before him, and gave the serpent a deadly buffet. When the lion saw that, he made him all the cheer that a beast might make a man, and fawned about him like a spaniel, and stroked him with his paws. And about noon the lion took his little whelp, and placed him on his back, and bare him home again, and Sir Percivale, being left alone, prayed till he was comforted. But at eventide the lion returned, and couched down at his feet, and all night long he and the lion slept together.

VI

As Lancelot went his way through the forest he met with many hermits who dwelled therein, and had adventure with the Knight who stole his horse and his helm, and got them back again. And he learned from one of the hermits that Sir Galahad was his son, and that it was he who at the Feast of Pentecost had sat in the Siege Perilous, which it was ordained by Merlin that none should sit in save the best Knight in the world. All that night Sir Lancelot abode with the hermit and laid him to rest, a hair shirt always on his body, and it pricked him sorely, but he bore it meekly and suffered the pain. When the day dawned he bade the hermit farewell. As he rode he came to a fair plain, in which was a great castle set about with tents and pavilions of divers hues. Here were full five hundred Knights riding on horseback, and those near the castle were mounted on black horses with black trappings, and they that were without were on white horses and their trappings white. And the two sides fought together, and Sir Lancelot looked on.

At last it seemed to him that the black Knights nearest the castle fared the worst, so, as he ever took the part of the weaker, he rode to their help and smote many of the white Knights to the earth and did marvellous deeds of arms. But always the white Knights held round Sir Lancelot to tire him out. And as no man may endure for ever, in the end Sir Lancelot waxed so faint of fighting that his arms would not lift themselves to deal a stroke; then they took him, and led him away into the forest and made him alight from his horse and rest, and when he was taken the fellowship of the castle were overcome for want of him. "Never ere now was I at tournament or jousts but I had the best," moaned Sir Lancelot to himself, as soon as the Knights had left him and he was alone. "But now am I shamed, and I am persuaded that I am more sinful than ever I was." Sorrowfully he rode on till he passed a chapel, where stood a nun, who called to him and asked him his name and what he was seeking.

So he told her who he was, and what had befallen him at the tournament, and the vision that had come to him in his sleep. "Ah, Lancelot," said she, "as long as you were a knight of earthly knighthood you were the most wonderful man in the world and the most adventurous. But now, since you are set among Knights of heavenly adventures, if you were worsted at that tournament it is no marvel. For the tournament was meant for a sign, and the earthly Knights were they who were clothed in black in token of the sins of which they were not yet purged. And the white Knights were they who had chosen the way of holiness, and in them the quest has already begun. Thus you beheld both the sinners and the good men, and when you saw the sinners overcome you went to their help, as they were your fellows in boasting and pride of the world, and all that must be left in that quest. And that caused your misadventure. Now that I have warned you of your vain-glory and your pride, beware of everlasting pain, for of all earthly Knights I have pity of you, for I know well that among earthly sinful Knights you are without peer."

VII

Sir Gawaine rode long without meeting any adventure, and from Pentecost to Michaelmas found none that pleased him. But at Michaelmas he met Sir Ector de Maris and rejoiced greatly.

As they sat talking there appeared before them a hand showing unto the elbow covered with red samite, and holding a great candle that burned right clear; and the hand passed into the chapel and vanished, they knew not where. Then they heard a voice which said, "Knights full of evil faith and poor belief, these two things have failed you, and therefore you may not come to the adventure of the Holy Graal." And this same told them a holy man to whom they confessed their sins, "for," said he, "you have failed in three things, charity, fasting, and truth, and have been great murderers. But sinful as Sir Lancelot was, since he went into the quest he never slew man, nor shall, till he come into Camelot again. For he has taken upon him to forsake sin. And were he not so unstable, he should be the next to achieve it, after Galahad his son. Yet shall he die an holy man, and in earthly sinful men he has no fellow."

"Sir," said Gawaine, "by your words it seems that our sins will not let us labour in that quest?" "Truly," answered the hermit, "there be an hundred such as you to whom it will bring naught but shame." So Gawaine departed and followed Sir Ector, who had ridden on before.

VIII

When Sir Bors left Camelot on his quest he met a holy man riding on an ass, and Sir Bors saluted him. Then the good man knew him to be one of the Knights who were in quest of the Holy Graal. "What are you?" said he, and Sir Bors answered, "I am a Knight that fain would be counselled in the quest of the Graal, for he shall have much earthly worship that brings it to an end." "That is true," said the good man, "for he will be the best Knight in the world, but know well that there shall none attain it but by holiness and by confession of sin." So they rode together till they came to the hermitage, and the good man led Sir Bors into the chapel, where he made confession of his sins, and they ate bread and drank water together. "Now," said the hermit, "I pray you that you eat none other till you sit at the table where the Holy Graal shall be." "Sir," answered Sir Bors, "I agree thereto, but how know you that I shall sit there?" "That know I," said the holy man, "but there will be but few of your fellows with you. Also instead of a shirt you shall wear this garment until you have achieved your quest," and Sir Bors took off his clothes, and put on instead a scarlet coat. Then the good man questioned him, and marvelled to find him pure in life, and he armed him and bade him go. After this Sir Bors rode through many lands, and had many adventures, and was often sore tempted, but remembered the words of the holy man and kept his life clean of wrong. And once he had by mischance almost slain his own brother, but a voice cried, "Flee, Bors, and touch him not," and he hearkened and stayed his hand. And there fell between them a fiery cloud, which burned up both their shields, and they two fell to the earth in a great swoon; but when they awakened out of it Bors saw that his brother had no harm. With that the voice spoke to him saying, "Bors, go hence and bear your brother fellowship no longer; but take your way to the sea, where Sir Percivale abides till you come." Then Sir Bors prayed his brother to forgive him all he had unknowingly done, and rode straight to the sea. On the shore he found a vessel covered with white samite, and as soon as he stepped in the vessel it set sail so fast it might have been flying, and Sir Bors lay down and slept till it was day. When he waked he saw a Knight lying in the midst of the ship, all armed save for his helm, and he knew him for Sir Percivale, and welcomed him with great joy; and they told each other of their adventures and of their temptations, and had great happiness in each other's company. "We lack nothing but Galahad, the good Knight," Sir Percivale said.

IX

Sir Galahad rested one evening at a hermitage. And while he was resting, there came a gentlewoman and asked leave of the hermit to speak with Sir Galahad, and would not be denied, though she was told he was weary and asleep. Then the hermit waked Sir Galahad and bade him rise, as a gentlewoman had great need of him, so Sir Galahad rose and asked her what she wished. "Galahad," said she, "I will that you arm yourself, and mount your horse and follow me, and I will show you the highest adventure that ever any Knight saw." And Sir Galahad bade her go, and he would follow wherever she led. In three days they reached the sea, where they found the ship where Sir Bors and Sir Percivale were lying. And the lady bade him leave his horse behind and said she would leave hers also, but their saddles and bridles they would take on board the ship. This they did, and were received with great joy by the two Knights; then the sails were spread, and the ship was driven before the wind at a marvellous pace till they reached the land of Logris, the entrance to which lies between two great rocks with a whirlpool in the middle.

Their own ship might not get safely through; but they left it and went into another ship that lay there, which had neither man nor woman in it. At the end of the ship was written these words: "Thou man which shalt enter this ship beware thou be in steadfast belief; if thou fail, I shall not help thee." Then the gentlewoman turned and said, "Percivale, do you know who I am?" "No, truly," answered he. "I am your sister, and therefore you are the man in the world that I most love. If you are without faith, or have any hidden sin, beware how you enter, else you will perish." "Fair sister," answered he, "I shall enter therein, for if I am an untrue Knight then shall I perish." So they entered the ship, and it was rich and well adorned, that they all marvelled.

In the midst of it was a fair bed, and Sir Galahad went thereto and found on it a crown of silk, and a sword drawn out of its sheath half a foot and more. The sword was of divers fashions, and the pommel of stone, wrought about with colours, and every colour with its own virtue, and the handle was of the ribs of two beasts. The one was the bone of a serpent, and no hand that handles it shall ever become weary or hurt; and the other is a bone of a fish that swims in Euphrates, and whoso handles it shall not think on joy or sorrow that he has had, but only on that which he beholds before him. And no man shall grip this sword but one that is better than other men. So first Sir Percivale stepped forward and set his hand to the sword, but he might not grasp it. Next Sir Bors tried to seize it, but he also failed. When Sir Galahad beheld the sword, he saw that there was written on it, in letters of blood, that he who tried to draw it should never fail of shame in his body or be wounded to the death. "By my faith," said Galahad, "I would draw this sword out of its sheath, but the offending is so great I shall not lay my hand thereto." "Sir," answered the gentlewoman, "know that no man can draw this sword save you alone"; and she told him many tales of the Knights who had set their hands to it, and of the evil things that had befallen them. And they all begged Sir Galahad to grip the sword, as it was ordained that he should. "I will grip it," said Galahad, "to give you courage, but it belongs no more to me than it does to you." Then he gripped it tight with his fingers, and the gentlewoman girt him about the middle with the sword, and after that they left that ship and went into another, which brought them to land, where they fell upon many strange adventures. And when they had wrought many great deeds, they departed from each other. But first Sir Percivale's sister died, being bled to death, so that another lady might live, and she prayed them to lay her body in a boat and leave the boat to go as the winds and waves carried it. And so it was done, and Sir Percivale wrote a letter telling how she had helped them in all their adventures; and he put it in her right hand, and laid her in a barge, and covered it with black silk. And the wind arose and drove it from their sight.

X

Now we must tell what happened to Sir Lancelot.

When he was come to a water called Mortoise he fell asleep, awaiting for the adventure that should be sent to him, and in his sleep a voice spoke to him, and bade him rise and take his armour, and enter the first ship he should find. So he started up and took his arms and made him ready, and on the strand he found a ship that was without sail or oar. As soon as he was within the ship, he felt himself wrapped round with a sweetness such as he had never known before, as if all that he could desire was fulfilled. And with this joy and peace about him he fell asleep. When he woke he found near him a fair bed, with a dead lady lying on it, whom he knew to be Sir Percivale's sister, and in her hand was the tale of her adventures, which Sir Lancelot took and read. For a month or more they dwelt in that ship together, and one day, when it had drifted near the shore, he heard a sound as of a horse; and when the steps came nearer he saw that a Knight was riding him. At the sight of the ship the Knight alighted and took the saddle and bridle, and entered the ship. "You are welcome," said Lancelot, and the Knight saluted him and said, "What is your name? for my heart goeth out to you."

"Truly," answered he, "my name is Sir Lancelot du Lake."

"Sir," said the new Knight, "you are welcome, for you were the beginner of me in the world."

"Ah," cried Sir Lancelot, "is it you, then, Galahad?"

"Yes, in sooth," said he, and kneeled down and asked Lancelot's blessing, and then took off his helm and kissed him. And there was great joy between them, and they told each other all that had befallen them since they left King Arthur's Court. Then Galahad saw the gentlewoman dead on the bed, and he knew her, and said he held her in great worship, and that she was the best maid in the world, and how it was great pity that she had come to her death. But when Lancelot heard that Galahad had won the marvellous sword he prayed that he might see it, and kissed the pommel and the hilt, and the scabbard. "In truth," he said, "never did I know of adventures so wonderful and strange." So dwelled Lancelot and Galahad in that ship for half a year, and served God daily and nightly with all their power. And after six months had gone it befell that on a Monday they drifted to the edge of the forest, where they saw a Knight with white armour bestriding one horse and holding another all white, by the bridle. And he came to the ship, and saluted the two Knights and said, "Galahad, you have been long enough with your father, therefore leave that ship and start upon this horse, and go on the quest of the Holy Graal." So Galahad went to his father and kissed him, saying, "Fair sweet father, I know not if I shall see you more till I have beheld the Holy Graal." Then they heard a voice which said, "The one shall never see the other till the day of doom." "Now, Galahad," said Lancelot, "since we are to bid farewell for ever now, I pray to the great Father to preserve me and you both." "Sir," answered Galahad, "no prayer availeth so much as yours."

The next day Sir Lancelot made his way back to Camelot, where he found King Arthur and Guenevere; but many of the Knights of the Round Table were slain and destroyed, more than the half. All the Court was passing glad to see Sir Lancelot, and the King asked many tidings of his son Sir Galahad.

XI

Sir Galahad rode on till he met Sir Percivale and afterwards Sir Bors, whom they greeted most gladly, and they bare each other company. First they came to the Castle of Carbonek, where dwelled King Pelles, who welcomed them with joy, for he knew by their coming that they had fulfilled the quest of the Graal. They then departed on other adventures, and with the blood out of the Holy Lance Galahad anointed the maimed King and healed him. That same night at midnight a voice bade them arise and quit the castle, which they did, followed by three Knights of Gaul. Then Galahad prayed every one of them that if they reached King Arthur's Court they should salute Sir Lancelot his father, and those Knights of the Round Table that were present, and with that he left them, and Sir Bors and Sir Percivale with him. For three days they rode till they came to a shore, and found a ship awaiting them. And in the midst of it was the table of silver, and the Holy Graal which was covered with red samite. Then were their hearts right glad, and they made great reverence thereto, and Galahad prayed that at what time he asked, he might depart out of this world. So long he prayed that at length a voice said to him, "Galahad, thou shalt have thy desire, and when thou askest the death of the body thou shalt have it, and shalt find the life of the soul." Percivale likewise heard the voice, and besought Galahad to tell him why he asked such things. And Galahad answered, "The other day when we saw a part of the adventures of the Holy Graal, I was in such a joy of heart that never did man feel before, and I knew well that when my body is dead my soul shall be in joy of which the other was but a shadow."

Some time were the three Knights in that ship, till at length they saw before them the city of Sarras. Then they took from the ship the table of silver, and Sir Percivale and Sir Bors went first, and Sir Galahad followed after to the gate of the city, where sat an old man that was crooked. At the sight of the old man Sir Galahad called to him to help them carry the table, for it was heavy. "Truly," answered the old man, "it is ten years since I have gone without crutches." "Care not for that," said Galahad, "but rise up and show your good will." So he arose and found himself as whole as ever he was, and he ran to the table and held up the side next Galahad. And there was much noise in the city that a cripple was healed by three Knights newly entered in. This reached the ears of the King, who sent for the Knights and questioned them. And they told him the truth, and of the Holy Graal; but the King listened nothing to all they said, but put them into a deep hole in the prison. Even here they were not without comfort, for a vision of the Holy Graal sustained them. And at the end of a year the King lay sick and felt he should die, and he called the three Knights and asked forgiveness of the evil he had done to them, which they gave gladly. Then he died, and the whole city was afraid and knew not what to do, till while they were in counsel a voice came to them and bade them choose the youngest of the three strange Knights for their King. And they did so. After Galahad was proclaimed King, he ordered that a coffer of gold and precious stones should be made to encompass the table of silver, and every day he and the two Knights would kneel before it and make their prayers.

Now at the year's end, and on the selfsame day that Galahad had been crowned King, he arose up early and came with the two Knights to the Palace; and he saw a man in the likeness of a Bishop, encircled by a great crowd of angels, kneeling before the Holy Vessel. And he called to Galahad and said to him, "Come forth, thou servant of Christ, and thou shalt see what thou hast much desired to see." Then Galahad began to tremble right hard, when the flesh first beheld the things of the spirit, and he held up his hands to heaven and said, "Lord, I thank thee, for now I see that which hath been my desire for many a day. Now, blessed Lord, I would no longer live, if it might please Thee." Then Galahad went to Percivale and kissed him, and commended him to God; and he went to Sir Bors and kissed him, and commended him to God, and said, "Fair lord, salute me to my lord Sir Lancelot, my father, and bid him remember this unstable world." Therewith he kneeled down before the table and made his prayers, and while he was praying his soul suddenly left the body and was carried by angels up into heaven, which the two Knights right well beheld. Also they saw come from heaven a hand, but no body behind it, and it came unto the Vessel, and took it and the spear, and bare them back to heaven. And since then no man has dared to say that he has seen the Holy Graal.

When Percivale and Bors saw Galahad lying dead they made as

much sorrow as ever two men did, and the people of the country and of the city were right heavy. And they buried him as befitted their King. As soon as Galahad was buried, Sir Percivale sought a hermitage outside the city, and put on the dress of a hermit, and Sir Bors was always with him, but kept the dress that he wore at Court. When a year and two months had passed Sir Percivale died also, and was buried by the side of Galahad; and Sir Bors left that land, and after long riding came to Camelot. Then was there great joy made of him in the Court, for they had held him as dead; and the King ordered great clerks to attend him, and to write down all his adventures and those of Sir Percivale and Sir Galahad. Next, Sir Lancelot told the adventures of the Graal which he had seen, and this likewise was written and placed with the other in almonries at Salisbury. And by and by Sir Bors said to Sir Lancelot, "Galahad your son saluteth you by me, and after you King Arthur and all the Court, and so did Sir Percivale; for I buried them with mine own hands in the City of Sarras. Also, Sir Lancelot, Galahad prayeth you to remember of this uncertain world, as you promised when you were together!" "That is true," said Sir Lancelot, "and I trust his prayer may avail me." But the prayer but little availed Sir Lancelot, for he fell to his old sins again. And now the Knights were few that survived the search for the Graal, and the evil days of Arthur began.

MADOC THE DOOR WARD

Douglas Carmichael

*The friction at Arthur's court as the final days draw near is never
more evident than in an episode where Guinevere is charged with
murder. It was the episode that inspired Phyllis Ann Karr's novel*
The Idylls of the Queen *(1982). The following version is by Douglas
Carmichael (b. 1923), an American professor of philosophy, and
comes from his unpublished novel* Last of the Dragons. *This was
a sequel to* Pendragon *(1977), a powerful historical novel which
traces the rise to power of the young Arthur.*

By ones and twos and threes the cataphracts of Artorius, the mail-clad
warriors who rode the big armored horses, came drifting back from
their quest for the goddess Coventina's Holy Platter of Plenty. Burrus
and some of the other Christians among them rather surprisingly
claimed it as the dish or wine cup used at the last supper eaten
by their Christ. Gwalchmai had actually seen it and said it was a
platter. Peredur must have seen it too, since he had stayed at the
remote and mysterious fort where it was kept.

Artorius listened to the different tales and laughed. "Whatever
god it belongs to, it seems to be holy, all right. There's been better
weather for the crops ever since Gwalchmai glimpsed it, and better
yet since Peredur asked what seems to have been the right question
about it. And if Peredur can let his uncle Pellam die in peace, he'll
be busy there at Caer Bannog for a while, and that's one less

of Pellionarius' brood to be cutting down Loth's." He paused a moment in reminiscence, and then went on, "Of the fathers, though, I preferred Pellionarius. I just hope enough men come back so we don't have to train too many new cataphracts this year. More than thirty and we'll have trouble horsing them all."

His wife Vinavera smoothed her gown and moistened her lips. "No word yet of Lance?"

Artorius smiled. "Not yet, but the fame of his latest exploits usually comes two or three days before he does. Listen for the bards."

Lanceolatus returned to Camulodunum, however, well before there were any new songs about him. It didn't matter to Vinavera; there was song enough soaring through her thoughts when she saw the curly, still-dark hair and the smooth-cut features once more at the Table. The inner music reached a crescendo in the middle hours of the night when a familiar scratching sounded at the door of her chamber. She whispered to her serving-maid Gwgon to draw the bar, and in a moment Lanceolatus' arms had reclaimed her. She sank into their depths and drew his face to hers.

His hunger matched her own, and in the following days they met frequently in her chamber when the fire in the hall burned low, in a honeysuckle thicket below the southwest rampart, and once or twice at his house, two hundred paces across the hill, when it was dark and there were no passers-by to recognize her as she slipped in. How many knew of their love, Vinavera had no idea. Certainly her chamber women did, tactfully burrowing into the rugs on their pallets and snoring when Lanceolatus entered. His servants also, who met her at the door with faces set like masks and lit her to his chamber. Artorius? It was many years since the period when he'd avoided her bed, after that unwitting and damnable encounter with his half-sister Morgause, but he came to it only with a certain regularity, assuring himself by a word in advance that she would be receptive. She never caught glances pass between him and Lance when he made such appointments, though they has been the closest of friends since early manhood and Lance had never had to make a hasty departure to avoid him. As for other people, Vinavera was sure some guessed, but she doubted that any knew for certain.

She sighed one night as she laid her head on Lance's firm shoulder. "It's all the monks say of Heaven to have you back again, Lance."

"I doubt it's quite *what* they say. You are married to Bear."

"Bear" was the nickname they both used for and to Artorius.

Arthyr was his name in British, derived from *Artza*, the name in the fairy tongue that Myrddin had given him in his infancy and which meant *bear* in that language.

"Yes, I *am* married to him, but don't they say that in heaven there is no marriage or giving in marriage?"

"You make it sound like the unbelievers' Isles of the Blest. But here on earth there is marriage." He fell silent a moment. "Perhaps it's because of your marriage that I never saw the Platter unveiled."

"Gwalchmai is no maiden. Nor Peredur, from all I hear. Don't take your lapse to heart as Bear did, or you might condemn me to the arms of still a third man."

Lanceolatus eased himself away from her and swung his feet to the floor. "God keep you from anyone else's, but perhaps you are too much in mine. Three weeks I've been back, and ten times we've come together. I'm afraid some tongues will be wagging."

"The brave Lanceolatus knows fear?"

"My sword can't cut into words when I don't even know who speaks them."

Vinavera sat up with a frown. "Who would dare to talk about us?"

"Agrippinus has always had an open mouth for gossip, and I saw him eyeing you speculatively at the Table yesterday. When his eyes met mine, he dropped them to his wine cup."

"We can't have people voicing all their guesses. Maybe you should challenge him to *gornest*?" Though she was speaking in her usual Latin, she used the British word for the judicial combat for which the Romans' law had no equivalent.

"On what pretext? Shall I say in public that he slanders the empress by linking her name with mine? For *gornest* I must make a clear accusation, or God might shield him from my sword. Besides, he's Bear's nephew, and there's nothing I've actually heard him say. Perhaps I should divert attention by courting some other woman." He pursed his lips a moment. "Helena of Astolat has skin like a lily."

Vinavera almost snapped at him. "How do you know?"

"Only from appearance."

"Any girl's skin at sixteen will be like a lily compared to the bark of a forty-year old tree."

"Well, how about Helena of Gododdin?"

"Gwalchmai's sister? There are too many Helena's. Don't run through the list, or I'll take you for a common lecher eager to get rid of me."

"If you won't let me find some other woman to screen myself with, maybe I should simply absent myself from court a while."

"And how will you explain that?"

"An errant disposition."

Vinavera tossed her head. "Two can play at screens. While you're gone, some time when Artorius is away too, I'll give an intimate dinner for just a dozen or so selected warriors. You're not the only sturdy man with scars in attractive places."

He laughed. "Between us we'll give the rumour-mongers something to puzzle over. Just let me come back by the Calends of each month."

"How could I keep you away? Bear needs you. Where will you go? Your Fort of Joy, up there on the Wall of Hadrian?"

"I'll keep in couch with Burrus, but if any other people know where I am, they'll think I'm just watching my chance to return. I'll simply disappear."

The idea left Vinavera vaguely dissatisfied, but she supposed it was for the best. She didn't even give the gossips a treat by going to the ramparts to watch Lance's departure. Two days later, when Artorius left with a troop of cataphracts to inspect the garrisons shielding Londinium from the new settlements of the East Anglians among the Iceni, she bade him an affectionate public farewell. The next day she summoned Caius, the Emperor's steward and foster-brother to help her plan a private dinner.

"Where would you like to hold it?" he asked. "It's warm enough now to clear everybody out of the hall, if you like. They can visit friends till your guests are gone."

"I don't want to inconvenience so many. Can't you bring tables enough into my chamber?"

"The trestles will fit below the bed. What shall we serve on them? Young ducklings, pheasant, and grouse for the first remove?"

"I leave it to you, Caius.

Whom shall I invite?"

The steward smiled. "If you're having Gwalchami, we'd better bring out the last of last year's apples. It's not dinner for him without at least one apple to end it."

"Lord of the Apples, don't they call him? Very well. Gwalchmai and some good apples. His brothers, too."

"All of them?"

"Even Medraut. Though perhaps we'd better have some wild apples for him." Vinavera felt free to show her feelings to her husband's foster brother.

"Whom else?" asked Caius.

"Some of Lanceolatus' kin – Hector, Burrus, and Leonillus. Brian of the Isles, Astamor, and that new Hibernian, Padraic."

"That cousin of Madoc the Door Ward's? That might cause difficulty. He claims he's been the lover of four different queens in Ireland."

"So now with any encouragement he'll try to add an empress to his list? He'll find there's a difference. Queens are six for a penny there, but he's handsome enough to decorate the room. And then let's ask Peasant, and Aliduc, and Pinel – what do they call him? Pinel the Wild Man?"

"He might be too wild to have at the same dinner with Gwalchmai. He's a cousin of Lamorac's, you know."

"And the feud still smoulders, doesn't it?" Vinavera shook her head. "He wouldn't get violent in my presence, I think. Artorius has bound them all to keep the peace. If the Gododdin clan didn't dare kill Pellionarius till they caught him two days' march away, Pinel won't try anything here, and he has a good turn of phrase. Besides, if Dyfed and Gododdin get squeezed into the same room often enough, maybe they'll find each other such charming company they'll make peace."

Caius appeared dubious, but Vinavera liked the idea of peace-making, even if she had to make her guests swallow more gorge than dainties.

She was glad she had begged Artorius to build her a private room there at the end of the great hall in Camulodunum. The place still fell far short of the many-chambered villas of her girlhood, but at least she could talk cosily to small groups without being watched by half the soldiers lounging in the hall. She could understand the strategic advantages for Artorius in using the old hill-fort at Camulodunum as his main base, but she was always happy when something took them to Caer Leon – or any other place where civilised quarters had survived from the days of Rome. Artorius bore a Roman name and title, and he tried to maintain the ways of the City, but the people of Britain had fallen sadly away from its customs, even since her father's time.

On the day of her special feast, Vinavera greeted her guests at the door of her chamber, trying by her manner to show any watchers in the hall that she took as much delight in all of them as she did in Lanceolatus when he was present. She hoped she wasn't being too effusive. With those she had known as long as Gwalchmai, Caius, or Burrus, the right note came easily. When the burly Madoc arrived with his cousin Padraic, though, the half-smile on the latter's lips broadening almost to a smirk as his eyes swept her from the toes upwards, she bridled slightly.

"We can't boast as many queens as Ireland, Padraic, but I hope our hospitality will recompense the lack."

He bowed. "Britain keeps showing me it has new things to boast of." His glance lingered on her as he passed, till she saw Madoc dig an elbow into his ribs. The preening cock pheasant! How did he keep that pretty face so unscarred through all the wars those Irish queens were supposed to have stirred up over him?

Vinavera re-arranged her expression for young Astamor, nearly as handsome as Padraic, but with a becoming shyness. If she needed a mild flirtation to divert attention from Lanceolatus, he might do. "Are you posted to a troop yet, Astamor, now that you've finished your training?"

"To the lord Gruffydd's, lady, at Luguvallium. I leave on the Ides of September."

A pleasant youngster. Behind him came Pinel, his eyes roaming the room till they fell on Gwalchmai, then shifting quickly to her as he murmured a respectful greeting. He wore voluminous sleeves from which he almost had trouble extricating a hand to bring her fingers to his lips. He started towards the end of the table where Gwalchmai stood talking with Peasant. Vinavera wondered for a moment if he were going to live up to his sobriquet of the Wild Man, but he halted some feet away, his baggy sleeve brushing a bowl of fruit that stood at the edge of the table.

"Pinel!" she called. "From this window you can see the recruits practicing archery! Didn't someone tell me you pride yourself as a bowman?"

Before she could pursue the matter, Caius was bowing to her, and Vinavera took her place at the head of the table, signing to her women to intersperse themselves among the soldiers. She had placed herself between Pinel and Burrus, whom she began asking about Peredur's crippled uncle at Caer Bannog. Burrus was quaintly embarrassed, she noticed, at describing Pellam's long-festering wound. "A spear thrust through the thighs," he called it. And all that lay between?

Caius' slaves brought the dishes on promptly and in good order. Three removes of well-seasoned meats they shared, and the time came for the fruits and sweets. "Padraic!" she called, to where he sat near the far end. "Let the Lord of the Apples initiate the fruit course! Pass the bowl to Gwalchmai!"

"I must levy tribute on all goods that pass," the impudent

Hibernian retorted, and took a large golden apple from the top of the mound in the silver bowl.

Pinel, Vinavera noted from the corner of her eye, looked startled. "At least take one from the lower slopes, Padraic," he interjected, "and let the Lord of the Apples claim the summit!"

"Only if his lips are quicker than mine," laughed Padraic, and as Gwalchmai scowled he took a large bite from the apple, following it quickly with several more.

He passed on the bowl, but before it reached the end of the table he gasped and clutched at his throat. Grabbing at his wine cup, he gulped down a large draft and choked, spewing red wine and gobbets of apple halfway across the table, then collapsed on the floor with inarticulate screams. Vinavera watched in horror, her thoughts flashing back to the serving wench who brought the lethal tunic his half-sister Morgana once sent Artorius and donned it herself at her insistence Vinavera wished she'd invited Nimu to the feast. The priestess of the lake-goddess had been a good source of lore in the days since Myrddin's disappearance.

Padraic's vomiting passed quickly into rigidity as he lay in the centre of an awed circle. Burrus knelt to sniff his lips. "Wolfbane," he said.

"Poison," breathed Madoc, then shouted, "Who killed my cousin?"

"Whom would the poison have been meant for but me?" cried Gwalchmai. "Everyone knows I love fruit, and I'd have taken that apple myself if Padraic hadn't levied his tribute, as he called it." He turned to Vinavera. "You told him to pass it to me, lady."

"And you planned the feast," urged Madoc. His words came in a rush. "I don't know why you wanted Gwalchmai dead, lady, but your scheme miscarried, and I have a cousin killed by it!" The door ward's hand was on his sword as he glared around the circle of warriors. "Empress she may be, but I charge her with Padraic's murder, and I'll repeat that charge to the Emperor!"

It was Vinavera's turn to look around the assemblage. She had thought them all her friends, but to her amazement no one voiced a protest. "Gwalchmai," she faltered. "Twenty years I've known you. Can you believe I'd—"

He looked at the floor. "Gladly I'd disbelieve it, lady, but I know the making of the feast was yours. Either you or your slaves must have dealt in poison."

"Why not one of the slaves? Or even Caius? Couldn't some slave in the kitchen have done it?"

Caius shifted his feet. "Kitchen slaves don't know who will eat from a dish, and the ones who serve them rarely fill them."

Gaeris was looking at the other apples in the bowl, sniffing them one by one. "No others," he said.

"Why would I do it?" cried Vinavera. "Doesn't anyone believe me? Garedd? Persant? Somebody?"

"How do we know it was even an accident?" shouted Madoc. "You couldn't hide your scorn for Padraic when we came!"

Wildly Vinavera looked again around the group. Some met her glance accusingly. Others shuffled or looked away. None spoke in her defense. With a cry she rushed to Artorius' chamber next door and flung herself on the bed, sobbing.

Artorius returned four days later, hastened in part by a frantic letter from Vinavera but also, no doubt, by an official report from Aristius, the justiciar. Vinavera had expected to meet him at the gate and explain to him the absurdity of Madoc's accusation when they were alone together, but he sent her word by Aristius to remain in her chamber until it was time to make formal reply to Madoc's charges. He even sent a new serving woman, Morfudd of Cilgerran, to vouch that there was no communication between their chambers.

"What does he think I am?" she exclaimed. "Some woman of the streets? Artorius is Emperor, and I am his wife!"

"The Emperor is Caesar," said Aristius, "or even above the Caesars, since they started using that title for sub-emperors, and there's a saying of our fathers that Caesar's wife must be above suspicion."

"And I'm suspected by all my guests," she added bitterly.

"The lord Artorius has tried to restore justice to Britain. It would hardly be even-handed for him to confer privately with one party to a suit before hearing the plea."

Artorius always took a special pride, she knew, in preparing his public appearances to dispense justice. She remembered the stake erected for her burning when Melwas accused her of adultery. Only Lance had saved her then. If she'd had more confidence in Artorius' arriving at justice in this case, she could have better savored the irony of being once again its likely victim. When he summoned her the next morning, she found him in his purple robe and diadem seated on his chair of state. At the call for pleas, Madoc stepped forward and repeated his accusation from the dinner. "I say that the lady Vinavera served poisoned apples at her banquet and that my cousin Padraic died from eating one. I demand that she be condemned to death by fire, lest her evil contaminate the earth."

Vinavera remembered women she had seen burned at the stake, and she shuddered. Artorius was speaking to her. "Lady, how do you respond to this charge?"

She looked straight at Madoc and tried to load her eyes and voice with contempt. "That Padraic ate a poisoned apple from my table, lord, I admit. That I knew it was poisoned and that I intended his or anyone's death at that dinner, I deny."

"There is a contradiction between plaintiff and defendant," said Artorius, with stiff formality. "Does the plaintiff offer evidence in support of his charge?"

"What evidence is needed?" demanded Madoc. "My cousin Padraic lies poisoned!"

Vinavera saw her husband's knuckles whiten as they clutched the arms of his throne, and she felt a moment's hope. Artorius whispered briefly with Aristius and Gwythyr, his advisers on Roman and tribal law respectively.

"In the absence of witnesses to the implanting of poison into the apple," he declared, "we have only the assertion and denial of the criminal act by the word of the parties. If the defendant were a warrior, it would be, under the customs of the Dumnonii, an occasion for *gornest*, with the truth to be revealed by the outcome given the combat by the gods. Since the defendant is a woman, she may be represented by any warrior who will swear to the truth of her statements. I would take this oath and fight in my wife's cause myself, but as judge I may not take sides. I assume, however, that she will not be wholly disdained and that some good warrior will risk his body in her behalf."

There was a silence in the hall, broken by Madoc. "None come forward, lord, and there were twenty-four at that dinner! Silence gives consent!"

"They aren't all here!" cried Vinavera. "Someone will give you the lie!"

"It would be a disgrace to me if none did," said Artorius. "I doubt you'll be friendless. Madoc, be ready for *gornest* on the field of the cataphracts in fifteen days. The Empress will be ready then for judgment. If a champion appears for her, the gods will decide the right. If none comes forward, then the law demands that she be burned. Until then, avoid my court, lest my justice waver."

Madoc left after a final glare. As the assembly broke up, Artorius took Vinavera by the hand and led her into his own chamber, next to hers. Alone together, he held her at arm's length and shook his head. "*How* did all this happen?" he asked her.

"I don't know," she said. "You heard as much in there as I know of it."

He dropped his hands and went to the window. "I don't want you burned, and I don't believe you did it, but after twenty years of bringing the land back to order I don't want to admit before everybody that there's one law for my wife and another for all others."

Vinavera produced a weak smile. "If burning wasn't such a particularly terrible death, I might tell you to do whatever you think just. Why must queens burn? Common folk just get hanged."

"Myrddin explained it to me once. There's so much magic to a king or queen that when it turns bad, only fire will wipe it out. Lest it contaminate the earth, as Madoc said."

"You haven't yet burned Morgana for trying to kill you three times, and you've held her a prisoner since the sack of Caer Loyw."

Artorius looked uncomfortable. "Had she attempted anyone else's death, I'd have torched her without a qualm, but when I'm the aggrieved party and she's of my own blood, I'm reluctant."

"She sought her husband Urien's death, too."

"And small waste it would have been. He was at least consenting to mine."

"I've never heard of a king burning."

"We're lucky. We can always die in battle before anyone can light the faggots. Where's Lanceolatus off to? He'd fight for you if he were here."

"His cousins aren't even sure if he's still in Britain."

"He'd have told me if he were going to Gaul." He spoke with some vexation. "What's the matter that you can't keep him by you?"

How much did Artorius know? Vinavera was on the verge of telling him of their agreement to see each other less often, but he continued speaking. "Twenty-four men and women at your dinner when Padraic died, and if none of them take up arms for you, it's a gross slander." He stood drumming his fingers on the table. "Burrus. It's not for nothing they call him Burrus the Dog. He's brave, faithful, and able. We'll ask him."

Lanceolatus' cousin was summoned, and Vinavera asked him to represent her in combat. Burrus tightened his lips. "You ask a lot of me, lady. I don't fear Madoc, but I was present at that dinner myself, and how can I swear to your innocence unless I know who the guilty person is? And if I don't reveal his name, they'll think I'm in league with him."

"You do think I'm innocent, don't you?"

"I do, but Lanceolatus would say it more forcefully. He would—" Burrus glanced at Artorius and fell silent.

Vinavera threw herself to her knees before him. "If you don't help me, Burrus," she said quietly, "I shall die in pain and disgrace." Quickly Burrus drew her up. "I'm none to kneel to, lady."

Artorius spoke. "Take pity on my empress, Burrus, and on me. Fight for Lanceolatus' sake even if not for hers."

Burrus sighed. "It's a large request, lord. Many of your other captains will be angry with me if I represent her. But since you ask it of me, I'll take up her cause unless some better champion comes along."

"I shall be satisfied," said Vinavera. "There could be few better."

Looking embarrassed, Burrus withdrew.

For the next two weeks the shadow of the approaching *gornest* hung over the court. Vinavera sent men searching for Lanceolatus in all the places she could think of, and kept a close watch on Burrus' health. If he so much as sneezed, she felt the heat of the flames.

"What if Madoc strikes him down and puts his sword to his throat?" she asked Artorius. "Won't he have to yield?"

"If he wants his life. And if he's on the ground, it would prove nothing different of the gods' will. The laws of the City are better on such matters. They demand human evidence."

"When Gwalchmai fought that *gornest* in Rheged years ago, you had Gruffydd ready to interrupt it with an alarm from the picket line. Can't you do something like that here?"

"We aren't at war now, and there's no likely enemy, but don't think I haven't thought of it. Clodius is commander of the decury on duty. I've told him to watch from the door of the hall, and if Burrus is failing, he's to sound the alarm for fire."

"Won't people suspect, if they see no flames?"

Artorius' face became grim. "He'll be alone, and he'll have a torch ready to fire the thatch. I"d rather lose my hall than my empress."

For the *gornest* Vinavera was escorted to the drill field below the hill of Camulodunum by old Baldwin, the Frank who had first come to Britain as a mercenary for King Uther and had held the post of constable since Artorius first ascended the throne of his original petty kingdom of Glywyssing. Today he led her to a railed enclosure beside Artorius' dais. Inside it stood a stake with bundles of brushwood piled high around it.

Vinavera walked more stiffly, lest any should think her shuddering, and looked for Burrus. Modoc was apparently looking for him too. Already before the dais, he kept shuffling his feet and looking towards the road down form the fort. "Where is her champion?" he burst out to Artorius. "Tell him to come out if he dares!"

"He will come," said Artorius calmly. As he spoke, Burrus appeared at the gate of the fort, riding at his leisure down the curving road, reining in his horse to exchange words with various people along the way.

"He dallies, lord!" shouted Madoc. "Don't let his dying take him any longer than Padraic's!"

"Madoc gets hot when he's angry," whispered Baldwin. "Burrus will be delaying him on purpose."

"To give his strokes more power?"

"With less accuracy." Baldwin spoke like a connoisseur, and Vinavera envied his detachment.

Before the Emperor, Burrus dismounted. Madoc was already on foot. Artorius discouraged *gornests*, and he insisted that even if any of his men wished to kill each other they shouldn't imperil any valuable war horses. The two warriors knelt before him and took their oaths to Vinavera's guilt and innocence respectively. At that moment, there was a pounding of hooves, and all eyes turned to see a warrior galloping out of the woods to the northeast. Vinavera's breast swelled with joyful recognition.

"I accepted this combat only if no better warrior should undertake it," said Burrus. "Now one comes, as he promised me."

Artorius shaded his eyes to make out the newcomer's posture in the saddle. "Lanceolatus! You knew where to find him?"

"He would not put himself beyond all reach, lord."

Lanceolatus was now swinging himself to the ground. He came forward and knelt. "I swear by God to the Empress Vinavera's innocence of the death of Padraic, and I shall prove it upon the body of any who deny it."

"She's still a poisoner though there were ten of you!" cried Madoc.

"Let us fight," said Lanceolatus.

Artorius lowered his staff, and the combat began. Vinavera had seen Lanceolatus many times demonstrating strokes and parries on the drill ground, she had heard of his deeds in battle, and she had seen him in full action to save her reputation from Melwas, after the latter had abducted her. Madoc apparently had not. He must have judged from Lanceolatus' fame that his own best chance was to overwhelm him with the sheer frequency of his blows, hoping that by some chance at least one would find an opening. Lanceolatus retreated steadily before him, moving ever to his left to keep his shield between himself and the strokes that Madoc launched, while circling to his own right to outflank the shield.

At length one of Madoc's slashes cut through the iron rim of Lanceolatus' shield to split the wood beneath. For a moment it caught his sword, and Lanceolatus swung his own. Madoc warded it with his shield, but the mere force of the stroke drove him to his knees. Lanceolatus stepped forward to drive him to the ground, but Madoc wrenched his sword loose and delivered a cut to the back of Lanceolatus' left thigh, below the mail hauberk. The blood gushed out fiercely, and while Lanceolatus collected himself, Madoc scrambled to his feet. At that, Lanceolatus struck him to the ground, face down, brought his wounded leg onto Madoc's outflung sword arm, and brought the point of his own sword to the back of the Door Ward's neck.

Madoc begged for his life.

"The Empress is innocent of Padraic's death?"

"I—I must have made a mistake. Somebody else must have poisoned the apple."

Artorius made a gesture to Baldwin, who lifted the rail to let Vinavera come to him. He met her at the foot of the dais and kissed her lingeringly. "I knew you were innocent, but the doubters had to be convinced too."

Vinavera gestured at the stretched-out Madoc. "What's to do with this scrap of putrescent flesh?"

"He looks capable of living. Send him back to soak in the peaty water of some Hibernian bog?"

Vinavera managed a smile. "If you want to keep your post, it takes courage to charge your lord's wife with wrong-doing. Let him stay. But what if that stroke had cut Lance's leg off?"

"Let us thank him."

Lance was sitting on the ground gritting his teeth while a surgeon applied a tourniquet and stitched the edges of his wound together. His eyes met Vinavera's. She bent down to kiss him. "It feels good to be alive, Lance. I never did like the smell of burned meat."

"I was sure if you wanted someone dead, you'd ask Bear or me to arrange it, instead of bothering with poison. Who did kill Padraic, I wonder?"

"It was Pinel the Wild Man, who's now on his way to the hills"
They looked up and saw Nimu standing with a wry smile a little
way off.
Artorius whirled on her. "Why didn't you speak before? Why
make me risk burning Vinavera?"
"I didn't know before. But as Lanceolatus' leg bled, I saw it in
the stains on the sand. Pinel is Lamorac's cousin. He wanted revenge
on Gwalchmai for Lamorac's death, and he knew that Gwalchmai
loves apples. He stuck wolfbane in one, sealed it over with wax,
and managed to put it on top of the bowl. I didn't see just how.
It was mere chance that Padraic took it first."
Vinavera remembered Pinel's drooping sleeve trailing over the
fruit bowl, and his suggestion that Padraic leave the apple on top
for Gwalchmai. It would fit. She had almost lost her life to the feud
between Gododdin and Dyfed. How many more would it cost? Her
left hand still held her husband's, and with her right she reached
for Lance's. Only between her two men did she feel safe.

GUINEVERE AND LANCELOT

Arthur Machen

Until this point we haven't really touched upon the relationship between Lancelot and Guinevere, but it now becomes central to this story and the next. The two stories complement each other, since they are both retellings of the traditional legend, though each is overlaid by a personal interpretation and image of the Arthurian world. Arthur Machen (1863–1947) was fascinated with Arthurian lore, particularly that pertaining to the Holy Grail which he explored in a number of esoteric articles plus two works of fiction, The Great Return *(1915) and* The Secret Glory *(1922). The following tale provides the whole story of Lancelot's relationship with Guinevere in as compact a format as you could wish.*

Upon a morning in May a man kept his master's sheep on the hills that are above the Forest of Dendreath, in the midst of the dole of Britain. It was very early in the morning when the man came out of the shelter that he had made between two rocks, and the dew was thick upon the short grass, and at the sun rising all the land glittered as if it had been the Shining Isle beyond the waves of ocean, and an odor of sweetness rose up from the regions of the leaves. Then the sun ascended in his splendour, and the mists in the forests vanished away, and the shepherd saw before him all the wonders of the Forest of Dendreath. In the west he beheld the

Road of the Eagle that issues from the waste land of Cameliard; and suddenly he was amazed, for far away he saw a red flame and a white flame advancing side by side along the alley of the wood.

Now, these flames were indeed nothing but that famous knight of high worship, Sir Lancelot, the principal warrior of the Order of the Round Table, and beside him Guinevere, that was to be Arthur's queen. When the shepherd far on the wild hill had seen them they had but come forth from a shade of beechen leaves, and as they appeared suddenly in the open glade the sunbeams smote upon them, and so bright was Lancelot's armour made that it was as if it spouted fire, and Guinevere was as the burning of vehement flames. Upon her head she bore a cap of golden cloth, curiously adorned with jewels such as rubies and carbuncles and chrysoprases, and her cotehardie was of red samite. And about her she held a cloak of flame-coloured satin, and her belt was of gold and crystals. Golden was the glory of her hair. So they rode through the alleys of the forest in the sweetness of the May morning, amidst the glittering of many leaves stirred by the winds of heaven. And at their passing by all the choir of the birds of the wood exulted. Deep from the shade in the heart of the forest Eos the nightingale chanted the melody of lovers with unwearied antiphons; to him gladly replied the blackbird, a master of song; the blackcap was of their chorus; from the throats of smaller birds there rose a sweet sound like that of the pipes of faerie. So journeyed Sir Lancelot and the lady by the ways of the happy forest, one glancing gently on the other as they rode at a merry pace.

Now, when Sir Lancelot brought Guinevere from her father's castle in Cameliard, they rode for a day and found no adventure. But as night fell, and the sun went down, and it grew dark, they heard a noise as of crackling flames, and the sky grew red; and they saw a high hill before them, and on the height of it a fair castle was built, with lofty walls and many springing towers and pinnacles. But a black smoke swelled up from it, and great flames encompassed it, and as they looked there was a roaring and a riving as of thunder; and then that fair and goodly place fell apart, and was dashed down into the dust, being consumed with fire. "Alas, fair lord," said Guinevere, "what castle was this, and who was the lord of it? What evil chance hath so piteously destroyed it all?" "Lady," replied Sir Lancelot, "that I may scarcely tell. Let us be awhile, and it may be that we shall fall in with some men who shall advise us." And then they pressed a little forward, and Sir Lancelot found a poor man hidden amongst the thorns and bushes by the way, and he asked the man what enemy had come upon the castle, and for what cause it had thus been burned and ruined. "Sir," said the poor man, "ye are to understand that this castle was the castle of Sir Sagramour of the Fair Mount, that was a knight of great worship, and a noble warrior, and the lord of all these lands. And it fell out by evil chance that he saw Eglaise, the daughter of King Ryon of the Rugged Island, as she went forth from her chamber to hear mass, and the hearts of these two became inflamed with love, and so they fled away together and dwelt happily at that castle for a year and a day. Then cometh King Ryon against Sir Sagramour and taketh his castle and burneth it as ye have seen, and Sir Sagramour is slain, and his wife with him, and no living man is left therein." Then Sir Lancelot and Guinevere, the queen that was to be, marvelled, and went on their way; and said Guinevere: "I see very well that this love is both piteous and cruel, since by it husband and wife are slain, and a fair hold has its portion with ashes and destruction." "Will ye say so, lady?" answered Lancelot. "Consider well that by this same love is all the round earth ordered, with the shining of the stars at night, and with all the sphere of the heavens, and with the perpetual choirs of Paradise. And without this love ye are to understand right as the doctors teach us, that there were no brightness of the sun at all, nor any light of the moon, nor should there be any green thing upon the earth, nor any bird of the wood, nor beast of the rocks, nor fishes in ocean; nay, when love shall pass, then passeth man also. And ye shall not say that this knight and his sweetheart were unhappy nor of an ill end, for to our lord Love they did great worship and great honour, and were well rewarded of him, so that they dwelt for a year and a day in the estate of gladness, and now praise God in Paradise, in the bliss that is perdurable and everlasting." "Oh, knight," said then Guinevere, "I see well that ye are a great lover and a high master – yea, a very doctor of love; and well I wit that in the King's court at Camelot ye have the love of many ladies and bear the palm of all amorous knights." "Lady, ye judge falsely, since never yet have I loved maid nor wife." "Is this as ye say, of very truth?" "It is as I have said, lady, and ye must know that I am none of the knights of the bower, but of the stricken field, where I do battle for my lord, King Arthur, against his enemies, and against the foes of all the land." "Nevertheless, sir knight, of love ye speak very honestly and fairly, and ye hold love in great worship, as is plain to see, and so at last ye shall doubtless receive the high guerdon and reward of that lord Love whose lauds and offices ye so well recite." And then that fair lady looked on Sir

Lancelot with right good liking. And as they passed on their way they came to a lake, and all about it there were yew-trees set as a high hedge, and from the shadow of these trees they heard issuing a noise of lamentation. "What is this?" said Guinevere. "Let us delay and listen." And there was a sound of a man who wept, and after his weeping they saw him take a lute, and he sang this melody:

I make an incantation against the brightness of the sky:
I make an incantation against the shining of the sun:
I make an incantation against the wind of heaven.

I utter a spell against the boughs of the oak,
Against the aspen and the alder, the willow and the birch,
Against the budding of every tree that is in the wood.

I bind a charm against the rose that it blossom not:
May my magic bring darkness on the generation of the flowers:
May blackness consume the grass of the fields.

Let there be a mighty spell upon the melody of the birds,
Let the green perpetual choir be silent,
Let the song of fairyland be heard no more.

For in Gwenllian was the brightness of the sky,
She was the splendour of the heavenly sun,
She imparted sweetness to the breeze from on high.

In her were contained the delight of the woods,
The sweetness of the rose, the pleasure of the flowers.
Her voice gave rapture to the song of the birds.
The joys of the world have departed with her to Paradise.

And Guinevere and Sir Lancelot went on their way, considering the sad estate of this desolate lover, and again the lady spoke and said: "What say ye, sir knight? Will ye still be so hardy as to praise this love that bringeth men into so piteous a case? Heard ye not how he spoke, saying that all joys had departed with the lady that death has taken from him?" "Lady," said he, "there shall come a day when ye shall understand well that, albeit lovers may die and perish, yet love remaineth ever immortal, since no pangs of death may ever assail him." And a second time, Guinevere looked gently on Sir Lancelot, and in her heart she had him in right good liking.

After this fashion Sir Lancelot and Queen Guinevere passed through the regions of Britain, till they drew near to Camelot, where King Arthur held his court with his Knights of the Round

Table. And as they passed through the Forest of Dendreath they could see through the boughs of the trees the open country shining before them, and Sir Lancelot said, "Lady, in a day's journey we shall come to Camelot, and there we shall find King Arthur and all his Knights of the Round Table, and the ladies of his court, and the saint that shall make you King Arthur's queen." And she knew not what she should have said to this, and her heart grew sad; and then she bethought her of an old tale and matter of wizardry, or so men say. And she gazed at the trees of the wood, searching for a tree that she knew of; and as they came to the wood's verge she saw her desire, and broke off a little bough from a wych-elm that grew by the way. Then she has broken this bough in twain, and one she has hidden about her, and the other she has given to the knight, saying: "I wit well that all of my lord's knights are men of truth and gentle dealing, and I think that of them all ye be not the least. Wherefore, whatsoever ye swear to me, sure am I that ye will perform your oath and keep it, and never gainsay it not so long as ye live." "Ye say rightly, lady. What will ye that I swear to you?" "I will have you swear that evermore while ye be quick and in this life ye keep this bough that I give you, for to be a token of this wayfaring and of my wedding of my lord, King Arthur." "So shall it be, very willingly," and Lancelot swore this by holy rood. Then at the end of their way they came to high Camelot, the golden and glorious city of King Arthur, and by the high saint were King Arthur and the Lady Guinevere made man and wife.

There was a day when Queen Guinevere, that now is married to King Arthur, sat with her ladies in her bower, and they were at sport, devising of certain flowers, that were their lovers, and of their divers properties. Said one damosel: "I know a rose-tree that rises not too tall, and it grows in a low garden, and four shining waters are about this garden, and five lions keep watch over this garden, and six thorns there be on this rose-tree, and one blossom only. Tell me where my rose is hidden." Then, by computing of numbers, the other ladies made out a name of a knight and spoke it, and they all laughed with glee; and so sped their sport very merrily. But all the while the Queen sat silent, and she looked out of the window of the high tower, and saw far away the green trees in the wood, and the road by which she had passed from Cameliard to Camelot. And whereas her ladies spoke of flowers and of the knights their lovers, so her thoughts fell on the bough of the wych-elm which she had broken with Lancelot; and fervently did she desire the love of this knight in her heart. Then did she wholly burn, then did her heart become as a coal of fire, and forthwith she went apart and wrote a scroll, and sent the writing to one that dwelt in Camelot, being a man reputed a sorcerer and a great clerk in the art magic. So it fell out that Guinevere stole away in the night-time, and came to a hidden place in a wood that was near to Camelot, and there the wizard had already his cauldron of sorcery and incantation. And he had made set about this cauldron a ring of fires, and a shining smoke went up from the vessel as it were quick glass, and within the ring you might see divers puppets and images in wax and in wood, shamefully devised and foully wrought, having on their foreheads and their breasts the signs and marks of the devils of hell and of the cursed gods and goddesses of heathen men. And with the wizard there was a lad that all the while made the fires to burn with spices and gums of Satan, and a black smoke rose up from these flames. Then came the Queen into the ring, and at the wizard's bidding she doffed all her clothes and stood naked by the cauldron, and so she dipped the elm wand into the bubbling of the cauldron, right as the wizard commanded her. Forthwith ye might hear a noise and a rushing sound amongst the black branches and thickets of the wood, the great boughs of the trees tossed one on other, and said the wizard: "Now, madam, the Hosts of the Air draw near; now is at hand the Army of Tzabaoth." Then, in the shimmering and in the shining of the glassy smoke that rose from the cauldron there showed the shapes of the Mighty Ones, and to the Mightiest did Guinevere there make offering of herself; and, this done, "Now," said the wizard, "is the time come." Then drew forth Queen Guinevere the wych-bough from its place and again dipped it down three times into the cauldron of incantation and drew it forth, saying –

> One was one in the wood,
> On the tree of old enchantment;
> One was made twain in the wood,
> A word of wisdom was uttered.
> Now, one calleth to one,
> One tree cannot be dissevered.
> By the sign of union
> Let the parted be joined together.

Then, with the great word of incantation, the lady made the sign, and forth came flying in the air Sir Lancelot, in his ghostly body.

And from that night Sir Lancelot, that was the flower and crown of all King Arthur's warriors, durst not deny the Queen Guinevere in anything, but loved her from that time forth.

Now at that time it is to be understood that Camelot was the wonder and prize of all the cities in the Isle of Britain, nay, of the whole world. For, like that city of Syon, it was set on a high hill, and encompassed on every side by rich gardens and bowers of delight and orchards and pleasure places. And on high were the palaces of the warriors and the choirs and altars of the saints, and the most lordly palace of the Emperor Arthur, as it were a mountain on a mountain. And here were assembled all the rarities and precious things of the whole world, and all the instruments of wisdom, and all the books in which the secret things were written, which Merlin had gathered together from all the coasts of the world. In this city did Sir Lancelot and the Queen have their pleasure and delight and dalliance, and by art magic no eye could discern their pleasures, while they lived in wantoness. And even Sir Lancelot, that was a loyal knight in his heart, must grieve and mourn for his piteous transgression against his lord, and ever must he weep and lament in his chamber for this mortal sin, and ever must he strive that it be put from him. Yet, by virtue of the spell and by the cauldron of incantation, he was without succour and relief, and what the Queen would that must he do. And it fell out that one night he strove against the word of incantation and magic, and it was as if his heart was bursten within him, and down fell he on the floor of his chamber, as though he were stark dead. Then came his squire, and to him it seemed that the spirit was departed from Sir Lancelot, and he made a lamentable crying, and still Sir Lancelot lay there like a dead man. And when the life returned to him, he that was the mightiest of all King Arthur's knights of the Round Table was, as it were, a little child, and no strength nor virtue was there left in his body. And while he lay there, there came without his window one of Guinevere's damsels, taught by the Queen, and thus she sang to him:

All through the nightertale I longed for thee,
In loneliness, and harkened for the door
To open, or a footstep on the floor.

O lief sweetheart, I pray thee pity me,
I hunger for thy kisses evermore;
All through the nightertale I longed for thee.

Delight is turned to woe, and misery
Is my solace, certes, my heart is sore,
Yet these poor lips a smile at morning bore,
Though all the nightertale I longed for thee.

Wherefore henceforth Sir Lancelot strove no more, but lived deliciously in the golden meshes of the Queen's desires. And so to them twain the fruits of the orchards of Camelot were as apples of Avalon and golden delights, and the gardens were as walks of Paradise, and the feasts in King Arthur's hall were like the perpetual entertainment of the Blessed and Venerable Head of Bran Vendigeid, and the singing of the birds was as the song of the Three Fairy Birds of Rhiannon.

And one year King Arthur kept the feast of Pentecost at Camelot, as his custom was for the most part, and thirteen churches were set apart wherein King Arthur and his court heard mass. And afterwards, when they were in hall, suddenly there fell a silence, and each man looked on other and was afraid. Then there was a noise like thunder, and the roof was all afire; and then they heard in that place a melody as of the choirs of Paradise and the rejoicing of the angels, and ye would have said that there was an odour in that hall as of all the spicery of the world. And all the knights fell down on their knees together, and they saw as it were a hand pass from one end of the hall to the other and go forth; and the hand bore up the holy and blessed Vessel of the Sangraal, wrapt about in veils of red samite, and there was a shining of light that made the sun darkness; and to Sir Lancelot, because of his deadly sin, it was as if a sword had pierced his body, for his flesh began to tremble when he beheld the spiritual things. Yet he might not put his sin from him, but ever again returned to his dalliance with the Queen, for the spell that she had set upon him could not yet be broken.

Now, with the passing of the years, it happened that the bough of wych-elm that Queen Guinevere had severed in the wood withered and shrank, and, though the Queen and Sir Lancelot might keep each other their portion never so well, the leaves that were on the boughs fell off. And when a leaf fell off then it vanished away, and as it vanished there flew forth a great bird, black as a coal; and these birds perched on the trees of the wood, and cried out as men passed by, "Guinevere is the leman of Sir Lancelot." And so this sin could no longer be covered, and all the court of King Arthur had knowledge of these birds and of what their message was, and some believed it and some not, but all looked strangely on Sir Lancelot and Queen Guinevere. And it fell out at last that Guinevere took out her portion of the bough and set it before her, counting the leaves that remained; and suddenly she must go forth from her chamber to sit in hall; and by ill chance she had forgotten the bough, so that one of her damsels cometh in, and seeing it, casteth it into the fire. And in that moment was Sir Lancelot set free from the virtue of the enchantment and the wizardry that had been done upon him; and in that moment came the lad that had prepared the fires of the sorcery, and confessed all to the King, and the report of this was made known to all the city of Camelot. Then the anger of King Arthur was like to burning of fire and he sent ten knights, that were the mightiest that he had, to waylay Sir Lancelot, that they might slay him forthwith and hew his body in pieces. So these knights went forth, and they came upon Sir Lancelot as he walked in his garden, and he had no arms, but only a short sword, upon him. Then they cried: "Now shall ye surely die, thou foul and disloyal knight, for the deep dishonor that ye have done our lord the King," and they ran at him to kill him. But, for all their mail, five of them did he leave for dead in that garden, since he was the most valorous and most mightiest of all the knights that ever have been in this world; and so the five knights that were left in life fled away from before Sir Lancelot. Then would Sir Lancelot endeavour to bring forth the Queen harmless, but he might not, she was so closely kept; and so Sir Lancelot fled north from Camelot, and gathered his kinsfolk about him, if haply he might deliver the Queen from prison. For Arthur swore that for wizardry and disloyalty she would be burnt. But afterward King Arthur repented his oath, and Guinevere dwelt, as all men know, in an abbey of nuns at Amesbury, and in due time was Sir Lancelot hallowed Bishop of Canterbury. And so, having repented of their sins, they both departed from this life: on whose souls may God have pity.

THE PRETENDER

Stephen Dedman

This story is one of the more recent treatments of Arthur's fate covering the events leading up to the Battle of Camlann. Stephen Dedman (b. 1959) is the author of the urban fantasy novel The Art of Arrow Cutting *(1996). He and his wife live in Western Australia and he has worked as a video librarian, game designer, actor, and manager of a science-fiction bookstore.*

The knight stood before the King and Queen, still in his armor. His face was flushed, except where it was scarred, and his close-cropped black hair glistened with sweat in the lamplight. Despite his youth, the scars were plentiful – it had been the custom of the court in less peaceful times that no knight without a face wound was permitted to sit at the King's table – and his face would not have been beautiful even without them. But his body was muscular and powerful, and even in armour he moved with the grace of some mythical beast, part cat, part dragon. He had been the Queen's lover for four years, and was also dearly loved by the King. He drew a deep breath, feeling as out of place in their chamber as a dead rat on a banquet table.

"We were on our way to Mass, and we saw an old priest praying at a great tomb outside the chapel," he said. "He greeted us, calling us the two most unfortunate knights who ever lived. We were unarmored and afoot, with only our swords and daggers, and I thought he meant we'd walked into a trap."

"Did he know who you were?" asked the Queen.

The knight nodded. "Mordred asked him why we were so unfortunate, and the priest told him that," he hesitated, "that he was the son of the greatest king England would ever know, and that he would destroy him."

"How did Mordred take this?" asked the king, softly.

"He laughed; he told the priest his father was the late king Lot and that he'd had no hand in his destruction, and the priest laughed back. He said Mordred was no more Lot's son than water was dry; he named *you* as Mordred's father." He resisted the urge to stare down at the fresh rushes on the floor, and looked the King squarely in the face. "He then said that you'd had all the baby boys born that May-day cast out to sea in a boat that sank, drowning all but him."

There was a long silence in the small chamber, and then the Queen asked, "And what did the priest say to you, Lance?"

"Nothing," replied the knight. "Mordred was standing nearer the old man than I was, and he drew his sword and slew him before I could prevent it. I wish now that I'd killed him there and –"

"No," said the King, his face grey. He tried to smile, but only succeeded in grimacing. "Nothing else the old man said was true; why should the prediction that Mordred would destroy me be different?" He stared at the horn window, watching it grow dark, then reached for the Queen's hand.

"Mordred does not favour Lot," said Guenever, quietly. "It has often been remarked on –"

"Neither do Agravaine or Gareth," replied the King, wearily. "I wouldn't swear that any of them are Lot's sons, except perhaps Gawaine; Margawse has long had a passion for young knights. Apart from their other obvious attractions, it kept them loyal to her rather than to Lot." He shook his head. "I don't know who Mordred's father may have been, but it wasn't I. I've never lain with a woman in my life, Guen; you must believe that."

"And the story about the boat?" asked Lancelot.

"That may be true; I've heard it before," replied the King. "But it was none of my doing; even had I wanted to, my arm wasn't so long as to reach to Lothian and Orkney, not with Lot and Margawse still alive. Lot might have done it, or it might simply be a slander."

"What would you have me do, sire?"

"Nothing."

"But if Mordred believes these tales –"

Arthur shrugged his mighty shoulders. "Mordred is an intelligent young man, and I have no other heir . . ."

Guenever stared. "Arthur!"

"You may go, Lance," said the King, his voice betraying his weariness. "If you would, watch Mordred for me, and tell me who else he tells about this, and see that he comes to no harm."

Lancelot bowed his scarred head. "Yes, my liege." They watched him walk out and close the door, then Guenever said softly, "Mordred was born on May-day?"

"Or the night before. It's difficult, now, to find anyone who was there and might remember. Why?"

Guenever's lips moved slightly as she calculated. "So he was begotten the summer before. Was that during her time as ambassador from Lot's court?"

"Yes," replied Arthur. "Lot must have known that the child wasn't his, but that doesn't make him mine. Margawse had her own knights there to protect her, and there were many others at court who she could have seduced easily enough. Oh, she wiggled her eyelids and chest at me while she was here, but only succeeded in making herself look foolish. Neither of us knew then that she was my sister; Merlin did not tell us who my father was until much later." He sighed. "I wish he were still here."

"Your father?"

"No, Merlin. He warned me about Mordred before he was born – he even said it would be better if he died as young as possible, though he never suggested a massacre of boy-babies. If I'd done that so soon after being crowned, it would surely have destroyed me; no knight would have sworn allegiance to a murderer of children."

He closed his eyes. Merlin had also advised him not to marry Guenever, warning him that she would fall in love with Lancelot, but he'd ignored his counsel. Though he was fond of Guenever, their marriage had been politically motivated. Guenever's father Leodegrance had been a staunch ally of Uther Pendragon's, and Arthur had badly wanted his support. Unfortunately, Leodegrance had also shared the Pendragon's hatred of sodomites – and he was offering a dowry of a hundred knights and the great round table, the wheel of a giant's chariot that Uther had given him.

The Queen had remained virgin until her thirtieth year, when Lancelot had come to Camelot. Like Arthur, she had soon fallen in love with the young man, and the king had appointed him her champion and bodyguard as a gift to both of them. Occasionally, Lancelot's conscience would trouble him, and he would leave

Camelot on quests, but always returned to Guenever. His King he loved without desire, just as Arthur had come to love Guen, and none of the ill that Merlin had predicted had come to pass.

"Mordred is your sister's son; you *can't* acknowledge him as your own."

"No," replied Arthur. "But I need an heir, Guen, or all we've achieved will melt away like snow as soon as I'm dead. You don't remember what Britain was like between my father's dying and my becoming King, with no one to unite the baronies and lesser kingdoms, and Cerdic and Claudas and . . . if you were to marry Lance after I die, then it might gain us a few more years, but even he would need a successor eventually."

"And what about Mordred?"

"If he should ask any of us, we can tell him the truth; what more can we do?"

Sir Dinadan lay across Arthur's bed and mused. "Finding the father of a child of Margawse's would be like going on a quest for all the splinters of the true cross."

Arthur snorted, and removed his crown – a thin circlet of gold, designed to be worn inside a helmet, but which somehow felt heavier than his jousting armor. Dinadan, better known as a satirist than a fighter, had been his friend for many years, and his lover since Camelot had been built. "Don't say that in front of her sons, for Jesu's sake."

Dinadan looked up innocently. "So she had a passion for young men, and indulged it when she could; where's the harm in that? And what did they think that fool Lamorak was doing in her chamber every night? Who do *you* think Mordred's father was?"

"I don't know. I think she actually wanted a child who would give her power; she tried hard enough to seduce me." Dinadan laughed aloud, and the King grudgingly smiled. "I could ill afford to be amused at the time. I'm afraid Leodegrance was still alive and very influential and I was terrified of being unmasked – we all believe Lot had sent her down here as a spy, but Margawse never used that against me," he said, as though it had just occurred to him.

"Probably too upset that anyone could resist her."

"Perhaps, but it gave her a weapon, one that neither she nor Lot ever used . . ." He shrugged, collapsed onto the bed next to Dinadan, then turned on his side and kissed him. "Who was the second most powerful man in court twenty-three years ago?"

"Merlin. Not exactly a youngster, but he always liked pretty women. So has Kay; pity few of them return the liking. I think it's his tongue, myself; too sharp, and he likes using it too much, it could do someone a lot of damage . . ." Dinadan looked Arthur up and down. "Kay was young then, too, and as seneschal and your brother, he might have enough influence to interest Margawse. But Mordred doesn't exactly look like any of you."

"No." Mordred was tall and handsome, and his hair was golden, as Arthur's had been in his youth – but there the resemblance ended. He didn't resemble Margawse, either; she'd been tall, wide-hipped and full-breasted, with green eyes, a powerful laugh and long hair the color of fresh blood. Sir Kay was brown-eyed and running to fat, and his thinning hair was brown; Mordred, though well-muscled, gave an impression of slightness, of hunger. Partly it was his narrow face and his dark eyes – deep and intense, like those of his grandfather Gorlois, or his Aunt Morgan.

"Perhaps he doesn't believe it . . . and even if he does, why should he love you less for thinking you're his father?"

There were seats for a hundred and forty-one knights at the Round Table, several of them never used except by the palace cats. Margawse's sons watched silently as the name of Tristram magically appeared in gold letters on the seat that had previously belonged to Sir Marhaus.

"They say that Lancelot was barely able to defeat him," murmured Mordred to Gawaine a few hours later when the feast had ended and the brothers had retired to Mordred's chambers. It had been two years since his encounter with the priest near Peningues, though he had never mentioned the incident. "Do you remember that Merlin predicted that the two greatest knights and best lovers would fight beside Colombe's tomb?" Gawaine merely grunted from behind his cup of wine. "Strange, when we consider how many ladies you and Gaheris have loved . . . everyone knows that Tristram is loved by Mark's wife, La Beale Isoud, but who do you suppose Lancelot's lady might be?"

"I neither know nor care," replied Gawaine, quietly.

"Fitting, though, that he has taken the seat of a man he killed." He glanced at Agravaine and Gaheris, then into his cup before saying, "I wonder whose seats ours were, before we came to sit in them. Do you remember, Gawaine?" No answer. "Weren't you once the second greatest of Arthur's knights, or was that Lamorak?"

"Hold your tongue," replied Gawaine, as the ageing Agravaine's once-beautiful face turned pale. "The King already has a fool, he doesn't need another,"

"And the fool he has, he loves dearly," said Mordred. "Gods, but we are a sad and sorry lot."

"If ye're talking about our father, now –" said Gaheris, unsteadily getting to his feet and reaching for his belt knife.

"*Your* father," snapped Mordred. Gaheris froze, then fell back down on his stool, almost upsetting it. The others stared in silence, and then Gawaine said, "So that's it."

"Yes," Mordred turned to Gareth. "Get out of here, keep your pretty hands clean." Gareth turned to Gawaine, who nodded, then walked unsteadily out of the room.

"You knew?" asked Mordred.

His eldest brother shrugged. "I was old enough when ye were born to count the months, even if *they* weren't. Gareth was the only one still at home; I don't know what he may have heard. Who told ye?"

"A priest, near Peningues. He's dead now."

"Did he say who your father was?"

"Arthur."

Gawaine snorted. "That's ridiculous."

"Why? Because he's a sodomite? Our mother could have seduced a coil of rope."

"*You dare!*" snapped Gaheris. Gawaine, moving with surprising speed and precision for a man so obviously drunk, grabbed Gaheris's right wrist and twisted it, forcing him to drop his knife. "Hear him out."

"You know it's true." Mordred sneered at Gaheris. "You murdered her, not for lying with your father's killer, but out of jealousy because she wouldn't lie with you. You would have murdered Lamorak, too, but even naked and unarmed and half asleep he was too quick for you, so you let us think *he'd* murdered her."

Gawaine let go Gaheris's arm as though it were something indescribably foul. "*Is this true?*" Gaheris glared at him, but said nothing, and Gawaine slapped him across the face with all his strength.

"Oh, excellent," said Agravaine, the colour slowly seeping back into his face. "How's he going to talk with a broken neck?"

Mordred laughed bitterly. "Well, that's Lothian justice for you, isn't it?"

"I didn't mean to kill her," said Gaheris, sullenly. "It was Lamorak I wanted dead, not her; anyway, it was Agravaine's idea, but *he* didn't have the courage. *You've* killed women who were trying to save their men, Gawaine, you must understand . . ."

"Then you have what you wanted," said Mordred. "Strange how everyone wants something. Pretty Gareth wants to be Lancelot in battle, pretty Agravaine wants to be Lancelot in bed . . . it seems almost everyone wants to be Lancelot, except Arthur, who'd rather be pretty Guenever. I wonder what it is that Lancelot wants? To be King, perhaps?"

"And that's what ye want, isn't it?" growled Gawaine.

"I'm the King's son; who better?"

"You're no son of Arthur's, boyo," said Gawaine, advancing on his youngest brother like a great tree slowly falling. "I don't know who or what your father was, but it –"

"I *am* his son," said Mordred, thumping his chest and staring into Gawaine's blazing blue eyes. "I feel it. I know it, in here."

Gawaine spat precisely into his wine cup. "Ye'll feel the point of my spear in there, come morning. I may not be the greatest knight in court any more, but I can still –"

"Kill your own brother?"

"Half-brother." He glowered down at Mordred, then shook his head. "Arthur would pardon me."

"Arthur pardons everyone," replied Mordred. "He's pardoned more murderers than you could count; he'd pardon Lancelot and Guenever for adultery if anyone ever had the guts to accuse them – but there's one person the King can't pardon."

"And who's that?"

"Himself. If the people and the priests knew about his lust for the great Lancelot –"

"What a man *wants* isn't a sin," snapped Gawaine. "Anyway, ye have no proof."

"How he and Dinadan amuse each other, then."

"And what good would that do ye? Ye don't remember what the land was like before Arthur's day: I do. He's been the best King we've ever had."

"I agree," said Mordred, calmly. "I have no wish to usurp Arthur, merely to succeed him. Swear that you will not hinder me, Gawaine, and I'll accuse no one of anything."

Gawaine considered this, then drew his dagger from his belt. "You will swear to this, too?" he asked.

"Of course," replied Mordred.

That was remembered as the year that Arthur defeated Claudas; that Brumant l'Orgilleus was consumed by flames while sitting in the Siege Perilous; and that Lancelot first saw his bastard son Galahad, and went mad.

Galahad was sixteen when his name appeared on the Siege Perilous, the seat reserved for the greatest knight in the world; he was also the most beautiful young man anyone had seen since the arrival of Gareth Beaumains more than twenty years before. He was loved, and hated, as his father had been, and by the same people.

He had a gracelessness about him, the result of a cloistered upbringing, and soon acquired a reputation for churlish manners. He declined all offers of love, courtly and otherwise – even those of Guenever – as politely as he knew how. Dinadan may have been the first to recognize that the young knight was in love with his King – or it may have been Mordred, but Mordred spoke to few people in court, and never to Galahad.

That was the year of the quest for the Grail, and so it was that the young knight and the grey-bearded satirist were riding together through the South March. "The King and Queen love my father well, don't they?"

"In their own ways, yes," replied Dinadan. "And your father loves them as he can. He loves the King, but does not desire him; he both loves and desires Guenever. The Queen loves your father, but she needs to possess what she loves; she believes he betrayed her by lying with your mother all those years ago, and may never forgive him. Almost everyone loves the King and your father – except for Sir Agravaine, who desires Guenever but loves only himself. Sir Kay loves no one but Arthur and Guenever, not even himself – and I love gossip, and have already filled your ears with too much of it. Who do you love, young sir?"

Galahad blushed. "The King is a great man."

"That he is – but he is also the king, and his kingdom is more to him than his own happiness, which is why he may not always do as he pleases, no matter how much he may love you. He fears that if you were to become his heir after being his lover, you might find it difficult to keep the allegiance of many of his knights."

Galahad considered this. "Me, his heir? Is this one of your famous jokes?"

Dinadan smiled; it was well known that Galahad lacked a sense of humour. "Arthur may seem eternal, but he's as mortal as any man, and has already seen some sixty summers. When he dies he expects your father to marry Queen Guenever and become King – and you, being your father's only son, will be next in line for the throne."

The two knights rode along in silence until sunset, when they set up their pavilions. Mordred and Agravaine found them there an hour before dawn and slew them both in their sleep.

Lancelot returned to Camelot a year and a day after setting out on his quest for the Grail, and found the King alone, staring northwest over the battlements. It seemed to Lancelot that Arthur had aged a decade or more since Galahad had come to court; there was now more silver in his hair and beard than gold, and he moved without his old vigour. "I'm glad you're back," he said, softly, without turning around. "It seems the best of my knights have gone, and many may never return. There's been no word of Galahad in three months. Your cousin Bors said he dreamed that Galahad found the Grail and has been taken bodily to heaven, but I suppose I'm the only one who's dreamed of Dinadan. Old fool should have stayed here. How did you fare?"

"I was found unworthy," replied Lancelot as quietly. "Where is Bors?"

"He went searching for Galahad and Percivale. I wish him every success."

Lancelot nodded. "How is the Queen?"

"Not happy. She spends most of her days beating Kay at chess. I'm glad you're back," he repeated. "We all are. This is as much of my realm as I've seen in more than a year, and there are people who need to see me, but I haven't dared leave Guen with no one to defend her. Even Gawaine is gone, doing penance for killing Yvonet in a friendly joust." He shrugged. "I've made Gareth king of Lothian and Orkney; Gawaine was pleased to let him have it, and his other brothers made no protest, but it means I'm losing yet another good knight."

"When are you going?"

"In a few days. London, then Oxford, Caerleon, Cardiff, and back again before it begins to snow. Go and see Guen; she's missed you as sorely as I have."

Lancelot was asleep in Guenever's bed when Mordred and thirteen knights, armed and armoured as for battle, came to the door. "Traitor knight, Sir Lancelot of the Lake!" called Agravaine, loudly enough for his voice to be heard throughout the castle. "Come out of the queen's chamber for, know you well, you shall not escape."

"Who is it?" whispered Guenever.

"It sounds like Agravaine," Lancelot replied softly, "but smells more like Mordred." He looked around the dark room. "Is there anything in here that I might use as a weapon or shield?"

Guenever shook her head. "How many of them do you think there are?"

"Ten, at least." He glanced at the furniture, finding nothing that would make a dent in armur or hold against a sword for more than a few buffets, then reached for his robe and began winding it around his right arm and hand.

"Traitor knight, come out and fight!" yelled Agravaine.

"They're going to kill us, aren't they?"

"Me, yes. They may want you alive."

"Why?"

"Because you're the Queen, and you have a better claim to the kingdom than –" He stopped.

"Arthur's dead, isn't he?"

"I don't know. If he is, Mordred can't very well accuse us of adultery . . . but Mordred will have to convince people of his death before he can claim the throne. He'd have a far better claim if you were to marry him than he would as Arthur's bastard. I suspect that's the choice he'll offer you." He bit his lip. "If I'm killed, pray for my soul, and my kin will come to save you." Before she could speak, he padded over to the door. "Fair lords, leave your noise, and I shall open this door and admit you."

There was a moment's silence, and then Agravaine replied, "A wise choice. You could never defeat us all."

"First, I will have your word that the queen is not to be harmed."

"You have it."

"I must hear it from Sir Mordred." Silence. "Or is he such a coward that he has sent you to do what he dares not?"

"The Queen shall not be harmed," replied Mordred, his voice barely audible through the solid door.

"I can't hear you!"

"The Queen shall not be harmed, and you shall both be brought alive before the King."

"Before *Arthur*."

"Before Arthur. I swear it."

Lancelot smiled slightly, then opened the door, just wide enough for one man to enter. Sir Colgrevance charged in, and Lancelot slammed the door shut behind him and barred it, plunging the room back into darkness, and hit the knight across the face so hard that his helm was knocked askew. He caught the blade of Colgrevance's sword in his right hand, wrenched the weapon from his grasp, and thrust it through his visor. As quickly as possible, he and Guenever stripped him of his armor, which Lancelot then donned. There came a sound of splintering wood from the corridor outside.

"Someone's thought to fetch an axe, at last," muttered Lancelot, picking up Colgrevance's shield.

"Can't you take me with you?"

Lancelot shook his head. "I would need more knights to protect you, and a horse for you to ride. Bar the door when I'm gone; stay in here as long as you can." He kissed her, then donned his helmet and strode towards the door.

"Traitor knight, come out and –" Agravaine fell silent as the door opened and he saw a knight in full armor before him; before he could speak again, Lancelot brought his sword down between his neck and his shoulder, cleaving through his chest.

He heard the door slam shut and the bar slide home behind him. He held his ground, so that his foes had to climb over their fallen allies to reach him. The corridor was narrow, so that only two knights could meet him at a time, and he quickly mowed his way through them: Sir Gingalin and Sir Astamore, Sir Mador de la Porte and Sir Gromer Somir Joure, Sir Petiphase of Winchelsea and Sir Galleron of Galway, Sir Florence and Sir Lovel, Sir Meliot and Sir Melion.

When only Sir Curselaine and a barricade of dead knights remained between himself and Lancelot, Sir Mordred turned and fled. Curselaine fell a moment later, his helmet and skull in two pieces, and Lancelot clambered over the pile of armoured corpses to give chase. He saw Mordred banging on the door of a chamber, and dash in as soon as it was opened. Lancelot hesitated outside for a moment, then ran to the stables.

"Is Arthur dead, then?"

Mordred stared sullenly through the rain at the empty road, until Gaheris repeated the question. "I don't know. Aunt Morgan sent me a message to say she saw a vision of him killed on Salisbury Plain, but that may be to come, or she may be lying."

Gaheris nodded. "What will you do if he returns?"

Mordred scowled at him, but there was a knock on the chamber door before he could speak. "Yes?"

"Sir, the Queen would speak with Sir Kay."

"Then she will speak with me," replied Mordred. "Tell her I shall attend her presently."

"Do you want me along?"

"No. Keep an eye on the road, and be sure that if Gawaine or Gareth return that they speak only to us. Tell them Lancelot has slain Agravaine, Lovel, and Florence, no more." He stood.

"Not that you hid in a lady's chamber while Lancelot was killing him?"

"Not unless you want Gareth to know who murdered our mother," replied Mordred, "and who let Lancelot ride out unchallenged."

"He was wearing Colgrevance's armour, and Colgrevance –"

"Lies dead in Guenever's chamber. I'll call you if I need help bringing him out."

"Where is Sir Kay?" asked Guenever. She had dressed in her best robe; several others were strewn over the dead knight near the door-way. Four of her ladies, including Mordred's lover Landoine, attended her.

"In his chamber," replied Mordred, smoothly, "awaiting punishment for the foul crime of sodomy. What would you with him?"

"He is seneschal of this castle; he, not you, rules in Arthur's absence." She did not refute the charge; the portly Kay loved beautiful men as well as women (he'd been one of the many men lured into Margawse's bed during her visits to Camelot), and it was well known that his sarcastic tongue lashing of young knights was often the spite of a scorned or abandoned lover. She wondered who they'd used to entrap him.

"Do you expect my knights would follow such a man – such a sinner?"

It was an obvious trap, one that Guenever avoided easily. "And your claim to the throne, Mordred? Arthur has other nephews."

"But no other sons."

"He has no sons," Guenever responded. "I don't know who your father was, Mordred. Have you asked your Aunt Morgan? I'm sure she knows."

Mordred bristled. He had asked Morgan le Fay, and he was sure she'd used her magic to look back to his conception though he was also aware of the rumors that Queen Margawse had often enjoyed three or four lovers in a night. "I do not need Dame Morgan to tell me what I already know."

"Then perhaps you will believe the Lady of the Lake. Arthur

told me he would visit her, and ask her, when he came to Caerleon."

If this rocked Mordred, he contrived not to show it. "And if he does not return, Lady?"

"Do you believe he will not?"

Mordred opened his mouth to answer, then glanced at the Queen's attendants. "Lady, I would speak with you alone."

Guenever hesitated, then nodded. "Don't shut the door," she warned Landoine. "I would not wish to be accused of entertaining knights in my chamber."

"If Arthur is dead, my Lady, would it not be better for the kingdom if we were to marry?"

"For the kingdom?"

"The land must have a King; marrying you would strengthen my claim greatly."

"I am already married," said Guenever, softly. "To marry another while the King lives would be treason."

"I could have you burnt for treason tomorrow," Mordred snarled.

"If the King were dead," continued Guenever, "Lancelot's presence here would *not* be treason. But I am prepared to wait for Arthur to return."

"How long will you wait?"

Guenever smiled sweetly. "Have you heard the bards sing of Odysseus and Penelope, Mordred? I've always admired Penelope."

Suddenly, there was a shout from the corridor outside. He turned around to see a page, breathless, holding onto the door frame. "My lord, Sir Gaheris sent me to tell you that your brother Sir Gareth has returned."

Mordred glared at him, then turned back to Guenever without his expression changing, "You have fifteen days," he whispered. "On the morning of that fifteenth day, if Arthur has not returned, you will be burnt or married." And he hurried out of her room.

The stake was set up in the square outside St. Stephen's Church, and Guenever was led towards it clad only in her smock, while Mordred watched from the safety of a balcony. "Lancelot will rescue her," murmured Gareth, behind him.

Mordred flushed. Sir Kay had escaped the night before he was to be burnt, and he suspected that Gareth – though never a friend of Kay's – had been involved. He could ill afford another embarrassment; too many knights had already ridden out of Camelot, supposedly to search for Lancelot or Arthur or Gawaine, leaving him barely enough to maintain a guard. He had yet to appoint a seneschal to replace Kay, and the castle stank. The only good news was that no one had – as yet – risen to challenge him. "He may try," he growled. "I want you and Gaheris waiting by the gate."

"I won't fight him," replied Gareth.

"Then go unarmed, and hope he doesn't fight you, but stop him!" He turned to Gaheris. "You may arm yourself, or not, as it please you, but go with him." His half brothers stared at him coldly, but obeyed. Mordred watched as Guenever was tied to the stake, and then a horn sounded from the castle's tallest tower; four blasts, signifying four riders.

The rescue was swift, but bloody; twenty knights were slain by Lancelot and his three kinsmen, and many more fled from them before Lancelot slashed through the ropes holding Guenever to the stake. He handed the Queen a gown and kirtle before lifting her onto his horse, then rode at full speed towards the gate. Gareth stepped aside to let him pass; Gaheris did not, but was knocked senseless with a buffet from Lancelot's shield. Mordred, watching in rage from the balcony, drew his sword and ran towards the gate.

An unknown defender of the Queen had ensured that the bundles of wood at the base of the stake were green and damp, producing little flame but much smoke. In the confusion, no one saw Mordred murder Gareth and Gaheris – and their deaths, like the others, were blamed on Lancelot.

Arthur walked across the battlefield at Camlaun, his horse having been slain beneath him hours before. Gawaine's ghost had appeared to him the night before, warning him to delay the fighting until Lancelot had arrived, but an argument between two of his young knights and two of Mordred's Saxon allies – supposedly someone had drawn a sword to slay an adder spotted in the grass – had escalated into a battle which killed thousands.

Gawaine had gone to France to avenge his brothers and had died there from wounds received in a duel with Lancelot; his last action had been to write a letter begging Lancelot to return to Britain to fight at the King's side. Arthur scanned the field looking for movement, and saw a man standing near the body of Sir Kay's unmistakable blood-red horse. As fast as his armour and his wounds would allow, Arthur ran across the plain towards him,

"Kay!"

The man turned, revealing a black shield with a silver bend.

Mordred's shield. Arthur continued to charge towards him, drawing Excalibur as he ran.

"Father!" yelled Mordred, mockingly. He walked delicately between the bodies, his own sword drawn. "Why have you forsaken me?"

Arthur stopped a scant ten paces from him. "Do you want to know who your father was, Mordred? I asked the Lady of the Lake, and she told me. I warn you, you may not be pleased by the answer."

Mordred took a step towards him. "Tell me, then. Who do you blame for my begetting, and your downfall?"

"Agravaine," said Arthur. "Your pretty brother. Your mother may have the excuse of having been drunk, but he wasn't. I didn't believe it, either, until the Lady showed me their images in her crystal."

Mordred staggered slightly, and the blood drained away from his face. "You lie. I know I'm your son; the first time I saw you, I knew it, I felt it here." He thumped his breastplate with the pommel of his sword. "I could not have loved you as I did had you not been my father –"

"If you loved me, it wasn't because you wanted me as a father," replied Arthur, grimly. "But you couldn't admit that, even to yourself; you've never had that sort of courage."

Mordred advanced slowly, his face contorted by hatred. "You lie," he repeated. "I've had women, nearly as many as Agravaine or Gaheris. I have sons; I don't love you and I am nothing like you!" He rushed at Arthur, and swung his sword with all his strength. The king parried with Excalibur, and the inferior blade shattered, one fragment piercing Arthur's helm and skull. Arthur thrust once, piercing Mordred's shield, left arm, breastplate and chest, and both men collapsed onto the bloody plain.

Some say that Arthur died and was buried, with Guenever, in the Isle of Avalon. Others say that he sleeps with his favorite knights in a hidden cave, waiting for a champion to awaken him. No one knows what befell the bodies of his enemies, nor praises the wisdom or courage of the pretender.

THE PASSING OF ARTHUR

Alfred, Lord Tennyson

One of the most atmospheric moments in the Arthurian Mythos is when Bedivere casts Excalibur into the mere and a hand rises above the water, catches the sword, and withdraws back into the lake. When I first encountered the Arthurian stories forty years ago it was that scene that remained in my mind, and which still can create a shiver of wonder even now. This episode, however, was not part of the original Arthurian stories. It emerged in what is called the Vulgate Cycle, a series of prose romances adapted by a long forgotten author (or authors) in the early thirteenth century. In that version it was Sir Griflet who returned the sword, but in Malory and most later versions it was Sir Bedivere, Arthur's life-long companion.

I have read many versions of this scene and the final passing of Arthur. It is difficult for anyone to write it poorly, but for pure atmosphere I don't feel anyone has yet surpassed that in the Idylls of the King (1870) by Alfred, Lord Tennyson (1809–92). Tennyson had a life-long fascination for the Arthurian legends. He wrote his first Arthurian poem. "Sir Launcelot and Queen Guinevere" in 1830, though he never completed it to his satisfaction and turned instead to "The Lady of Shalott" (1832). He returned time and again to different aspects of the Mythos, publishing his first sequence of Idylls of the King in 1859. As we have seen soon after that he became acquainted with James Knowles who had written his prose version of the stories, and Knowles encouraged Tennyson to explore the legends further. As a consequence there emerged The Holy Grail and Other Poems (1869) and further expansions of The Idylls of the King until the final complete edition in 1886, though he wrote

one further poem, "Merlin and the Gleam" in 1889. Tennyson's
version had a strong appeal to the Victorian establishment and it
was he more than anyone else who popularised the modern concept
of King Arthur.

That story which the bold Sir Bedivere,
First made and latest left of all the knights,
Told, when the man was no more than a voice
In the white winter of his age, to those
With whom he dwelt, new faces, other minds.

For on their march to westward, Bedivere,
Who slowly paced among the slumbering host,
Heard in his tent the moanings of the King:

"I found Him in the shining of the stars,
I mark'd Him in the flowering of His fields,
But in His ways with men I find Him not.
I waged His wars, and now I pass and die.
O me! for why is all around us here
As if some lesser god had made the world,
But had not force to shape it as he would,
Till the High God behold it from beyond,
And enter it, and make it beautiful?
Or else as if the world were wholly fair,
But that these eyes of men are dense and dim,
And have not power to see it as it is:
Perchance, because we see not to the close;
For I, being simple, thought to work His will,
And have but stricken with the sword in vain;
And all whereon I lean'd in wife and friend
Is traitor to my peace, and all my realm
Reels back into the beast, and is no more.
My God, thou hast forgotten me in my death:
Nay – God my Christ – I pass but shall not die."

Then, ere that last weird battle in the west,
There came on Arthur sleeping, Gawain kill'd
In Lancelot's war, the ghost of Gawain blown
Along a wandering wind, and past his ear
Went shrilling, "Hollow, hollow all delight!
Hail, King! to-morrow thou shalt pass away.
Farewell! there is an isle of rest for thee.

And I am blown along a wandering wind,
And hollow, hollow, hollow all delight."
And fainter onward, like wild birds that change
Their season in the night and wail their way
From cloud to cloud, down the long wind the dream
Shrill'd; but in going mingled with dim cries
Far in the moonlit haze among the hills,
As of some lonely city sack'd by night,
When all is lost, and wife and child with wail
Pass to new lords; and Arthur woke and call'd,
"Who spake? A dream. O light upon the wind,
Thine, Gawain, was the voice – are these dim cries
Thine? or doth all that haunts the waste and wild
Mourn, knowing it will go along with me?"

This heard the bold Sir Bedivere and spake:
"O me, my King, let pass whatever will,
Elves, and the harmless glamour of the field;
But in their stead thy name and glory cling
To all high places like a golden cloud
For ever: but as yet thou shalt not pass.
Light was Gawain in life, and light in death
Is Gawain, for the ghost is as the man;
And care not thou for dreams from him, but rise –
I hear the steps of Modred in the west,
And with him many of thy people, and knights
Once thine, whom thou hast loved, but grosser grown
That heathen, spitting at their vows and thee.
Right well in heart they know thee for the King.
Arise, go forth and conquer as of old."

Then spake King Arthur to Sir Bedivere:
"Far other is this battle in the west
Whereto we move, than when we strove in youth,
And brake the petty kings and fought with Rome,
Or thrust the heathen from the Roman wall,
And shook him thro' the north. Ill doom is mine
To war against my people and my knights.
The king who fights his people fights himself.
And they my knights, who loved me once, the stroke
That strikes them dead is as my death to me.
Yet let us hence, and find or feel a way
Thro' this blind haze, which ever since I saw

One lying in the dust at Almesbury,
Hath folded in the passes of the world."

   Then rose the King and moved his host by night,
And ever push'd Sir Modred, league by league,
Back to the sunset bound of Lyonesse –
A land of old upheaven from the abyss
By fire, to sink into the abyss again;
Where fragments of forgotten peoples dwelt,
And the long mountains ended in a coast
Of ever-shifting sand, and far away
The phantom circle of a moaning sea.
There the pursuer could pursue no more,
And he that fled no further fly the King;
And there, that day when the great light of heaven
Burn'd at his lowest in the rolling year,
On the waste sand by the waste sea they closed.
Nor ever yet had Arthur fought a fight
Like this last, dim, weird battle of the west.
A deathwhite mist slept over sand and sea:
Whereof the chill, to him who breathed it, drew
Down with his blood, till all his heart was cold
With formless fear; and ev'n on Arthur fell
For friend and foe were shadows in the mist
confusion, since he saw not whom he fought.
And friend slew friend not knowing whom he slew;
And some had visions out of golden youth,
And some beheld the faces of old ghosts
Look in upon the battle; and in the mist
Was many a noble deed, many a base,
And chance and craft and strength in single fights,
And ever and anon with host to host
Shocks, and the splintering spears, the hard mail hewn,
Shield-breakings, and the clash of brands, the crash
Of battleaxes on shatter'd helms, and shrieks
After the Christ, of those who falling down
Look'd up for heaven, and only saw the mist;
And shouts of heathen and the traitor knights,
Oaths, insult, filth, and monstrous blasphemies,
Sweat, writhings, anguish, labouring of the lungs
In that close mist, and cryings for the light,
Moans of the dying, and voices of the dead.

Last, as by some one deathbed after wail
Of suffering, silence follows, or thro' death
Or deathlike swoon, thus over all that shore,
Save for some whisper of the seething seas,
A dead hush fell; but when the dolorous day
Grew drearier toward twilight falling, came
A bitter wind, clear from the North, and blew
The mist aside, and with that wind the tide
Rose, and the pale King glanced across the field
Of battle: but no man was moving there;
Nor any cry of Christian heard thereon,
Nor yet of heathen; only the wan wave
Brake in among dead faces, to and fro
Swaying the helpless hands, and up and down
Tumbling the hollow helmets of the fallen,
And shiver'd brands that once had fought with Rome,
And rolling far along the gloomy shores
The voice of days of old and days to be.

Then spake King Arthur to Sir Bedivere,
And whiter than the mist that all day long
Had held the field of battle was the King:

"Hearest thou this great voice that shakes the world,
And wastes the narrow realm whereon we move,
And beats upon the faces of the dead,
My dead, as tho' they had not died for me? –
O Bedivere, for on my heart hath fall'n
Confusion, till I know not what I am,
Nor whence I am, nor whether I be King.
Behold, I seem but King among the dead."

Then spake the bold Sir Bedivere: "My King,
King everywhere! and so the dead have kings,
There also will I worship thee as King.
Yet still thy life is whole, and still I live
Who love thee; but who hates thee, he that brought
The heathen back among us, yonder stands,
Modred, unharm'd, the traitor of thine house."

Then spake the King: "My house hath been my doom.
But call not thou this traitor of my house
Who hath but dwelt beneath one roof with me.
My house are rather they who sware my vows,

Yea, even while they brake them, own'd me King.
And well for thee, saying in my dark hour,
When all the purport of my throne hath fail'd
That quick or dead thou holdest me for King.
King am I, whatsoever be their cry;
And one last act of kinghood shalt thou see
Yet, ere I pass." And uttering this the King
Made at the man: then Modred smote his liege
Hard on that helm which many a heathen sword
Had beaten thin; while Arthur at one blow,
Striking the last stroke with Excalibur,
Slew him, and all but slain himself, he fell.

So all day long the noise of battle roll'd
Among the mountains by the winter sea;
Until King Arthur's Table, man by man,
Had fall'n in Lyonesse about their lord,
King Arthur. Then, because his wound was deep,
The bold Sir Bedivere uplifted him,
And bore him to a chapel nigh the field,
A broken chancel with a broken cross,
That stood on a dark strait of barren land:
On one side lay the Ocean, and on one
Lay a great water, and the moon was full.

Then spake King Arthur to Sir Bedivere:
"The sequel of to-day unsolders all
The goodliest fellowship of famous knights
Whereof this world holds record. Such a sleep
They sleep – the men I loved. I think that we
Shall never more, at any future time,
Delight our souls with talk of knightly deeds
Walking about the gardens and the halls
Of Camelot, as in the days that were.
I perish by this people which I made, –
Tho' Merlin sware that I should come again
To rule once more; but, let what will be, be,
I am so deeply smitten thro' the helm
That without help I cannot last till morn.
Thou therefore take my brand Excalibur,
Which was my pride: for thou rememberest how
In those old days, one summer noon, an arm
Rose up from out the bosom of the lake,

Clothed in white samite, mystic, wonderful,
Holding the sword – and how I row'd across
And took it, and have worn it, like a king;
And, wheresoever I am sung or told
In aftertime, this also shall be known:
But now delay not: take Excalibur,
And fling him far into the middle mere:
Watch what thou seest, and lightly bring me word."

To him replied the bold Sir Bedivere:
"It is not meet, Sir King, to leave thee thus,
Aidless, alone, and smitten thro' the helm –
A little thing may harm a wounded man;
Yet I thy hest will all perform at full,
Watch what I see, and lightly bring thee word."

So saying, from the ruin'd shrine he stept,
And in the moon athwart the place of tombs,
Where lay the mighty bones of ancient men,
Old knights, and over them the sea-wind sang
Shrill, chill, with flakes of foam. He, stepping down
By zigzag paths, and juts of pointed rock,
Came on the shining levels of the lake.

There drew he forth the brand Excalibur,
And o'er him, drawing it, the winter moon,
Brightening the skirts of a long cloud, ran forth
And sparkled keen with frost against the hilt:
For all the haft twinkled with diamond sparks,
Myriads of topaz-lights, and jacinth-work
Of subtlest jewellery. He gazed so long
That both his eyes were dazzled as he stood,
This way and that dividing the swift mind,
In act to throw: but at the last it seem'd
Better to leave Excalibur conceal'd
There in the many-knotted waterflags,
That whistled stiff and dry about the marge.
So strode he back slow to the wounded King.

Then spake King Arthur to Sir Bedivere:
"Hast thou perform'd my mission which I gave?
What is it thou hast seen? or what hast heard?"

And answer made the bold Sir Bedivere:
"I heard the ripple washing in the reeds,
And the wild water lapping on the crag."

   To whom replied King Arthur, faint and pale:
"Thou hast betray'd thy nature and thy name,
Not rendering true answer, as beseem'd
Thy fealty, nor like a noble knight:
For surer sign had follow'd, either hand,
Or voice, or else a motion of the mere.
This is a shameful thing for men to lie.
Yet now, I charge thee, quickly go again,
As thou art lief and dear, and do the thing
I bad thee, watch, and lightly bring me word."

   Then went Sir Bedivere the second time
Across the ridge, and paced beside the mere,
Counting the dewy pebbles, fix'd in thought;
But when he saw the wonder of the hilt,
How curiously and strangely chased, he smote
His palms together, and he cried aloud:

   "And if indeed I cast the brand away,
Surely a precious thing, one worthy note,
Should thus be lost for ever from the earth,
Which might have pleased the eyes of many men.
What good should follow this, if this were done?
What harm, undone? Deep harm to disobey,
Seeing obedience is the bond of rule.
Were it well to obey then, if a king demand
An act unprofitable, against himself?
The King is sick, and knows not what he does.
What record, or what relic of my lord
Should be to aftertime, but empty breath
And rumours of a doubt? But were this kept,
Stored in some treasure-house of mighty kings,
Some one might show it at a joust of arms,
Saying, 'King Arthur's sword, Excalibur,
Wrought by the lonely maiden of the Lake.
Nine years she wrought it, sitting in the deeps
Upon the hidden bases of the hills.'
So might some old man speak in the aftertime
To all the people, winning reverence.
But now much honour and much fame were lost."

So spake he, clouded with his own conceit,
And hid Excalibur the second time,
And so strode back slow to the wounded King.

Then spoke King Arthur, breathing heavily:
"What is it thou last seen? or what hast heard?"

And answer made the bold Sir Bedivere:
"I heard the water lapping on the crag,
And the long ripple washing in the reeds."

To whom replied King Arthur, much in wrath:
"Ah, miserable and unkind, untrue,
Unknightly, traitor-hearted! Woe is me!
Authority forgets a dying king,
Laid widow'd of the power in his eye
That bow'd the will. I see thee what thou art,
For thou, the latest-left of all my knights,
In whom should meet the offices of all,
Thou wouldst betray me for the precious hilt;
Either from lust of gold, or like a girl
Valuing the giddy pleasure of the eyes.
Yet, for a man may fail in duty twice,
And the third time may prosper, get thee hence:
But, if thou spare to fling Excalibur,
I will arise and slay thee with my hands."

Then quickly rose Sir Bedivere, and ran,
And, leaping down the ridges, lightly, plunged
Among the bullrush beds, and clutch'd the sword,
And strongly wheel'd and threw it. The great brand
Made lightnings in the splendour of the moon,
And flashing round and round, and whirl'd in an arch,
Shot like a streamer of the northern morn,
Seen where the moving isles of winter shock
By night, with noises of the Northern sea.
So flash'd and fell the brand Excalibur:
But ere he dipt the surface, rose an arm
Clothed in white samite, mystic, wonderful,
And caught him by the hilt, and brandish'd him
Three times, and drew him under in the mere.
And lightly went the other to the King.

Then spoke King Arthur, drawing thicker breath
"Now see I by thine eyes that this is done.
Speak out: what is it thou hast heard, or seen?"

And answer made the bold Sir Bedivere:
"Sir King, I closed mine eyelids, lest the gems
Should blind my purpose, for I never saw,
Nor shall see, here or elsewhere, till I die,
Not tho' I live three lives of mortal men,
So great a miracle as yonder hilt.
Then with both hands I flung him, wheeling him;
But when I look'd again, behold an arm,
Clothed in white samite, mystic, wonderful,
That caught him by the hilt, and brandish'd him
Three times, and drew him under in the mere."

And answer made King Arthur, breathing hard:
"My end draws nigh; 'tis time that I were gone.
Make broad thy shoulders to receive my weight,
And bear me to the margin; yet I fear
My wound hath taken cold, and I shall die."

So saying, from the pavement he half rose,
Slowly, with pain, reclining on his arm,
And looking wistfully with wide blue eyes
As in a picture. Him Sir Bedivere
Remorsefully regarded thro' his tears,
And would have spoken, but he found not words;
Then took with care, and kneeling on one knee,
O'er both his shoulders drew the languid hands,
And rising bore him thro' the place of tombs.

But, as he walk'd, King Arthur panted hard,
Like one that feels a nightmare of his bed
When all the house is mute. So sign'd the King,
Muttering and murmuring at his ear, "Quick, quick!
I fear it is too late, and I shall die."
But the other swiftly strode from ridge to ridge,
Clothed with his breath, and looking, as he walk'd,
Larger than human on the frozen hills.
He heard the deep behind him, and a cry
Before. His own thought drove him like a goad.
Dry clash'd his harness in the icy caves
And barren chasms, and all to left and right
The bare black cliff clang'd round him, as he based
His feet on juts of slippery crag that rang
Sharp-smitten with the dint of armed heels –

And on a sudden, lo! the level lake,
And the long glories of the winter moon.

Then saw they how there hove a dusky barge,
Dark as a funeral scarf from stem to stern,
Beneath them; and descending they were aware
That all the decks were dense with stately forms,
Black-stoled, black-hooded, like a dream – by these
Three Queens with crowns of gold: and from them rose
A cry that shiver'd to the tingling stars,
And, as it were one voice, an agony
Of lamentation, like a wind that shrills
All night in a waste land, where no one comes,
Or hath come, since the making of the world.

Then murmur'd Arthur, "Place me in the barge."
So to the barge they came. There those three Queens
Put forth their hands, and took the King, and wept.
But she, that rose the tallest of them all
And fairest, laid his head upon her lap,
And loosed the shatter'd casque, and chafed his hands,
And call'd him by his name, complaining loud,
And dropping bitter tears against a brow
Striped with dark blood: for all his face was white
And colourless, and like the wither'd moon
Smote by the fresh beam of the springing east;
And all his greaves and cuisses dash'd with drops
Of onset; and the light and lustrous curls –
That made his forehead like a rising sun
High from the dais-throne – were parch'd with dust;
Or, clotted into points and hanging loose,
Mix'd with the knightly growth that fringed his lips.
So like a shatter'd column lay the King;
Not like that Arthur who, with lance in rest,
From spur to plume a star of tournament,
Shot thro' the lists at Camelot, and charged
Before the eyes of ladies and of kings.

Then loudly cried the bold Sir Bedivere:
"Ah! my Lord Arthur, whither shall I go?
Where shall I hide my forehead and my eyes?
For now I see the true old times are dead,
When every morning brought a noble chance,

And every chance brought out a noble knight.
Such times have been not since the light that led
The holy Elders with the gift of myrrh.
But now the whole Round Table is dissolved
Which was an image of the mighty world,
And I, the last, go forth companionless,
And the days darken round me, and the years,
Among new men, strange faces, other minds."

And slowly answer'd Arthur from the barge:
"The old order changeth, yielding place to new,
And God fulfils himself in many ways,
Lest one good custom should corrupt the world.
Comfort thyself: what comfort is in me?
I have lived my life, and that which I have done
May He within himself make pure! but thou,
If thou shouldst never see my face again,
Pray for my soul. More things are wrought by prayer
Than this world dreams of. Wherefore, let thy voice
Rise like a fountain for me night and day.
For what are men better than sheep or goats
That nourish a blind life within the brain,
If, knowing God, they lift not hands of prayer
Both for themselves and those who call them friend?
For so the whole round earth is every way
Bound by gold chains about the feet of God.
But now farewell. I am going a long way
With these thou seest – if indeed I go
(For all my mind is clouded with a doubt) –
To the island-valley of Avilion;
Where falls not hail, or rain, or any snow,
Nor ever wind blows loudly; but it lies
Deep-meadow'd, happy, fair with orchard lawns
And bowery hollows crown'd with summer sea,
Where I will heal me of my grievous wound."

So said he, and the barge with oar and sail
Moved from the brink, like some full-breasted swan
That, fluting a wild carol ere her death,
Ruffles her pure cold plume, and takes the flood
With swarthy webs. Long stood Sir Bedivere
Revolving many memories, till the hull

Look'd one black dot against the verge of dawn.
And on the mere the wailing died away.

But when that moan had passed for evermore,
The stillness of the dead world's winter dawn
Amazed him, and he groan'd, "The King is gone."
And therewithal came on him the weird rhyme,
"From the great deep to the great deep he goes."

Whereat he slowly turn'd and slowly clomb
The last hard footstep of that iron crag;
Thence mark'd the black hull moving yet, and cried,
"He passes to be King among the dead,
And after healing of his grievous wound
He comes again; but – if he come no more –
O me, be yon dark Queens in yon black boat,
Who shriek'd and wail'd, the three whereat we gazed
On that high day, when, clothed with living light,
They stood before his throne in silence, friends
Of Arthur, who should help him at his need?"

Then from the dawn it seem'd there came, but faint
As from beyond the limit of the world,
Like the last echo born of a great cry,
Sounds, as if some fair city were one voice
Around a king returning from his wars.

Thereat once more he moved about, and clomb
Ev'n to the highest he could climb, and saw,
Straining his eyes beneath an arch of hand,
Or thought he saw, the speck that bare the King,
Down that long water opening on the deep
Somewhere far off, pass on and on, and go
From less to less and vanish into light.
And the new sun rose bringing the new year.

THE LADY OF BELEC

Phyllis Ann Karr

These final stories look at the final days of Arthur's knights and the aftermath of the dissolution of the Round Table. Phyllis Ann Karr (b. 1944) is a noted authority on Arthur, having compiled The King Arthur Companion *(1983), recently revised as* The Arthurian Companion *(1997). She is also the author of* The Idylls of the Queen *(1982) and a number of short stories. In fact she is the only author to appear in all five of my previous Arthurian anthologies as well as this one.*

Until after the birth of their third child, her lord had locked her into a chastity belt each morning, hanging the key around his neck before opening the door of their bedchamber. At night, he would relock the door with a large key and hide the key somewhere about the chamber while she undressed by rushlight, with her back to him, her eyes seeing only his shadow moving on the tapestry. When all was ready, he would summon her to the bed, unlock the chastity belt, and pull her under the linen sheets and the covers of animals furs to him.

The Lady of Belec did not complain. The chastity belt was a symbol of his love for her. She was his jewel, to be guarded as carefully as a soft, white pearl from the depth of the sea, or the golden amber that hyenas emitted from their bodies and buried jealously in the sand to keep it from mankind, or a great ruby like the Heart's Blood of Jesu, crystallized in the holy chalice. She might have asked to wear the belt on the top of her gown, as she heard some of the high Ladies did at court, especially when it became fashionable after the goblet of Queen Morgan le Fay showed the unfaithfulness of womankind in the courts of King Mark and King Arthur. But the Lady of Belec was not quite clever enough with her fingers to make the slits that would be needed in order to fit the metal through her skirt, nor quite bold enough to have worn a gown so perforated. Sufficient that the Lord of Belec wore the small iron key in plain sight against the murrey brown cloth of his surcoat.

Nevertheless, the symbol of his love was not comfortable, and she was glad each time he laid the belt aside for a few months in consideration of a child swelling within her.

The first two babes were daughters, coming little more than a year apart; and, after the birth and the churching, the chastity belt. The third child was, at last, a boy; and, after his birth, the Lord of Belec brought out the belt no more, except when he left the castle to hunt or to visit some old friend or kinsman. It was as if by giving him a son she had at last proven her faithfulness, as if only now did the Lord of Belec consider their marriage fully sealed.

She rejoiced in the freedom with which she could now move by day – freedom all but forgotten since her girlhood years. And yet, conversely, now that he seemed satisfied with their union, she felt less secure, and thought wistfully sometimes of the old nightly rituals . . . as she thought wistfully of so many things in her past.

Once, when she was a girl not quite fifteen, Sir Gawaine had visited this castle of Belec, her father's castle then. Sir Gawaine of Orkney, Sir Gawaine of the golden tongue, Sir Gawaine the favorite nephew of the King himself, Sir Gawaine with the golden pentangle, the symbol of perfection, on the crimson of his shield and surcoat. The great Sir Gawaine, in his early manhood then, looking to her mature, strong, ageless, and, with his fine golden hair falling to his shoulders, his fine golden beard, his kind brown eyes and ready smile, seeming to her much as she thought sweet Jesu must have been when He walked among the unbelieving Jews of the Holy Land. Gawaine's voice seemed to her like Jesu's also – or at least, since Gawaine spoke in pleasantries instead of holy parables, like the voice of an angel fay.

The Damsel of Belec waited on her father and Sir Gawaine as they sat at table and talked of things she could not understand, things she could partly understand, and things she might have understood if she had not had to pour ale or replenish a platter of meat and bread. Often enough to nourish her, though not enough to sate her, Sir Gawaine had looked in her direction, either full in her face or with a soft, sliding glance that showed his awareness of her and appreciation of her efforts, and spoken of matters she could perfectly understand, comparing the flow of life to the flow of the seasons . . . or telling short tales of the bravery, fellowship, and love at court . . . or likening glory to the sun and the sun to the King, love to the moon and the moon to the Queen and the Queen to all good and beautiful womankind.

The old minstrel of Belec had been sick that week with the beginning of the fever that was to kill him, but Sir Gawaine had shown her a few new bransle steps as well as he could without music. Afterwards, they sat together by the fire in her father's chamber (a rare honor for her, to be allowed to sit here with a guest). Sir Gawaine had drawn out Excalibur to show them, holding him up full in the firelight, hilt flashing like the sun and blade gleaming like the moon, and told them the tale of how Arthur had received the great sword from the Lady of the Lake and later given it in trust to his nephew.

Before the Damsel of Belec left them, Sir Gawaine had taken her in his arms, in sight of her father, and kissed her gently on the forehead. For a few moments, her hands felt the beat of his heart beneath the crimson silk of his surcoat; for half a heartbeat, his lips touched her skin.

He had left the next morning before daylight; but often, during the months that followed, she pressed her fingers to her forehead and then to her own heart until she seemed to feel him again, as clearly as when it had truly happened. And, indeed, those few heartbeats had never truly ended for her.

A few years later, feeling his end draw near, her father arranged her marriage with the third son of an old friend. Thus she would gain a lord and protector, and her husband would gain a wife and the castle and the lands of Belec. So far as she knew, only one obstacle had threatened the union.

Her father used to boast of the occasion when they of Belec had entertained the greatest knight of the land and favorite nephew of the King. Her bridegroom-to-be seemed to find displeasure rather than satisfaction in the account. Once the Damsel had heard angry words between her father and her future lord, the younger man hotly demanding proof that his bride was unstained, the older as hotly protesting her honor and his own. This happened in the garden, and they seemed not to be aware she sat in her arbor, enjoying the thick green of summer.

"If any other," she heard her bridegroom say, "*any* other – even the King himself – were to touch . . ."

Her father began to interrupt with a shout, but it turned into choking. Hearing another fit in his cough, the Damsel rushed from the arbor where she had sat innocently concealed. Her future bridegroom did not seem embarrassed.

Her father recovered. The marriage was read and sealed. The next morning her new lord pronounced himself satisfied of her virginity on the bridal night. Yet quarrels continued, long and heated, between her husband and her father. Those which she overheard seemed to be of foolish matters, and she tried to beg her husband not to cause her father more fits. Her husband seemed sincerely to repent of his hot temper; but he could not control it. Some of the folk of Belec whispered that the new lord's temper hastened the old lord's death, and perhaps it was so. But her father was old and ill, and would have died soon in any case.

Once, shortly after the birth of their first son, she ventured to ask her lord, "What would have you done, that first night, had you not found me . . . to your taste?"

"Had I not found you to my taste," he replied, kissing her and trying in his way to make a pleasantry, "I would still have done my duty and given you children, but I would also have taken a paramour."

She suspected he had a paramour already, in the castle of one of those old friends he visited thrice or four times yearly; but all men could not be like holy priests or knights of the King's court, sworn to perfection. "If I had been otherwise to your taste, but not a virgin, my Lord, would you have abandoned me?"

"I would have taken a burning brand from the fire," he said, "and thrust it through your foul body."

She did not mention such things again. Nor did she ever give him cause to quarrel with her. When he sought to quarrel, she was silent, or answered him only with agreement, even when he abused her. Sometimes he would stalk out and quarrel with another; several times over the years there were servants with cracked heads to mend, and three or four times there were dead knights to bury, after her lord indulged his temper. But never did he beat her, as she heard some lords beat their wives. And if sometimes, in temper, he put sword or spear through a retainer or a passing knight-errant, that was less than she heard of other knights doing in sport and honor.

On the whole, she did not regret her marriage. She was practical enough to realize that not everyone could go to court, and that not all loves were for wedding, nor even for bedding. Her lord seemed a good husband to her, in most ways; and even if he were not, he would still have been her father's bequest to her, and precious on that account. She was faithful to him in body and intent; and, when she noticed that those servants and retainers to whom she spoke most often were those with whom her husband was most like to quarrel violently, she learned to keep her eyes lowered at all times except when alone with her husband and children, and to give what few orders she issued through the lips of one of her two damsels.

Always, however, she kept just below the skin of her breast, where he could not see it, a thin line in the shape of the golden pentangle that Sir Gawaine of Orkney wore on shield and surcoat. The five-pointed star was to her more than the symbol of all perfection and all true love, as the memory of the sword Excalibur shining silver and brilliant summed up more than beauty and honor. Together, the sword, the pentangle, and especially the man reflected a glory too bright for the world, a perfection that, being too noble to remain on earth, must rise to Heaven of itself, and in rising draw all the rest of mankind up with it, at least partway. She thought of the other knights, of Sir Gawaine's brother Sir Gareth Beaumains, of his favorite cousin Sir Ywaine of the Lion, of the great Sir Lamorak de Galis, or of Sir Lancelot, of whom Sir Gawaine had spoken as his special friend, giving Lancelot praise that in the opinion of the Damsel of Belec could belong only to Gawaine himself. All other great knights, the King himself, even Jesu in her prayers, all had Sir Gawaine's face, above their various shields and surcoat which her imagination could not quite fill in from the descriptions she had heard.

For thirty-five years, the feel of Sir Gawaine's lips upon her forehead and Sir Gawaine's heartbeat beneath the silk of his surcoat never faded, though the skin that remembered was growing wrinkled and mottled.

From the time of his visit until the time of her marriage, she had counted the days and months, hoping he would come again. Even after marriage, though her mind willed him to stay away – for her husband's sake, not for Sir Gawaine's, who could have defended himself at need against any three other knights who dared attack him in enmity – her heart raced and her hands trembled when she heard of his being anywhere within two day's ride of Belec. But the King's knights must do the King's good work; and the greater the knight, the more he must do. It had been a priceless gift that he came even once, all the more precious in that he came so early in her life, leaving her so many years to cherish the memory.

Belec lay on the way between London and Dover. Surely, she thought, the King's work must bring one of his knights past them here again sooner or later. Whenever, from crenel or thin, deep-set window, she glimpsed some strange knight or party of knights ride by, the blood throbbed in her neck. Even a visit from some lesser companion of the Round Table or the Queen's Knights would be a thing to savor, a second glimpse of the great, noble world beyond the walls and fields of Belec.

No other knight was Gawaine, but another knight could, perhaps, tell her news of him. She was old enough now to sit as mistress, helping entertain visitors; and surely not even the Lord of Belec could grow jealous of hospitality offered to one of Arthur's own good knights.

The Lady of Belec realized unbelievingly that she had been old enough for most of her life, now, to sit as mistress in her father's hall, and never another knight from Arthur's court had she helped to entertain, nor any strange knight at all – only, from time to time, a minstrel, or a wandering holy man, or an old friend of her husband's. Her children, those who had survived childhood, were grown and gone, the last daughter married at an earlier age than her mother had been, the last son killed in the great tournament at Winchester. Unlike their mother, the daughters had left Belec for the castles and manors of their own husbands, where, perhaps, some of them might entertain knights from Arthur's court, or see tournaments. The Lady of Belec had never seen a true tournament, only a small one her father staged at his own castle even before the visit of Sir Gawaine. The thought that her sons had died in the exercise of glory somewhat eased the pain of their deaths. She had never, in any event, felt as close to her sons as to her daughters.

She thought, sometimes, of holding another tournament at Belec. Perhaps it would bring back Sir Gawaine for a day or two. But her lord would never have permitted so many strange knights so close to her; and, moreover, a tournament at Belec could only be a tawdry mockery of such great tournaments as those of Winchester, Lonazep, Surluse, or the Castle of Maidens. Better not to lime the twig for Sir Gawaine at all, than to lime it with such bait!

And then, too – she looked at herself in the water of her small garden pond – she was growing old. If he came now, he would be disappointed in her. Then she remembered that he would have grown old, too . . . ten years older than she. Perhaps it was best that he never return, best to keep the memory of him always as he was thirty-five years ago.

But no. He could never grow old, any more than Jesu in her book of hours could grow old. Or, if he did grow older, it could only ennoble him still more.

The Lady of Belec heard rumours sometimes, news that was months or years old and distorted beyond measure. There was talk that King Arthur's great court was not as it should be, that adultery was more common than faithfulness, that the Queen herself had taken a lover, or several. Now love, now jealousy of the Queen was said to have driven Sir Lancelot mad more times than once. An angel, or several angels, had appeared in the guise of knights and led the companions of the Round Table in search of the Holy Grail; only half these knights had returned to the King, but none had come past Belec.

Then Lancelot had actually been found with the Queen, in her chamber. The Queen had been burned at the stake and Lancelot driven into exile across the sea. Then the Queen had not been burned, but cast off and put into a convent. Then the King himself had crossed the sea, shipping with his host from Cardiff or another port far to the north, to make war on Lancelot for stealing the Queen from him. Then the Queen had not been put into a convent, nor carried over the sea with Lancelot, but was to marry the King's nephew, Prince Mordred, in London; and folk said that Prince Mordred was trying to raise the country to his own banner and soon would be here in the south.

The Lady of Belec sat in her small garden, enclosed by the walls of her father's castle, watching the spring herbs turning into summer herbs and the summer ones into fall, and trying to reconcile the reality of Sir Gawaine's visit thirty-five years ago with the impossibility of what was said to be happening now. All her life she had lived within an area of land that she could have walked across in half a day. One time only had the greatness of King Arthur come into her life. Sir Gawaine's visit was truth to her, and all the rest was falsehood.

Then a great host passed by on its way south to Dover, and folk said it was the new King, Prince Mordred, and that he would have come aside to claim more men from the Lord Belec, but was in too great haste.

Three days went by, then four, and there came rumors of a great battle at Dover, half on the land and half in the sea, with ships sinking for the weight of the blood that was spilled within them.

Close on their heels of these newest rumors, Sir Gawaine came again to Belec.

He came in the night, and he came with thirty men around him, knights, squires, and yeomen. He came with a crowd of country folk following him. The Lady of Belec heard their voices and woke before her husband. She rose, climbed to the narrow window, looked down and saw their torches on the other side of the moat. She did not see Sir Gawaine. She only saw six men carrying a long litter, and a throng of men and torchlights surrounding them. She woke her husband.

The Lord of Belec would not permit her to come down to greet the party of knights. He shut her in the bedchamber, and she heard the heavy bolt fall on the other side of the door.

She could not return to bed. With great care, she dressed herself in her best gown. It was more than twenty years old, older than her youngest daughter, who was not three years away from home; but she rarely had occasion to wear it, and it was still unfrayed, though somewhat faded, like her hair. She plaited her hair slowly, noticing by the firelight that there were still a few strands of black among the long, gray ones. She twined it up on top of her head, and she rubbed her face and neck with the precious, perfumed ointment she used only on the highest feast-days. Then she sat beside the fire and waited.

Soon she heard the bolt withdrawn. She stood, her blood throbbing, wondering what she would say, how she would persuade her lord to allow her to descend to the hall, why it even seemed important that she go.

There was knocking on the door. The Lord of Belec would not have knocked for permission to come into his lady. She called out that whoever was without should enter.

He entered, a strange knight, almost as old as her lord, with an animal she thought might be a lion or a gryffon embroidered on his surcoat. Its colors were hardly visible for the dust. "My Lady?" he said.

"I am the Lady of Belec."

"My cousin visited your castle once, my Lady. He spoke highly of it. Perhaps that was before you came here . . ."

"I have always been here." She would not ask who this knight was, nor who was his cousin; but she thought she could trace a faint resemblance, through the years and the shadows. "Is your cousin below?"

He nodded and stepped aside. She crossed to the open door, and the strange knight, the cousin, escorted her down. Was this, she wondered, the courtesy that fine ladies enjoyed at court? No, it was the poor shred of an ancient garment that the last wearers were trying vainly to hold together in the face of a freezing wind. The spirit . . . aye, she could feel what must have been the old spirit of the cousin knight, struggling to walk steadily beneath grief and weariness. But the grace was lacking.

He led her into her own hall as if she, and not he, were the stranger. She knew her husband must be here, frowning at her. She wondered, very briefly, how the strange knights had persuaded him to allow her presence, to permit her to be brought down by one stranger. Then she forgot the Lord of Belec. For the table was raised on the trestles, and on the table lay a tall man in a crimson surcoat.

She stepped forward. His hands were folded in prayer, the fingertips partially covering the golden pentangle on his breast. No man, how saintly whatsoever, slept with his hands folded in such rigid, motionless prayer. She moved her gaze slowly up to his face.

The silver did not show so clearly in golden hair as in black, but the face was sunken and withered with more than age, the lips were beginning to pull back despite a cloth tied around the jaws, and a gold coin weighed down each eyelid. The Lady of Belec screamed.

Then she stood for several moments, panting, listening to the echoes of her shriek die away in the high beams of her hall. Sir Gawaine of the golden tongue had returned to her at last, and brought with him the reality of all the rumors of these later years.

"Where is the sword Excalibur?" she said. "He should be holding the cross of the sword Excalibur."

"He gave the great sword back to the King when he was dying," said the cousin of Sir Gawaine. "During the battle at Dover, a wound he had from fighting Sir Lancelot reopened."

"Sir Lancelot? He would not have fought with Sir Lancelot." That much remained of the old vision, a memory of how Sir Gawaine had praised Lancelot as his truest friend. They could not have fought, unless in friendship and mere testing of arms.

"Lancelot had killed Gawaine's brothers, rescuing the Queen from the stake."

She screamed again, a longer scream, and fell to her knees, clutching the table, not quite daring to reach farther and touch his hands.

Footsteps approached her. Her husband's voice came down from somewhere above her, angry, but low – unusually low, for his anger. "Stand up. You disgrace my hall."

She stood, but she did not turn to face the Lord of Belec. She gripped the edge of the table and stared down at her other lord, the lord of thirty-five years of hope and trust. "Ah my lord Sir Gawaine!" She reached out at last and seized his folded hands. "Ah my Lord, my noble Lord, the only Lord I have ever loved in all my life!"

It was not only for the death of one man alone that she cried, but for the death of honor and glory and nobility, for the decay of every true and good ideal from within, for the loss of the calm center of her soul.

The sudden shuddering pain in her neck seemed for an instant merely the natural extension of the storm within her. But the strange, dizzy angles at which her eyes met the whirling walls and floor – Mercifully, her consciousness was extinguished before she fully realized what had happened.

Gawaine's cousin, Sir Ywaine of the Lion, and his companions had among them some of the finest of those few who remained to Arthur and all of the Round Table. They cut down the Lord of Belec with immediate justice.

Then they carefully bound the head of the Lady of Belec back to her body. The top bandage was a band of crimson velvet, tied with threads of slightly tarnished gold. They carried her body back with that of Sir Gawaine. Thus, at last, the Lady of Belec came to court with the lord of her true soul, to be buried beside him in the same tomb.

RAVEN'S MEAT

Fay Sampson

*In my introduction to the stories "The Winning of Olwen" and
"John, the Knight of the Lion" I referred to Owain the king of
Rheged who was killed in the Battle of Catraeth in AD 595, and
also to the Celtic tale collected in* The Mabinogion. *We return to
Owain and his legend in this story which uses as its starting point
the tale "The Dream of Rhonabwy", which was probably first
told in the early thirteenth century, but which survives in* The
Red Book of Hergest, *produced a century later. "The Dream of
Rhonabwy" is a surreal story which seems surprisingly advanced
for its period. Rhonabwy is a soldier seeking the renegade Iorwerth
ap Maredudd. He sleeps in an old house and has a dream featuring
many of the great Arthurian heroes which includes a scene in which
Arthur and Owain play chess while Arthur's soldiers fight Owain's
ravens. It is this dreamworld that Fay Sampson uses as her setting
for the following story, which takes that same surreality to explore
the facts versus the legend. Fay Sampson (b. 1935) is the author
of the* Daughter of Tintagel *sequence about the life of Morgan le
Fay:* Wise Woman's Telling *(1989),* White Nun's Telling *(1989),*
Black Smith's Telling *(1990),* Taliesin's Telling *(1991) and* Herself
(1992).

"You don't look comfortable," said the Raven.
"How can I?" Owain shifted his perch on the sword-edge bridge

over a fathomless abyss before a turreted castle. "I'm in the wrong story, aren't I?"

"You've got the chequerboard, though . . . You *have* still got it, haven't you?"

"Oh, that." Owain felt between his medieval surcoat and a full suit of armour. It occurred to him that the gaming board, though inconvenient to carry on a quest, might be more comfortable to sit on here, if he could balance it. "Yes."

"You needn't say, *Oh, that,* in such a particularly irritating tone of voice. It's not every prince who has a gaming board which can make whole armies fall apart when you move the pieces."

"It doesn't make any difference, does it? Arthur always wins. If he doesn't like the way the game is going, and the battle with it, he just tips the board over and crushes my pieces in his fist."

"You've got us, though." Meddwl sidled closer. "Meddwl and Cof."

Owain steeled himself not to shift away, in spite of the fact that a drop to the lions roaring in the chasm was his only available move. "Ravens are bad news."

"Not necessarily. Not if they're *your* Ravens."

"There are times when I wish Gwendoleu had left you to somebody else." Owain wondered immediately if that was a wise thought to have voiced.

"It wouldn't have mattered whether you said it aloud or not," Meddwl clashed his beak in the corvine equivalent of a laugh, "since my specialised function is to collect the thoughts of the world and bring them back to you. It would be no trouble at all to deliver your own in the next consignment."

"But what am I supposed to *do* with thoughts?"

"Ah," said Meddwl. "I was forgetting. You're a Knight of the Round Table now. Thinking is definitely not recommended. It gets in the way of dressing yourself up in a full suit of armour, sallying forth through trackless forests until you spy another suit of armour, then cleaving both helm and brain pan before you realise it was actually your best friend."

"I don't *want* to be a Knight of the Round Table. I wasn't born to it. Look." He dragged a much-thumbed poetry book out of his hauberk and flipped it open. The Raven perched on his shoulder and read.

"*Where is the grave of Arthur? A mystery.*"

"And this?"

"*In Llan Heledd is the grave of Owain.*"

"See? There's a question mark over Arthur. I definitely exist."

"It's charismatic movement," Meddwl said. "The power of outstanding heroes to attract legends of lesser figures from other eras into their orbit."

"Lesser?"

"Sorry. But you did ask."

"Dammit. Dad and I had Taliesin for our royal bard. That's *history*. Have you heard my elegy? He used to practise it tactlessly enough. Intoned it from every hilltop in the North West while he fine-tuned the alliteration."

His voice boomed from the sides of the abyss.

"Buried below is
rich-sung great renown
the wings of white dawn
like shining spears."

A keen wind sang over the sword-bridge. Next moment, Owain was sitting on the knife-edge of Helvellyn. He swung round, dangerously disbelieving the shining panorama of Derwentwater, Coniston Water, Windermere, Ullswater, the far, fair sheen of the Irish Sea.

"It's magic!" he gulped. "No, I mean, it isn't magic. This was it. The real Rheged. Where I was king."

"Taliesin, eh? You're a lucky man." The Raven wiped away a tear with a wingtip. "Very good at laments, the Celts. I wish I had an elegy like that to look forward to. I know what they'll say when Cof and I turn belly up: *One of the Three Fortunate Assassinations.*"

"Can you die?" said Owain, twisting round on the unstable equilibrium of the chequerboard with dangerous enthusiasm. "I didn't think . . ."

"You don't often, do you," snapped Meddwl. "I've seen the inside of your head often enough No, you know the Rules as well as I do. Ravens don't *die. People* die. Some of them get turned into Ravens for ever. We have to spend the rest of time perching on branches, croaking in a sinister way, pretending to be ourselves when actually we're some long-dead mythical hero, Brân or Arthur . . ."

"*Arthur?* But I thought he . . ."

"Ssh." Meddwl nudged him and looked swiftly round. "Not so loud. Remember Clust son of Clustfeinad. Were he to be buried forty feet underground, he would hear an ant fifty miles away when it stirred from its bed in the morning. Forget the . . ."

He scratched on the rock with his beak a cave full of sleeping warriors.

"And the . . ."

A lightning sketch of a dusky barge with three tall queens wearing crowns of, presumably, gold.

"It's going to be one of us when he goes. It's different for *her*." His sly bright eyes lifted to distant speck winging its way up the Lake District towards them. "It's not the dead she's in danger of being taken over by. It's the living. Your mother."

Owain brought his gaze back from the dazzle of that black speck in the clear spring sky to the *Corvus corax* shuffling scaly claws on his shoulder. "My historical mother?"

"Don't act the fool. You know I know you know. Your legendary dam. Morgan le Fay."

"Ah," Owain enunciated carefully.

"Exactly."

The black speck had grown to a spearhead, then a jagged wing-spread. It darkened the sunlit sky in front of Owain unnecessarily close before flapping down to a ledge below his feet. Meddwl picked up the end of a golden chain trailing from her and snapped it round his own leg.

"Lunch," said Cof, cocking her head at him.

Meddwl on Owain's shoulder twisted his neck so that the beak was just under the prince's chin and an eye reflecting the first lambswool cloud danced out of focus in the corner of his vision.

Owain looked away. "Do you have to?"

"Your uncle never missed."

Owain dislodged the leaning Raven from his shoulder and stood up cautiously, retrieving the silver chequerboard from its unstable balance. The vision of peaks and lakes swam round him. The hedge of magic mist was closing in, eliminating it.

He slipped the game board into its pouch. "We'd better get down before it's sword-bridge time again and the lions get us."

In an anticipatory scramble of wings Cof hopped up closer.

Owain picked up his limewood shield, with three black birds crudely painted on it. "I'm sick of this. Could I become a Raven?"

The beating feathers fell still. "You?"

"You've got your warhost, Owain's Ravens."

"But you're . . ."

"I mean, in your case, it's metaphorical."

"Not in the Dream of Rhonabwy, it isn't." Owain started

to stride down Striding Edge. "That was real Ravens picking
Arthur's warriors up off the ground, tearing them limb from limb
and scattering heads and eyes and ears on the ground."

"Not you, though." Meddwl was flapping alongside his left
ear.

"You and Arthur were having a contest on the gaming board,"
Cof croaked in his right ear.

"And I was winning at last," Owain broke into a run down the
steepening track, "until Arthur kicked the board over."

"And you think that if *he* was a Raven . . ."

"And *you* . . ." suggested Cof.

"Only once he's dead," Meddwl said.

"My mother doesn't need to die first."

The two Ravens landed on the stones in front of him.

"He has a point."

"If it's in the blood."

"Oh, *blood*."

"Lunch?"

They entered the mist. The bare black cliff rang round Owain
as he based his feet on juts of slippery crag that rang sharp-smitten
with the dint of armed heels. And on a sudden, lo! the level lake.
The wrong lake. No map of Cumbria would ever show this.

Owain strode along the margin of the enchanted mere into his
high-roofed hall and surveyed the guards. They stood straight-faced,
staring in front of them, trying not to make eye-contact. The Ravens
eyed the lines hungrily, while Owain made his selection. In his haste
to form an inconspicuous unit in the ranks, one of the men had
trodden in a wolfhound's turd. A louse crawled across the sweating
forehead of another.

"Him," said Owain. "And him."

The men shuddered, and went outside to get the waiting
corpses.

The Ravens settled to enjoy their rations.

"Now," said Owain, when they had finished. "Do it."

The boards of the floor appeared disconcertingly close, the filth
among the trampled chaff disgustingly detailed. Owain did not
like this sudden foreshortening of his height. It was not a pleasant
feeling to be below the knees of guards he had looked down on
from the saddle, as he rode at their head into battle, or from his
superior table on the dais, while they drank to his victories. He
fought to restrain the impulse to stab their legs with the black beak
he saw extending a considerable way in front of him. It looked a

serviceable weapon, with a heavy curve to the upper mandible and a sharp point.

He flapped, ran awkwardly and found himself airborne. Or smoke-borne. The atmosphere in the hall was thick. The men dodged back from his uncertain circling. The women crouched over the benches, watching through their clutched hair. The rectangle of shining air and water called to him. He darted out over a magic, mist-hung mere. Just for a moment, it bore a painfully unfair resemblance to the real Ullswater.

He was not alone. A flutter of black to left and right showed Meddwl and Cof flying just behind him. They made a dark chevron, more suited to ducks than ravens. Performing a ragged somersault to see more clearly behind, he spotted that the other two were still looped together by the golden chain.

"You don't fool me," he grunted. "Enchanted princesses you two are not."

"The important thing," Meddwl called back, "is to get the timing right."

They flew south over a barren fastness of zig-zag paths and juts of pointed rock.

Several weary hours later Owain grunted. "Somebody should signpost this as a long-distance Way."

At last the contours softened. The ravens descended into billowing forest. Through the trees a river flowed deep and dark, except where it bubbled silver over stones to form a ford. No one was about. Owain landed and hopped nearer. Thirst had become intense.

"Better not," Meddwl advised. "Your mother might not like it. At best, you could end up as the next champion guarding the ford. At worst . . ."

"*That* ford?"

Cof nodded. As Owain looked, an invisible castle shimmered into three-dimensional architecture across the river. A knight, eager to lend him shield and lance, could not be far away.

"I'm not a complete fool. I've no intention of blowing any horn or scattering water from a silver bowl or anything in that line of provocation. Away from this ford, it's probably a perfectly ordinary river, suitable for drinking purposes."

Meddwl ruffled his shoulder feathers in an avian shrug. "Have it your own way."

The water was cold enough to shock, intensely refreshing. It made Owain think of May Day dew, of the first wild plums, or fresh-killed frogs. He jumped at the last thought, scattering a spray of drops on the stones. As his wings flapped to regain his balance, an unseen horn slung from the branch above him began to hum.

"I didn't do it," gabbled Owain. "I never touched it."

The undergrowth crackled. Thunder rent the sky. Rain hurtled down on them like a volley of arrows. As the stormburst switched itself off a knight in sable armour came crashing down the track from the castle.

Owain's wet wings sagged. "Sorry, Dad. Wrong romance. I'm looking for Arthur."

Urien Rheged pushed up his helmet, so that it balanced like the jaws of a porpoise straining to swallow his head. He leaned down from the saddle to peer at the bird. "My family always said you favoured your mother. I see the resemblance now."

"What time is it?" cawed Owain. "Is Arthur dead?"

"Fighting time." Urien snapped his helmet shut. "Since you don't look as if you could hold a shield and spear, we might as well begin."

Meddwl and Cof flew up hastily to the tallest tree, snapping off a shower of twigs as the golden chain snagged.

Owain leaped sideways. "No, Dad. All I want is a re-match with Arthur. Be reasonable. I forgot the legends had got you too. Perhaps I can get both of us out of this."

"No son of Urien Rheged runs away from battle."

"But you really want to get back to Rheged, don't you? The homesteads among the apple trees in the dales, a king's mantle of heather on the hills, the poignant cry of the gulls and the waves washing our horses' tails. Remember? The real Rheged, where you were King of the Baptised World, Battle-Goad, Anchor of the Kingdom?"

"Right now, your mother's set me to defend this fairy ford. Have at thee."

With a little groan, Owain launched himself into the air and darted in, straight past Urien's guard. While his father beat wildly with his wooden shield at the storm of black feathers in front of his face, the Raven Prince tore at his plumage and stuffed up the eyeholes of Urien's helmet. The blinded king tumbled backwards out of the saddle on to the stones of the ford.

"Ouch. I bet that hurt," said Owain, landing on his father's breastplate.

"Mmemm omm omm mme," came the answer through a mouthful of feathers.

"I want that boy next," boomed a female voice from the castle.

The sky darkened with a flight of carrion crows.

"Hail, Prince," screamed their leader. "This year's champion."

"I haven't got time to defend fords," Owain snapped. "I only stopped for a drink."

There was a shriek from the castle, a crash and a tumult of smoke. Thick darkness fell. Out of the darkness the crows fell on Owain.

He fought back with beak and wings, slashing and striking at the smaller birds. They ripped the primaries from his leading edge, tore the down from his throat, stabbed for his eyes. But it was Owain's beak which pierced the breast of a crow. A comely young damsel tumbled on to the bank. As she fell, a wail rang from the ruins of the castle.

"I say, I'm frightfully sorry," gasped Owain. "I'd no idea. Are you all right?"

The blood spread over her breast while her face turned marble white. The black birds swooped down and scooped her up into the clearing sky. Half of them turned back and started to lift Urien too, where he lay on his back in the shallows still spitting black feathers.

"Not me, you idiots," he groaned. "I've no wish to go to Avalon. My son's your client. He wants to follow Arthur."

"I do *not*," grunted Owain through gritted beak, "want to follow Arthur. That is the whole point. I am trying to recover my real self."

Urien sat up in the ford and stared at the dripping feathers of the indignant Raven. "Really? You could have fooled me."

A crooked-winged crow hopped round Owain and examined him critically. "Avalon? Are you sure? He's lost a few flight feathers. But he doesn't look very dead to me."

"I wasn't asking for stately forms, black-stoled, black-hooded, like a dream, to bear me away in an agony of lamentation, like a wind that shrills all night in a waste land, where no one comes, or hath come, since the making of the world. I just want to meet Arthur. After he's dead."

The limping crow edged alongside her leader. "Do we give return flights to Avalon?"

"The Isles of the Blest beyond the setting sun?"

"It's getting a bit late for that. Glastonbury's nearer. Most people can't tell the difference."

"We heard that," said Meddwl. The chained Ravens had taken the risk of coming down from the treetops.

"As long as he meets Arthur," called Urien, tipping the water out of his greaves.

"That's the one thing he doesn't have to worry about," the leading crow screamed. 'Arthur's not going to let him get away. Alive or dead. Ready?"

It was as if he had flown too close to the vortex of a waterspout. The power caught him helpless. The crows lifted the damaged Raven in a spiralling rush and then steadied to a straight flight path towards the setting sun. Meddwl and Cof flew yoked by their golden chain behind him. Owain was sucked onward in the slipstream of the spearing crows. Then he was spinning again, on a giddily shortening radius closer and closer to the focus through which he must plunge into oblivion.

There was rock rushing up under him, geologically real as the summit of Helvellyn he had felt beneath him for an aching moment that morning. It was almost sunset. They dropped him to flutter down on to Glastonbury Tor. The level golden light was striking towards him along drainage channels and meres, ringing the Tor with shining spears. A funeral psalm was rising from the abbey below.

"Nearly suppertime," said Cof. "Two British corpses, twice a day. You know the Rules."

"I don't know why you can't eat Saxons. It would be more patriotic."

"I spy a graveyard down there," said Meddwl. "It might save you trouble."

The crows were preparing for take-off. "Enjoy the rest of your trip." They spiralled into the lemon glow of the eastern sky.

The sound of the abbey bell precipitated a crisis of confidence in the Raven Prince.

"Is this honourable? Ought I, at this point, to change back into a human? Meet him man to man, should you think?"

"Stick it out," croaked Meddwl. "You always played him in human form before, didn't you? Look what happened."

Owain saw again the golden gaming pieces crushed in Arthur's fist, the upended board. He looked at his own black claw hooked on the rock. He clenched it experimentally.

"You're right," he cawed. "Ravens it is."

Owain could barely fly. He flopped on torn wings down the hill, with Meddwl and Cof a watchful flap behind. The monks were filing out of the cemetery towards the abbey church. Two stayed behind, shovelling newly-dug earth into the grave. Owain staggered on to the branch of a thorn tree with his companions.

"Looks a big one," said Meddwl.

"You're sure it's British?" Cof nearly overbalanced as she peered down.

Owain fluttered down to a lower branch. Over the humped back of the nearer monk he saw a lead marker lying in the long grass. He read the inscription aloud.

"HIC JACET INCLITUS REX ARTURIUS IN INSULA AVALON."

"Come again?"

"HERE LIES BURIED THE RENOWNED KING ARTHUR IN THE ISLE OF AVALON."

"We'll buy it," said Meddwl. "We're a legend too."

Cof's beak gaped like a ravenous nestling. "So that's Arthur? That's all right, then. They don't come much more British than him."

"Hang on." Even Meddwl looked shocked. "I mean. Arthur? For supper? It's not even a feast day, is it? Pentecost or anything."

"He was a big man, by the look of that coffin." Cof had her head on one side. "You wouldn't need seconds."

"I don't like the way this conversation is going," Owain croaked. "I mean, I know from a Raven's point of view it's just carrion. And Arthur's got a lot to answer for to my family. We were making a perfectly good job of defending Rheged against the Saxons without his help. We won Wensleydale. We flattened flaming Flamddwyn. We lambasted them the length of the land to Lindisfarne. What help was Arthur to us then? He was seventy years dead . . . if he existed at all."

"There you are, then. If he's dead, he's fair game. Fairly gamey, too, by now."

"You've missed the point. They've only just buried him today. I'm out of my time. That's why it's got to be Ravens this round."

"Have it your own way. A gwyddbwll game instead of a gourmet dinner. As long as you realise you still owe us one."

The earth was thudding on the oak-log coffin from the monks' shovels.

"Better be quick," said Meddwl. "Or he'll be nine feet under."

Owain lifted his beak. The sky was still steeped in lemon.

"Do you have a suggestion?"

Meddwl and Cof looked sideways at each other. They rattled the gold chain between them. From the Tor came an answering tinkle, as of a handbell. The monks straightened up at once and began to intone the evening psalm. The sound above them swelled.

The far-off tinkling deepened to an unmusical clanking. Down the
hill, bounding across the levels of the spiralling maze, came a round
object throwing off metallic gleams where it caught the last sunrays.
It leaped the boundary bank of the abbey, heading straight for the
cemetery. The two gravediggers in its path dropped their shovels,
hitched up their skirts and sprinted for the church door.

Meddwl and Cof flew down to the grass. They separated in
front of the open grave, so that the golden chain stretched taut
as a finishing line, and braced themselves. Owain stood well clear.
The rolling missile rang as it hit the first gravestone. With a louder
clang, it bounced over the next one. Striking the third, it gave a huge
bound, cleared the finishing chain, and landed on three short legs.
The handle clanked and fell still. A huge, empty, bronze cauldron
stood beside Arthur's grave.

"Right," ordered Cof. "Hoist him in."

"Look," said Owain. "We've been through this before. I draw
the line at eating kings."

"Think *cauldron*," explained Meddwl patiently. "This is the Celtic
legend bit. As in: nine maidens fanning it with their breath? Won't
boil the meat of a coward? Raises slain warriors to fight again?

"Oh, *that* sort of cauldron."

"I knew Gwyn ap Nudd was bound to be up there getting his pots
and pans together for May Day. The King of the Fairies doing battle
to win his lady-love. Happens every year, regular as the new moon,
till the day of doom. He always has a cook-up afterwards."

Cof hopped into the hole. She shuffled piled earth from the
coffin with her claws. It was hollowed from a single tree-trunk.
Meddwl dropped to help her. With their broad beaks they prised
the lid open.

"There's two of them," said Meddwl. "And she's got yellow
hair."

"That'll be the sweeter one."

"I'm warning you," said Owain.

Meddwl tugged at the dead king's shroud. "The size of that coffin
wasn't lying. He's a big lad. Do you think we'll get him all in?"

"He's long past *rigor mortis*. He'll bend at the knees."

"Or break."

The three Ravens hauled Arthur's corpse out of the grave and
heaved his head over the edge of the cauldron.

"What about her?" said Cof, still looking at Guinevere.

"Forget it. She was always trouble."

"You've been talking to my mother," said Owain.

"Morgan's one of us."

Arthur's toes hung over the rim of the full-crammed cauldron, imperially purple. Owain watched.

"What happens now? I've a feeling we left something out. Shouldn't I have blown a horn to rouse him from slumber? Or banged a drum?"

"You're too early for Francis Drake."

"Well, we seem to have a bird."

In the shadows of the cauldron Arthur's shroud was darkening, the purpled toes contracting into claws, loosened limbs flapping. A large black carrion bird exploded into the air and balanced just over their heads.

"Is that him? I was expecting an armed warrior, in full fighting mode, only speechless."

"I told you. Morgan lets him leave Avalon in the form of a Raven. It's what you wanted, isn't it?"

The fourth Raven took up position in the thorn tree above them. He was considerably larger than the others.

"I summoned you," cawed Owain, "to settle some unfinished business. There was a little matter of a gwyddbwyll game. You weren't a very good loser."

The royal Raven puffed out his feathers, though it was a warm evening.

"I think," translated Meddwl, "he means he's Arthur the King. He doesn't lose."

"Did anybody bring the gaming board?"

Meddwl lifted one ragged wing. A silver square slipped to the ground. It was smaller than the board Owain had perched on over the moat, but it was chased with sixty-four chequered squares and it had a miniature set of the same golden pieces. Untouched by anyone's beak or claw, these took up their starting positions. The little king stood ready, opposed by the hunt.

Owain hopped closer. The royal Raven clapped his wings and landed heavily on the opposite side of the board. Under their bright black eyes the pieces began to move.

The game flooded and ebbed across the squares. Arthur's king dashed for freedom and was driven back. Owain's concentration was driving the hunt. They were closing in.

Shrieks split the air. A young squire, who had not shaved that morning, wearing a white and purple tunic slashed with gold, and a gold cap hung with tassels of purple and scarlet, with white and black chequered stockings above boots of purple leather and a cloak of gold fringed with white and black, carrying a bleeding spear of gold tipped with a polecat's head, came running up and cried out,

"Sire, Sire! Owain's Raven Band are attacking your warriors. They are carrying them up into the air, and arms and legs and noses and teeth and other essential bits are dropping off all over the place."

The black mandibles of Arthur's beak clashed together.

"I think the general idea is, he'd like you to call off your Raven Band," Meddwl prompted.

"Play on," snapped Owain.

The crowned gold piece lunged for the boundary. Three smooth moves later, Owain scooped the trapped king off the board.

"My game, I think."

Owain's eyes sparkled across the squares. Before he could issue another challenge, Arthur's furious look sent the gold figures leaping back to their starting positions. The next game began. Owain's side rushed to the attack.

"Just remember," Cof looked up at the fading sky and gave a gentle cough, "it's the *last* game that counts."

The hunt faltered. Back and forth they jumped between the squares, but the king went racing past unharmed.

A freckled, squint-eyed lad came dashing into the graveyard on a piebald pony with trappings of orange and crimson, an emerald bonnet on his head from which floated a rose-pink scarf over the diamond-weave of his crimson and yellow tunic that ended above bare legs, with his feet shod in pointed shoes of orange leather buckled with gold, and a mantle of pink chaffinch feathers tasselled with yellow silk over the lot.

"My lord Owain," he gasped. "Is it by your leave that Arthur's men are hacking your Raven Band to pieces? There's guts and claws and feathers enough to stuff a castle-ful of cushions."

"Sire," rasped Owain. "Call off your warhost."

Arthur did not so much as glance up from the board. His bird stare sent the golden king shooting across the remaining squares, heading for the margin of the board that would mean victory. Owain's hunt changed direction and staggered after him, without conviction. His king reached freedom. The royal Raven gave a bound of triumph that sent the defeated pieces jumping from the silver board into the grass.

"All square." Meddwl jigged up and down, twitching his chain, until Cof tugged at her end so sharply she almost throttled him.

The pieces disentangled themselves from the herbage and took up their places again.

"Now." The word hissed through Meddwl's beak.

Owain's black eyes met his opponent's across the board. "Let me go, Arthur. Please. It's all I want. Just to be King of Rheged, the Men of the North, as I really was. I want out of your legend."

Wings lifted regally.

Now it was the turn of Owain's king to circle this way and that, looking for a way out. Arthur's hunt moved ahead of him, behind him, cutting him off. Like the tide ebbing out through the rocky defences of a coast, the game fell back, crept forward, began to turn. The little king was within one square of freedom.

A lank-haired boy came galloping up on a high-mettled glossy black pony with a royal blue saddlecloth and harness of silvered leather, wearing boots of the same over hose of striped sky blue and green, with a tartan kilt in green and scarlet and black and a plaid of seven hues from lime to lavender surmounted by a turban of lilac and bottle green with a gilded ostrich feather fastened by a square-cut garnet in a silver cruciform brooch and a . . .

"Get on with it," said Meddwl. "Who's winning now?"

The boy fingered regretfully the gloves of griffin leather stitched with peacock blue and buckled around the wrist with leviathan's teeth, which there had been no opportunity to describe. "Owain," he scowled.

Arthur lifted a massive black claw over the board. Owain cocked his head and watched. He would have smiled if the shape of his beak had permitted it.

"You can't smash the pieces this time. You're just a bird. The ghost of a bird. You have to let me go."

"Careful," Meddwl said swiftly. "Just because he doesn't speak, it doesn't follow he's not dangerous."

The claw descended. Owain's pieces went flying in all directions. Some of them tumbled into the open grave. Owain lunged forward. He snatched up Arthur's king. It had just occurred to him that the broad black beak was a stronger tool than his claws.

Breath whistled from Cof. "Can he really do it? Can he break Arthur?"

"I bet he can't," said Meddwl.

Owain's beak grated on sculptured gold. Arthur advanced a step, pinions raised, spreading. The board scraped under hooking claws.

"It's Owain's turn," pleaded Cof. "He was winning."

"Not now," said Meddwl. "He never will. The legend's got him."

Arthur hopped heavily to the centre of the board. The silver squares rocked. Owain's beak was rasping, trembling on the gold of the king-shaped gaming piece. No word came from the royal Raven's throat. The black eyes refused to let the Prince of Rheged go.

The golden robes in Owain's beak wobbled.

"Hold on," groaned Meddwl.

"Gold's not that tough to cut. You can do it. Bite." The golden chain between the birds jangled with Cof's agitation and broke apart.

The royal Raven heard it. His eyes snapped alarm, but he did not look round. One black claw lifted. His gaze did not leave Owain's.

Owain Rheged's – Sir Owain's – eyes never blinked. But like a tear in the sunset the little golden king slipped from his slackened beak, tumbled down over his breast feathers, fell on to the squares. Silver clashed against gold. Arthur snatched up his king and set it in the winning position on the cleared board.

"Caw," he broke his silence at last.

"Sire," begged Owain. "I was winning. Let me go. I *loved* Rheged, damn you. The Mabon Stone on the Solway Firth. The red walls of Carlisle. There were daffodils gilding Ullswater every Lent. I rode the dragon spine of the Roman Wall from coast to coast. It was all Rheged. Our land. The snow piled up in breakers on Shap Fell. The dales dancing with red squirrels. Jet on the beach at Whitby and black-faced lambs. I was the real Owain. My father was really Urien. We had the real Taliesin playing his real harp to us. Listen. Can you hear it? The actual harp of the living Taliesin, in a genuine, physical mead-hall. Mine. Shall I sing you one of his very songs?"

"*Owain, scourge of the Saxons,*
Defied Flame-Bearer.
"*Coel's kin would be a weak warrior*
Before he gave you a hostage."

Cof gave a stifled squawk. Owain's feathers were fading. The strong shapes of buckskin boots, chequered tunic and silver bound scabbard were beginning to show through.

". . . The sands to Holy Island, like silver smoke. Salmon leaping up the pebbles of the Ribble. We shed real blood at Catterick for that land."

Arthur's claw pinned his little king to its winning square. The twilight opposite him began to shudder. The bush of Owain's beard was sinking back into a black-downed, throat, the woollen breeches contracting to scaly legs, the sweep of his cloak to a wedge-shaped tail.

"Told you," grunted Meddwl.

"Is that it, then? That's all you've got to say? I've lost it all, have I? Rheged. Reality. You're going to force me back to your Round Table that never was. And what do I get in exchange? Stopping my mother stealing Excalibur and killing you? A magic fountain? A ring to make me invisible? A portcullis that cuts my horse in half? It's not a fair exchange. I was a real king, of a real country, fighting real Saxons. Can't you understand? I *really* loved my land."

"Caw," said Arthur. "Kneel."

The dusk blossomed. Black feathers rose into a white surcoat blazoned with a scarlet cross, over silver armour. King Arthur bestrode the board, a mighty monarch wearing the crown of England. He was taller than ordinary men. His hair was as fair and his eyes as blue as any Saxon's. His hand played with the jewel-rich hilt of Excalibur at his hip. Blue eyes flashed scorn at the bedraggled Owain.

"Tough," translated Meddwl. "History is what people want to believe. He's King Arthur. There's no contest."

The twilight shimmered on the other side of the board. There was a struggle of feathers, a cry of anguish, before a lesser knight of the Round Table materialized in full medieval armour, his visor down.

"You're jealous. I was a king. I'm talking fact."

King Arthur toyed with Excalibur. The ruby eyes of the dragons on the hilt sparkled warning. Owain's voice boomed.

"The grave of Arthur, question mark?" His pain was hidden in the hollow of his helmet. "My father was Urien Rheged. We're in all the king-lists. Does your legend count more than the true history of Britain? The King Arthur Experience?"

The sun dipped below the Somerset Levels. The last ray caught the sparkling coronet round Arthur's helmet. He settled his hands on his hips and his smile broadened. What need was there for him to answer this knight?

Owain's knees were buckling. "Warleader, at the most, you. If you ever existed."

The dusk was silent.

Dew was falling through the holes of his helmet. "Let me go home."

The hero towering over him half drew Excalibur from its scabbard and fondled the blade.

Sir Owain knelt before him, head bowed. He held out his own quivering sword in homage to King Arthur. "Please . . . Sire!"

"The sun's set." Cof said to nobody in particular. "Suppertime. Two British corpses?"

THE QUIET MONK

Jane Yolen

And so we return from the world of Arthur back into recorded history, to the time of the rediscovery of Arthur and the birth of the legend. Jane Yolen (b. 1939) is a prolific writer of books for adults and children, and is arguably the greatest modern exponent of the fairy tale. She has written several books and stories based on Arthurian themes and characters including Merlin's Booke *(1986) for adults and* Merlin and the Dragons *(1995) and the* Young Merlin *trilogy for younger readers.*

Glastonbury Abbey, in the year of Our Lord 1191
He was a tall man, and his shoulders looked broad even under the shapeless disguise of the brown sacking. The hood hid the color of his hair and, when he pushed the hood back, the tonsure was so close cropped, he might have been a blonde or a redhead or gray. It was his eyes that held one's interest most. They were the kind of blue that I had only seen on midsummer skies, with the whites the color of bleached muslin. He was a handsome man, with a strong, thin nose and a mouth that would make all the women in the parish sure to shake their heads with the waste of it. They were a lusty lot, the parish dames, so I had been warned.

I was to be his guide as I was the spirest of the brothers, even with my twisted leg, for I was that much younger than the rest, being newly come to my vocation, one of the few infant oblates who actually joined that convocation of saints. Most left to go into trade, though a few, it must be admitted, joined the army, safe in their hearts for a peaceful death.

Father Joseph said I was not to call the small community "saints," for sainthood must be earned not conferred, but my birth father told me, before he gave me to the abbey, that by living in such close quarters with saintly men I could become one. And that he, by gifting me, would win a place on high. I am not sure if all this was truly accomplished, for my father died of a disease his third wife brought to their marriage bed, a strange wedding portion indeed. And mostly my time in the abbey was taken up not in prayer side by side with saints but on my knees cleaning the abbot's room, the long dark halls, and the *dortoir*. Still, it was better than being back at home in Meade's Hall where I was the butt of every joke, no matter I was the son of the lord. His eighth son, born twisted ankle to thigh, the murderer of his own mother at the hard birthing. At least in Glastonbury Abbey I was needed, if not exactly loved.

So when the tall wanderer knocked on the door late that Sunday night, and I was the watcher at the gate, Brother Sanctus being abed with a shaking fever, I got to see the quiet monk first.

It is wrong, I know, to love another man in that way. It is wrong to worship a fellow human even above God. It is the one great warning drummed into infant oblates from the start. For a boy's heart is a natural altar and many strange deities ask for sacrifice there. But I loved him when first I saw him for the hope I saw imprinted on his face and the mask of sorrow over it.

He did not ask to come in; he demanded it. But he never raised his voice nor spoke other than quietly. That is why we dubbed him the Quiet Monk and rarely used his name. Yet he owned a voice with more authority than even Abbot Giraldus could command, for *he* is a shouter. Until I met the Quiet Monk, I had quaked at the abbot's bluster. Now I know it for what it truly is: fear masquerading as power.

"I seek a quiet corner of your abbey and a word with your abbot after his morning prayers and ablutions," the Quiet Monk said.

I opened the gate, conscious of the squawking lock and the cries of the wood as it moved. Unlike many abbeys, we had no rooms ready for visitors. Indeed we never entertained guests anymore. We could scarce feed ourselves these days. But I did not tell *him* that. I led him to my own room, identical to all the others save the abbot's, which was even meaner, as Abbot Giraldus reminded us daily. The Quiet Monk did not seem to notice, but nodded silently and eased himself onto my thin pallet, falling asleep at once. Only soldiers and monks have such a facility. My father, who once led a cavalry, had it. And I, since coming to the abbey, had it, too. I covered him gently with my one thin blanket and crept from the room.

In the morning, the Quiet Monk talked for a long time with Abbot Giraldus and then with Fathers Joseph and Paul. He joined us in our prayers, and when we sang, his voice leaped over the rest, even over the sopranos of the infant oblates and the lovely tenor of Brother John. He stayed far longer on his knees than any, at the last prostrating himself on the cold stone floor for over an hour. That caused the abbot much distress, which manifested itself in a tantrum aimed at my skills at cleaning. I had to rewash the floor in the abbot's room where the stones were already smooth from his years of penances.

Brother Denneys – for so was the Quiet Monk's name, called he said after the least of boys who shook him out of a dream of apathy – was given leave to stay until a certain task was accomplished. But before the task could be done, permission would have to be gotten from the pope.

What that task was to be, neither the abbot nor Fathers Joseph or Paul would tell. And if I wanted to know, the only one I might turn to was Brother Denneys himself. Or I could wait until word came from the Holy Father, which word – as we all knew full well – might take days, weeks, even months over the slow roads between Glastonbury and Rome. If word came at all.

Meanwhile, Brother Denneys was a strong back and a stronger hand. And wonder of wonders (a miracle, said Father Joseph, who did not parcel out miracles with any regularity), he also had a deep pocket of gold which he shared with Brother Aermand, who cooked our meagre meals. As long as Brother Denneys remained at the abbey, we all knew we would eat rather better than we had in many a year. Perhaps that is why it took so long for word to come from the pope. So it was our small convocation of saints became miners, digging gold out of a particular seam. Not all miracles, Father Joseph had once said, proceed from a loving heart. Some, he had mused, come from too little food or too much wine or not enough sleep. And, I added to myself, from too great a longing for gold.

Ours was not a monastery where silence was the rule. We had so little else, talk was our one great privilege, except of course on holy days, which there were rather too many of. As was our custom, we foregathered at meals to share the day's small events: the plants beginning to send through their green hosannahs, the epiphanies of birds' nest, and the prayerful bits of gossip any small community collects. It was rare we talked of our pasts. The past is what had driven most of us to Glastonbury. Even Saint Patrick, that most revered of holy men, it was said came to Glastonbury posting ahead of his long past. Our little wattled church had heard the confessions of good men and bad, saints of passing fairness and sinners of surprising depravity, before it had been destroyed seven years earlier by fire. But the stories that Brother Denneys told us that strange spring were surely the most surprising confessions of all, and I read in the expressions of the abbot and Fathers Joseph and Paul a sudden overwhelming greed that surpassed all understanding.

What Brother Denneys rehearsed for us were the matters that had set him wandering: a king's wife betrayed, a friendship destroyed, a repentance sought, and over the many years a driving need to discover the queen's grave, that he might plead for forgiveness at her crypt. But all this was not new to the father confessors who had listened to lords and ploughmen alike. It was the length of time he had been wandering that surprised us.

Of course we applauded his despair and sanctified his search with a series of oratories sung by our choir. Before the church had burned down, we at Glastonbury had been noted for our voices, one of the three famed perpetual choirs, the others being at Caer Garadawg and at Bangor. I sang the low ground bass, which surprised everyone who saw me, for I am thin and small with a chest many a martyr might envy. But we were rather fewer voices than we might have been seven years previously, the money for the church repair having gone instead to fund the Crusades. Fewer voices – and quite a few skeptics, though the abbot, and Fathers Paul and Joseph, all of whom were in charge of our worldly affairs, were quick to quiet the doubters because of that inexhaustible pocket of gold.

How long had he wandered? Well, he certainly did not look his age. Surely six centuries should have carved deeper runes on his brow and shown the long bones. But in the end, there was not a monk at Glastonbury, including even Brother Thomas, named after that doubting forebear, who remained unconvinced.

Brother Denneys revealed to us that he had once been a knight, the fairest of that fair company of Christendom who had accompanied the mighty King Arthur in his search for the grail.

"I who was Lancelot du Lac," he said, his voice filled with that quiet authority, "am now but a wandering mendicant. I seek the grave of that sweetest lady whom I taught to sin, skin upon skin, tongue into mouth like fork into meat."

If we shivered deliciously at the moment of the telling, who can blame us, especially those infant oblates just entering their manhood. Even Abbot Giraldus forgot to cross himself, so moved was he by the confession.

But all unaware of the stir he was causing, Brother Denneys continued.

"She loved the king, you know, but not the throne. She loved the man of him, but not the monarch. He did not know how to love a woman. He husbanded a kingdom, you see. It was enough for him. He should have been a saint."

He was silent then, as if in contemplation. We were all silent, as if he had set us a parable that we would take long years unraveling, as scholars do a tale.

A sign from his mouth, like the wind over an old unused well, recalled us. He did not smile. It was as if there were no smiles left in him, but he nodded and continued.

"What does a kingdom need but to continue? What does a queen need but to bear an heir?" He paused, not to hear the questions answered but to draw deep breath. He went on. "I swear that was all that drove her into my arms, not any great adulterous love for me. Oh, for a century or two I still fancied ours was the world's great love, a love borne on the wings of magic first and then the necromancy of passion alone. I cursed and blamed that witch Morgaine even as I thanked her. I cursed and blamed the stars. But in the end I knew myself a fool, for no man is more foolish than when he is misled by his own base maunderings." He gestured downward with his hand, dismissing the lower half of his body, bit his lip as if in memory, then spoke again.

"When she took herself to Amesbury Convent, I knew the truth but would not admit it. Lacking the hope of a virgin birth, she had chosen me – not God – to fill her womb. In that I failed her even as God had. She could not hold my seed; I could not plant a healthy crop. There was one child that came too soon, a tailed infant with bulging eyes, more *mer* than human. After that there were no more." He shivered.

I shivered.

We all shivered, thinking on that monstrous child.

"When she knew herself a sinner, who had sinned without result, she committed herself to sanctity alone, like the man she worshipped, the husband she adored. I was forgot."

One of the infant oblates chose that moment to sigh out loud, and the abbot threw him a dark look, but Brother Denneys never heard.

"Could I do any less than she?" His voice was so quiet then, we all strained forward in the pews to listen. "Could I strive to forget my sinning self? I had to match her passion for passion, and so I gave my sin to God." He stood and with one swift, practiced movement pulled off his robe and threw himself naked onto the stone floor.

I do not know what others saw, but I was so placed that I could not help but notice. From the back, where he lay full length upon the floor, he was a well-muscled man. But from the front he was as smoothly wrought as a girl. In some frenzy of misplaced penitence in the years past, he had cut his manhood from him, dedicating it – God alone knew where – on an altar of despair.

I covered my face with my hands and wept; wept for his pain and for his hopelessness and wept that I, crooked as I was, could not follow him on his long, lonely road.

We waited for months for word to come from Rome, but either the Holy Father was too busy with the three quarrelsome kings and their Crusades, or the roads between Glastonbury and Rome were closed, as usual, by brigands. At any rate, no message came, and still the Quiet Monk worked at the abbey, paying for the privilege out of his inexhaustible pocket. I spent as much time as I could working by his side, which meant I often did double and triple duty. But just to hear his soft voice rehearsing the tales of his past was enough for me. Dare I say it? I preferred his stories to the ones in the Gospels. They had all the beauty, the magic, the mystery, and one thing more. They had a human passion, a life such as I could never attain.

One night, long after the winter months were safely past and the sun had warmed the abbey gardens enough for our spades to snug down easily between the rows of last year's plantings, Brother Denneys came into my cell. Matins was past for the night and such visits were strictly forbidden.

"My child," he said quietly, "I would talk with you."

"Me?" My voice cracked as it had not this whole year past. "Why me?" I could feel my heart beating out its own canonical hours, but I was not so far from my days as an infant oblate that I could not at the same time keep one ear tuned for footsteps in the hall.

"You, Martin," he said, "because you listen to my stories and follow my every move with the eyes of a hound to his master or a squire his knight."

I looked down at the stone floor unable to protest, for he was right. It was just that I had not known he had noticed my faithfulness.

"Will you do something for me if I ask it?"

"Even if it were to go against God and his saints," I whispered. "Even then."

"Even if it were to go against Abbot Giraldus and his rule?"

"Especially then," I said under my breath, but he heard.

Then he told me what had brought him specifically to Glastonbury, the secret which he had shared with the abbot and Fathers Paul and Joseph, the reason he waited for word from Rome that never came.

"There was a bard, a Welshman, with a voice like a demented dove, who sang of this abbey and its graves. But there are many abbeys and many acres of stones throughout this land. I have seen them all. Or so I thought. But in his rhymes – and in his cups – he spoke of Glastonbury's two pyramids with the grave between. His song had a ring of Merlin's truth in it, which that mage had spoke long before the end of our tale: *'a little green, a private peace, between the standing stones.'* "

I must have shaken my head, for he began to recite a poem with the easy familiarity of the mouth which sometimes remembers what the mind has forgot.

A time will come when what is three makes one:
A little green, a private peace, between the standing stones.
A gift of gold shall betray the place at a touch.
Absolution rests upon its mortal couch.

He spoke with absolute conviction, but the whole spell made less sense to me than the part. I did not answer him.

He sighed. "You do not understand. The grave between those stone pyramids is the one I seek. I am sure of it now. But your abbot is adamant. I cannot have permission to unearth the tomb without a nod from Rome. Yet I must open it, Martin, I must. She is buried within and I must throw myself at her dear dead feet and be absolved." He had me by the shoulders.

"Pyramids?" I was not puzzled by his passion or by his utter conviction that he had to untomb his queen. But as far as I knew there were no pyramids in the abbey's yard.

"There are two tapered plinths," Brother Denneys said. "With carvings on them. A whole roster of saints." He shook my shoulders as if to make me understand.

Then I knew what he meant. Or at least I knew the plinths to which he referred. They looked little like pyramids. They were large standing tablets on which the names of the abbots of the past and other godly men of this place ran down the side like rainfall. It took a great imagining – or a greater need – to read a pair of pyramids there. And something more. I *had* to name it.

"There is no grave there, Brother Denneys. Just a sward, green in the spring and summer, no greener place in all the boneyard. We picnic there once a year to remember God's gifts."

"That is what I hoped. That is how Merlin spoke the spell. *A little green. A private peace.* My lady's place would be that green."

"But there is nothing there!" On this one point I would be adamant.

"You do not know that, my son. And my hopes are greater than your knowledge." There was a strange cast to his eyes that I could just see, for a sliver of moonlight was lighting my cell. "Will you go with me when the moon is full, just two days hence? I cannot dig it alone. Someone must needs stand guardian."

"Against whom?"

"Against the mist maidens, against the spirits of the dead."

"I can only stand against the abbot and those who watch at night." I did not add that I could also take the blame. He was a man who brought out the martyr in me. Perhaps that was what had happened to his queen.

"Will you?"

I looked down the bed at my feet, outlined under the thin blanket in that same moonlight. My right foot was twisted so severely that, even disguised with the blanket, it was grotesque. I looked up at him, perched on my bedside. He was almost smiling at me.

"I will," I said. "God help me, I will."

He embraced me once, rose, and left the room.

How slowly, how quickly those two days flew by. I made myself stay away from his side as if by doing so I could avert all suspicion from our coming deed. I polished the stone floors along the hall until one of the infant oblates, young Christopher of Chedworth, slipped and fell badly enough to have to remain the day under the infirmarer's care. The abbot removed me from my duties and set me to hoeing the herb beds and washing the pots as penance.

And the Quiet Monk did not speak to me again, nor even nod as he passed, having accomplished my complicity. Should we have known that all we did *not* do signaled even more clearly our intent? Should Brother Denneys, who had been a man of battle, have plotted better strategies? I realize now that as a knight he had been a solitary fighter. As a lover, he had been caught out at his amours. Yet even then, even when I most certainly was denying Him, God was looking over us and smoothing the stones in our paths.

Matins was done and I had paid scant attention to the psalms and even less to the antiphons. Instead I watched the moon as it shone through the chapel window, illuminating the glass picture of Lazarus rising from the dead. Twice Brother Thomas had elbowed me into the proper responses and three times Father Joseph had glared down at me from above.

But Brother Denneys never once gave me the sign I awaited, though the moon made a full halo over the lazar's head.

Dejected, I returned to my cell and flung myself onto my knees, a position that was doubly painful to me because of my bad leg, and prayed to the God I had neglected to deliver me from false hopes and wicked promises.

And then I heard the slap of sandals coming down the hall. I did not move from my knees, though the pains shot up my right leg and into my groin. I waited, taking back all the prayers I had sent heavenward just moments before, and was rewarded for my faithlessness by the sight of the Quiet Monk striding into my cell.

He did not have to speak. I pulled myself up without his help, smoothed down the skirts of my cassock so as to hide my crooked leg, and followed him wordlessly down the hall.

It was silent in the dark *dortoir*, except for the noise of Brother Thomas's strong snores and a small pop-pop-popping sound that punctuated the sleep of the infant oblates. I knew that later that night, the novice master would check on the sleeping boys, but he was not astir now. Only the gatekeeper was alert, snug at the front gate and waiting for a knock from Rome that might never come. But we were going out the back door and into the graveyard. No one would hear us there.

Brother Denneys had a great shovel ready by the door. Clearly, he had been busy while I was on my knees. I owed him silence and duty. And my love.

We walked side by side through the cemetery, threading our way past many headstones. He slowed his natural pace to my limping one, though I know he yearned to move ahead rapidly. I thanked him silently and worked hard to keep up.

There were no mist maidens, no white robed ghosts moaning aloud beneath the moon, nor had I expected any. I knew more than most how the mind conjures up monsters. So often jokes had been played upon me as a child, and a night in the boneyard was a favorite in my part of the land. Many a chilly moon I had been left in our castle graveyard, tied up in an open pit or laid flat on a new slab. My father used to laugh at the pranks. He may even have paid the pranksters. After all, he was a great believer in the toughened spirit. But I like to think he was secretly proud that I never complained. I had often been cold and the ache settled permanently in my twisted bones, but I was never abused by ghosts and so did not credit them.

All these memories and more marched across my mind as I followed Brother Denneys to the pyramids that bordered his hopes.

There were no ghosts, but there *were* shadows, and more than once we both leaped away from them, until we came at last to the green, peaceful place where the Quiet Monk believed his lost love lay buried.

"I will dig," he said, "and you will stand there as guard."

He pointed to a spot where I could see the dark outlines of both church and housing, and in that way know quickly if anyone was coming toward us this night. So while he dug, in his quiet, competent manner, I climbed up upon a cold stone dedicated to a certain Brother Silas, and kept the watch.

The only accompaniment to the sound of his spade thudding into the sod was the long, low whinny of a night owl on the hunt and the scream of some small animal that signaled the successful end. After that, there was only the soft *thwack-thwack* of the spade biting deeper and deeper into the dirt of that unproved grave.

He must have dug for hours; I had only the moon to mark the passage of time. But he was well down into the hole with but the crown of his head showing when he cried out.

I ran over to the edge of the pit and stared down.

"What is it?" I asked, staring between the black shadows.

"Some kind of wood," he said.

"A coffin?"

"More like the barrel of a tree," he said. He bent over. "Definitely a tree. Oak, I think."

"Then your bard was wrong," I said. "But then, he was a Welshman."

"It is a Druid burial," he said. "That is what the oak means. Merlin would have fixed it up."

"I thought Merlin died first. Or disappeared. You told me that. In one of your stories."

He shook his head. "It is a Druid trick, no doubt of it. You will see." He started digging again, this time at a much faster pace, the dirt sailing backwards and out of the pit, covering my sandals before I moved. A fleck of it hit my eye and made me cry. I was a long while digging it out, a long while weeping.

"That's it, then," came his voice. "And there's more besides."

I looked over into the pit once again. "More?"

"Some sort of stone, with a cross on the bottom side."

"Because she was Christian?" I asked.

He nodded. "The Druids had to give her that. They gave her little else."

The moon was mostly gone, but a thin line of light stretched tight across the horizon. I could hear the first bells from the abbey, which meant Brother Angelus was up and ringing them. If we were not at prayers, they would look for us. If we were not in our cells alone, I knew they would come out here. Abbot Giraldus might have been a blusterer but he was not a stupid man.

"Hurry," I said.

He turned his face up to me and smiled. "All these years waiting," he said. "All these years hoping. All these years of false graves." Then he turned back and, using the shovel as a pry, levered open the oak cask.

Inside were the remains of two people, not one, with the bones intertwined, as if in death they embraced with more passion than in life. One was clearly a man's skeleton, with the long bones of the legs fully half again the length of the other's. There was a helm such as a fighting man might wear lying crookedly near the skull. The other skeleton was marked with fine gold braids of hair, that caught the earliest bit of daylight.

"Guenivere," the Quiet Monk cried out in full voice for the first time, and he bent over the bones, touching the golden hair with a reverent hand.

I felt a hand on my shoulder but did not turn around, for as I watched, the golden skein of hair turned to dust under his fingers, one instant a braid and the next a reminder of time itself.

Brother Denneys threw himself onto the skeletons, weeping hysterically and I – I flung myself down into the pit, though it was a drop of at least six feet. I pulled him off the brittle, broken bones and cradled him against me until his sorrow was spent. When I looked up, the grave was ringed around with the familiar faces of my brother monks. At the foot of the grave stood the abbot himself, his face as red and as angry as a wound.

Brother Denneys was sent away from Glastonbury, of course. He himself was a willing participant in the exile. For even though the little stone cross had the words HIC JACET ARTHURUS REX

QUONDAM REXQUE FUTURUS carved upon it, he said it was not true. That the oak casket was nothing more than a boat from one of the lake villages overturned. That the hair we both saw so clearly in that early morning light was nothing more than grave mold.

"She is somewhere else, not here," he said, dismissing the torn earth with a wave of his hand. "And I must find her."

I followed him out the gate and down the road, keeping pace with him step for step. I follow him still. His hair has gotten grayer over the long years, a strand at a time, but cannot keep up with the script that now runs across my brow. The years as his squire have carved me deeply but his sorrowing face is untouched by time or the hundreds of small miracles he, all unknowing, brings with each opening of a grave: the girl in Westminster whose once blind eyes can now admit light, a Shropshire lad, dumb from birth, with a tongue that can now make rhymes.

And I understand that he will never find this particular grail. He is in his own hell and I but chart its regions, following after him on my two straight legs. A small miracle, true. In the winter, in the deepest snow, the right one pains me, a twisting memory of the old twisted bones. When I cry out in my sleep, he does not notice nor does he comfort me. And my ankle still warns of every coming storm. He is never grateful for the news. But I can walk for the most part without pain or limp, and surely every miracle maker needs a witness to his work, an apostle to send letters to the future. That is my burden. It is my duty. It is my everlasting joy.

The Tudor antiquary Bale reported that "In Avallon in 1191, there found they the flesh bothe of Arthur and of hys wyfe Guenever turned all into duste, wythin theyr confines of strong oke, the boneys only remaynynge. A monke of the same abbeye, standyng and behouldyng the fine broydinges of the womman's hear as yellow as golde there still to remayne, as a man ravyshed, or more than halfe from his wyttes, he leaped into the graffe, xv fote depe, to have caughte them sodenlye. But he fayled of his purpose. For so soon as they were touched they fell all to powder."

By 1193, the monks at Glastonbury had money enough to work again on the rebuilding of their church, for wealthy pilgrims flocked to the relics and King Richard himself presented a sword reputed to be Excalibur to Tancred, the Norman ruler of Sicily, a few short months after the exhumation.

Afterword:
THE ISLE OF AVALON

Phil Carradice

The temptation to include this afterword was just too great. Our fascination with the Arthurian world makes it all too easy to accept the standard interpretation of the legend. It's refreshing when someone turns it on its head and challenges our thinking. Phil Carradice (b. 1947) is a writer, poet, broadcaster and social-work consultant who has produced a number of special interest books on Welsh history and life including The Book of Pembroke Dock *(1989) and* Welsh Shipwrecks in Camera *(1992) plus countless magazine articles and radio features. He also has a fascination with revisiting history and exploring how events might really have happened, which is what inspired the following story.*

From the old drovers' track across the eastern edge of the marsh, Glastonbury Tor with its tall and ancient tower reared like a giant's tooth out of the mist. The hill was still some six or seven miles distant, a good hour's ride across evil smelling fens, picking our way around deep lagoons and pools of stagnant water. Already the November afternoon was beginning to chill and darken into evening.

"A curse on this damned place!" snarled Kei as his horse shied and snorted beneath him. "It's more like an island than a bloody hill."

I smiled at his words. Local people still called Glastonbury the Island of Apples or, occasionally, Avalon. Over the years I had seen the fruit trees, dozens upon dozens of them, which the monks cultivated and the place was, indeed, well named.

Now Ambrosius Aurelianus, last of the great Roman cavalry leaders, had come here to die. As if sensing my thoughts Kei glared at me and inclined his head.

"Come, story teller. Time is short."

I followed him along the narrow path, grey marsh mist coiling around our horses flanks. Kei had found me two days before. Apparently he had been searching for some time, following my trail from monastery to ruined villa, from ancient hill fort to communal village hut. He finally ran me to ground in the old legionary camp at Caerleon-on-Usk.

"Ambrosius Aurelianus is dying, story teller," he had announced.

It was a typical Kei statement – short, sharp, to the point. Despite all the years they had been together, despite the battles and long campaigns – the shared moments of discomfort and fear – I had always felt that Kei did not really like. Ambrosius. Feared him, perhaps; respected his power, certainly. But there was never affection.

"What happened?" I asked.

Kei threw himself down onto a pile of furs and loosened the fibula which held his cloak. He drank deeply from a flagon of wine and smiled at me, the scars of recent battle still livid on his arms.

"We won a great victory at Mount Badon. The power of the Saxon is broken at last. They will not come again, not for many years. But Ambrosius was hurt, grievously hurt. We've carried him to Avalon – to the monks at Glastonbury. He is asking for you, Aneurin."

And that was how I had heard. Riding, now, towards the abbey – following the broad rump of Kei's workhorse – I was still amazed at myself. Why had I ever agreed to come? Kei might dislike Ambrosius but I hated him, despised him with every ounce of my soul. So it was indeed, strange that I, Aneurin the Bard, the greatest story teller and poet of all the Celtic peoples, should abandon my comfortable winter quarters at Caerleon and chase off into the unknown at the behest of some bloodthirsty warlord who had only ever caused me pain and sorrow. I really didn't know why I had come except, deep inside, there was the faintest beginnings of an idea – if the bastard was going to die then I, sure as hell, wanted to be there when it happened.

They saw us approaching long before we reached the foot of the hill. Soldiers with flaming torches rushed to light the last half mile. Bedwyr, I noticed, had also come to greet us.

"Are we in time?" Kei called.

"Aye. Just."

Bedwyr's voice was deep and resonant. He stared at me, eyes blazing with distrust. He and Kei were Ambrosius' chief lieutenants and I knew the way he was thinking. If Ambrosius was dying, one of them would probably take his place as leader of the warband. So now, for Ambrosius to suddenly demand my presence at the deathbed? Just what did that signify?

"Where the hell have you been?" Bedwyr demanded as we came up to his position at last. "You've been gone nearly ten days. Do you know what it's like trying to keep somebody alive with wounds like that?"

Kei shrugged and spat onto the mud. Carelessly he leapt from his horse, stood facing his comrade. They were an ill matched pair, Kei short and fair skinned, Bedwyr looming huge and dark in the gathering gloom.

"I came as quickly as I could. Our little story teller did not leave an easy trail to follow."

Bedwyr grunted and turned away as Kei pushed me roughly through the gateway. Inside the courtyard soldiers stood expectantly, their lances and battle axes close to hand. The air of tension was almost tangible.

Bedwyr lead the way into the Abbey, thrusting aside the monks who came forward with meat and drink. I cursed him soundly to myself – I would have murdered for a mug of ale. We walked down a passageway, coming to a halt outside the door of a darkly curtained chamber. What seemed to be a bundle of rags – half human, half malformed creature – lay across the entrance. Coldly, deliberately, Bedwyr drew back his foot and slammed it into the bundle. Instantly it came alive, leaping and screaming across the corridor.

"Arthur. Hold!"

Kei's voice was harsh, his words bringing the creature to a sudden halt. As he shrank back warily into the shadows I recognised the scrawny half starved features of Arthur, Page and whipping boy to Ambrosius Aurelianus. God knows how he kept himself alive; beaten and abused by every brutal warrior who crossed his path, the boy was a born victim. Ambrosius treated him worse than

anybody – even the kitchen dogs lived better than Arthur. Little
wonder, then, that the boy was half saint, half idiot. Yet there was
no denying his love for Ambrosius – and anybody would have to
be demented to care about that vicious bastard.

"Have you come to heal him?" Arthur asked, urgently. "My
master needs healing."

I stared at his vacant face, his mouth hanging open, spittle dripping
from the lower jaw. Hugging his arms to his side, Arthur jogged
impatiently from foot to foot.

"Get out of the way, fool!" barked Bedwyr suddenly.

He gathered himself and smashed his fist down across the boy's
head. Arthur fell sideways, slumping to his knees and staying there.
He made no sound.

"There's no healing for your master, boy. No hope. He's dying.
And soon as he's gone you're next."

He leered at the fallen boy but the significance of the remark was
lost on him. At that moment only one thing registered in that poor
simple mind. I felt his fingers clawing at my ankle and, looking
down, saw tears in Arthur's eyes.

"Cure him, lord. You must help him. Please?" Gently I eased his
hand away and pulled him to his feet.

"I'll do what I can, Arthur, but I have no healing arts."

Even as I said it I cursed myself for the lie. Help Ambrosius? By
God, I'd as soon slip in the knife myself.

We went through the chamber door and immediately the stench
filled my nostrils. The stale stench of death. Ambrosius Aurelianus
was lying on his back on a low couch, seemingly asleep. His once
handsome face was twisted in pain, covered with deep cuts and
bruises. His beard was matted with dried blood. The death wound,
however, was to the stomach, a long spear thrust which had pierced
his mail and lanced upwards into the vital organs of the body. Seeing
the wound it was astonishing to think that the man was still alive.
How long had he been like this, I asked myself? Ten days? Two
weeks?

"Ambrosius," Kei whispered. "I have brought you Aneurin.
As you asked." The eyes of the dying man flickered open and
swept around the room. Gradually they focused and came to
rest on me.

"At last," he said.

The words took effort, immense effort, and I suddenly realized
the sheer will power with which Ambrosius had kept himself alive

over the past days. Kei and Bedwyr eased him into a sitting position. It was easily done. Ambrosius seemed to have shrunk since the last time I had seen him. But then, that had been a long time ago, at night, by the light of burning buildings, and the blood on his hands and sword had given him a fiercer, more terrifying appearance. Now he was little more than a frail, dying man.

"Come close," he gasped. "I want to talk to you. Alone." His eyes swept towards Kei and Bedwyr. Weak and helpless as he was, something of his power remained. They lowered their heads and shuffled out of the chamber. I moved towards the bed side.

"I need your help," Ambrosius said. I shook my head.

"I don't have the power to heal you. I am a story teller, a bard, you know that. Besides, there is only one person who can help you now." Cursing, Ambrosius tried to ease himself into a more comfortable position. Pain lanced through him and he fell back onto the bed.

"I know that, you damned fool. I'll face my maker soon enough. I have nothing to regret – I've done my duty, that's all. I've saved this God forsaken country. Me. Not the Legions of Rome. Me – Ambrosius Aurelianus. Single handed I've beaten the Saxon raiders. They won't come again."

I shrugged. The speech seemed to have drained him and his eyes closed. For several minutes there was silence in the room, only the rasp of his laboured breathing to disturb the peace.

"Maybe. Maybe not," I said, at last. "You did what you had to do. But sometimes much more."

His eyes shot open and he glared at me.

"What do you mean by that? No matter. There's no time for debate. I need your skill, your very particular skill."

"What for, warlord?"

"I want you to tell a tale, Aneurin, a tale more thrilling than any you have yet told. My tale, my life. I want you to weave your spell, to tell the story of Ambrosius Aurelianus, the last of the Roman generals. I may be dying but I want the world to remember what I have done. When the Legions left – left us to the mercy of the Norsemen – it was me, me and my warriors, who defended this island. Defended it and beat them off. I want my glory as a general to live forever."

Exhausted, he slumped back, eyes closed. When he spoke again his voice was weaker and he kept his eyes shut. The effort of his words brought huge beads of sweat to his forehead. The end was not far away.

"I want posterity to remember me. I want people in a thousand years from now to know the name of Ambrosius Aurelianus, to know and wonder at my deeds. That's not too much to ask, is it?"

Desperately, his hand shot out and clutched my arm. His grip was still vice-like and I felt my skin crawl at his touch. Somehow, somewhere deep within his pain – filled world, Ambrosius Aurelianus felt my repulsion and, with a supreme effort, turned to face me.

"What is it? What's wrong? Why do you shrink away, Aneurin?"

I told him then, quietly and quickly, in short brutal sentences. I had held the pain so long that I thought spilling it out would bring relief, like water pouring over the river bank in winter. In truth I just felt empty, empty as the day Ambrosius and his warband had ridden through our village. We had expected to pay homage – food and drink, and maybe a few of the less choosy village girls might bestow their favours. After all, he was protecting us from the Saxon raiders. We couldn't do that ourselves, not ordinary farmers and tradesmen. Warriors fought the Saxons for us, so we were prepared to pay our dues.

But Ambrosius took more than food and drink. He took our lives and our livelihood. He burned our houses, ravaged our crops, raped our women. Above all he took my reason for living. He killed my wife, raped her and ran her through because she spat in his face. I watched, helpless, while he laughed and then rode away.

Now, when I told him, he was unsure, uncertain even of the time or place. "I . . . I don't remember," he stumbled. "So many villages. It's been so long. There's been so much war."

Anger blazed in my belly and suddenly I wanted to kill him. I grabbed him and shook him like a child's ragdoll. "It wasn't war!" I spat. "That was murder. You were supposed to protect us, not hunt us down like the damned Saxons. We looked to you for protection. You gave us death."

He turned his face away and said nothing. I let go of his tunic but stood there above him, watching and waiting for him to speak again. He didn't.

When Kei came back, maybe half an hour later, we were still there, in exactly the same positions – him flat on his back, me towering over him, rigid as a footman's lance. Ambrosius Aurelianus was dead and I wasn't even sure that he had understood what I had said.

"What did he want of you?" Kei asked, staring almost in disbelief at the body of his leader. "Whatever it was, it must have been damned important – to keep him alive in his condition." I shrugged.

"He wanted me to create a story. His story. The story of his life." Kei smiled and turned to face me. Those all seeing eyes knew far more than I sometimes gave them credit for.

"Will you do it?"

For the first time I dragged my gaze away from the dead body. Kei was staring at me intently.

"Perhaps."

The door to the death chamber suddenly burst open and the boy Arthur hurtled across the room, shrieking in torment and fear. Throwing himself upon the body of Ambrosius, he wailed and pummelled at the corpse. "Why have you left me?" he cried. "What's to become of me, now? Who will look after me?" Kei gathered him around the shoulders and, surprisingly gently, pulled the boy away.

"It's over, lad. Come away now."

They took his body and laid it in the chapel. I spent a restless night, thinking and turning ideas over and over in my mind. Too many ghosts had been disturbed, too many phantoms from the past. I slept very little. Eventually, however, towards dawn, ideas began to harden and I suddenly knew what I had to do.

That morning we walked, all of us, in long procession to the water that they call the Mouth of the Severn. There Kei and Bedwyr laid the body of Ambrosius in the shallow hull of a longship and solemnly cast it adrift.

"What will you do now, story teller?" asked Kei as we stood watching the silent vessel drift away towards the sea.

"I shall go back to Wales, to Caerleon. Just a short walk from here. And Arthur – if you will allow – can come with me. I take it nobody here wishes to look after him?"

Bedwyr snarled and turned towards me.

"Take the idiot. It'll save me the trouble of putting a dagger into his belly."

The three of us – Kei, Bedwyr, me – glanced, in unison, towards Arthur. Clad in a huge leather jerkin that had once belonged to Ambrosius – at least three sizes too big – he was staring after the distant boat. He had not heard my words and it was probably just as well as they had not been uttered from affection or even compassion. Arthur was important to me and to my plans, but I didn't really care about him.

An hour later we were several miles distant, Arthur and me, free at last from the warband which was, even now, beginning to argue about their new leader. Poor addled Arthur skipped along beside me, happy to be out in the cold November air. Already Ambrosius Aurelianus was just a memory.

Beyond the Severn the blue slopes of the Welsh hills reared huge and solemn in the morning sunlight.

"Your home, Arthur," I said, pointing. "Your home from now on."

He grinned at me and gleefully wiped the spittle from his chin. "Yes," he said. "Home."

Suddenly his head swung around, staring intently inland. I followed his gaze. Grey bellied hunting birds – hawks and falcons – were wheeling and dipping over the edge of the moor.

"Birds," whispered Arthur. "Pretty birds."

I smiled.

"Merlins, Arthur. They're called merlins. They're hunting for food for their families. Taking it home, to their nests."

"Merlins."

He repeated the name over and over again, relishing and tasting its sound. Then he smiled and I could have sworn there was cunning in the expression.

"You are my Merlin. You're taking me home. You are my Merlin, aren't you?"

I raised my eyebrows at him and slowly nodded my head.

"If you like, Arthur. I shall be your Merlin."

He danced gleefully down the track ahead of me, singing "Merlin, Merlin" at the top of his voice.

"And you," I whispered to myself as I walked after him, "shall be my king."

Posterity didn't need Ambrosius Aurelianus but it did need his story. We would all need something to cling to in the dark days and nights that undoubtedly lay ahead. Britain required a legend – the legend of a warrior king, a noble man who was merciless to the enemy but compassionate with the weak. That certainly hadn't been Ambrosius.

Yet I would give Britain that legend, and I would base it on his deeds. I would embroider, I would improve. And this Arthur, this simple idiot boy, would become my hero, my warrior king. The name of Arthur would live forever. I would do that with my skill, with my words, with my gift for story telling. In a hundred years they would have forgotten Ambrosius. Few would even know he had existed. Arthur, on the other hand, would be exalted as the king for all times, now and in the future. That was my revenge and sweet revenge it was too.

We walked on across the moor. Behind us merlins flashed and darted and far, far away the sun shone on the Isle of Avalon.